At The Dark Hour

John Wilson

Clink Street

London | New York

Published by Clink Street Publishing 2018

Copyright © 2018

First edition.

All characters in this novel are fictititious and any resemblance to real persons, living or dead, is purely coincidental, apart from Barry and Jean Funge. Because Barry asked to be included and I could not have Barry without Jean.

ISBNs: 978-1-912262-88-5 paperback
978-1-912262-89-2 ebook

For Sue

And in memory of Gerry Farrell (1951 – 2003)

Acknowledgements

First of all I would like to thank my wife, Sue, who was not only read through this manuscript on many occasions, both when it was a work in progress and after it had been completed, but also had to live through the novel's very long gestation and provided some excellent plot suggestions when things were not progressing as I wanted them to.

I would also like to make specific mention of my excellent editor, and fellow writer, Martin Ouvry who put long hours into a very thorough editing of the novel as well as providing enthusiastic encouragement to me.

I could not have got this far without the enormous assistance I received from Authoright (aka the Clink Street Press) so I would like to say a special thank you to Gareth Howard, Hayley Radford and Elaine.

I am also indebted to the excellent writing of Sol Stein and, in particular, his books "Solutions for Writers" and "Solutions for Novelists" which I can heartily recommend.

Finally, I would like to thank all of my friends who have taken the time and trouble to read the novel, either as a work in progress or as a final draft, and have given me much encouragement and useful criticism. I apologise for any names that I have left out:

Tim Amos QC, Craig Barlow, Becky Bailey-Harris, Julian Beard, Cheryl Bell, Eléonore Berthelsen, Bruce Blair QC, Jane Bradley, Tom Braham, Emily Brand, Caroline Bridge, Michael and Mary Brown, Jane Campbell, Rebecca Carew-Pole, Andy Carty, Philip Cayford QC, Jane Chapman, Ken Collins, Louise Cowen, Barbara Davidson, Jo Delahunty QC, Anne Donald, Simon Edwards, Carol Ellinas, Barbara Ellington, Dave Eva, Fr

James Finnemore, Kate Fitzpatrick, Victoria Francis, Jean Funge, Nicholas Garthwaite, Angela Green, Michael Harris, Kate Hernandez, Mike and Clare Hooper, Ross Hooper, Mike Horton, Ann Hussey QC, Frances Judd QC, Veena Kanda, Camini Kumar, Emma Kurzner, Val Le Grice QC, William Longrigg, Jan Madden, Linda Malcolm, Jane McBennett, Nigel McNelly, Norman Miller, Duncan Morum, Lily Mottahedan, Norman Moss, Catriona Murfitt, Tim O'Brien, Kathy O'Connor, Michele O'Leary, Julie Okine, Katherine Oliver, Sarah Palmer, Alison Plouvin, Heather Rabbatts, Lynn Robinson, Peter Robinson, Sara Robinson, Georgina Rushworth, Janys Scott QC, Thoweetha Shaah, Ines Sdouk, Alastair Sharp, Hannah Sharp, Katherine Sharp, Caroline Sheldon, Samantha Singer, Candida and Robin Spencer, Jan Stockdale, Amy Sugden, Emma Sumner, Lucy Theis, David Thompson, Richard Todd QC, Gus Ullstein QC, Christine Vaughan-Edwards, Hugo Walford, Grant Walker, Martin West, Jenny and Louise Wilson, Philip Wilson, Catherine Wood QC, Ben Wooldridge and John Zieger.

The essence of being human is that one does not seek perfection, that one is sometimes willing to commit sins for the sake of loyalty, that one does not push asceticism to the point where it makes friendly intercourse impossible, and that one is prepared in the end to be defeated and broken up by life, which is the inevitable price of fastening one's love upon other human individuals.

At the Dark Hour

Our love was conceived in silence and must live silently
This only our sorrow, and this until the end.
Listen, did we not lie all of one evening
Your heart under my hand

And no word spoken, no, not even the sighing
Of pain made comfortable, not the heart's beat
Nor sound of urgency, but a fire dying
And the cold sheet?

The sailor goes home singing; the lamplit lovers
Make private movements in a public place.
Boys whistle under windows, and are answered;
But we must hold our peace.

Day, too, broke silently. Before the blackbird,
Before the trouble of traffic and the mist unrolled,
I shall remember at the dark hour turning to you
For comfort in the cold.

PAUL DEHN

Prologue

(Monday 21ˢᵗ October 1940)

Adam opened the window, lit a Woodbine, and gazed down onto Green Park. He had reserved a bedroom on the second floor and left the details in a note within the shield of a knight over a week ago. Julia's note in reply expressed a reluctance that was more and more evident in her correspondence, but he was insistent. Eventually, on the previous Friday, she had agreed to come. He had signed under his real name and asked that a bottle of champagne be brought up to the room. It was sitting in a bucket of ice on a table near the window. There were two iced flutes. A cold wind blew in and he pulled his overcoat closer to him. The barrage balloons floated eerily in the sudden stillness of the late afternoon. He ran a hand down the side of the bottle. It was still slightly warm and there were no drips of condensation on the glass so he pressed it further into the ice and twisted it down so that the ice made a crunching sound. He looked at his watch. It was a quarter past three. He had suggested three o'clock.

His knowledge of her movements was diminishing. Whereas in the past there would be a note in the church every weekday, now they were frequently absent. He wondered whether she would even show up. How many afternoons had they spent in the Stafford? He had no idea. They had kept no records and any communications were always destroyed. If he had been accused of a crime of which he was innocent – a murder perhaps – and the time and date of the crime was one of these afternoons, he would not be able to prove his alibi. This lack of any evidence meant that it would be difficult to prove any case against them. But it also meant that, on one level, nothing ever happened. Nothing could be verified. If she were to deny that she loved him, that she had ever even met with him privately, he would not be able to prove the contrary. He looked at his watch again. Three thirty. *Well this has been a waste of money,* he thought. He would stop leaving her notes. It was causing him too much pain.

Then there was a knock on the door and he rushed over to open it. Julia was wearing a long black coat and had a headscarf with a peacock motif, *probably from Liberty,* he thought. Stray curls of blonde hair escaped from under it. She gave him a warm but distracted smile and they kissed in greeting.

 – Ooh, it's cold in here. Can't you shut the window?

He stubbed out his cigarette and did as she had asked and then turned back into the room to look at her.

 – Champagne? Are we celebrating something?
 – As a matter of fact, we are. Can you guess what?
 – Oh, Adam! I'm not in the mood for silly games.

Adam turned around, looked back down onto Green Park and said morosely over his shoulder:

 – It's four years to the day since we spent the night together in the Feathers. This is our fourth anniversary.
 – Four years … our lives are flying away from us.

He heard her approach him as she said these words. Her tone was sad. And then her hand was on his shoulder and she stood beside him and leaned her head into his side.

 – I'm sorry, Adam. I didn't mean to sound ungrateful. I'm under a terrible strain, that's all.

They stood together in silence for a long while gazing out into the place where their affair had most of its origins. At last she said, more brightly,

 – Come on then. Let's have some of that scrumptious bubbly.

She took off her overcoat and scarf and laid them neatly across an armchair. He studied what she was wearing underneath: a dark blue tweed twin-piece and a cream-coloured blouse.

– I know what you're thinking. That it's rather dowdy for an assignation, especially on our anniversary – but I can hardly draw attention to myself.

They moved over to the table, Adam poured and they each took a chair. Tiny bubbles rose to the surface and popped in long unbroken chains. He lifted his glass and tilted it towards Julia.

– To us.
– Yes. To us.
– What's upsetting you?
– I got a lovely letter from Agnes this morning. Well ... not so much a letter ... but she had drawn a picture of a house, a boxy thing, with a line of blue crayon at the top – that was the sky – and a line of green crayon at the bottom which was the grass.
– When did you last see them?
– And she had written, scrawled really, "To Mummy and Daddy, love Agnes", and then put a line of crosses under her name.
– They'll be able to come back soon, I'm sure.
– I couldn't bear to lose them, Adam
– Why should you lose them? They're much safer where they are.
– I've been sleeping very badly. I'm so tired.

She turned away from him, wiped her eyes and drained her glass.

– Top-up please ... Thank you ... So much has changed in the last four years.
– We haven't changed though.

Julia didn't answer and stared out of the window. They finished their second glass in silence. Adam didn't know what to say.

– Would you like some more?
– Let's leave a glass each for afterwards.

And she rose and walked over to the window. He followed her and, standing behind her, he pulled her close to him. Her body arched and she pressed her bottom against him. He raised his hands to her breasts and began to caress them.

– Oh, Adam!

He began unbuttoning her jacket and she shifted her arms and shoulders so that it could fall to the ground.

– Are you sure I should be doing this in front of the window?
– We are not being watched yet, Adam.
– Yet?
– My blouse?

He undid the buttons and with the same fluent movement she allowed it to fall to the floor.

– And my brassiere.

She was naked from the waist up and still staring into Green Park.

– I could close the curtains?
– Not today, Adam. My skirt?

He closed his eyes and let his fingers stroke her neck and then slide down her torso, caressing her breasts and twisting her nipples before moving down to her tummy and reaching for the top button of her skirt.

– And my suspenders.

He unclipped them and she reached down to pull off her stockings until all she was wearing were her panties.

– Shouldn't we move away from the window?
– No, Adam. Put your hand inside.

****

He led her naked to the bed and she pulled back the blankets and climbed under them. He hurriedly removed his clothes and climbed in next to her. Pressing against her so that they touched at every point, he savoured her body's warmth. He looked into her eyes. Longing, desire and sadness. The sky was beginning to darken. She stroked his face.

- I want this to be memorable.
- I love you so much!
- I love you too. I mean it, you know.
- Why should I not believe you?
- I mean it, you know.

And they made love. Adam had never known Julia to be so passionate. She gripped his wrists with such force that the bruising didn't go down for days – he had to pull his frayed cuffs down over the contusions. She kissed his neck in a way that made him feel she was trying to eat him. She groaned and howled. When at last their bodies went limp, the bed was in ruins. They lay still for a long time afterwards.

- Let's have that last glass of champagne.
- Do you want me to cover you with a sheet?
- Come to the window, Adam.

And the two sat naked at the same little table.

- Julia. What's wrong?
- I don't think we can carry on any longer.

His heart lurched.

- Why ever not?
- It's this war. We're taking enormous risks.

She started to cry. Adam did not know what to say. He needed to persuade her not to give up.

- Do you remember that time when I asked you whether, if we weren't

5

both happily married with children, you would marry me and you said yes?

She was sobbing.

- Yes.
- Do you think that will ever happen?
- Not now, one day perhaps.

And she sobbed again.

- When?
- Maybe in twenty years.
- Twenty years?

He didn't think that he could live that long. He was overcome by violent coughing. Still sobbing, Julia said she wanted to go back to the bed. She climbed into the ruins and immediately fell asleep. She was still naked and had her right hand behind her head and her left across her breast. Her right leg, bent at the knee, touched the floor and her left was at an acute angle, with her foot resting on her right upper leg. She looked defenceless. He pulled up a chair and watched her gentle breathing as the sky darkened into night and she became no more than a silhouette. Then he closed the curtains.

The time came when he had to wake her. She roused herself, pulled herself off the bed and, almost mechanically, dressed herself, picked up her overcoat and scarf from the armchair and put them on. Then she opened the door to leave.

- Goodbye, Adam.
- Please don't leave me!
- Goodbye, Adam.

And she turned and was gone.

PART ONE

Chapter One

(Friday 13th December 1940)

Bateman was angry:

- What's his name again?
- Falling. Mr Adam Falling.
- Is he really the best you can offer me?
- He's very good, you know.
- Well. Why wasn't he on the original list that you gave me?
- They're all away, I'm afraid.

Bateman knew what that meant. He said:

- Oh God! So, either he's a conchie, a cripple or drawing his pension?
- His clerk recommended him highly to me. And Stirrup Court is a very good set of chambers.
- Right. So what can you tell me about him?
- Not a lot, I'm afraid. But he is very sharp. Went to Cambridge. Destined to do very well. And not that old. Probably only in his late thirties.

Being no fool, Bateman read it right.

- You don't know anything about him do you? You're just parroting what his guvnor told you?

Jones laughed awkwardly and shifted in his seat, looking around the waiting room. Black curtains had been nailed over the window. The room was murky and a heavily shielded lamp cast shadows over the law books lining one of the walls. His mouth was dry and he wished, not for the first time, that barristers would offer tea or coffee, or even water.

– And why did we have to come here after dark? It's a rabbit warren. I'd have had trouble finding the place in daylight, let alone during the blackout!

– Mr Falling is a Judge (sort of) – said Jones sensing a way out – and we had to wait until he'd finished … his business.

Jones and his client had been obliged to pick their way down from Fleet Street into the Temple and past Cloisters after night had fallen. Notwithstanding war, the old conventions remained and it was still normal to wait until 4.30 p.m. or later to see one's barrister. The edge of an early moon had given a silver sheen to the Temple Church and the white stone of Cloisters' arches glowed fluorescent beyond them. But for the rubble, Jones could have done it blindfold. He'd been doing it for years. They had stumbled past the wreckage of Fig Tree Court on to Stirrup Court and then up cold stone stairs, where they were shown to the waiting room by Arthur, the senior clerk.

– Sorry to keep you. Mr Falling won't be a minute. He's just popped out to Temple Church for a quick pray.

And they found themselves in the gloomy room. Nothing but the day's *Daily Mirror* to sustain them. They'd both read it earlier.

– What's he praying for, then? And if he's only in his late 30s, what's he doing here? He should be off with the rest of them defending the country.

– If he wasn't here, I don't know where I would have found a barrister for you.

They lapsed back into silence. Jones didn't like his client's mood. Ungrateful bastard! He'd spent an age phoning around trying to find someone who would take the brief. Bateman had no idea how difficult it was to find anyone. Let alone anyone good. Arthur had never put Falling forward before, even though he had been around – so he said – for over fifteen years. He had no idea what to expect.

Presently, Arthur came into the room again.

– Mr Falling will see you now.

And he led them up a further set of stairs. Bateman could not help noticing the fine cut of the clerk's suit as the small fastidious man led them to their counsel.

****

Falling's room was narrow and cold. The windows were heavily curtained but a warm light emanated from his desk. He looked like a barrister, though not a very well one, thought Bateman. He was about five eleven and a little older than Bateman himself. Certainly not forty. He wore a black jacket and white shirt. His black hair, which was slightly too long, flopped down over his forehead. He slipped a piece of notepaper under a small crystal paperweight, then steepled his long thin pianist's fingers in front of him. Bateman noticed that his right cuff was fraying white. On the shelf behind Falling, Bateman saw a row of books – mostly Penguin paperbacks.

– Good day at the Tribunal, Mr Falling?

Jones asked, a little too cheerily and with no interest in the answer. Falling's voice in reply was mellifluous but slightly breathless and broken:

– The usual business. Very good to meet you at last, Mr Jones. Good evening, Mr Bateman.
– Hello.

There was a pause whilst everyone considered whether any further pleasantries were required. Then:

– Well, Mr Bateman. I have read the instructions that Mr Jones has so carefully prepared on your behalf and it looks as though you may be in a spot of bother.
– I was fine until I received those papers. Or as fine as you can be these days.
– Yes. You were served two days ago as I understand it?
– In the office, would you believe?

- Does your wife know about these allegations?
- She's dead.
- I'm sorry.
- Died three months ago. Run over by a car during the blackout. Found out she died when I got back from work.

Jones interrupted:

- Yes, I'm sorry. I should have mentioned that in my instructions. Mr Bateman is a widower.

It was a common story at the time. Strict imposition of the blackout and the prohibition on torches, streetlamps and headlights had meant that by December 1940 about forty people were being run down and killed every night on the streets of London.

- Anyway – said Bateman, forgetting that perhaps he should look more grieving – it's bad enough as it is. I still have my reputation. And Jones here says it could be all over the papers.
- Yes. I'm afraid so. If this goes to Court I will have to wear my wig and gown – he motioned to a blue bag with his initials on it hanging in the corner – and the press likes a ... a bit of fun (*I'm afraid*) at times like this.
- Fun!?
- I'm sorry. But that is how it will be seen. With bombs landing all around us and people dying all over the world it's rather comforting to discover that men and women are still having sex with people they shouldn't be having sex with. Gives things an air of normality.
- But I wasn't, you know ... having sex with Mrs McKechnie.
- Mr Jones has told me what you say. But why would Mr McKechnie make these accusations against you?

There was a long pause. Adam had time to study his client. A small red-faced man in a loud pinstripe with wide lapels, fidgeting in his chair. He knew the type.

- You understand, Mr Bateman, that anything said in this room is privileged and need be known to no one else. But if you tell me one thing is true and expect me to proceed on the basis that the truth lies elsewhere I will be obliged to withdraw from your case?

Jones had warned Bateman about this question.

– I know. There's nothing in it. I don't know why he's done it. But I knew it was coming. Did Jones tell you how he set about me in the office about three weeks ago, in front of everyone, accusing me of screwing Victoria?

Adam knew about this. It was in his instructions in lurid detail. Graham McKechnie was Bateman's immediate superior in an insurance office in the City. Without warning in early November he had approached Bateman loudly during the morning tea break and accused him of carrying on with his wife. He was waving her diary around and pointing to various entries, shouting "ABC."? Don't you think I know what that means?

– Tell me about the diary?
– Nothing to tell. Nothing I know at any rate. The four of us were friends and lived local to one another round Ilford. Victoria keeps a diary – I knew that much – and apparently she'd been putting these "mysterious" references to ABC in it. Well, I'm Arnold Bateman. Don't know what the "C" could stand for. Could be the pictures or the teashop for all I know. Well, Graham thinks she's acting oddly, looks at her diary and comes up with the answer that it's something to do with me.
– Is there anything else?

Again, a long pause.

– Not that I can think of.
– What does Victoria look like?
– What's that got do with anything?
– It's helpful to have a mental picture.
– I suppose she's rather beautiful really. About five foot six with blonde hair in a curly frizz round her head. Slim … she's got blue eyes … is that enough?

- Have you been sleeping with Victoria?
- No! I've told you that and I've told Jones that. Why would I be here if I had?

Adam could think of a number of reasons. He was overcome by a coughing fit before he could reply and it was over a minute before the conference continued. Wiping his mouth with a large white handkerchief, he said:

- Money, Mr Bateman.
- I thought we'd get onto that subject sooner or later.
- Money. If Mr McKechnie is telling the truth and you've been sleeping with Victoria, he'll sue you for substantial damages and he'll get his costs. It could be hundreds or thousands of pounds.

Bateman blanched, then went red. Adam waited for him to say something but he remained sitting in stunned silence.

- You've come to me for advice about your legal position. You have been cited as the Co-Respondent in divorce proceedings. The allegation is that you have committed adultery with Victoria McKechnie. Mr McKechnie is the Petitioner. If he succeeds in proving that then he will be entitled to recover money from you for breaking up his marriage. The proceedings will be contested in open court and the press will be there. It will be embarrassing for everyone. And not a little distasteful, I'm afraid. I will be representing you in Court if it comes to that. I am bound by the facts. If you say you did not do it then we will proceed on that basis. If you said you did do it we will have to adopt another tack. Perhaps that Victoria was an awful wife and he really has lost nothing by being relieved of such a dreadful person. That will cut the –
- How dare you!
- I'm sorry, Mr Bateman?
- Nothing. Carry on.
- If we can satisfy the Court that in any event Mrs McKechnie is no loss to her husband, that will certainly cut down on the amount of damages you will have to pay, but you will still have to pay his costs. If you have been sleeping with … Victoria … then we better try and

cut your losses now. Have you been sleeping with her or having sex with her? I'm sorry to be technical but "sex" in this context means "actual penetration of her vagina by your penis".
– This is disgusting!

Adam wanted him off balance.

– Have you been sleeping with her or have you had sex with her?
– No.
– Do you know what she says to these allegations?
– Yes ... I mean no. Of course I don't know. But I know that she will deny them.
– How do you know?
– Well ... because we haven't.
– Have you discussed the petition with her?

Long pause.

– No. Anyway, why would she deny it if she had been?
– Well. She may not want to be divorced and left to fend for herself. How would she support herself if he divorced her?
– I hadn't thought about that.
– I see she has children. Ernest and Susan?
– Yes. But they've been evacuated. They may never hear about it anyway.
– But she loves them, doesn't she?
– Yes, and they love her, and always will, I'm sure. What's that got to do with it?
– Well, she wouldn't want to lose custody of them, would she?
– Why should she lose custody of them?
– If it is proven that she has been having adultery with someone then her husband will be entitled to their custody. She will probably still be able to see them from time to time.
– This is bloody madness. They've always been with her, ever since we met them. Why should he have them? He's never there.
– That's the law, Mr Bateman. So you see, this could be extremely serious. If she is a good woman – and you aren't giving me much encouragement that she is not – and you have been committing adultery it

could cost you an awful lot of money and possibly bankrupt you. I wouldn't think he's doing it for the money. He probably knows you can't afford it. He just wants to humiliate you ... and humiliate his wife.

Jones coughed before interrupting.

– Actually, Mr Bateman probably can afford it.

Adam raised an eyebrow and took another look at Bateman.

– You work in an office in the City?
– Mr Jones is talking about my compensation.
– For what?
– For Marjorie's death. She was insured. I got £10,000. I think that McKechnie wishes it was his wife that died. So that's why he's coming against me, I reckon.
– And according to the petition, he is saying that you've been having an affair since January of this year, at least, on the basis of the diary?
– Yes.
– So he's alleging that you were unfaithful to your own wife before she died?
– That's about the sum of it I suppose.

Adam sighed to himself. So many of the cases he had to deal with came down to secret, yet commonplace, acts in dark rooms. They all ended up in bedrooms or cars or on office floors. He thought of Victoria, with her blonde halo, letting her dress drop, or Bateman's little red face getting redder. And the panting and groaning. Victoria bending backwards or forwards. The words of love and the promises that may – or may not – have been made. The act itself was ultimately uninteresting. It was how people got there – or how they got accused of being there – that was so infinitely various. Why did he ask what the women looked like? He told himself that it was a purely professional thing. Damages were lower for a scrofulous dwarf than they were for Aphrodite. A man would be more likely to commit adultery if a woman was beautiful – or if he thought that she was beautiful. He pictured Victoria, whom he had never met, bending forwards – or backwards. Little red-faced Bateman's penis entering her vagina.

- And there is no other evidence, as far as you know, apart from these three letters from time to time in Victoria's diary?
- I don't know of any.
- Is there anything else you think you ought to be telling me?
- No.
- How long have you known McKechnie?
- About five years.
- When did you first meet Victoria?
- About four years ago.
- Where?
- At an office party in 1936. It was about December the 22nd.
- Did you see her after that away from the office?
- The four of us would go out to the pub or the pictures and things like that from time to time?
- Did you see her alone?

Long pause.

- I may have been for a walk in the park with her once or twice. That's about it.
- Sure?
- That's about it.
- So your instructions are that you have not committed adultery with Victoria McKechnie but if you had you cannot say in mitigation that she was a bad wife to her husband.
- I suppose that's my case.
- Very well.
- So your advice is that if McKechnie proves that I've been having it away with his missus, I'll have to pay him thousands of pounds and she loses her children and almost any financial support. And I'll have my pictures in the papers?
- That's about the sum of it.
- I hope one of those bombs lands on him!
- Mr Jones, I'll draft a request for further and better particulars. I

think we ought to try and find out the dates of all the occasions when it is alleged that intercourse took place. And where. And I'd like to see the diary if at all possible.

Adam then gave some further technical advice about the pleadings and tactics from here on, and drew the meeting to a close. It was getting on for six and he wanted to get to his wife before the bombing started. He led them to the door to see them out.

- By the way – he said as they were heading down the stairs – if there is anything more to this than you've told me, you'd better watch your step. If McKechnie hasn't got the evidence he needs yet, he may be working on you to find it.
- I'll bear that in mind, Mr Falling. Good night.

*****

- Can't say that I enjoyed that experience very much, Mr Jones.
- I think, at least, that Mr Falling knows what he is doing. I was rather impressed by him. I don't think we need worry about your being properly represented.
- Certainly knew a lot about adultery. I think he's a pervert saying things like that.

The two climbed down the stairs and back into the little courtyard, then edged their way back up towards Fleet Street. Behind them a shadow moved against the shadows, and a large man, hat pulled down low, slanted after them. He seemed to have a lot of people to follow from Stirrup Court. But he knew where Falling was going that evening and decided, tonight, to track Bateman.

Chapter Two

Adam would have been unsurprised to be thought of as a pervert. Medical students juggled with brains in the autopsy rooms; divorce lawyers inevitably found themselves wondering about their clients. Commonplace. It was going on all around the city even during the war, even during the blackout. Especially during the blackout. All over the city life went on as it had to. Mostly in private, intimate and unspoken, men and women coupled and uncoupled. The divorce law, like a terrier in a badgers' set, brought them out from time to time, blinking into the torches of their pursuers. And then he would become involved.

He lifted the small obelisk of crystal from the sheet of notepaper, unfolded the note and re-read it:

"Destroy this."

Destroy this? He always did. He didn't need to be reminded. "Destroy this": there was an uncharacteristic urgency in the writing. He placed the note in the ashtray and put a match to it, watched it blacken and crumple, and then broke it up with the nib of his pen. Destroyed. Almost destroyed. Only someone who knew the writing paper would see the clue that remained as to its provenance.

He took down a paperback to read on the tube, then left the room. Closing the door behind him, he edged down the stairs. The blackout had been in force for over a year and no gas lamps were lit to guide him. It had been difficult at first to find his way but by September he could have walked to Temple tube with his eyes shut. Then the bombs started to fall and familiar landmarks disappeared or were reduced to splinters and broken stone. In mid-September the clock tower of the Library was hit by high explosive and the tower and staircase were almost completely destroyed. The Benchers' Smoking Room and the Treasurer's Room were badly damaged, as were the Committee Room and the Ladies' Room. A few days later the west end of Inner Temple Hall was hit. A high explosive bomb fell through the roof and musician's gallery and burst outside the door of the Buttery. The whole of the interior was badly wrecked and enormous damage was done to windows, panelling, furniture and the pictures on the walls. Adam and his colleagues, who had taken lunch there for many years, were forced to move on to Lincoln's Inn and then to Niblett Hall, behind the Alienation Office.

That same night Crown Office Row was badly damaged and a gas main outside was shattered. He had watched the escaping gas blaze furiously for a time before it was tamed. And so the war edged closer, moving from the East and into the City and the Temple. 13, King's Bench suffered damage, and then, on the 16th October, a night Adam would never forget, incendiaries fell by parachute onto Elm Court and exploded on the roof. Adam and a few others had taken cover in the shelter under nearby Hare Court. The dark room shook and they felt the air being pulled from their lungs and a rush of intense heat, and they prepared to die. Instead they lived and emerged blinking and hungry after the "all clear", into utter desolation.

The blast and fireball had destroyed Fig Tree Court and Crown Office Row completely. Adam's room had overlooked the former, and in idle moments he would look out at that beautiful little seventeenth century building, flat-fronted and serene, and see in it timelessness. All gone. Later that morning he saw familiar faces, drawn and desolate, picking through the rubble for books and briefs, their practices as shattered as their buildings. He had thought of all the colleagues of similar call, fit enough to fight and away on active duty, and was thankful for them that they did not have to see this.

As the year moved on, more buildings were destroyed, more men picked through the rubble and more craters opened up in what had been to him so comforting and familiar. Barrage balloons loomed out of the darkness above. His journey to Temple tube followed a similar route to before but now he had to pick his way past broken stone and splintered timber, sometimes still smouldering. And the sadness that had been growing in him for eighteen months grew greater. A spiritual darkness had descended upon him well before the order for "lights out" was given, and month by month the familiar landmarks of his inner life were being destroyed. He had lived, relatively comfortably, with his comparative failure as a barrister. But when the call-up came and he was rejected on health grounds whilst those who had always bettered him professionally moved with ease into the ranks of officers a greater gloom had entered. His civilian clothing marked him out from the soldiers as someone who had chosen not to fight. He saw disdain in the uniformed eyes around him. The fact that Arthur was now obliged to give him more work provided only a little comfort.

Reaching the tube, he picked his way past the sandbags and the touts selling shelter, and made his way to the platform. He was meeting Catherine at a pub off Sloane Square. She didn't want to go to the Pembertons' party as she didn't like Pemberton or his wife, or, for that matter, the other members of his Chambers. Their wealth and success left a stain for her on Adam. No doubt, also, she would bring up the cat and call him a murderer again.

The pub was already crowded by 6.30. People looking for a skinful of weak beer to see them through the raids that would almost inevitably follow. Adam hoped they had shelters with toilets. Many did not, and one had to make do with "piss buckets". Alongside the civilians there were soldiers in a medley of uniforms, Polish, Canadian, Free French, and a fug of black-market cigarettes hung blue over everything. Catherine was sitting by the bar in her blue dress, her dark brown hair pulled up. She was holding a half of mild, her gas mask by her feet. He kissed her hello and got himself a beer.

- I tried to call you earlier but Arthur said you were in the church again.
- I was only there about fifteen minutes and then it was straight into my con. Sorry.
- Since when have you become so religious?

Adam had been making regular visits to the church for over four years but it only seemed to have come to Catherine's attention in recent months.

- It's a lovely old building even after the Victorians ransacked it and filled it with modern rubbish. We've lost so many good buildings and that is one to cherish.
- It's funny. You always talk about the building and never about the God whose supposed to be inside it.
- Enough people go there for God. I go there because it's quiet. To be away from everyone for a while.
- I was ringing to say I didn't want to come tonight and you should go on your own. But as I couldn't get hold of you …

– It'll be all right. Makes a change from suburbia and there should be some good food and drink, and it's not often that he has bothered to invite us. They know how to entertain and Pemberton gives no sign that there's a war on at all. He and Arthur have some sort of thing going on.

Catherine winced at the mention of Adam's clerk. She had heard all Adam's tales of the contraband that Arthur regularly brought in and left on Pemberton's desk.

– I really don't like that man. Who else is going to be there?
– The usual crowd from Chambers and there are one or two back on leave. And some of Jeremy's friends from Belgravia, I suppose.
– And Julia, I suppose?

The repetition jarred. Adam looked into her face for any hidden meaning but her brown eyes gave away nothing.

– Yes, of course. She is his wife, after all. If her "war work" will allow it. She works irregular shifts.
– Her "war work"! I suppose the rest of us are doing nothing. We don't all have servants and it's not as though she has to worry about the children. All packed off to the Cotswolds for the duration.
– I know. I'm not saying she makes a big thing of it. She works irregular shifts.
– And at least she has her cats to keep her company.

Adam had wondered how long it would take her.

– I'm sorry about Socks.
– Saying sorry all the time won't bring her back.
– We made a decision about it together.
– You told me I had no choice. Our "contribution to the war effort" – she added bitterly.
– It seemed to be the right thing to do at the time. I'll get you another one.
– You can't bring Socks back.

Adam lapsed into silence. It was almost a year since they had their cat put down. Catherine had been very distressed about it, as had their daughter, and it was right to say that he pretty much forced her into doing it. Although it wasn't as if he was acting in isolation. At the outbreak of war the government had advised Londoners to have their pets destroyed on the grounds of economy. Four hundred thousand cats and dogs – but mainly cats – across London had been killed and incinerated in the first few days. The furnaces of the RSPCA had to be damped down at night, because of the blackout, and could not cope with the demand. Then it was decided that this was all something of a mistake. And Catherine did not let him forget that. She returned to the party.

- I suppose Preston will be there?
- Probably
- And his wife.
- Inevitably.

Preston was the new silk. He had been made up to KC only that spring. Just a little older than Adam, he was known for his driving ambition. His wife, Cara, was a good twelve years younger than he. Most people never knew what he truly thought; Adam, however, had learnt long ago not to listen to what he was saying but to watch the reactions of his wife. Less political than he, her face or the odd comment mirrored Preston's inner thoughts. As a result Adam was pretty sure that he always knew exactly what Preston thought of someone by watching his wife by his side. Catherine prickled:

- He thinks we're all fools but he's not the only one with a university education.
- He respects you, sweetheart. He knows you're not stupid.
- He didn't need to use his hands to show respect for my intellect!
- You made sure he got the message.
- At least he's got himself a decent war job, I suppose. Why couldn't you get something in Whitehall?
- I didn't get asked.
- Anyway, don't let me get stuck with them, please.
- I'll do my best.

– And please can we go at a relatively early hour? They are all far too relaxed about this blitz. I'd like to try and get the 10.08 at the latest.
– The bombing's eased over the last month … but of course. We'll leave early.

They finished their drinks and headed out into the street. Sandbags were everywhere around them and they had to make their way by what light the moon afforded. Bands of white paint had been applied to kerb stones, trees, pillar boxes and lamp posts as an aid to getting about in the dark.

– You've forgotten your gas mask again.
– I don't think it would be much help. I have enough trouble breathing without shoving one of those over my head.
– I think you're just trying to be fashionable. Because it's not the done thing to carry them anymore. Either that or you don't particularly want to live.

– Maybe the latter.

Adam said this under his breath, stifling another coughing fit.

Chapter Three

They made their way slowly to Eaton Square. The further to the west of London one went the less seriously the blackout was taken and progress became easier. Partly because the richer people had less concern about offending the ARP officers. Partly because either they were also the magistrates charged with enforcing the law or they knew the people who were. Half the houses were now empty, their owners having fled to country estates. Many of them were on the market for sale but it wasn't a sellers' market. The Pemberton home was on the north side of the Square. Light seeped from the blackout curtains across the ground floor. It was darker on the upper levels. Samuels, the butler, opened the door to them and ushered them into the reception rooms. Light flooded in on them. All the chandeliers were alight and liveried servants were gliding around carrying silver trays laden with crystal glasses full of champagne. Canapés sat on trays placed strategically around the room.

Jeremy Pemberton KC came over to greet them, a tall man with silvering hair and lines of worry and age around his blue eyes. He wore black tie. Adam was nervous as to how he would greet them, but Pemberton gave nothing away. Perhaps things were not as he feared?

- Adam! Catherine. Very pleased you could join us. Have some champagne. Samuels will take your coats – and your gas mask, Catherine. Couldn't let the Christmas season pass us by without at least trying to celebrate it. It would all be too ghastly if we simply sat back and let it happen.
- Good to see you, Jeremy. And thank you for inviting us. This is quite a bash. Glad to see you're not letting the privations of rationing get to you.
- Just a matter of planning. Saw all this coming from a long time ago. "Reasonably foreseeable", as we lawyers say. You know that the Inner

set up an Air Raids Precaution Committee about eighteen months ago; I'd say I'd seen it coming from about a year earlier than that.
- Very good. But how did that help?
- Forewarned is forearmed as they say. Very simple when you think about it. And I had a lot of time to think about it. I remembered the last time this all happened and just asked myself what there were shortages of, then stocked up.
- But what about perishable things like eggs and milk? You can't stock up on those.
- Of course not. I stocked up on things that last. Don't drink anymore. And I've never smoked. Bad for the health in my view. Don't care what they say in their advertising. But the last time around cigarettes were better than money. Filled the cellar with them. That and wine and champagne … silk stockings and brandy. Stretched the Exchequer at the time but it's paying dividends now.

Catherine was far less tactful.

- So you give cigarettes and brandy to Arthur and he exchanges them on the black market for things that you want and then he takes a cut for himself? Is that it?
- Catherine!
- Don't worry, Adam. Yes, Catherine. That *is* it. Arthur is a bloody barrow boy when it comes down to it. But he knows where the action is. You must have seen it over the years, Adam. If there was a pie Arthur had a couple of fingers in it.

Adam had seen it. When he was looking to find a house to rent in Dulwich, Arthur told him that he had a friend who could help out. Although initially disappointed when he discovered that Adam had gone ahead without him, he turned immediately to the task of fitting him out with curtains and carpets. He had friends who could supply both.

- You're right. I remember telling him he would sell his own mother. Said there wasn't a market for her.
- That's Arthur. I think he clerks for us as a sideline for his real activities. Maybe we're his "front". He's wealthier than any of us you know.

And he knows everything. Speaking of which, I understand that you may be getting involved in the McKechnie case?
- He told you! He really shouldn't have done.
- Well. I am sure no harm's been done.
- How long have you been involved?
- A month or so. Perkins is my junior. And as I know about your conference this evening I'll tell you that we met with Mr McKechnie a good three weeks ago. Nice man. I think you're going to have big problems on this one. Still. All good money for us at a time of need.

Adam tensed. He knew Pemberton of old. If he had been on the case for that length of time it was inevitable that he would have put his snoop, Jackson, onto following Bateman. He was glad now that he'd told Bateman to watch his step.

- So you recommended to Arthur that I should have the brief?
- Wanted Bateman to have good representation. And there are few better, Adam. Eh? You could always bring Preston or Storman into lead you if you find me intimidating.

He couldn't quite keep the disdain from his voice. But Adam didn't react. He knew that Pemberton, as his Head of Chambers, held all of the cards. The burnt-out note was a serious warning.

- And anyway. I thought you needed some light relief from what's left of your work on that Tribunal.
- Yes. Well, thank you for getting me on to it. I had a day of it today actually. And thank you, I suppose, for recommending me to Arthur. I've never been instructed by Jones before. Seems a nice chap.

It was Pemberton who had got him the job on the Aliens Tribunal. He treated it as his little joke. Adam wasn't sure how much it was fellow feeling that had led him to make the gesture. He knew that Pemberton didn't really rate him. He knew now, also, that Pemberton may have reason to hate him. War, and the threat of war, coupled with Nazi persecution of the Jews over a number of years had led to an influx of refugees from across Europe. The trickle that began in 1933 had turned into a deluge by the time of the declaration of war when there were almost thirty thousand enemy nationals of sixteen and upwards seeking sanctuary in London alone. It had always been very difficult to obtain licences to come to Britain. No one would be admitted without a guarantor, and, save for domestics or those with special expertise, all immigrants were precluded from employment. Those who came from Germany were not allowed to bring any of their assets beyond their personal luggage and furniture. Sometimes these were sprayed with acid by the German authorities to render them worthless. Things were not often better when they arrived in England. They were not wanted and there was widespread antipathy, to the Jews particularly. When war broke out they were often regarded as the reason Britain was involved in an unnecessary conflict. Or worse, as spies and fifth columnists.

When, in September 1939 over a hundred tribunals were set up to consider whether, on the grounds of national security, Germans and Austrians in this country should be interned or, if not interned, subject to restrictions, Pemberton put Adam forward and he got one of the posts of chairman. In addition to deciding for or against internment he had to consider whether applicants should be exempted from the various restrictions placed on enemy aliens by the Aliens Order of 1920. Was the man or woman before him, usually poor and ill dressed, a "refugee from Nazi oppression"? A procession of stateless persons and those of dubious nationality – ten to fifteen cases a day at first – would come before him to plead their cases, from all parts of Germany, Austria, Czechoslovakia. And from all walks of life. Some had been long settled in London and were married to British nationals.

By April of 1940, however, fear of a fifth column led the authorities to intern everyone anyway regardless of the decisions of Adam and his colleagues, so all that work was rendered pointless. Tribunal work was less time-consuming now and less remunerative accordingly. He was glad of it all the same.

– You haven't asked me about Julia.

Pemberton's eyes gleamed.

– Sorry. Yes. How is she? I haven't seen her about much. Is she here

tonight? I don't think I've seen her.
- I'm sure you haven't seen her (*again the gleam in his eyes*). She is out with her "war work" but she should be back before the party's over.
- What exactly does she do?

Catherine had been very curious about this from the first time it had been mentioned. Adam knew but could say nothing.

- Ah! Classified I'm afraid. Apparently Julia, with her connections … is regarded as being entirely trustworthy (*again looking at Adam*). Important work but rather sensitive. She'll be here soon, I'm sure. She's been looking forward to it. Had her dress dry-cleaned for the occasion. Had all her dresses cleaned actually. We must keep up appearances. I must be off to say hello to a few other people. Enjoy the party. Adam, I know you like a smoke. I'll get one of my people to give you a packet while you're here.

And he glided away. Adam didn't like the look on Catherine's face. Her eyes had narrowed and clouded, as though she was completing some complex mathematical equation, and he knew well that was a bad sign. She fiddled with her hair.

- Well. He was a bit queer just then.
- How do you mean?
- All that heavy emphasis. As though he was saying something very important when it was only the same old self-important tripe. Or was he trying to say something else?
- I'm sure that was just old Pemberton being himself (*Adam tried to keep the anxiety out of his voice*). I wish he wouldn't rub it in about the Tribunal. We didn't all get the chances that he got.
- Hmm.

He beckoned a waiter and obtained a refill of champagne for them both and then suggested to Catherine that they take a turn around the room to see who else was present. It was crowded now. Little groups of people had gathered around the trays of food and were talking animatedly. Pemberton's eldest glittered in a red dress. He saw various members of his Chambers and noticed, with the usual shame, that those of his age or a little older or younger were all in uniform. In fact, the majority of those bordering his age group were in uniform. There was no need for uniform at a cocktail party but it carried its own kudos and marked the wearer out from people like Adam. In fact, it was worse than when he passed people in the street and caught their disapproval, for here he was captive to it, naked before their badges of valour. He'd joined the Home Guard but it would have looked plain ridiculous to turn up in ill-fitting khaki.

The room was spacious. Elegant, as were the people who filled it. He saw one or two High Court Judges in their ill-fitting dinner jackets. His work-suit was shabby by comparison. The women sparkled in diamonds and silk and the war seemed an eon away. He looked at Catherine, standing defiant by his side in the blue dress. It had seen many seasons and he hoped that people wouldn't recognise it. Or at least be too kind to say anything cutting. All members of his Chambers who weren't at war were there. His was a moderately sized set but, as Jones said, well respected. They were about sixteen in number. Only about eight of them had avoided active service. Although he had thought of himself earlier that evening as a divorce lawyer, he – and they – did anything that would come along. Crime, running downs, contract cases. It was all money after all. Apart from Adam they could rely on age or Whitehall responsibilities or something equally grand for the absence of a uniform. They could usually rely also on a private income and a trust fund as well.

He could see Preston and his wife taking centre stage and talking confidently to someone who looked like a Cabinet Minister and Perkins (*also working in Whitehall when not at the Bar*), gathered with the younger, and uniformed, members of Chambers. He suddenly felt out of place and the desire to socialise left him. Stipples of sweat pricked his face and neck. He wondered when Julia was going to arrive. He had calculated that she would be here by about 8.15 or 8.30 but that was a good forty-five minutes away. He pulled out his Woodbines and shucked a cigarette. His smoke joined the comfortable smog floating over the crowd and he relaxed a bit.

– Adam! How are you? Glad you could make it. Hullo Catherine.

Adam relaxed further: it was Jack Storman KC, one of his favourite people in Chambers. Now approaching fifty, he had been in silk for about eight years and had somehow achieved that without making any enemies. Or none that Adam was aware of. He had a bluff, common-sense approach to life and was free from the pettiness and pomposity that annoyed him in too many of his colleagues at the Bar.

- Good do, this. Must have cost old Jeremy a small fortune. Still, he can afford it. Glad to see you're both here. Haven't seen you at one of Jeremy's functions for quite a while.
- I don't think we're on his 'A' list. It's a bit of a relief to see you here.
- Oh. Don't let all that bother you. Mostly, they're a bit of a bore. The usual people sounding off with the usual stories. You seemed to be having quite a conversation with the old boy. He doesn't usually give his guests that amount of time. Pretty serious, too, from the look on your face.
- Oh not really. Rationing. Work. The black market. Usual sort of thing.

Storman was unconvinced. Of that Adam was sure. He hoped that he wouldn't start cross-examining him. His skills were well known.

- Jeremy's been acting a little oddly lately. Can't quite put my finger on it. But he seems a bit, well, preoccupied. Made a point of mentioning that you were coming when I asked who would be here.
- We're in a case against one another. When I mentioned "work" that's what I was talking about.
- Ah! Well, that solves that then. Surprised that Julia isn't here. Still (*motioning to the girl in the red dress*) Jenny's doing a good job as stand-in.
- Julia will be along later apparently.
- Good. Always liked her. And she does keep the old boy young. He was a real misery before she came into his life.

Adam hadn't seen Storman's wife.

- Where's Margaret?
- We all of us react differently to what's going on, Adam.
- Has she left London?
- Nothing like that. She wouldn't leave me behind here. She just doesn't like coming into the centre. Did I tell you about that time I broke my

right wrist and Margaret came with me to court *every* day so she could take a note for me?

And then Storman went on to tell them a number of stories about his early days at the Bar – and went out of his way to compliment Catherine on her dress. Peter Preston KC and his wife made their way over to join them. He had the polish and gleam of a marionette, fresh from a good rub with the chammy leather. He leaned over Catherine and gave her a courtly kiss on each cheek, and then nodded a greeting to Adam. Adam looked at his watch and lit another Woodbine.

- Lovely to see you, Catherine. How's Deborah?
- She's very well. We sent her back out to Edenbridge when the bombing started. She didn't want to go but Adam was insistent. I suppose he was right to be.
- Absolutely right. We've been doing our best to get people to see sense but they're ignoring the posters and taking no notice of our radio broadcasts. Don't want to be taken for mugs again.
- Do you think we're past the worst of it now?
- I'm afraid not. This is just a respite. They'll be back in force. Have you managed to fix her up with a school up there?
- We got her a private tutor. An old lady who lives on the farm. She's doing very well. We hope she'll be able to follow us up to Cambridge in due course. The war should be over by then.
- Beauty and brains. She takes after her mother.
- She didn't get blue eyes from me. And her hair is darker. I want her to go to Girton but Adam thinks she should apply to somewhere more accessible, like Newnham. He always found Girton something of a trek.
- He's never been one for much physical exertion, have you, Adam?

Adam shook his head affably, dragged on his Woodbine and turned to Cara. She'd been watching Preston with mild amusement and was in no hurry to speak. She took a sip of champagne and ran her fingers across a blue velvet fleur de lys on her right hip. He was about to speak when he felt a surge of sputum rising with the smoke from his lungs. Somehow he got his handkerchief to his mouth before the coughing started. Catherine and

Preston carried on talking. He recovered his composure and folded the handkerchief away. Only Cara noticed the large splash of crimson spreading against the white. She spoke more gently than she usually did.

- We've not seen much of you lately, Adam. Are you very busy?
- Not really (*a stifled cough*). Busier than I was. Home Guard work fills up some of the time.
- Peter's running all over the place. I think he enjoys an emergency. Most people would be content to be close to the levers of power and forget the Bar, but he wants to have both. He wants to come out with a good war.
- I'm surprised the Ministry lets him.
- Oh, he's very persuasive. He's already looking beyond the war to his position in the peace. Is it possible to be a High Court Judge and a Cabinet Minister at the same time? Peter usually gets what he wants.

But not always, thought Adam – and remembered Catherine's entreaty earlier.

- I don't think so. But you're right: he does still seem to make it down to the Bailey on a regular basis, though he's pretty cagey about what he's up to.
- That's Peter. Loves a bit of intrigue. Don't know why he's so secretive about it. Careless talk costs lives, I suppose.

He sensed her indiscretion.

- What exactly is he doing?
- I suppose I'd keep quiet about it too if my powers of advocacy were sending men and women to their deaths on a regular basis.
- What?!

Cara's voice sank beneath the hubbub:

- Spy trials. Treason. Our people pick them up, put the papers in order and give them to Peter. He does the rest. Says it's as easy as shelling peas. He's got a one hundred per cent conviction rate, which he's rather proud of. He must shut his mind to what happens when they're taken below.

– How long has he been doing this?
– Oh. Most of this year. He probably started last year but it took a little while to winkle it out of him. He says it dovetails nicely with his other Government business.
– It must be a lot of work.
– Not really. I've seen the briefs. They're wrapped in white tape and marked secret but they're never very bulky. It seems that we're catching them as soon as they land so they're usually red-handed. I don't know how we're managing to find out about them so quickly. Peter says it's just good luck but I think there's more to it than that. That's one thing I haven't been able to prise out of him. Doesn't Jenny look lovely this evening?

She motioned towards Pemberton's daughter as she floated from group to group and he sensed that she wanted to move the conversation away from these disclosures. Jenny had come out the previous season into a world of war and uniforms, but she seemed to be thriving on it. Adam saw Preston ushering Catherine towards the parliamentarian.

– Let me introduce you to Sir Henry.

Adam saw the pleading look in her eyes.

– Yes, she's coping well. Not quite the season Jeremy had anticipated.
– She'll probably net a Brigadier. She can look after herself … I think the dress she's wearing belongs to Julia. I recognise the pattern of sequins.
– The two of them seem to get along very well.
– It was difficult at first. But she's very fond of the children. I think she misses them almost as much as Julia does.

No one missed them as much as Julia did, of that Adam was sure. She wrote to them several times a day and cherished the scribbles in reply.

– I believe they both drive out to see them quite frequently.

– Anything more than that?
– I don't know.

The conversation faltered. Adam delved into his pocket for the handkerchief, felt the familiar viscous slide and discreetly removed his hand. It was 8.35. He saw Catherine in animated conversation with the Minister and looked around at the spinning room … the cawing crowds. No air raid sirens so far. Preston probably knew when and where they were likely to hit. They were probably safe. Where was Julia? The sweat was cold. Cara sensed the lull and gazed around the room running her hand over crimped brown hair.

– We'll have to go soon. Peter's due at the Dorchester. He's cultivating
    that man Channon over there. Are you going on somewhere?
– Just home.

He caught Catherine's eye. A slight tilt of her watch hand told him she wanted to leave. Cara saw it and read it. He warmed to her.

– Peter *does* go on sometimes. Poor Catherine. What a lovely dress she's
    wearing

Adam was sinking. He had nothing left to say. He was saved by Samuels announcing that Mrs Pemberton had arrived.

Chapter Four

Conversations stopped and all eyes turned when Julia entered the room. She wore the attention lightly. In dowdy skirt and serge top she didn't look out of place amongst the satin and lace. An enormous smile broke open her angular features. Adam felt physically sick.

- Sorry I'm late everyone. Don't mind me and enjoy the party. Merry Christmas! I've got to get changed.

But rather than leave the room she circulated. Adam turned back to Cara and tried to resume their conversation but was as conscious of her movements amongst the guests as one would be of a breeze that moved from tree to tree fluttering the leaves behind one. She came nowhere near him. 8.45.

- Forgive me, but you have an awful cough.
- I'm sorry. I hope I haven't been hitting you with it.
- I don't remember it being so bad.
- It's worse in the winter. It doesn't like December. Catherine and I went to Marrakesh a couple of years ago and that seemed to help. But it always comes back.

Adam reached into his pocket, reordered the handkerchief and then used it to wipe his mouth and to wipe away the persisting sweat. He was conscious of a rattling in his chest.

- Have another cigarette. That should get the stuff out of your lungs.

Adam shucked another Woodbine, lit up and breathed in deeply.

- We'll have to go soon. Catherine wants to catch the 10.08.
- You really don't look at all well.
- I'll be fine.

But Adam could feel his gorge rising and knew that what was left of his handkerchief would not help him. The sweats were back and he felt cold and vulnerable. Catherine was still laughing with the Cabinet Minister. His vision blurred and conversational noise undulated around him. Nausea.

- Would you excuse me, Cara, I'm terribly sorry.

Samuels directed him to the first floor. He collapsed in front of the toilet bowl and retched. His eyes were closed and streaming ... When he opened them the bowl was streaked red. The harsh, antiseptic toilet paper was no use and so he wetted down his kerchief and used that to clean himself, checked for stray spots of blood, and then pulled the chain. His eyes in the mirror were bloodshot and pained so he splashed his face with cold water and reordered his hair. 9.05. He needed to talk to Julia; but this was a disaster. Everyone wanted to talk to her. The written word was enigmatic and would keep him awake. They rarely saw one another now. Better to stay silent than to take risks.

He emerged onto the landing and paused before heading back down. Photographs filled an alcove. Jeremy and Julia on their wedding day: she looked so young clutching his uniformed arm. Black and white with a hint of sepia. Julia with Stephen. Julia with Sebastian. Julia with Stephen, Sebastian and Agnes. Carefree. That was probably 1936. Julia and Jeremy posing for the society photographer at the 1936 Middle Temple Ball. She was wearing a low-cut backless white dress. He'd already known her for ten years by then – she'd been terribly young when Jeremy first introduced him to her as the new junior tenant – a marquee had been set up near the rose garden and he and Catherine had attended. They'd been married eleven years and she was still fresh-faced. Free from the disillusionment that now affected her. As always, all eyes were on Julia. But he managed to mark her card and had one of her ten dances.

Margaret Storman had also been at the Ball but with a tall elegant man, whose face he did not see, rather than her husband. The man had ushered her towards the photographer and left her to have her picture taken alone. Jack's wife had been radiantly beautiful as she struck the necessary pose. Adam and Catherine had decided that they could not afford a picture.

Adam knew that he had danced too close, but that had been his first opportunity in ten years. It was a slow waltz. He let his hands slip onto her bare back. His fingers typed their message. Pressing and kneading in a way that could be explained on the drink or the scents in the air – or as nothing. Longing and desire. Morse which, if you didn't understand the language, meant nothing. Julia, inevitably, understood. When the dance ended she took his hand and led him outside. A foxtrot was starting up inside. Alone, they rounded the corner of the marquee, and, clear of the crowds with the Thames shimmering, she turned into his arms and they were kissing. Astonished and delighted, he let his arm move up to her breast and caressed it through the silk. A body desired seems all the more fragile and ... human ... when first touched. Then it was over.

– I've wanted to do that for years.

He glanced up and saw, through the gloom, a slim figure in white tie leaning against a tree. The man slipped away. "Probably a drunk taking some air," Adam had thought.

– We'll be missed.

And she led him back inside like a co-conspirator. The following morning he wasn't sure it had actually happened. He could have dreamt it. There was no evidence to substantiate it. Four and a half years on, he remained unsure. Unsubstantiated memories are blown away like dust. If he had wanted to prove it he would not be able to do so. He had no alcove of photographs. No letters. No cards. No outward thing to connect him with her. Nothing. No one would believe it anyway. The record was as clean as his conscience. Nothing.

He turned to descend and then heard familiar footsteps on the stairs above. Julia was wearing a long black velvet dress. A diamond necklace shimmered at her neck. She hadn't expected to see him there.

– Adam! You look terrible.

– Julia. It's good to see you.
– I can't talk. I'm late. I've got to rush. The party's breaking up.

That familiar evasion was there. For obvious reasons he knew her capacity for deception. They needed to talk and he could see that she wasn't prepared to do so.

– I got the note. He can't possibly know.
– I can't talk, Adam.
– He couldn't possibly know.
– Did you destroy the note?
– Of course I did. How could he possibly know?
– He's my husband, Adam. He's not a fool.
– But there's nothing.
– There's always something, Adam. We could never hide everything. I can't see you anymore.
– I need to talk to you.
– Things are going to move more quickly than you know. I can't speak with you.

Adam remembered Pemberton's professional tactics.

– Look. This is important. Do you know a man named Jackson?
– I'm in a hurry, Adam.
– Jackson. Tall, corpulent. Late forties. Tends to wear a low-brimmed fedora.
– I don't think he's part of my social circle.
– He's a private detective. Jeremy always uses him. If he suspects anything you can be sure that Jackson's been watching us both.

Julia had been attempting to pass him and head on down the stairs, but at this she froze.

– Oh God!
– You recognise the description?
– Someone like that has been hovering around the Temple. I've seen him loitering when I go to morning communion.

– Has he been coming into the church?
– No. I'm sure he hasn't. But over the last few weeks someone like that has been there when I go in and when I come out.
– Christ! Does Jeremy know about the church?
– I don't think so … I don't know anything anymore.
– We need to speak.
– I really must go. I'll be missed. We can't be seen together. We can't meet again.

There was no way Jeremy could know about them. Nor would Julia tell him or even hint to him. She had far too much to lose. But Adam knew her ability to dissemble. If she wanted to end it, this would be as good a way as any to do so. A surfeit of caution to protect her marriage and her family. He had watched the door closing over many months and now the last chink of light was disappearing.

– I don't think you love me anymore. I don't think you ever loved me.
– If it makes you happier to believe that, then believe it.
– We've got to talk
– We can't.

They had been talking for five minutes and time was running out. It was his last hope:

– Okay. I understand. But listen. If you're right that something is brewing we need to be sure that we are saying the same things. Can't we just meet once so that we can deal with all those points where we are vulnerable? I accept it may be dangerous. But it's more risky not to.
– I'm late, Adam … but I'll think about it.

And then she was gone. He watched her dash down the stairs and noticed, bleakly, that the black dress was backless.

****

Adam allowed her a few minutes. When he returned to the reception rooms the party was indeed coming to a close. There was a drift towards the door, where Pemberton stood with Julia at his side, their backs to him as he re-entered. He squeezed past the farewells, taking care not to acknowledge either Julia or her husband, and re-joined his wife. She was still speaking with Preston and Channon. Cara stood silently by them and continued to smooth imaginary creases in the blue velvet.

- Are you all right? You dashed off rather suddenly.
- Yes. I'm sorry about that. I'm fine.
- You were gone a long time, Adam.
- Was I? Just cleaning myself up. We ought to be going, Catherine.
- Peter's going on to the Dorchester. Sir Henry's promised to take him and Cara onto the Café de Paris afterwards. Such insouciance.
- Don't be such a prude, Catherine. I wish we could persuade you and Adam to join us. Life can't come to a standstill because the Germans are dropping a few bombs. Trust me on this. I don't think London's their main target at the moment anyway. Chips knows Poulsen and he can get us in. The Café de Paris is probably the safest place to be during a raid.

Chips Channon wore white tie and glowed with self-confident assurance:

- Poulsen knows his market. We need more entrepreneurs like him. He's been laying down the champagne all year. They reckon he's got 25,000 bottles of the stuff and I think we should relieve him of a few magnums.

Adam had heard of Sir Henry "Chips" Channon. He'd been in the news earlier that year over the Halifax affair but was as well known for his social life. He knew also of the Café de Paris. Martin Poulsen had re-opened it the previous month to considerable fanfare – "the safest and gayest restaurant in town, twenty feet below ground". It was beyond Adam's pocket.

- It's very enticing, Sir Henry. But I think we'll take our chances in Dulwich. Come on, Catherine, or we'll miss the train.

He was anxious to be gone. He knew that the mention of trains and Dulwich told Channon all he needed to know about them.

   – Perhaps we'll be able to persuade the Pembertons, then, Peter?

Adam ushered Catherine to the door and they said their goodbyes. Pemberton's arm rested stiffly on Julia's waist. They seemed brittle.

   – Thank you both for coming. Samuels will get your coats. And your gas mask, Catherine. Perhaps we can have a discussion about the "ABC mystery" on Monday, Adam?
   – Goodbye Catherine. Goodbye Adam. Thank you for coming.

Was there more warmth in the word "Catherine" than in her utterance of his own name? Adam wondered. A glassiness in her eyes? A momentary veil of sadness over her features before she brightened for the next guest? They pulled on their coats and headed out into the darkness. Air raid sirens began sounding as they made their way to Victoria.

✳✳✳✳

Sixteen letters. Four words – three and a half words. How could so little change so much: "J knows. Destroy this." They sat in silence on the train and the letters and the words spooled and shifted through his mind: "this knows J. Destroy." "J knows this destroys." "Know J destroys this." "Destroy. Destroy. Destroy."

Chapter Five

(Monday 16th December 1940)

Adam emerged from Temple tube at 8.15 on the Monday. Fifty-eight hours since he was last there. Fifty-five and a half hours since they had left the Pembertons. Three thousand four hundred and eighty minutes. He felt as though he had been awake through all the hours. Heard the seconds of every minute. Sleep was never easy when bombs were falling, even at a distance. But the dreams weren't usually so bad. Images in his mind blended with the noise overhead. Some droned above him incessantly. Others fell like strings of incendiaries through his mind. Planes left the imprint of their sounds in his memory long after the raids had ended …

… Julia, in her backless black dress, descending a never-ending stairway away from him. "Goodbye Adam." Veils over her eyes.

– I don't think you love me anymore. I don't think you ever loved me.
– If it makes you happier to believe that, then believe it.

"Destroy this." A glass ashtray with blackened paper in it. "J knows." A sheet of white paper with a red heart shape in the middle of it, flames curling up the edges. Blackness heading for the heart.

– There's always something, Adam. We could never hide everything.

And around every corner there was Jackson. The corpulent detective rooting out petty secrets.

"On the evening of the 21st October 1936 at about 7 p.m., acting on information received, I made my way to the Feathers Hotel in Chippenham. In the car park I saw a blue Bugatti motor vehicle, Type 49, registration number IPF 262, which I knew to be registered in the name of Mrs Julia Pemberton. By telephone enquiry I established that she was staying the night in Room

Four which was on the first floor at the front of the building. At about 8 p.m. I saw the lights go on in Room Four and a person I recognise as Mrs Pemberton drew the curtains. At about 8.30 p.m. I saw a man I recognised as Mr Adam Falling arrive by taxi and enter the hotel. I know Mr Falling as a barrister and I have given evidence in cases in which he has acted.

At about 6 a.m. I saw a taxi arrive at the hotel. Mr Falling emerged from the hotel and got into the taxi. I followed the taxi back to Chippenham station. Discreet telephone enquiries confirmed that no one by the name of Falling had checked into the hotel that night."

He'd seen many of the man's reports. But he couldn't have been there, or at The Stafford, or any of the other places. Pemberton couldn't have known. And that thought droned overhead all weekend: How could Pemberton know?

– There's always something, Adam. We can't hide everything.
– I can't see you anymore.

Flames advanced across the white paper and the red heart turned brown, then black, then disappeared.

Destroy this.

****

He picked his way past the ruins and through the Temple to Stirrup Chambers. People were filing into the Church for the morning service. Julia was probably in there already. He wanted to go in and sit with her. Speak to her. But the image of Jackson, lurking somewhere unseen, restrained him. It must wait. If he busied himself with preparing that morning's hearing at the Westminster County Court, that would pass the time.

Pemberton was in Adam's room and seemed unsurprised when Adam entered. He was standing languidly before Adam's shelves surveying the books, his gold spectacles set at a raffish angle.

– Ah. Good morning. Adam. Thought I'd come up and see you about our ABC mystery. Interesting books. I tend to keep my literature at home. No time for anything but law when I'm in Chambers.

- I like a bit of reading when the work is slow.
- All sorts of interesting authors here: Evelyn Waugh … Conan Doyle … even some Aldous Huxley. Altogether avant-garde. Wilfred Owen. Siegfried Sassoon. I like the war poets. My sort of era. It was as black as they painted it. All that death. Never got round to getting any of the books myself though. *Down and Out in Paris and London*. Now I'd never come across this Orwell chap.
- He's a personal favourite of mine. More for his journalism.
- Interesting. Interesting.

Adam didn't know where this was leading but felt vaguely uneasy. Pemberton had never shown any interest in his literary tastes before. He wasn't the literary sort. He glanced at his ashtray and saw, with a little shock, that it was empty.

- Thank you for inviting us to the party on Friday. Catherine and I very much enjoyed ourselves.
- Oh. Not at all. It was a great pleasure to have you there. Bit of a risk with the date of it, eh? Friday the thirteenth. "Unlucky for some."
- Did Peter persuade you and … Julia to go onto the Café de Paris?
- He had a very good try. As did that Channon chap. But Julia was fairly whacked and we had an early night. Jenny and a few of the officers went along though. Had a very good time by all accounts. Did you have a good weekend?
- Usual stuff: Catherine did her WVS and I was on duty with the Home Guard. Pretty uneventful. And you?
- Rather disruptive actually. Julia's been very preoccupied lately. She hides it fairly cleverly. Only someone who knows her well would notice (*said with emphasis*). Says she's worried about the children so she absolutely insisted on driving out to see them on Saturday. Still there actually. Probably won't come back until tomorrow. Changed her shifts around.

Adam hid his disappointment.

- Ah well. At least you can be sure that she and the children are safe. Look, Jeremy, I would like to discuss this McKechnie case with you

45

but I'm due in Court fairly soon. Can it wait until this afternoon?
–   Yes. Of course. Come down and see me when you've a minute.

He made for the door.

–   Oh. By the way. I took the liberty of cleaning your ashtray for you. I know there's a war on but we must still try to keep up appearances.
–   Thank you, Jeremy.

Pemberton opened his hand to reveal the blackened paper.

–   It's funny, you know. You can burn a piece of writing paper but somehow, sometimes, the water mark survives.

A pale ghost of the letter "P".

Chapter Six

The Temple Church, consecrated in 1185, was one of the oldest "round" churches in England. The rounded shape of the nave, fifty-nine feet in diameter and standard for the churches of the Knights Templar, was based on the Holy Sepulchre Church in Jerusalem where the Templars were founded. An enlarged chancel was consecrated in 1240. Dark purbeck marble was used extensively inside the church and marble tomb effigies lined the inner walls. In the nave itself several prominent knights were buried. Over their tombs, marble sculptures of the dead soldiers, their helmets still in place, a sword and a shield still ready across the body, protected their remains. Some had their legs crossed in supplication, an indication that they had died in the Christian faith. As if to be buried on sacred ground would absolve them of their many sins. Legs crossed at the ankle indicated that the dead knight had been on one crusade. Two crusades if crossed at the knee. Three if crossed at the thigh. Well, that was what was said anyway. They had lain there silently since the thirteenth century. The discovery of America. The dissolution of the monasteries. The Great Fire and the plague all came and went and still the knights remained. They had survived all the wars untouched and continued to lie in silent supplication awaiting the final judgment, whilst under the marble the bones turned to dust. Now an air raid shelter had been established in the crypt beneath them.

Regular visitors to the church hardly noticed them. There would always be time to study them more carefully. Marble soldiers lying silent. Some with their legs crossed. Inevitably, it had been Julia's idea. Communication had been difficult. He could not telephone her at home. Samuels would always answer the phone. She could not call him at work. It would be even more dangerous to call *him* at home. Letters were out of the question. Their arrival at home or chambers would be noted even if they were destroyed after they had been read. There could be no evidence of any kind. It could not be known that they communicated with one another. That they met. Adam had desperately wanted to know what that first kiss meant. What licence it gave? Whether that was all? What should he do next? What more, if anything, did Julia want? But whenever he saw her, which was infrequently, she was with Jeremy or the children. There was nothing in her demeanour that gave anything away. She was the dutiful wife, the loving mother. But for someone who was watching there was the slightest whisper of unspoken desire. Then, in the early autumn of 1936, as he was on the way to the library, he saw her emerging from the morning service.

– The crossed-legged knights!

And before he could reply or question her, she went on her way. He watched her disappear up Inner Temple Lane and then, edging past Lamb Building, went on to find the books he needed. Unable to concentrate, he went back to the church. The knights lay there as they had always lain. Grey and dark. He looked at them anew but they were unchanged. He understood.

The following day he listened for the bells chiming the hour and, when he felt that the service would be long over, he crept out from his room and went to the church. Rays of light from the upper windows, under the coned roof, penetrated the gloom of the nave. He was alone. The knights lay as still as dead time, as they had lain when lawyers would conduct important interviews with clients in their presence. Grey and quiet. He walked from knight to knight. From grey to grey until he saw a flash of white within a stone shield. Thick white paper folded into a small square. The note was unsigned. He had never seen her writing before. Black ink in strong curved lines:

– Green Park. Next Wednesday. 12.30 p.m. Destroy this.

Destroy this. She was only to write those words once more, and that would be over four years later.

He rushed back to Chambers to check his diary and saw to his dismay that he was booked to be in Court in Edmonton all of that day. His one chance seemed to have gone. He took a plain piece of paper and wrote a hurried note:

– Can't do Wednesday

And he gave details of his diary for the following two weeks. Following her example, he did not sign it. He knew, if she read it, she would destroy it, so he did not repeat that injunction. Folding it up, he took it and placed it where her note had been. Then he waited. A complex set of papers sat on his desk but he could not concentrate. He moved the papers around. Read the lease, making desultory notes. Read the correspondence. Went to the library and shuffled around the books. Went back to the church. The note was still there. That was the pattern for the day and, by home time, he was no further forward with the lease. The note was still there within the shield. Should he remove it? This was madness. He took it out. Unfolded it. Re-read it. Crumpled it up and left. Halfway to the tube he changed his mind, smoothed it out, took it back and replaced it.

The following morning he was in early. He noted the times of the early morning service posted outside the church. In Chambers he resumed playing with the lease. At 8.45 a.m. he went to get a newspaper and read it until nine. At 9.15 he went back out to get some Woodbines and noticed the churchgoers dispersing, the chaplain at the door saying his farewells. He didn't see Julia amongst the crowd. He opened the Woodbines and smoked one by Fountain Court. At 9.30 he went back towards Stirrup Court and then diverted at the last moment back into the round church. It was empty again. He saw his folded square of paper still there under the marble ankle and sat down heavily in the rear pew, pretending to pray.

Looking down the chancel, he tried to think about his actions. What did he want? This was madness! She had wanted a private moment with him to explain her actions, and he was giving her a check-list of his dates. He was happily married. He had an eight-year-old daughter. He was making himself available to a married woman. Two weeks of his available dates and times. Asking for intimacy. Using the church as his go-between. Madness. He went to the effigy and removed the paper, crumpled it up without reading it, went back to his lease and got down to work.

He thought no more of it until he was heading back to Temple tube. If Catherine found it in his pockets it would be difficult to explain. Passing a litter-bin he paused, removed it from his pocket and threw it in. Madness.

He slept badly that night. "Why?" was the bell-beat of his dreams. He didn't know why. He couldn't even remember exactly what he had written.

The note was still there when he passed by the following morning, gleaming white amongst the other rubbish. He took it out and unfolded it. What exactly had he written?

– It works! Next Thursday, then. Green Park. 12.30.

The same curved writing. Black ink. He read it and re-read it. Had she been following him, and replaced her note for his in the bin? He wanted to keep the note forever. To frame it. But instead he crumpled it up and put it, almost reverently, back in the bin. The morning service had already begun. Julia would be inside saying her prayers. He was too late to reply. But Thursday was a week away. In Chambers he wrote a series of notes and rejected them all, throwing them away. His pen paused over his fifth attempt. And then:

– Yes!

And so Adam returned to the Christian fold. Julia wrote a short note in reply which said simply, "Thursday, then," and their correspondence began.

Chapter Seven

Arthur was particular about the Chambers' Diary. A big red book with a black leather spine. Entries would be made in pencil at first, and then, when the booking was confirmed, he would painstakingly over-write in ink next to the initials of the barrister concerned. He was at this work when Adam returned from Westminster County Court. Seeing Adam, he put down his Parker:

- Ah. Mr Falling. Mr Pemberton asked if you would go and see him about the McKechnie case when you returned from Court.

He pulled out a large gold watch.

- He said 3.30 would be a good sort of time.
- Thank you, Arthur.

Adam returned to his room and put down his papers. How could he explain the watermark? Why hadn't he noticed it? Was it peculiar to Pemberton's note paper or could he use a broad-based excuse? He needed to talk to Julia. He needed a cigarette. He pulled out the packet to shuck one out but fumbled so that they all fell to the floor. Scrabbling on the carpet to pick them up, he was unable to get them back into the packet. He broke two matches before he succeeded in getting a light, and then drew the smoke deep into his lungs.

Twenty-five past three. Time for one more cigarette.

Pemberton was reading a three-page typed document, holding it between his finger and thumb, when Adam entered. He put it down carefully, obscuring all but the signature with his blotter. Adam recognised Jackson's spidery writing.

- You've been smoking.
- I like a cigarette after Court.
- I can always tell, you know. The smell of Woodbines sticks to the clothing. I don't suppose you even notice it after a while.

Adam thought back to the party:

She's been looking forward to it. Had her dress dry-cleaned for the occasion. Had all her dresses cleaned actually. We must keep up appearances.

And:

There's always something, Adam. We could never hide everything.

- You wanted to discuss the McKechnie case with me?
- Mrs McKechnie ... Victoria, as I'm sure Bateman calls her ... has gone to see Farquarson at 3, Paper, so it looks like we'll be having a good punch-up. Can't see how the two of you are going to get anywhere with it though.
- You've brought Jackson in, no doubt?

Pemberton allowed his finger to trace slowly across the spidery signature and took a sip from a glass of water.

- Yes. Good man, Jackson. I can always count on him to dig up the dirt somehow. He's remarkably ... *unobtrusive* – for such a big man. You never know he's there until it's too late.
- Well, Bateman will be denying adultery.
- Yes. Of course he will. Don't they always?
- There's absolutely no evidence and if there's nothing to dig up, Jackson won't be able to help you (*Adam hoped that Bateman was being sensible*).
- It's the little things that catch people out, Adam.
- You can't build a case on three letters written from time to time in a diary.
- Bateman will have to explain where he was on each of the ... the "ABC days". People think they can get away with lying about the seemingly insignificant, but they soon get tangled up. Inconsistencies emerge.

A big lie to hide a smaller lie ... and so on. It's one thing for a man to tell a lie in the comfort of these rooms but quite another in the Royal Courts of Justice ... when ... he's under oath. Serious matter, perjury.

Adam didn't reply immediately. He needed time. In the silence, Pemberton slowly unscrewed the barrel of his Mont Blanc and held the pen over the glass of water. He pressed the pressure bar against the sac and a bubble of black ink emerged onto the nib, then dropped to the bottom of the glass. Wisps of black swirled upwards until the filigree dissolved and the ink infiltrated all of the water.

- One lie, Adam. That's all I'm going to need.
- This is all about money, Jeremy. If poor old Bateman's wife hadn't died, none of this would be happening.
- Ah, yes. The money. Poor old Bateman. All that money for the death of a woman he was being unfaithful to. Wonder what she would make of that. I expect she would be rather pleased to see it going into McKechnie's pockets. And yours and mine, for that matter.
- What do you say the letters "ABC" stand for?

Pemberton gazed out of his window onto the ruins of Fig Tree Court.

- Why do people do it, Adam? When they have so much to lose? Take Bateman. He sleeps with the wife of someone who is in a position of superiority to him at work. Forget about the insurance money for a moment. If I prove adultery against him, he could lose his job. Even if he doesn't lose his job, things will be pretty uncomfortable for him at work.
- That's precisely why he wouldn't be sleeping with McKechnie's wife.
- You're right, I suppose. It would be uncommonly foolish to carry on an affair right under her husband's nose. One small slip and McKechnie would be able to study the man at his leisure. Uncommonly foolish.
- Mrs McKechnie will deny it. It's not just Bateman. It will be their combined word against his.
- She'll be worrying about her children. Should have thought of that earlier. If I were McKechnie I'd make sure she saw as little of them as possible.

Suddenly Adam felt very cold.

– Anyway, with Arthur's help I intend to get this matter into Court as quickly as possible. Petition in December, contested hearing in early April. All these wartime reconciliations are clearing out the Lists. I can move extremely quickly when I want to.

Things are going to move more quickly than you know. I can't speak with you.

– Anyway, Adam. I am sure you will protect your client's interests. I expect a Request for Further and Better Particulars from you in the next few days. No doubt you'll be seeking chapter and verse.

He was relieved that he had managed to predict at least one thing.

– It will be with you by tomorrow.
– Good. Perkins will give you the dates when we say adultery took place by Friday. Poor Bateman. His dear wife is lying dead in the road and he's in bed with Mrs McKechnie.

Chapter Eight

(Monday 16ᵗʰ December 1940)

Julia wouldn't be back until Tuesday. She wouldn't make the morning service prior to Wednesday. There would be no note. No flash of white within the marble shield. Arthur would be suspicious if he didn't go. And he didn't trust Arthur. Every evening since late 1936, if at all possible, he had spent a quarter of an hour in the church at around four. "Praying", he told his clerk. Irrational, the idea of prayer. But people wanted to believe you. Just as they wanted to believe in God. Irrational and harmless. They would no more question you about your habits of prayer than they would ask after a mad aunt. Catherine knew him too well to be taken in by talk of God. Too many earnest undergraduate conversations on the subject. But the aesthetics of the building – timelessness in the face of war – satisfied her.

He was badly shaken. He had felt that Julia's attitude to him had been cooling over the months since the declaration of war and that her note, the attitude on Friday, were her way of distancing herself from him. Pemberton had no evidence. But there was ... there seemed to be ... an edge to everything he said. Perhaps it was his imagination.

The church was cold and empty. The knights lay still. He pulled out his Woodbines and then thought better of it. In his mind he attempted to count the number of notes he had left with them. Had picked up. Life had been so comfortable then. Julia would attend the morning service and leave him a letter. He would pop in during the afternoon and replace her note with his. It was quieter before the war and often he could write a reply there and then. Primarily, their notes set out their movements for the day or week ahead and they would plan their time together around their respective diaries. It was even possible to arrange times when it would be possible to speak by phone. As time went by a little more affection, and then love, crept into them. But they would all be destroyed before the day was out.

He had gone to Green Park that Thursday. Not knowing the park; not knowing what to expect. Where in the park would she be? He'd looked at the A to Z and saw that it was not small. He needn't have worried. She was waiting by the gates near the tube, a baby at her hip. She saw him coming and smiled broadly. His heart leapt. All the reserve he had witnessed over recent months was gone. She wore a nondescript blue dress: a mother, amongst other mothers, enjoying the afternoon with her baby. She kissed him openly on the lips:

- Meet Agnes.
- Hello, Agnes.

She was very pretty. Like her mother. Big blue expressive eyes and a garrison of blonde curls.

- I rarely come here. I'm not known, I don't think. Let's walk.

And she headed off, past the deckchairs, towards the trees. The autumn sun was warm. He followed, pulling out a cigarette as he walked. And they disappeared into the innocent crowds. Deep into the park she leaned against an anonymous tree.

- Have you met Agnes before?
- She's very beautiful.
- The boys are very fond of her. I was worried they'd be jealous.

She stroked the child's face and rearranged her curls. Agnes smiled at them delightedly and made some incomprehensible affectionate noises.

- Little dear. This is Uncle Adam.
- Hello, Agnes.

He gently squeezed her cheek between his finger and thumb.

- Jeremy says that she resembles me as much as Jenny resembles *her* mother.
- She must be fifteen now?
- Just. I think she accepts me at last. Such an awful thing. She was very

young when it happened, so she never really knew Joan. I think that probably helped.

- I never knew her. She died before I joined Chambers. Jeremy was such a grump then. He must have loved her very much. He was so lucky to find you.
- Oh, he loves ... he loved her a lot. Every day Jenny grows more like her.
- Beautiful little Agnes.

Adam didn't know what to say. This wasn't what he had expected. He didn't know what he expected. He leaned out across Julia and ruffled the baby's curly head. Soft. Like gossamer. Julia was so close, the crowds so distant. The smell of fresh cut grass hovered in the air. Something else ... intangible ... was drawing him, like iron to a magnet. He felt her cool hand on his neck as she pulled him towards her, and the metallic cold of her wedding ring, and they were kissing. And Agnes looked at him with those big blue eyes and gurgled.

- Don't worry. She can't talk yet. And she won't remember. It will be more difficult when she gets older.

A promise of years ...

In the weeks that followed, Adam found the time to go to Green Park once or twice a week. Usually Agnes was with them, and in a sense that made it easier: a happy married couple out with their baby. Julia told him all about her children. Stephen was five and Sebastian three. Hardly begun in life, but each day was chronicled to him. She talked about Agnes as well, but somehow he felt he knew the little girl anyway. She was beginning to talk and he knew that this time must now draw to a close. He was beyond explanation. Julia stopped calling him by name in her presence. And their letters flowed.

She told him, too, about Jeremy. His successful campaign during the Great War. His medals. His wife Joan left behind. Armistice Day and the great reunion. The birth of Jenny. Then the influenza. Joan dying and Jeremy's world falling apart. The drink, the collapse, the slow recovery, and then her arrival on the scene. A fresh-faced debutante as his angel of mercy.

There was an Indian summer that year, and in early October they were lying on the grass. Julia gazed at the sky, a misty distance in her eyes:

- What are you thinking?
- Nothing much.
- You can tell me.
- I was wondering whether it was possible to love two people at once. It's not that I don't love Jeremy ...
- I'm very fond of you. What would Jeremy do if he found out?
- He can't find out.
- But if he did?
- He'd be very hurt ... disappointed ... I think he would be very angry.

He felt a strange elation. They had talked about everything. But they had never talked about love. Never talked seriously even about affection or fondness. He had been spending secret happy hours in her company, but all they had done was talk. Love was the great taboo. But, by grandmother's footsteps, they had been edging nearer to it. It didn't seem real. Why should she be interested in him? He was, comparatively, a failure, albeit a happy failure. Thin and feeble with a weak chest. He lit another Woodbine:

- Why do you see me? What can you possibly see in me? Why not someone like Preston?

She shuddered.

- I've never liked him. And I wouldn't trust him. Those hands every-where. He did try to start something. Suggested that he book a room in a hotel somewhere so we could meet during the afternoons. How grubby! I don't trust him ... I trust you.

And so, talking and sitting in the sun, the smell of fresh cut grass around them, they edged nearer to the abyss.

****

As well as talking about her children, and about Jeremy, Julia would talk about her aunt Beatrice. Beatrice was her father's only sister and had never married. Rumour had it that the man she loved had died at the Somme. Other rumours suggested that she had established a home with another woman. Julia said she was never sure. Certainly she shared a small house with another woman outside Chippenham and ran a bookshop there. Beatrice had been ill since early summer and from the start of their correspondence Julia's visits to her in the nursing home had punctuated her timetable of availability. She charted her aunt's swift decline. And then, suddenly, she died. Julia was distraught. The funeral was to take place ten days after the death. The children were deemed too young to attend and Jeremy was defending a murder in Manchester. So she made arrangements to attend alone. It turned out that there was only one bedroom in her aunt's home after all, and so she decided to stay the night before at the Feathers Hotel in Chippenham.

Chapter Nine

(Wednesday 18ᵗʰ December 1940)

There was no note. On the Tuesday evening he'd left one inside the shield for her to collect after the Wednesday communion. He'd taken a sheaf of unacceptable drafts and scrunched them into the bin near Temple tube before taking the final version to the church.

– Must talk to you. J recognised the watermark.

And after the morning service it was gone. No answering note replaced it. He returned to the church on the hour, as though, by some alchemy, a note would appear later in the day. Perhaps it had blown away or been found by someone? But there was nothing. He checked the bins around the Temple in case she had written a note, thought better of it and then disposed of it. Nothing again.

It was dark now. He returned slowly to Chambers and, climbing the stairs, he heard a commotion coming from the waiting room and the sound of Arthur shouting. An unusual thing: his clerk was usually able to get his own way quietly. There was another voice as well, unfamiliar and guttural but equally determined, though not as loud. Adam was too preoccupied to be other than mildly curious.

Arthur was standing with his back to the door, his luxuriant grey hair out of place, and it seemed almost as though he was begging. Before him sat a man Adam did not recognise. He looked poor and out of place and he was clutching an old brown leather briefcase to his chest. Adam would guess he must have been about fifty-five. A small man, he wore a wispy intellectual beard and a look of quiet defiance.

– For the last time. You must leave here. You haven't got an appointment and you haven't got a solicitor. I can't let you talk with my barristers.
– I will not be leaving. I am used to waiting. I can wait.

– For God's sake, go!
– I will not be leaving. I must see him.
– I'm not going to go round in circles with you any longer. I shall call
  the police.

A look of alarm crossed the man's face. Then:

– I will not be leaving. I am used to waiting.

Arthur seemed to have met his match. Adam could see that the man
shared not only an ethnic background with his clerk but also his obstinacy.

– What's going on here, Arthur?
– I'm very sorry about this, Mr Falling. But this ... gentleman is insis-
  tent that he must speak with you. I can't get him to leave.
– Well, I'm afraid it's out of the question.

At the mention of Adam's name the man's face lit up.

– Mr Falling, I must have a speak with you.
– It's out of the question, I'm afraid, Mr ... ?
– Hoffer.
– Mr Hoffer. You heard what Arthur said. We are simply not allowed
  to see members of the public without appointments and without
  solicitors.
– But I have come a long way today to see you.
– If you want advice you must contact a solicitor and then the solicitor
  can make an appointment for you to see me.
– I do not want advice. I want help. And it is not help for me.

This was getting out of hand. Adam did not have the mental energy for
riddles, and other thoughts were swimming through his mind.

– I really don't follow. Why do you want to see me?
– I thought you would recognise me.
– Why on earth should I recognise you?
– You dealt with my case on the tribunal.

Adam looked at the man afresh and tried to place him. He had dealt with hundreds of cases. Hoffer had risen to his feet and put down the briefcase. He squared up to Adam and stood as would a man before a tribunal, smoothing down the fronts of his jacket pockets as though awaiting the passing of a sentence. Yes, there was a vague familiarity now.

- You are from Czechoslovakia?
- You remember me? Yes. I am a doctor. You were very good to us. Friends said to us to expect Grade "A" or "B" but you graded me "C".

It was coming back to him now. Hoffer and his wife had been before him at around the turn of the year. They'd boarded a boat in Gibraltar, swung out into the Atlantic to avoid the mines, and eventually swung back to land at Liverpool. From there a train had taken them to London where they were put up at the Empress Hall in Earls Court pending their appearance before Adam. He had the power to grade them "A" which would have meant internment, "B" – restrictions on their freedom, travel bans and a prohibition on the ownership of cameras or large scale maps – or "C" – friendly and to remain at liberty. Adam did not like the xenophobia of the popular press at the time, and saw the man for what he was: harmless and scared; his dignity almost off him.

- I'm afraid that I was acting in a judicial capacity then. I cannot act for you in connection with that. You must go.
- I have taken days to find out where you worked. You have a very nasty cough.
- Why have you come to me?
- Because you were kind to us.
- I can do no more for you. Your case is over. I have graded you "C". You should be grateful that I did so.
- I do not come for myself. I come for Tomas Novak.
- Why can he not come and speak for himself?
- He is in prison. He is in very great danger.
- He has been interned?
- No. He is in prison. They say he is a spy. But he is not a spy. They took him away three days ago. He has told some silly little lies.
- Shall I call the police, Mr Falling?

– No, Arthur. Mr Hoffer. I will speak with you but there is little that I can do.

Adam was grateful, in a way, to find someone who had more serious problems than he himself, and so he invited the man up to his room.

– You shouldn't be doing this, sir.
– I am not seeing him as a client, Arthur. I won't be charging anyone for my time.

Hoffer told him about Novak. They had met soon after his tribunal hearing. Hoffer had managed to find work in a bookshop and Novak used to frequent it, browsing the shelves but never buying. The two Czechs became friends. He soon learnt that Novak had evaded the immigration authorities and had not declared himself. Buoyed by his own experience at Adam's hands, Hoffer had attempted to persuade him to declare himself. Novak would not. He feared that he would inevitably be interned or deported. When Churchill came to power in May 1940 and much of Adam's work was undone, he was confirmed in that view, and with each passing day it became more difficult for him to come forward. He found what work he could from black marketeers and received pauper's wages. And then in mid-December the knock came at the door and he was taken into custody. The authorities appeared to have very specific information that a Tomas Novak had entered the country a few days earlier and was living in the street he in fact lived in. His first lie was to say that he had indeed just arrived in the country, thus confirming official suspicions. When he tried to change his story to say he had been in the country for some ten months, that simply increased his unreliability in police eyes. It had been impossible for him to get any alibi evidence as, should any others come forward, they would have to explain why they had not informed the authorities of him earlier. Hoffer did not know where the original intelligence leading to his arrest had come from.

– It has to be a mistake. Tomas is harmless. All the time I knew him he did nothing wrong. He is a fool but he is not a spy.
– As a tribunal chairman Adam had to know about the Treachery Act, passed when Churchill came to power:

"If, with intent to help the enemy, any person does, or attempts or conspires with any other person to do any act which is designed or likely to give assistance to the naval, military or air operations of the enemy, to impede such operations of His Majesty's forces, or to endanger life, he shall be guilty of felony and shall on conviction suffer death."

Novak was in very serious trouble. There was no alternative to the death penalty on conviction. No pleas for leniency could be heard. Adam thought of Preston and his little briefs wrapped in white tape. An hour or two's reading before bed. Easier than shelling peas. Hundred per cent success rate. Preston, polished and gleaming. A quick trial at the Bailey and then off to the Café de Paris.

- But what do you want me to do about it?
- Will you represent him?
- I've never done a spy trial before. There must be others who would be able to provide more help than I.
- I trust you. I know you will be fair.
- You will have to see a solicitor for Mr Novak.
- He won't be able to pay you much. I can try and collect some money to cover your fees … I don't remember your chest being so bad.

Adam should have stopped him there. His mind was beginning to wander back to the church, to Julia. But he was tired and it was easier to say yes to the man. He needed distraction. Distraction? Not the right word.

- Do you know when he is likely to be tried?
- About four weeks' time.

Four weeks! He would probably be in need of his own solicitor by then. He gave Hoffer the names of three solicitors whom he thought might be able to assist, and then said his goodbyes. It was late and he should be getting home. Instead, he went back to the church.

Chapter Ten

(21st October 1936)

Julia had opened the door to him, smiling. She was wearing the white silk backless dress and looked more beautiful than ever.

- I had to wrap it in my weeds to smuggle it out. It didn't look very funereal. I *couldn't* have explained it to Jeremy.

Over her shoulder he saw two glasses of champagne sparkling on the dressing table, long blue velvet curtains pulled almost closed, and a large double bed.

- You're lovely. Thank you. I thought I was never going to get through to your room, you were permanently engaged.
- I'm sorry. I was saying goodnight to the children. Usually I'm there to tuck them in. Did you have any trouble with reception?
- No. They were fine. It was as you expected.
- I'm not known here. Come in so I can shut the door. It's good not to be known.

Adam slipped in and put his coat – and the overnight bag concealed beneath it – down on the floor near the bed. She brought him a glass of champagne and they toasted themselves, she in the white dress, he in his striped trousers, his hair still slicked back from the wig. At their feet his coat and overnight bag. They kissed. Her tongue hard. Hard, her tongue. His hands explored her back and her sides. Time stood still and he told himself to remember every moment (although the following morning he could not). When eventually they drew apart she motioned to a silver platter of sandwiches over by the bathroom.

- That nice Mr Forsyth on the desk got us some supper. We must do things properly.

- I've never done anything like this before.
- Neither have I ... I'm scared, Adam.
- I'm scared too.
- I don't know how I'm going to feel in the morning. I may never want to see you again.
- That's what scares me most of all.
- Did you have a good journey across?
- No problems at all. Disentangled myself from the others, messed up my bed to make it look slept in, and caught the first inconspicuous train I could out. Travelled first class so there was no chance of seeing anyone I know. There's a train back at 6.30 tomorrow and I'll be back in Bristol well before eight.
- I'll ring down later to book you a cab. Six a.m. should be fine. We have nearly nine hours then to ourselves. Let's have some sandwiches.

They sat down on the side of the bed, eating sandwiches, talking and drinking the champagne. Taking their time. By good fortune Adam had been on circuit at the time of the funeral. There had been little planning. Each knew the other's movements. A word here, a sentence there sufficed. Impressionist brush-strokes. Wisps of paint creating the full picture of what they wanted to do – what they had to do, bringing them both to the Feathers. There was no talk between them of what was to happen during the nine hours of privacy they would have. No talk of love or tomorrow. Adam watched her as she ate, the silk shifting as she moved her arms, until presently they had finished. She brought her arm up behind him, caressing his hair, and they moved towards one another and kissed again. A gentle, familial embrace. He felt an urgency, like a migraine, in his skull and began pulling at her, trying to bring her fully onto the bed. But she resisted and rose to her feet.

- Everything should be done properly, Adam.

And standing before him, she brought forward her shoulders and shrugged her way out of the dress until she was standing naked except for a golden locket around her neck. He began unbuttoning his clothing until he was dressed only in his underwear, and getting to his feet he walked her round to the pillows, conscious of his obvious arousal. Julia looked at him with a warm, slightly amused smile as he made a courtly gesture and beckoned her to lie down.

And then the phone rang. Julia picked it up in her usual voice and he could hear the tinny sound of Pemberton coming from the earpiece. After the usual courtesies – asking after her journey and the hotel –

- And what are your plans for the evening, darling?
- Well. I wasn't sure what I should do. At first I thought I would go down and eat in the restaurant. But then I decided that sandwiches in the room would be much more pleasant in the circumstances.
- Were the sandwiches good?
- Oh. Very good. Cucumber ... and salmon.
- And what of the rest of the evening? It's still quite early.
- Well, I think I'll turn the light out soon. It's going to be a difficult day tomorrow.

And so, without a beat, Julia spoke truthfully to her husband. Adam hoped that the conversation would end there but it did not. Jeremy had had a hard day in court and wanted commiserations from his wife. She gave them, speaking gently and with the right degree of concern or encouragement as necessary. As the conversation continued she climbed onto the bed to make herself more comfortable. Silently, to ensure he was not heard, and still wearing his underwear, he laid his head on her breast. He noticed that she had a little tummy that he had never seen when she was upright or dressed. She fondled his hair and carried on talking until Adam thought that the conversation would never end and he gradually drifted away.

- Oh! He didn't! I don't know why anyone let him become a Judge ...
- But Jeremy, I'm sure you did everything you possibly could ...
- But how long could he possibly have cross-examined your client for? How very unfair ...
- I'm sure you did everything you possibly could ...

And gazing down at her nakedness, feeling her hand on his hair and half listening to one side of a conversation, he fell asleep.

She was gazing down at him and rearranging his hair – as once he had seen her playing with Agnes's curls – when he awoke. She smiled at him as he opened his eyes.

- You really do need a haircut ... and you look tired. I think you should come to bed.

And she pulled back the blankets so that they could both climb inside.

****

Hours later he awoke. It was very dark, and at first he was only aware of her breathing beside him. Slowly, as his eyes adjusted, he could see her, lying on her back beside him with the covers down. A line of silver from a thin moon gave her whole body a sheen. He reached over so that he could run his hand gently from her breasts down to her toes, and then watched her as she slept. Silent now, he remembered the sounds they had both made earlier. His alarm would go off at 5.15. Only four and a half hours' sleep at most. And he did not want to sleep. He ran his hand up her side again and rested it on her and lay watching, willing himself to stay awake.

The alarm caught him sleeping. He flailed about before finally stopping it. Julia was still where he had been gazing at her, and the ringing brought a fuzzy wakefulness to her. She didn't speak as he got up and bathed quickly. He had fifteen minutes before his cab was due. She lay there, unmoving, watching him. As beautiful and as naked as she had been all night. Before dressing he leaned over her to kiss her. Looking down at her he tried to imagine that she was still wearing her dress, so that in future when he saw her dressed he would be able to imagine her naked. She raised a languid arm and put it around his neck.

When he looked back on that moment he could never really remember what had happened next. Did he climb onto her or had she pulled him down? It was as though she had engulfed him and he was lost in her, their bodies touching at every point. Her hips shifted beneath him and he felt her ankles edge out around and over his feet to lock them together, pinioning him to her, her arms tight around his shoulders. He had a sensation of searing heat throughout his body, of being turned inside out. And then a deep sense of release. And peace.

Five minutes perhaps, and then they lay quietened and still. His head against hers. Her hair wrapped around his face as he lay into the pillow. She whispered:

– I love you.
– I love you, too.

And it was said. Adam felt his words in reply coming from somewhere unexpected. The words themselves were unexpected. And although they had spent a long night together, it was as though that last was the first time.

****

It was an early funeral. The party attending was small. Julia wore a black woollen dress with a high collar and long sleeves. A small black hat with a long veil covered her features entirely. She introduced herself to Beatrice's companion and the two of them led the cortege. She bent her head and prayed during the service.

Remembering her aunt. Thinking of her children. Of how soon she must introduce them to death. An onlooker would see only grief worn with dignity. Under the veil she was smiling:

– I don't feel any guilt. I don't feel guilty at all.

She said it to herself over and again.

Checking out of the hotel, Mr Forsyth on the desk politely handed her a brown paper bag containing Adam's underwear. They had found them wrapped up inside the blankets of her bed. She disposed of them on the way back to town.

****

The sirens were beginning to sound. In the darkness of the Church the knights lay still and unsubstantial. Adam was thinking back on how he had felt as he climbed into the cab for Chippenham station that morning. Changed. Utterly changed. When Julia told him, subsequently, that she had felt no guilt, he realised that he hadn't felt guilt either. He was so much without guilt that the possibility of it never struck him. In fact, there had been a deep joy, an elation to be lying against her as she, naked, spoke to her unsuspecting husband about the mundane evening that lay ahead of her.

But it was an elation tinted dark from the start, for he had seen how easily she could dissemble and feared that one day she would lie to him. But then, after that night, he would know as and when she was doing so.

He looked in the direction of the knights. No message. No indication of where she was. London in the blackout. Millions of people, and Julia moving somewhere amongst them, threatened by the same bombs and shrapnel. Would she be alive in the morning? She did not know where he was either, but she didn't seem to care. At least, she knew whether the places he was likely to be frequenting were being or had been bombed.

He thought back to the vision of her naked and moon-tinted during that night. It was over four years ago.

They had not spent a night together since.

He lit a Woodbine (it was only a building after all) and made his way to the bomb shelter in the crypt.

****

The sirens sounded more faintly in south London but were still audible. Catherine looked across at the bakelite telephone crouching silently in the corner of the room. He had not rung. He would not be home now. Was he safe? She switched off the radio and changed into a nightdress and dress-ing-gown. Only the distant rumble of aircraft and the sound of explosions broke the silence. She folded up her day clothes and placed them carefully in a drawer.

What to do now? He promised always to ring if he was likely to be caught out in a raid. She wandered about the empty house, picking up his clothes and putting them away. She polished his shoes, went up to bed and turned out the light.

She got up an hour later and switched the light back on. Opening her wardrobe, she got out her clothing for the following day and arranged it neatly over a chair. No word. She went down to check that the phone was properly on the hook. What to do? Opening a drawer in the kitchen, she took out a pile of letters:

– Dear Mummy and Daddy ...

But the words blurred for her and she could not read on. She sat down to write to Deborah but could think of nothing that was capable of being said.

Yes, one of millions of people in London under the Blitz that night. Adam knew where she was and how to contact her, but had not done so. He thought instead of Chippenham and how Julia had betrayed her husband.

Chapter Eleven

(Wednesday 18th December 1940)

Few bombs fell around Westminster that evening and Julia and Antonia found time to wander into the room containing the Permanent Record Map. Eric, the Plotting Officer, was busy preparing a consolidated list of blocked roads. It should have been sent to the various fire stations almost twenty-four hours ago and he hardly noticed them as they entered the room. He was a rotund man who looked permanently baffled. He scratched at the few wisps of hair left to him and wrote in spasmodic bursts. Eric was the keeper of the maps, and he was as busy after the "all clear" as he was during the raids.

Julia was an "in" telephonist at the Westminster Report Centre. Antonia, an old friend, was a Utilities Clerk. It was glorified secretarial work for both of them. Julia would receive and record all reports of air raid damage from Wardens' Posts, Fireguards, Gas Identification Officers and others. Standing orders emphasised the need to use the right form and the importance of a well-sharpened pencil. All messages received had to be read back to the person reporting, in the interests of accuracy, and all messages would be kept on a clip and then passed onto a messenger for onward transmission. It was nowhere near as glamorous as Jeremy had made out at the Eaton Square party. But one did need to be trusted. Information about where bombs had fallen and the extent of any damage, human or material, was extremely sensitive, as was the whereabouts of the Report Centre itself. Julia had to differentiate between calls on exchange lines, on direct lines and those on TEM 0111 extensions. In all cases it was necessary to obtain details of the identity of the caller before giving out any information about herself or her whereabouts. Calls on exchange lines were answered giving her number. Direct lines were answered with "Westminster Control", and calls on extensions with "Report Centre".

Each bomb that landed generated a secondary explosion of paperwork. All incidents were reported to Julia or the other "in" telephonists in the Report

Centre and it was necessary for there to be multiple copies of every message received. There were standard instructions about the replacement of worn carbon paper. The messages would be passed on to the Plotting Officer, the Operations Officer, the Tally Board Officer, Special Action Officer, the Fire Clerk or the Utilities Clerk, depending on the nature of the report. Antonia's job, as Utilities Clerk, was to receive supplementary reports notifying damage to gas and water mains, electric cables, sewers and telephone lines. Then she had to pass on the necessary intelligence to the utilities companies concerned, particularly if the damage was impeding rescue work. If a bomb fell within fifty yards of utilities services she had to ensure that the relevant company was notified. She, like Julia, had to hand all her message forms to the Plotting Officer both during and after raids.

The pre-war sexual hierarchy was more resilient than the buildings and people being bombed. Women in the work place, particularly moneyed women, remained an anachronism. Duties were distributed according to gender rather than intelligence or initiative. The Plotting Officer's role was pivotal. Antonia would have been more than able to cope, as would Julia, but the job had gone to Eric, a retired bank clerk who lived in Pimlico. It suited a clerical mind. He would give each new "incident" a number and mark its position on the Operations Map with a large pin. The incident number would then be marked on all the messages that related to it. It was his responsibility to distribute the message to the various officers and clerks affected by it. Smaller pins were placed on the Operations Map to denote fires (red pins), complete road blocks (blue pins), partial road blocks (pink pins), poison gas (yellow pins) and unexploded bombs (green pins). These were his duties during the raids and he had many others after the "all clear".

Eric did not look up. He was a shabby man of sixty-seven wearing last week's shirt. He was having trouble cross-referencing the reports and looked more perplexed than usual. Julia or Antonia could have made a better fist of it and would have had a better understanding of what it meant for the capital. Perhaps that was in itself a good reason to disqualify them from the work.

The Permanent Record Map was crowded with details of the bombings. Each mark was accompanied by a handwritten incident number. There were now almost twelve hundred of them. Eric's delicate bank-job italic had become increasingly cramped as the raids continued. The Permanent Record Map had a bad case of measles. Public morale had been boosted by the increased noise from anti-aircraft guns in recent months, even though they had done little good and probably more harm than good. The damage to confidence if the Permanent Records Map, with its evidence of the bomb virus, had been made public would have been incalculable. Press reports were strictly censored and only those members of the public fortunate, or unfortunate, enough to work in the Report Centre knew how bad it really was.

Antonia's hair was pulled back under a colourless turban. She said:

- I'm thinking of having an affair.
- Is it anyone I know?
- Just generally. Why should it be anyone in particular? It's always dark and I wouldn't have to know him. He'll probably be dead after a few mornings anyway. Or *I* might be, clutching at my handbag.

Julia's interest was pricked. Antonia was conventional but she might have meant what she said.

- Why have an affair with anyone?
- It's the dark. All this darkness. I'm lonely. I need to be held by someone new. Anyone new, I suppose.
- They're all pretty useless out there.
- But they're scared of dying.
- I really don't know why. This just accelerates things.
- If everything is getting faster, then we have to act more quickly.
- To achieve what?
- I'm lonely. There must be so many lonely people out there. One of them might hold me. Just for a night. I don't expect anything of them.
- You'll wake up the day after and you'll still be lonely. We're all lonely at the end. At the end we're all alone.
- How long do you think it's going to last? Could I fall in love with a German?
- You can fall in love with whomsoever you want to. It's a rational choice with irrational consequences.
- But would it be wrong? To fall in love with a German, I mean?
- If you do decide to fall in love with someone you must try and be sensible about it.

- I only want to have an affair. Everyone else seems to be.
- It's all dust and wreckage. Not like the pictures.
- I'm bored.
- I wouldn't have an affair.
- Why?
- You'd be swapping one boring man for another boring man.
- He'd be boring in a different way and that would be something.
- You'll more than double your problems. The lying. You start by lying to your husband but it can never end there. If you lie to him you must lie to other people too. Sooner or later you'll have to start lying to your lover – and somewhere along the way you begin lying to yourself. It's inevitable.
- Would you lie to your husband?
- He'd never forgive me ... and there's everything else of course.

Antonia paused and studied her fingernails, splaying her right hand out in front of her. The nails were long and bright red – the only part of her private life she brought to work. She adjusted the turban covering her long brown hair. Most women wore such headwear to conceal a lack of grooming, but Antonia's hair was sleek and clean.

- Do you mind if we make another pot of tea?
- Not at all. I'll go and put the kettle on.

Julia reached down into her bag and pulled out a bag of tealeaves and her little flask of milk.

- It's one of the few consolations of this job – that you bring in your real tea and fresh milk; it's a relief to get away from the powdered stuff. How do you do it?
- Jeremy's very clever like that.
- Well, you know what I think of Jeremy ... but he is very good with the provisions. That was a lovely party last Friday, even if we turned up late and I was dressed like a menial.
- I did suggest that you bring along a dress to change into. I'm sure nobody noticed.

Julia immediately regretted that. Antonia loved to be noticed. She and Julia had married in the same year and everyone agreed that, in marrying the Honourable Reginald, she had made a good match. But with their respective marriages and their successions of children they had drifted away from one another. It was an unspoken drift; the unsaid truth was that neither of them liked the other's husband. Antonia thought Jeremy an old, self-important and pompous bore. To Julia, Reginald Badenoch was a shallow, worthless rich man.

Antonia was still beautiful but it was a beauty blurred with sadness. Where once she was high-spirited and forthright, she had become acerbic and cynical. Yes, she was still beautiful, but it was true to say that she made very little impression at the Pembertons' Christmas party.

- Perhaps I should have worn one of your dresses. Jenny looked ravishing. She's turning out to be quite a bright spark. She's so different – forgive me – from Jeremy. Joan must have been very beautiful.
- Oh. She was. Jenny is beginning to look more and more like the photographs of her mother.
- Don't you find that difficult?
- Not really. I'm not Joan and I think Jeremy understands that. I can quite understand why he keeps photographs of her around the house.
- I'd hate that. I know that you don't like Reggie and I can understand why. But at least I'm not competing with a dead person. Don't you find the age difference a bit of a bore?
- Jeremy's all right, you know. Although his circle of friends is a bit on the crusty side.
- If I were you I must confess I would be tempted ...

But then Antonia checked herself and changed the subject.

- It's hard to believe that this time next week it will be Christmas Day.
- Are you staying in town?
- Probably. And you?
- I'm hoping we can get out to spend some time with the children.
- This is such an odd job to be doing. Don't you ever wonder about the things we're charting? Who's under the bombs? If anyone we know has been killed? That sort of thing?

- I try not to.
- I find it so hard not to talk to people about it. I do think that they should know just how bad it is getting.
- You just like to gossip.
- Maybe. But when I read the papers and see all the things that they don't say it makes me angry.

Julia let the conversation drift over her. A nagging anxiety that had been scratching at her all day had returned. Jeremy always locked his study and his desk, but several years ago she had taken the opportunity to have spare keys cut. She kept them under a loose board in the pantry. That morning, after he'd left for work, she had used them.

The study was as orderly as Jeremy's mind. She knew why he had always locked it. A large partner's desk with a red leather top dominated it. This was his space. There was a large photograph of Joan on the corner of it. A photograph of the two of them nestled amongst his books on a shelf at eye height. His reading was mostly political autobiography with the odd memoir from some long-forgotten silk. A long clock ticked in the corner, the golden pendulum swinging languorously. She looked around to see if he had a picture of her on display but could not see one. There were pictures of their children however.

She had waited until the servants were busy downstairs. It was unheard of her to enter this room and it would be difficult to explain. At a distance she heard Samuels giving instructions. His loyalty, at the end, was to her husband.

The desk key was slippery in her hands. She had never used it before. It caught in the lock. The central drawer was the obvious place to begin. With a wrench the barrels turned. There was a cache of letters, addressed to him in France in faded blue-black ink, and tied together with barristers' red tape. She recognised Joan's elegant hand. For a second she considered untying them and reading but thought better of it. More importantly she saw a large buff envelope of recent postmark next to them. Before removing it she looked carefully at its position in the drawer. She held her breath as she slipped the contents out and then read with growing alarm. It was a report from Jackson. Jeremy, through Jackson, knew far more than she had realised. How much more did he know than was contained in this summary? On a first reading, Adam was in very deep trouble. She seemed to be in the clear at one level, but her options were being closed down. She knew that she too was being targeted.

Under the enquiry agent's report was another envelope. It was from his solicitors. She had been in the study fifteen minutes now. With every minute the danger increased. But she couldn't risk waiting until another day. She heard Samuels climbing the stairs. The study door was closed and the waste bin empty. There was no obvious reason why he would come in.

– Gemma! Did you clean Mr Pemberton's study?

She saw the door handle turn down. There was nowhere to hide. In the distance she heard a muted girl's voice replying. The handle wavered and then returned to its usual position.

– Very well.

And she listened, holding her breath, as he mounted the stairs to the next floor. She would not be able to leave the room in any event now until he had reached the next landing and moved on. She really had little choice but to read his solicitor's letter. The envelope was made of expensive paper, as was the sheet within. The signature had an exotic flourish:

The timing of the petition must, ultimately, be a matter for you. My advice is that there is sufficient evidence available for you to succeed, albeit that you do not, as yet, have a cast iron case. If you are correct in your assessment that Mr Falling and Mrs Pemberton are aware of your suspicions, then it is likely to become increasingly difficult to obtain conclusive evidence. My own view is that there is good cause for waiting at least a few days longer. I say this because, in the first instance, it may be that Jackson will be able to obtain something damning. My second reason is more pragmatic and human. Next Wednesday will be Christmas Day. I know that you are particularly concerned about the effect that this will have on Jenny. I acknowledge, also, that you are concerned about Mrs Pemberton's children who, whilst young, will be very affected by the course that you are intending to follow. A petition before Christmas will affect all the children, probably for the rest of their lives, far more than a petition in early January. My own advice ...

"Mrs Pemberton's children"? That hurt her more than the imminence of the petition and the catastrophe that awaited her. She did not need to read further. She had known and accepted that she would have to take second place in his affections to Joan. But they were his children too. They were in no way inferior to Jenny. And he wanted to take them away from her.

She took a deep breath and then lost control. An enormous sob broke from her, so loud that she was convinced that Samuels must hear it; her shoulders shook and tears fell onto the solicitor's letter, staining the signature. She pawed it in an effort to clear away the damage but the signature just became more smeared. She bit her lip in an effort to stop the noise, and then held her breath. That was supposed to stop hiccupping. After a minute she drew her fingers across her eyes. There was a mirror in the corner of the room and she made for it. She was still beautiful. Her long blonde hair was less curly than Agnes's. Her eyes were still blue but they were red-rimmed and bruised with tears. Dark shadows lay under them. It was not just the lack of sleep from the Blitz. The tears were still visible. She could not leave the room unless she was sure she had time to reach her own dressing room.

She looked at herself and remembered what she was and how she had made herself into what she was. An old determination entered her. A battle lay ahead but she would win it. She knew what she needed to achieve. She knew what her priorities were. If Jeremy … if Adam … had to suffer … so be it. She wiped away the remnants of her tears and went back to the desk, replacing the letter in its envelope. She was careful to replace it beneath the enquiry agent's letter. She locked the drawer again, struggling once more with the barrels of the lock. Her self-possession restored, she stood beside the study door and, satisfied that there was no one around, left the room, locking it behind her, and returned to safe territory …

– Julia?!
– I'm sorry.
– Have you been listening to me at all?
– I drifted. I'm sorry.

Antonia sensed weakness in this distraction and, perhaps out of some intuition, returned to the theme that really interested her.
– I know we have very different tastes in men. And you know what

I think of Jeremy. But I am surprised that you wouldn't think of having an affair with anyone. Surely the thought must have crossed your mind?

– Antonia!

– I mean, we're good friends after all. And we have no secrets. I tell you what is going on in my mind. Is it really the truth that you've never thought of straying? I mean straying in a quiet way. One that wouldn't be found out? On one level I don't think that Jeremy would mind if you did. He's so old! It must have crossed your mind?

– You know my views on these things. You shouldn't equate my feelings with yours.

Again Julia shuddered at the reproof implicit in what she had said. But Antonia ploughed on as if she hadn't understood (*though surely she had*).

– I've set myself a little puzzle. Just to while away the time. Who would you have an affair with if you were given the chance? I thought about Preston. But then again he is rather creepy. And if he said he loved you it would be like moving his queen across the chessboard. Storman's too in love with his wife. Perkins? Now I wondered about Perkins but ultimately I think he is a bit of a bean-counter. Then I thought of Falling. I've always thought he was rather good-looking. But on the other hand, he smells of failure. And of death. So I couldn't see any obvious candidates within Jeremy's chambers.

– You do talk such nonsense.

– So I began thinking about Jeremy's other friends. But they are all so old and predictable.

– Julia moved the question back to her friend:

– So you want an affair but you have given me no clue to who it might be that you are thinking of.

– I just want to hold someone. I want to be comforted in the cold. I don't want anyone bringing baggage along.

– Have you thought of the consequences?

– I think that's all that's stopping you. I never thought you would be so … so … conventional, Julia. I thought that you wouldn't let that sort of thing get in the way of happiness…

– I didn't think you were expecting *happiness*?

80

   – You know what I mean. We could both be dead in days. Why carry on as we do?

   – I feel very old. I have my children. I'm married. I made promises.

And she let the conversation die, suddenly incurious as to Antonia's agenda, as to what Antonia would say or think if she knew the truth. Her earlier thoughts once more intruded and she thought again of Adam's note. The watermark. Jeremy had commissioned the paper himself. It was unique – something metallic in the letter "P" that allowed it to survive fire. She could not see Adam again. But she would have to. Just one more time. Everything was crumbling.

Chapter Twelve

(18th December 1940)

Bateman's face was framed irregularly behind shoulders and elbows. The fug of cigarette smoke descended around him like a mist so that he was seen in soft focus. He was talking and laughing and every so often his arm, in loud pinstripe, raised a pint glass to his mouth. Jackson, breathless, was too far away to hear what he was saying over the chatter – or to whom he was saying it. Bateman's face had a sheen on it suggesting one too many, and he had the air of one enjoying a private joke in public. It was too risky to get any closer but, with any luck, he would soon be able to make out the man's companion.

He felt the familiar thrill of the chase. He had been tailing Bateman for several weeks now but the little man had given him nothing. Usually he would moon about after work, having the odd drink in one of two or three pubs before going home, and staying home. But in the last few days, since the weekend really, he had been going all over the place from pub to pub. Never staying for more than one, or at most, two drinks in each. It was as though he wanted to try each pub in London before it was bombed out of existence. The effects of the blackout and the need for Jackson to remain inconspicuous had meant that on Monday and Tuesday evenings he had lost him either on the third or the fourth pub and been obliged, after one or two inconsequential drinks in other pubs, to resume surveillance out-side Bateman's home. Somehow, he couldn't work out how, Bateman had already been at home by the time he had got to the little house in Seven Kings. Bateman complied with the blackout regulations and so it was impossible to see whether he was there alone or in company. Jackson had been around long enough to recognise the air of anticipation in a man, and that Bateman definitely had. It was just a matter of time before he got a proper sight of the woman.

He felt for the small black and white photograph in his pocket. He did not need to take it out. He could picture Victoria's dimples with his eyes shut.

And, of course, he knew what she looked like – he had followed her more than once. After a while he had realised that she was a more difficult person to trail even than Bateman was. Instead, now, he relied on McKechnie to tell him of her movements. And her movements were irregular. Not surprising, he thought: the atmosphere at home with her husband would not have been easy. At home? Not really: they had been bombed out early in the German onslaught and so were staying with a family near to where their own home had been. That couldn't have been much of an encouragement for her to stay at home either. He knew that, when he reported back to McKechnie, his client would confirm that Victoria had not been with him that evening. Now, if he could just get a confirmed sighting of Victoria with Bateman he would have the beginnings of the evidence that Pemberton would need.

Keeping his pint glass close to his mouth, he focused again on Bateman across the other side of the bar. He was sure he himself hadn't been spotted. The shifting crowd of people between him and his man made it difficult to keep him in sight, but he was determined not to lose him this time. It was Bateman's fourth pub of the evening and he was beginning to look quite drunk. Perhaps, on this occasion, he would give himself away. And all the while Jackson was aware that there was someone *with* Bateman, just out of sight. Bateman's face was angled towards him, so the woman (*it must be a woman*) would be angled away. He just needed one or more people to get out of the way and he would be able to see her. He didn't want to wait until they made to leave, as he had taken the precaution this time, and at the other pubs earlier that evening, to station himself by the main door. It meant that Bateman couldn't give him the slip so easily. But it also made it increasingly likely that he would be noticed. He prided himself on not being noticed.

And then his luck changed. A large man who had been obscuring his view moved out of the way and he was able to see Bateman's companion. She had her back to him but he was able at once to make out her halo of golden hair. He was in business. Although she was standing it was impossible fully to guess at her height, but he would put it at about five foot six. She was responding to Bateman's jokes and she threw her head back at one of his punchlines. He found himself mentally preparing his report and the usual warm glow of professional pride in a job well done descended upon him:

"On the evening of Wednesday 18th December 1940 I followed a man I know to be Arnold Bateman over a period of about two hours. Mr Bateman went first into the Crown and Sceptre where he had two pints of beer. As far as I could ascertain he was alone at that time. Mr Bateman then left the Crown and Sceptre and made his way by an indirect route to another public house, the Mitre, about five hundred yards away. I was able to follow him unnoticed. Here he had only one pint of beer. From here he moved on and, again taking a roundabout route, made his way to the Eagle where he stayed for a pint and a half of beer. I was again able to follow him unnoticed. Finally, at about 9.30 p.m. Mr Bateman entered the Rising Sun public house. This was a very crowded place and observation was difficult but I was able to ascertain that Mr Bateman was with another party. Eventually, the crowd cleared a little and I was able to get a clear sighting of Mr Bateman's companion. It was a woman about five foot six in height. She had blonde shoulder-length hair. And I am now able to confirm that she was Victoria McKechnie, a person whom I have been directed to in the past and whom I recognised from previous sightings and from her photograph, a copy of which I attach to this statement ..."

But it wasn't Victoria.

As he was making his mental note to himself the woman had turned so that he could see her. He could have sworn that she had looked directly at him but that was probably a trick of the light and the cigarette smoke. She was laughing. Although from behind it could have been Victoria, when he saw her face full on it was more than apparent that she was not the person he had expected her to be. She was looking directly at him. He tried to look impassive, and concentrated on his pint, using it to shield the lower half of his face, and his low-brimmed hat to conceal the rest of him. Bateman's mouth was wide open in his red face and his shoulders were heaving. He must have been laughing loudly but the din of the pub drowned out the sound.

****

Bateman raised his pint glass to his lips again and took a large gulp. Silently, he toasted Adam Falling. He obviously wasn't as bad as he had feared. On Monday morning he had telephoned Jones and given him a precise description of Jackson to pass on to his client. He had suggested, perhaps mischievously, that it would do Bateman's case no real harm if we were to lay a few false trails. Bateman had set to, taking peculiar pleasure in watching the big man in the low-brimmed hat trying to avoid his eyes when they passed near one another, or, looking behind him down the dark streets, seeing the large shadow of a man trying to press himself out of sight along the walls as he followed. On the first two nights an extended pub crawl was sufficient to amuse him. On the Wednesday night he had the brilliant idea of arranging to meet someone with a passing resemblance to Victoria. He had plenty of money to play with, and if he could increase McKechnie's bills from the enquiry agent and have a little fun himself, then why not?

No. Falling wasn't such a fool. He just wished that he hadn't started getting so interested in how, where and when his wife had died.

Chapter Thirteen

(Thursday 19th December 1940)

Bateman took great pleasure in reporting his movements back to Jones, who in turn passed them onto Adam. He would have been less impressed with his barrister if he had known that Adam had his own reasons for keeping Jackson as busy as possible and a long way from him and from the Temple. For his part, Adam found grim amusement in the fact that his solicitor and his client were effectively keeping tabs on the man who had been trying to follow him.

He was sticky and dirty, his mouth as stale as an ashtray. By the time the "all clear" had sounded it was impossible to get home, so he had taken advantage of one of the bachelor flats over 2 Dr Johnson's Buildings. The owner had been away for some months although no one knew precisely where. He had notified the Inn that his flat would be available to whomsoever might need it to help the war effort. A small bedroom with limited facilities. There had been no hot water and, with little access to the black market, he had no razor blades. How had he sweated so much when it was only a week to Christmas? His shirt stuck to him and he was overly conscious of the shadow of growth on his face. He had made his excuses by telephone to Catherine, but she had been monosyllabic in reply. He had washed his hair in cold water from the basin and it had dried awkwardly, giving him a Mohican aspect. Fortunately, he was not busy and did not expect to see any clients that day.

He had bumped into Pemberton on the stairs. He, as always, looked immaculate.

- No blades, Adam? Have a word with Arthur. I'll sub you. Can't have you seeing clients like that.
- Thanks, Jeremy. Got caught out by the sirens. My razor is at home.

He didn't want his Head of Chambers to know he had no access to shaving materials.

- I'm unemployed today so that shouldn't be a problem.
- Speak to Arthur ... Didn't get home to Catherine last night? Tongues will be wagging. What have you been up to?

Adam told him, in as prosaic a way as possible, emphasising that he had been alone.

- Ruddy war! Julia was out late last night as well. But perhaps you knew that? Didn't get back until after ten. Don't know why. Wasn't much bombing around our way. Don't really see the point of documenting the bombs – *I'm sure you know that's what she's up to*; once they've fallen they've fallen. We've got to get on. It's like this Mass Observation nonsense.
- I didn't know. I didn't know anyone was doing that. I'm sure there are good reasons for it. Was she all right?
- Perfectly. Kept me up half the night talking about her children ... but I'm sure it must be the same for you and Catherine and ... and ...
- Deborah.
- Ah yes, Deborah.
- We do worry. It's not seeing her that is so difficult. I think Catherine feels it more keenly than I do.
- Jenny is in London, which is a comfort. I don't think she takes this war nearly as seriously as she should. But, I suppose she *is* still under twenty. Joan and I had such plans for her season. Not quite what we had anticipated. Then, we had thought Joan would be there for her season, and that didn't happen either.
- We're going up to Suffolk next week so that we can at least spend Christmas together.
- Splendid! Julia has decided that we should bring the children back over Christmas and the New Year, so we shall all be in London. It makes it easier for her to keep up her "war work". Her children should stay evacuated as far as I'm concerned.
- Maybe they'll give up on bombing London?
- Oh. I don't think so, Adam. Talk to Preston. They'll be back in force.

He's right about the need to evacuate. I've tried to get Julia to join them but she won't. Don't know what's keeping her here.

- Well. It's less than a week to Christmas. That's something to look forward to.
- Yes. Christmas. But, between you and me, Adam, I think the New Year is going to be infinitely more exciting. I don't think you or I will forget 1941! Give my regards to Catherine … and Deborah.
- And mine to … to Julia … and the children and to Jenny.
- Merry Christmas, Adam.

And he slipped off up the stairs and into his room. It had been the first time he had seen Pemberton since their uncomfortable interview on the Monday. In truth, he had been doing his best to sneak in and out of Chambers unseen. It was now 10 a.m. Adam felt for the note in his pocket with a mixture of pleasure and consternation. He couldn't bring himself to borrow a razor from Arthur, and in any event there was the problem with his hair. It was a waste of money and something he had never done before but he decided to go to the barber's for a shave. That meant going to his bank in Chancery Lane and a paying-out slip. If he was having the cut-throat applied to his neck, it was little added cost to have his hair cut and washed.

*****

Afterwards he felt considerably smarter and less self-conscious about his old suit and smelly shirt, and he turned to the matter in hand. Bateman was proving very difficult about a fairly innocent request on his part. He had slept very little over the previous six weeks. It was, primarily, Julia. His thoughts of her were like a ball bearing rolling round and round and across a baking tray. Why wouldn't she speak with him? What was she holding back? What had he done or said? Had someone said something against him, and if so, who? Was she seeing someone else? The thoughts rattled and rolled in his head. But in the gaps, in the silence when the ball bearing was still, other thoughts troubled him. It was something Bateman had said:

- *Died three months ago. Run over by a car during the blackout. Found out she died when I got back from work.*

He'd been thinking about this. His first thoughts were embarrassment. It was Jones's fault. He should have briefed him on her death. Then he found himself thinking about Bateman's ... Bateman's matter-of-factness. Whilst it was not relevant to the forensic process Adam, in his own mind, was convinced that Bateman was having an affair with Victoria McKecknie. And something did not ring true about what Bateman said. "Three months ago." September 1940? "Run over during the blackout." British Summer Time. When would the sun have gone down? "Found out she died when I got back from work." He works in an insurance office. What time did he finish work? How long would it have taken Bateman to get home?

– *Poor Bateman. His dear wife is lying dead in the road and he's in bed with Mrs McKechnie.*

Pemberton's throw-away comment had awoken him to the potential significance of Mrs Bateman's death. Finding out the time and place of her death had been easy. Bateman could not easily avoid surrendering that information. Two days after the Blitz began. There would have been an inquest. If Bateman was telling him the truth the evidence at the inquest could have been decisive. The obvious thing to do was to commission the inquest notes. Bateman had the money to pay for a copy-typist to prepare a record of them. There was a lot at stake financially for him. If he was to be believed, there was no truth in the case against him, yet when he asked Jones over the phone to get Bateman's approval for a transcript it was not forthcoming. Bateman, apparently, had become angry. Jones had phoned him back with the news:

– Yes, Mr Falling. There was an inquest. At Romford Town Hall. But I'm afraid Mr Bateman won't authorise me to spend the money on getting a record of it.
– Doesn't he understand why I want it?
– No, frankly. He doesn't. Says it's a waste of money ... intruding on his private grief ...
– Well. He must have been there. Wouldn't he at least tell you what happened? Who gave evidence?
– Says he was in a state of shock. Doesn't want to talk about it.
– If it helps him win his case he'll get the costs of it back from McKechnie.

 – I told him that. But he won't budge.
 – Romford Town Hall?
 – Yes.
 – Okay. Well, we'll have to leave it there. But I'll want to ask him about why he's being so difficult.

Adam had hung up. He would get no further with the case for the time being. Pemberton had promised the answers to the Request for Further and Better Particulars by Friday so that they wouldn't come through until tomorrow. He felt again for the note in his pocket:

 – Hamleys. Friday. 1 p.m.

That was all it said. He had gone into Temple Church resigned to there being no note. There hadn't been one since the previous Friday – the one he had burnt but Pemberton had retrieved. The note was folded up in the same place but it was not of the usual creamy paper but rather a nondescript piece from Woolworth's. The writing, too, did not look like Julia's. He wondered whether it might be a trap, but then decided that it couldn't be. No one could have known about the trips they had made to Hamleys together – or the time of year at which they had made them – or of the note Julia had left just before Christmas 1936:

 – Meet me at Hamleys at 11.30. I have some Christmas shopping to do. Perhaps we could steal lunch afterwards?

What better excuse for going somewhere, unaccompanied by family, than buying presents? If they were seen together it could always be coincidence. He had slipped out of Chambers at around eleven and taken the Underground to Oxford Circus. Passing down Regent Street, he had entered the store. It was crowded with shoppers and decked out in seasonal decorations and he thought he would never find her. Starting at the ground floor he worked his way around the displays and up the stairs. It was impossible. Young women and families were everywhere. Music and the scent of oranges. But she was there somewhere. He decided that when he reached the fifth floor he would begin the search again in reverse.

Then, on the third floor, amongst the dolls and the dressing-up, he heard familiar laughter sounding above the laughter of others. He made his way towards her. At first he could see only a bubble of blonde curls behind a large dolls' house, and then he realised that, somehow, she was holding it in her arms, as though for a dare, so that it almost engulfed her. She had not seen him and he was able to move round so that he could see her in profile, wearing a dark blue woollen dress and a bright red scarf, her head thrown back and her eyes twinkling as she teetered under the weight of the toy, the shop assistants laughing along with her.

- Adam! What a surprise seeing you here! What do you think of my dolls' house?

Julia was shining like a child. She lowered the dolls' house back onto its stand.

- I always wanted one. I hinted and hinted but Daddy said they were silly.
- I wanted to get Deborah one but Catherine said they were too expensive and that she'd grow out of it.
- Oh, there were all sorts of other things going on with Mummy and Daddy. It wasn't the money. I think they sometimes forgot I was there.
- Is that why you don't see them anymore?
- I never really think about them, even at Christmas. I'm not sure I even have their addresses anymore.

The shop assistants had gone back to their duties. She ran her hand over the roof and pulled open the façade to look inside at the toy furniture.

- Are you going to get it?
- Not this year. Agnes is too young yet. But she's going to have a dolls' house and we'll be able to play with it together.

They moved off and began exploring for presents, she for her three and he for Deborah, looking, to anyone that might have thought about it, like a young married couple getting ready for Christmas. Afterwards Julia hailed a taxi and they went and had lunch at Quaglino's. It was busy enough to be anonymous and, with a post-prandial stroll through Green Park, it was to become a staple of their time together. As they crossed the park Julia put her hand in his and passed him something that felt cold and multi-faceted. He looked at it with surprise. It was a piece of crystal, shaped like a tiny obelisk but mined with cracks and small faults:

It's only a little paperweight. I wanted to give you a Christmas present but couldn't get anything too ostentatious obviously. I found it in Portobello Road. It cost less than a shilling. You can say that you bought it for yourself and keep it on your desk in Chambers to remind you of me.

It's beautiful.

He turned it over in his hands and watched as weak sunlight prismed off it. No one would take a second glance at it but he meant what he said. He hadn't thought of Christmas presents and felt embarrassed at his lack of forethought. He wanted to give her something in return but all he had on him was the current paperback he had been carrying, out of habit, for his tube journey. He pulled it from his pocket:

– Merry Christmas. It's a good book and it's not marked in any way.

And he handed her his copy of *Down and Out in Paris and London*. He would have to buy a replacement. It was the first of many books that he would buy her in the following four years.

"Hamleys. Friday 1 p.m." Adam played with the note in his pocket as he headed to his room in Chambers.

"Idiot"

Nearly every one of the books on his shelves there had its mirror in those on the shelves in her dressing room. He remembered Jeremy's exaggerated interest in his library.

– Down and Out in Paris and London. *Now I'd never come across this Orwell chap.*
– *He's a personal favourite of mine. More for his journalism.*
– *Interesting. Interesting.*

– *How could he possibly know?*
– *He's my husband, Adam. He's not a fool.*
– *But there's nothing.*

— *There's always something, Adam. We could never hide everything. I can't see you anymore.*

He lit a cigarette and shivered. He took down a book at random – *Antic Hay* by Aldous Huxley – his hand shook as he held it. He had given her a copy for her birthday in 1938. *Vile Bodies* – an Easter present in 1937. The list went on. He had thought he was being discreet, when in fact he had been giving her a body of evidence against them to keep right under her husband's nose. "Idiot!" Why had he kept his books in Chambers? The mistake, once seen, was so obvious.

He tried to pull himself together. What had Jeremy actually got against them? A burnt fragment with a watermark and the coincidence of their literary interests. It couldn't be enough. But there was plainly more. Last Friday Julia had said that she could not see him anymore. But by the following Thursday she was arranging a meeting. Perhaps she wanted some form of reconciliation with him? Maybe she wanted to work together with him to thwart her husband's plans? Surely they were still on the same side? Surely he could trust her?

He did not know what to think. He put back the book and lit another cigarette. Pemberton's words from Monday came back to him:

— *It would be uncommonly foolish to carry on an affair right under her husband's nose. One small slip and McKechnie would be able to study the man at his leisure. Uncommonly foolish ...*

"Jackson!" It had to be Jackson. How much had he found out? What else did Pemberton know? There must be more. They were never going to be able to hide everything. If Julia wanted to see him it must be because there was more. He remembered the thoughts that had plagued him the previous Friday night as he lay awake. How long had Jackson been following him? What had he seen or heard or learnt?

That morning he had received formal instructions from Jones in the case of Tomas Novak. A conference had been arranged for 10 a.m. the following morning in Wandsworth prison. Oh God! Friday! The papers were not thick but he could not concentrate, reading the opening paragraph again and again. He no longer felt comfortable in Chambers. Whether the word was out or not he felt the smoke of rumour seeping under his door, swirling around the staircases and rising from colleagues that he met on the stairs; as though his reputation was on fire in the basement and the flames were rising. He had to get out. He needed to leave a note in the church saying that he might be late.

It was very cold and Adam was without his overcoat. He came out of Stirrup Court and walked across to the church. Lamb Building squatted between it and the Hall leaving only a little room on either side to pass it by. His exit from Chambers had taken Jackson by surprise and he caught the big man lumbering out of view, trying all the while to look invisible.

"Bugger!"

Bateman had clearly made it all too obvious. His cover blown, Jackson had returned to concentrating on Adam. It was too dangerous to leave a message for Julia. He scrunched it up in his pocket and made for the library. There was nothing for it: he would have to collect his papers and go home, and then directly to the prison in the morning. Anything rather than try and work in Chambers.

Chapter Fourteen

(Friday 20ᵗʰ December 1940)

The evidence was pretty damning. The police raid at three in the morning had clearly been based upon specific intelligence. They knew who he was and where he was living. There could have been no other reason for ten officers to swoop in on a small bedsit in Leytonstone. Specific intelligence was required to know which floorboard to lift. A cylinder of cardboard contained maps and plans of London's reservoirs and basic bomb-making instructions.

He hadn't helped himself either. Undisclosed intelligence sources indicated that Novak had entered the country only a matter of days earlier. He had confirmed that this was so. However, according to Hoffer, he had been in London since February. The lie, if it was a lie, was an obvious one. If he had indeed been in the country that long he should have presented himself to the authorities, as Hoffer had done. There was no record that he had; nor was there any form of corroborative evidence. Hoffer was unwilling to come forward formally – he should have reported Novak's presence if he had known of it – and his landlord was faced with a similar dilemma. When Novak changed his story and said he had been in London far longer, this only served to confirm police suspicions. His landlord, having said that the man had only just arrived and pleading ignorance generally, was hardly going to help. It was obvious who the police – and the security services – were going to believe. After all, they had been led directly to him and to the stash of maps.

– You have my statement, Mr Falling. I don't need to repeat myself.

His English was good. He had been a physicist in Prague.

– I have read your statement. I have also read the statements of the witnesses for the prosecution. They do not tally.
– We know why that is.

- I know why you say it is.
- Hoffer knows how long I have been here.
- Hoffer won't give evidence. You can't blame him for staying away from the police. You should be glad he is giving you the help he is giving you.
- Hoffer is not so intelligent.

It was unhelpful, but Adam instinctively disliked the man. At the Bar intellectual arrogance was all around him. But he did not like to see it in his clients – particularly in the present circumstances. Novak was tall and slim and held himself with exaggerated straightness. He was almost able to make the prison serge look fashionable. His piercing eyes were a slightly paler blue and prematurely silvery hair made him look like a portrait. He was too relaxed:

- Without Hoffer you would probably have no proper representation.
- I am not sure how good my representation is going to be.

Arrogant and offensive.

- You are fortunate that he has been able to raise sufficient money for you to have any representation … even from someone like me.

He felt more worthless than he had been feeling before arriving at Wandsworth.

- He has done everything wrong for me.
- What are you talking about?
- I am not a spy. I am a Jew. Why would I be helping the Nazis?
- Why would you be having plans to blow up our reservoirs?
- I'm sorry, Mr Falling. But I do not trust you. I do not trust Mr Hoffer. Why should I trust you?
- Mr Hoffer is a Jew as well.
- Huh!

This was not what he had expected. It was as though he carried an odour of failure about him. He was struggling. The interview had begun late and it was now 11 a.m. Meeting Julia was more important than this man's story … his defence … his life. He stopped himself. He could not concentrate. It had taken until 7 a.m. that morning to begin reading the papers. And he had a hangover. An undrinkable bottle of sloe gin was all that was available to shield him from the wrath of his wife. Catherine had been understandably difficult and a dreadful silence had permeated the house. Sleep was impossible. He kept thinking of Julia.

- You have problems because you did not report to the authorities on your arrival. Why didn't you report yourself? How did you get here?
- You are asking two questions of me. Which one would you wish me to be answering first?
- How did you get here?
- With Hoffer of course. Surely he has told you this?
- No.
- We boarded the same boat from Gibraltar. I liked his wife very much.
- He made no mention of this.
- It was his wife who helped me. Not so much Hoffer.
- Why didn't you report with them?
- She was called Katya.
- You should have reported.
- It was Hoffer who said that I should not do so.
- Don't be ridiculous.
- Doctors would be treated differently from physicists, he said. I made a mistake. I should not have trusted him. How can I trust you if Hoffer has sent you?
- He wanted you to report yourself but you would not be persuaded.
- Hoffer has told you this? He is not to be trusted. Why should I not report myself?
- Perhaps because you were intending to bomb our reservoirs?
- Hoffer told me not to report myself. Hoffer arranged my accommodation. If I had only just entered the country, how would I have come by the maps?

The story was all wrong. Hoffer had made it clear in their recent meeting that he had not met with Novak until after his tribunal hearing. Novak had browsed, without buying, in the bookshop where Hoffer was working.

Hoffer, so he said, had attempted without success to persuade Novak to report himself. Someone was not telling the truth.

- I'm afraid your story is completely at odds with what we have been told by Mr Hoffer. I can see no reason for him to lie to us.
- Katya spoke to me about you after the Tribunal. She said that you were a gullible man. I see that she was right.
- Mr Novak. You are facing charges under the Treachery Act. The Crown says that you were attempting to do something that was likely to endanger life in this country. If they prove that, you will be executed, probably just around the corner from this interview room. Is that what you want?
- I don't believe that you have met with Katya. You must talk with her. I do not trust Hoffer. And so I cannot trust you. So you must talk with Katya. Katya. Katya, I trust.

It was hopeless. Adam had tried to make Novak speak around his statement so as to tease out any inconsistencies or – if he was speaking the truth – to give his story some colour. His blank refusal was plainly based on genuine mistrust of his counsel's motives. He was being paid practically nothing to be there (although to someone living on the fringes it may have seemed like a lot). His defence was simple and incredible: he had come over with the Hoffers via Gibraltar. He had been persuaded by Hoffer not to report himself. Hoffer had arranged his accommodation and he knew nothing about the plans beneath the floorboards. He was not going to be believed. Novak continued:

- There is no point in this interview continuing. I do not see the point in further elaboration. You have my explanation. Until such time as you have spoken to Katya I cannot see us progressing...

Novak had taken control of the situation. Adam wondered at his ability to do so with the noose so close to him. This insistence. This faith in a woman whom Adam had never met triggered doubts in him.

- And, anyway. I see you have a more pressing... more urgent engagement that you must attend to rather than to be troubled by my... my little … problem. You must be on your way. Speak to Katya. I hope that perhaps we can meet again very soon. Preferably when you are not so preoccupied.

- I take your predicament very seriously. Jones and I will be doing all we can to ensure that you are properly represented.
- You are very concerned by your watch. I can assure you that it has not stopped. There is a clock behind your head. They are both moving. Speak to Katya. It may be then that we can have a meaningful meeting. I think that our meeting is over for now.

And he flicked his hands in dismissal.

Adam looked at Jones as they made their way out through security.

- He's headed for the gallows.
- You want to wash your hands of him, I can tell.
- Have you taken a statement from Katya?
- Didn't know she existed. Hoffer made no mention of a wife when he was interviewed for his statement. Novak hadn't mentioned a woman either. But he seemed a bit obsessed by her. Odd, if she doesn't exist.
- I'm sorry to have got you involved in this.
- Novak seems to have a death-wish.
- Did you prepare his statement?
- No. But I will try and get in to see him early next week. Find out more about this Katya. And I'll interview Hoffer next time and press him on his "wife". I don't know why I'm bothering.
- If you can it would be useful to try and arrange a further conference for the early part of next week. Something about all of this doesn't ring true. I'm beginning to wonder whether either Hoffer or Novak is telling us the truth.

They were back on the road and standing under the shelter by the bus-stop outside the prison. It was twelve fifteen and the sky was moody. Adam began coughing and could not stop. He had learnt the taste of blood as it rose, and he suppressed it. He felt that his world was ending. Who needed high explosive? Some red escaped, but he didn't think that Jones had noticed.

– I want to carry on with this one. He's too calm about things. I can do it for nothing. We haven't been given the full story. I don't know what my fee is supposed to be, but you can have it.

– That's really not ...

– Take the fee. I'll speak to Arthur. Perhaps we can speak on Tuesday. I'm afraid I've given you rather a lot to do.

– You should go home to bed. Until Tuesday then.

And they made their farewells. Adam hailed a cab that he could not afford. He needed to be at Hamleys by one o'clock. But before that he needed to go to his bank on Chancery Lane.

Chapter Fifteen

He went straight to the third floor. He knew she would be amongst the dolls' houses – or, at least, be where the dolls' houses used to be. The store seemed threadbare. Where there had been an abundance of toys there were now boxes covered in coloured paper and exhibits of things that strived, but failed, to hide the huge gaps in supplies. This was not a happy time to be a child. He looked around at the rationed artefacts and wondered whether the place would ever entrance a child again. He tried to imagine it as a warehouse of delight but he could not. Perhaps one day the notices would be in German, or, at best, bi-lingual. Hamleys was crowded enough; but the crowd was listless. Shopping when there was nothing to shop for.

He was already fifteen minutes late. His business at the bank had taken longer to transact than he had anticipated, and then there had been a false alarm on the tube. But it had been a necessary detour. He needed to be clear about this before he spoke to her. His shirt was sticking to his back and he could feel the familiar crackle in his oesophagus. It seemed a long time since they had been together and there was so much he had to say. He wished he was calmer. He rubbed his forehead with the back of his hand and wiped the moisture off onto his overcoat.

Shoppers were milling about the floor and there was a hubbub of voices. He panicked that she had been and gone. He remembered her laughter as she held up the dolls' house four years ago, and listened, without hope, for its sound again. No laughter. It was lunch-time and it was impossible to make out individual people in the throng. He was beginning to despair – and then he saw her. Amidst all the movement she was still. She had her back to him and was wearing a long black coat. Strands of blonde hair, pulled back, emerged from beneath an elegant emerald and crimson headscarf. She did not move and seemed fixed in thought. The world slowed down as he walked towards her. People seemed to be walking at half speed past and around her and the colours of their clothing seemed to detach themselves and swirl around the still black form so that he saw her through a miasma of fabric. And still she did not move. The sounds of the store died away and all he could hear was his own breathing. His own heart.

He touched her on the shoulder and she turned towards him. He saw with a shock that she was ugly. Her face was closed and shuttered as if she had folded in on herself. Her eyes were like two dull blue beetles and there was a rash of acne spreading across her right cheek. She had pulled her hair back so tightly that it distorted her features. There was no warmth. He sensed her thoughts: *Here I am. I am not attractive. I don't love you anymore. This will make it easier.*

- I'm sorry I'm late. I had to go to Wandsworth prison this morning and I couldn't leave you a note yesterday. Bateman was prowling around outside the church. And I've been to the bank. I am so pleased to see you. There's so much I need to say ...

The words came out in a rush and not in the order that he intended, but there was no reaction.

- Were you followed?
- I'm pretty sure not. I got a cab from outside the prison. I checked around me and didn't see anyone. I haven't been back to Chambers. I've been to the bank.
- Jeremy knows about the Stafford.
- But we haven't been there for months!
- He knows about you. But he can't be sure about me.
- That's impossible!
- We were stupid.
- We need to talk. I've drawn out some money. We can go to Quaglino's and discuss our tactics –
- Adam!!

She shouted at him and he was sure that everyone must have heard her. But the crowds continued milling. He felt the colour draining from him. He had not known what to expect but this was far worse than he had anticipated. The room was spinning. The rash on her face had darkened. The

102

beetles that were her eyes had narrowed further. When she spoke again her voice was low and controlled.

– He will be serving you and me with a petition in the New Year. He intends to prove adultery. I can't be seen with you. Even this is too much of a risk … Quaglino's!

He had been half expecting this and had rehearsed what he would say.

– Julia. Julia. I don't care. I love you. I've been to the bank –
– Will you stop going on about the bloody bank!

Her language startled him but he pressed on.

– I've been to the bank and I've checked on my account. Look. I've got two hundred pounds. I know it's not a lot. But it's a start. Let him divorce you. You can have everything I've got. We could start again together. I'll move Chambers. I don't need money. I don't need my career. I just want to be with you. We'll manage. I'll look after you. I'll …

He stuttered and the words ran out on him. He was holding twelve large paper notes in his hand and Julia was watching him. Her eyes had widened and he saw emotion there for the first time in so long. It was anger still, but tinged with pity … with incredulity. Her voice was soft and she touched his sleeve when she spoke.

– I don't want to be divorced, Adam. I don't want to be with you. Two hundred pounds! It's not going to pay your legal costs. You won't be able to meet the damages you're going to have to pay Jeremy for breaking up his marriage. Put your money away.
– So it's the money! That's what it comes down to. You don't want to lose the money! You cheap … !

He'd gone too far and he knew it. He saw her wincing and she seemed to shrink further. This wasn't how he had foreseen things.

- I don't want to be divorced, Adam. This must be the last time we meet. I had to tell you about the Stafford.
- I said I loved you ... and I meant it ... You said you loved me once and I think you meant it.
- If you love ... loved me ... you'll tell the world you hate me. If you love me you'll understand why I must tell everyone that I have never cared for you. You will find a way to explain why all the bloody books on my shelves are the same as the ones you have in chambers ... to explain why you were going to the Stafford on free afternoons. A way that doesn't involve me. New Year's Day is on a Wednesday. We'll both receive the Petition on the Thursday. I can't see you again.

And she turned to leave.

- Stop! Can't you find the time at least to come for a cup of tea?
- I can't see you again, Adam. Goodbye.

And as she said it he noticed her eyes soften. A vague look of regret suffused with relief that she had said what she had to say, they had not been seen and she was leaving. And she walked away. Shoppers were still circling around looking for presents. His eyes lost focus and, vaguely, he was aware of a black coat sliding out of view through the crowds. A final question formed in his mind. But she was gone. And he would never be able to ask her it.

Chapter Sixteen

(Friday 20ᵗʰ December 1940)

He found himself at the gates of Green Park. He had stood for an age after she had gone, unnoticed by the throng around him. He had made half-hearted efforts to find a Christmas present for Deborah … but could not concentrate. He didn't remember descending the stairs or making his way down Regent Street towards Piccadilly. At some level he had known that there would be no hope of a long lunch in Quaglino's or a drift through Green Park afterwards. It was always going to come to an end. But he had hoped otherwise.

From Piccadilly it was a short walk to the park. He had not known what to expect or what he was looking for. His memories were of candy-coloured deckchairs billowing in the late September sun … greens and yellows and reds … and couples sauntering nonchalantly amongst the slanting shadows. The green verdure of late summer. It was all gone. It was scarcely two and he hadn't eaten but he didn't feel hungry anymore. He lit up and stepped through the gates. His breath misted and mixed with the smoke from his cigarette. A sheen of frost glistened on the grass and the trees were bare. The ground was pockmarked with trenches, each one surrounded by sandbags. There were no deck chairs. No lovers drifting into anonymity. The young men had gone. Their women had been evacuated or were working. The park was barren. It mirrored him.

When did you stop loving me? That was the question he had not been able to ask. Not "why?" "Why?" was how the question had started during those long, lidless nights. But he had realised that "why?" was a stupid question. It was as pointless as asking someone why they began to love someone else in the beginning. The question was unanswerable. Or, rather, there was no simple answer. It was the way he tied his shoelaces. The fact that they kept coming undone. His stutter when trying to express things that mattered. The thinness of his chest. His cough. His frailty. A shot of sunlight across his hair when the clouds were dark. Things he was totally oblivious of. Had no control over. These, he knew, had been part of the "why?" Not all. Not the inexplicable all. Not logical reasons for loving. If there was no good reason to love, no explanation as to why one loved, there could no good reason why one person ceased to love another. Explanations were impossible and did not work.

That was why "when?" was a better question. It had a chronological – perhaps a geographical – nexus. There was a point in time, a place, where it happened. And that was always the best that one could do. But even this was imprecise. A person stops loving before they realise that they have done so. The "when?" also remains imprecise. The crossroad arrives before the crossroad is reached, even though the change of direction does not happen until the latter point. He thought again of John Donne's "Lecture on the Shadow": the poet's contention, charting Love's day in one circuit of the sun, that until love be at its full noon and its shadows be underfoot the lovers hide it from those around them. But:

> *Except our loves at this noon stay,*
> *We shall new shadows make the other way.*
> *As the first were made to blind*
> *Others, these which come behind*
> *Will work upon ourselves, and blind our eyes.*
> *If our loves faint, and westwardly decline,*
> *To me thou, falsely, thine,*
> *And I to thee mine actions shall disguise.*
> *The morning shadows wear away,*
> *But these grow longer all the day;*
> *But oh, love's day is short, if love decay.*
> *Love is a growing, or full constant light,*
> *And his first minute, after noon, is night.*

So it had happened and he did not know why. He had hoped at least to find out when, but the question had gone unasked and unanswered. But even if asked it would not have been answered. And even if answered it would not have been answered truly. Truth dies first in the death of love.

And why had he, did he, love? He had seen her and she was ugly. There had been no warmth. A cold, cut-off end to things. She neither wanted, loved or needed him. Everything was collapsed in a love of money. She did not love Jeremy. Jeremy did not love her. They were together. He was alone. The logical thing was to close this off but he could not. If he could not understand why he loved, how could he possibly understand why she did not? Only the "when" was tangible. Even the "when" only provided something of a road map.

It was half past two. He walked down into the empty park. It was a long way past noon. He found the tree where first she had put her hand upon his neck and pulled him towards her. Before Agnes could speak or understand. He retraced their steps and found the benches they had sat upon, the places amongst the grass where they had been; but the cold and empty spaces gave no hint that they carried memories.

****

It had been their talk of Preston whilst they were lying in Green Park that had sparked the idea. Preston had suggested to Julia that they meet during the afternoons in a hotel and she had mentioned this to Adam in her disparaging way. But the idea had taken some sort of root. The Feathers in Chippenham had been a one-off and could not easily be repeated though they had both wanted it to be. They contented themselves instead with walking or sitting in Green Park.

One day, in the early spring of 1937, they had been walking the curtilage of the park when, on the eastern side, Julia had spotted a small opening in the wall. It led to a footpath which in turn led to the Stafford Hotel. A little more exploration showed that one could reach the Hotel from the park, but equally one could reach it from St James's Street. And so the plan was hatched: Adam would enter from St James's Street and book a room under the name of Wilson, a common enough name, and make his way to the second floor. Julia would detour from her walk around the park and come in some twenty minutes later. There was nothing to connect them. There was an old man – George – on reception who could see what was happening but Adam felt confident that he would say nothing, that he enjoyed the intrigue. It was no more than two hours once, maybe twice a week. He paid in cash.

Then the war began. Julia began to withdraw. Still they would go, when they could … or when he could persuade her … to the Stafford on a midweek afternoon. Sometimes, still, she would bring a picnic. In May of this year Churchill became Prime Minister and the war effort took on a more determined line. One consequence of this was that anyone booking into a hotel had to provide identification. Julia and Adam had their first argument, and – even then – he felt the beginning of the end. She said it was too dangerous. He said that she was a coward who didn't have her priorities right – if she loved him, that was. And he won. And now, as he walked around the park in late December 1940, he began to wonder whether that was the "when" point of their relationship.

A compromise had been reached. He would continue to book the room but he would do so under the name of "Falling". George would smile indulgently as he checked in. He knew Adam was not a spy. But it was in the records and now Jackson had found them. He only had to succeed in following him once and then he could uncover the whole pattern, at least from the point when he stopped calling himself Wilson. Adam had calculated, from what Julia had told him, that although they knew he was staying at the hotel on a regular basis, Jackson had not been able to prove that she had been with him. But surely they had enough? He understood, now, Julia's alarm. She knew about the watermark and, now, the books he had given her – and they could prove that he visited a central London hotel on a regular basis during the afternoons … and she wanted him to come up with an explanation that would put her in the clear.

Why did he love her? He no longer knew. He felt a cough rising in his chest and readied himself with his handkerchief. A wave of nausea hit him and he had to lean against a tree. She had asked that he prove to her that he loved her. He had no choice. He didn't want to love her anymore. This was not how he saw things turning out. He had no choice: he would find a way of absolving her, whatever the consequences for him or for Catherine or Deborah. He would find a way through. He wiped some blood from his lips and gazed at the handkerchief. He didn't think he would live much longer in any event.

Chapter Seventeen

(Saturday 21st December 1940)

Weak sunlight trickled through the stained glass tulips of the front door onto the early Saturday post. Panels of pink, green and yellow on the envelopes. Adam stooped to pick them up: some Christmas cards, a letter from their landlord and a letter from Deborah. The Edenbridge postmark was smudged and there was some soot on her big curly writing.

Breakfast was scrambled eggs made from reconstituted powder and tasting of little more than water. Weak tea with powdered milk and some slightly stale toast. They read the letters as they ate:

- I've forgotten to pay the rent again. I'll write a cheque on Monday. Deborah's getting very excited about our visit. She wants us to bring up some of her books.
- I'll dig them out before I go off to Home Guard.

Catherine was opening the Christmas cards and arranging them across the kitchen table. Theirs was a comfortable, well-proportioned house built in the late nineteenth century on a plot carved out of the Thurlow estate, part of the second ripple of plot sales that spread out in concentric circles of increasingly diminishing size. They could probably afford to buy their own home but there seemed little point with the bombs falling.

- Adam?

Her tone put him on edge.

- Yes?
- I know we weren't planning to go up to Edenbridge until Tuesday but isn't travelling on Christmas Eve leaving it a little late? Can't we go up on Monday? I do miss Deborah and she is so anxious for us to come.

He froze.

– No! It's out of the question. It can't be done.
– Why on earth not?
– I … I … I need to be in London on Monday.
– Don't be ridiculous. Why?

This is going to be the best I can come up with.

– There's some urgent work on the Bateman case. It can't wait. Something doesn't make sense. I need to go to Romford.
– Romford?! Why can't it wait until the New Year?
– We can go first thing on Tuesday. I promise.
– Adam! I'm getting tired of this. It's not as though you're busy. You're spending more time in the Temple than you are with me. Why didn't you come home on Wednesday night?

He had managed to avoid talking about this during the uncomfortable silences of Thursday evening.

– It wasn't deliberate. I got caught out by the raids. We'll go first thing on Tuesday, I promise. I still have some Christmas shopping to do.
– Oh, do what you like! I'm going up on Monday!

She stood suddenly and swept up the cards.

– Don't forget to read your daughter's letter to you! She names the books she wants us to bring.

Her eyes were bright with the luminosity of tears and she grimaced – holding back her thoughts and her emotions; then she turned away and left the kitchen.

****

The khaki shirt rubbed at the back of his neck. His daughter's room was almost as she had left it. He made a pile of the books named in her letter and ran his fingers over her curly handwriting:

- Oh, Mummy and Daddy. I can't wait to see you. I've missed you so and I'm so looking forward to Christmas …

He stood by her bed and looked around him, forcing himself to try and remember everything about it: the pale blue walls, her little bookshelf and the smell of lavender. There was a sheet of paper pinned to the wall that he had never noticed before: a little painting of a black and white cat curled up on a bed. She'd written the word "Socks" underneath it …

He looked out of her bedroom window at the sparse rectangle of garden. Everything seemed to be retreating from him.

****

Bright sunlight lay in bands across the bed, broken up by the curtains at the hotel window. Julia was covered only by a sheet. It was a bright April day during the Phoney War and the last time he would be able to sign himself in as Wilson. He sensed an uncomfortable edge to things:

- May I ask you a hypothetical question?

A narrowing of her eyes – hesitancy and apprehension.

- … Yes.
- If we weren't both happily married in our thirties and with children, would you marry me?

She started then, her eyes widened and she threw back her head and laughed.

- Yes! Of course! Yes …Yes …

Chapter Eighteen

(Monday 23rd December 1940)

Bateman had lied to him.

How, when and where had Marjorie Bateman died?

These were the questions that had brought Adam to Romford Town Hall on Monday morning. That and the need to spend one more day in London. He sat under the watchful eye of a town hall official with the contents of the manila file spread out before him – five sheets of hurried clerical writing chronicling Mrs Bateman's last hours. A one-pound bribe had bought him an hour with the notes of the inquest.

How, when and where?

Bateman had lied about the when and the where. He might even have lied about the how.

The story had emerged prosaically. There had been four witnesses: Bateman himself, who identified the body, and Graham and Victoria McKechnie. The fourth witness was a police officer. Bateman and the McKechnies had all apparently been in the vicinity of the accident. He'd said nothing about this in conference. If there had been the level of animosity between them that Bateman had described, why were they all together?

The "how" of the accident seemed to be clear. It was as Bateman had told him in conference. Marjorie had been run down by a car after the blackout. He and the McKechnies were at one in their description of what had happened. They had gone to the cinema together and then visited a public house afterwards for a drink before home. They had all been a little tipsy and they had been laughing and joking together when Marjorie made to cross the road. The next thing they heard – they were all clear about this

– was a heavy thud and a scream and then the sound of a car accelerating away. The driver was never traced.

But the "how" played havoc with the "when". Bateman had told him that the accident occurred when he was on his way home from work. He hadn't been there when it happened. And yet, his evidence was quite clear on this. Marjorie had died at the scene. The coroner's verdict put the time of death at about 11.15 p.m. So Bateman had lied to him about the time of death, about his whereabouts and about the precise circumstances of his wife's demise.

How? When? Where?

Adam took the crystal obelisk from his overcoat pocket and turned it over in his hand examining the faults deep inside it. He had been careful to check his instructions as to where Bateman lived. A small house in Seven Kings. But the accident had apparently taken place in a street near the centre of Ilford. It may only be a matter of about a mile away from her home but a mile during the blackout was a long way. Perhaps that was where they had all gone to the cinema?

Where did the McKechnies live? There was another surprise. They had been bombed out. They had given their address as a school hall. Bateman had said nothing about this either. There was nothing in his instructions to suggest this. What had the petition said? He was sure there had been no mention of a school hall. Adam remembered what Pemberton had said the previous week:

Poor Bateman. His dear wife is lying dead in the road and he's in bed with Mrs McKechnie.

He felt in his overcoat pocket for the Further and Better Particulars picked up from Chambers that morning, and unfolded them. The date of Marjorie's death was there as a date when adultery took place. Although he hadn't seen it he felt sure that Victoria's diary would contain the letters ABC on that day. It didn't make any sense. If Graham McKechnie thought his wife was committing adultery on the day in question, why had everyone, apparently, behaved in the way that the inquest notes seemed to suggest? If they had been at the pictures and then the pub in the hours leading up to the tragedy, how could it be that Bateman would have had the time – or the opportunity – to commit adultery?

Adam had been there for forty-five minutes and the clerk was beginning to drum on his desk with a pencil. He had had little time to take in Marjorie Bateman's injuries so he took some hurried notes about these and details of the address of the accident and the school hall, then he handed the file back and left the building. It had been a worthwhile exercise – insofar as anything was worthwhile now: Bateman had been lying to him. The "when" and the "where" did not fit with the "how". The "when" and the "where" had been confirmed by the police officer. Of course, Bateman could have been lying about the "how". And if he had been lying about the "how", then Graham and Victoria McKechnie had been lying as well. And why would Graham McKechnie be making these allegations of adultery and running up these legal costs if what he was saying through his lawyers was untrue? He was a bombed-out insurance clerk. The more he thought about it the less sense it made.

****

Jackson was still outside the Town Hall doing his best to hide behind a tree. He was reading an old copy of the Sunday Express. Adam saw his eyes in the gap between the paper and his hat and felt a strange fondness for this absurd man.

After he had comprehensively given him the slip the previous Friday, Adam knew that the private detective would be waiting to follow him when he arrived at Chambers that morning and – beyond a detour into the Temple Church to leave a note under the cross-legged knights when Jackson wisely stayed outside – that had been the case.

Adam had made no attempt to lose him as he walked briskly out of the Temple and onto Fleet Street before making off towards Liverpool Street station. There had been crowds at the station as he made his way to the ticket counter and he felt Jackson's presence grow closer behind him and shivered slightly as he asked the old man behind the glass for a return ticket to Romford. His voice was so loud he surprised himself. Jackson could not have failed to hear that. He headed towards the platforms and when he was far enough way, looked back to see the corpulent detective leaning over the ticket desk as he bought his own tickets. It had all been far too easy.

He had remembered to check an old railway timetable before he left home so that he could count the number of stops before it was time for him to get off. The absence of station signs was intended to confuse the enemy but it also made things very difficult for commuters. Jackson hadn't had the opportunity to plan ahead and at every stop Adam would look out of his window to see the low-brimmed hat leaning out as Jackson anxiously scanned the platforms for his quarry. He breathed more deeply. If the man had managed to stay with him this far he could ignore him – certainly until the afternoon. It was imperative that he was still following him during the afternoon. The afternoon! Suddenly his plan seemed not only deranged but far more destructive than he was able to imagine. He tried not to think of the consequences, but the nausea returned and he felt his gorge rising. He had remembered a clean handkerchief. Beads of sweat prickled out on him despite the cold.

As he had stepped down from the train he told himself to ignore Jackson and trust him to continue following. It was a relief nonetheless to see him being conspicuously inconspicuous behind an oak tree. He thought he would take him on a walk through Romford market. He had some Christmas shopping to do. He had just over eighty pounds left from the money withdrawn from his bank on Friday. Almost half of the life savings that had so manifestly failed to impress Julia in Hamleys. Ten pounds had been given to a sullen Catherine for her journey up to Edenbridge and other sums had been spent on train fares and bribes. He would need to spend a lot more during the afternoon.

****

In the market he bought a black and white kitten for his daughter and a cage to put it in – and a straw hat for Catherine. It was a bit summery but it was the best he could do given what was available. Jackson was standing behind a clothing stall pretending to examine some shirts. It was all too easy.

Chapter Nineteen
(Monday 23rd December 1940)

Jackson could feel the beginnings of an erection. It was all too easy. The only tricky bit had been the train journey, but fortunately Falling had been as lost as he was without the station signs and had to look out of the window at every stop to check where he was. He felt a growing excitement. Falling was behaving erratically. He was prickling with tension, and Jackson had noticed a decided tremor in his left hand when he was paying for his train ticket. He was carrying an awful lot of money. Long experience had taught him that these were all the signs of a man about to make a mistake. And something was out of the ordinary – if Falling had thought that a detour to Romford would give him the slip, he was wrong. Clearly he felt safe now. It was only a matter of time.

He was also clearly developing something of a religious mania. He had gone into the Temple Church before the journey and now, on his return to Chambers, he had visited again. It was only three thirty and there were no services on. Only guilt could explain his behaviour.

Jackson had used the train journeys to write up his notes. Pemberton was going to be very pleased with him. And now Falling was off again. Jackson watched as he trudged back up Inner Temple Lane. His overcoat was too big for him and he had a blue notebook sticking out of one pocket and a set of papers – red ribbon hanging down – out of the other. And he was carrying a kitten in a cage in one hand and a straw hat in the other. Jackson wondered whether the man was going mad. It didn't matter – a deranged man was easier to follow.

They had a long wait on Holborn station and it was past four thirty when they reached Green Park. Jackson had known that sooner or later they would end up there. Pemberton had ostentatiously announced to his wife that he would be stuck in court all day and would then be working late in Chambers in preparation for the Christmas break. They hadn't worked out how Mrs Pemberton was able to communicate with Falling, but somehow she did. She would think that she was going to be free to go to the hotel. They already had enough evidence, but to have an eye-witness account of the two of them meeting would leave them with no way out.

On the tube journey Falling had balanced the straw hat on his head and was talking to the kitten, pushing his fingers through the bars – and chain-smoking. The tremor in his left hand was more pronounced and there was visible sweat breaking over his face. Watching from behind his newspaper Jackson almost felt sorry for him. He was painfully thin and engulfed by his overcoat. As the day had gone on he had been seized by ever more frequent coughing fits and would hold a bloodied handkerchief to his mouth – to cover his embarrassment as much as anything else.

Dusk had fallen by the time they emerged outside Green Park station. Blackout covers were going up on the shop windows. Jackson relaxed – it was going to be even easier to follow Falling now that darkness had come. It was a short walk down to the Stafford from here. Then he would give them a few minutes to settle down before going into question the Reception clerk.

But Falling didn't head for the Stafford. He was going in the wrong direction altogether. Jackson felt a puzzled disappointment rising in him. Falling was walking down Piccadilly towards Hyde Park Corner, slightly swinging the cat in its cage and carrying the straw hat again in his left hand. He didn't seem to care if he was followed. Perhaps they met some-where away from the hotel? Suddenly, Falling was gone.

Jackson panicked and began to run. So far he had gathered nothing of real value and his whole day may have been wasted. Falling must have turned into one of the side streets. He reached the point where he had last seen his suspect and realised with a sigh of relief that the man had turned into White Horse Street. He could see him again drifting up the lane. And then he realised, with a mixture of disgust and disappointment, where Falling was going – and what that meant. Shepherd Market.

He edged his way up the street behind his man, hugging the walls. A strange fascination overcame him. So intent was he on watching the retreating silhouette – the cat cage and straw hat swinging by his sides – that he tripped over a foot protruding from a doorway.

– 'Ere! Watch it mate. What do you think you're doing?!

A young woman with too much make-up was leaning there smoking a cigarette.

- Very sorry. Didn't see you.
- You should bloody well look where you're going.
- Please. Keep your voice down.

The wrong thing to say.

- Don't tell me what to do! I'll be as loud as I like!
- Please. I'm a private detective. I'm trying to follow someone.
- Private detective!

She was shouting now.

- Now I've heard it all. I know what you are! Well, I'm not impressed. It'll cost you the same as it would cost anyone else!

Out of the corner of his eye he could see Falling disappearing out of sight. Further argument with the woman would be pointless. It was better to get away from the source of the commotion. Jackson hoofed it to the other side of the street and resumed the chase – there were other women to avoid and he was more careful in his progress along the wall.

It was getting very dark. The street was narrow and no light emerged from the houses. Falling was no more than a black shape ahead of him. He had put down the cage and balanced the straw hat on top of it, and he was talking with a woman. Jackson could see that she was slender and that her clothes appeared to be well cut, but other than that she was beyond identification in the darkness. Surely Mrs Pemberton would not choose to meet him here? Falling was reaching into his inside pocket. Jackson saw him produce his wallet and rifle through it. He was sure now that it was not Mrs Pemberton. But surely this was just as damning …? If it didn't get Mr Pemberton a divorce it would surely end Falling's marriage.

They were coming back towards him – walking slightly apart from one another – the cat cage and the straw hat swinging again in Falling's hands. He heard mewlings of hunger. Jackson retreated back onto Piccadilly ready to resume following his suspect. But he'd already guessed where the man was heading.

Falling and the woman walked back up Piccadilly and then crossed the road, passing the Ritz before passing down into St James's Street and then into St James's Place. They were going to the Stafford Hotel.

Jackson waited for ten minutes before entering the hotel. Subdued lighting and an air of dilapidated elegance greeted him. There was no one there except an old man in a liveried uniform studying the *Racing Post* behind the reception desk. Jackson approached him waving a ten shilling note.

- Sorry to disturb you but do you mind if I ask you a few questions?
- Sure mate. Ask away.

The old man took the note from him.

- A man came in here with a woman a few minutes ago. He was carrying a kitten in a cage.
- It's not against the law.
- Can I have a look at the register?
- Help yourself.

Falling had written his name and his address there just as before.

- Has Mr Falling been here before?
- Oh yes. He's a regular.
- Does he always come with a woman?
- Yes sir.
- And is it always the same woman?
- Yes sir. Every time.
- What's her name?
- Betty.
- Why hasn't she signed in?
- He's the one with the money, sir.
- Right! Well, thank you very much. I'll be off. Many thanks. And Merry Christmas.
- And a happy Christmas to you too, sir.

****

The old man watched as the corpulent man shambled out of the hotel, his large hat drooping down over his head. Thirty bob! Not bad for a few minutes' work. He looked at the red banknote and then put in his pocket with the green one given to him by Adam.

Chapter Twenty

(Monday 23rd December 1940)

Betty could tell that it was his first time. Something about his hesitancy, the way he had approached, speaking with the other girls on the way. He had seemed interested in the whole way that she looked, and that was telling. Men usually only wanted one part of her – and that didn't show easily through her clothing. He was particularly interested in her clothing. It may well have been that he would have passed her by as he had the others but for an altercation down in the street behind them. That seemed to galvanise him into making a choice.

She did not have the luxury of choice and would have turned him away if she had. Painfully thin and in a coat that was too big for him. And he was carrying a cat in a cage, and a straw hat. She could not make out his features. She could see his money, though, and there was a lot more of it in his wallet. She sensed the beginning of a lucrative franchise. But things had taken an odd turn: she had a perfectly serviceable room to take him to but he had insisted that they go to a hotel. Then, having installed her in a room, he had disappeared off again back to the concierge leaving her with a newly liberated black and white kitten. Returning he had told her that he'd been to order some tea, with extra milk, some Dundee cake and a large jug of water.

It was definitely his first time. Such men, she knew, wanted to talk about their lives and their families before getting down to business. The tea, cake and water had arrived before conversation had really started between them and he immediately drank back the water and began devouring the cake. There was a jug of real milk to go with the tea and he placed far too much of this in a saucer to give to the kitten. Real milk! Somehow, over her outrage, she began to warm to him. Then he offered her a cup of tea. She knew he was going to ask her about herself. It was, after all, the first time. So she was ready.

- I'm a seamstress.
- I was attracted to you by your clothes. They're well cut.
- Shoddy material though.
- But well cut.

She looked at him properly for the first time. It was his eyes: dark hollows lay beneath them ... and crow's feet ... and there were blood lines across the veins. But they were so blue. Piercing and blue. And somehow calm.

- How long have you been doing this?
- None of your business.
- No. But how long? It's important to me.
- Why?
- Please. Answer me. Trust me.

She saw a tremor in his left hand and he began coughing. His handkerchief was thick with blood.

- How long have you been doing this?
- Since September.
- Have you given up as a seamstress?
- Not much call for it now.
- Why did you start?
- Money. I need the money.

After his eyes it was his voice. It was cultured and mellifluous. Later, when she thought back on it she would say it was mesmerising. She was not surprised when the dailies confirmed that he really was a barrister. There was a persuasive vulnerability about him.

- Why do you need the money?
- The bloody war.
- What happened?
- A bloody bomb fell on us. Killed my mum and dad. Killed my husband.
- I'm sorry.
- So I've got no home and no one to support me. And so here I am. Can we get on please?

- What did your husband do?
- He was home on leave. Survived Dunkirk! I thought it was a bloody miracle. He should have stayed at the front.
- Listen, I –
- It wasn't as though Joe hadn't tried to provide for us. Took out an insurance policy on his life. Didn't cover enemy action though. And so that was that.
- Look … I'm sorry but –
- Or was it Act of God? Interesting, these policy exclusions, aren't they?

She sensed, belatedly, that he was trying to say something and so she shut up.

- Listen, I've paid you thirty shillings to be with me now and we both know that is a lot of money.
- An awful lot of money for just talking!
- That's all I want to do. But I have something important to ask of you.
- Look, I don't want to get involved with anyone. Certainly not a punter.

She was beginning to feel nervous. He was clearly deranged, for all his fine language. He was reaching into his jacket again. He pulled out his wallet and then removed some notes from it.

- Look. Ten pounds. It could be yours.
- I don't want any funny stuff you know. Here's your money back. I want to go home. Leave me alone.
- When you leave here you will be followed.

Betty was becoming very scared and her accent started to slip.

- Are you a spy or sumfink?

The kitten was playing with the edges of the curtains and jumping and pouncing on imaginary prey.

- I'm not a spy. But I need your help.
- Ten pounds?

- When you leave here you will be followed. But don't worry. He's a fat, hopeless detective who's trying to catch me in bed with his boss's wife. All I need you to tell him is that you have been coming with me here since May.
- I only started in September!
- A small expansion on the lie.

He waved the notes at her in a way that was more pleading than perfunctory. His voice was calm and controlling. It made her relax.

- That's it. I give you ten pounds and you tell some little lies. Will you do it?

She looked again at the money. It was very inviting.

- That's all I have to do?
- That's all you have to do.
- All right then.

He reached over to her with the money and placed it in her hand. She made to take it but he held on.

- There's one added condition?

She knew it.

- What's that then?
- There is a possibility that the fat man's boss will take me to court over his wife. If he does that I'll need you to repeat to a court what you tell the fat man. It probably won't happen. But if it does you'll have to give evidence.
- It's one thing to lie to this fat man. It's another to swear on the bible!

His voice was like velvet:

- I do understand. If it comes to that I'll give you another ten pounds. Do we have a deal?

He was still holding onto the notes as they sat in her hand. She was uncertain, but she felt that she could trust him.

    – All right. You have a deal. But it isn't going to come to court is it?
    – I'm almost certain.

He let go of the notes.

    – Now. I need to know all about you. And you need to know something about me. We both need to be ready to answer any questions that are asked ...

And for the next surreal hour they talked like young lovers – committing as much to memory as they could and creating a past for themselves. She learnt then that he was a barrister. That he had a degree from Cambridge and lived in south London with his wife and that they had a daughter of twelve called Deborah who was in Edenbridge for the duration. She learnt of his affair with Julia (though he held back her name), and the nemesis that was heading for him. He in turn learnt that she was from Islington, that Joe had been an electrician who had joined up and went with the BEF before being successfully brought back. That they had been living with her parents when the bomb blasted everything away. They had had no children. He had her address and a telephone number. When an hour had passed Adam allowed her to leave, giving her a description as she went of the private detective who, he had little doubt, would be waiting outside. As she left the hotel room she looked back on the funny thin man on the bed, his overcoat still on him, as he played with the black and white kitten; and she thought – to her surprise – that she would not have minded making love to him.

****

A similar thought had passed through Adam's mind as she closed the door behind her. But he was utterly incapable of the act. His innards felt like loose molasses and churned on internal tides within him. Waves of nausea had been sweeping across him with growing frequency as the day progressed and in the quiet moments when he stopped to think what he was doing. His chest had a double wheeze now and he felt his body whistling at him. He took out his handkerchief and re-folded it – trying to make it look white again – then looked back on his day: he had bribed a council official, picked up a prostitute, bribed a hotel clerk and finally bribed the prostitute and persuaded her to join him in a conspiracy to pervert the course of justice. And it was only six in the evening. Worse than that, he had created an alternative truth that would reflect more badly on him than the reality. It would probably end his marriage. The only person it helped was Julia, who would not even speak to him now.

Why had he chosen Betty? The cut of her clothes had been important. He didn't know how difficult it might be to take someone off the street and into the Stafford. And she was pretty, in a girlish way, and blonde. He thought it might help in the long run if she were to be blonde. The racket Jackson was creating further down White Horse Street had helped him make his final choice.

He thought again of Julia: there had been no note in the church when he returned from Romford. She had taken the one he left there but had not replaced it with one of her own. He had originally intended to write only two words but he couldn't prevent himself from continuing. It would mean nothing to her, of course, and would probably just irritate. But he had to say it one last time. He put the kitten back in its cage and made to leave the hotel. Sometime over the course of the next few days he was going to have to tell Catherine that he frequented prostitutes and was going to be Co-Respondent in an unrelated action brought against him by his Head of Chambers. Christmas was unlikely to be happy this year.

****

Julia kept a bowl of hyacinths in the window of her dressing room. During the day they were framed by views of Eaton Square but now the blackout shades had come down. She unfolded the note and read it again:

"TRUST ME"

And then, in much smaller, more hesitant writing:

"I love you."

She folded and unfolded it and then reached for the Swan Vestas. She should burn it. *"Destroy this."* But she read it again and told herself that the smell of smoke would be equally incriminating. She folded it up again, went over to the window and nipped a hyacinth between finger and thumb, just above the bulb, pulling it from its pot. Then she placed the folded piece of paper deep in the bowl, replaced the bulb and tamped down the soil.

There would have been many other ways to get rid of the note but for some reason she chose to keep it.

Chapter Twenty-one

(Tuesday 24ᵗʰ December 1940)

"The war brought this to a head."

Catherine stood before the mirror and examined her eyes. The reflection of an oil lamp on the dresser behind her glowed and gave the glass a golden edge; her face a coppery chiaroscuro. Dusk was falling. She had good eyes, dark and brown with flecks of gold. Her mother's eyes. She thought of her mother's eyes in those last days: how the depth went out of them and the gleam in them died. The colour in them had remained the same but it was if it had been painted on parchment. She wondered if that would happen to her; if her eyes would get set with age and die while she was still alive. For now they remained deep and dark.

She closed out the sound of her daughter sobbing beyond the door and began to apply the kohl. Appearance was going to be important. She had applied a home-made foundation cream recommended by the gipsy, and it had hidden the dark rings under her eyes. The kohl, applied to the lower eyelids, would accentuate her eyes. The first impressions would be the important ones. She raised the makeshift pencil carefully to begin the application when there was a sudden hammering on her door which startled her so that a black line ran from her eye down to her cheek.

– I want to come too, Mummy. Why can't I come too? It's not fair!

Catherine threw down the pencil.

– I've told you. We've been through all this. You can't come with me. You'll see Daddy soon enough.
– But why can't I meet him with you at the station? I wanted to come for a ride in the car.
– Mummy and Daddy need to talk. You'll see Daddy soon enough.
– It's not fair! It's not fair!

128

She turned back to the mirror and, with a handkerchief, began repairing the damage.

"The war brought this to a head."

That thought passed through her mind again. Something had not been right for a long time but she had not been able to pin it down. A collection of small, disparate things had been gathering, like dust over time, in the corners of her mind. She saw, too, that the occasional moments of insight that came to her, like sudden sunlight, revealed that the air was thick with dust, glinting and gleaming around everything. Illumination. Revelation and illumination had been slow. But she trusted her instincts and had been patient. And now it was as though she was able to look into her own thoughts as one who looks into a room that was once clean and has now become dirty.

She inhaled deeply. It had not been her fault. It could not have been her fault. The war had quickened an existing process, had allowed her to become aware of its progression: two years? Three? Four possibly? At some point he had detached himself, or become detached, from his orbit around her. But they had remained happy. Life itself had not changed. Evening conversations and the daily intimacies of their lives together had lost little or nothing of their tempo. There was just the odd "wrong" note; the occasional missed beat. The moments when she had asked what he was thinking and he had said "nothing" when he had been too deep in thought to be thinking of nothing – or to be thinking of nothing important.

And then war was declared and something changed. *When* had it changed? She had done her best to articulate for herself something that still remained beyond her words. Evacuation! It came to her suddenly like a shaft of sunlight: it was at about the time, or soon after the newspapers started to be full of ministerial advice that the children should be evacuated. But the change – the acceleration – couldn't be connected to their daughter, could it? She was as sure as she could be that it was not. It was as though whatever new orbit he had been on had been lost gradually. As if he had begun to drift inexorably through the empty spaces in their lives.

She thought of him over the last six months or so: detached ... uncoupled ... disengaged ...

They were undergraduates at a time before wireless. She had a gramophone and they amassed a collection of 78s which they would dance to or simply have on in the background – quietly, to avoid the College curfew and the porters. She would always have to go down to his College in the heart of the University. He didn't like the exercise that a trip to Girton entailed. He could listen to the same 78 again and again – she tired of their records more quickly than he did. He didn't like it when there was no music, as though, she thought at the time, he didn't like to be alone with his thoughts. She supposed that she was more at home with herself than he was with himself, but she didn't mind that.

And so, as the music palled for her, they would play chess. She had concluded that he was moderately intelligent and she liked that in him, though she saw, even then, the limitations to his intellect. They would play chess. And she would always win. You can learn a lot about a man if you play chess with him regularly. He was impulsive and would panic and act precipitately. He made silly mistakes. Beating him was easy. In all the permutations of a game of chess she would know how he would react when pressure was applied – when things went in unexpected ways. And she was always capable, in chess, of the unexpected.

He was moderately intelligent. But intelligent enough, she thought, to become a success at the Bar. His comparative failure irked her, if only because she felt that she could have made a better fist of it. But it was still a Man's World and she had settled into her expected place as a housewife and a mother. If she regretted anything it was that. And he would come home and tell her of his cases and the advices he had written, and time and again she would ask him the perceptive question only for him to say that he hadn't thought of that. And she had studied English!

Deborah was still sobbing beyond the door. She was more like her father than her mother. She was emotional and impulsive and lacked self-discipline. She would do well. She could get to Cambridge. After the war, when the world changed, as it had to, she would find it easy to establish herself in a profession. She ought to do better than Adam – but not, she thought without arrogance or conceit, as well as she herself would have done given a better chance.

She missed the fact that they no longer played chess together – even though she would always win. But in a sense she was embarking on a game of chess of sorts ... It was not like the chequered board: there were no blacks and whites anymore and they could not take it in turn to move their pieces. But she knew, at least, how he was likely to react to her moves – sometimes as a rook would move, sometimes as a knight – sometimes as a pawn. A game of chess of sorts. But this was one game that she knew she could not win. The best that was left to her, if she chose her own battle-ground and attacked, was a draw that was an honourable draw of sorts. The very best she could hope for – she allowed herself a dry and bitter chuckle as the thought came to her – was a stale mate.

****

The gipsy had prepared the car for the journey to Lowestoft and wanted to ride with her, but she held him off and told him that she was perfectly capable of getting there under her own steam. She had ignored Deborah's entreaties and threatened her with an early bed before leaving. In her pocket she had two freshly laid eggs. They were brown and she had care-fully washed the farmyard dirt off them. She was taking them with her in the hope that, perhaps, things would go well and there would be something to talk about on the drive back to the farm.

It was getting dark as she climbed into the car. She had ensured that there was sufficient time for her to make the five-mile journey to the sta-tion in good time for his arrival. The air was crisp and her breath turned to frost around her. She struggled with the clutch and, as the engine splut-tered into life, wrenched the car through the gears – with the change from second to third she broke a nail. She rarely had, or needed, the opportunity to drive in London. The roads were empty and she drove slowly, partly in deference to the blackout and partly because a journey without headlights was inherently hazardous.

"What is a defining moment? What is being defined?"

She tried to work out in her mind how she found herself driving to a railway station in the middle of nowhere on Christmas Eve in wartime to confront her husband over something that was so ill-defined and yet, in her mind, with growing clarity, so certain. The temptation to say nothing grew with every telegraph pole she passed. And with every mile that dis-appeared behind, her doubts increased. She had no evidence of anything. There was nothing definite. Only the certainty that she had always had when she knew she was right. The knowledge that the future was now, subject to errant bombs, broadly determined.

"If I choose to act – to say something – it is I who am seeking some sort of defini-tion. I will be defining myself. My past. My future. My marriage. My relationship

with Adam. If I say nothing, then events will probably occur in much the same way but I will lose the ability to put my stamp on them. I'll be a passenger on this train of events."

And so she wrestled with her dilemma and decided, ultimately, that her one chance of some autonomy required action.

****

The platforms were empty. It was nearly four o'clock on Christmas Eve and most sensible people were at home preparing for an attenuated Christmas. Catherine looked around her. Two platforms. Railings. A sign swinging languidly in the light wind. All the lights had been extinguished. The solid shapes were turning into shadows. She took a seat on an empty bench and rearranged her hair under her scarf. The chill of the wind crept under her cuffs and she thought of the fire burning back on the farm. Her cheeks were cold. This station. This platform was her chosen battleground.

****

She heard the train before she saw it – a shooshing noise as it slowed – and then it was pulling in with large clouds of steam rising from the locomotive and cab, half obscuring them. She took a photograph in her mind: the train rushing towards her and filling her view – steam rising – and the noise – and told herself that she would remember this. A few passengers filed off and she looked, without anxiety, for Adam. Finally, she saw him: a straggler at the back in his heavy overcoat, lugging a suitcase and carrying some sort of cage – a hint of cigarette smoke rising over his shoulder. Another photograph for her memory bank as she watched him turning into a silhouette. He looked thinner even than forty-eight hours ago.

"Lost,"
she thought.
"Detached, uncoupled and disengaged."

Chapter Twenty-two
(Tuesday 24ᵗʰ December 1940)

- Where's Deborah? I thought she would be with you. I was looking forward to seeing her.
- If you'd come up with me you would have had a whole extra day with her.
- Didn't she want to meet me?
- You'll see her soon enough.
- What's wrong?
- You haven't been eating properly. You never did know how to look after yourself.

Catherine smelt stale smoke on him and looked instinctively for his handkerchief but it was out of sight.

- You've been smoking all the way up, haven't you?
- A small luxury I allow myself. It clears my catarrh for me.

And as if to prove his point, he let out a long and retching cough. Catherine noticed how he reached for his pocket and then held back from producing his handkerchief.

- I know that we have about two hundred pounds in savings – I checked with the bank last week – but it isn't much; I don't like watching it go up in your smoke.
- Why did you go to the bank?

Her first move and it had produced the reaction she had expected. He began coughing again and this time pulled out his handkerchief, making no effort to hide the blood that coated it.

– You're looking beautiful this evening. It's really good to see you. I can't wait to see Deborah. I've brought her a present.

He was swinging the cage and she noticed for the first time that it contained a kitten. She would not be distracted.

– What's going on, Adam?
– What are you talking about?
– We're not going home until you tell me.
– It's Christmas, Catherine.

Find the pressure point and apply the pressure. Don't let up until you get what you want.

She looked into his eyes, knowing that hers were looking beautiful and seeing that his were bloodshot and red-rimmed. He could never hide from her eyes. And she saw something break, and a glitter of resignation, and his thin shoulders slumped.

– Look. It's not good and I'm very sorry. But it is not as bad as it may seem.

She knew at once that it was worse than she could ever imagine, but kept her voice calm.

– What's going on, Adam?
– Look …

He put his suitcase and the cage down at last and opened his arms in entreaty. He looked, she thought, like the silhouette of a scarecrow and would have been almost comical but for the blood-stained rag in his right hand. She watched as he struggled for breath. She was not to know that he was debating in his mind whether or not Julia had been right when, in Hamleys, she told him how things were going to unfold.

– I think I'm going to be cited in a petition for divorce.
– What?!

Catherine was genuinely shocked and could not control her reaction. She felt as though she had, perhaps, moved her pieces too well. There was a pause and she tried to make a mental picture of this for her memory as well: a man and a woman in their thirties caught in a ghastly tableau on an anonymous station platform as the darkness fell around them. She imagined an omniscient eye, rising from them and circling around, watching them in their predicament from every angle – shadows frozen in time with the ghosts of their breath rising.

- But, it's not what it looks like.
- Tell me what it is before you tell me what it looks like, Adam.

She was surprised at how quickly she had regained herself.

- What do you mean?
- Just tell me what you think is going to happen.

She watched him as he appeared to shrink before her. He took an ostentiously deep breath before continuing:

- I think Jeremy Pemberton is going to divorce Julia. I think that he is going to cite me as the Co-Respondent ... I think that I will be served soon after New Year.

Now Catherine was struggling for breath. She wondered to herself whether, if she had not forced the issue, he would have confessed.

- What makes you think this is going to happen?
- I don't know. It's just a feeling.
- You don't expect me to believe that do you?
- I don't understand.
- You don't expect me to believe that you would tell me something as ... as ... horrible as this because you have a *feeling*?
- I ... I –
- Who told you this, Adam?
- It's just a feeling. Honestly. You saw how Pemberton was behaving at his party the other week. Why did he invite us when he has never

135

shown any interest in me – or us? That anxiety to talk to me? Getting me the Bateman case? And all that innuendo? All those references to Julia?

Catherine did recall now her curiosity at the circumstances of the party, but was not satisfied with this explanation.

- Is that it?
- Well ... no ... it wasn't just at the party. There have been all sorts of snide little remarks. It's as though he saw parallels between the Bateman case and the case he's trying to build against me and Julia ... I mean against me.
- So he told you, did he, that he will probably be serving you with a petition in the New Year?

She could not keep the contempt from her voice.

- No. No. It's not like that, it's just that ...

Adam slumped down and sat on his suitcase and said nothing. Just sat there with his head bowed, looking at the ground.

- So, what makes you so sure there will be a petition in the New Year?

She sensed that things were about to get a lot worse.

- Catherine. I'm really sorry. I don't know why I did it. Truly I don't.
- Did ... what?

He had put his handkerchief away and his head was in his hands.

- You see. I've been seeing a prostitute ...

She opened her mouth to speak but could not.

- I've been seeing this prostitute and taking her to the Stafford Hotel off Green Park ...

Her mind filled with obscene images and she looked at her husband again and began to retch uncontrollably.

– I'm sorry Catherine. I'm so sorry.

She found again her ice and her steel.

– How much have you been spending?
– I don't know. I haven't been keeping records.
– And why did you have to take a prostitute to an expensive hotel?
– I … I don't know. I think I was trying to impress her.
– So you are telling me you have been taking the same prostitute, again and again, to the Stafford Hotel?
– I'm so sorry, Catherine.
– Stop saying that! What's her name?

She could see that the question threw him and he struggled for too long before saying that she was called Betty. His hesitation was enough for her.

– And what has this got to do with being cited as a Co-Respondent in the Pemberton divorce?
– Pemberton always employs the same snoop. I had to sign the register and Jackson found out. The man on reception let me know about it. It had to be Jackson from the description he gave – told the man that he was working on a case for an important barrister; in a personal capacity. What else could it mean – with all those hints that Jeremy's been throwing at me?

Catherine looked at the crumpled man.

– So you're telling me that you've been taking the same prostitute to an expensive hotel over a period of months – or is it years? – and Pemberton has found out about it and has jumped to the conclusion that you've been taking his wife there?
– I suppose that is what I'm saying, yes. I'm so sorry.
– And what does … does Betty look like?
– Oh, I don't know … I mean … she's blonde and about five foot four.

– She does seem to look rather like Julia. But why would you need to see prostitutes, Adam? We had a better marriage than that, surely?
– I don't know … I just don't know.

And as she looked down at the man she had married some fifteen years ago, she began to see.

– You bloody fool!

Her voice was a mixture of anger and frustration and something approaching love.

– You bloody fool. Tell me the truth. We can get through this. I'll give you a chance. Have you any idea what you're unleashing? Tell me the truth and I'll stand by you.
– But I'm telling the truth.
– I'm offering you a lifeline, Adam. If you don't accept it you're on your own.
– I'm telling you the truth. Please believe me. I haven't been having an affair with Julia. I promise to stop seeing Betty. Thank you for standing by me on this.
– I'll stand by you if you tell the truth. You're running out of time.
– Catherine, please! We're two articulate adults. Surely we can talk this through?
– *I'm* articulate, Adam. You're merely eloquent. There is a difference. I think that your time is up.

She reached into her pocket and pulled out the two brown eggs.

– I brought these with me in case things turned out differently. So we could have something nice to talk about on the way back to the farm. I haven't seen a real egg for so long. I thought that we could bake something special with them – for Christmas. Deborah was looking forward to helping me with the baking.
– We can still use them in the cooking.

She took the eggs and smashed them, one by one, on his face.

– We shall have a civilized Christmas, Adam. For Deborah's sake. And then you will take the first available train back to London.

He was wiping the albumen and yolk away with his handkerchief.

– Please, Catherine!
– And when you return to London you will take steps to move out of our house into some other place. I don't want you under my roof.
– But I have nowhere to go.
– You will find somewhere, I am sure. Perhaps you can stay wherever you stayed when you didn't come home last Wednesday.

He pulled himself to his feet and picked up the suitcase and the cage.

– I hope Deborah likes the kitten I've brought for her.
– Socks had four white paws. This one only has three. You can take the cat back with you as well.

And so they made their way to the car for the journey back to a very uncomfortable Christmas Day.

– Oh, and Adam?
– Yes?
– I suppose you have thought through the implications of your Head of Chambers citing you in a petition for divorce against his wife?
– What do you mean?
– You do realise, don't you, that you won't be able to continue to practise from Stirrup Court? That you will be without Chambers?
– I ... I hadn't thought of that.
– No, Adam. I'm sure you hadn't.

Chapter Twenty-three
(Sunday 29th December 1940)

Inner Temple Lane is accessible through a large wooden gate fronting onto Fleet Street. In a matter of steps one leaves behind the rush and dirt of the Strand and Chancery Lane and enters a world of almost monastic calm. Adam had been in his early twenties when he had first entered the Temple that way after dark. And he felt as though he had been entering paradise. There was a full moon, which washed everything in silver, and all the gas lamps were alight – a bearded man in blue overalls would go round every evening at sunset with his lamplighter applying a flame. All was peaceful and quiet and the glow of lights from windows in Dr Johnson's Buildings, Goldsmiths Buildings and, at the bottom of the lane, Hare Court, testified to the industry of members of the Bar as they prepared for the following day in Court. That first moment had always been special to him, and in his memory, it was as if the whole lane was phosphorescent with all the different kinds of light. It was then that he knew for certain that this was where he wanted to live and work – among the tangle of sixteenth and seventeenth century buildings in a place where the twentieth century had not penetrated. He had been in his first few months of pupillage, and with a decent degree from Cambridge the opportunities available to him and Catherine seemed endless and intoxicating.

But that was in the autumn of 1923. As he made his way down the lane on Sunday morning, carrying two suitcases and balancing the kitten in its cage, everything was very different. Blackout shades were still in evidence and there was a thick layer of dust over everything. He hadn't been able to get a train back from Suffolk until the Saturday, and the days between his confrontation with Catherine at the station and his return to the same station, driven by the gipsy, had been slow and very painful. Catherine had made him hide the cat in a barn so Deborah would not see it, and as a result he had no Christmas present for his daughter. They had put on a pantomime of marital harmony for her benefit whenever their daughter was present, but when she was not a curtain of ice fell between them. Catherine seemed to be revelling in the play-acting and went out of her way to humiliate him in subtle ways whilst at the same time ensuring that he realised what he was on the verge of losing. If she had brought him a present she did not give it to him. He gave her the straw hat and she mimicked gratitude in front of Deborah but then threw it to one side with disdain when they were alone in their bedroom that night. And Deborah just looked miserable. She did her best to show her father all the things she had found to do and see on the farm, but it was plain that she knew that something was very wrong. The only relief for him was that every day he and Deborah would be able to go off for long walks in the morning after breakfast, and then again after lunch and before dusk.

- Mummy says you're going back to London on Saturday.
- I'm sorry, sweetheart, but I'm afraid I have to.
- But you've only just got here. Why do you have to go?
- It's the war, darling. We can't always do what we want to do.
- Can't we all go back together then?
- Deborah. We'll all be together soon. But, for now, I have to go back on my own. I'm going to have to live apart from Mummy for a little while – because of the war – just like you've had to be living apart from Mummy and me.
- Are you going to be a soldier?
- No, darling. I'm not going to be a soldier. I'll be in London. But a different part of London. Will you look after Mummy for me until she comes back to London?
- Mummy can look after herself.
- But keep an eye out.
- Mummy says that you're weak. That you're the one that needs looking after.
- What else has she been saying?

Deborah looked away.

- She says you don't eat properly. And you've got a bad cough. She thinks you spend too much on cigarettes.
- I'm sorry I forgot to bring your present with me. I promise to send it up from London in the next few days.

– Oh. That's all right. There aren't any good presents at the moment anyway.

– Look after Mummy – and Deborah, if you hear bad things about Daddy don't worry about them. Everything is going to be all right.

****

Catherine had allowed him one night at their home in Dulwich to pack his things. She was unmoved by his entreaties, and he supposed he should have expected that. However, he had nowhere to go. And so he found himself back in the Temple in the hope that he could borrow the flat in Dr Johnson's Buildings again, just for the short term. Whether he would find someone around with a key between Christmas and New Year was another question altogether. He dropped his bags and the cat in the entrance to Stirrup Court and decided to have a look around the Temple for signs of life.

He stepped out through the rubble, dust and broken glass. He hadn't allowed himself the time to look at the devastation wreaked on the Temple in the preceding months. He had been too preoccupied with his own problems, and anyway, when he emerged from Chambers the blackout would be in force and it was not possible to see everything. He walked back through the arches of Cloisters towards Lamb Building. Today, under a sky heavy with rain clouds, he had his first proper chance to look around. The Clock Tower of the Library had gone, and the associated buildings of the Benchers' Smoking Room and the Treasurer's Room were largely demolished. A large part of the Dining Hall had been destroyed by high explosives. Elm Court and Fig Tree Court, of course, had also gone. Beyond the Hall, down towards the gardens, most of Crown Office Row had disappeared, and looking east towards King's Bench Walk he could see that many buildings there had sustained significant damage. Weak sun glinted off broken glass in the window frames and there were craters in Inner Temple Gardens.

But the bombing had eased over Christmas. Stirrup Court was still in one piece, as was the Master's House, the Temple Church and Lamb Building. Dr Johnson's Buildings also, to the west of Inner Temple Lane, was still intact. And so was Cloisters. He allowed himself a quick inventory. Paper Buildings was still there, and Pump Court, Harcourt Buildings,

Hare Court and Mitre Court Buildings. All was not lost. The worst may have passed.

As he completed his tour he saw a group of men assembling on the Terrace staircase in front of what remained of the Hall and Buttery. He recognised them as employees of the Inner Temple. From July 1940 the Inn had provided a nightly fire guard that had been stationed in the Buttery to the west of the Hall. They were often to be seen sitting on the stairs at what had been nicknamed the "Golden Gates" – large Victorian iron gates which had been built in 1870 but, prior to the Blitz, had rarely been open.

– Hullo, Mr Falling.

One of the men was walking across to him – greying and in his late forties but as good-natured as ever –

– Hello, Barry. What are you doing here?
– Could say the same for you. We're keeping an eye out for your buildings, sir. Shouldn't you be celebrating Christmas somewhere?
– Barry. I need a favour. Is that flat in Dr Johnson's Buildings still available? I need somewhere to stay for a few days.

Barry took him by the shoulder, led him away from his colleagues and looked at him keenly through blue-grey eyes.

– Where're your things, mate? I'll see what I can do.
– They're in Stirrup Court. It should only be for a few days.

****

Barry looked at the cases and cage containing the kitten.

– Wait here. I'll go and get the master key.

And on his return he helped him up to the third-floor flat and opened the door onto a small bedroom with a kitchen off to the side.

– I don't know how I can thank you. It isn't as it may seem you know.

– Don't worry, mate … sir, whatever. You're not the first, if that's any
help. I don't think you'll be thanking me so much if they start drop-
ping bombs on us again.
– Is there any chance you could find me a bit of milk – for the kitten,
I mean?
– I'll see what I can do.

And he was gone. Without fuss or questions.

✳✳✳✳

It was five o'clock on Sunday 29th December 1940. The blackout shades were
down and the room was lit only by a small oil lamp that Barry had con-
siderately provided. The nameless kitten was lapping up a small saucer of
milk. Adam put his crystal paperweight on the bedside table and thought
back. It was only sixteen days since he had seen Bateman in conference –
since the Pembertons' party. On Wednesday or Thursday of next week he
would be served with the petition. He would start clearing out his room
in chambers on Monday morning, beginning with his paperbacks. The air
raid sirens started sounding, and gradually he began to hear the dull roar
of planes. They seemed to be saying *"We're coming … we're coming … we're
coming …"* over and over again and he knew he should be making for the air
raid shelter but, really, he just couldn't be bothered. He'd lost Catherine,
Deborah, his home, and soon his profession. And worse would follow. He
would be the subject of ridicule amongst his professional colleagues and
might find his way into the newspapers – *"the nearest I'll ever have got to
being in the law reports!"* What little money he had left would not go far, with
the legal costs and the damages.

The drone of planes was getting louder and closer but he chose to ignore
it. The kitten had finished the milk and was licking itself clean. He picked
it up and it mewled contentedly as it balled up in his hands and tried to
push its face against his.

– I should give you a name.

The little cat pripped and mewed and looked into his eyes.

– What's a good name for a little cat like you?

He rubbed his knuckle on the cat's nape. The planes sound as if they were almost overhead and the whistle of shells started, rattling the window frames. The cat started, its pupils narrowed, and it dug its little claws into his forearm.

"One direct hit. Just one direct hit. That's all we need."

And almost before the thought was complete there was an enormous explosion just outside his window. The oil lamp went out and the whole building began to shudder.

"This is it."

And then there was a frantic hammering on the door. It was Barry shouting through the darkness and the noise.

– Incendiaries! They're dropping bloody incendiaries! The whole bloody place is going up in flames! Open the bloody door! We need help!

PART TWO

Chapter Twenty-four

(Monday 30th December 1940)

Jack Storman KC lowered his umbrella as he passed through the Tudor Street Gate and into the Temple. The rain was beginning to ease but the hissing sound that had accompanied him from Blackfriars grew louder and more sinister as he walked past King's Bench Walk. The sight that greeted him was dumbfounding. He let the umbrella drop to his side and was oblivious to the drizzle landing on his head and shoulders. There was freshly broken glass and rubble all around him. The acrid smell of burning. To his right the remains of 5, King's Bench Walk were still smouldering. Ahead of him he could see that the Temple Library had been virtually destroyed and smoke continued to rise from two sets of chambers. Water damage to what remained of the library testified to the intense fire-fighting that had gone on overnight. Rain on hot ash was causing the hissing noise. In the distance he could hear glass being swept away.

All our books ...

A few dazed individuals had begun the task of sifting through the new destruction and he saw some members of the Bar he recognised picking through the broken stone for what remained of their possessions. He tried to picture the battle against the bombs that must have taken place during the night but his imagination faltered at the task. He and Margaret had lain awake in their Anderson shelter as the bombing continued and, as always, he wondered whether Stirrup Court would still be there for him to go back to in the morning. The signs were not good. He took a last look at King's Bench Walk and then headed towards Lamb Building, seeing with relief that it had survived untouched. Beyond it the white pillars and columns of Cloisters also remained. His hopes were rising as he turned the corner into Stirrup Court and saw it standing as it always had done. He made to go inside.

– Mr Storman! Mr Storman!

A bedraggled man was running towards him, his clothes and face black against the white pillars of Cloisters.

– Barry! What is it?
– Come quick. It's your Mr Falling. He needs help.
– What's Adam doing here? I thought he'd gone out to Suffolk.
– He's in 2, Dr Johnson's. Come quickly!

Storman forgot about going into Chambers and followed the man as he dashed back up Inner Temple Lane. Barry gave a garbled account of the fall of the incendiaries the previous night as they climbed the stairs to the third-floor flat.

– There were fires everywhere and we had to work flat out with the hosepipes. Mr Falling was staying in Dr Johnson's and came to help.

Barry turned the key and they entered the little flat. Adam was lying unconscious on the bed, his trousers covered in soot. His white shirt, stained red, was soaking wet and open to the waist. A sheen of perspiration glistened over the dirt on his chest and face and his breathing was laboured and uneven. Storman could see the bump of his ribs under the shirt. He seemed a lot thinner even that a week or two ago. His crystal paperweight was by the bed. This was not the time to ask him what he was doing there. Barry took a towel and wiped the dirt and sweat away from his face.

– What happened?
– There was so many fires in and out of the Temple that we ran out of water.

He gestured at the figure on the bed.

– He was like a madman, sir. Running in and out of buildings and trying to beat on the flames with whatever he could get his hands on. I'm surprised he didn't kill himself. I told him to be more careful but he took no notice. When the fires spread to the Library he really went doolally. You'd have thought he owned it.
– How did he get hurt?

– That's the funny thing, sir. I got him to calm down after a while and we started relaying the water up from the Thames. He was passing the full buckets to me and I was taking them up to the next man in line.

He paused and wiped Adam's face again.

– Then at about three in the morning. Just before it started raining. I came back to him with an empty bucket and he was collapsed on the ground with blood coming out of his mouth. I had to half carry him back here. He was raving again when I got him to his feet.
– How long has he been unconscious?
– About seven hours, I think. He's been talking in his sleep.
– What's he doing here, Barry?
– Arrived last night with two bags and that kitten. Said he needed a place for a few days. I didn't ask any questions, sir.

Storman hadn't noticed the kitten until then. It was sleeping in its cage in the corner of the room. More questions were forming in his mind but he decided it would be better if he kept them to himself.

– By the way, sir. Who is Julia?

Storman was startled by the question, but before he was able to think of an appropriate answer a stirring from the bed distracted them both.

– Jack?

Adam was trying to raise himself into a half seated position. His eyes were dim and out of focus.

– Is that you, Jack?
– Adam. Are you all right?
– I haven't got any cigarettes. They all got soaked. Do you have any cigarettes, Jack?
– Never mind cigarettes. We need to clean you up and put some fresh clothes on you.

– Have you got any more milk for the kitten, Barry?

Before Barry could answer Adam sat bolt upright and grabbed Storman's arm, a look of panic in his eyes.

– What day is it Jack?
– It's Monday.
– But what's the date?
– 30th December. Why do you want to know?

Adam fell back onto the bed and became calm again.

– Not the New Year yet. Not the New Year.
– Come on. Let's get you out of those clothes.

Storman put his arms round Adam and brought him gently back into a sitting position. He weighed almost nothing. He started to ease his arms out of the blood-stained shirt but the exertion was too much. Adam began to retch horribly and his thin chest began to heave. He let out a ghastly cry and then vomited blood. Storman let him lie back down again and Adam began to cry. There was brick-dust in the blood.

– I think we'd better get him a doctor.

Chapter Twenty-five
(Monday 30ᵗʰ December 1940)

It's the little things that give us away: unusual warmth – uncharacteristic harshness. For Storman, forced politeness was the most cracked of the masks: people not being entirely themselves. It was like a wrong note on a frequently played 78 – the sensation we feel when a key which had always turned smoothly in the lock inexplicably catches. We tremble when the sense of things is wrong, and lie awake at night looking for logic.

Storman thought of detection – which was a job for the police – and cross-examination – which fell to him – and he saw how they overlapped like circles in a Venn diagram. He thought of those "join the dot" puzzles in the Saturday penny dreadfuls: a blank sheet of white paper covered in black spots. You joined the dots together to find the image concealed. But on Saturdays you could cheat: the relevant dots had numbers next to them. The rest remained anonymous as snow.

In life – in the courtroom – there were very many dots and very few numbers. No road map. The facts were jumbled up, with little facts taking up more room than big facts and sometimes obscuring them entirely. And some of the dots were not flat and black but glittered with three-dimensional significance like diamonds. There was no cause and effect on the face of it, beyond those evident within the facts themselves. Observable facts, facts that would make up the dots on the landscape, paper-white or otherwise, tend to be physical. Emotions and feelings – the human factors – cannot easily be distilled into facts. The random magnetic impulse drifting beneath things, attracting or repelling and moving men and women in inexplicable ways, they were the dye that coloured a scene. The frame that gave a picture its proper perspective.

The police, or the solicitors, would collect the random dots that were the facts and place them before Storman on a blank piece of paper. And they would ask him to persuade a judge or a jury how the dots joined up – to persuade him, or them, about cause and effect. He had thought much about detective work, and about cross-examination particularly, when joining the dots together in the Saturday puzzle. Sometimes he would ignore the numbers altogether and see what he could produce without them. He realised, using different coloured pencils, that he could make the same random scattering of dots resemble, on the one hand, a Duchess riding in her coach and, on the other, the same Duchess being pleasured by her coachman. The two images lay across one another in different colours. He found them vaguely erotic. And he realised through the exercise how important the joining of the dots was. How important were cause and effect. How invisible in the equation were feelings, emotions … and motive.

He shivered. After they had cleaned Adam up he'd put his overcoat back on. He moved over to the window and gazed down on the Norman steeple of the church. His breath frosted the glass. Barry had been gone for almost two hours. He hugged himself and found comfort in the warmth of the cashmere. Behind him Adam slept in fresh clothes and under additional blankets. The kitten was curled up at the bottom of the bed and the bloodied shirt was soaking in the sink.

He turned from the window, his overcoat silhouette partially blocking the light, and looked down at his friend. He was glad he hadn't been talking in his sleep. He thought about the joining of the dots. We all see things in different ways. It could be dangerous to join the dots.

He thought back to the previous Monday: approaching Chambers from the Gardens he'd seen Jackson loitering around Cloisters and he'd hung back. Jackson was Jeremy's favourite detective – Storman wasn't sure why – and he'd noticed him lingering around Chambers with increasing frequency over recent months – his stomach sticking out from pillars or the brick of buildings. And then, three weeks ago, when looking at his own diary entries, he saw that Jeremy was marked for a private appointment. It was Jackson. He saw him slipping in. A barrister never met a witness without a solicitor present. There was no case name in the diary. Storman was not stupid, but he didn't know where this particular trail was leading. He wasn't sure he wanted to know.

And then there was Jackson, loitering in Cloisters. Storman had hung back. The detective looked like a dog with a scent. His excitement betrayed him. He was oblivious to Jack's presence. He shifted in the shadows around the columns. Storman followed his eyes to the doors of the Temple church. Adam emerged and headed up Inner Temple Lane. And Jackson had followed.

Storman thought back to Pemberton's party. He had known Jeremy for twenty-five years. Adam for fifteen. He could see where the key was catching in the lock. Jeremy had never invited Adam and Catherine to one of his soirées before. And he was agitated, in a way that Storman had never previously noticed. Too keen to speak with Adam. He had watched the exchange between the two when the Fallings had arrived. Adam and Jeremy facing one another. It was like a still life against the glittering tableau of champagne, chandeliers and candles. Jeremy speaking to Adam, outwardly courteous. Catherine to one side in that blue dress, her eyes flitting around and taking stock. Something had troubled him at the time and he cast a fly with Adam, to no effect. What was it? And then it clicked; and the lock turned.

A crackle of menace. Something defensive in Adam. Catherine sniffing the air. And at the end of the party, as he said goodbye to the Pembertons, there was something that did not fit. He was not to know that Adam had thought them "brittle". But "brittle" was apposite. There was an air of static around them.

****

Adam was still asleep, his breathing stertorous. What was he doing in a flat on the third floor of Dr Johnson's Buildings on the approach to New Year? Why was he so perturbed by the year ahead? The mix was volatile. Jeremy or Catherine or Adam or Julia could have drawn wrong conclusions. Emotions were on hair-triggers. To intervene would be to complicate. He would wait. And he would watch. When he addressed a jury he would often call upon Shakespeare: time would unravel what plighted cunning hides. Patience was a virtue. He would watch and he would wait.

But if a proper interpretation of all this was that Jeremy was going to petition his wife and to cite a member of Chambers as Co-Respondent, that would have consequences. It would affect Chambers. And it would affect him. Adam, wherever the truth might lie, would have to leave.

****

Night was beginning to fall. Storman brought down the blackout and lit an oil lamp by the bed. Fragments of light glittered out from the fractured paperweight.

155

– Jack? Is that you? You're still here?
– How are you, Adam?
– I'm done in, Jack.
– Barry's gone to find a doctor. You'll be all right.

The kitten uncurled with the voices, stretched and began moving towards Adam with the starched prance of the newly woken feline.

– What do you think I should call her, Jack?
– Haven't a clue.
– I was thinking of "Jules".
– I don't think that's a very good idea.

Adam had raised himself on an elbow but slumped back. He looked hurt and puzzled.

– What do you suggest?
– How about Cordelia?
– Why?
– It has a certain alliterative resonance. The name was going through my head. You could call her Delia for short if you were in a hurry.

And so Cordelia – or Delia – became the name of the cat. Storman stood by the blacked-out window. The lamp threw his shadow against the walls. It flickered behind him. Cordelia nuzzled up to Adam and he stroked her.

– Is there any more milk, Jack?
– I don't want to ask any questions, Adam; but you shouldn't be here alone. You're not well. Come and stay with us.

Adam's eyes levelled on Storman's. Ice blue, they had regained their depth.

– That's very kind. But I wouldn't be good company. I need to be on my own. I want to be near the church.

There was steel in the answer. Jack let it hang in the air. The kitten had fallen asleep. He was cold. Adam was looking at the cat.

– Jack?
– Yes?
– Hypothetically ... I mean ... if I found myself ... involved in a divorce case ... would you act for me?
– It would depend who else was involved. I'd be happy to ... but I know Catherine rather well and ...
– It's nothing to do with Catherine ... Catherine will stand by me.
– It depends who else is involved, Adam.

Adam flickered. He was not a fool.

– But if you couldn't act for me. Who would you recommend?

Like the balls in a bagatelle board, the pieces were falling into place.

– There is a man I know who, I think, would be able to help.
– Who is it, Jack?
– We're talking hypothetically, Adam, I don't want to put any names into the mix.
– Please, Jack. If you can't tell me who he is can you at least tell me something about him?
– I can't say much, Adam. It would not take much for you to recognise him.
– Please Jack. Tell me something.
– He's my call but he's never taken silk. I don't think he ever will. But he's a better barrister than I'll ever be.
– Why has he chosen not to take silk?
– The choice is not ultimately his. Let us just say that the Lord Chancellor does not look on him with favour.
– What's he done wrong, Jack?
– He's done nothing wrong in my opinion, which might be a minority view, but his lifestyle is somewhat ... unconventional.
– Why would he be the right man then?

Adam's eyes had narrowed and his gaze was like a splinter of ice. Storman could see him thinking. Anything more and his friend would work it out.

– Adam! This is all hypothetical, isn't it? I'll say more if it's absolutely necessary.

He looked at his watch. It was getting dark. When would Barry arrive with the doctor?

Chapter Twenty-six

(Monday 30th December 1940)

Across London Jeremy Pemberton KC entered his study and locked the door behind him. Samuels had put the blackout shutters in place and lit his desk lamp for him. There was a sheaf of his writing paper squared off on the red leather top. This marked the end of Christmas for him and the beginning of something far more serious. He had left Julia and Jenny with Agnes in Julia's dressing room, and as he closed the door the sounds of their voices receded to nothing. He picked up the photograph of Joan as he made his way to the desk and gazed at it for long minutes before replacing it reverently. His notepaper glowed under the green shade of the desk lamp, and his spectacles, similarly, gleamed gold as he sat down.

He picked up a sheet of writing paper and held it up to the lamp to remind himself of the distinctive "P" in the watermark. Monday the 30th December 1940, only two days until the New Year. He had followed his solicitors' advice and done his best to make Christmas seem as normal as possible for Jenny – and for Julia's children. Julia had given nothing away. There had been no sign that she was in any way perturbed and she just seemed pleased to have her children back with her in London. Jenny had seemed to him oblivious to what was about to happen. He must speak with her in the next few days and explain to her why he had to do what he was doing.

He took out his key and unlocked the side drawer of his desk, taking from it a carefully folded silk handkerchief. He placed it on the leather next to his writing paper and unfolded it carefully so as to disturb the ashes as little as possible. The ghost of the letter "P" was still plainly visible and, holding up a fresh sheet again to the lamp, there could be no doubt that it was a burnt-up piece of his own writing paper. Only Julia had access to it and she had made no mention of using it or of writing to Adam. There could be no acceptable reason for her to write to him. It was a small piece of evidence. But in Pemberton's view, in the right hands, it was damning.

He unlocked the middle drawer and pulled out a small pile of buff envelopes – reports from Jackson. The last of these was dated the 24th December. Jackson had been very pleased with himself and brought it to the house personally. Pemberton read again the detective's account of his adventures the previous Monday. Jackson's clever pursuit of Falling as he attempted to shake him off by taking a train to Romford; the trip to Green Park, and the extraordinary turn of events as Falling went to Shepherd Market to pick up a prostitute and then, in an even more surprising twist, took her to the Stafford Hotel. Jackson had done well. It was only disappointing that the evidence, as a whole, suggested that Adam had been in the habit of taking the same girl back to the hotel and that there was nothing to connect Julia with the Stafford. He wished they had been able to dig out the fact that Falling had frequented the Stafford earlier in the year but, unfortunately, Jackson had only been able to discover this after weeks of leg-work.

It had been Pemberton's idea: he knew the sort of hotels that Julia would be prepared to go to, if his hunch was right; and he had made up a list of those that were within a certain circumference of Eaton Square. It had only been on Monday the 16th December that Jackson had hit the jackpot: Falling had been going there regularly, sometimes more than once a week from the May of 1940 until about October, and then had stopped. Pemberton assumed that prior to that he had been signing in under a false name. It was a pity that the sordid truth was that he was seeing some prostitute – the girl had confirmed it to Jackson – rather than Pemberton's wife, but it didn't spoil the general thrust of his case. Here was a man who was unfaithful to his wife. The fact that a member of his Chambers had taken to consorting with prostitutes was a sufficient reason to give him notice to leave. Falling was finished.

But something was nagging at him: why, after a two month abstinence and when Falling ought to have known better, had he gone back to the Stafford at all? Pemberton had started to apply the pressure and it was clear to him that it was beginning to get to Adam. He thought back to his exchange with him on the Monday after his party, when he had dropped heavy hints about his choice of books. More importantly he remembered Adam's reaction when he showed him the burnt paper and the watermark – the uncontrollable tremor in his left hand. Pemberton had almost gone as far as to accuse him of an improper association just by showing him the burnt note paper. He had made even heavier hints that afternoon when Falling had returned from Court and it was plain that Falling was very nervous. Why compound things for himself? At that stage on the Monday morning Pemberton himself was unaware of the fact that Falling had been going to the Stafford. And by the following Monday Adam had gone back there. It wasn't possible that he could have found out what Pemberton knew.

He put the report back in the envelope and placed all the buff envelopes next to the silk handkerchief holding the ashes. He took the letter from his solicitors out of the drawer, unfolded it, and was running a cursory eye over the advice they had given when, on reaching the final page, he froze. There could be no doubt about it: the flourish of the signature was smudged. He placed the page down under the lamp and took out a silver magnifying glass – a gift from a grateful Countess. Under the light it was clear: a small initial smear had been made worse by the attempt to clear it. He could picture Julia reading the letter – saw her tears falling – it could only have been Julia. It was a pity we didn't have the science to link a person to their tears. So Julia had known about the Stafford, had known that he was planning to petition her in the New Year and cite Falling. He thought of the way in which she had mimicked marital harmony to all over the previous ten days and he felt a surge of rage.

If she had known, it was possible that she had alerted Falling. That would explain why he would have behaved in the way that he did. But he was certain that she had not been in contact with Falling. He had briefed Samuels discreetly, as he had Arthur, his senior clerk, and both had made it clear to him that there had been no unexplained phone calls or letters. If they were communicating with one another it must be in some other way. He threw the magnifying glass across the room. He wasn't prepared to wait until the New Year. He would arrange for Julia to be served tomorrow. Jackson could go up to Edenbridge on New Year's Day and serve Adam in front of his wife and daughter.

Pemberton picked up the photograph of Joan again. She had been so lovely and intelligent. Long dark hair and a beautiful pale complexion with a hint of roses. And every day Jenny was looking more like her – it was almost as if Joan was growing up again before his eyes. He missed her so much.

He took out his Mont Blanc and began to compose a letter to Falling – giving him notice to leave Chambers. He would have to change the locks to his study.

****

- How does it look?
- They all look good on you!
- I'm going to try the green one on again. I'm so excited.
- Are you sure it's safe to be going out?
- It's one of the safest places in London – and that coloured man and his band will be playing.

Jenny let the red dress fall from her so that she was wearing only her underwear. In her haste her brassiere had fallen slightly so that Julia could see the trace of a nipple, rosebud pink, before she adjusted herself.

- We took such a pounding last night. They could well be back tomorrow night.
- Oh don't be silly. And besides, there's this young captain who has an eye on me.
- You'd captivate him in any of these dresses.
- It's so good of you. They all fit me so well. We could be sisters.
- Yes.

The truth was that Julia regarded her step-daughter more as a sister than anything else. When she first met Jeremy Jenny had only just started crawling. Jeremy always referred to her as "our daughter" but Julia always found it awkward to call her that. As far as she was concerned Agnes was their daughter and Jenny was Jenny. She was very fond of her. Puberty had been kind. She had never been an ugly duckling. Her limbs had lengthened and her body had filled out without acne or lack of proportion. Her teeth had been, briefly, too big for her mouth but now she had the most wonderful smile and her eyes were deep and brown.

- What's wrong with Daddy?
- What do you mean?
- He's such a fool. He doesn't think I notice things.
- Jenny! What *are* you talking about?
- You've both been behaving oddly lately and I can't put my finger on it.
- What do you mean?

- You weren't like this when I was younger.
- We haven't changed.
- You're both stiffer. It's like you're both acting.

Sometimes it takes someone who knows you and is observing you to bring home the little truths. Julia was shaken. She had been trying so hard to be natural.

- You look more and more like your mother every day.
- Do I? What was she like?
- I never knew her. I meant the photographs of her.
- Daddy keeps saying that to me. You're beautiful too.
- I wish we had some colour pictures of her. I can't really picture her moving and laughing.

Jenny held the green dress in her left hand. She looked so vulnerable as she stood there in her underwear, the weight slightly on her right hip. There was a puzzle in her eyes. If Joan was half as kind, half as sympathetic, as her daughter, Julia could understand why Jeremy missed her so much. With every year of her step-daughter's life she understood more why her husband missed his first wife. And why, every year, as Jenny grew, the memory of Joan grew stronger with him. Julia was sure it was this as much as anything else which powered his animus. That pushed her away from him. Jenny would know any day now.

- You look so sad.
- Daddy misses your mother.
- What's happening with you and Daddy?
- I think that something's about to happen. But you *must* understand. If it does, it's not your fault. It's nothing to do with you.

Jenny dropped the dress. Agnes was chattering to herself amongst the discarded outfits. The air was heavy with the scent of hyacinths. Stephen and Sebastian were up in the nursery with the nanny playing chess together.

- What do you mean, it's nothing to do with me? What's happening?

– I'm sorry. I didn't mean it *that* way.

Jenny had sagged down onto a chair. Her eyes were troubled.

– Listen. Daddy has got an awful lot on his mind. When we get older
we think a lot more than we did when we were young. We sit and
stew and sometimes we get it wrong. We can look back and wish that
things were different.
– What's happening?
– Do you know a man called Adam Falling?
– Never heard of him.
– He's a member of Daddy's chambers. He was at the Christmas party.
– Daddy's never spoken of him.
– He was the very thin man who wasn't wearing a uniform. He kept
coughing.
– Oh, him! Has he upset Daddy?
– Listen. Jenny. I'm sorry. This is all so absurd. But I think Daddy thinks
I've been having an affair with that pathetic little man.
– But that's so stupid!

Julia could see that the whole idea was fantastical to her step-daughter –
as she had hoped it would be.

– Please don't tell Daddy I've told you this. If nothing comes of what I'm
saying he'll think I'm being pathetic and silly myself.
– But you've never mentioned him. If I was in love with someone I'd be
talking about them all the time.

Jenny had been talking incessantly about this captain who she was going
with to the Café de Paris in recent weeks and Julia knew that what she was
saying about herself was true. Age teaches us camouflage. She wished she
could be young again.

– I know. I know. That's why it's so silly.
– What do you think he's going to do?
– Well, darling. Please be calm about this. I think he is going to try to
divorce me over it.

– What!?

There were tears in Jenny's eyes.

- Please don't tell Daddy I told you this. I'm sure he is plucking up the courage to tell you himself. The silly man!
- You haven't been having an affair with him, have you?
- Look me in the eyes, Jenny. Of course I haven't. I love Daddy. It's just that he misses your mother.
- I think you were the best thing that could have happened to Daddy after mummy died.
- I've tried so hard.
- I'm going to speak to him about it!
- Please don't! Not unless he tells you he's going to divorce me.
- I don't want you and Daddy to separate. It's so unfair!

Jenny was half sobbing but she pulled herself together and Julia's heart went out to her. Agnes was gazing up from the discarded dresses with a puzzled look on her face. Before they could continue with their conversation there was a ring of the doorbell. Julia excused herself and went to the landing. Samuels shimmered over to the front door and opened it to Jackson.

- Good evening, Mr Jackson. Mr Pemberton is expecting you. I will show you up.

So Samuels was in on it as well. Was there no one she could trust? She fixed herself with a smile and went back into her dressing room.

****

Bateman was sweating. He was late and had been running for about twenty minutes. He'd reached the gates of the park. Or rather, he had reached the place where the gates used to be – they'd all been taken away and scrapped as part of the war effort. He had thought Jackson would never stop trailing him and so he had led him as far away from where he had intended to be as he could. Then, suddenly, he had seen Jackson look at his watch, turn around and lumber off in the opposite direction. Bateman lit a match to look at his own watch. He was very late. He hoped she had waited.

Victoria was in their usual place against the trunk of an old oak tree.

- I'm freezing!
- I'm sorry I'm late. That bloody snoop has been following me.
- Graham will be suspicious if I'm out much longer.
- I'll be quick. We need to have our stories straight. I'm going to ask my solicitor to sort out another meeting with the barrister.
- Is it worth it, Arnold? Why don't you give him some of the insurance money?
- I've got a good barrister. I think he can get us out of this.
- How much have you told him?
- No more than I have to. Odd bloke but very good. I'll bet he's working on the case as we speak.

****

- Kerthunk!

Novak lay back on his bed and looked down on his blue serge outfit. He wished they would stop practising.

- Kerthunk!

It had been going on since sunset. Almost an hour now. Tomorrow was New Year's Eve. Why execute someone on such a day? He heard the warders lifting the sack back into place.

- Kerthunk!

So someone was going to drop through the trapdoor tomorrow at 6 a.m. Someone was not going to see 1941. Someone was going to die without a death certificate – one of the smaller indignities of execution as a spy. He thought it was probably the Pole. No one liked him. A bad day to go, but then again was there ever a good day? Would he be next? His trial had been set for Monday 3rd March – nine weeks away. He was lucky. It was further away than he had been told it would be. They had to talk with Katya. She was his only hope. He missed her so! He thought of his barrister. A bit weak. Gullible. But sincere. He was probably working on his case as he, Novak, lay there in his bunk.

– Kerthunk!

Chapter Twenty-seven
(Monday 30th December 1940)

Storman had pulled down the blackout shades and lit the oil lamp. It threw his elongated shadow along the walls as he paced up and down. He looked, for the umpteenth time, at his watch. It was well past six. The air raid sirens had begun sounding over twenty minutes ago and already he could hear the throbbing of aeroplanes above to the east and to the west of him. A third-floor flat in the Temple wasn't a clever place to be. Margaret would be worrying about him. He had been out for over nine hours. Adam was sleeping fitfully again, curled like a baby. There were still traces of blood on the blanket and sheets, but thankfully he had lapsed into silence and then dozed off. Cordelia was balled up at the end of the bed.

Before pulling down the shutters he had taken one last look from the window. As night advanced the flickering of still burning fires around the Temple – and in the wider city – had become brighter. They were sitting ducks. If Goering chose to attack again as he had done the night before there would be little they could do to stop him. The flames of last night's bombings made the targets stand out like beacons and they were running out of water. If only Adam had a wireless. Where was Barry? Perhaps he should wake Adam and pull him down into one of the shelters? He looked at the vulnerable figure and decided against it. Barry would never find them if they moved on and Adam clearly needed urgent medical attention.

He needed to ring Margaret. Checking that Adam was still sleeping, he went over to the door and let himself out silently so as not to wake him. He would go down to Stirrup Court and try and use one of the telephones there. He felt his way down the unfamiliar stairs. Reaching the ground floor, he fought off the temptation to go one floor further down into the shelter and stay there for the night. It was little more than twenty-four hours since the incendiary strike. Emerging into the cold night air, Storman caught the smell of burning; the whiff of cordite. There was brick-dust still, floating in the air around him. No one was about. He inched his way down Inner Temple Lane towards Cloisters.

The sky was dull above him and no stars shone. A barrage balloon drifted high over the Thames. The sound of planes was getting louder. Ack-Ack guns were firing into the sky, and not far off he could hear the crump of falling bombs. So far none were landing on the Temple. He wanted to get back home. He edged down towards Cloisters, resisting the growing temptations of the shelters under Hare Court and in the church.

And then he heard voices and hurrying footsteps – he saw two shadows moving quickly through the white columns of Cloisters. Barry was running at a crouch, dragging a small man holding a briefcase along with him.

- Barry! Over here!
- Mr Storman, sir. This is Doctor Hodgson. I found him over near Ludgate Circus. He was patching somebody up. It's a right bloody mess out there. There's fires everywhere. It's all been flattened, so far as I can work out, between Cannon Street and Moorgate. He's been doing running repairs for people all the way over. I'm done in. He is as well.

Both men looked exhausted. There were purple circles under Barry's eyes and a fresh accumulation of grime on both of them. As they got closer Storman was able to get a better look at the doctor. He was a slight man. His smart gabardine was creased and soiled. His eyes were glinting behind round wire spectacles and he was breathing heavily.

- I'm just going off to Stirrup Court. I need to ring my wife. Then I'll take you up to Falling.

The doctor gave out a large sigh.

- Have you any idea of the devastation out there? I haven't rested all day. I'm very tired, Mr Storman. I want to get home to my own family. Can we make this quick? We will go and see your friend now or not at all.

Reluctantly, Storman turned and led the men back up Inner Temple Lane.

****

169

– Shall we wake him?
– Not yet. Barry has told me the circumstances of his collapse. It sounds to me as though he has been haemorrhaging. But what is he doing here?
– I'm not sure. I think he may be having marital problems.

Storman kept his voice as neutral as he could.

– I see there is some blood still on his blankets.
– We've cleaned him up as best we can.
– Put handkerchiefs across your mouths.

Doctor Hodgson took off his coat and picked up the oil lamp. He went over and, taking out a magnifying glass, looked more closely at the traces of blood on the counterpane. He took a spatula from his briefcase and began probing the blood stains.

– As I suspected.
– What?
– There is the brick dust but this ... this was what I thought I might find.

Doctor Hodgson held up his spatula. Barry and Storman closed in to examine it.

– What?
– Can't you see? Look more closely.

Some small white specks ...

– What are we looking at?
– Necrotic tissue. If I am not mistaken these are the granulomas of tuberculosis.
– Necrotic tissue?
– These are the remains of dead cells from your friend's lungs.
– What are you saying?

Doctor Hodgson stepped backwards and his shadow leapt in the lamp-light across the walls. He put his handkerchief across his mouth.

- Mr Falling has a tubercular infection. It is probable that he has had it for some time.
- How long? How?
- Bad diet. Cold housing. Your friend does not look after himself. They used to call it consumption. The illness that consumes from within. That is why he is so thin. I must examine him. Make him ready.

Storman woke him and, gently, he and Barry lifted him into a sitting position and opened his shirt. Hodgson reached into his case and pulled out a stethoscope, breathing on it to warm it up.

- Jack? Are you still with me?
- You're all right, Adam.

Hodgson was probing his chest. In the distance the sound of bombs could still be heard and, across the shutters, the metronomic sweep of searchlights.

- Mr Falling. How long have you had problems with your chest?
- I don't know. There isn't much wrong with me. A bad cough. That's all.
- Barry tells me that you vomited blood earlier today. Has this happened before?
- From time to time. If I don't think about it, it goes away. It's nothing. Really. It's nothing.

Hodgson used his handkerchief to wipe away the sweat on Adam's forehead.

- You are married?
- My wife and my daughter are in Suffolk.
- Why are you here?
- Jack? Jack? Were you able to find me any cigarettes? I need a cigarette.
- Mr Falling. You must sleep. Cigarettes are not what you need now.

The doctor turned to Barry and Jack.

- He has a tubercular infection. He is lucky that it has not advanced to the full-blown disease. If it did, his chances of survival would be less than fifty per cent.
- What should we do?
- Mr Falling. Mr Storman has told me that perhaps you have some marital difficulties. Can you tell me about these?
- Jack!? ... Mr Storman has it wrong. My wife and I are very happy. It's just the war. Jack?
- Calm down, Adam. We should get you into a shelter.

Adam's eyes were clear and blue.

- I don't want to go down to any shelter. I'm happy where I am. You can go if you wish.

Barry had been sitting quietly in the armchair in the corner.

- Mr Storman, sir. I'm sorry. But I haven't slept for over twenty-four hours, and if last night was anything to go by I won't get much sleep tonight. Do you mind if I leave you?
- Yes. I'm sorry. Yes. Of course. Thank you Barry. And good night.

Barry hauled himself upright and headed for the door.

- Good night, Mr Storman ... Jack ... Doctor Hodgson.

And he was gone.

- Thank you, Doctor. I do appreciate everything you've done. I should let you go home now.
- Your friend is in a bad way. I'm not sure he should be left on his own.

Adam stirred.

- Go home, Jack. I'll still be here in the morning.

Cordelia stretched and began to move across the bed towards Falling. Storman picked her up and began to stroke her.

- You must go home, Doctor. What must we do to help Adam?
- He needs plenty of food and more warmth. An extra fire would help. He is a heavy smoker. I do not think that is helping. The brick dust and ash in his lungs probably precipitated his current problems. He is also under other pressures. Try and get him to talk about them. I am not a psychiatrist, but whatever the burden he is carrying it would be easier if it were shared.
- Thank you, Doctor. Send your invoice to me at Stirrup Court. It will be met.
- I'll write him a prescription. Morphine may assist. If any can be found.

Storman watched as the doctor packed up his things and then made for the door.

- It would not be a bad thing, Mr Storman, if your friend did not go the shelter tonight. He may well be infectious. We would not be thanked for allowing such an infection to spread.
- I will speak with him.

****

It was getting on for eight in the evening. Storman calculated that he could just get the last train home.

- Adam. Come home with me. We can look after you for a few days.
- Have you told anyone I'm here?
- What's going on?
- Have you told anyone where I am?
- Why aren't you in Suffolk?
- Don't tell anyone where I am, Jack.
- People will find out soon enough. But no, I won't tell anyone. If you won't confide in me though, I can't help you.
- You know more than you're letting on to me.

– I must go. I'm going to miss the last train.
– Come and see me tomorrow, Jack.
– It will be New Year's Eve. It will be difficult.
– Thank you, Jack. Whatever happens. Thank you.

Chapter Twenty-eight

(Tuesday 31st December 1940)

Samuels balanced the tea tray in his right hand and carefully made his way down the stairs into the cellars, using his left hand to steady himself as he descended. Reaching the bottom, he threw a switch and light flooded out before him creating stark shadows and pools of darkness amongst the wine racks. The space below the Pembertons' house was deceptively deep and spacious. Pemberton had not been exaggerating when he said that he had filled the cellar with wine and champagne. Like the bookcases in a library the wine racks rose up to the ceilings all around the butler as he made his way through the labyrinth. The arc lamp behind him threw his distorted shadow against the brickwork and it danced ahead of him.

When the air raids started to gain in intensity Pemberton had given orders for beds to be made up in the cellars. Makeshift rooms were arranged, with sheets and blankets being used to create walls. He had arranged for the load-bearing walls to be reinforced with steel girders. Those members of staff who lived in – namely Samuels himself and the housekeeper, Annie – were also granted space down there. To that extent, in Eaton Square, the war had brought the classes down to the same level. It was dry but cold and so a network of electric extension cables had been laid down and electric fires would be lit on those afternoons when it was anticipated that the cellars would be used. In a way that seemed to Samuels uncanny: Pemberton always seem to know when there was likely to be a big raid. On the night of the 29th December, for example, he had arranged for the whole family to camp in the cellars even though there had been relative calm over the Christmas period. Samuels thought it was probably something to do with Preston, who frequently telephoned the house.

There were no toilets in the cellars, of course, but that was an inconvenience the Pembertons had to put up with for the sake of the war effort. Samuels had been surprised, before he knew more, when Pemberton had asked that two separate single beds be installed for him and his wife.

Undoubtedly this was an easier task than it would have been to dismantle and reassemble a double bed, and for that he was grateful. But it was unlike Jeremy Pemberton KC to give any particular regard to the convenience of his servants.

A large space had been curtained off amidst the racks of champagne for Mr and Mrs Pemberton. Samuels knocked on adjacent wood before moving the large blanket to one side. The Pembertons' beds had been moving gradually further apart in recent weeks and he noted that there was perhaps two feet of space between them now. He laid the tray down on a side table. They were both awake.

- Good morning, sir. Your newspaper. The "all clear" sounded an hour and a half ago.
- Thank you, Samuels.

The butler turned to leave.

- Samuels.
- Yes, sir.
- I would be very grateful if you would ensure that Mrs Pemberton and I are not disturbed. We have some important business to discuss.
- Very good, sir.

And he pulled the blanket into place behind him and went back upstairs.

****

Julia had been lying on her side with her head cushioned against the pillow. But with Jeremy's last words to the butler she hauled herself into a seated position and fixed her husband with a stare. She was wearing a blue night-dress that set off her blonde curls but her hair was awry and her face, with-out make-up, was washed out. There was sleep in the corners of her eyes.

- Jeremy! What's going on?
- My dear, I think you know only too well what we need to talk about.
- I think you're going mad. You've been acting so strangely over the last ... I don't know ... few months.

176

- Don't pretend to be ignorant. The only surprise for you is that I want to have our little talk today rather than in the New Year.
- What ... is ... going ... on?!

Jeremy took a sip of his tea and looked across at his wife, a sardonic smile on his lips.

- I have instructed my solicitors to issue proceedings for our divorce. The petition was issued before Christmas and I mean to have it served today. I thought it only civil to advise you of it in advance.
- But this is preposterous. On what possible basis?
- You know very well, my dear. Don't tell me that when you have been prying around my study and rifling through my drawers you didn't read my correspondence?
- You've never given me keys to your study. I have never understood what secrets you needed to keep from me there.
- I'm having the locks changed.
- So that strange man who called last night, Johnson? Is your solicitor?
- Jackson is a private detective.

Julia had half climbed out of bed. She made a movement with her hands to bring unruly curls under control.

- You've been having me followed? I can't believe you would do such a thing. I'm sure this Jackson can tell you nothing unseemly about me.
- We will see.
- I want to hear from you what you are intending to do.
- Very well. I believe you have been unfaithful to me. I am citing Adam Falling as Co-Respondent and he will be served tomorrow in Suffolk.

If Julia had been expecting this she gave no sign of it. Instead she threw back her head and let out a peal of laughter.

- Oh, darling! You are so ridiculous! Adam Falling?
- Don't pretend to be surprised. You know that my solicitors think I have a good case.
- I don't know what you're talking about.

– Can you explain to me why I would find a piece of my writing paper burnt out in Falling's ashtray?

Pemberton watched his wife carefully and took another sip from the cup.

– Oh that! Yes of course I can.
– I'm waiting.
– I'm your wife. I notice things. You've been acting so strangely recently and it took me a while to work it out. You can tell a lot about what's going on in a man's mind by listening to what's coming out of his mouth.
– What are you implying, my dear?
– This man has been a member of your chambers for, what, fifteen years and you've hardly mentioned his name. And then, all of a sudden, you can speak of no one else and you've been giving me funny looks when you do mention him.
– I don't see how that explains the writing paper.
– I wrote him a very polite, apologetic, letter explaining my concerns. I sent it to him in Chambers by first-class post. I didn't even mark it "private and confidential". You've probably read it so you will know what it said.
– He destroyed it as I'm sure you asked him to.
– I was embarrassed; of course I asked him to destroy it. It was so humiliating even to be writing it. Have you any idea what torture these last months have been for me?

Pemberton was taken aback. The letter had been one of his trump cards but Julia appeared not to be at all discomfited when he played it. If she had asked him to destroy the letter she would presumably have felt safe in denying that she had sent it. That is what he had expected her to do. After the discovery of the ashes and the watermark he had ensured that an especially careful watch be kept on both her and Adam and he was sure, as far as he could be, that there had been no communication between them. A seed of doubt entered his mind. But then he remembered how, despite these months of "torture", Julia had been able to hide her feelings so well, even when he was watching her carefully. He thought of her books, of the Stafford Hotel ... and of Falling's evident nervousness in his presence.

- I'm sorry, my dear. You will have to convince a Court of your story. I'm afraid I don't believe you're telling me the truth.
- Jeremy. Please. I love you. Let's stop this nonsense.
- I'm going to speak with Jenny later today and explain to her what is happening with us. I'll leave it to you to tell Sebastian, Stephen and Agnes.
- Have you any idea what you're doing? Do you want our names to be in the newspapers? What will our friends think?
- You should have thought of that before you embarked on this adventure. Anyway, the press has more ... pressing ...matters to report on. I intend to have this resolved before Easter if at all possible.

Julia allowed her shoulders to slump. She fingered her wedding ring and ran her hand through her hair again.

- Think of our children. It will be horrible for all four of them.
- I've always thought you've loved your children more than you love me. More than you love Jenny.
- That's not fair! And they're *our* children. If I loved them more than I loved you, why do I allow myself to be parted from them? I belong by your side.
- I have asked Jackson to be ready to serve you with the papers. I thought he could either serve them on you here or at my solicitors' offices. They're only a short ride away.

Julia sighed and her eyes filled with tears.

- You're really going ahead with this aren't you?
- I don't feel I have a choice, my dear.
- May I at least choose where I am to be served?
- Of course. I will allow you that dignity.
- Where am I supposed to have committed adultery anyway?

****

Gazing across Piccadilly to Green Park on New Year's Eve in 1940, an observer would see the remains of the gates. Banner headlines with the latest from the air raids posted behind the wire mesh as usual. The usual flurry of people climbing the steps from the underground and rushing backwards and forwards about their business. If such an observer had been standing there at about midday on New Year's Eve he would have seen a tallish man with a large belly waiting by the entrance to the park, his hat pulled down low and a long brown envelope in his hand. An elegant lady in a long black coat, blonde hair pulled back under a peacock scarf, approached him and he lifted his hat in greeting. He handed her the envelope and they shook hands. Then she disappeared down into the park, looking for a bench amongst the trenches where she could sit down and read.

****

It was about six in the evening and Jenny was in her bedroom on the second floor. She had chosen the green dress and some matching shoes. She sat at her little dressing table and opened a lipstick. Dark red always brought out the best in her complexion. The atmosphere around the house had become unbearable and she kept thinking back to her conversation with Julia the previous day. It all seemed so preposterous. Perhaps it would all go away? In the meantime, she busied herself with preparations for a night out. Simon would be calling for her at seven thirty. He had arranged a car for them. She knew she looked beautiful. There was a knock on her door. It was Samuels.

  – I'm sorry to disturb you, Miss Pemberton, but your father has asked that you come and speak with him in his study.

Jenny left her room and headed down the stairs. Julia was standing on the first-floor landing with her back to her step-daughter. She was holding one of the photographs from the alcove – Jenny could see that it was of Julia with all three of her children. Julia turned as she heard her approach. Her eyes were red-rimmed and full of tears.

  – Julia! What's wrong?
  – Help me, Jenny. Please help me! Get him to stop this!
  – Oh, Julia. I'm so sorry. I'll try.

And she crossed the landing and knocked on her father's door.

****

Pemberton was sitting at his desk. The green lamp glowed and his spectacles shone. He was holding the photograph of her mother. He asked her to take a seat. Jenny remembered what Julia had said to her the night before: don't tell what you know; don't reveal your sources. She came to listen to what her father had to say. She would do her best to talk him out of it.

****

It was eight thirty by the time the car dropped Jenny and Captain Jenkins in Coventry Street. Simon was on leave and wore full uniform. He had never been to the Café de Paris before. Jenny had booked a table weeks ago and was looking forward to showing it off to him. They had ignored the air raid sirens. There were few places safer than the Café de Paris. Those who were less well-off envied them, sometimes vociferously, but if they had had the money to go there, they would have gone themselves.

A concierge welcomed them at the doorway and they made their way down a very long steep staircase. The room at the bottom was far smaller than the club's reputation and it was already thronging with officers in uniform and girls in their best dresses. On a stage at the rear a band was playing and a tall young black man was singing "Oh, Johnny". He wore an immaculate white suit with an exotic buttonhole and swung his hips fluidly as he sang.

- – This is quite a place!
- – I knew you'd like it.
- – You'd think it would be a lot hotter down here with all these people dancing.
- – Oh, there's plenty of air. That man, Preston, from Daddy's chambers, told me that they've got a large air shaft so that we don't all suffocate.
- – Would you like a dance before dinner?
- – And a glass of champagne. I want to have a good time tonight.

And having obtained a bottle and an ice bucket, they danced. Jenny felt a flood of euphoria fill her as she mixed with so many happy young people. So many people who were in love. She put her interview with her father out of her mind and tried not to think of Julia's face, tear-stained and full of entreaty, when she emerged. She had not been successful in her attempts to dissuade her father. He was resolute. He was also awkward and strange. More than once he had called her "Joan" before correcting himself with an apology. He wished her the many years of happiness that had been denied to her mother.

She smiled at Simon as he led her round the dance floor. Love didn't need to be so complicated. She would have to work on her father. If anyone could talk him out of this, she could. A plan was forming in her mind.

The sound of the air raid going on outside faded to nothing and on the stage Snakehips Johnson launched into "The Sunny Side Of The Street".

Chapter Twenty-nine

(Wednesday 8th January 1941)

Roland Blytheway shimmered up from past Garden Court towards Fountain Court. As always he was dressed impeccably, wearing a long, almost Edwardian, frock coat over his tailored suit, with an elegant white cashmere scarf thrown over his shoulder in a way that appeared, but was anything but, casual. Blytheway stepped over the rubble and broken glass rather as a nanny would step over the toys in an untidy nursery, tip-toeing daintily in his well-polished shoes, so as to avoid any possibility of dust taking away their gleam. He was like a matinee idol stepping through a film set of war.

For the third day running Falling watched him discreetly from a bench behind the trees in Fountain Court. He pulled on a cigarette, savouring every mouthful of smoke. Adam had put on a little weight and there was some colour again in his cheeks. It was almost a week since a rather uncomfortable Jackson had arrived at the flat in Dr Johnson's Buildings to serve him with the petition and the letter terminating his tenancy at Stirrup Court.

Storman had been able to visit him, very briefly, on New Year's Eve with the doctor's prescription, and Barry, a good night's sleep behind him, had ensured that Adam was provided with extra blankets and an additional electric fire. He had also restored hot water to the flat. He had brought from the Temple kitchens bread and soup and significant quantities of beef and sausages. Adam was sure the man had been breaching rationing regulations to do so but he was too grateful to him to ask questions. He was still sleeping badly, however. Storman had not been able to visit him on New Year's Day and Adam was secretly relieved. He did not want his friend to be present when Jackson turned up with the petition. The day was spent in an agony of anticipation. But the detective did not turn up.

The evening of New Year's Day had also been bad. A landmine hit Harcourt Buildings during further raids and caused a great deal of damage. Despite

Adam's entreaties Barry would not allow him to help with the fire-fighting. Despite Barry's entreaties, Adam had refused to go down to a shelter and spent the night instead in the third-floor flat, listening to the bombers and the ack-ack and waiting for a direct hit. It did not come. He slept poorly.

Storman had come to visit again on the 2nd January in the early afternoon. Barry had brought food and drink and Adam was propped up in bed when Storman entered.

- Adam! You're looking a lot better. The prescription seems to be working.
- Thank you, Jack. Barry's been very kind. You've both been very good to me.
- How's 1941 been treating you so far?
- Were you able to get me any cigarettes?
- They aren't doing you any good, you know.
- You haven't got any cigarettes?

Adam sighed and pulled the blankets up over his chest.

- How long do you intend staying here?
- A few days. That's all. I'm happy here for now.
- I'll make us some tea.

Storman went over into the little kitchen and put the kettle on. There was a small jug of milk and so he poured some of it into a bowl for the kitten. He put two generous spoonfuls of tea in the pot. During his preparations, he looked over at Adam with questions in his eyes. But he said nothing. Adam heard the kettle begin to rattle and then the sound of boiling water being poured. Eventually, Storman emerged holding two mugs. He put one down by the bed and cradled the other.

- Adam...

There was a knock at the door.

- Good afternoon, Mr Jackson. This is a pleasant surprise. Happy New Year.

There was acid in his voice.

- Mr Storman, sir. Happy New Year, sir. I'm sorry, sir. I'm ... I was looking for Mr Falling. I've been wrongly informed.
- Oh no, Mr Jackson. Mr Falling is here. He's sick.
- I'll come back another time.
- I'm sure, Mr Jackson, that, subject to what Mr Falling has to say, he won't mind me being present.

Adam, from his bed, said nothing. A long pause and then Jackson edged his way across the room.

- Mr Falling, sir.

And he had handed over the petition and a separate letter and then turned and almost ran for the door. Nothing was said. Adam listened to his footsteps clattering down the stairs and looked up at Storman. The questions he had noticed in his eyes were gone.

- Would you like me to leave you?
- There's no need now.

Adam read the petition and then handed it to Storman. Whilst the latter was reading it he turned his attention to the letter. It had been sealed and there was an ostentatious "P" stamped into the wax. The writing paper inside carried the Pemberton watermark that had become so familiar to him over the previous four and a half years. Its contents had, thanks to Catherine, been anticipated. The only surprise was that Pemberton had dated it the 30th December 1940. Adam couldn't understand why it had taken Jackson until the 2nd January 1941 to get round to serving it on him.

It wasn't until the following day that he received a letter, sent by his daughter care of Stirrup Court, which described the strange events of New Year's Day: how a peculiar fat man had turned up in something of a lather at about four in the afternoon. She had been riding with the gipsy on his pony at the time. Deborah described how she'd watched, from the far side of the paddock, a confrontation between him and her mother: Catherine's body hunched forward, her finger pointing – the sound of unintelligible shouting drifting across the meadow – whilst Jackson leaned away from the verbal onslaught before turning, head down, and sloping back to his car. "Mummy didn't tell me what she said to him or what it was all about, but she was terribly angry." There was no word from Catherine herself but Deborah said that she, at least, missed him and she asked him to take care of himself.

Storman had finished reading the petition. As anticipated, it had alleged that Adam had committed adultery with Julia Pemberton on a number of dates, on each of which – according to the hotel records – he had checked into the Stafford. If Storman had been surprised by its contents he did not show it. Adam passed him Pemberton's letter and watched his friend read in silence.

- Adam. How much truth is there in any of this? We need to talk.
- I'm very tired, Jack. I will talk with you about it. I promise. I'm very tired. Can we talk tomorrow please?

And Storman had let him be. Adam lowered himself down into the bed, curled up and pulled the blankets over his head. An enormous tired-ness came over him and he fell asleep. It was twenty-four hours before he awoke again. If there had been another air raid he had not been aware of it. When, finally, he woke up he felt infinitely better than he had done for a long time. His secret was out. He knew that, already, the talk would be all over the Temple, and in a funny way he felt as though he had been freed from something. As if the poison in the suppurating wound of his enforced silence had been brought to the surface and released. He'd been able to sleep. He was warm and he'd eaten better than for some time. Both Barry and Storman had insisted he remain in the flat and rest. He had been without cigarettes since the raid on the 29th January but the pain in his chest had eased.

He realised that Storman was now compromised. Although the notice period expired after seven days – the 6th January – Storman had persuaded Pemberton that, as it had not been formally received by Falling until 2nd January, he should have a further seven days to remove himself. Subject to that he and Adam were no longer members of the same chambers. Without an address from which to practise he could not take instructions, so he had asked that Storman contact Jones and let him know of his circumstances and of the fact that he could no longer act for Mr Bateman or for Novak. Storman had initially protested, but in the end accepted that without Chambers Falling could no longer hold himself out as a practising barrister. And as always with the weights that we do not appreciate that we are carrying, the fact that he no longer had to worry about Bateman and the McKechnie divorce or Novak and the gallows, Adam was, to his own surprise, able to relax further.

When eventually he emerged from Dr Johnson's Buildings into the Temple it became immediately apparent to him that the news was about. He had written a letter to Pemberton acknowledging his notice and delivered it by hand to Arthur, who received him with cold formality. Preston, whom he had known since he had been a pupil in chambers some sixteen years ago, had once said to him that in times of adversity one's true friends would stand by you. On seeing Adam in the Clerk's Room he turned on his heel and, with a look of disgust, walked out again, thus, with commendable economy, proving the truth of his dictum and the falsity of his friendship. With Barry's assistance, Adam moved the contents of his room into the flat.

Storman, however, did not desert him. Instead he had returned to the half-conversation that the two men had had on that first evening in the Temple.

****

And so, for the last three days, Adam had been watching Roland Blytheway glide up through the Temple towards Lamb Buildings. He thought back over the years: Blytheway had been making his progression from Temple tube through to his Chambers near the Temple Church for over fifteen years. He had seen him move from being a man in his late thirties to one in his middle fifties – although he still had the svelte figure and dandyish demeanour that he had always had. He had not changed. Adam had long been aware also of his louche reputation – of the snide little jokes made about him behind his back in the robing rooms around the Assizes – and he had assumed him to be a dilettante of dubious ability. But Storman, whom he respected, had repeated again that the man was a better barrister than he would ever be – and that if anyone could save Adam's reputation it was Blytheway. That Blytheway might even be prepared to allow him to have a place in his Chambers in Lamb Building. That Blytheway was his only hope.

****

There had been another thing that had, perhaps inexplicably, raised his spirits. That day, after the morning service, he had crept into the church as always, and saw to his delight a glimpse of white under the purbeck marble heel. The paper was rough and anonymous:

"The note you destroyed was sent by ordinary post on the 11th December. The envelope was not marked 'Private and Confidential'. It read as follows:
  'Dear Mr Falling ….
  …Yours sincerely, Mrs J. Pemberton.'
  Memorise its contents and destroy this."

Of course he would destroy it. It was for her protection rather than for him at all. But she had spoken to him through it. What joy!

****

The tall, self-contained barrister sashayed his way around some more rubble, tipped his hat to an elderly bencher who was heading his way, and then disappeared up Middle Temple Lane.

Chapter Thirty
(Wednesday 15th January 1941)

Eric Jones put the phone down. He was running late. A lengthy and ulti-mately pointless conversation with his wife was the last thing he had needed. She had spent two hours queuing for their meat ration only for the butcher to run out three customers in front of her. What was he sup-posed to do about it? He took his overcoat from the stand and buttoned up. He had a medium-sized office on Fetter Lane, and although it would look untidy to the casual observer he knew where everything was. Rummaging through a large pile of files arranged along one of his shelves, he pulled out a slim buff folder and made for the door. As he went to open it he saw through the frosted glass the silhouette of a vaguely familiar little man hurrying towards him, the voice of his secretary following in his wake.

– Stop! You can't just burst in like this. You need an appointment!

But Bateman had pulled open the door and positioned himself chest to chest with his solicitor.

– You've not been answering my calls. What's going on?
– I'm terribly sorry, Mr Bateman. I'm in a great hurry and, as Sonia says, you need an appointment.
– I want to see Falling. I rang almost a week ago. And I've sent a letter.
– Yes. I'm sorry. I'm dealing with it.
– When can I see Falling?
– Soon. I'm going to speak with him ... with his clerk ... as soon as I get back from my meeting.
– I'm paying you both good money.
– I'll sort it out. It's difficult. I can't call you at work and be put through the exchange. Call me tomorrow.

189

Bateman continued to block Jones's way.

- What's going on?
- Look, I'm already late. I have other clients.
- Something's happened to Falling?
- He's been a little poorly. That's all. He's getting better.
- When can we see him?
- By the end of the week ... the beginning of next week.
- Are you telling me the truth?
- Falling wants to talk to you about the inquest into your wife's death.

Bateman faltered, his mouth open.

- I told you. We don't need to go into that.
- Falling knows what it says. You've been lying to us
- He had no right ...

Jones pushed his way past the little man.

- Look, speak to Sonia. Arrange an appointment for tomorrow. At your convenience – though I've got a conference in the evening. I'll explain everything then. I'm sorry. I've got to run.

And he moved quickly past his secretary and left her to deal with a rather bemused Bateman.

****

He walked briskly to Chancery Lane tube station. If he had tried to explain the whole picture to Bateman, it would have led to a series of further questions and he would never have got away. The truth was that he himself did not know what was going on. Rumours that Falling had been ejected from Stirrup Court had reached him towards the end of the previous week – a day or so after Bateman's letter had reached him. Then Jack Storman KC had telephoned him to say that Falling felt obliged to withdraw from the case. But before he could contact Bateman he had received a call from Falling himself who had asked him to hang fire as everything might yet change; that he should carry on as though nothing had happened and stall Bateman. He also swore him to silence and made him an extraordinary offer. He couldn't really believe it. The implications of what he had been told were truly incredible.

And so he was heading off to his meeting. He had been putting it off. Falling had insisted that it needed to be carried out by someone of his seniority and experience. He should have dealt with it over a week ago but the trial timetable had been extended and he had let matters drift. It was not going to be an easy journey: he had to take the Central line to the final stop at Liverpool Street and then go overland to Leytonstone. Travel was slow and difficult. Even though there had been nothing to match the bombardment of 29th December transport links remained unreliable. Falling's instructions had been precise as to what should happen at the interview. No advance warning of his visit was to be given. He couldn't be sure they would even be there.

The train rumbled towards Liverpool Street. Jones didn't understand what was going on. Adam had already indicated that he was going to waive his fee on the case. But more than that he had promised Jones that, if he did this for him, he would instruct him on his own case and pay him well for it. At the time he had thought Falling was going mad, but, already, rumours were beginning to circulate: that Jeremy Pemberton was divorcing his wife and citing Adam as the Co-Respondent. The story seemed incredible but it would explain Adam's precipitate departure from Stirrup Court. It was going to be a big case. It was only a matter of time before the newspapers got hold of it. Jones had a good practice and was well regarded. But this was the sort of high-profile litigation that came up once in a lifetime. Half the solicitors in London would sell their mothers for it. It was too good an opportunity to miss.

****

It was getting dark by the time the solicitor stepped onto the platform at Leytonstone. He had brought a map. Old King's Road was a ten minute walk away. There were many bomb-damaged buildings along his route. Where was Falling now? What was going through his mind? How could he continue to act if he was without Chambers? And how was Jones going to get back home once this interview was over?

191

The road was cloaked in darkness by the time he reached it. He walked silently up to the first front door he came to so that he could get an idea of the numbering. He was looking for number 11. It was six doors down. Reaching it, he knocked hard and waited. Eventually he saw shadowy movement through the stained glass and a slight oldish man with a wispy beard opened it to him. Jones saw anxiety glinting out from behind his spectacles.

– Yes?

– I'm looking for a Mrs Katya Hoffer.

As he said it a tall, dark-haired woman, some fifteen to twenty years younger than the man who had answered the door, swept passed him. She had high cheekbones and a large, sensuous mouth. A bohemian shawl was draped over her shoulder.

– I am Katya Hoffer.

Chapter Thirty-one
(Wednesday 15th January 1941)

As Jones began his journey to Leytonstone Adam had been sitting at the back of the Temple Church. A weak sun penetrated from outside and bands of light fell across the wood and marble, casting an unearthly glow on the interior. Looking towards the altar he saw the morning service end and the worshippers depart into nothingness. A solitary figure remained on her knees. When the church had emptied she got to her feet and, satisfying herself that she was alone, went over to the knights and placed a folded piece of paper under an ankle. Then, making sure it was secure, she headed for the door. But the image of her faded to nothing before she reached it and he realised again that he was alone.

Why did he keep coming here? She would not be back. Not in the same way. No more notes would be left for him. His life and his thoughts circled around this place. It had happened. There was a time when she had wanted to be with him. The ghosts of the living inhabit the places where we knew them, or imagined them best. She had been here and, on her knees, she had thought of him. She still came to morning communion, walking up from Temple tube. He knew her route, and ever since taking up residence in Dr Johnson's Buildings he would find a way to watch her, to remember what she was wearing. He tried to imagine what was going on behind that closed face. Did she remember at all? Why had she changed? What had he done?

He would listen for the end of the service and creep in when he was sure the church was empty. But there was never a note. So he would sit there at the back, out of sight. They had never been in the church at the same time so he did not know where she would sit. There was no place there which he could know had been hers. He would pick up the order of service and read it through, for this was something that she had read less than an hour earlier. But she eluded him.

In the autumn he had watched the planes over London, vapour trails following them through blue skies. They were white and well defined but the planes flew away and the clear white lines were broken up by the wind, became ragged and disconnected before disappearing altogether, leaving only blue heaven. That was what had happened to their love. The fire somehow had gone. Things fell apart and now there was nothing left but the empty inexplicable sky.

He was not sleeping again. There was no reason for it. Lying awake solved nothing. His thoughts were rutted deep and no new insights came to him. He would wait until it was late enough and then go to bed. He had no interest in the shelters. On 11th January a high explosive bomb had destroyed 2, Mitre Court Buildings and the adjacent Barristers' Common Rooms together with the whole of the eastern part of the Master's House. It stood just to the east of the church and was regarded as one of the most beautiful houses in London. The church itself had survived with only a few broken windows but was covered in dust. Incendiaries had caused fires at 1, Paper Buildings.

Adam was unconcerned by the continued bombardment. In a strange way he welcomed it. Instead, he longed for the morning so that he could watch Blytheway make his way to his Chambers and then watch her going to communion. Then he would sit at the back of the church. But as his strength returned to him a sort of boredom had set in. Storman had said there was a possibility that he would be able to obtain a place at Lamb Building. He had two cases that mattered to him: Bateman and Novak. There was his own case also. Inexplicable rejection had made him call into question his own worth. What had he got left? Nothing. Not quite nothing. He had a little money. He was still a barrister. Perhaps, he told himself, if he could succeed for Bateman and Novak and see off Pemberton's action, he might still win her back. He had nothing to lose. If Pemberton succeeded he would, he had no doubt, be bankrupted and disgraced. He had no choice but to fight back.

He reached into his wallet. He had sixty pounds left of the money he'd withdrawn before Christmas. He needed to pay Catherine and Deborah something. Jones was going to be expensive and, on top of that, he had to fund Blytheway's fees. It had become clear to him that Blytheway had always lived well and was a connoisseur of the finer things in life. He would not be cheap. Not for the first time he found himself questioning Storman's judgment on the man. Such views as he had been able to glean about him were mixed. He didn't fit in. Storman had tried to persuade him that adverse views of him were born of envy at his talent, but he was not satisfied that this was right.

He got up from his bench and made for the church door. Looking at the effigies of the Knights Templar, he thought of their remains lying somewhere beneath his feet. They were dust. But once they too must have been filled with all the longings that now engulfed him. How could any of this matter? When he was gone his love and longing would die with him. For now he would have to find ways to endure.

The blackout had been brought down on Lamb Building. Inside, he knew, Roland Blytheway was due to begin a conference. Tomorrow he would be in court. It had been Blytheway's commitments that had prevented an earlier conference taking place. Tomorrow evening was the earliest he could manage. Tomorrow he would meet him for the first time. He would be able to make up his own mind about him.

The sirens began to sound again and he returned to Dr Johnson's Buildings, climbed into bed and, as the sound of bombs and explosions grew nearer, he fell asleep.

Chapter Thirty-two

(Thursday 16th January 1941)

Adam and Jones followed Blytheway's clerk up the cold stone steps to his room. He couldn't help noticing that, compared to Arthur, the man's suit was bagged and ill-fitting. If his clerk was not as elegant as Adam's, Blytheway's room was in a different league. It was spacious and bright behind the shades of the blackout. Adam noticed that his windows looked out over the church. He counted four Tiffany lamps arranged around the room, stained glass images of dragonflies and dogwood illuminated by the electric bulbs within. An electric fire was burning in the corner of the room and gave a comforting warmth. There was a Japanese Shoji dressing screen in another corner. Adam noticed that there were natural leaves embedded in the mulberry paper.

Blytheway rose to greet them, shaking hands, before sitting again. He had an immense desk, and on the corners of it were two Chinese vases, each filled with peacock feathers. Close up his face resembled that of a goat and there was a warm twinkle of amusement in his eyes. He saw Adam staring at the feathers.

- Thank you for seeing me Blytheway
- Call me Roly, Adam, all my friends do. Do you keep peacocks?
- I live in Dulwich.
- They have such beautiful feathers and it is so difficult getting a regular supply of pretty flowers for my room these days.
- You have a lovely room.
- Of course, I've had to hide my peacocks in the depths of Wiltshire for the time being. They do make a ghastly racket and I didn't want the neighbours eating them.

At that moment the door to the room opened and Blytheway's clerk entered with a large tray loaded with fine china, a teapot and milk. Blytheway began pouring as his clerk left.

- I'm afraid I can't offer you sugar. It's not good for you, you know.
- You can't do this!

Adam was flabbergasted. It was against all professional ethics to offer tea to professional or lay clients – tantamount to touting or advertising.

- Oh, don't be a silly billy. It's a foolish rule. I like a cup of tea after Court, and if I want to have one I don't see why my ... my guests shouldn't have one as well.
- You'll be hauled over the coals ...
- Tush. It can be our little secret. And besides, can the Benchers really think that my clients come to me for my tea rather than for my advice?

He handed Adam a cup and saucer.

- See. Real Spode bone china. I have so few opportunities to invite people to salons chez moi these days so I thought I would bring it into Chambers.

In spite of himself Adam found the tea refreshing.

- Now. Where were we? Ah yes. A question. Do you believe in God?
- What?
- Are you a Christian?
- I'm not sure what that has to do with anything.
- Just idle curiosity. I, for my part, cannot believe there is any such thing.
- You have read Mr Jones's instructions?
- Yes. There is an allegation that you have breached the seventh commandment. That you've breached, I suppose, the tenth, by coveting your neighbour's wife. If you can call a man like Pemberton your neighbour.
- Well, I don't believe in God if you must know. I'm more concerned about allegations that I have breached our temporal laws.

Adam was confused. He remembered how he had attempted, successfully, to unsettle Bateman by reference to the physical definition of intercourse and wondered if this was what Blytheway was up to.

- But, you see. That is my point. As I understand the overall effect of
  the speeches in Bowman v Secular Society, almost twenty-five years
  ago, we are no longer part of an Old Testament Christian society.
- What's this got to with my predicament?
- I suppose it means that you are unlikely to be stoned for your crime
  if proven.
- I don't believe you are taking this seriously.
- Oh, but I am. You see, I believe that the whole process in which you
  are embroiled is a farce. An expensive one of course. Whether or
  not you have committed adultery should be a matter of considerable
  indifference to our courts. Twenty or thirty years from now I am
  sure it will be. Too late for us, particularly for you. So, I suppose we
  must make hay whilst we can.
- This is all very interesting but, as you say, my difficulties are temporal not spiritual.
- Forgive me, Adam. But you are an intelligent man and I get so few
  opportunities to have such discussions. My views – as is so much of
  my life – are in a minority. It is good to have a chance to speak with
  someone who may be able to engage in the issues. Particularly as it
  would be in your interest to be able to agree with me. More tea?

Blytheway reached over and poured out another cup. Jones sat quietly
next to him, his pen poised over a still empty notebook.

- What exactly are you saying?
- Simply that, in my view, the law has no significant place in areas of
  private morality. For my own reasons it is something that I have been
  forced to grapple with.
- So you would get rid of divorce, of marriage, altogether?
- Oh, not at all. It is just that I believe that the law should do the bare
  minimum to regulate our conduct. We must have our lives and our
  property protected, of course. But women ... men for that matter ...
  are not property. I believe that a person should keep his word and be
  bound by his contracts.

Adam was becoming angry. He had not intended to pay this man good
money for a philosophical debate.

- This is more about trying to justify your own way of life than anything more honourable. I've heard all the stories …
- But of course you have. You would have to be deaf not to have. But
  I don't believe I have breached, in my own life, any code of private
  morality. As you will be equally aware, I am unmarried and have no
  intention to be so. But I would not dream of stopping others from
  doing so. It is just that so many people become blinded by what they
  think of as love and make unfulfillable promises. I don't believe they
  should be shackled to such promises. Love is like water or dust. It
  flows and blows away.

Jones intervened.

- I'm sorry to interrupt. But we've been here for half an hour now and
  I haven't written down a word. I didn't get in till very late last night. I
  want to be on my way home before the sirens sound.

Blytheway sighed.

- Very well, Mr Jones. I will move on to more pertinent matters. Tell
  me, Adam, I understand that you holidayed in Marrakesh a few years
  ago?

It did not seem as though anything that either Adam or Jones could say
would make Blytheway get to the point.

- How did you know that?
- I have two eyes and two ears and a very good memory. I think we all
  have. It's just that most people don't use them properly. Did you enjoy
  Marrakesh?
- Well, yes. The weather was temperate. It did my chest good.
- Ah, yes. Your chest. You have been suffering poor health. I love
  Marrakesh. This beastly war makes it so difficult to travel. The Bahia
  Palace … Djamaa el Fna … the snake-charmers and story-tellers. And
  the Medina of course.
- Tell me what you think of my case?

It seemed as though, at last, Blytheway was going to cooperate.

– Yes. Very well. We must rely upon the petition. That suggests you
have been in the habit of committing adultery with Mrs Pemberton
at the Stafford Hotel on a given number of dates between the summer
of last year and September. Your defence is that you were at the hotel
but you were with a prostitute called Betty, who bears a passing
resemblance to Mrs Pemberton. As yet (*looking at Jones*) no one has
obtained a statement from this woman. I don't know, of course, what
evidence Pemberton is going to rely upon. We will only find that out
at trial.
– You know about the writing paper in my ashtray with his private
watermark on it.
– And your explanation for it. What else is there?
– I've been followed by Jackson, Pemberton's snoop.
– And has he got anything on you?
– Apart from the fact that I went to the Stafford, no.
– Is that really all there is to it?

Blytheway looked deep into Adam's eyes and he could not but be aware,
for the first time, that a ferocious intellect was trained upon him.

– Yes.

Blytheway said nothing and continued to look at him, as though he
could divine his deepest thoughts. The silence lasted over a minute. Jones,
who had been writing furiously for the first time in the conference, found
himself caught up in the tension, his pen raised.

– Is that really all there is to it?

There was another long pause. A short distance away sirens began to
sound.

– Yes.

Let me put this another way. I have, of course, your instructions that there is nothing in these allegations. But if you, as an intelligent and educated man, had to make a guess at what other evidence there might be, what would you pluck out of the air?

Adam hesitated.

- Well …
- Yes?
- As an educated guess, you understand?
- Of course.
- I think there may be an unusual coincidence that Pemberton intends to rely upon.

Blytheway leaned forward.

- Go on.
- Well, a couple of weeks ago – the day Pemberton found the writing paper in my ashtray – he was taking an inordinate interest in the collection of paperbacks in my room.
- And …
- Well … I think … and I'm only guessing of course …
- Of course …
- That Mrs Pemberton has a very similar collection of books to the ones that I have.
- Is that all?
- My tastes are rather esoteric.
- I see.
- It's just a guess of course.
- Of course. I will be able to check its accuracy, discreetly of course, with Mrs Pemberton's counsel.

Blytheway ran his finger around the rim of his teacup.

- What do you think of my case?
- Well, there is precious little evidence against you. But …
- But what?
- If I were the judge I would find the explanation for Mrs Pemberton's

letter to you less than convincing. It is – subject to learning more about your books – the big hole in your case.

- I've told you the truth.
- A little piece of evidence can make a big hole. I fear that this one lies below the water line. It could sink you. Forgive me for asking, but how much money have you got?

Adam was shocked. If there was one thing barristers never spoke about, certainly to their faces, it was the wealth of their clients. Although customs would change over the decades they certainly did not discuss, face to face, the wealth of another member of the profession.

- I have enough to pay your fees, if that is what you're worried about.
- My dear Adam! I'm shocked! The very thought! I know I am thought of by my peers as unconventional but there is one convention I do adhere to. I would never expect to be paid for acting for another member of the profession.

Tears pricked the back of Adam's eyes.

- That is too kind.
- There are so few beautiful things to buy these days.
- Why do you want to know?
- I really think you ought to invest in a new suit. It hasn't escaped my attention that you have been getting scruffier and scruffier lately.
- A new suit is the last thing I can afford.
- One needs style as much as substance, Adam. One without the other is quite useless. I know that I have both. You need style.

The sirens were getting louder, and somewhere, not far away, the sound of a bomb exploding rumbled towards them. The previous night's bombardment had caused serious damage to Middle Temple with direct hits on New Court, Essex Court and Pump Court.

Jones was becoming agitated.

- I don't know about you two but I want to get down to a shelter.
- Adam doesn't like the shelters, do you, Adam?

- How do you know that?
- Be a sweetheart and come to the shelter with us – for Mr Jones's sake – there's one under the church that I've used in the past. I had to break into a run once. I think we had better adjourn this conference until sometime tomorrow.

They all rose and Blytheway extinguished all but one of the Tiffany lamps and put out the fire. Outside his room all was in darkness and they were forced to feel their way. Blytheway waited until Jones was out of earshot.

- Are you sure you don't believe in God, Adam?
- Can't we just go down to the shelter and wait until tomorrow to discuss theology?
- I just find it so hard to believe that you don't believe in the Almighty.
- What on earth are you talking about?
- You see, I've occupied the same room in Chambers now for over fifteen years and over the past four or so I couldn't help but notice that you would go into the Temple Church every working day. But not during communion. In fact, usually just after everyone had left.
- What?
- But then again, maybe you're not a Christian after all. I mean, you would hardly stay inside long enough for a Hail Mary.
- You've been spying on me! How dare you!
- Not at all. Mere idle curiosity. As I said, I have two eyes, two ears and a very good memory. As for spying, I couldn't help but notice that, if anything, you have been spying on me since New Year ... hanging around Fountain Court ... it's quite all right of course. In your position I might be tempted to do the same. Then again, why you should also be following a woman, who looked to me as though she might be Mrs Pemberton, as far as the church before veering off up towards Fleet Street, I find more difficult to fathom.

By now they were heading down the stairs into the crypt. Blytheway's voice dropped to a whisper.

- I must say it was quite amusing watching that oaf Jackson trail you up Inner Temple Lane. I found it hard to believe you were unaware of him. Hey ho.

It was pitch black in the shelter and Adam was vaguely aware of other people huddled down there. He lowered his voice.

- I'd like to tell you a little more about that.
- No, Adam. It is always wise, at the dark hour, to keep one's own counsel.
- Please?
- Absolutely not. This is not the place.

Before Adam could reply another voice spoke.

- For once the old dandy is absolutely right you know, Adam.

Across the crypt there was the scrape of a match against a box. In the flickering light Adam made out the grim face of Jeremy Pemberton, wreathed in shadows.

Chapter Thirty-three

(Thursday 16th January 1941)

The match went out and all was darkness again. A bomb landed a little distance away shaking the floor of the crypt. Small bits of stone were dislodged from the ceiling and went down Adam's neck. He felt a surge of panic and tried to turn and run back up the steps. Blytheway caught him as he turned, and, with surprising strength, turned him back to face into the blackness. Then, with almost womanly tenderness, he put his hand on his shoulder and eased him forward.

–   Oh. It's only you, Jeremy. I'm quite happy to carry on my conversation with Adam in your presence. You may even be able to help. Just give me a second.

There was the scratch and flare of another match and Adam half turned to see Blytheway, his face flickering in the light, pulling a large candle from his trouser pocket and lighting it. A warmer glow lit the low-roofed room as the flame took. Adam saw that there were seven or eight people already in the crypt.

–   Beeswax, you know,

said Blytheway.

–   I keep a little supply just inside my room for these eventualities. I never come down here without one. Slipped it into my pocket as I was leaving.

He placed the candle in the middle of the room so that its light was shared, then looked around for somewhere to sit, beckoning Jones and Adam to follow suit. He found a place opposite Pemberton and wiped the seat with his finger. Outside, the sound of sirens and explosions was intensifying.

– I do wish they would give this place a proper cleaning. I abhor dust.

And he carefully spread the tails of his frock coat before sitting down, and brushed his hand down his lapels.

– Now. Where was I? Ah yes. I was going to talk to Adam about his tailor. I was telling him that he really ought to smarten himself up. Wouldn't you agree, Jeremy?
– You're as frivolous now as you were thirty years ago, Blytheway. I'm not surprised that you never took silk.
– Oh do call me Roly. All my friends do. Thirty years! Is it as long as that? And still calling me Blytheway. I thought you might be able to give us some hot tips on haute couture.
– I have no interest in Falling's clothing. Is he getting ready to have his picture in the papers?
– Oh, not at all. Adam is a man of substance. All he needs is a touch of style.

He turned to Adam.

– Don't worry, sweetheart. I'll give you the name of my man in Jermyn Street. He regards me as one of his more valued patrons, even in these dark days. If you mention my name he'll give you a ten per cent discount.

Adam saw Pemberton's features darken and his mouth turn down. His spectacle frames gleamed gold in the candle light against the silver of his hair. No one else had spoken. The heavy drone of planes overhead, the scream and whine of falling bombs and the staccato ack-ack was intensifying. Adam recognised some familiar faces from Chambers around the Temple. There could be no doubt but that they were aware of the drama that was unfolding before them.

– Did you have a good Christmas, Adam?

The menace in his voice was unmistakeable.

– Not really, I'm afraid. I was rather ill.
– Ah. That must have been why you came back from Suffolk early. I can't *imagine* any other reason. I must say that move was rather unexpected.
– I'm sorry that I didn't let you know of my change of plans, Jeremy. It must have been an inconvenience to you.
– Oh, not at all. A wasted journey for Jackson. No more than that. Our Christmas was mixed. Julia spent far too much money on commissioning a dolls' house for Agnes, and they spent most of their time up to New Year's Eve playing with it. I think Julia was getting more pleasure out of it than her daughter was … She should have made better use of her allowance.

At the mention of her name, Adam was engulfed by an uncontrollable flood of memories. Her bubble of blonde hair and her laughter in Hamleys as she held that dolls' house aloft …

– *I always wanted one. I hinted and hinted but Daddy said they were silly … there were all sorts of other things going on with Mummy and Daddy. It wasn't the money. I think they sometimes forgot I was there …*
– *Are you going to get it?*
– *Not this year. Agnes is too young yet. But she's going to have a dolls' house and we'll be able to play with it together.*

Adam felt his eyes stinging and held back his tears.

– How is Julia?
– Oh. She's seen better days. She took the children back to the Cotswolds yesterday and will be gone for a few days.
– What you have done is very cruel.
– Oh. She's pretty thick-skinned under her foundation cream. And Adam, I don't think that you are well placed to speak of cruelty. How are Catherine and your daughter faring?

All the shame and remorse that had gripped him on Lowestoft station flooded through him again. He opened his mouth but before he could say anything Blytheway took over.

- I *do* think that was a rather bitchy remark, Jeremy.
- What *are* you talking about, Blytheway?
- I mean, speaking openly about your wife's foundation cream.
- Oh, for God's sake!
- I think we all need a bit of help as we get older. I confess that *I* use it from time to time ...
- You are insufferable!
- You see. You are comparing the present with the past and that is never sensible.
- What *are* you talking about!?
- I'm old enough to remember your lost years. Those nights when you were in your cups and lamenting the loss of her alabaster skin ...
- How dare you bring Joan into this!
- The past is never as perfect as we remember it, Jeremy. And the present is better than it seems. You don't bring back the past by getting rid of the present.

Blytheway's apparently insouciant intervention had been highly effective and now Pemberton was reeling. But he had upped the ante. The tension was mounting. The sound of the war outside seemed to be fading away but the crypt was getting hotter and hotter and Adam sensed sweat trickling down his back.

- What business is any of this of yours?
- Now that's a very interesting question. But you *musn't* blame yourself for what happened almost twenty years ago. We were both very ambitious and worked long hours. You couldn't be at home as much as you may have wanted to be. I only had myself to look after of course.
- You're still sore at failing to get silk. That's it, isn't it?
- Oh. Not at all. The ways of the Lord Chancellor are more mysterious than those of God. He seems to be positively wilful when I look at some of his appointments. It would have been nice to have the clothes that go with it all the same. I would have liked silk – as a material that is.

Blytheway seemed to be enjoying himself and Adam sensed that, under the surface of these exchanges, some other conflict was being played out. He was becoming increasingly uncomfortable. He heard muffled shouting from beyond the safety of the crypt.

- You seem to forget that His Majesty's Counsel are expected to show high moral standards as well as learning in the law, Blytheway.

Blytheway sighed.

- I *do* wish you'd call me Roly, Jeremy. As to morality, my conscience is absolutely clear. Didn't we study Hume's *Treatise of Human Nature* at about the same time?
- It's not just a matter of morality. It's a matter of law.
- Do you know, that's strange. Adam and I found ourselves having a similar debate in my Chambers just over an hour ago. But speaking of "law", did you read that report in the *Times* the other week? That Labour MP. Joseph Clynes, was it? He described the black market as "treason of the very worst kind".

Blytheway's tone of voice had not changed at all from his first observations on coming down into the crypt, whilst Pemberton was becoming increasing fractious. He changed the subject.

- I take it from your last remarks that you will be representing Falling?
- If it pleases him.
- I have retained Sir Patrick Tempest.
- As I expected. Ah. The "all clear" is sounding. I think we can all now go home. Do you mind if I take my candle with me?

And he rose elegantly, brushed himself down again, and picked up the candle.

- I trust you are content to represent a member of the Bar who is without Chambers?
- Oh, but he isn't, Jeremy. You see, Adam is joining me in Lamb Building. I think he'll make a splendid addition to our numbers.

- He'll do your Chambers' reputation no good at all.
- Oh, don't be silly. People should move Chambers more often in my opinion. Particularly if they are unhappy or their set has its failings. It will come to pass. Mark my words.

Adam felt a sigh of relief as he followed Blytheway out of the crypt. The tension in the room behind him began to dissipate. Pemberton's voice followed after him.

- I hope you managed to move all your books safely, Adam?
- Yes. Thank you, Jeremy.
- I made an inventory of them, just in case there were any problems.
- There were no problems.

Jones had kept very quiet. If anything, he felt more uncomfortable than Adam.

- I think you'll regret this retainer, Jones.
- Good night, Mr Pemberton, sir.

And they were back outside the church. It was covered in a fresh coat of dust and smoke was rising from the roof. A fresh breeze blew over them. There was dust and ashes in the air. Blytheway nipped the wick of his candle and bowed to Adam and Jones.

- Well then, Adam. That was fun wasn't it?
- I don't know what to say.
- As you see, sometimes saying nothing is the best thing to do.
- Those things we were discussing when we left chambers …
- Sometimes saying nothing is the best thing to do.
- What do you think of Sir Patrick Tempest?
- We'll have to be very careful with him, my dear. A dangerous opponent. I must speak with Alnwick about him.
- Francis Alnwick?
- Oh, didn't I mention it? Mrs Pemberton has retained him. I think she has been sold a pup by that husband of hers.
- Don't you rate him?

– Oh, he's competent enough. But I doubt that mere competence is going to be sufficient here. What's needed here is honest cruelty. Few of us have that.

– What do you mean?

– Forgive me, Adam, but I suspect that it is something that you do not possess. Please don't take this the wrong way but I don't think you are entirely honest, with yourself or with others for that matter. Nor do I think you are entirely cruel. If that's any consolation?

– I don't understand …

– I fear that you are, for all your undoubted substance, insufficiently ruthless. Believe me. If a forensic dagger comes into my hands I shall not hesitate to plunge it in and twist it … courteously of course.

Footsteps were sounding on the stairs from the crypt and Blytheway ushered Adam and Jones around to the other side of Lamb Building out of the view of Pemberton and the others as they emerged.

– Well. We'll have to see if we can find time to meet again tomorrow.

– Are you sure I can join your Chambers?

– Consider it done. I have more influence than perhaps you realise. Now Mr Jones can instruct you properly on those other two cases you're worried about.

– How do you know about that!?

– Eyes and ears, sweetheart. Eyes and ears. Tempest will be a worthy opponent. Goodnight, gentlemen.

And he turned crisply and headed back up to his room in Chambers. Adam and Jones walked together through Cloisters. Smoke was rising from extinguished fires at 3, Hare Court. They walked on up to Dr Johnson's Buildings, where they parted. The air was crisp and the sky clear. Silvery clouds drifted east and there was a hint of cordite on the wind. Snowflakes of ash were floating around in eddies, and from beyond the Temple the red glow of fires around the docks.

****

Jones watched Adam disappear up the stairs into Dr Johnson's Buildings and then headed back towards Fetter Lane. As he left Fleet Street and made his way north back to his offices, he pondered the events of an extraordinary day. He had hoped to have an opportunity to talk to Adam about his meeting with Bateman earlier that afternoon but, when he saw Pemberton in the crypt, thought better of it. Instead he had been playing over, again and again, in his mind the strange interview the previous night with Katya Hoffer.

Chapter Thirty-four

(Wednesday 15ᵗʰ January 1941)

There had been a moment's pause whilst Jones looked at the Hoffers and
they in turn had looked back from their doorstep to him. With a vague air
of timidity about her, Katya Hoffer broke the silence:

- How can we help you, Mr …?
- Jones, Mrs Hoffer. I am the solicitor for Mr Novak.

But before he could finish what he was saying – and at the mention of
Novak's name – Katya Hoffer let out a scream and pushed at the front door
so that it almost closed in his face. Beyond the stained glass he heard her
speaking loudly in what must have been Czech, with murmured responses
also in a foreign tongue coming from Mr Hoffer. Jones stepped back onto
the path. Katya had left a light on in the kitchen and it projected their silhouettes onto the door panes – hers was rearing up grotesquely whilst her
husband's seemed to cower and shrink; her hands flitted around like the
shadows of giant butterflies as she made her points. It felt like an age but
was probably less than five minutes before the front door opened again.
Jones had no intention of leaving before he had achieved what he had set
out to do.

It was a timid and vulnerable Katya Hoffer that re-opened the door, her
husband standing meekly behind her.

- I'm very sorry. You surprise me very much by coming so late. I was
  angry that Milo had not told me you would be coming, but he says to
  me that he did not know.
- It's true. I gave him no warning that I would be coming. I apologise.
  May I please come in?

Jones was beginning to feel very cold. It was mid-January and there was a hoar frost on the ground. A northerly wind was beginning to rise and it slipped fingers of ice inside his overcoat. Katya opened the door wider and allowed him to enter. She ushered him into a small room to the left of the entrance.

- You can speak with Milo here. I can make some mint tea for you.
- I've come to see you, Katya.

Her eyes widened and she looked over her shoulder to her husband for reassurance.

- But ... but ... I know nothing ...
- I just want to hear your story. That's all. I would like to speak with you alone.

The solicitor's voice was soothing and he made calming gestures with his hands, as though he were a conductor stilling his orchestra.

- But I would very much like some mint tea. I will wait here for you.

Jones found himself an armchair and sat down. From the little kitchen he could hear the murmur of voices as husband and wife conversed urgently in a foreign language until their conversation was drowned out by the whistle of the kettle. He looked around him. The room was sparsely furnished but someone, presumably Katya, had covered every available surface with brightly coloured fabrics and throws. A lamp in the corner had been draped with a square of white and purple silk and it gave the room rather an exotic colouring. Bohemia was part of Czechoslovakia and Jones felt that it would be entirely appropriate if the Hoffers had come from that part of the country. But the room was very cold. Eventually Katya returned with a tray and two cups of mint tea.

- I am sorry we were so rude to you ...
- That's al –
- In our country to receive a knock on the door like that – at night – is very bad sign. And when Milo said that you were not expected I thought you must be secret police.

214

Her voice was lightly accented but rich and warm now. She sat down on the couch opposite him, pulled up her legs and clasped them around the knees. He noticed, for the first time, that she was wearing several layers of clothing to keep her warm. His first impression was that she had been tall but well-built, but that was an illusion of garments hiding her slenderness. Whether it was art or accident, he could make out the contours of her body from the way she held herself on the sofa. And her hair was dark and luxuriant. Her eyes were deep almonds. But it was her mouth that fascinated him. That large sensuous mouth opening and closing. White, white teeth and a little pink tongue, like that of a kitten, flickering between her lips. And he realised that she had been talking but he hadn't heard a thing.

- I'm sorry. What were you saying?
- It is so good of you to come so far to see us. I am very happy to help you. But you know so much already. I see you are clever man. Good man.

And she fixed him with a broad smile that strayed between bashful and alluring.

- If you tell me what you already know then I will know how I can help you.
- I would much rather you simply told me your story (*Adam had been quite clear about this*).
- But it is so late and you will be wanting to be going home.
- Just tell me what you know about Tomas Novak. Please, Mrs Hoffer … Katya.
- But I know so little. I have so little to say. Please tell me what you know. Please …

Her eyes widened. He saw the dark hollows under them and thought she was about to cry. It was late, after all. He had come unannounced and he had given her quite a fright. There could be no harm in it. So he relented and she smiled at him as a reward. He told her, in brief summary, all that Novak had told them in the interview room at Wandsworth Prison: how he had travelled with the Hoffers on the boat from Gibraltar; how he had liked Katya very much and trusted her because she had helped him. How her husband, Miloslav Hoffer, had found him the rooms in London and told him not to report himself to the authorities. The more he spoke, the uneasier he became, but Katya just looked at him with innocent wide eyes and nodded encouragement. Novak had said that she had described Adam as gullible, and Jones was on the point of repeating this as well when he brought himself up short. He was talking like a fool and, when she spoke, he was not listening but just gazing at her like an idiot. He shook himself and looked at her again. He had thought her to be in her mid-thirties but if anything she was a fair bit younger. She had called Adam gullible. Perhaps she would be saying the same about him when he had gone. He took a deep breath.

– So, Katya. I have done as you asked. Now please may I have your story?

And he took his notebook out from the buff folder he had been carrying and unscrewed his fountain pen. She smiled at him apologetically, as if unwilling to let him down.

– But I am afraid that all what he has told you is wrong.
– What?
– I do not know him. Only Milo knows him. I may have met him once or twice maybe but that is all.
– But why would he say these things?
– I do not know. It is true that Milo advised him not to report to the authorities. I did not understand that. It is true also that Milo found him his rooms. But the rest of it?

And she waved a hand in dismissal of the whole fairy tale.

– You and … and Milo came to this country by boat from Gibraltar to Liverpool. Is that correct?
– Yes.
– And Tomas Novak was on the boat as well?
– I do not know. It may be that he was. I did not know of him then.
– He says that you were kind to him.
– If I was kind to him it was because I wanted to be kind. Not because I

wanted to be kind to *him*. It may be that he remembers something ... some happening ... that I do not remember
- Have you met him or spoken with him since he came to London?
- I think so, yes. Maybe a few times. Milo wanted to raise some money to help him when he was arrested and I helped with that.
- And that is all?
- Yes.

It was beginning to look as though Adam had sent him on a wild goose chase, but, having come so far, he decided to persist.

- How long did it take to sail from Gibraltar to Liverpool?
- Ten days ...

Katya paused a long time and stared at the silk-covered lamp. Jones waited, then she began again, as though something she had buried was being uncovered.

- Ten days. I thought we must be going to America not England after all. It was so beautiful. I felt so free ... then we changed direction and headed north ... and my heart sank. They had travelled out to sea just to avoid the mines and submarines. It was very crowded but the skies were so blue. Milo. Poor Milo. He did not travel well. He was most of the time in the sick room. So I was alone mostly. At night time I would sleep on the deck. I found a private place under a life-boat, wrapped myself in canvas and looked at the stars. There were three nights when they said there were German submarines around. And the engines would stop and everyone was very quiet and nobody moved. And I would look at the stars and I would listen to the sea. And I was *so* happy!
- And was Tomas Novak there?
- I was *so* happy ...

It was as though she was dreaming.

- And then we were approaching Liverpool and the sky was dark and raining. Milo had family in this part of London and we wanted to come straight here. But they put us on trains and took us to Empress Hall in Earls Court and looked at our papers and we had to go to the Tribunal.

– Didn't you know about the Tribunals?
– There was a rumour on the trains, and some of us were frightened and ran away.

Her eyes widened in recollection as she told her story.

– We had to be wary for spies, Katya.
– But we were not spies! I hate the Germans! We came here to escape. They are holding my brother and I am very scared for him. Why would we help the Germans?
– Tomas Novak has been charged with treason. Our government thinks that he is a spy.
– But that is so ridiculous, Tomas would not ...

She caught her breath.

– You called him Tomas?
– Milo calls him Tomas. That is all.
– If Tomas is found guilty he will be executed.
– No!
– And he will be executed. We do not have the evidence to save him.
– But this is stupid. Why should he die because they find old plans in an old house?! ...

She bowed her head and was silent. Jones looked at her for a long time. Her shoulders slumped and she loosened her grasp on her knees. He spoke quietly.

– I never said anything about plans, Katya.
– Well, I must ... someone ... I heard that from somewhere. I can't remember. Maybe Milo ... I don't know.
– Have you been telling me the truth, Katya?

But she had regrouped.

– Yes … I do not know him. I only know what Milo has told me. I have
met him maybe once or twice.

And she would not be shaken. She would not change her story and she
refused to sign his hastily written notes. It was getting late. He would miss
the last train.

****

He caught the last overland train back to Liverpool Street. He felt no further forward. Milo Hoffer had admitted to him that he had told Novak not
to report; that it was he who had found him the rooms; that Katya hardly
knew Novak. But, when pressed for an explanation for his earlier lies, he
just shrugged his shoulders and looked up helplessly at Jones.

– I am trying to save him now.
– He doesn't trust you.
– I am doing what I can to help him.
– It's too late.

The blacked-out train trundled back towards the city, and in the blue
half-light Jones opened the buff folder and looked again at his evidence so
far. If it had been dark when he made his way to Old Kings Road the night
was impenetrable when he left. He was forced to check each street sign as
he made his way back. Something had jarred. And looking at his accumu-
lated notes he saw it. Tomas Novak had been arrested in the street that ran
parallel to Old Kings Road. He and the Hoffers were near neighbours. But
neither Milo nor Katya had made any mention of this. Why would they
withhold that piece of information?

He put away the buff folder and closed his eyes. His mind filled with an
image of white, white teeth and a pink kitten tongue, darting in and out
of Katya's mouth. He hated to think what Mrs Jones would have made of
it all.

Chapter Thirty-five
(Thursday 16th January 1941)

Pemberton took his jacket off and hung it on the back of his chair. Samuels had prepared his study for him as usual and the greenish light glowed out from the middle of his desk. It had not been a good day. The encounter with Blytheway had not pleased him and he came away feeling that the man had got the better of him again. They had known one another for thirty years and had studied Law together but he had never liked him. He couldn't put his finger on precisely why that was. There was his effortless insouciance; that air of the clever student who affects not to work at all but always comes top of the class; his wordplay and wit and his indifference to what others might think of him. That was probably it. Pemberton had always had ambition and he wanted to make an impression on the world. But he made no impression on Blytheway. Put shortly, Blytheway was unimpressed.

For all Blytheway's student brilliance there could be no doubt that Pemberton's practice took off more spectacularly. Blytheway proved to be more of an acquired taste. By 1914 Jeremy was a successful junior and married to one of the most beautiful debutantes of the season. Blytheway seemed just to be pottering along. He had not married. It was some years before Pemberton understood why. Pemberton had joined his father's battalion on the outbreak of the Great War and saw action on the Western front. He led a charmed life and if a spray of machine gun fire was directed at him and his men when he made a charge it would be they that were cut down whilst he remained unscathed. He was decorated several times and kept his medals now in a glass case in his study. Blytheway had opted to work on the ambulances. Their paths had crossed for only a short time towards the end of the war and they had a terrible argument.

****

Pemberton had tried to suppress those memories but they came back to him now.

Muriel Armstrong worked on the ambulances with Blytheway. She didn't need to be there. She was a woman after all. Blytheway let her do the driving. She was a twenty-three-year-old suffragette and would bang on about the rights and the equality of women. A starched bluestocking with no understanding of Class. There was a young private, whose name he had long forgotten, to whom Blytheway and Armstrong had taken a shine. They would let him into the back of their vehicle to play cards. The war was nearly over and Pemberton had survived. He congratulated himself by drinking the better part of a bottle of whisky – his luck couldn't last for ever.

He had slipped in the mud and fallen over, and when Muriel Armstrong started shouting at him he saw double. Blytheway was shouting too. Muriel was a very attractive woman. Long dark hair and a mouth with a natural pout. She was covered in mud. She picked up another handful of it and matted it into her face and hair so that all he could see were here blazing eyes.

– You bloody cowardly drunk! You could help us save him.

He slurred:

– We can't help him. He's going to die and there's nothing we can do.
– You could go out there with Roly. There has to be two of you.
– I'm an officer and he's only a private. It's too great a risk.
– You bloody, bloody coward!

And then she had rushed at him, hitting him with her muddy fists until Blytheway, caked in mud and slime himself, pulled her away.

– M. M., there's nothing to be done.

And in the black distance, out in No-Man's Land, the private with whom Blytheway and Armstrong played cards was screaming and moaning.

****

After the war Pemberton's world began to fall apart. His joy in the birth of Jenny turned to despair when Joan succumbed to influenza and died. She had only been twenty-nine. He realised too late that he had put his work and his career first and that his assumption that his wife would always be with him had proven to be wrong. He turned to drink and became a fixture in El Vinos, where he would talk for hours about Joan, her beauty and his loss to anyone who was in range, including Blytheway. And Blytheway was initially sympathetic but after a while became impatient with him and chided him for wasting his life. He would speak to him roughly and try to shake him out of it, and Pemberton's old antipathy, through the haze of drink, regret and guilt, returned. And slowly Blytheway's stock rose until it could be fairly said that he was at least as successful as Pemberton if not more so. Rumours of the drinking meant that his solicitors became less loyal and Blytheway and others cleaned up.

Then he had met Julia and his life began to turn around once more. She was barely twenty years old and her youth restored him. He became tee-total and slowly a zest for life returned. He was able to turn his practice around and, although he never really got over the loss of Joan, he attempted to be a better husband than he had been before: dutiful and attentive. Then the children had come along and Julia was happy. He even toyed with removing the photographs of Joan from his study. But this was a step too far. Pictures of him with Julia and her children were given a place in an alcove on the stairs. He knew, too, she kept photographs in her dressing room. His study he kept sacrosanct and Julia understood, in the unspoken way of married couples, that it was out of bounds. As a quid pro quo – though, again, nothing was ever said – he would keep out of her dressing room. As to Blytheway, Pemberton's memories of those lost days left an antipathy that grew darker as the years passed.

And then he had taken silk and succeeded where Blytheway, despite several attempts, failed. He rejoiced in the other man's failure almost as much as he enjoyed his own success. Yet Blytheway affected not to care and Pemberton was left with nagging doubts as to whether his elevation reflected a real superiority in ability. For all Blytheway's "front", his apparent lack of concern for what others thought of him and the louche stories repeated in the robing rooms, Pemberton felt he knew the man little better than he did all those years earlier.

And so the encounter in the crypt was doubly unwelcome. He had reason to fear Blytheway's abilities and would have much preferred it if Falling had turned to some fashionable silk. Someone he could impress. But he knew he could not impress Blytheway. There was another reason: Blytheway's casual and cutting reference to Joan and to his drinking days had hurt him deeply and reopened a wound that had never really closed. But more than that it reminded him of Blytheway's legendary memory. He had a fearsome reputation as a cross-examiner, and in Pemberton he had a victim he knew only too well. He knew Pemberton's past and his weaknesses. He had no deference. If Pemberton had made a greater effort to be friendly to the man, who had always put on a façade of amiability to him, Blytheway might perhaps have been obliged to recuse himself. But that was not the case. Pemberton felt the man had shown a glint of pleasurable anticipation in what lay ahead. It was just as well that he felt confident in emerging victorious. Otherwise he might have allowed himself to worry a little.

The journey home from the Temple had been difficult that night and he had some work to do before he retired. He opened his briefcase and arranged a set of papers across the desk. Before he could begin there was a knock at the door. It was Jenny. He beckoned her into the room and motioned to a chair across the desk from him. She looked extremely beautiful and was wearing a dress that he recognised as being one of Julia's. Her hair was immaculately coiffed and she had a hint of make-up which made her pale skin glow. She also looked nervous.

– Jenny, my dear. You look entrancing tonight. How can I help you?
– I want you to look at this, Daddy.

And she handed a small red leather-bound book across to him. It had a little brass padlock clasping it closed and the key was in the lock. Pemberton recognised it as the diary he had given her for Christmas in 1939.

– But Jenny? What's this all about?
– It's very private, Daddy. But I want you to look at it. Please open it and look through it. But don't read the entries. They're private.

Pemberton turned the key, opened the book and flicked through the pages. They were all filled with Jenny's neat but girlish handwriting and he was sorely tempted to stop and read what she had been writing. But he remembered her injunction.

- But darling. What is the point of leafing through your diary if you don't want me to see what you've written?
- It's not the words that I have written that are important.
- What do you mean?
- Look at my entry for the 31st May 1940. But *don't* read it.

Pemberton looked down the page and his eyes blurred as he attempted not to read the words.

- What am I looking for Jenny?
- There's a little cross next to the date.

And so there was. In the same ink as the rest of the entry.

- And what of it?
- Look at the entry for the 4th June.

The same little cross next to the date.

- You see, Daddy. Those little crosses marked the days when I spent the afternoon with Julia. She's been so good to me and there are certain things that, well, you know, I feel more comfortable talking about with another woman.
- What sort of things precisely?

Pemberton did not like the direction that this conversation was taking.

- Oh. You know, women's things. I know I'm still only a girl really but it's not easy growing up and it's nice to have someone to talk to. Julia's always been so understanding.
- Well. I'm very pleased that you and she have been able to get on so well in the past, but you must understand I have made my decision.

He was touched at his daughter's attempts to paint a sympathetic portrait of his wife, but on this thing, at least, he would not allow himself to be bowed to Jenny's wishes that he and Julia should stay together.

– But Daddy! You're missing the point!
– What point?
– The dates! Julia let me see the petition. Those are dates when you've said that she was with Mr Falling. But she couldn't have been. She was with me. She wasn't there!

Pemberton felt his mouth drying and an awful cloud growing in his mind. He flicked more quickly through the diary and the crosses kept on appearing. On through September and beyond. They did not cover every date when he had alleged that his wife was with Falling. But there were enough of them to cast a doubt on his theories. He was troubled. He could see now what his daughter was leading up to. If there were to be a contested hearing, Julia intended to call Jenny in her defence. Sir Patrick Tempest would have to cross-examine Pemberton's own daughter and call her a liar. He felt a chill shiver through him and he thought again of facing Blytheway in the witness box.

****

Jenny watched her father with a mix of nervousness and fascination as he leafed through her diary. He ran his fingers through his hair and polished and re-polished his gold-framed spectacles. He must never find out the truth. It was only a white lie after all. And it would keep Julia and her father together. The use of the diary was her idea. At least she thought it was. In truth Julia and she had been meeting and chatting regularly over the last nine or ten months and Julia would take her step-daughter out to tea at the Ritz on occasion so that they could have some privacy. Jenny had no one else she could talk to about the things that troubled her. And more recently, those little chats had intensified. For Jenny was in love. Simon, the officer she had taken to the Café de Paris, had occupied much of her thoughts and scarcely a day would go by without her talking to Julia about him.

In the course of one of these conversations the previous week in Julia's dressing room, Jenny had asked again about the divorce proceedings. Julia had recovered much of her poise since the day the petition was served, and, although she affected to demur, she allowed Jenny to see the allegations that had been made against her. The first had been dated the 31st May 1940.

– But isn't that one of the days that you and I were together?
– I really don't know Jenny.

She had fetched her diary but the entry for the day didn't spark any memory.

– I can't remember whether it was or wasn't.

She was downcast.

– Oh, don't worry, Jenny. Thank you for trying anyway. It was a good idea. I suppose it could have been. Isn't it a pity we didn't keep any records of when we had our little meetings. It could have been so helpful.
– I suppose. If it *was* one of the days that we met up, I could try and add in a line to say that we did. But it wouldn't look right. It would be all squashed up and you'd be able to tell I'd added it in afterwards … even if it *was* true.
– Never mind. And anyway, you wouldn't put in your diary the things that we've been talking about in case someone else read it.
– That's true.

Jenny sighed again. Julia continued:

– I suppose the most you would have done would be to put some little mark next to the date. Like a cross or an asterisk …
– That's it!
– What? What do you mean?
– I could put a little cross next to some of the dates. I can't be sure now of when we met but they could easily have been those days. Because you weren't seeing that man Falling were you?
– No, I wasn't. Of course I wasn't. But what a *clever* idea, Jenny. I would never have thought of that.

– And even if the dates aren't exactly right. It would only be a *white* lie. Wouldn't it.

Beseeching uncertainty. There was a long pause.

– Jenny. That's really kind. But I wouldn't want you getting into any trouble ...
– I wouldn't be getting into any trouble. And anyway, if a little lie helps bring out a big truth, it's got to be the right thing to do hasn't it?

Ever since the night at the Café de Paris, on the evening when Julia had begged her to help, Jenny had been looking for a way to do so. And now it had come to her. She knew Daddy would be upset. But he would be grateful in the end. And he and Julia would be able to stay together.

Pemberton shut the diary so that it made a small slamming noise and made to hand it back to his daughter. He looked weary.

– Well. Thank you, Jenny. That is most kind of you. You must have your diary back. Now, please forgive me. I have some work that I must do. We shall talk about this again very soon.
– No, Daddy. Please keep the diary. For now at least. I'm on my new one now. But please don't read the entries.

Jenny went round the desk to her father, leaned over him and kissed his cheek. Her dark hair fell across his face and an unmistakeable perfume drifted across him loosing flower-bursts of bittersweet memory. She squeezed his shoulders, then headed for the door. He saw the ghost of another woman merging with her as she left, and felt tears forming in his eyes.

****

He was alone. The green light glowed out. The little red diary, still unclasped, with the key next to it, lay in the middle of his desk. He reached out a hand to it, then drew back. His papers lay to one side, forgotten. He reached out again, picked up the diary and held it to his face. The smell of leather and perfume. He secured the clasp, locked the diary and put diary and key in his middle drawer, closing it gently. He tried to return his attention to his work but the words would not stay still before him. It was half past eleven and beyond the closed door of the study a silence had descended and all was dark. He opened the drawer again.

He opened the diary from the back. It would do no harm to look at just the last few entries. Jenny would understand ...

31ˢᵗ December 1940

This has been a lovely day and a horrible day all at the same time. Julia was right about Daddy. The atmosphere in the house has been getting worse and worse and I couldn't wait for Simon to pick me up and take me out. I've been so looking forward to showing him the Café de Paris. I won't be able to see him for months and months after tonight. I decided on the green dress Julia lent me and put my dark red lipstick on. Oh, and some matching green shoes. Then Samuels came and told me Daddy wanted to see me. Julia was on the landing looking at her pictures but when she turned round I was really shocked because she was crying and upset. I've never seen her cry before. And she asked me to help her. Daddy was really strange. He kept calling me "Joan" and he told me he was going to divorce Julia. And I couldn't persuade him not to. I had to go upstairs and start all over again with my make-up.

The lovely bit was with Simon. He loved the Café de Paris and he made me so happy. Snake Hips Johnson and his band were playing and Simon said he had never heard music like that before. And we danced and drank champagne and I wished life could always be so good and happy.

Pemberton felt himself reddening, at the reminder of how he had referred to Jenny as Joan, and at his breach of his promise to his daughter. He made to close the diary but could not prevent himself from peeping at the previous day's entry.

... Julia told me how much Daddy still misses Mummy and how he thinks too much and sometimes he gets it wrong. Then she said that she was scared that Daddy was going to try to divorce her for having an affair with someone from Daddy's chambers – I can't remember his name – I'd never heard of him before. In all the talks we've had she's never <u>ever</u> mentioned him! And

Julia said that it was untrue and she looked me straight in the eyes when she said it. And I <u>believed</u> her! I think she knows that Daddy still loves Mummy and it's getting harder and harder because I look so much like Mummy now. Julia's been so good for Daddy and I don't think he can see it anymore. I was so upset to see her so hurt but I think that she was trying to protect me and she was really worried about Daddy too ...

Pemberton read no more and locked the diary away. He was a man of few doubts. But the uncomfortable exchanges, with Blytheway and then with Jenny, and her diary had sowed a seed of uncertainty. Jenny wouldn't lie to him? He wasn't sure what he should do next.

****

Julia couldn't sleep. Something had not been right. She climbed up softly from the cellars, passing Jeremy's study on the way. She paused to look at the photos in the alcove. Flicking on the light, a warm glow suffused her dressing room. What was it? And then she realised. The bowl of hyacinths, once blue then turning to brown and fading, had gone.

Chapter Thirty-six

(Friday 17th January 1941)

Adam, cigarette in hand, looked down on the Temple Church from his new room in Lamb Building – his cigarette smoke left a trail from the window along the stone work. Blytheway had been as good as his word, and the day following the uncomfortable encounter in the crypt there had been a knock on Adam's door in Dr Johnson's Buildings. He answered it, cradling Cordelia, to find Blytheway's clerk who advised that a room was being made available for him. Together they carried his collection of paperbacks over to his new chambers and arranged them on the shelves. His pedestal desk – dismantled and piled in the corner of the room where he slept – was carried in stages around the corner into Lamb Building and reassembled.

He smiled to himself. It was entirely typical of Blytheway to ensure that he had a room overlooking the church. Now he could observe it from his bedroom *and* from the place where he was to work. A thin sun fell in a square on the carpet and scattered light over his books. Below him the church was coated in a thick layer of dust. Light glinted from the fractured panes. He gazed past the church to the remains of 2, Mitre Court Buildings and the Master's House. It was the only dwelling in the Temple where all the windows faced south. To the north side of it there was an unbroken brick wall beyond which lay the courtyard to Hoare's Bank. He had never been deemed important enough to be invited inside but it was well known to be an architectural gem, built in 1667 with panelling and a staircase from London's most gracious period.

Lamb Building, Dr Johnson's Buildings and Stirrup Court all survived still. But the destruction of the Blitz was encircling them and him. He vowed to himself that he would do everything in his power to save the buildings that were so dear to him. He turned away from the window and went to his jacket, hanging from a coat stand. Pulling out his wallet, he counted again the papery notes, putting them down with slow deliberation on the worn leather of his desk. Still sixty pounds. Catherine had returned

230

to London. He had received no word from her but Deborah had sent him another letter from Suffolk. He took ten pounds from the wad and put it to one side. He would send it to Dulwich for his wife and daughter. He returned the balance of his money to the wallet.

Blytheway was right. The sleeves and lapels of his suit were frayed and shabby. He could not expect to make the right impression, dressed as he was. He had been using and re-using the few clothes he had taken with him from Dulwich when he moved out. It didn't matter to him after he had been expelled from Stirrup Court, but if he was to return Blytheway's confidence in him – repay him for representing him without reimbursement – he would have to buy some new clothes. He removed a further twenty pounds from the wallet before replacing it in the inside pocket of his suit.

Blytheway had arranged through his clerk that the conference, interrupted the previous night by the air raid, should continue between 1.15 p.m. and 1.45. He was still wearing his bands. The pressure on his time effected a significant change in his approach and he was business-like to the point of being brusque. Jones was instructed to obtain statements from the prostitute, Betty, and from the concierge at the Stafford. Adam was told that he must prepare a detailed statement of his relationship with the prostitute and his relationship (or lack of it) with Julia and Jeremy Pemberton. As a final aside, before heading back to the Royal Courts of Justice for his resumed hearing, Blytheway passed Adam a card.

- My tailor. Go to him this afternoon. It's a horror, I know, but it is only a matter of time before they introduce *clothes* rationing! The things we must do!
- Thank you, Roly.
- Oh, and ... well, I can't say anything much as yet ... but I feel relatively confident that we shall have some helpful developments in the next few days.

Before Adam could question him further he swept out onto the stairs and headed back to court.

- I hope you like your new room.

And he was gone.

Adam examined the card. Apart from Novak and Bateman, he had no practice left to speak of. He decided to spend the rest of the afternoon in Jermyn Street.

Chapter Thirty-seven

(Friday 17th January 1941)

Bateman pushed a few coins across the counter, picked up his bottle, a beer glass and a glass of sherry, and headed to his favourite corner. The saloon bar was crowded and the familiar fug of cigarette smoke swirled around the ceiling. A heavy cloud cover hung over London that evening and the chances of a large-scale air raid seemed slight. He had his back to the room and knew he was virtually invisible. On the wall facing him was a large bevelled mirror advertising Watney's Pale Ale. He was below the sight line and he knew that whilst he could observe those who were behind him they could not see him. The mirror was dusty and gave off faint rainbows of colour around the edges. Framed in it was a mass of people, uniforms and civilians, thronging around the bar. Glasses of pale ale and porter. The off-licence door opened and closed. He was in a pub just outside Liverpool Street station. He thought back to the days when he could meet Victoria here regularly without danger. Below the sight line. Before those final few months when life became both simpler and infinitely more complicated. He took the stopper out of his bottle and carefully poured out the pale ale.

As he waited his thoughts turned again to his meeting with Jones the previous afternoon. This time he had not been kept waiting and the secretary, Sonia, ushered him to the frosted glass door. Beyond it he could see the hazy outline of his solicitor, sitting at his desk and organising his papers. Jones had his file out on the desk and, though he greeted him warmly as he entered, Bateman sensed an apprehension in his solicitor. He had been apologetic about his rudeness two days earlier. But he was also evasive and avoided looking Bateman in the eye. When Bateman asked what was going on with Falling, Jones half turned and looked out of the window. Already dusk was falling. Bateman had asked again after Falling.

– Well, that's been the problem. You see. There've been some … some developments …

– Can't Falling do my case?

He had sensed that something was up. Jones had always been punctili-ous in responding to him quickly in the past and the silence of the last two weeks had filled him with foreboding.

– No. No, of course not. It's just that you may not want to have him as your barrister anymore.
– Why? What's he done?
– Look ...

Jones shuffled his papers and looking out into Fetter Lane as he spoke.

– Well there's some good news and some bad news.
– Give me the good news first.
– Falling can do your case if you would like him to.
– And the bad news?
– He's no longer at Stirrup Court. He's moved chambers.
– What's the big deal? We all change jobs from time to time.
– Not at the Bar, I'm afraid. Falling has a black mark over him.
– So why's he moved?
– Well ... it's like ... I mean... You see ...

Jones took a deep breath.

– You see, Falling has been cited himself as a Co-Respondent in a divorce case.

Bateman was temporarily stunned, and then he let out a roar of laughter.

– That's rich! That's really rich! I told you I thought he knew a lot about adultery!

The words came out in a torrent of laughter and tears rolled down his cheeks.

– All that stuff about men and women having sex with people they shouldn't be. Giving things an air of normality! So we'll be seeing *his* picture in the papers!

And he had continued to laugh. But Jones wasn't laughing. Slowly, Bateman subsided.

- But why does that mean he had to move Chambers?
- You see, the man who is accusing him is his Head of Chambers. McKechnie's barrister.

Jones let this sink in. Bateman was aware that his mouth had fallen open, and with an effort he closed it.

- Mr Falling is denying the allegations of course. But it's likely that the trial will come on for hearing very soon after yours. You may feel that he might be distracted by his own problems.
- Does McKechnie know about this?
- Oh, I'm sure he does. In fact, half the barristers in the Temple know all about it. It's quite a talking point.
- And how's Falling coping with it?
- Oh, perfectly well I think. But I doubt it's going to be easy for him.
- I think I'll keep him. Give me some good reasons why I shouldn't.
- Well, first of all, it's likely to be all over the papers. It would've been anyway. But – think about it – the barrister who is representing you as Co-Respondent in a divorce trial is himself the Co-Respondent in divorce proceedings brought by the barrister representing Mr McKechnie.
- I think I can cope with that. Give me another reason.
- Well. It's bound to get personal between Falling and Pemberton. There's a risk that you, Victoria and Mr McKechnie could become pawns in a bigger game.
- Yes. I see that. But let's say I'm prepared to take a chance on it. Is there anything else?
- The inquest notes. You haven't been telling us the truth. Falling is onto it. He'll want to know what's really been going on.
- Hmmm.

And Bateman had paused, asked when his trial was likely to come on for a hearing and said he would think about it.

He looked at his watch. He'd been nursing his pint for almost a quarter of an hour. Where was she? He glanced up again at the large pub mirror and then he saw her. Victoria McKechnie was wearing a heavy dark coat. He saw a glimpse of the blue dress beneath it. Bateman had described her to Falling as being rather beautiful, and she was. A rich blonde curl had slipped out from under her scarf, there was a hint of rouge on her cheeks and her eyes were a deep blue. She caressed his shoulder lightly as she passed and took a seat opposite him. He motioned to the sherry.

- Were you followed?
- No. I came straight from work. Anyway, why does it matter?
- We mustn't be seen together.
- Who cares?
- When this is all over –
- Why don't you just stop it?!
- What are you talking about?
- Admit to the lawyers that we've been having an affair. Give him some money to go away. I love you.

And she reached out her hand to put it on his. He loved her and his heart expanded whenever he saw her. He moved his hand away.

- No physical contact in public. Remember?

She withdrew her hand.

- Oh darling …
- When this is all over. It won't be long now.
- But we don't need to have all the money. Please can't we end it now?
- He's bluffing. He won't dare go through with it.
- He's not bluffing! He's my husband. I know him.

They lapsed into silence. Bateman took a gulp of his beer. Victoria sniffed at her sherry. They stared into one another's eyes until Bateman looked away.

– What's wrong?
– My barrister's being having an affair with Graham's barrister's wife.
– What?
– But it's not that that worries me. He's been and looked at the inquest notes.

Victoria's eyes widened.

– But you said ... you and Graham *both* said no one would find out.
– Well, he has. And I don't know what to do about it.
– It's obvious isn't it? Let's admit it. *Please* let us end all these lies.
– Look. If he's clever enough to work that out I want him on our side.
– It's only money, Arnold. I want to tell the truth. I want everyone to know that I love you.
– Trust me, sweetheart.
– I don't want to go into that witness box, Arnold. God help me. I don't know what I'll say.

They were interrupted by a commotion at the entrance to the public house. Bateman looked up into the mirror. A tall man in his mid-forties, wearing a dark blue overcoat and muffler, was pushing his way through the drinkers towards them.

– Oi! Bateman! Don't think I can't see you. Bateman!

Bateman turned on Victoria and said, more loudly than was necessary:

– I thought you said you hadn't been followed?
– I didn't follow her, Bateman. I've been following you. Far easier!

Graham McKechnie was standing over them now. He wiped his brow and ran his hand through short brown hair.

– What do you want, McKechnie?
– Don't be stupid. You know what I want.
– I'll see you in Court!
– We all know the truth. You'll have to pay up!

- If you were so sure about it you wouldn't be following me ... and threatening me.
- It's going to be all over the papers. You'll both look like fools!
- People have got more important things to worry about than us.
- My barrister's going to crucify you.
- We'll see about that.
- Crucify your barrister too.
- Go home.
- I'll give evidence that I saw the two of you here.
- And ...?
- Well. It's evidence. Isn't it?

McKechnie swayed slightly and steadied himself on Bateman's chair.

- You could give evidence about a lot of things, Graham. But you wouldn't dare.
- Says who?
- My barrister's seen the Inquest notes. How are you going to explain that?

McKechnie faltered.

- We don't need to go into that. Just pay up and we can go our separate ways. I'll let Victoria keep Ernest and Susan.

Bateman had raised the stakes but he sensed an unlikely triumph. Victoria had her hands demurely in her lap. He reached across the table and took her hands in his own. Staring at McKechnie, he put them to his lips and kissed them. A trickle of sweat fell down his cheek.

- I think you'd better go, McKechnie.
- I want my wife back!
- It's too late. Come on, Victoria. Let's go.

And he took her by the hand, drained his glass and pushed his way past McKechnie towards the exit.

Chapter Thirty-eight
(Wednesday 22nd January 1941)

Dusk was beginning to encroach. Jack Storman KC sat unobtrusively at the back of a tea shop on the Strand, gazing at the blackout shades that had been drawn over the windows. He took a sip from his cup and again pulled out his fob watch. Ten minutes now. He should have brought something to read. He pulled the letter out from his inside pocket again and studied the envelope. Blue-black ink – his name and home address written in a cultured hand. He was not looking forward to the impending interview. He ran a finger under the flap and made to take out the writing paper within. He had read the letter so many times that he knew the wording by heart.

As he was removing the letter from its casing, the bell at the door tinkled and he looked up to see Catherine entering. She was wearing her blue dress under a dark overcoat. She peered into the gloom before spotting him and making for his table. Storman motioned to the shop girl and, with sign language, ordered a further cup of tea.

- Catherine! It's lovely to see you!
- Thank you for being here. I couldn't bear to go into the Temple …
- You're looking very well.

He regretted his observation almost as he made it. It was true that she was looking surprisingly composed. He noticed that she had taken great care with her make-up, and her eyes, always beautiful, looked larger and deeper than ever. But he sensed a paleness – a fragility – lying just below the surface. Dark shadows suggested many nights without sleep and he pictured the trouble that had gone into her appearance for their meeting. With a sense of shame and shock he realised, belatedly, that this interview was going to be more difficult for her than it was even for him. He reached out and placed his hand on hers. It was very cold to the touch.

– How's Adam?
– He's much better now. I think he's on the road to recovery.
– What are you talking about?

A hint of alarm. Storman realised, too late, that Catherine would not have known of Adam's illness, so he told her as prosaically as he could of the events of late December, playing down the seriousness of the condition. Her eyes widened as he unfolded his story and he sensed a mixture of anger and pity rising in her – each struggling for control of her reactions.

– Bloody cigarettes!

she said when he had finished.

– Actually. I think it was the brick dust. He was very brave that night.

Storman stopped short of telling Catherine of the provisional diagnosis of tuberculosis. It would have been unfair of him to try and evoke sympathy for Adam in the circumstances. A long silence ensued and they each concentrated on their cups of tea. Eventually, Catherine spoke again.

– I expect you have realised why I needed to see you?
– Catherine. There are limits to what I can say or do …
– I know that. There's no one left now that I can trust. Not one. I have come to you as a friend – not as a lawyer. I don't expect you to take my part. Just tell me what I should expect. I can work out myself what I must do.
– Adam asked me to act for him.

Catherine drew back shocked and began to rise from the table, pulling her coat more tightly around her.

– I'm sorry. I didn't think. I should be going …
– Catherine! Please! No! Stay …

Storman placed a restraining hand on her arm and caught her before she could stand.

– I told him I couldn't act for him. You are both my friends. He told me
that the allegations against him were all untrue and that acting for
him was not incompatible with my friendship with you. I refused,
however ...
– Then you don't believe his story any more than I do!

A hint of steel had entered her voice.

– I didn't say that, Catherine.
– Oh, come on! Don't treat me like an idiot.
– What am I supposed to do or think? He is a friend, as are you. I have
to rely upon what he tells me.

Storman felt uncomfortable hiding his own doubts in this way but it
was the best course that he could see open to him.

– He's made a complete fool out of me. I suppose you know that his
defence is that he wasn't seeing Julia but consorting with a prostitute
– at great expense – at the Stafford Hotel?
– I had heard. Yes.

This was an understatement. Pemberton had taken no steps to hide what
he had found and the word was all around the Temple. He could quite
understand why Catherine did not want to go in there.

– What is going to happen?
– Adam has secured the services of a very good barrister. His name
is Blytheway. I understand that he has agreed to act on Adam's
behalf for nothing. Adam is in good hands. If anyone can save him
Blytheway can.
– Will he be looking for a statement from me?
– I don't know. If he doesn't it won't be out of a failure to consider the
position.

Storman thought about Blytheway. He thought it highly unlikely that he
would be so foolish as to involve Catherine in the case.

- I know you can't advise me on what I should do. But you *can* tell me how the case is likely to unfold?
- Pemberton must show that Adam has committed adultery with Julia. He has pinned all his colours to that mast. Adam showed me the petition – I was there when he was served. A strange man by the name of Jackson turned up in Dr Johnson's Buildings.

Catherine remembered her encounter with the man on New Year's Day.

- And if he fails to prove adultery with Julia?
- Then his petition will fail and he will have to pay the legal costs of the exercise. Adam will avoid paying him damages.
- But Adam's defence depends upon him proving that he was having a relationship with a prostitute?
- Yes.
- And if he is believed? What does his defence do to our marriage?

Storman had anticipated – and dreaded – this question. There was no way to avoid it. He took a deep breath.

- Well. He is defending himself against an adultery petition by countering that he has been committing adultery with someone else.
- And that would give me grounds to divorce him?
- Yes.

Storman observed her as she considered this. She had known the answer before she asked the question. He had always thought her more intelligent than Adam; than most of his colleagues at the Bar for that matter. She seemed to shrink into herself as he watched her. He knew she needed little guidance. He calculated that she would work out what to do whether or not he advised her – and that the course he would suggest was for the best for her and for Adam.

- Look. Catherine. I know I said I couldn't advise you but I think you'll work it out for yourself if you haven't already. My advice to you would be to do nothing for now ...
- Yes. I think I understand.

- Divorce proceedings are very expensive. If Pemberton succeeds, his petition will also give you grounds to divorce Adam should you choose. If he fails and Adam has gone on record as saying he has had an affair with a prostitute, you would have grounds to divorce Adam … if you should choose.
- Thank you, Jack. That is what I was beginning to conclude myself. There's nothing I can do is there?
- I don't think there is, Catherine. Pemberton has set a stone rolling down the hill and all we can do now is watch – and try to keep out of its way.

She finished the last dregs of her tea and reached for her purse.

- No. Catherine. This is on me. I hope you don't mind if I ask but are you all right for money?
- Just about. For now. Adam sent me two five-pound notes through the post. He promised to keep me in funds.
- Well. If there is anything I can do just let me know. You have my home telephone number?
- Thank you, Jack. Yes.
- Margaret knows you might call.

She rose to leave.

- How's Deborah?
- Well. I think. I miss her, Jack. I want her to come back to London. Do you think it's safe?
- No. She's better off where she is for now.
- I hope so. I'm not sure. There's a man on the farm who worries me.
- What do you mean?
- Oh. It's probably nothing. I just miss her that's all.

She leant over him and kissed him on the cheek and her delicate perfume drifted over him.

- Thank you again, Jack. Oh, and how is Adam at the moment?
- He's well. He seems to be settling in well at Lamb Building. To be

honest I miss his presence at Stirrup Court. But I think I am in a minority on that front.

- Well. Goodbye, Jack. Please don't tell Adam that we met.
- Of course I won't. Goodbye Catherine.

The door tinkled as she left. Storman sighed and pushed some pennies across the formica. He had told Catherine what he felt he had to tell her. He had not told her that, as he left Stirrup Court that evening, Adam had been sitting in the Chambers waiting room, an unusually well-polished shoe tapping up and down as he and Jones, his solicitor, waited for a very uncomfortable meeting with Peter Preston KC.

Chapter Thirty-nine

(Friday 24th January 1941)

Adam put his wallet back in his pocket and headed up to his hotel room, as the liveried old man behind him pocketed the pound note. But he couldn't remember the number of his room. The corridors filled with misty smoke, back-lit by blue lightbulbs from the blacked-out over-ground trains.

The numbers on the hotel room doors had been replaced by metal grilles. He climbed ever higher up the stairs but nothing looked familiar anymore. He paused at an anonymous door and pushed back the grille. At the far end of the room was a small red-faced man in a loud pinstriped jacket with wide lapels. Pinstriped trousers lay round his ankles. Seeing Adam he shuffled over to the door, shouting, "I'm Arnold Bateman. Don't know what the 'C' stands for!" Adam felt hot breath on his face and a rising gorge of fear. He slammed the grille shut and moved on. Blue smoke was rising.

He reached the next door and cautiously slid back the grille. Catherine was waiting for him with an arm pulled back and a look of fury on her face. She screamed and lunged and he slammed the slat shut – but not before an egg sliced through the bars and splattered down his clothing.

He had no alternative but to carry on trying the doors. Through the next grille he saw Delia, his kitten, swimming in a bowl of fresh milk the size of a sombrero. An empty spotlight shone down on the middle of the room and just beyond that stood Betty with her back to him – an elegant silhouette. He put his key into a conventional lock and entered the room. Betty turned. But it was Julia.

– Socks had four white paws. This one only has three.

And then she was Betty again. The kitten climbed out of a bowl of milk that had become the size of a swimming pool. But it was Katya Hoffer who purred at him:

– You must listen carefully to everything ...

The blue mist coagulated into some sort of shapeless form and started to slide around the room, distracting his attention.

Now he was sitting down with Betty and she was telling him her story: how her husband, Joe, had gone to Dunkirk to buy her a dolls' house but the Germans had got there first and so she had to make do with a straw summer hat which he wired up with the lights he was going to put into the dolls' house, him being an electrician. And she'd put the hat on during the blackout and when Joe turned the switch so that the lights came on a bomb fell on him and killed him, leaving her standing there next to him in a flashing straw hat. But the insurance company wouldn't pay up because she'd been wearing that hat at the time.

Adam was about to tell her his story when he heard light footsteps marching towards the spotlight. Tomas Novak stood to attention in the circle of light. There was a shriek from Katya, who ran to him and entwined him in her arms. Then suddenly she was a kitten again rubbing herself up against his calves.

On the count of three, I will tell you everything. One ... two ...

And there was an almighty bang. Novak and the kitten disappeared through the floor. There was a sickening snap and all that remained in the spotlight was a black square hole in the ground and a thick rope, swinging slowly and creaking over the abyss with the weight it carried. Two white hands emerged and Katya pulled herself back into the room.

– You should have listened more carefully.

The blue mist coagulated into a human form and shimmered towards him.

– The evidence. Sweetheart. Always start with the evidence.

Said Blytheway's cobalt ghost.
Then everything went black.

****

246

Adam had taken at least some of Blytheway's advice to heart. As well as investing in a new suit and some fresh collarless shirts, he had his hair cut again. The starch of his collar rubbed uncomfortably against his freshly shaved neck. He ran his finger between neck and collar once more to ease the discomfort. It was Friday evening and he and Jones again found themselves waiting to be shown through security at Wandsworth Prison. He thought back to his last visit, just over a month ago, when he was scruffy, hung-over and distracted. When he still had some hope. It seemed so long ago. So much had changed. Nearly all of it for the worse.

And yet, he felt healthier, albeit weaker. His new suit had been made within days – business was slow in Jermyn Street – and he was wearing it now. The tailor had honoured the ten per cent discount and given him a couple of silk ties as a token of thanks for his custom. Although Blytheway had alluded to a potentially helpful development in his case over a week ago, he had not elucidated further. Instead, nearly all his comments were directed to Adam's appearance. He chided him on the state of his shoes, and one morning before he headed off to Court he entered Adam's room with a pair of horsehair shoe brushes and a tin of boot black and insisted that Adam polish his shoes there and then.

- I'll bring you some shoe trees this afternoon. You must take better care of your footwear. It's really embarrassing.
- I'm sorry, Roly.
- You can tell a lot about a man by the state of his shoes. I believe those are your only pair. Buy some Church's and alternate.
- But they're very expensive, Roly, and I have spent over twenty pounds already in the last week.
- One can't have enough pairs of shoes. I saw you wearing those at the weekend!

And then he left for Court. The nagging continued, however, whenever he and Adam were in the same room. He drew the line at buying a frock coat and Blytheway seemed, belatedly, to remember how little money Adam actually had and desisted from further scolding. And yet, wearing his new suit and shirt, his tie precisely knotted and his hair neat and in place, he reluctantly recognised that he was beginning to feel better about himself. His new appearance had been invaluable for his awkward meeting with Preston.

Roly had given him one piece of non-sartorial advice: that he must always concentrate on the evidence (sweetheart) when preparing a case. His insistence on this one point had begun to permeate his dreams. The previous Monday morning, as he came round from a restless sleep and Blytheway's blue ghost faded into the washed blue of the sky over the Temple Church, he knew he had to re-read the witness statement prepared by Jones for Katya Hoffer. He had cursed to himself when Jones told him that Katya had persuaded him to tell her Novak's version of events before she gave her own. Her statement was evasive. What did not come across from the document before him was any idea of the sort of person Katya was. Jones, however, had filled him in on this – an erotic kitten. He had plainly been captivated – beguiled – by her. She had dropped her guard only once:

> – But this is stupid. Why should he die because they find old plans in an old house?! ...

Adam had pressed Jones on the words he had written down but he was in no doubt that Katya had said more than she intended. "Old plans"? Why did she use the word "old"? There ought to have been no way that she could know what had been found in Novak's bedsit. But she had volunteered the fact that plans had been found. And she had gone further. She had described them as old.

Old plans!

He could have kicked himself. He had been ostensibly conducting Novak's case for over a month – protecting him from the gallows – and had taken no steps at all to see the evidence that the prosecution was going to be relying upon! As Defence Counsel surely he should be taking steps to see the plans, the bomb-making instructions, for himself. He had wasted over four weeks and the trial was now less than eight weeks away.

It had taken only a couple of telephone calls to establish, as he had feared, that Peter Preston KC was prosecuting Counsel. His next call was to Preston himself.

> – Ah, Falling. I wondered when you would get around to contacting me.
> – You knew I was representing Novak?
> – Everyone knows *everything* about you now, Falling.

His voice was laced with contempt.

- I want to see the evidence that the police picked up from Novak's rooms.
- Room, dear boy. I take it that you haven't advised your solicitor to visit the "scene of the crime".
- When and where can I see the plans?
- I really was beginning to think you were going to try and defend this man without any knowledge of the evidence at all.
- When and where can I see the plans?
- I take it you and your solicitor have signed the Official Secrets Act?
- I ... I, er ...
- You hadn't thought of that had you?
- Of course we will provide the necessary signatures.
- You're out of your depth, Falling.

And so, a meeting had been arranged at Stirrup Court so that Adam and his solicitor could sign the Act, reminding them of the need to abide by its terms when representing Novak, and to see the plans. Preston had received them with cold discourtesy and asked them to wait for Arthur to show them up. Adam forced himself to think of the man's wandering hands as a defence against this antipathy – Preston's attempts to get close to his own wife, and to Julia. They were to be allowed to take notes but not to take away the originals.

Jones looked around the waiting room. It was much as it had been the last time he had been there. The black curtains were still nailed across the window. The same heavily shielded lamp cast shadows over the rows of law books that lined one wall. However, when he had been there in December an irritable Bateman had been sitting next to him and they were waiting to see Adam Falling. Now, scarcely six weeks later, Falling was no longer a member of Stirrup Court – was not even welcome there. Falling was sitting where Bateman had plonked himself. Falling, whom he had never heard of in November 1940, was now his counsel in the Bateman and the Novak trials. Falling was also his client in what was set to be the most high-profile divorce of the legal term, if not the year. And now they were sitting together in the waiting room of Jeremy Pemberton KC's chambers.

– *I think you'll regret this retainer, Jones.*

Jones said a silent prayer that they would avoid bumping into Pemberton on the stairs. So far only Jack Storman KC, urgently buttoning his overcoat as he passed, had spotted them as he came out of the Clerks' Room, but he was in a hurry to get somewhere and did not acknowledge them as he went by. Jones looked over at Adam. Falling was deep in thought, rhythmically tapping a well-polished shoe and turning his blue notebook over and over in his lap. Even through the gloom it was possible to make out the expensive cut of his dark pinstripe, and his cuffs shone white and unfrayed at his wrists. Unusually, he was not smoking, although there was a faint aroma of Woodbines. Jones thought back to their meeting at Wandsworth Prison, Adam distracted and in mental and sartorial disarray. Falling's appearance had undoubtedly improved significantly after Blytheway's intervention. But there was something else, and as they waited Jones struggled to put his finger on it.

Arthur came into the room.

– Mr Preston is ready for you now

He led them up a flight of stairs and Jones realised they were heading towards what had once been Adam's room. Once again, he fixed his eyes on the fine cut of Arthur's suit as they climbed.

Arthur showed them into Adam's old room. It remained narrow and cold but now there was nothing other than a makeshift table with an Angle-poise lamp balanced on it, its light shining on a pile of documents and a long brown cardboard tube. Dust shadows marked where Adam's books had been. Preston emerged from the gloom holding a document and two pairs of white gloves. Jones felt that this had been orchestrated to make Falling uneasy, but Falling remained impassive.

– Falling. This is a register of the documents on this desk. I want you to go through it with me and confirm that all the documents are there. When you and your solicitor leave I will want you to go through it again so that we can be sure no documents have been removed. Is that understood?

Falling took the document from him, nodding almost imperceptibly. He and Jones studied it together. A Baedeker map, circa 1900, of the area between Victoria Park in Hackney and Walthamstow, a list of coded names, large photographs of handwritten bomb-making instructions, a short written history of Abbey Mills Pumping Station and, finally, a roll of plans giving the detailed layout of Abbey Mills Pumping Station itself. Adam ticked them off, signed the register and handed it back to Preston.

- – Thank you, Preston.
- – Wear the gloves when you are handling the evidence. If your fingerprints turn up on anything there will be hell to pay. Arthur will be waiting outside. I have work to do.

And Preston dropped the gloves on the table and left the room without a further word, closing the door quietly behind him.

Adam picked up the closest pair and squeezed his hands into them. The material was coarse and pulled at the skin on his knuckles. He couldn't understand why Preston was making such a fuss. Fingerprints were one of the weaker points in the prosecution case, no thanks to the police who handled the cardboard tube and enclosed documents liberally at the time of Novak's arrest. Numerous different prints had been found, and, although some remained unidentified once the police had been excluded, none matched those of Novak.

Gingerly, he placed one gloved forefinger on each end of the tube and held it under the lamp, turning it slowly and sliding the light along its length. It was old and slightly spongy to the touch. The spiral fold moved along its length as he turned it, and deep dust lay in the groove. There was a rectangle of damaged paper where, Adam assumed, an address had been taped to the side, and another area of adhesive damage where once postage stamps had been. Otherwise the cardboard was anonymous. The documents had been found rolled up inside it under Novak's floorboards.

He handed the tube to Jones and turned to the plans of the Abbey Mills Pumping Station and tried to roll them out flat under the light. But the plans, made of pale blue paper, kept rolling shut again until Jones was enlisted to hold one end open whilst Adam carefully unrolled the other end. Katya had been right. The paper was old and very thick. In the right-hand corner, with the other technical details, was the date that the plan had been produced: 26th January 1926. How could she have known that? And how could one man work easily with these large plans when the ends obstinately rolled over his hands as he tried to read what they contained? Adam looked for evidence of any man-made folds in the document, effected with the intention of stopping the plan from rolling up, but he found none. It looked as though the plans had rarely been removed from the tube over the previous fourteen years.

****

Albert Simms, an official of the Metropolitan Water Board, had provided a short history of the Pumping Station. In the 1840s and 1850s, before the creation of a modern sewage system, human waste was pumped straight into the Thames. This had led to numerous outbreaks of cholera and the deaths of tens of thousands of Londoners. In the late nineteenth century Sir Joseph Bazalgette, chief engineer of the London Metropolitan Board of Works, created a sewer network for central London. Central to his project was the construction of the Thames Embankment and the building of major pumping stations at Deptford, Crossness, Chelsea Embankment and, finally, at Abbey Mills in the River Lea Valley.

Adam picked up the Baedeker map. Not much had changed in the East End of London since 1900. The Abbey Mills Pumping Station was located around a mile west of Novak's flat in Leytonstone. Bands of blue, London's rivers, flowed around it, and to the north was the East Warwick Reservoir, where hundreds of millions of gallons of London's drinking water were stored. Several strategically placed bombs would cripple the sewage system and poison the water supply. This, said the prosecution, was what Novak had been planning to do at the time of his arrest.

– Oi!! Mr Falling! How long are you going to be? I've been standing here an age!

There was an angry rapping on the door. Falling and Jones looked at one another through the gloom and then at their watches. It was 7.30 p.m. You lose track of time in the blackout.

– Sorry, Arthur. Won't be long.

Adam was scribbling furiously in his notebook.

– I'm coming in!

Arthur burst into the room. His eyes were gleaming and his usually immaculate coiffure was awry.

– Have you any idea what time it is? I need to get home!
– We're finishing off … nearly there.
– I don't need to be treated like this. I'm not your clerk anymore … Thank God!
– The feeling is mutual, Arthur.
– Bloody cheek!
– Let's go through the inventory together. I'm sure it's not the first time you've done an inventory of the contents of my room.

They went down the list ticking it off, and when this was over Adam and Jones removed their gloves and placed them under the circle of light thrown by the Angle-poise lamp.

– All right. Now please leave, Fa – *Mister* Falling.
– If you don't mind, Arthur, I would like to have a few moments alone. I won't do anything illegal.

And Adam ushered Jones and a protesting Arthur out of the room and onto the stairs. He looked around the cold and narrow room. The last time he had had felt like this was in his daughter's room in Dulwich just before Christmas. A muted glow emanated from the lamp's cone of light. There had been his desk. That was where he had kept the crystal paperweight Julia had given to him. His paperbacks had been on those shelves. His blue bag had hung from a hat stand in that corner. Thirteen years. Here had been his daydreams and his hopes. He would never see this room again. How much of himself had he left behind here? He took one last slow look around him, and then switched off the lamp and everything went black.

****

That had been Wednesday evening. Now Jones looked across at Adam as they sat waiting to be shown through security at Wandsworth Prison. His well-polished shoe was still tapping and every now and then he would run a finger between his nape and collar or smooth down his hair. Otherwise his head was bowed as he looked down at the blue notebook in his lap, turning it over and over without opening it. Jones recalled his surprise when Adam had suddenly pushed him and Arthur out of the room, shutting the door behind them. A crack of light under the door, silence from within and a red-faced Arthur complaining loudly about the intrusion. Then the light disappeared and Adam emerged.

- Good night, Arthur. Please thank Mr Preston for his hospitality.
- You've no right –
- Good night, Arthur.

And Adam led Jones down the stairs and out of Stirrup Court. Once outside, as soon as they had made it to Cloisters he had reached urgently for his Woodbines and lit up immediately, regardless of the blackout. The flare of the match, followed by the glow of the cigarette, threw Adam's shadow into larger-than-life relief against the white column behind him. Behind Adam's shoulder, against the column, his magnified shadow-hand was shaking violently against the stillness of the rest of his silhouette. Jones looked into Adam's eyes. Through the darkness they seemed calm but the erratic flickering of the cigarette in his peripheral vision hinted at something else.

- Fine. Fine. Just needed a cigarette.
- We should be making tracks.
- Yes. Of course. But would you mind if I had one more before we go.

And Adam had thrown down the half-spent cigarette and lit another whilst the first still glowed against the flagstones.

In the waiting room earlier Jones had been struggling to pin down the change that had come over Adam and, at that moment, watching the shaking fingers and the flicker and flare of the cigarette as Adam drew deeply on it, it came to him. He had been like a swimmer getting ready to dive deep underwater – preparing himself, pulling all his resources together until the time when he could surface again. He was going through the same preparation now, as they waited in the prison. Would he be able to hold it together?

There was a loud clang as the metal door swung open. A lanky warder stood in the doorway.

– Novak is in interview room four. Follow me.

Chapter Forty

(Friday 24th January 1941)

The corridor walls were a dirty cream colour, lit badly by a line of unshaded lightbulbs running the length of the ceiling. It had a narrow emptiness and their footsteps echoed to the counterpoint of the warder's keys, rattling on his belt as he walked ahead of them. The blue serge of his jacket creased rhythmically with the movement of his shoulders as he marched.

Interview room four came into view. It had an ordinary household door with large plate glass windows on either side of it. Novak was sitting behind a rectangular table. He was oblivious to their approach. Adam could not recognise the straight-backed arrogant man he had met the previous month. His head was bent forward and, as they got nearer, Adam saw that he was rubbing his hands up and down his thighs in a repetitive, if not obsessional way. He seemed thinner and his hair, which had been so neat, had grown unruly and curled down over his ears. When the warder jangled the key in the lock he jumped out of his reverie, a startled look on his face. Seeing his visitors, he leapt to his feet, his head bowed.

- Mr Falling! Thank you so much for coming! I was beginning to think ...
- I'm sorry it has taken longer than I had intended, Mr Novak. I had not meant to keep you waiting this long.
- Then you have spoken with Katya?
- Mr Jones has seen her, yes. She refused to sign the statement he prepared for her.
- But ... but ... she told him that I came over on the same ship?
- She told us she did not know you. She did not recognise you from the boat. She first became aware of your existence after your arrest.

Adam had been rehearsing these lines to himself ever since Jones had reported back to him. Even so, he was not prepared for the dramatic effect they would have. Novak, who had still been on his feet, slumped, crumpled even, back into his chair and, his arms and elbows flat against the table, he buried his face in them.

– She has not visited me, nor has she written to me!

Minutes passed. Adam looked over at Jones, who shrugged his shoulders, a bemused expression fluttering across his features.

Eventually Novak raised his head from the desk and looked their way.

– I am sorry.
– That is all right, Mr Novak. Would you mind if we got on? There is a lot we must discuss.
– Please, do you have a spare cigarette?
– I didn't know you smoked.
– Usually I do not smoke. I need a cigarette please.
– Of course.

Adam pulled out his Woodbines, offered one to Novak and shucked one out for himself. There was a well-smudged saucer at the edge of the table and he pulled it across so that it lay between them. He tried to control the tremor in his right hand as he put the lighted match to Novak's cigarette. The Czech inhaled deeply and immediately had a coughing fit as the smoke invaded his lungs. Once recovered, he carried on smoking, giving no indication that he was going to say anything. Adam, smoking opposite him, looked into his red-rimmed eyes. The arrogance was gone. Instead there was, in their pale blue, entreaty, deep thought and … fear. Novak's skin, even without the coughing fit, was more pallid than before and he smelt stale. There was dirt under his fingernails.

They stubbed their butts into the saucer.

– As I was saying, Mr Novak. Katya does not know you and she does not support your story …
– Yes … Yes. Forgive me. I do not know why I tried to involve her. It was wrong of me. It was very foolish.

- What are you talking about?!
- It was foolish. I made up a story because I thought it would help me. I should not have been so selfish.
- I don't believe you, Novak.
- Why would I lie to you?
- Tell me about the documents that were found under your floorboards.
- What is there to tell?
- Well, describe them to me.
- They were … well, they were just documents.
- You know what they were. Describe them to me.
- Mr Falling, we have both read the police evidence.

A touch of the old arrogance returning.

- Tell me about the plans of the Abbey Mills Pumping Station.
- Yes. There were plans of the Pumping Station. And I am supposed to have been planning to blow it up!
- What colour was the paper?
- The colour? I … I cannot now remember.
- Mr Novak. This is important. Was it blue, white, brown or red?

After a long pause:

- Brown, I think … no white … I'm not sure.
- You don't know, do you?
- Mr Falling, I have other things to worry about than the colour of paper.
- Were the plans old plans or new plans?

Another long pause and a sigh.

- I do not know.

Novak slumped backwards in his chair, a look of helplessness in his eyes. Adam slammed his hand down so hard on the table that even Jones jumped. He heard the rattle of keys behind him as the warder came across to see what was going on.

- I want you to tell me the truth! Did you hide those documents under the floorboards?
- I told you before. I had never seen those documents before. I had never even touched them.
- So how do you say that the documents got there?
- I do not know.
- And how was it the police knew where to find you and them? They knew exactly which floorboard to lift.
- I don't know.
- Someone must have put them there. And someone must have tipped off the police. Have you any idea who that could have been?

I have no idea.

They were getting nowhere. Adam sensed that Novak was trying to help, was certainly more cooperative than he had been the last time. But he was holding something back. He sighed.

- The plans of the Abbey Mills Pumping Station were printed on blue paper. They had not been unrolled for a long time. And they were old. Katya knew that they had found plans under your floorboards. And she knew that the plans were old. How could she know that? Hoffer did not tell us anything about plans and we didn't tell Katya.

Novak sat bolt upright.

- Katya knew about the plans?
- It seems to me, Mr Novak, that this means one of two things: either she planted the plans there herself or she visited your flat and found them there. Or perhaps she planted the plans and *also* visited you there?

Novak began rubbing his hands up and down on his trousers as he had been doing when they had approached the interview room. He did not answer but his eyes betrayed wild confusion.

- You're not telling me the truth about your relationship with Katya.
- Why would I lie to you when my life is at stake?

- When we met in December you told me Katya thought I had been gullible at the Tribunal. Why ... how could you make such a thing up?
- Forgive me. I was being offensive. You see, I do not trust people easily. I trusted Hoffer and he betrayed me. I trusted ... I trust Katya.
- Tell me the truth! How well do you know her?
- Ah! I remember now. It was Hoffer who told me what Katya said about you. It was not Katya. I was mistaken.
- You're making this up as you go along.
- I remember. Hoffer told me that Katya was unhappy to be graded "C". She wanted to be graded "B" or even better "A". She was unhappy with your decision, Mr Falling.
- That doesn't make any sense at all.
- I do not say it makes sense. I do not understand it. Why would she want to be interned? I am only telling you what ... what Hoffer told me.

The trial was a matter of weeks away and they were getting nowhere. Novak was trying to protect Katya, of that Adam was sure. But he could not understand why. She obviously did not reciprocate this loyalty.

- Mr Novak. Do you know what a sub-poena is?
- What is this word suppeenah?
- It means witness summons. If we issue a sub-poena against Katya then she will be forced to come to court to give evidence. She cannot be forced to tell the truth but I believe she will. It may be the only way to save you. That is, if you want to be saved.
- I forbid it!
- I think that I might just instruct Mr Jones to issue a sub-poena against her. Your trial is only a matter of weeks away.
- But I forbid it. You are my lawyer. You must follow my instructions!

Adam shifted uncomfortably. Novak was right of course. If Adam acted contrary to his instructions he would be putting himself in serious professional jeopardy. However, if he followed Novak's instructions, Novak would undoubtedly be convicted. And hanged. Outside the room the warder was jangling his keys. Time was nearly up.

– So, Mr Novak. Just to recap. You knew nothing about the plans. You had never seen them before the police arrived. Hoffer found you the room and advised you not to report yourself. You did not know Katya before your arrest but you came over from Gibraltar on the same boat that they travelled on?
– That is so.

And Novak sat back and folded his arms, straightening himself into something like the posture he held on their last visit. It was hopeless. Then, in a flash of inspiration, Adam made one last roll of the dice.

– Tell me about your journey from Gibraltar, Mr Novak.

Novak jumped slightly. He looked over Adam's shoulder and a dreamy look entered his eyes.

– It was a beautiful journey. I thought we were sailing to America – we travelled so far west. But it was only to avoid the mines. The boat was very crowded. But the skies were bright and blue …
– Where did you sleep?
– I would sleep on the deck. I found myself a place under a lifeboat and wrapped myself in sheeting to keep warm … and I would look at the stars. I was very happy. I was oh, so very happy …

There was loud knock on the door.

– Time's up, gentlemen.

Jones and Falling got up to leave. Novak also stood.

– We must meet again, Mr Novak. I need you to see the original plans and documents. It may be that this will be just before the trial.
– Would you do me a favour, Mr Falling?
– If I can. What is it?
– Can you lend me any books? I have only three books that they have let me have from the library. I have read a novel by Sinclair Lewis four times now. *Main Street*. It is not a very good book. It has no plot.

Maybe America was not such a good place. It also has writing all over it. My fellow prisoners are illiterate!

Adam pulled out his current Penguin – *Brighton Rock* by Graham Greene – and made to hand it over.

– I'm sorry, Mr Falling.

The warder placed a restraining hand on his arm.

– I'll take that. All books have to be examined by the Librarian before being handed over. If he passes it I'll give it to Novak.
– That's very good of you.
– That's all right, Mr Falling, sir. Anyway, once Mr Novak here has been here eight weeks he'll be able to have four books a week. He should have plenty to read after the middle of February.
– One way or another I don't think Mr Novak will be here after the middle of February. Goodbye, Novak. I'll arrange another meeting.
– Goodbye, Mr Falling.

****

Standing under the shelter by the bus-stop outside the prison, Adam lit another cigarette. This time there was no incentive to catch a cab, and anyway after black-out they were hard to come by.

– That was all pretty rum, Falling.
– I beg your pardon?
– I was saying he was even stranger this time than he was last time.
– Oh yes … yes.
– I got a full note of it anyway – for what it's worth; didn't make a lot of sense.
– Good … yes … good.
– Do you want me to organise another visit?
– Yes … good idea … yes. Actually, Mr Jones, would you mind if we had a chat on the telephone on Monday? I've rather a lot on my mind at the moment.

262

- Oh! Well, all right. Anyway we're travelling back on the bus together so if anything comes to you ...
- Yes... of course.

They boarded the bus in silence and travelled slowly back to the city. Jones watched as Adam turned his blue notebook over and over in his hands, puzzled by this change of mood. Their meeting with Novak had certainly given him a lot to think about so it was no surprise, perhaps, that Falling too was deep in thought.

Adam had thought about Novak and Katya, and about Hoffer, as they walked from the prison gates to the bus-stop. But then memories of Julia returned. His journey to his last meeting with her began from this bus-stop and so it bore the imprint of her memory. He thought of Blytheway's reference to a potentially helpful development in his case and his throw-away invitation earlier that day to come "chez moi" for dinner the following week "as a friend and fellow member of chambers, sweetheart, not as a client. It would be good to get to know you better. Life can be *so* dreary!" What developments had there been? Did Blytheway have some sort of ulterior motive in inviting to dinner?

But most of all Adam had been thinking again about his strange dream

- The evidence. Sweetheart. Always start with the evidence.

Betty had said something to him – either in the dream or in the Stafford Hotel – which was extremely significant. But he couldn't remember what it was. And he could not work out why it was so important.

Chapter Forty-one

(Wednesday 29th January 1941)

Julia Pemberton was sitting at her dressing table. She looked into the reflected image of her eyes. She was no longer as beautiful as the photographs of her; even though they were in black and white. They looked better than she did. She felt far worse than they looked. Only an experienced observer would notice the slight sagging of her chin, the fullness of her cheeks. There were shadows under her eyes that had never been there before. Only an experienced observer would notice these things. But Julia *was* an experienced observer, and saw these things on a daily basis as they charted some sort of internal collapse. She thought, inexplicably, of her father. She never thought of her father! Weak chin. Lips that were too fleshy. He looked like an apology made flesh. How had he begotten her? Why had he never liked her? Why had she always hated him? She would start with some blusher.

When she had given her cheeks some artificial colour she turned to her lips. Bright red lipstick. And then onto her eyes. They had always been bright blue, like a summer's day, but now, as she looked into them, they seemed full of clouds and rain. A touch of mascara, but not too much. A little more blusher over her bags and she could almost fool herself. There was a knock at the door. It could not be Jeremy. There was an unwritten rule that he did not come in here.

– Yes?
– Sorry, ma'am. May I come in?

A sigh of relief. It was the housekeeper.

– Why, Annie! Yes of course! Do come in.

Annie bustled in carrying a bundle of clothing and a bowl of flowers. Julia looked at her with the eyes of someone for whom everything "everyday" might hide a curse. Annie was about fifty years of age and had been with the family almost as long as Julia had been married to Jeremy. Annie had never married. She was short and fat and rather self-important. Julia knew that the Pemberton family was her life. She sensed an inordinate pride in her when she learnt that she and Samuels would be sharing the basement with them during the blackout and the air raids. It put her on a level above the other servants. But she had always been kind and deferential and, so far as Julia was aware, had never said an unkind word about her. Then again, thought Julia, the same could have been said of Samuels. Who could she trust?

- I've brought you your clothes for this evening, ma'am. Shall I lay them out on the bed?
- How kind, Annie. Yes, please do.

And Annie arranged a dowdy skirt and a serge top carefully across the bed.

- Forgive me, miss. But I don't know how you can bear to wear that stuff. I can tell it's scratchy just by carrying it.
- Oh, don't worry, Annie. It would be quite wrong to dress up. Have you put aside the usual for later?
- Yes of course, miss. There's a little jug in the fridge and I've put together a packet of tea in the pantry.
- You are a treasure! Thank you so much.

Annie, with a hint of pride, held up a bowl of early-flowering tulips.

- And I've got these for you! I'm sorry it's taken me so long. You've been without flowers for over a week now.
- How very thoughtful! I'd noticed that my hyacinths had disappeared.
- Sorry, miss. I should have said something. But they were going brown. And they had started to lose their smell.
- Oh! Don't worry. That's quite all right.

Julia affected a casualness that she did not feel.

– Tell me. How on earth did you get these beautiful tulips to flower so early?

Annie expanded with pride.

– Well, ma'am. It wasn't easy. I've been moving the bowl around the cellars for two or three weeks now. I thought that, well, if the electric fires were on, there was no harm in putting the bowl near them so that the bulbs would think it was nearly summer. Well. It's worked.
– How it has worked! They look lovely! But, tell me. What about the hyacinth bulbs? Were you able to save them for next year?
– I'm sorry, miss. No. I know we ought to try. But I emptied them out and had a good look at them and they were done for.
– What a pity! Well. Thank you for trying. Were you able to do *anything* with them?

Julia had tried but, to her mind, failed to keep the tremor out of her voice. There was a pause, and she felt two long heartbeats through the pale linen of her shirt, before Annie replied. Her brightness contrasted with her mistress's inner feelings.

– Oh no, miss. Well, obviously, I tried. But there was nothing to be done. So I put the lot on the vegetable garden. Help the war effort at least.
– Exactly so, Annie. Thank you for trying.

Julia was repeating herself.

– Will that be all, miss?
– Sorry. Yes. Thank you, Annie. There's nothing else. Jenny and I will be going out for tea. But I will be back in good time to change for work. Thank you for organising the tea for later.
– A pleasure, miss.

And she was gone. Julia thought of her heart's beating. Two beats. How much could happen in two beats of the heart? She had tried to be good. She had tried to be rational and kind. But so often her heart had betrayed her. She returned to her mirror. She was beginning, again, to resemble her old photographs. But what lay behind her face now was so different from what lay there before. Where exactly was her heart? Of course there was that silly organ pumping blood around her. It sat where everyone else's hearts sat – well, almost. That couldn't be it. A muscle, at the core of her, feeding her troops. A playing card – the Ace of Hearts – expanding and contracting in her breast. How could sunlight on the trees – or across Adam's hair – affect her heart? Her heart had no eyes. It was buried deep within her blindly pumping blood. She looked again into the mirror. Her heart was behind her eyes. And it was hurting her.

Still in her slip she went to the wardrobe and chose a bright, peacock-blue, two-piece tweed. It should be warm enough. She always dressed brightly when she felt vulnerable. She smelt it for smoke but the Woodbines had been routed by her dry cleaner. She held up the golden locket that hung round her neck and clicked it open to look inside before closing it again and sliding it under her blouse. Opening the top drawer of her dressing table she took out a small velvet casket. It contained a ring, a giant emerald in a platinum setting. She had worn it for many years but it had not been on her finger when, for the first time, in Green Park, she had cradled Adam's head in her hands. Nor had she worn it since. She slipped the casket into the pocket of her two-piece.

Buttoning up the jacket she picked up her coat and headed for the door. Jenny's bedroom was just across the landing. Before entering, Julia stepped to the window and looked out on the garden. Prior to the war it had been a beautiful Victorian set-piece. But all that had changed and, in common with everyone else, the careful structures had been razed so that vegetables could be grown. Somewhere down there lay Adam's note. She prayed for rain.

Jenny was sitting at her writing desk, with her back to the door, wearing a silk dressing-gown – pink and blue and twenty years old. She jumped when Julia walked in, and instinctively her hands went to cover the paper in front of her.

– Julia!

– Oh, I'm sorry. I should have knocked. Forgive me.
– That's all right.

Hands moving away from the paper and shoulders relaxing.

– You gave me a bit of a shock.
– Are you ready to come for tea?
– Tea? Oh, I'm sorry, Julia. I quite lost track of time. I'm nearly there. Can I catch you up?
– Of course. The table's reserved for four o'clock.
– I'll run if necessary.
– Don't worry. I can wait.

Julia left the room and headed down the stairs. Jenny was plainly writing another letter to Captain Jenkins. There had been a succession of letters, in bold blue-black ink, addressed to her step-daughter, sitting on the silver tray in the hall in recent weeks. Julia paused at the alcove. The photographs were still all there. She picked up the one of her and her children and gazed at it for a long time. How long would these photographs remain here? Would Jeremy remove them if he succeeded? But she would not let him succeed. She thought of Adam, who had confronted her here just over a month ago, his eyes streaming and that wheezy cough in his voice. She thought of Jenny, who had seen her crying, exactly here, before she went to see her father. She looked down towards Jeremy's study. The new brass lock shone out like a reproach and there was a light under the door, although that didn't mean anything. Jeremy had said so many contradictory things about his movements in recent weeks that it was laughable. She couldn't believe a word he said.

And yet their single beds in the cellar were no longer moving apart and, if anything, somehow, they were moving closer together. And she knew that Jenny had caused him to doubt. He was less certain of himself and no longer made emphatic mention of the proceedings. But the petition remained alive. She could not help but be aware of Samuels's visits to Jenny's room. A knock on the door, a muffled communication, and then Jenny would head down the stairs to her father's study.

She descended to the ground floor. The reception rooms were empty now. She had not entered them since the evening of the party. The first and last time that Adam had been in her home. The only place she felt safe was her dressing room. Julia still had her coat over her arm. She slipped it on and began buttoning it up. The cashmere was warm and comforting to her touch. Putting a hand into the deep pocket, she felt for her purse. Jeremy had at least continued to provide her with her allowance. How was she to survive if he succeeded on his petition? She shivered and opened the front door to leave.

The cold air hit her and she pulled her coat more closely to her, lifting the collar so that it covered her cheeks. She turned suddenly to her right and glanced down the square. A familiar figure jumped backwards to hide behind a tree but the belly, protruding as it always did, gave him away. Despair mixed with grim amusement rose up in her. Until Adam warned her she had never noticed him. Now he seemed to be everywhere. Why was Jeremy bothering? Julia ambled off towards Belgrave Place before turning into Eaton Place and heading along Upper Belgrave Street. The doughty Jackson followed. Eventually she reached Constitution Hill and entered Green Park from its north-western corner. How thrilling this must be for the private detective on her tail!

It was a short walk along the Green Park footpath adjacent to Piccadilly but Jenny was running late and Julia had time to spare. She walked as far as the exit to Green Park tube and stood there for a moment. This was where it all began four and a half years ago. She had walked the same route pushing Agnes in her pram and then waiting for Adam to emerge from the sea of faces. And this was where everything ended: Jackson handing her a brown envelope containing the petition and doffing his hat. She had shaken his hand. It had been warm and clammy despite the cold.

Julia turned to look out over the park. Ugly trenches had been cut into its surface and a barrage balloon swung out overhead, its cables humming ominously. It had been so sunny that first day. And because she had been so happy it was as though everyone around her had been just as happy as she. She tried to picture the leisurely crowds, the candy-coloured deck-chairs, but she could not. She walked on in towards the centre of the park. Here was the bench where she read the petition, tears running down her face. This was the tree they had leaned against when first they kissed. Here was the second entrance to the Stafford. She glanced across the park and caught sight of Jackson attempting to be inconspicuous behind a tree and decided not to dally near the hotel. She took a deep breath and made her way to the Ritz.

She had asked for a table in the middle of the room. She had nothing to hide. Someone looking in would have seen, through prisms of crystal, a glamorous self-contained woman dressed in brilliant blue and green, daintily sipping tea.

Julia looked at her watch. Ten past four. She'd booked tea for four. Petit fours and biscuits were balanced delicately on the cake tray in front of her but she had not yet touched them. By the end of the month such treats would be almost impossible to find without breaking the law. There was a clattering of heels on marble and Jenny appeared, breathless, on the threshold of the room. Julia gasped.

Jenny steadied herself and flapped an elegant hand across her face to cool herself. Her cheeks were flushed. She caught sight of Julia, smiled broadly, and walked gracefully across the room, her dark hair bobbing gently on her shoulders as she approached. Men and women turned their heads to watch her. She was no longer a girl. But it was her dress that caused Julia to catch her breath. It was a deep crimson with flashes of mauve cut high to the knee in a Twenties style which on anyone else would have looked dated. She had seen that dress before but only in black and white. Jeremy had always told her that Joan had been beautiful, but black and white photographs told a limited two-dimensional story. It was as if Joan had come back to life and was walking towards her in glorious three-dimensional colour. Only Jenny's warm smile of recognition differentiated them. Joan had never known Julia and could not have recognised her. And Julia was afraid. In a flash she saw what Jeremy had been seeing for the last five years as Jenny grew and changed and became more like her mother. She could never have competed with that beauty. But Jenny, kissing her on the cheek and sitting down neatly opposite her, was oblivious to this.

– I'm so sorry I'm late. I needed to catch the post.

Julia smiled.

– Simon again?
– Yes. I know how upset he would have been if no letter was waiting for him tomorrow.

Julia knew all about Captain Simon Jenkins as he had been a staple of their conversations at the Ritz for the last several months. Jenkins was in his early twenties and had been an actor before war broke out. Although she had never met him, she had seen Jenny's photograph of him, which showed him to be dark-haired and good-looking. His eyes twinkled with amusement. According to Jenny he was also a "terrific" painter and this was borne out by the fact that he had been commissioned to work on camouflage development at Farnham Castle. Whether or not he should have told Jenny this – and whether or not Jenny should have told Julia – she did not know.

- I haven't seen him for *four weeks* and I do miss him so!
- The time will go by quickly enough, Jenny. And remember: you don't really know him all *that* well.
- But sometimes you just *know* about a person. Don't you believe that?
- Life gets far more complicated before it starts getting easier. I sometimes wonder if one can know *oneself*. Let alone those around us.
- Anyway, he feels the same way about me.
- How can you possibly tell?
- He told me. He put it all down in black and white.
- Really! Jenny! Don't you think that was a little bit … forward of him?
- But he did. Look. I'll show you.

And she brought her handbag up onto the table and started ruffling around inside it before pulling out a sheaf of letters tied with pink ribbon. Julia looked at Jenny's head as she shuffled through her letters. Her black hair gleamed with health and half masked her face. The envelopes were all creased and thumbed through regular re-reading, and Julia guessed that Jenny carried them with her everywhere.

- No, Jenny. Please don't show me. I'm sure Simon meant those letters for your eyes only. It wouldn't be proper to show me them.

And Julia put a restraining hand over Jenny's. She looked up, rebuffed, and her cheeks glowed pink.

- Well. He loves me. And I think I love him too.

271

- But, Jenny. You're still very young. You have your whole life ahead of you.
- But you were only about my age when you married Daddy.
- That was different.
- Why was it different?
- Well … uh … well, Daddy was a lot older and more worldly-wise than Simon could possibly be. Please don't think that's a criticism.
- You're not saying you made a mistake when you married Daddy are you?

Julia had fallen into a trap that she had always known lay hidden under the surface of these conversations.

- No! No … of course not. I was just trying to be helpful. I do apologise. Perhaps I was speaking out of turn.
- Well, I think he's going to ask me to marry him.
- How could you be so certain of that?
- I just know.

Julia trod carefully.

- I'm sure you know best, Jenny. But you are barely eighteen and he'll have to ask Daddy for permission.
- You don't think Daddy would refuse him?
- I really don't know.

A new cloud drifted over her features and her brown eyes looked troubled.

- You don't think Daddy would stop me getting married because of my diary, do you?
- Oh, Jenny, I'm sure he wouldn't. He knows you wouldn't lie to him. He knows you're telling the truth. And we have been coming here for many months now.
- I did put the crosses next to the right dates, didn't I?
- Yes. I'm sure you did.
- No. I mean I did put the crosses next to the days that we actually met and not just the days that Daddy put in his petition.

- Absolutely. I mean, it was your idea, remember. You were the one who remembered that one of the dates was a date when we had met.
- Yes. I know. It's just that I'm not sure anymore.
- What's Daddy been saying to you?
- I shouldn't say ...
- Please, Jenny. You and I have *never* had secrets. Have we?
- Daddy says that I'll have to give evidence in court.
- Oh, Jenny. Don't worry. I am sure it won't come to that. Daddy and I seemed to be getting on better now. I think that everything will just go away.
- But if it doesn't?
- Well. If it doesn't, I'm afraid you will have to give evidence. You've already met my solicitor, who is a very nice man, and he's prepared a statement that you will have to sign in front of a witness.
- Oh, Julia! I really don't think I could go through with it!
- I'm sure you won't have to. I'm sure Daddy will see sense. And even if he does press on I'm sure his barrister, Sir Patrick Tempest, and my barrister will be very kind to you when you're giving evidence. It's just that ...
- Just that what?!
- Oh. It's nothing. Never mind.
- Please. What else is there?
- Oh, I really don't want to worry you unnecessarily, Jenny.

Jenny had begun wringing her napkin in her hands. Her tea had not yet been touched. Her eyes filled with entreaty – and a hint of tears.

- Please!
- Very well. I am sure it is nothing to worry about but it's just that Mr Falling has employed a very nasty barrister.
- What do you mean?
- He's called Roland Blytheway and I know that Daddy really hates him.
- Why does he hate him?
- He's a *very* odd man and Daddy says that he can be very cruel. My barrister, Mr Alnwick, agrees.
- But how could he be cruel to me?

273

– He knows about your diary. He knows about the crosses you've put in it. And he knows what you've said about those crosses. Well, you can't exactly rub them out now, can you?
– Oh …

Jenny bit her lip.

– My barrister can't cross-examine you – that is ask difficult questions – but Blytheway can, and my lawyers have told me that he is likely to force you to admit that all the entries in the diary are true and, if you try and say that they're not, he'll ask you why you put them there in the first place. And accuse you of perjury and attempting to pervert the course of justice.
– Oh my God! Julia! No!

And Jenny crumpled up and began to cry, burying her head in the still crumpled napkin. Julia reached out a consoling hand and began stroking her sleeve. She whispered soothingly:

– Jenny. Please don't worry. It's not going to come to that. Daddy knows you wouldn't lie. He'll drop it all. I'm sure he is already thinking of dropping it. All you've got to do is tell the truth. We'll get through this together. We're like sisters, aren't we?
– Oh Julia. I'm sorry. It's so upsetting.

Jenny looked up into her eyes. She had stopped weeping and her normal complexion was returning. Julia thought of peach blossom. A thought struck her.

– Are you so worried because of something Daddy has been saying?
– I think he's going to carry on with it.
– What makes you say that?
– He's been calling me down for little chats. He told me about the books on your shelves. How they're the same as Mr Falling's. He told me that you had written to Mr Falling on his notepaper. You never told me that you'd written to him!
– But I explained all that to Daddy … Remember when I first

274

mentioned all of this to you and you said how stupid it was. Well, Daddy had been dropping all sorts of awful hints. I knew he was doing the same with this Mr Falling and so I simply wrote a short, polite letter apologising for Daddy's behaviour. Didn't daddy tell you this?

– No ... he didn't.
– I sent an ordinary letter to Mr Falling – it wasn't even marked "private and confidential" – and it reached him in his chambers some time before Christmas. I told Daddy all about it as soon as he raised it. I don't understand why he didn't tell you.
– Daddy says he can't trust you anymore.
– Look, Jenny, please trust me. Have I ever lied to you?

And she began to stroke Jenny's sleeve again.

– Oh. This is too gloomy. Let's change the subject to something far brighter. I've got something to show you.

And Julia reached into her pocket and pulled out the little velvet casket. She placed it on the table between them and opened it carefully so that the large emerald caught the light and sparkled.

– Oh. It's beautiful.
– It used to belong to your mother. Daddy gave it to me when we got married.
– Why don't you ever wear it?
– I used to wear it every day but as time went by and you grew older I began to feel that it had never really been meant for me. It was Joan's ring – your mother's ring – and as you grew up I stopped wearing it and told myself that, when the time was right, I would give it to you. Please. Take it.
– But I couldn't. It's so lovely!

But as she said it Jenny was already lifting it from its box and putting it on her finger. She held it up to the light, her fingers splayed.

– It was a little tight getting over my knuckle.

- You can wear it next time you see Captain Jenkins. I'm so sorry if I seemed to be interfering. I was only trying to help.
- Oh, Julia. You're right. Everything is going to be just fine, isn't it?
- Of course it is. Please don't worry. Carry on wearing it if you want to. Here. Take the casket as well. When are you next seeing him?
- He doesn't have any more leave until March. He'll be coming up to London to see me.

Jenny had calmed down now. But there was something else Julia needed to know.

- May I just ask you one little thing about home?
- Of course. What is it?
- I'm probably being really silly. But it's the servants. I've seen Samuels letting that private detective into the house and so I know that he's in on it with Daddy. I was really hurt when I found out. I'm right about that aren't I?
- Samuels is very loyal to Daddy. But I don't think he knows everything. He believes everything Daddy tells him.
- But what about Annie?
- Annie? I hadn't really thought about her. She's invisible almost.
- Do you think she's in on it?
- I really don't know. I don't think so. I hardly notice her. I do think she's a bit conceited – though she's always been very pleasant to me.

Jenny paused to think.

- There is something, I suppose. But it's probably nothing.
- What exactly?
- Well. It's just that she sometimes looks rather too pleased with herself. Sometimes it's as though ... as though she knows something that nobody else knows. Which is silly really isn't it?
- Yes. Very silly. I think that she just likes the idea of sharing the cellar with us during the air raids. I think it makes her feel important. I doubt that there's anything more to it than that ...

Suddenly the air raid sirens began to sound. It was nowhere near black-out time. There had been few raids over the previous few days but it looked like the bad times were coming back. The room filled with the sound of chairs being pushed backwards and the hubbub of voices grew louder.

– Come on, Jenny. We'd better go. I've got to get to work anyway.

Julia left her payment on the table and she and her step-daughter made for the exit.

– Thank you for coming, Jenny. It is always lovely to spend time with you. And don't worry. It's all going to be all right.
– Thank you, Julia. I'm sorry I got upset.
– Don't be. Now let's cut across the park and get home.

They hurried away. Julia's mind stretched to the weeks ahead – and then back to Annie. She had said that she had carefully examined the hyacinth bulbs to see if they could be saved. How could she not have noticed the note? If that note came to light she was finished. How could she possibly explain that to Jenny? Or to anyone else for that matter? It was raining by the time they reached the steps of the house. Perhaps the weather would save her?

Julia remembered the light shining out from under the door of Jeremy's study. Was he at home or not? She and Jenny went down into the cellars to await the "all clear".

Pemberton was not there. Several miles across London he was readying himself to begin a consultation with Graham McKechnie.

Chapter Forty-two

(Wednesday 29th January 1941)

Miss Emma Chapman raised her pencil and prepared to write. The sleeve of her jacket, burgundy herringbone tweed, slipped down to reveal the crisp white cotton of her shirt cuff. Across the room Arnold Bateman was shuffling buff-coloured files, picking them up, turning them over and putting them down again until at last he found the one he had been looking for. She adjusted the antique clip in her thick brown hair and looked out of the window down at what was left of Bank underground station. A giant crater, brick-dust, rubble and twisted metal, were all that remained. A direct hit on the 11th January – less than three weeks earlier – had killed over fifty people.

– Right, Miss Chapman.

And Bateman began dictating a letter, gabbling his words as he spoke.

– Mr Bateman. Please slow down, I can't keep up.

Bateman let out something between a snort and a sigh.

– What's wrong with you today? We have a lot to get through. How much did you get down?

She scrolled back through her shorthand. What was wrong with her *indeed*; he spends forever finding the right file, then starts jabbering at twice his normal speed.

– "I am sending out the necessary forms in tonight's post."
– Ah yes. "Please be assured of our utmost attention at all times. Yours, etc." Now onto the next one.

He looked at his watch and began scrabbling through the files again.

- Five more letters to go out before close of business.
- We've plenty of time, Mr Bateman. It's only half past four. I'll go and type this one up.
- No. I want to get on with my dictation. You can type all the letters up when I've finished.

Bateman was wearing his usual loud pinstripe but his tie was slightly awry and she could see red braces protruding from his jacket. She knew all about McKechnie's petition and the allegation that Bateman had been sleeping with Mrs M. Indeed, everyone knew about it. Ever since McKechnie had confronted him with his wife's diary and started yelling about "ABC" it had been the main topic of office gossip. And McKechnie had made no secret of the fact that he had petitioned for divorce and cited Bateman. Bateman looked at his watch again and started dictating furiously once more so that again she struggled to keep up. By ten to five she had taken down four more letters. Her wrist was starting to hurt. Bateman began rummaging through the folders on his desk again, picking them up and putting them down noisily. She put down her pencil and flexed her fingers; then, looking out of the window, she began planning her route home. A heavy fog was falling. The loss of Bank was a nuisance! Then she felt guilty because so many people had died there.

- Damn and blast!
- What is it, Mr Bateman?
- Where's the Bridges file?
- That's still in the main cabinet. Would you like me to go and get it for you?
- No. You stay here and get on with the typing. I'll get it. Save a bit of time.

And he jumped up from his desk and dashed out of the door. What peculiar behaviour, thought Miss Chapman, there was plenty of time to get everything done and posted.

The central filing cabinet was on the next floor up, as was McKechnie's office. Bateman rushed to the stairwell and began taking the stairs two at a time. Turning the second corner, he ran slap bang into McKechnie. The latter was buttoning up a dark blue overcoat as he went down. The two men looked at one another, then McKechnie snorted, brushed down his overcoat and went on towards the exit. Bateman looked at his watch. It was only five to five. Then he continued up the stairs.

He rifled through the main cabinet, found the Bridges file, and ran back down to his office. Through the frosted glass he could see the fuzzy maroon outline of Miss Chapman sitting at her typewriter. An industrious click-clacking greeted him as he came back in.

– On with the dictation. "Dear Mr Bridges ..."

And once again Miss Chapman struggled to keep up.

– "Yours etc." Right.

He picked up some office stationery and started signing his name at the bottom of the blank sheets.

– Now. Type the letters onto these and make sure my signature doesn't look out of place. If you mess it up you'll have to PP me.

He grabbed his coat and headed for the door again.

– But Mr Bateman. It's only five o'clock.
– When you've finished typing them put the necessary enclosures together and send them off. Leave the carbons on my desk and I'll look at them in the morning.
– But Mr Bateman ...
– Good evening, Miss Chapman.

And with that he was gone.

Gloom was descending by the time he reached the street. A real pea-souper. Under the brown fog of a winter dusk Bateman headed west towards Fetter Lane. He had gone no more than a hundred yards when the air raid sirens began to sound. The same sirens that, several miles away, abruptly ended tea at the Ritz for Julia and Jenny. He kept on going. He was already late. The sun wasn't due to set until after five forty and black-out did not begin till ten past six, but it was already getting dark. British Winter Time had been suspended yet again but it didn't seem to make much difference.

The "all clear" was sounding by the time Bateman, out of breath and sweating, reached Jones's offices in Fetter Lane. On this occasion he was shown in to his solicitor without delay or fuss. Jones was pacing up and down, his overcoat on and his gloves in his hand.

– I was beginning to give up on you.
– Sorry. Difficult to get away.

The two of them headed down towards Mitre Court. The last time they had gone to see Falling they had picked their way through the rubble on Inner Temple Lane. Since that time, of course, Adam had moved chambers.

– Blast! Damn! And buggery!

Bateman picked himself up and kicked the offending masonry.

– Bloody blackout!

He dusted down his lapels and thighs. He would have been happier about the darkness, however, if he had realised that at that precise moment McKechnie and his solicitor were picking their way carefully down Inner Temple Lane towards Stirrup Court to see Jeremy Pemberton KC.

Chapter Forty-three

(Wednesday 29th January 1941)

The waiting room at Lamb Building was no more spacious than that in Stirrup Court but far more attractive. Large blackout shades covered the window but someone had decided that they should be backed with a brightly coloured tapestry depicting a medieval lady emerging from a blue canopy covered in stars. The background was a russet colour and she was attended by a lady in waiting. A lion and a snow-white unicorn, holding red banners patterned with crescent moons, knelt in attendance on her. Oriental lamps were placed strategically around the room giving it an understated brightness. There were some law books but the shelves also contained leather bound volumes on the Renaissance, Syria and other esoteric subjects. There was no sign of dust or cobwebs and even the air smelt fresher. They must use different cleaners, thought Bateman.

If anything the journey down to counsel's chambers had been more perilous than the last time. There was no moon and the heavy smog obliterated all but the closest obstacles. Bateman had fallen heavily in front of Tanfield Court and skinned his knee. The pain made him let loose another stream of obscenities. Even Jones, who knew this place, had stumbled more than once. There was much new rubble and an acrid smell hung in the air. It was only when they entered the waiting room that Bateman saw that his trousers were covered in dust and ash, which he brushed off self-consciously.

He thought back to his last meeting with Falling. Being kept waiting because his barrister had taken it upon himself to go and pray in the Temple Church. Someone had placed a large jug of clear cold water on the side table and clean empty glasses had been left as an implicit invitation for them to drink. An invitation they had accepted. Neither man spoke. Jones was subdued and appeared to have much on his mind.

– Mr Falling will see you now.

Falling's new clerk poked his head round the door and, when they had risen to their feet, headed up the stairs. He needed a haircut and his suit didn't fit properly. Falling's room was on the second floor. Bateman heard coughing from behind the door. The senior clerk knocked and there was a muffled invitation for them to come in. In the widening rectangle of light as the door opened Bateman saw Falling rising to his feet, a handkerchief to his lips. Moving towards them, he made his introductions and shook hands. As they all sat down around his desk, Bateman heard the door closing quietly behind him.

Falling looked different – even thinner, and yet somehow taller. Bateman looked around the room in an attempt to work out what had changed. Falling's hair was shorter, tidier, and he wore a well-cut dark suit. His shirt cuffs were no longer frayed. The desk was the same, as were the chairs. Bateman noticed the crystal paperweight and recalled how, on their last meeting, Falling had folded a piece of paper and put the paperweight down on top of it. This evening there was nothing under the paperweight. There was an ornamental vase, containing peacock feathers, on the corner of the desk and two delicate lamps with stained glass shades. The room was certainly better lit than his last one. Falling's lips were moving as Bateman looked up at him but he did not hear what he was saying. He stared instead at the brightly coloured tapestry that adorned the blackout shade on the window behind him. All in all the effect was rather pleasing, though it did not fit with Bateman's preconceptions of Falling's taste.

- I'm sorry, Mr Bateman. Did you hear what I was saying?
- Oh! Sorry! I was miles away.
- Why have you been lying to me? To us?
- I've told you the truth about me and Victoria.
- You've lied about your wife. About Marjorie Bateman. Why?
- This isn't about me and Marjorie. It's about me and Victoria. And while we're on the subject, who gave you permission to go nosing around in Romford anyway?
- That's beside the point, Mr Bateman ...
- No it's not! You're supposed to be acting on my instructions. I didn't authorise you to do that.
- Well. It's out in the open now ...

- And, anyway, I thought you barristers were supposed to leave the legwork to the likes of Jones here. I thought you barristers were supposed to be too busy for this sort of stuff. Explain that to me will you?
- You weren't at work when your wife died. Why did you lie?
- And another thing. How did you get hold of the inquest notes? You can't just walk off the streets and pick them up?

Falling had opened his mouth to interrupt but pulled up short of speaking. Bateman saw a veil of worry cloud his features for a moment and realised that he was taking control of the conference. Had he known that Adam had been worrying for some weeks about the fact that he had bribed a council official to get the notes, he would have pressed home his advantage. But Bateman did not know of that. Falling took a deep breath.

- Mr Bateman! Either you want me to conduct your case for you or you do not. If you do not, then I think we had better bring this interview to an end.

Falling got to his feet and began to walk towards the door. Bateman noticed that his shoes gleamed brightly with a recent polishing. He and Jones were still sitting, bodies twisted towards the door, by the time Falling had opened it. He gestured for them to leave.

- How – hang on a minute! We've only just started.
- My way or no way, Mr Bateman. Which is it to be?
- How long is it to the trial?
- About eight weeks.
- And how long is it until *your* trial?

Falling closed the door again but did not move back to his desk.

- I'm not sure that is any of your business, Mr Bateman.
- What? You're being named as having it off with McKechnie's barrister's wife and you're saying it is none of my business?!
- Well. If you must know, it has been pencilled in for the week after your trial. I'm not sure of the precise dates but I am sure Mr Jones will be able to fill you in.

– And what's this about you carrying on with a tart round Shepherd Market?
– Who told you that?

Jones, notebook in hand, shuffled uncomfortably in his chair.

– It's nothing to do with me, Mr Falling. I don't know where Mr Bateman got this story from.
– Don't you worry, Jones, there was plenty of other places for me to get this ... "story" from. I think the papers will be more interested in you than they are in me, Falling.

Falling opened the door again.

– My way or no way, Mr Bateman. Which is it to be?

Bateman realised that his bluff was being called. He had already decided that he wanted Falling to represent him. The gossip about Falling was all over his office thanks to McKechnie. He was pushing his luck by dropping that one in.

– All right. Have it your way. What do you want to know?

Falling took his hand off the door handle and returned to his chair. Before he could speak he was overcome by another coughing fit and had to pull his handkerchief from his pocket and put it over his mouth. Worried about germs, thought Bateman. The spluttering subsided and Falling looked critically into the linen square before folding it precisely and returning it to his pocket.

– We all lie, Mr Bateman. You lied to me about Marjorie's death. You told me she was run over during the blackout whilst you were still at work. But you see, what troubled me was that, if she had been run over in September, you ought to have been home well before the blackout came into force. I haven't checked with the newspapers as to when the blackout started that night, but when I thought about it, your story made no sense at all. The rest was pretty obvious. We all

lie, Mr Bateman. We've established the fact of your lies. But I'm not particularly interested in those facts. I am not defending you on a murder charge. I'm more interested in the reasons why people lie. I want to know why you lied about Marjorie's death.
 – What did the inquest notes say?
 – You were there, Mr Bateman. You tell me what happened.

Inwardly, Bateman had realised that this would be one of the consequences of sticking with Falling. The trouble was that he could not remember exactly how much they had told the coroner. The inquest had served its purpose. None of them had seen the potential implications beyond the immediate consequences. He decided that he ought to tell as much of the truth as he could. He was not to know, at that time, that this was probably the best option he could have gone for.

 – Okay. We'd all gone to the pictures together, as a foursome. When the film finished we went for a pint. We didn't think it would be too dangerous. It was over a year since they closed all the cinemas and nearly a year since they opened them again. Nothing had happened. It didn't seem dangerous, even with the air raids of the previous nights.
 – What did you go and see?
 – *My Favourite Wife*. Cary Grant and Irene Dunne.
 – You're making this up!
 – As God's my witness. It's been showing at the ABC for the last two weeks. Proper corker it is.

Falling had steepled his fingers and Bateman could tell he was sceptical about his story. Why couldn't they have been to watch Lillian Russell or *Charley's Aunt?*

 – Why didn't you tell us this before? It would have given you an alibi. The night of Marjorie's death was one of the nights when you were supposed to have slept with Victoria.

Bateman had an idea. He would be the first to admit that he was not an intellectual, but he had always been cunning. Low cunning was a particular speciality. In retrospect, though, he would have been forced to admit that, in these circumstances, bare honesty might have trumped low cunning.

– Ah, well. Yes. That's it. You see. I thought I was being clever. I'm sorry, Mr Falling. I knew I had an alibi. But I thought I would save it up, like, for when I really needed it. You're right. I have an alibi. I thought it would be more dramatic if I held it back.

He could tell that Falling was unconvinced. By his side Jones was scribbling furiously. This was all going on record. He pressed on.

– Think about it, Mr Falling. What other reason could there be for holding back on my alibi? I know it's stupid but that's the way my mind works. I wanted to drop McKechnie in it.
– Forgive me, Mr Bateman. But why prolong this agony? If you had told me this earlier we could have nipped this whole thing in the bud. All I need to do is call Pemberton and all of this ought to go away.
– No! You can't do that!
– Why ever not?
– Trust me on this, Mr Falling.
– I don't see why I … or Mr Jones for that matter … should trust you about anything.
– Mr Falling. You told me last time we met that as long as I told the truth you would act for me but I couldn't expect to tell you one thing and then tell the world something else. Well, I'm telling you the truth. I didn't have an affair with Victoria and I lied about Marjorie's death. I didn't see that you needed to be interested in that. Anyway, if it comes up I'm not going to deny that we were all at the pictures. But I don't see why it needs to come up.

Bateman watched Falling closely. He had picked up the paperweight and was looking at the faults in its prisms. He looked at the lampshades through it and Bateman tried to imagine the broken images and colours he was seeing. Falling seemed to be conducting some internal dialogue, and Bateman wondered whether he was thinking about his own case rather than *his* problems with Graham McKechnie.

– Very well, Mr Bateman. I suppose, in fairness, it is your case. But you
  must understand that if this is all a pack of lies I will have to stop
  acting for you. You've lied to me ... to us, once. Any more lies and I
  am afraid I will not feel comfortable acting for you.
– Thank you for warning me about Jackson by the way.
– I beg your pardon?
– Jackson. That private dick.
– Oh yes. Not at all.
– Sticks out a mile once you know he's there.
– Yes, well I hope it helped. Pemberton's always using him. I hear from
  Jones that you had a little fun with him?
– Best part of this mess to be honest. I suppose he's been following you
  around a bit?

Falling allowed himself a smile.

– Oh. Up to a point. Know your enemy, eh, Mr Bateman.
– Mr Falling. I think that in other circumstances we might have made
  quite a good team.
– Yes, Mr Bateman. I think we might have done. Perhaps when this is
  all over we should have a pint somewhere. Perhaps in one of those
  pubs that you led Jackson such a merry dance around.
– I'll pay! One other thing, though, Mr Falling. Sorry to be serious for a
  second. But Jones has told me you've got another big case coming up.
  Some sort of spy trial. It's not going to get in the way is it?
– Oh, I doubt it.

Bateman felt he heard a flicker of worry in that broken voice.

– When exactly is that supposed to be happening?
– Well, Mr Bateman, I'm afraid I can't tell you much. Official Secrets
  and all that. But it should be over and done with in the next four or
  five weeks. Plenty of time between that and your trial. Nothing to
  worry about.
– Well. Just so I know. Well. I suppose that's it.

Bateman started to rise from his seat and Jones, closing his notebook, made to do likewise.

- – One more thing before you go.
- – Yes. What is it?
- – You've told us you have an alibi for the night of Marjorie's death. But what about all the other nights. All the other entries in Victoria's diary that refer to "ABC". What do they mean?
- – Ah yes ... well it's the same thing really. We all used to go to the pictures together. At the ABC. That's about it.
- – Why isn't this in your statement?
- – Didn't seem relevant. Sorry about that. But that's my case. And I wasn't sleeping with Victoria.
- – Tell me, Mr Bateman. Mr Jones tells me that you have been very anxious to see me over the last few weeks. Why was that? When you took so long to tell me ... the truth today?
- – Just needed to be sure of you. Seems like you're doing well here. A change has done you good. I have complete confidence in you, mate.
- – Thank you. I think we can call it a day, Mr Jones. For all those daylight sirens I think that the worst has passed. Would you mind if we had a brief chat about the ... the spy trial that Mr Bateman was referring to?

They all rose and Adam showed Bateman out of his room before beckoning Jones to sit again.

Jones watched as Adam closed the door, turning the handle with a precision that allowed him to hear the catch slip comfortably into place. As Adam passed him on his way back to his chair Jones smelt a perfume that was either eau de cologne or pomade. He was pulling at his pocket even before he resumed his seat and produced a packet of Woodbines, shucking one into his hand and lighting it in one gesture with a match that emerged almost magically from the other pocket. Jones noticed the slight trembling of his left hand.

- – Mr Falling, look, I'm terribly sorry about that reference to ... to ... Shepherd Market. Believe me. It was nothing to do with me. I never mentioned –

- Not at all, Mr Jones. Pemberton has been spreading it so thick around the Temple I feel as though I am walking through the gossip every time I leave my rooms. It's no wonder McKechnie knows.
- Anyway, I'm really sorry.
- Don't trouble yourself. Fortunately, it would appear that the only person who *hasn't* done me down over this is Roly Blytheway. Seems to regard it as an irrelevance ...
- Well. I need to speak with you about that. I presume that's why you asked me to stay behind?
- Not at all. I wanted to talk about Novak and our conversation yesterday.
- Well ... you see ... it's not like me to be pushy ... it's just that ...
- It's just like what?
- Well. It's Mr Blytheway. God knows he's a good barrister ... wished I'd known about him sooner really – all that talk about him – but he's been on my back for over a week now ...
- About what?
- Well, exactly. It's about this Betty woman. I could see he had a thing about it right from that conference, but he keeps telephoning me asking whether I've got a statement from her yet. And I can't keep holding him off. But until you give me her address there's not a lot I can do ...

Jones looked Adam in the eye. Adam looked away. His cigarette, hardly smoked, was sitting in the ashtray sending up blue plumes. Oblivious to it, Adam pulled out his packet and lit another. The shake was more perceptible now.

- Damn! I'm sorry, Mr Jones. I don't have her address on me. I'm really sorry. I've been meaning to deal with it. I'll try and get it to you by tomorrow.
- Don't mind me, Mr Falling. It's your case after all and you're a barrister. You should know how important – or not – this is. It's just that Mr Blytheway keeps on at me about it.

Jones watched as Falling alternated between his two cigarettes, apparently unaware of the fact that both were burning.

– I really wanted to talk to you about Novak and our chat yesterday.

It was only as that discussion was beginning that Adam realised he'd failed to ask Bateman about that cryptic comment Pemberton had made to him before Christmas. He cursed himself for his stupidity.

Chapter Forty-four

(Wednesday 29th January 1941)

– You say Bateman was in bed with *your* wife when *his* wife was knocked down by a car?

– Yes.

– How can you be sure of that?

– Well, I wasn't there, obviously, but I did see Marjorie lying in the road. She wasn't moving. I went over and touched her face. She was clearly dead … quite near her home … I dashed over there and started hammering on the door … but there was no answer … so I went inside only to find Bateman and Victoria coming downstairs. He was still shoving his shirt into his trousers.

– And that was the first you knew of any … goings-on?

Mr McKechnie sighed. Pemberton's eyes were glittering behind his gold-rimmed spectacles. The divorce pleadings – and Victoria's last diary – were arranged neatly across the desk in front of him. Bright light filled the room and a two-bar electric fire was burning against McKechnie's right leg.

– Look. We've been through all this before. I told Mr Collins all about it and we talked it all through at our last meeting.

– You must understand, Mr Mckechnie. This will probably be our last meeting before the trial and I need to be sure that you have told me everything of relevance.

McKechnie looked around the room. In addition to his KC there was Mr Collins, his solicitor, and a funny nondescript chap in his thirties – Mr Perkins – who was Pemberton's junior, sitting at a desk to the side, scribbling away and every now and again laughing at Pemberton's (unfunny) jokes. He resented Perkins more than he resented the rest of them. He couldn't see why he should have to pay for two briefs when one would do. Collins, however, was insistent: if he wanted to have a KC, a top barrister, then he would have to pay for a junior as well. What he resented most of all was having to pay up front. Collins not only insisted that they have this meeting (waste of time as far as he was concerned) but also insisted on being "put in funds" in advance of it. McKechnie believed in payment by results. What happened if he lost?

Then again, he knew he couldn't lose. He knew that Bateman had been having an affair with his wife. Pain now, pleasure later; all his costs and all his damages would come out of Bateman's pocket.

- I'm afraid you're not listening, Mr McKechnie.
- Sorry?
- Where were you when all this was going on?
- Oh ... er ... I was in the pub. Having a quiet pint.
- When there was an air raid going on?
- Well, it was early days, mate ... I mean, Mr Pemberton. No one was taking them seriously then.

It was only a little white lie, after all. As long as he told the truth about the main thing – about the fact that Bateman was in bed with his wife – the other bits and pieces didn't matter really. He also held back something else. Because, to him, it didn't seem important.

- And you are telling us that, before that night, you had no idea that your wife was conducting a relationship with someone who worked under you at the office?
- Well ... I had no reason to suspect anything.
- So when did you discover all these "ABC" notes in her diary?
- Our house got hit that night. Everything was spilled out all over the street. We got moved into a shelter and I was tidying up our furniture for the move when it fell out of a drawer in her bedside table.
- I'm sorry about the loss of your home.

McKechnie gazed at his ever-so-proper barrister and imagined Mrs Pemberton taking off her clothes to sleep with someone else.

- What does "ABC" mean, Mr McKechnie?
- I've no idea. Something to do with Bateman's initials perhaps?

A variation on the same little lie. But it was hardly important. Pemberton was fiddling with one of Jackson's reports and turning it over and over in his hands.

- Collins. I've been reading Jackson's latest letter. It looks as though Bateman's been leading him a merry dance. Have you any idea what's going on?
- How do you mean, sir?

Pemberton stared into space and tapped his figures up and down on a buff envelope.

- One minute he can follow Bateman with absolutely no trouble ... and the next ... the next ... he's pulling him round the city like a puppet. When did things change?

Pemberton pulled a buff envelope from the shelf behind him and started to scan the private eye's reports.

- The 18th December last year. That's when it all changed ...

Pemberton gazed at the law books on the shelves opposite his desk. Ornate, leather-bound with gold lettering – and a deep silence pervaded the room. Only the tapping of the silk's fingers on the leather top of his desk disturbed it.

Then Pemberton brought his fist down on the table with a crash that made everyone, even Perkins, jump.

- Blast! Falling! Damn him!

The colour rose swiftly in his cheeks. Collins bubbled like a goldfish:

- What is it, Mr Pemberton?
- I've been a bloody fool!

– I don't understand.
– Falling must have alerted Bateman. That explains a lot!

McKechnie eyed his barrister – his barristers – with alarm. Falling, that so-called no-hoper, had got one over on them. Falling, who had been having it away with Pemberton's wife without him knowing. A lizard of fear began scaling his spine and he felt the cold crawl of its toes. Only deference prevented him from shrieking:

– What's going on?!
– It's nothing. Nothing. Mr Falling has clearly alerted Bateman to Jackson's presence. That explains it. Collins, we must stand Jackson down and get someone else onto the case.

Pemberton was rubbing his right temple with the stub-end of his wrist. McKechnie saw something being rearranged in his features as he puzzled things out. He wasn't even sure that Pemberton was thinking about his case anymore. Then it came to him:

– Have you been using Jackson to trail Falling?
– What on earth are you talking about?
– I'm sorry, Mr Pemberton, sir, but I couldn't help but hear that ... well ... you know ... you and me have got similar problems, like.
– How dare you!

Red face, the knuckles shining whitely around his black pen. McKechnie took a deep breath.

– I'm sorry, Mr Pemberton, but after all I'm employing you – and paying good money – and, well, it's all over that you're going for Falling over your wife. That's true, isn't it?
– Yes ... Yes ... but I assure you, Mr McKechnie, that it does not in any way affect the way in which I am conducting your case.
– So have you been employing Jackson?
– I was, yes, he's a very good man. One of the best. But his involvement in your case – and my own – is now ended.
– How good is Falling?

– Falling is a scoundrel! A reprobate! I would go so far as to say he is dishonest, if his dealings with my wife are anything to judge him by.

McKechnie looked around the room again: Pemberton sitting opposite him, the colour slowly fading from his cheeks as he put down his pen; Collins affecting a blank stare; Perkins keeping his head down and concentrating on his notebook. The light was bright and his right calf was beginning to burn with the electric fire. He rubbed it slowly and looked at the leather-bound legal books on the walls. This was not his world. He would be glad to be out of it.

– I think that we have covered everything we need to before the trial. Now, is there anything else that you think I should know?

McKechnie thought about his encounter with Victoria and Bateman in the pub, and decided against speaking of it. It wasn't strictly relevant after all. And he didn't want a load of questions about the inquest. He shook his head. He kept something else to himself as well. Two related things really. They didn't really matter, after all, and were insignificant in the grand scheme of things.

Pemberton and Perkins rose to say their goodbyes and he and Collins left to head out into the darkness. The meeting had unnerved him. Were it not for the fact that he knew about Victoria's adultery, he would be getting worried.

Had McKechnie appreciated the true significance of the things that he had withheld, he would have been a very troubled man.

Chapter Forty-five

(Wednesday 5th February 1941)

Jones emerged from Chancery Lane tube station and, briefcase in hand, set off along High Holborn. He was late and, although he did his best to run, the crowds slowed him down. A news-vendor was calling out the headlines:

"Victories in Libya! Victories in Libya!"

He didn't stop for a paper. Sonia always bought one on her way in and left it on his desk. Mrs Jones and her blasted ration book! All she ever seemed to talk about these days was queuing up, her little successes with oranges or apples, her defeats in the line-up for meat. And last night she had gone on and on about making an early start today and then, as he was about to leave for work that morning, she announced that she had lost their ration book. And he had wasted half an hour helping to find it before she discovered it in her special hiding case at the bottom of her jewellery box!

He made his way down Fetter Lane and then up to his office. It was twenty-five to ten. Sonia stood as he entered and came towards him with an armful of post for him to open and sort.

– Not now, Sonia. Bring it in at lunch time. I'm running late.
– Mr Blytheway called again. He wants you to ring him back.
– Get him on the line for me then.

With that, he bustled into his office and closed the door behind him. Hanging up his overcoat he sat down at his desk, pushed the day's newspaper to one side and opened his work diary. The previous seven days had been very busy, not just with Adam's cases but with the rest of his workload. It had been seven days since the conference with Bateman at Lamb Building. Seven days since the post-conference discussion with Falling about Novak's case, and to his embarrassment he had found time to do nothing about either in the days that followed. And here he was late for work.

He looked through his diary at what the coming weeks held. Novak's trial had been fixed for the 3rd March – less than four weeks away. The McKechnie case was fixed for 31st March, shortly before the end of Hilary Term when the Courts would close for Easter until sometime in late April. Adam's own case had not been fixed until Monday 28th April, so for all Pemberton's threats of getting it on before Easter he had not succeeded in doing so. Jones had almost twelve weeks in which to get the case ready, which was just as well as Adam still hadn't given him an address for this Betty woman.

And Blytheway. Whilst he was sure he was a good barrister he wished he would leave him be. For all his insouciance Adam's counsel was clearly troubled about the prostitute angle to the case. The man had actually taken to telephoning him at his office, which was unheard of for a member of the Bar. Jones felt sure that it must be unprofessional of him to do so. His telephone rang.

– I have a line to Lamb Building for you, Mr Jones.

But when Jones got through to Blytheway's clerk he was told that he had left to go to Court for the day. Jones left a message and returned to his diary. Novak's case was closest to trial so he should start with that. Adam had told him to prepare a sub-poena to be served on Katya Hoffer: that would be his first task of the day. He felt distinctly uncomfortable about it.

Adam had discussed the case with him on two occasions: once on the 28th January, the day before the conference with Bateman, and then again in considerable detail after Bateman had left chambers on the 29th. Adam had plied him with the questions that had clearly been forming in his mind as they had travelled back from Wandsworth together:

Novak plainly didn't know about the plans. He didn't know what colour paper they were on. He didn't know whether they were old or new. Novak's fingerprints were nowhere to be seen on the documents, although other unknown fingerprints were. Novak said he didn't know Katya Hoffer when previously he appeared to be very close to her. Katya seemed to know far more about the documents than he did. And how did Milo Hoffer fit in? Novak told him that it was Hoffer who had advised him not to report himself, whereas Hoffer, initially at least, had said that he had tried unsuccessfully to persuade Novak to report. What possible motive could Hoffer have had for dissuading him from reporting? And if he *had* dissuaded him, why then go out of his way to try and get him legal representation? It was Hoffer who had found him the accommodation. A flat with suspicious plans under the floorboards. A flat only a street or two away from where Milo and Katya Hoffer lived, though no one thought to advise Jones of this.

Then there was the whole issue about the ship from Gibraltar. Novak said that he was on the ship. Hoffer said that he did not meet him for the first time until after he had been through the Aliens Tribunal and was working in a bookshop when he tried to persuade him to report. Katya, similarly, denied any positive recognition of Novak on the ship. And yet Novak had been very clear about their meeting on the ship. It was Katya, he had said, who had helped him then. Katya who could help him now. And then there was Novak's strange reverie when asked about the trip from Gibraltar. He had gone into a dream when talking about it. Jones scrabbled around for his notes of that last conference.

"I would sleep on the deck. I found myself a place under a lifeboat and wrapped myself in sheeting to keep warm ... and I would look at the stars. I was very happy. I was oh, so very happy ..."

It was this that had excited Adam, and when he had called Jones on the 28th January he had asked him to dig out his notes of the interview with Katya Hoffer. Jones had asked her how long the voyage from Gibraltar had taken.

"Ten days. I thought we must be going to America not England after all. It was so beautiful. I felt so free ... Then we changed direction and headed north ... and my heart sank. They had travelled out to sea just to avoid the mines. It was very crowded but the skies were so blue. Milo. Poor Milo. He did not travel well. He was most of the time in the sick room. So I was alone mostly. At night I would sleep on the deck. I found a private place under a lifeboat, wrapped myself in canvas and looked at the stars. There were three nights when there were German submarines around. And the engines would stop and everyone was very quiet and nobody moved. And I would look at the stars and I would listen to the sea. And I was so happy!"

Jones had asked her whether Novak had been there and she had just said again that she was *so* happy. It was the similarity of description that had caught Adam's attention. Sleeping under a lifeboat and being *so* happy ... with submarines prowling around under them and trying to sink them.

Why had Katya Hoffer screamed on her doorstep at the mention of Novak's name? Why had she wanted to be interned rather than graded "C"? Jones thought again about that first encounter with the Hoffers. What an odd couple they made, with Katya decades younger than her husband. Why had neither Novak nor Hoffer mentioned Katya's existence when he took statements from them? He remembered her description of Adam Falling as gullible – did Hoffer tell Novak that she had said that? – and he cursed himself for being beguiled into telling her his version of events before she gave hers.

So Adam had concluded that Novak was telling the truth and that he – and possibly Milo Hoffer – were protecting Katya for some reason. And he advised Jones to issue a sub-poena. He would force her to give evidence at Novak's trial. It was completely improper of course – Novak had given express instructions that it should not be done. However, despite Jones's protests, Adam was insistent. And Jones had put it off. Until today. He could not afford to put it off any longer.

He busied himself with the necessary drafting for the remainder of the morning and broke for lunch at 1.30, removing his foil-wrapped sandwiches from his briefcase and opening the day's paper. He buried himself in an article about the bombing of two hospitals the previous evening, and chewed absent-mindedly on his sandwich.

Sonia knocked and entered with the post. He had completely forgotten about it and, reluctantly, he put the newspaper down and, still munching, took the armful of envelopes from her. Two letters stood out from the rest of the pile. One was a letter from Pemberton's solicitors. The other was from the Court. He opened the solicitors' letter first and as he read, stopped eating and dropped his sandwich onto the desk. Somehow Pemberton and his legal team had succeeded in bringing forward the hearing to the 10th March, barely five weeks away. The letter from the Court confirmed the change of date. How had they managed to do that? Hadn't Pemberton been having second thoughts about going ahead? Suddenly he had lost seven weeks of preparation time. And still they hadn't got a statement from Betty.

He put a call through to Lamb Building immediately but Blytheway was still at Court and Adam had just left to go to Court himself. Neither was likely to be back in Chambers before tomorrow morning. This changed everything.

Chapter Forty-six

(Wednesday 5th February 1941)

Adam moved away from the window and back to his desk. It was a clear, bright morning and Julia had just disappeared out of sight, walking through Cloisters down towards the Embankment. Services in the Temple Church had been suspended in January with one final celebration, the Te Deum, soaring out across the rubble and the Sunday peace, but still Julia came at the usual time and stayed inside for the allotted length of morning communion. Adam did not know why she persevered but he was glad that she did. He would leave no notes now as he knew they were unwelcome. He felt Blytheway's eyes upon him whenever he passed the entrance, whether he was being watched or not.

His morning ritual over, he went down to the Clerks' Room to see what, if anything, the day held for him; a fellow barrister greeted him surprisingly warmly on the stairs. In his tray he found a cheque for two guineas, and two small briefs – rolls of white paper wrapped in red tape with his name calligraphed across the front with, beneath his name, a modest (but acceptable) fee inked in. Money and work! Blytheway had done more than merely provide him with a seat and a room in his chambers. It was plain that he had been recommending Adam's work to the senior Clerk, who had been able to push some cases his way. There had also been another unexpected development.

Unexpected by all but Blytheway, that is. Perhaps his long personal experience of notoriety had attuned him to the vagaries of human conduct, but he had, during one of his several conversations with Adam, spoken enthusiastically about the unusual benefits of Adam's predicament.

– There is an indefinable advantage of being the subject of gossip, you know…

he had said.

– It attracts people to you the way the scent of lavender attracts bees –
and other insects for that matter; I get the prettiest butterflies fluttering about my garden in the country as well as the odd dragonfly
skimming away from my pond to have a taste. If your experience is
anything like mine has been over the years you will have the most
unexpected people showing an interest.

And he had been proven right. Word of his shame had spread throughout
the Temple and there had been several scurrilous pieces in the popular press,
rich with innuendo and slavering over imagined details. And whilst a significant number of his contemporaries affected to avoid him, there was no doubt
that some of the solicitors who had been motivated to send him work did so
out of a curiosity to meet this unlikely celebrity, if only to give themselves a
slightly risky allure, or to provide conversational fodder for their social lives.

And not all of his contemporaries shunned him. It was not possible to
know the popularity – or unpopularity – of those one shared chambers
with when one was part of the same close-knit band. Outsiders would not
press about the merits or demerits of one's professional colleagues. On his
expulsion from Stirrup Court, though, the shackles of omertà were loosened. Jack Storman was universally respected; however, Adam quickly
learned that Pemberton was not liked generally in the wider professional
world. He was perceived as an aggressive bully, arrogant, self-regarding
and possessing a lesser ability than he (and by extension the members of
his chambers) supposed. There was sympathy, of course, for the tragic loss
of his first wife, and muted admiration for his impressive war record, but
Adam heard, from Blytheway and others, about his lost years: the heavy
drinking, the uncontrollable rages and the frequent descents into violent
and sentimental self-pity before Julia appeared to save him from himself.

Julia, with her regular visits to the church, was well-recognised by many,
although no-one appeared to know a great deal about her as a person. The
impression that she gave was broadly a good one and, whatever the truth of
the rumours about her alleged relationship with Adam, some members of
the Bar were quietly impressed that Adam could attract such allegations.
Pleased, too, at the humiliation that this implied for Pemberton.

Blytheway had made a point of getting to know Adam better in the days
and weeks after his belongings were moved to Lamb Building. When his
work commitments allowed, he would pop into Adam's room for a chat,

advising him on décor and lending him prints and vases as well as giving him some of his peacock feathers so as to provide some colour to his desk. Sometimes he would invite Adam to his room for tea at the end of the working day. It was plain that he already knew a lot about him, and Adam wondered from time to time whether this omniscience applied to all who fell within his gaze. Frequently he would be surprised by Blytheway's perspicacity. Towards the end of one such conversation he said, out of the blue:

- So your father came from Bury in Lancashire and your mother came from Edinburgh?
- How could you possibly know that?
- It's a little trick of mine. I have always been (though I say so myself) extremely good at discerning accents, and the more we talk the more you relax. The more your *received* vowels emerge. Our voices are a palimpsest of our histories. Your history has been gloss-painted by Cambridge and now the Bar. The Lancastrian ingredient was relatively simple to place but it was only today that I was able to pin down the Scottish element.
- But why do you say that my father was from Bury and not from Edinburgh?
- Guesswork, I'm afraid. The stronger inflections belong to the place where you grew up, and I fancied that, as your father would have been working and your mother not, it was she who moved to live with him rather than your father moving down from Scotland to find work.
- And what else do you say you can "discern" from the inflections of my voice?

Adam was sceptical – and slightly alarmed at the same time – about how much he apparently gave away simply by talking.

- Well. Now I am *really* guessing. However, I would say that you are probably not the product of one of our illustrious public schools, probably not even a minor one, and that you were fortunate enough to obtain a scholarship from the elementary schools to a local grammar school and thence a scholarship to Cambridge. I hesitate to use this expression but I would venture to suggest that your parents were "lower-middle class".

- What on earth gives you that impression?
- The Woodbines you smoke. A very cheap cigarette that, unusually, one can buy one at a time.
- My father did smoke them until they became too expensive and then he gave up.
- I would conclude that your parents were not rich but were themselves (or your father at least) fairly well educated and understood the value of education ...
- My father was a school-master.
- When did he die?
- I didn't say that he was dead.
- I am sorry if I was wrong about that.
- When I was eighteen.

And after a twenty-minute conversation Adam would feel that Blytheway knew a great deal more about him whilst he, Adam, knew little more about his mysterious new friend.

Adam signed the receipt and pocketed the cheque before taking the two new briefs out of his tray: a contract case in Bromley County Court and a road traffic accident in Shoreditch, both listed for the following week. Blytheway was shimmering down the stairs, his red bag in one hand, a sheaf of papers in the other, as Adam mounted the stairs.

- Morning, sweetheart. Sorry about tonight. Hey Ho. Until next week!

That morning Blytheway was starting a high-profile libel case. His clients were the Renshaws, a trio of literary but eccentric siblings of some fame who had taken exception to a review of an anthology by one of their number in which the reviewer had attacked all three of them as publicity-seeking mediocrities whom oblivion had now claimed. The brothers and sister had interpreted the article as meaning that they were people of no literary ability whose arrogance and conceit constituted their only claim to prominence. They took great exception to the suggestion that they had been consigned to oblivion: on the contrary they were only now reaching the peak of their respective powers. As for the book in question, the only two comments that the reviewer deigned to make were that it was too heavy to hold as a bed-book, and secondly, that the part under review, being Miss Renshaw's 150-page introduction to the anthology, would have greatly improved the book if it had been omitted altogether. The Renshaws had thus, they alleged, suffered serious injury to their character, credit and reputation. An open offer of £150 to be shared between the three of them had been turned down. The case, set as it was against the backdrop of the continuing Blitz, had achieved some publicity in the press and was admirably suited to Blytheway's mixture of frivolity and high seriousness. The failure of the case to settle, however, meant that his invitation to Adam to dine with him that night had to be postponed.

In reality, Adam was relieved. In all of their various conversations Blytheway had conspicuously avoided discussing Pemberton's petition. It had been hard enough to get him to focus on it in their conference, and Adam knew that his counsel would only raise the issue in his own good time. Instead he spoke of Marrakesh or Italy, or Dresden china and Jermyn Street – nagging him to buy more suits and shoes. Or else he would lecture him on the proper use of his receipts: a third for himself, a third for his wife and daughter, and a third on buying clothes and beautiful things before rationing took away all pleasure. Although, a week or so earlier, he had expressed confidence in "some helpful developments" in the case, he would not thereafter be drawn on what those developments might be. Adam's curiosity about this throwaway remark was tempered by the fact that he was also likely to be quizzed on the prostitute, Betty. Jones's demands for details of her address were becoming more strident, and although they emanated ultimately from Blytheway, the man himself never raised the subject directly with Adam, but spoke instead in fripperies and riddles.

Adam desperately needed to make contact with Betty and the longer he left it the more precarious his position was likely to be. If he was to protect Julia he must present his legal team with Betty. To do so, however, would be to damage irrevocably (if it was not already so) his marriage and to move his acts of conspiracy to pervert the course of justice from the merely preparatory to the full-blown crime itself. It could be put off no longer, and he had decided that today he had to go and find her.

He had been instructed on behalf of a landlord in Clerkenwell County Court that afternoon and planned, having dealt with the case, to catch her at home before she went out to work.

As he was leaving the Clerks' Room he caught a snippet of a telephone conversation:

– Sorry, Mr Jones. I am afraid Mr Blytheway has left for court ... probably not back until the evening. Yes. I'll pass that on.

What did Jones want? Adam guessed it concerned Betty and was glad that he had decided to tackle the problem later that day.

****

Clerkenwell County Court was in Duncan Terrace just off Islington High Street. Betty had given an address in Sheen Grove and Adam calculated that it would be no more than a twenty-minute walk from the Court. He had forgotten, however, that he would be carrying the blue bag that contained his wig and gown – with his initials stitched onto the outside – and all his papers and books from the hearing.

He set off from the court at about 4 p.m. heading across to Upper Street. He had fastened up his overcoat over his suit, hooked his thumb through the thick rope of his robes bag, and slung it over his shoulder. He was carrying his papers in both hands before him. At first he made good progress, but the further he went into this working class area, bomb damage and rubble everywhere, the more conspicuous he felt in his expensive suit and shiny shoes. He walked down Theberton Street and then up Liverpool Road to Richmond Avenue. This was a mistake. What had he been thinking of? If he were to be seen in these circumstances with Betty he would be drawing attention to both of them. What if someone other than Betty answered the door? How would he explain himself? Sweat trickled down between his starched collar and his neck and the bag and the papers became heavier the further he walked. He felt the weight of his wallet shifting against the inside of his suit as he walked. He had wanted to have his money in case an extra bribe was to be necessary. But now he felt vulnerable as well as conspicuous. It contained the remains of the cash he had drawn out from the bank before going to see Julia at Hamleys. If he were robbed now he would have virtually no money at all.

Then he remembered: he had her telephone number as well. He would find the address and then telephone her from the nearest phone box and arrange to meet her somewhere, in a pub or in the nearest park. He had brought a street map with him but it was of little assistance. Many of the street signs had been taken down and some streets seemed to have vanished altogether. When he felt that he was as close as he was going to get with the aid of the map he decided that he had better ask for directions. It was beginning to get dark. A man of about sixty was walking slowly towards him so he stopped him and asked how he might find Sheen Grove.

– Sheen Grove?

The man laughed.

– Sheen Grove? Well it's down there on the left – he said pointing vaguely – Sheen Grove.

And he laughed again and hobbled on his way.

Turning the corner into Sheen Grove Adam knew, almost before he saw it, what would confront him. Almost the whole of the terrace had been destroyed: broken houses like gaping mouths spewed out timber and broken stone. Either Betty was dead, or homeless again, or she had given an address that had already been demolished. In his heart he knew it was the latter. She had not wanted him to find her, even as she had taken his money.

Had he left for Court five minutes later he would also have known that Pemberton's petition was only five weeks away.

Chapter Forty-seven

(Thursday 6th February 1941)

Julia had been unaware of Adam's eyes following her as she left the church. Why did she still go there when there were no services? She had no clear answer to this question. It was a time of peace away from Eaton Square. It was part of her routine. It reminded her of happier and easier times. It was all those things. She stepped through the white arches of Cloisters and made her way through Pump Court across Middle Temple Lane and on to Judges' Gate.

Devereux Court was thick with dust. Julia brushed against a wall and a smear of soot attached itself to the peacock green of her shoulder. She stopped and tried to rub it away but the smudge simply spread. Standing outside the Devereux Arms, Julia looked around her before taking the solicitors' letter from the inside pocket of her coat. The paper was thick and creamy. Received in the last post the previous evening, it had told her of the new hearing date and had summoned her to an urgent meeting in Lincoln's Inn Fields. It was half an hour until the appointed time.

Julia emerged onto the Strand. Across the road from her the Royal Courts of Justice, in all its grimy Victorian splendour, rose into the sky. In a matter of weeks she would be giving evidence inside this building; and all of her future hung upon the outcome of that evidence. Early lawyers were crossing the Strand towards the Courts. She joined the throng and then slipped sideways towards Bell Yard and Carey Street.

Walking along the western side of Lincoln's Inn, she saw a crowd gathered by the gates of Lincoln's Inn Fields. A VIP brandishing an oxy-acetylene burner was making a speech. As Julia passed, the dignitary lit the flame and applied it to the railings surrounding the central park area. They were being dismantled for scrap.

It was 9.25 when she walked up the imposing steps leading to her solicitors' offices, entered the architectural gem and presented herself to the tweedy matron on reception. She took a seat as requested, and flicked through an old copy of *Country Life* as she waited. Large windows looked down onto the Fields and a hazy sun penetrated the clouds and threw a half-hearted light onto the trunks and bare branches. Julia glanced out at the black-coated lawyers strolling up and down, seemingly oblivious to the sound of hammers against metal as the two-hundred-year-old railings were dismantled.

– Good morning, Mrs Pemberton!

a voice boomed out, and Julia started involuntarily before rising to her feet.

– Lovely day. Good to see you. Sorry about the short notice. Let me take your coat.

Said almost as a litany. The bonhomie was not so much forced as practised over many years. Mr Purefoy took her coat, slipped it over his pin-striped arm, and walked briskly towards his room beckoning Julia, with a slight turn of his head, to follow him. His office was at the rear of the building and he held the door open so that Julia could precede him into it. An unfashionable chair had been placed in front of his large partner's desk, and he took it by the top rail and tilted it slightly, inviting Julia to sit. A slim buff file lay in the middle of his blotter. That, she thought, was her life – her false life.

Mr Purefoy was a tubby man. His suit, although expensive and well-cut, could not hide that fact. He slipped behind the desk, took his seat, and then picked up her file. With pudgy fingers he removed the contents and spread them out in front of him. He had a signet ring on his little finger. Julia was more than a little suspicious of this middle-aged "hail-fellow-well-met", his greying hair slightly too long and curling down over his starched white collar.

When Jackson had served the petition on her just before the New Year she had been in a state of panic and despair. The strain of pretending that nothing was wrong had been too much and she had cracked in front of Jenny. Jeremy came from a more rarefied social circle than her own, and had been a practising barrister since she was a young girl. She had immersed herself in his life to the extent that no one would imagine their backgrounds were so different. But when it came to lawyers and the law she had not known where to begin to find decent representation. Even Adam Falling was better placed than she in that regard. None of the popular women's magazines or periodicals touched upon the subject, and she did not dare ask her female friends about such a taboo topic. She certainly couldn't ask Jeremy. And so she had looked for a respectable address and a firm of some longevity and had alighted on Randall, Beams and Purefoy in Lincoln's Inn Fields, established 1895.

And Mr Purefoy had, in turn, instructed Francis Alnwick as her barrister. Julia knew nothing about him. They had met with him in chambers in the first week of January. He was a ponderous and pessimistic man who moved slowly about his room and had a look of disappointment on his face. He did not inspire confidence. That meeting had taken place before Jenny had doctored her diary, and Alnwick's advice was to the effect that she was likely to lose.

Certainly, Jeremy did not seem daunted by the prospect of Francis Alnwick, or of Frederick Purefoy for that matter. It could have been her imagination but her husband seemed to breathe a sigh of relief when she told him who was to be representing her. The name of Roland Blytheway, on the other hand, caused him visible agitation. The evening when Jenny had shown Jeremy the diary was also the evening when Julia, unable to sleep, had gone up from the cellars to the dressing room to discover that the bowl of hyacinths (with their dangerous message) had disappeared. She had returned to her single bed in the cellar more awake than ever, although when Jeremy eventually came down to sleep she lay very still and tried to breathe deeply and evenly. Jeremy tossed and shifted on his narrow bed and, thinking she was asleep, spat out the words "Blasted Blytheway!" with such venom that she felt herself start with surprise. But he hadn't noticed, and in the darkness she listened as he turned, wriggled and pulled at his blankets. Until finally she fell asleep.

- Mrs Pemberton?
- I'm sorry, Mr Purefoy. I was miles away I'm afraid.

Purefoy was holding up a document.

- I don't know why Pemberton did it but he has and so it is very important that this is signed and witnessed.

- Oh do I *have* to Mr Purefoy? Can't it wait? I still think this will all go away.
- I was prepared to sit on my hands when we had twelve weeks to play with, but really you don't have the luxury of time anymore.
- But does that mean Jenny will have to give evidence?
- Not necessarily at all. When Pemberton sees this, signed off and everything, he may just drop the whole thing.
- *Please?* – she drew out the middle vowels and there was a note of entreaty in her voice.

Jenny knew nothing of this draft statement. She had allowed Julia to see where she had marked the crosses, and Julia had taken a note. She handed these to Purefoy on a scrap of paper and he had worked them up into a short statement to be signed by Jenny. This did little more than to make reference to her diary and the crosses it contained and then to confirm that Julia had been with her throughout the afternoons in question. All Jenny had to do was sign it before a witness and it would blow a huge hole through Pemberton's case. Purefoy could not understand Julia's reluctance. The diary had been volunteered by Jenny after all.

- I really can't see any advantage in delay, Mrs Pemberton.
- It's just that I think that Jeremy will drop it anyway.
- Well, bringing forward the hearing is a funny way of seeking a reconciliation.
- I *know* my husband.
- At least take this home with you – I have copies.
- Tell me about Roland Blytheway.
- Mr Falling's barrister?

Julia had learnt for herself that Blytheway had a reputation for cruelty, but she wanted to know what her own lawyers thought of him. Mr Purefoy blinked and ran his hand over his thinning scalp.

- Why do you want to know about Blytheway?
- I think my husband's scared of him.
- Blytheway's a *very* odd man. My firm has never used him. We don't approve of him.

- Why? Is he not very good?
- No. Quite the contrary. But he has a … a reputation. It simply wouldn't do for me and my partners to be linked to that man.
- Is he dishonest?
- Not as far as I am aware.
- So, if he is good at his job and honest why won't you use him?

Purefoy went very red and began rubbing his scalp with renewed intensity. How could he explain Blytheway's failings?

- He never married you know.
- Never married?
- He's never even been engaged.
- Oh … I see.

Julia blushed and they sat in silence across the desk from one another avoiding one another's eyes. Then Purefoy began gathering the papers together and slotting them back into the file. He handed Julia the unsigned statement.

- Is that all that we needed to discuss?
- We'll need to go and see Mr Alnwick again nearer the time. Please get Miss Pemberton to sign the statement. And remember to have it witnessed. You mustn't witness it yourself of course.

Julia got up to leave and took the overcoat Purefoy proffered. She folded up the draft statement and placed it in a pocket of the overcoat, then shook Mr Purefoy's hand and headed back to reception unescorted. She wasn't prepared to argue about the statement any more but she didn't intend to show it to Jenny. Not yet. Jeremy wouldn't go through with it. Of that she was certain.

The truth was that a rapprochement was happening. Julia had little doubt. The two single beds in the cellars had continued their imperceptible move closer together and Jeremy was more like his old self again. He had been shaken by Jenny's diary. He was frightened of Blytheway, of that she was sure, and he had too much to lose.

She thought of her children living safely, she hoped, in the Cotswolds. Jeremy hadn't got as much to lose as she had.

She crossed reception, nodded goodbye to the receptionist and was about to leave the building when Purefoy came scurrying after her.

- Mrs Pemberton! Mrs Pemberton! I'm sorry. There was one important thing that I forgot to deal with. Would you mind coming back to my office for a few minutes?
- Really, Mr Purefoy! Can't it be dealt with here?
- It's a bit delicate.

Mr Purefoy was rubbing his hands together in an agitated manner. She looked over at the receptionist who was affecting not to listen and decided it would be more sensible to follow the man back to his room.

- Well. What is it?
- Um ... you see ... it's about money.
- Money? I've paid you a significant sum of money in advance already.
- It's just that, with the trial being brought forward, Mr Alnwick's brief will be delivered any day and ... I must be in funds for him.
- How much do you want?
- I'm afraid I'll need another fifty guineas.
- Fifty guineas!

Julia had little money of her own. A small marriage settlement, but that had already been diminished by the cost of lawyers.

- With any luck Mr Falling will have to pay it at the end of the day ... I mean (*realising his mistake*) Mr Pemberton – if ... when he loses.

Julia laughed mirthlessly. She had far more to lose than Jeremy. If he succeeded in divorcing her she would lose her children and would be penniless.

- I'll see what I can do, Mr Purefoy.

Chapter Forty-eight

(Wednesday 12th February 1941)

Blytheway had won his libel case. Judgment was handed down on Tuesday 11th February. The Judge found the review of Miss Renshaw's anthology defamatory not just of her but of her brothers as well. A defence of fair comment was rejected and the Judge was particularly critical of the publisher's attempts to portray the Renshaws as conceited snobs. Nor did he accept the defence's rather forlorn suggestion that the action was a waste of time in the midst of the Blitz of London. "So long as the doors of the Law Courts remain open for litigation there is no reason why they should be closed to those who wish to defend their professional reputation." And that was that. He awarded each of the siblings £350 as well as their costs, and the case made headlines across the tabloids as well as in the quality press. Blytheway's name was at the forefront of the reports and an editorial in the *Times* drew attention to the case as a shining example of the continuation of the British spirit and way of life against incalculable odds. There was praise too for Blytheway's rhetoric in ridiculing his legalistic opponents and eulogising the importance of art, literature and high fashion no matter how dark, dull and dangerous everyday life was becoming. Adam had sensed that these causes were closer to Blytheway's heart than mere professional interest warranted.

He had not been able to speak with Blytheway since seeing him on the stairs almost a week before. On the rare occasions that he ventured into Blytheway's room the man was immersed in the collected works of the Renshaw siblings, which ran to many volumes. And after the judgment he failed to return to chambers. Rumour had it that he had gone with the Renshaws and their solicitor to a private club in Soho where one could still find, at a price, vintage champagne. However, Blytheway had found time to leave Adam a note reminding him of the invitation to dinner the following night, giving directions to his home and asking that he attend at 7.30 p.m. In fact, it suited Adam not to see Blytheway that Tuesday, as he had, surveillance permitting, his own task for that evening.

****

It was 5 p.m. on Wednesday afternoon when Adam and Jones emerged for the final time from Wandsworth Prison. Dusk was falling and the streets were turning to monochrome. Adam lit a cigarette as they reached the bus-stop and let the smoke – and the solicitor's silence – envelop him. Then:

- Are you sure you know what you're doing?
- It's his only chance.
- He doesn't want us to do it. He's forbidden us to do it.
- But he hasn't sacked me.
- He was too furious to think about sacking you.

And then, apart from the stamping of their feet against the cold, there was silence again as they waited for the glow of the bus.

They had been shown to the same interview cell, but Novak's condition had deteriorated since their last visit. He had scarcely raised his head when they entered the room. His shoulders were hunched and he was tracing circles around the surface of the table with his right index finger. When he shook hands the grip was weak and clammy. He took the cigarette that was offered to him without a word of thanks and the first five minutes of the meeting were spent in silence whilst he smoked it. Attempts at general conversation were met with incoherent grunts or no reply at all.

Jones watched Adam with new eyes. If he had been confident on their last visit, on this occasion he was almost reckless. His suit was as sharp as before and his shoes had been newly polished. His relationship with Novak had changed palpably since their first meeting in December. One by one he took Novak through the inconsistencies between what he had said at the outset and what he was saying now. And then he turned to the inconsistencies in what had been said by Milo Hoffer. And slowly Novak's grunts were replaced by monosyllabic answers and then by loud and increasingly vehement denials. There were no inconsistencies. He had insisted and, with a touch of his old arrogance, he began to shout at his two lawyers, accusing them of incompetence and stupidity. But still Adam, chain-smoking, ploughed on, as though he was oblivious to the insults. Jones didn't know where this was heading but he fancied that Adam knew what he was doing and so kept silent, taking a note when Novak's replies slipped into coherence.

Then Adam had turned to the unsigned testimony of Katya Hoffer.

- You didn't know anything about the plans under your floorboards did you?
- Of course I did not. I have said that to you many times.
- How did Katya know about the plans?
- I don't know what you are talking about.
- She knew, didn't she?
- How could she know?
- Katya had been to visit you in your flat, hadn't she?
- This is preposterous (*raising his voice*). Of course she had not!
- Are you saying that she came to your flat when you were not there?
- She would not do such a thing!
- I thought you hardly knew her.
- I do not.
- She has a key, doesn't she?

Novak brought his fist down on the table with such force that the saucer-cum-ashtray jumped into the air spilling ash everywhere. The warder looked in at the window to see what was going on.

- Why must we talk about this Katya Hoffer? She has nothing to do with my case.
- There is no need to shout … Katya found you the flat, didn't she? It was she who told you not to report?
- I am sick of this. You must leave now.
- Whose fingerprints are on the plans?
- I do not know.
- Why did you say that Katya told you I was gullible?
- I did not say such a thing.
- Mr Jones took a note, Mr Novak. I can show it to you if you like.
- It was Milo Hoffer who told me what she said.

Jones stole a glance at his watch. The time allotted for their visit was running out and Novak had not made any positive statement as to his defence. This was their last opportunity to get Novak to help himself. He looked at the man as he faced off Falling's questions. There were dark bags under his eyes and a broken red capillary ran across his left eyeball. He was blinking rapidly. Adam continued relentlessly on.

- Mr Novak. We are running out of time. Your trial will begin in less than three weeks. How can I help you if you won't help yourself?
- I have told you the truth. I know nothing about the plans. I did not put them there. I do not want to help the Germans. I am a Jew.

This was going nowhere. Adam faltered. Suddenly he looked haggard and Jones noticed how deep the rings were under his eyes. He had had less sleep than Novak by the look of it. Then Falling suddenly changed tack.

- Tell me what happened on the boat from Gibraltar.
- There is nothing to tell.
- Why did you say Katya was kind to you on that trip?
- I have said. It was foolish to involve her.
- You only changed your story to fit it in with hers.
- That is not true!
- You told us you slept under a lifeboat. Who else was under the lifeboat with you?
- It was a very big ship. Many people slept under the lifeboats.
- Why was Milo Hoffer in the sick bay?
- He was a poor sailor.
- So you knew who he was.
- No. I did not. This was a guess.
- Was Katya with you on deck?
- No! I did not know her.

There was a rattle of keys behind them as the warder knocked on the door. Adam looked at his watch. The session was over. He took a long drag from his cigarette and tipped the ash into the saucer.

- So you did not know Katya and you have no reason to be trying to protect her?
- Of course I do not. I hardly knew her at all. I wish I had never met Milo *or* Katya Hoffer.

– So you would not mind, then, if we forced her to give evidence at your trial?
– No. I forbid it! I forbid it!

Novak half rose from his seat and grabbed Falling round the throat and squeezed so that the cigarette fell from his lips. He banged the table with his other fist and started to yell.

– I forbid it! I forbid it!

Jones ran round behind him and started pulling at his arms. The warder rushed in and grabbed Novak's wrists from the front, prising him off Falling's neck and forcing the man into handcuffs.

– I forbid it! I forbid it!
– Time's up, sirs. I'll take Mr Novak back to his cell.

Adam retrieved his cigarette and rubbed his neck with his free hand before taking a long drag.

– You are making our job very difficult, Mr Novak.
– I forbid it!
– I will try and arrange for Mr Jones to see you one more time before the trial.

But Novak, struggling with the warder as he was hauled out of the interview room, was no longer listening.

*****

It was almost 5.30 before Jones saw the muted lights of a bus approaching. An hour to blackout. Falling was lost in thought. As they boarded the bus Jones saw in the light from the driver's cabin red finger marks across Adam's neck. He took a deep breath.

– About the … er … Betty. I really do need an address. The trial is only four weeks away.

Adam looked at him absent-mindedly.

– Yes. Of course.

And he handed him a slip of paper.

– I thought you said she lived in Islington.
– She got bombed out. I had to go and find her.
– And how did you go about doing that?
– It's a long story, Mr Jones (*Falling looked dog-tired*) – can it wait?
– You ought to get yourself to bed.
– Not yet I'm afraid (*he said lighting up another cigarette*); I have a dinner appointment tonight.

Chapter Forty-nine

(Tuesday 11th February 1941)

Betty Sharples lived in Mayfair. That was the address on the piece of paper that Adam passed to Jones. Not a particularly salubrious part of Mayfair, however. The previous day, as Blytheway was taking judgment and then celebrating his triumph, Adam had to deal with a small contract case in Bromley, O'Grady versus M.K. Simkiss Limited. He was representing an employee who sought payment for a period of time when he was unable to work through ill health. His employers said that there was no entitlement to sick pay and that the plaintiff knew this as he had not sought such pay until he discovered that a different worker was getting it. It was a simple question of fact as to the terms of the contract. And a guinea was a guinea.

Adam had set off in good time from Lamb Building and headed down to Temple Tube. From there he would travel to Victoria and take the overland. He had not seen Jackson hanging around for a week or so and guessed Pemberton had realised his cover had been blown. However, he remained alert to the possibility that he was being followed. Walking through Cloisters, he saw an unfamiliar man in a gabardine loitering around the arch leading into Middle Temple Lane. Adam walked slowly, without looking behind him, through Fountain Court and down past Garden Court. On reaching the westbound platform he put his blue bag on the floor and made to read his newspaper. An echoing rumble heralded the approach of the train and only at that point did he look up and to his right. The man in the gabardine was leaning against the wall near to the stairs, a newspaper up to his face. Adam knew that he could ignore him for the rest of the journey.

Arriving in Bromley, Adam made his way up the High Street and when he was a decent distance from the station he stopped and looked behind him. The man with the gabardine was walking slowly up the road. Adam looked through him and continued on his way to court. It was a long but not particularly strenuous day. Mr O'Grady was a pleasant old man who didn't look as though he could afford the guinea. The employer was represented by an elderly member of the Bar, armed with textbooks and legal authorities. After final submissions on both sides the Judge found for the employer. On early occasions when Mr O'Grady had been off work sick he had not claimed sick pay. It was only when he had heard of a report in another case that he sought payment. There was no express term that he was entitled to sick pay, so such a term would have to be implied. The Judge refused to imply such a term. If it had indeed been part of the contract the old man would have sought payment the first time he was ill. Judgment for the company with costs. Adam had the unpleasant task of explaining to the bewildered plaintiff that he had not only lost but would have to pay the defendant's lawyers for their time. Not his best day in court.

As expected, on regaining the High Street there was no sign of the man in the gabardine. He had no doubt satisfied himself that Adam was gainfully employed and taken himself back to London. Adam popped back into Dr Johnson's Buildings to feed Delia and change her litter. He was back in Chambers by 5.30 p.m. when he learnt of Blytheway's success and found the note in his tray reminding him of dinner the following evening. Dusk was falling by the time he emerged again from chambers. There were still quite a few people about. The bombing had been abating as February progressed. Gaberdine was standing half out of sight in the archway leading towards King's Bench Walk.

Adam lit a cigarette and walked slowly up Inner Temple Lane and then made his way to Chancery Lane tube station on Holborn. It was a cold evening and he pulled his overcoat more tightly around him. Crowds were pouring down into the underground from the southerly pavement and Adam joined them, vaguely aware of the private detective on his trail. The concourse around the ticket office was teeming with people, and on a whim Adam forced his way up through the throng coming down from the northern pavement, leaving his tail stuck down below. He broke into a run and within seconds was within the boundaries of Gray's Inn. The blackout had begun. He felt his way further away from the entrance to the Inn – the brick of the buildings was cold and grainy against his fingertips – and, when it lay seventy-five yards or so behind him, took up a place to watch. If Gaberdine were to try and follow him, his silhouette would show as a separate shadow against the dark. Adam waited for twenty-five minutes and, satisfied that he had lost the man, he lit another cigarette and headed slowly through the Inn and up to Theobalds Road. The devastation there was terrible.

He pulled his coat sleeve back and tried to read his watch; too dark. He calculated that it must now be around 7.30. He would walk west. Public transport was fickle and uncertain in the dark and he was in no particular hurry. His progress was slow and halting. He cupped the glow from a stream of cigarettes. Gradually he made his way along to Oxford Street. This was no brighter but the pavements were wider and he was able to make slightly swifter progress. John Lewis, as was well known, had been blown out. And the trestle tables from which they now conducted their business had long been packed away.

He marked off the tube stations as he passed them – so far no air raid warning sirens had sounded – Tottenham Court Road, then Oxford Circus. He turned down into New Bond Street and headed south. The darkness was getting deeper and he was forced to use his hands again to feel his way, occasionally crashing into pedestrians going in the opposite direction, with mumbled apologies on both sides. At Bruton Street he headed west again, past Berkeley Square and finally down towards Shepherd Market.

The last time he had come to this place he had been anxious to be followed. He never thought then that he would have to come back. This time it had been imperative that no one who knew him saw him. He slowed as he approached the place where he had picked up Betty less than two months earlier. It was, he guessed, about nine in the evening now. The side streets were busier here, with men standing against the walls, watching from street-corners or fumbling their way down to Shepherd Market itself. Last time, he had walked up White Horse Street from Piccadilly. His current route was far less straightforward. He didn't know where Betty Sharples lived. But he knew where she worked.

– Fancy some fun, sir?

A voice beckoned to him from a doorway but he ignored it and stumbled onwards.

– Suit yourself!

Finally he was within fifty yards of where he had first met Betty. He found an anonymous stretch of wall, leaned against it and strained to see through the darkness. Rubbing his hands together against the cold, he could feel the dust on them picked up on his journey. Shadows moved against shadows. People clung to the anonymity of the place so that a shadow would rarely leave the wall for long enough to permit a recognisable outline. There were occasional mumbled exchanges, the words impossible to make out. Now and then, shouting and an altercation. Obscenities and threats. How could he expect to make out her shape against all the other people milling around in the darkness? What if she did not work that night?

He had been standing there motionless for over half an hour when at last he saw her, in her well-cut coat, moving from the direction of Clarges Street back to her station. He fought an urge to go over to her, take her by the arm and pull into a doorway. She had deliberately misled him and he felt a surge of anger mix with his relief at finding her again. He stayed where he was. If he lost her this time he might lose her forever.

After about ten minutes a man approached her and there was an inaudible exchange between the two before they headed off together, Betty leading the way, back towards Clarges Street. Adam followed the two shadows as closely as he could, aware that if he let them get too far ahead of him he might lose them. Halfway along Clarges Street Betty stopped at a door, fumbled for a key and let herself in. A hall light brushed briefly across her face and he saw the half-familiar profile, the blonde hair showing under her scarf. Then the man followed, the door closed swiftly behind them and all was dark again. Adam edged towards the front door. There were six separate bells – bed-sits – one of which had her name against it. He memorised the number of the house and the bell and faded back into the shadows to wait.

About fifteen minutes later the door opened and the man came back out into the street and disappeared into the darkness. Barely enough time to take her coat off, Adam thought. A few minutes after this Betty emerged and headed back to Shepherd Market. Adam resisted the urge to follow her: he knew where she was going, and he knew where she lived. If he stopped her outside her door she might disappear again, and he needed to talk to her, to remind her of their deal. He patted his breast and felt the comforting shape of his wallet. It was getting late. He lit another cigarette.

Dropping the fag-end and twisting out the embers with his toe, he came to a decision. He pulled out his wallet and felt for the texture of a one-pound note. He needed her to help him. His mind made up, he strode back to where he knew she would be standing. His eyes were becoming more accustomed to the gloom and he was able to pick her out almost immediately, a frail silhouette wrapped in the well-cut curtain material that was her coat. A sudden transitory glow lit up her lips and nose. She was smoking. He realised that his right hand had balled into a fist, crumpling up the one pound note. He was sweating despite the cold. He needed to look into her eyes.

Shadows upon shadows as people moved around. He saw the arc of her discarded cigarette and a splash of sparks as it hit the ground. She was fumbling in her coat as he made his way over to her. She had reached a cigarette and was groping for her matches when he reached her and struck a match from his own box. She looked up at him in surprise, her eyes widening as she looked him in the face. He saw her pupils dilate. The flame hovered moth-like around the tip as she sucked in hard on the filter then looked away.

– Hello again, Betty.

She looked at him and then looked away again, a mixture of pleasure and foreboding playing across her features.

– I wondered when you'd be back.

He shook the match until the light folded, and dropped it to the floor.

– I've come for your time,

he said, holding out the pound note.

She breathed in and then blew smoke out at an angle, avoiding his face. She looked harder and sadder.

– Go away, old man.
– Why are you doing this?
– You know why I'm doing this.
– Please take me back to your room. I need to talk.
– The bombing seems to have eased off. D'you think it's seasonal? Only bomb us when it's cold.

– Why did you lie to me?

– What do you mean?

– I went to Sheen Grove. There was nothing there ...

– I thought you might. You're not so stupid, are you.

– Why did you give that as your address when it wasn't?

– It *was* my address!

Betty was shouting at him now and he sensed shadows turning around onto him. Harassment wasn't appreciated. He lit another match and held it to her face. The angles between cheek and chin flickered as she stared angrily into his eyes. Her gaze dropped and quietly she repeated:

– It *was* my address.

– Is that where Joe died?

– They never found him, you know. Not even a piece of him.

– I'm sorry ... I'm really sorry

The flame from the match had reached his fingers and he let it drop so that they were both in darkness once again. A firework-flare of her eyes was embedded on his retinas so that he wanted to light another match and see her again. See her now. In her pain.

– Please take me back to your place. I only want to talk again. Talk some more. I promise.

– No.

– Please, Betty.

– No. Why should I?

– I'm offering twice the asking price and I promise not to hurt you.

– No one gives more than the asking price.

He admitted defeat. In that private admission he saw the uncertain structures of the future collapse upon themselves. He could not force her. If she was not willing she was dangerous. Perhaps the portent of helpful developments from Roly (whatever they were) would save him. The imprint of her eyes in the darkness, the sadness of her situation, overwhelmed him.

– You're right. I must go. I'm sorry ...

And he began to walk away … then turned as if struck by a thought.

– May I have just one kiss? Please? You can have the pound for it.

He walked towards her and in the darkness she folded into his arms and before he knew it he felt the salty warmth of her tongue on his. A kiss that seemed to go on and on. And then, as though she was reaching for breath, it was over. He passed the pound note across, looked at the fragments of her that were visible, and, using touch, smoothed her skin and stroked her hair. He knew from her kiss how lonely she was – and how alone.

– Thank you, Betty. Thank you for everything. I'm so sorry. Goodbye.

And he headed off into the darkness.

– Wait! Wait! Come back. I'm sorry. Come back!

And she invited him back to her room.

****

She unlocked the door and moved inside. He saw the same light illuminate her features as she entered and he felt a pang of something that he thought might be love. Her room was on the second floor. It was small, modest. There was a bed, the sheets rearranged to hide recent activity, a wash basin and a small chest of drawers by the wall. There was a framed photograph on it, turned to the wall – the dearly departed Joe, he thought. All other facilities were obviously communal. They had been draped in one another's arms all the way back to Clarges Street but, adept as he increasingly was in the ways of deception, he didn't allow himself to read much into that. The weight of her head on his shoulder – too close and too trusting – struck a wrong note on that, however. She didn't offer him tea.

– Why did you come back?

The memory of her tongue impeded logic. How could one tell from the feel of a tongue so much about someone?

– This is a really beautiful room …

He stumbled into silence.

– I've thought about you a lot you know. How is the cat – sorry, kitten?
– Oh. Fine. Fine. Cordelia. She's called Cordelia.
– Do you see how stupid this is?!

He was taken aback by her vehemence. He nuzzled her neck and kissed her hair.

– I need your help, Betty. I need your help.

She twitched him off her, as though he were a cobweb.

– You want my help? I'll give you my help. I've been thinking about this. You ain't been telling me the truth. Fact is, you've been having it off with your boss's wife and you want me to give you an alibi. But it's not much of an alibi is it? Cos if you convince all of those idiots you're telling the truth, your marriage will still be fucked (*he was shocked at the obscenity*) and you'll still be fucked with everyone else. So, I ask myself, why is he doing it? And do you know what, I found only one answer that fits.
– And what's that?

Adam was dreading the answer, although he had already guessed it. He needed her too much not to go along with her train of thought.

– What's that?
– Because you love her. You bloody fool! You love her.

And she looked up at him and her eyes were full of tears as she said:

– You bloody fool!
– Please help me?
– I don't know … Why are you doing this? She doesn't love you. If she did, she wouldn't make you do this.

- I don't know why. I don't know anything anymore. I just need your help.
- Why should I help you? Why should I help anyone?

His voice was as she remembered it. She had fallen asleep remembering that voice. The war would be over within a year, one way or another, and then everything that she, anyone, had done to survive would be forgotten. With a rare recklessness that betrayed her buried Presbyterian roots, she gave in.

- All right, all right. I'll stick to our story.
- Thank you.

The crisis over, she put her arms back around his neck and kissed him in memory of their early slight intimacy. She felt his neck yield to her caresses. He stroked her breast through her overcoat and she realised that they had taken no steps to conform to the orthodoxy of such situations.

- But I still think you're mad. She doesn't love you. You must of gone all the way to Islington to find me, and then, when you couldn't, you come all this way. It doesn't make any sense.
- Well, I could say the same for you.
- There's no need for that. I don't need your help. You're the one begging.
- Why are you doing this, Betty? You're beautiful, you're intelligent, why?
- Now don't you go passing judgment on the one person who might save you, if that's the right word.
- But why?
- Look! I'm here cos Joe died. I didn't want him to die and I loved him very much. And if he wasn't dead I wouldn't be here. But he is dead, silly sod. And no insurance. I can't help it but at night when I can't sleep I think, why can't he still be alive? And then I think, if he has to be dead why did he have to die under a bloody bomb? Why couldn't he of had a heart attack, or been killed in a piss-up or been run over by a car?
- You won't move again will you?
- No.

328

And that one word carried so much regret and meaning that he felt he would never be able to read a word of literature without trying to excavate the meaning buried in the shortest outburst.

   – Thank you.
   – You're mad, you know?

She extricated herself and arranged herself across the bed.

   – You can have more for your money if you want to?
   – No. No thank you. And thank you at the same time.

He left her there, putting the sweaty one-pound note on a dish by the door.

It was now well after midnight. As he began the long walk home he thought about what Betty had to say. She was right. He was taking ridiculous steps to protect someone who didn't care for him. It was illogical. Then he thought of Novak. That was the only explanation. Novak was in the same position. There was no other explanation. He had to be protecting Katya. He would press him on this the following day. It would take him an hour or more to get back to Temple. He lit another cigarette.

But there was something else that Betty had said. Something about her own situation. It had something to do with that dream. He tried, as he walked, to untangle that mystery. But nothing worked. And so he walked on home, oblivious to the shadowy people, the dark and their mutterings. Betty had said something important. But he couldn't work out what it was.

Chapter Fifty

(Wednesday 12th February 1941)

The bus was already crowded by the time it reached Adam and Jones. They climbed on board and were able to find two seats downstairs at the front. Adam fell asleep almost before the bus moved off, his head sagging against the side window. Jones hadn't the heart to wake him when the conductor came round and so paid for tickets for the two of them. He had a host of questions to ask about Betty but it seemed that, for the time being at least, they would have to go unanswered. Instead he contented himself with looking out of the front window as the bus chugged slowly into town. But the windows were soon all steamed up and, in the gathering dusk, it was impossible to make out much about their surroundings. He wiped a hole in the condensation and saw that they were heading over Wandsworth Bridge. Another forty minutes from here. Then, eventually, he recognised the turn of the bus as it headed onto the Strand. He nudged Adam awake as they passed the Royal Courts of Justice and they got off on Fleet Street just by Fetter Lane. It was just past 6 p.m. They shook hands and said their goodbyes. Jones headed back to his offices and Adam turned down into the Temple.

Delia was curled up asleep on the corner of his bed. She was still little more than a kitten. She stirred as he closed the door and stretched out yawning. There was a little jug of milk on the side and Adam said a quiet thank you to Barry. Since the night of his collapse he and Barry had become friends. In addition to bringing him extra food from the kitchens, Barry had taken to looking after the cat when Adam was out at court or away from the Temple. When Adam was obliged to leave the house in Dulwich, that had created difficulties with his Home Guard duties. He simply lived too far away. So, with surprisingly little difficulty, he had been able to resign from his local regiment on condition that he took up some other form of war service. He had volunteered for the Inner Temple's Fire Watch and was spending two days in seven as a part of a trio of men, armed with a stirrup pump, on the rooftop of Hare Court. Barry was part of his team. They had been provided with heavy blue overalls and a belt to carry the axe and torch that each were issued with. Doing more than forty-eight hours per month also meant that they were provided with the loan of a steel helmet.

Adam poured some milk into a saucer and stroked the cat as it drank. The blackout was approaching. He filled the basin with cold water and splashed it over his face. Looking at himself in the mirror, he saw dark circles under his eyes. He smoothed down his hair, patted his pockets and made to go out again. His torch. He had better take that along with him. He forced it into his overcoat pocket, retied his scarf and headed out into the night.

It was little more than a mile to Bloomsbury but it was more than an hour before Adam found himself on the west side of Bedford Square, using his torch to check surreptitiously the house numbers. Finally, he found the address he was looking for, the windows all dark and no shred of light escaping. Wrapping his overcoat more tightly around him against the cold, he gave one long press on the large brass bell next to the letterbox.

Within seconds the door swung noiselessly open and Adam found himself face to face with a tall man in his early forties, blond hair greying, dressed in black tie.

– Good evening, Mr Falling. Mr Blytheway is expecting you.

He stood aside to let Adam enter and, as he passed, Adam noticed a long, faded scar running down the man's cheek. The large hallway was discreetly illuminated and, as the outside door closed behind him, he took in the black and white tiled floor and an elegant side table, a hat and umbrella stand beside it, which glowed in the subdued light. Wall lights shone gently on Japanese prints and small Impressionist paintings. Blytheway, also dressed in black tie, emerged from a door to the left and moved towards him, right hand outstretched. His handshake was firm but gentle. Foundation powder could not quite conceal a black eye. He was smiling.

– Good evening, Adam.
– What happened to your eye?
– That's a story for another day, sweetheart.

He ran a finger round his left orbit and flakes of powder fell to the floor.

— I'm sorry. I didn't realise it was going to be so formal.

— I hadn't said. Go with Caldwell. I'll be waiting in the Salon.

He gestured towards his butler who was already marching, with a pronounced limp, towards the stairs. Adam followed. Caldwell took him to the first floor.

— This is Mr Blytheway's *spare* dressing room.

It was relatively small. There was a built-in wardrobe along one wall and, facing it, a full-length mirror, a small chest of drawers standing next to it. Caldwell extracted a dinner suit draped in cellophane and teased the jacket out from the hanger, proffering it to Adam to try on. The fit was good, though slightly loose on him.

I'll leave you alone to try on the trousers. There's a black tie in the top drawer. If they fit you comfortably Mr Blytheway would be obliged if you would wear them down to the Salon. I will take care of your suit and overcoat.

A pair of braces had been hitched to the buttons in the trousers, and by adjusting them Adam could keep the trousers from sliding down over his shoes. He checked his appearance in the mirror and made his way downstairs to Blytheway's reception rooms.

****

The "Salon" was a spacious sitting room with a chaise longue against the far wall, two large armchairs, a long mahogany coffee table, a cocktail cabinet and a rococo table which Roly would subsequently identify as being the work of Meissonier. The remaining walls were lined with glass-fronted bookcases. There were two three-bar electric fires, one on either side of the room, which targeted the area around the coffee table and armchairs. Candles were burning on almost every surface, beeswax no doubt. Blytheway was half sitting, half lying across the chaise longue as Adam entered. He rose to his feet in one fluid movement and advanced across the room, put his hands out and squeezed Adam's shoulders through the dinner jacket. Then he placed his forefinger in the front of his trousers and pulled them slightly outwards from Adam's stomach.

– Three inches,

he said, almost to himself, before turning Adam round so that he could look at the cut of the suit from the rear. Adam felt his eyes moving down his back and legs, and then the touch of Blytheway's hands against his sides. The door to the Salon had been closed after he entered and he felt slightly uncomfortable ... vulnerable. Blytheway turned Adam to face him again and, with a flourish, produced a white silk kerchief which he arranged artfully in Adam's breast pocket.

– Slightly loose around the torso and the trousers are a little roomy. But not bad. *I've* not been able to wear it comfortably for years now; even keeping myself trim it was beginning to pinch. But it was in far too good a condition simply to throw away. It will do.

Then he moved towards the armchairs.

– It's not enough, of course, to have a good wardrobe. Clothes must *fit* properly and one *mustn't* bulge. One only has to look around on Dining Nights to see how many have allowed themselves to go to seed. Champagne!

Caldwell entered with an ice-bucket and two crystal flutes which he set out on the table, returning seconds later with a bottle of Taittinger. Rotating the bottle, he eased the cork off with a sigh rather than a pop and filled the glasses – waves of bubbly yellow under a snowy mousse that gradually subsided into streams of bubbles rising to the top and bursting. He handed each of them a glass and then retired.

– Take a seat.

Roly motioned to one of the armchairs as he settled into another. Adam wanted to get on to the business of the evening, which, he assumed, was his case, but he remembered Blytheway's discursive performance in conference and so held his tongue.

– A toast!

said Roly, clinking his glass to Adam's.

– To the triumph of substance over shadows … Dinner isn't for another forty-five minutes so we have a little time to talk. Feel free to smoke.

In the manner of all addicts Adam had transferred his cigarettes to the dinner jacket. Roly slid a lacquer dish over to him as he lit up.

– So. You've been with us now for almost four weeks. It seems to be suiting you.
– The clerks are recommending me for work. I'm sure I have you to thank for that.
– Not at all. Not at all. I put it down to your new suit. And to the exotic little reputation you have earned for yourself.
– I'd like to talk to you about why I used to go into the church.
– I'd rather you didn't.
– You do believe me, don't you?
– Adam. Adam. Sweetheart. We both know that an advocate's job is to deal with the evidence that is presented. It is not a matter of whether I believe you or not. And besides. I don't want to talk about your case at the moment. It is *not* a subject for polite pre-prandial conversation.

There was an unexpected edge of steel in his voice and Adam recoiled from the rebuke. Roly continued in a more conciliatory fashion.

– Tell me about those other two cases that you are so concerned about.
– I'd rather not. Your Renshaw case sounds a lot more interesting.

Adam decided that he had to try and learn at least a little more about this strange man who, whilst apparently courting controversy and a high profile, had told him so little about himself.

– Oh. It was certainly good fun. But rather easy money in the end. Do you know that *none* of the other barristers had actually read the Renshaw oeuvre? Rather a fundamental error in my view. I had advised that this was critical. Not only because it *was*, but also because I could be paid for reading it all. It was a bit recherché for my tastes

if I'm honest. But I suspect I learnt something on the way through.
- And the party afterwards?
- A very *gay* affair. We all trooped off to the Dorchester in the end. All sorts of strange creatures tagged along. Our contemporaries would *not* have approved of them at all. Some interesting writers amongst them though. Do you know, I don't think enough people appreciate the importance of parties. One learns so much. But enough of that, tell me about your case against Pemberton – McKechnie isn't it?

Adam told Blytheway about the developments in the case. His certainty that Bateman had indeed been having an affair with Mrs McKechnie, the "ABC" jottings in the diary, the trips by the foursome to the cinema and the inexplicable circumstances surrounding Mrs Bateman's death. Bateman had told him that his wife had been run over by a car after the blackout whilst he was on his way back from work but that couldn't be right because the blackout would not have started by the time he got home from work. He also decided that he could trust Blytheway with the story about the inquest notes. Of the fact that Bateman and Mr and Mrs McKechnie had given corroborative stories to the coroner. And then the fact that Bateman had come into £10,000 by way of life insurance on his wife's death. Blytheway, who had been listening in a languid, almost bored way stiffened at the story of the inquest notes.

- How *very* interesting.
- It's a bit of a mystery to me, I'm afraid. All I know is that Bateman seemed determined to prevent me from finding out what happened, and yet, now that I know, what with all my other problems, he seems equally determined to continue to instruct me.
- A mystery indeed! And when *I* am faced with a mystery I tend to set my bloodhounds onto it.
- Your bloodhounds?
- Oh. I have a whole *pack* of them. But my favourite two are called "Cherchez la femme" and "Follow the money". And I say to myself, "It's not the lie that counts. It's the reason for the lie."

Blytheway paused and looked into space. The candles flickered their reflections in his eyes. Adam waited. Finally, the mist fell away from Blytheway's eyes, he took a sip from his second glass of champagne and

then looked directly at Adam, just as he had done in conference. And again
he felt the ferocity of that intellect.

> – Well. I've only had a few minutes to think about it. And, of course,
> you know so much more about the details of the case. But my instinct
> would be to follow the money. Now, about this treason trial. What
> can you tell me about that?

Adam gave him a brief resume of Novak's case, the contradictions and
the lies culminating in the unhappy meeting with Novak in Wandsworth
earlier that day and Adam's decision to issue a witness summons against
Katya Hoffer. At this juncture Blytheway tutted loudly.

> – I really wouldn't do that, Adam.
> – Novak's clearly protecting her. And he'll pay for it with his life.
> – But Adam. That is his choice. You have clear instructions not to do it.
> You should not.
> – If we don't do it the truth won't come out and an innocent will die.

Blytheway chuckled.

> – Adam! I'm surprised at you!
> – What?
> – "The truth won't come out"? What has *that* got to do with anything?
> – Doesn't the truth matter to you at all?
> – It matters to me enormously. I would never lie. Nor would I mislead
> the court. But you should know by now that the courtroom is not a
> theatre for truth. Or for justice for that matter. Would *you* really want
> the truth to come out in *every* case? And anyway, let us assume that
> Novak loves this woman. Is he not entitled to say to himself I will
> sacrifice my life for that love even if the truth must remain hidden?
> Assuming he actually *knows* the truth. People do the strangest things
> in the name of love, as we all know.

At that moment Caldwell entered to say that dinner was ready.
Blytheway rose, brushed out the creases in his trousers and finished his
glass of champagne.

– Enough of that for now. I am sure we shall return to the subject of love over dinner.

****

Caldwell led the way into the dining room. A Regency period dining table was in the centre of the room, leaves removed to make dinner a more intimate affair. There was a candelabra in the middle of the table and the candles glinted on the silver cutlery. Subdued wall lights made the paintings glow. Spode china bowls lay on their place mats. When they had seated themselves opposite one another Caldwell poured out two glasses of claret from a decanter and then brought in a small tureen and ladled out soup for them.

– Oxtail. Tinned,

said Blytheway, by way of explanation, as he dipped his spoon delicately into the first course.

– I've got gallons of the stuff down in the cellar. Bought it all before the rationing started. Completely legal and should last until Domesday.
– You don't approve of the black market do you?
– I have many issues with Jeremy Pemberton but I object in particular to his vainglorious boasting about flouting the rules that apply to everyone else.

For the first time in all of his conversations with Blytheway, Adam heard a note of genuine anger in his voice. He had reflected frequently on the exchange between the two men in the crypt of the Temple Church, and Blytheway's reaction betrayed the existence of an acrimonious relationship between the two.

– What is there between you and Pemberton?
– Not now, sweetheart. Not while I'm dining. Have another glass of claret. I've been looking forward to the next course all day. Caldwell went to Billingsgate specially.

Caldwell cleared the soup and brought in two plates, each with a piece of steamed white fish of a kind Adam had never seen before. Then he rolled in a heated trolley bearing bowls of boiled potatoes and boiled green beans and carrots. The oxtail had been surprisingly delicious. Warming and with a hint of spice. Adam had wiped the plate clean. But the fish was a revelation. The glowing white flesh came away in firm flakes and melted in the mouth.

- This is wonderful. What is it?
- Cod, would you believe. Very cheap and very tasty … and *not* rationed! You've probably eaten it as fish and chips from time to time. Such a barbarian dish.

As Caldwell cleared away the main course and there was a pause in the dining, Adam felt the time was right to try and get Roly to talk about his own case. The decanter was almost empty and Caldwell removed it and replaced it with a second.

- Roly, you said a little while ago that you thought there would be some helpful developments in my case within a few days …?
- Yes. I'm sorry about that. I may have been a bit premature.
- Can you at least tell me what they were?
- I'm not sure it is a good idea. I can see little point in getting your hopes up for something that does not, in the end, materialise.
- Is that why you've said no more about it?
- My dear Adam, in every case it is the *evidence* that is important. I do my best to concentrate on that and leave to one side that which I observe or surmise – unless it helps me! *You* should be doing the same.
- *Please* tell me, nevertheless.

Blytheway sighed and took a sip of claret.

- Very well. You are a grown man, I suppose. And it is your case. At the time of that last conversation a report reached me to the effect that Jenny Pemberton was going to provide her step-mother with an alibi that would be sufficient to defeat the petition.

– An alibi?

Blytheway looked long into Adam's eyes, watching for a reaction.

– Her diary apparently. On practically every occasion when you are alleged to have been visiting the Stafford, Julia was having tea with Jenny in the Ritz and discussing, well, women's things.

Adam felt his mouth drop open and pursed his lips to hide the slip. He looked down at the napkin on his knee, conscious of those eyes upon him. A wild mixture of confusion, relief and foreboding boiled in his mind.

– Well, that's excellent news! … What's the problem?

He drained his glass and Blytheway solicitously refilled it.

– The problem, Adam, is that it seems too neat to me. But, more importantly, Jenny has yet to file a statement confirming what her diary apparently says. And the entries in the diary, though I have not actually seen it as yet, consist of no more than a number of convenient crosses on the appointed days. They could have been added afterwards for all anyone knows.
– But it's a complete answer. It proves that I was telling the truth …

Blytheway let Adam's declaration hang in the air and looked at him with a mixture of amusement and concern.

– It isn't evidence at all until such time as we have a signed and witnessed statement from Jenny Pemberton. Of course, once we have that I will press her hard on the truth of what she has deposed to, whether or not I actually believe personally that she is telling the truth.
– Why shouldn't she be telling the truth?
– It's a matter of instinct. My instincts have *never* let me down … and the more I have pondered on this the less happy I have become.
– Instinct? But you've said yourself that it is the evidence that one must concentrate on.

- Perhaps instinct isn't the best word then. You see, Adam, one of the advantages I have in my work is my memory. If I were to read a statement – a book even – it is as though I have taken a photographic image of each page, and each image gets filed away in my mind. I have, as it were, a photographic memory. And every new piece of information that comes my way gets filed. But sometimes that new information is discordant with what I already know. Sooner or later I sense that discord as clearly as I would a wrong note in a piano recital. Then I must find the source of that dissonance. It sometimes takes a little time but I always get there. And this information strikes a wrong note. So, instinct is too poor a word to use, I would accept.
- Then have you worked out why it does not ring true?
- Yes ...
- Are you going to tell me?
- No ...
- Why ever not?
- It would assist neither you nor me to do so.

Blytheway took another sip of his claret and looked around the room as though waking from a slumber.

- Caldwell should be here in a minute with our bread and butter pudding. I bought an enormous bag of sultanas and I think I've found a way of making sure they don't go off.

It was clear that the conversation was over and Adam knew better than to press him. He was coming to trust Blytheway's judgment on such things. His sense of foreboding increased as his relief at the revelations evaporated. They ate dessert in silence and after Caldwell had cleared everything away Blytheway suggested that they return to the Salon for coffee and port. It was getting late now and Adam felt his eyes drooping. He stifled a yawn. Blytheway, on the other hand, seemed as frisky as a four-year-old.

- Come on, Adam. There's still an awful lot to talk about.
- I'm sorry, Roly, I'm fading rather.
- Nonsense! A cup of coffee will restore you.

340

- I need to be getting back to Dr Johnson's Buildings ... it's not an easy journey.
- Then you must stay the night. I've taken the precaution of having a room prepared for you, just in case. Please feel free to smoke.

Adam felt a sense of vulnerability returning. He didn't know where this evening was heading. But the coffee had arrived and he could at least drink that before taking any decisions. He lit up.

- Now that the meal is over, we can talk a little more about your case. Why haven't you provided Jones with Betty's address?
- I have. I gave it to him earlier this evening.
- And are you prepared to tell me where she lives?

Adam gave him the address and watched as Blytheway assimilated this new piece of information.

- You *do* look very tired, Adam. Did you have a *very* late night last night?
- Quite late, yes.
- Well. It can't have been Mr O'Grady's case that kept you awake. I took the liberty of looking at the papers. Rather straightforward if anything. You lost, I assume?

Adam was too tired to effect shock at this latest breach of protocol.

- Yes.
- Quite unfair. But inevitable. Can you describe the man who was following you?
- How do you know I was being followed?
- Adam! Please!
- A small man wearing a gabardine coat.
- Richards. I don't want to ask what you were up to last night. But did you give him the slip?
- Yes.
- Are you sure?
- Yes.
- Good. Well, that's an end of that discussion. Have some port.

Whatever was going to happen later that evening, Adam realised that it was in his interests to stay and speak for as long as possible. The meal was over. Now Roly might be prepared to loosen up about Pemberton. Blytheway read his mind.

- Jeremy Pemberton and I were exact contemporaries as it happens. We studied law together.
- What was he like?
- Rather good-looking actually. In a dashing sort of way. But not my type. Bright, too. Very bright. But not as clever as he thought he was. Perhaps because he was handsome ... and clever ... I kept an eye on him from the start.
- So you liked him to begin with?
- For a matter of days. He was too *narrow* for my tastes ... too ambitious. He wanted to *win* everything, wanted to be cock of the run. And he soon had his coterie of admirers and hangers-on ... I wasn't part of it. To be honest I don't think he noticed that I existed until I beat him in the scholarship examinations. That *really* riled him. And to be honest that's why I did it. So, then he saw me as someone he had to beat ... but he never succeeded. And the harder he tried the more evident were his flaws.

Adam stubbed out another cigarette in the lacquer tray. It was overflowing. It was the first time Blytheway had spoken of his past.

- And after student days?
- Well, it's fair to say that he was significantly more successful than I was. *He* certainly had style though the substance was somewhat lacking. So, I just carried on my merry way and let him get on with it. He went from strength to strength whilst I paddled in the shallows.

He got up and emptied the ashtray into a nearby bin and smiled at Adam as he returned to his seat, a look of wry amusement in his eyes.

- Tell me about his first wife ... about Joan.
- Ah yes. Joan. Well. Even *I* could see that she was an absolutely breath-taking woman. She came out in 1913 and could have had the

pick of the bunch. And she chose Pemberton. It was all over the society pages of course. A beautiful rich debutante and a dashing and successful young barrister. If it had been in my nature I could have become embittered and envious of the man. A successful career and a beautiful wife whilst I was overlooked and had to navigate my way around a lot of perverse and unjust laws that would condemn me just for existing. No "married and lived happily ever after" for me!

– Were your ... your leanings well known at that time?
– *My leanings?* What sort of euphemism is that? Well, there were whisperings ... which I did my best to ignore. But one had to be careful. It wasn't long since the trials of Oscar Wilde, which, I confess, I read avidly. One of the reasons I decided to try the Bar actually.

Adam glanced at his watch. It was past one in the morning. Blytheway betrayed no signs of tiredness. He wondered how often he had spoken of those days. Not frequently, if at all, he suspected. Why had he chosen to tell him all these things?

– So they must have got married at about the time the Great War started?
– Yes. Bit of an upset, that was. He signed up at the first opportunity and I will have to give him credit for that. Leaving the delightful Joan behind. Led a charmed life out in the trenches ... medals, mentions in despatches, that sort of thing.
– So that was it between you and him for a few years?
– Oh, not at all. We served on the same front, albeit in different capacities. He was an officer in the infantry whereas I volunteered to work with the ambulance corps. It was during one of those battles that I truly came to dislike the man. Then finally the war was over, we both survived and we both returned to working in the Temple. Then Jenny came along and then Joan died. The poor thing was only twenty-nine.
– And Pemberton started to drink?
– He was in a terrible state and one could understand that. He had lost a truly lovely wife. She was, by all accounts, a very good woman. He was forever getting drunk in El Vinos or other less salubrious places, and boring everyone who came within shooting range with his loss. And his practice went downhill as mine began to take off. So, I took

pity on him and befriended him. But his rages were unbearable and eventually I lost patience with him and told him that he was becoming a self-pitying bore – which he didn't appreciate – and that was the end of my attempt at friendship.

Blytheway paused and looked up at Adam.

- Well. That's enough of the history of my relationship with Jeremy Pemberton.
- What was it that made you really dislike him during the War?
- That, I'm afraid, must be a story for another time, if it is told at all.
- Does any of this explain why you decided to take my case?
- Storman is a good man and when he asked me about it that was one of the things that interested me. Now. It's time you went to bed. It's the second door on the right on the first floor. Caldwell has prepared it for you and your suit and coat are laid out for tomorrow. I'll stay down here. I have a little more work to do for tomorrow.

Adam got up and said goodnight. As he was heading for the door, he remembered his strange experience in the church on the day before he was first introduced to Blytheway. He had seen Julia rise from her prayers and walk towards the door and then she had vanished into nothing.

- Do you believe in ghosts, Roly?
- I don't believe in an afterlife or that we carry on as disembodied spirits when our bodies die, if that's what you mean. But, yes, I believe in ghosts. That we can be haunted by those who have left us whether they are still alive or not. And they can haunt us in the places where we, perhaps, loved them or remembered them, or in faces that remind us of them. Are you haunted, Adam?
- No! I mean … I don't think so.
- Jeremy Pemberton is a haunted man. I saw it in his eyes in the crypt. His ghosts are all around him. He reminded me of how he used to be in the weeks and months after Joan died.

Chapter Fifty-one
(Thursday 20th February 1941)

Storman had been caught in a light afternoon shower as he made his way across Trafalgar Square to the restaurant. He lowered his umbrella as he entered, and his first glimpse of her as he emerged from under it was of two shapely legs crossed at the ankle under the table. Catherine was engrossed in a thick book and did not become aware of him until he was almost in front of her. She gave a little "oh" of surprise and jumped to her feet smiling broadly – beaming, he thought.

- Jack. I'm sorry. I was miles away.
- That looks rather a weighty volume?

Catherine glanced over at it and stroked the cover, slightly embarrassed. She was elegantly dressed and Storman could not remember the last time she looked so poised. She also seemed slightly slimmer than when last they had met, although in a good way. She held up the book to him as they both sat down: *The General Theory of Employment, Interest and Money* by J.M. Keynes.

- It's frightfully interesting, but rather expensive to buy. One of the girls in my department lent it to me.
- How's it going? Or is it too early to say?
- Oh Jack! It should be boring but it's not. There are so many interesting people around and such fascinating conversations. Thank you so much!
- I hadn't expected the work to be so fulfilling.
- Well, the typing and all that isn't really. But they let me do other things as well. And there are women who were at university at the same time as I was and we've got a lot we can talk about. I'd forgotten how much I enjoyed using my brain, even if it is mainly on trivial things.

She was in much better spirits than the last time they had met. After their cup of tea in January Storman had telephoned her and suggested that they have a bite to eat together. They had met in a down-at-heel place in Covent Garden that had known better days. He was able to bring her up to date with developments in the case against Adam and to listen to her worries. The house in Dulwich was cold and dark and she was lonely. Deborah was away in Edenbridge and Adam was, of course, in the Temple. There had been no communication between them other than a short letter containing a further ten pounds and assuring her that he was well. It had contained no mention of his illness.

Her daily routine was meaningless to her, and when the day ended she would make sure that the blackout screens were in place and then turn on the wireless and move the dial across the frequencies looking for news bulletins in English and avoiding the German language stations beaming in. But the news was depressing and, above all, censored so that she ceased to be able to believe in it. She would re-read yesterday's paper after reading today's, and spot the inconsistencies in the reports. And, finally, she had given up trying to listen to the news and instead, alone, cold and lonely, she worried about money, about Deborah and about their future. Catherine had wept as she spoke.

Storman had sympathised and told her he would do what he could. And, several days later, Catherine received a letter from someone in the Board of Trade offering her a secretarial position. She had jumped at it. Storman had allowed her a week or so to settle in before suggesting this further lunch.

– So, it's not all rationing and scrap metal then?
– There *is* all of that. Did you know that there's a shortage of alarm clocks and that means that miners are oversleeping and missing their shifts? But I feel that I'm doing something productive now. There's a sense of purpose – even though everyone hates the Board of Trade – and they seem to know what they're doing.
– How's the pay?
– Forty-eight shillings a week, which isn't bad really. It's just good to have an idea what's going on. And to feel *useful* after so many years. Did you know that they'll be introducing clothing rationing soon? They're working on a slogan for it, and as for my boss, *she's* interested in my ideas.

- She?
- She was at Oxford at about the same time as I was at Cambridge and went into the administrative side of the Civil Service. I'm sure I could have done that if I hadn't got married.

They ordered some food – steak and kidney pie with boiled potatoes – and Storman told her that the meal was on him. The place had filled up, and though the food wasn't particularly good it was clear that this was a popular venue for the Civil Service. Catherine ate delicately, the brick of a book balanced on her side plate.

- So. What do you talk about other than work?
- All sorts. There are quite a few intellectuals and ... leftists I suppose. But not at all like the caricatures you read about in the *Daily Sketch*. My boss knows the Bloomsbury set and talks about "free love". She doesn't believe in marriage, you know.

Storman listened as she spoke, her face animated and her eyes alive again.

- It seems to be doing you good.
- How's Adam?

He had wondered how long it would be before she raised the subject.

- A lot better. He's put on a bit of weight and seems to be better dressed than he used to be. I think Blytheway's behind it. He seems to be busier work-wise than when he was with us. I don't think Arthur went out of his way to help him along.
- Arthur always was a snob.
- It's funny, you both seem to be doing much better since ...

Storman stopped himself but it was too late. He had hoped to build the conversation towards the possibility of some sort of reconciliation. Catherine coloured.

- I'm sorry. I didn't mean it to come out like that.

347

- What's happening with the trial?
- To be honest, I don't really know. Pemberton's getting jumpy about it. I can't imagine Adam's particularly calm at the prospect. Have you been asked to be a witness?
- No.
- I didn't think Blytheway would want to call you, and as the hearing's only two and a half weeks away –
- Two and a half weeks?!
- I'm sorry. You haven't heard. Pemberton got the date pulled forward. He'd been boasting that he could get it over with before Easter.
- Two and a half weeks? But that's only a fortnight on Monday.
- It means it's nearly over. One way or another.
- What's Pemberton got to be jumpy about anyway?

Storman had realised that he shouldn't have mentioned Pemberton as soon as the words left his lips, but he had still been recovering from his earlier gaffe. There was no way of distracting Catherine from her question and so he decided to tell the truth.

- Well ... it may be that Adam has a defence to Pemberton's allegations.
- A defence?!

A mixture of confusion and cautious relief crossed her features.

- It's not good news, I'm afraid, Catherine.
- I thought it couldn't be.
- It seems that Jenny Pemberton is going to provide her step-mother with an alibi. Apparently, she is likely to say that on the days when Adam was supposed to be at the Stafford Julia was having tea at the Ritz with Jenny.
- Oh.
- So. To put it bluntly, Adam has a defence against the allegations about Julia; but that still leaves him in the hotel with a prostitute.
- That's *utter* nonsense!

Catherine spat the words out so vehemently that the lunch-time chatter from surrounding tables died away. Storman was embarrassed and looked down at his now empty plate. When he looked up again Catherine was staring at him defiantly. He reached over and took her hand, then whispered:

  – Look. Catherine. I know that you want to see the best in Adam but the evidence is all pointing one way.

She allowed his hand to stay on hers. Her eyes were smouldering.

  – It's complete rot! Adam's a bloody fool. But he's not such a fool as to take a prostitute to a hotel, provide his identification and sign himself in. That's putting a bulls-eye on his chest or on his … on his … nether regions.
  – But what other explanation could there be, Catherine?
  – I know my husband, Jack. There's only one person this benefits. And that's Julia.

Storman saw the point without the need to argue it further. Once the provision of ID became compulsory, why did Adam persist in going to an expensive hotel and checking himself in?

  – Anyway. There's no guarantee that Jenny will actually give evidence. I think that's what Pemberton is counting on.
  – Why shouldn't she? If she's gone this far?
  – She still hasn't provided Julia's lawyers with a statement. Without that the whole alibi is likely to fall away.
  – Either way I'll be entitled to a divorce.

Catherine, still looking into his eyes, was breathing heavily now. She withdrew her hand from his and, with her forefinger, traced figures of eight across the cover of her book. Storman listened to the diminishing hum of fellow diners and the sound of plates and cutlery being collected and stacked, and motioned for two cups of tea and the bill.

  – How's Deborah?

She came back from her trance.

- All right. Well, not really.
- Why not?
- I miss her, Jack … and the bombing has eased off in the last month or so.
- It's still not safe to bring her back.
- It's not just that.
- What then?
- That man I mentioned to you. I have a bad feeling about him.
- Is that all it is?
- Something in Deborah's letters doesn't sound right. I need to go and see her. Talk to her. But it's impossible to get away before Easter.
- Can it wait until Easter? We'll be a bit clearer about the bombing by then. And at least we know she's safe from that out there.
- I suppose it can wait until Easter.
- And it should all be over by Easter.

He bit his lip a third time. He hadn't been talking about the war or the Blitz.

Chapter Fifty-two
(Thursday 27th February 1941)

Julia emerged from the church and headed down through Cloisters. From his window in Lamb Building Adam watched her as she went. He picked up his cigarette by the pin speared through the filter and sucked hard until he felt his lips burning, then pulled it away and inhaled deeply before blowing a long trail of smoke out of the open window. The last edge of it caught in his throat and set off a spasm of coughing. He eased the butt off the pin and added it to an overflowing ashtray. Stubs and ash. No wasted tobacco. He opened a desk draw and pulled out a paper bag, then carefully tipped the contents of the ashtray into it before depositing it in his litter bin.

Cigarettes were a luxury and his intake was increasing. He had started buying Turkish brands. He pulled out a Pasha, put the pin in place, and lit up again. Acrid smoke soon surrounded him before being caught on a slip of wind and slithering out of the window. It was cold outside but even he could not bear the noxious smell. He looked at his watch. Time for the next part of the day's timetable. Blytheway was striding past the church and up Inner Temple lane, a notebook in hand as he headed over to Court. A clerk would follow with his papers. Once the Court began sitting he would probably go and check for a note from Julia, more out of habit than any expectation.

He had begun to fit into an almost comfortable routine in his new chambers, and the first time he had recognised this he had felt a shudder as he realised how easy it must have been for Blytheway to watch him each day as he went into the church. He had seen very little of Blytheway since the evening of their dinner. He had been woken the following morning at about 8 a.m. by Caldwell, who brought him a cup of tea.

- Thank you Caldwell. Is Mr Blytheway still here?
- I'm afraid he's left for the morning, sir. He asked me to draw him a hot bath at 6.30.
- He was up very early!

– I don't believe he went to bed, sir. I have taken the liberty of pressing your suit for you.

Blytheway was striding off to Court by the time Adam made it into chambers that morning. He gave his usual cheery greeting and then was on his way. And that had been the pattern for the following two weeks. Blytheway would come in early, head off to Court most days, and then in the evening a conference would be waiting for him in another case. He had had little time for small talk.

Adam brushed some cat hairs off his lapels and looked over at the chair in the corner where Delia was sleeping. He had taken to bringing her into chambers when he wasn't particularly busy. No one seemed to mind. He would only ever do so, however, when wearing one of his old suits. The Jermyn Street one Blytheway had persuaded him to buy was kept for the days when he had clients. He didn't want to get cat hairs on it. He was going to need it more than ever in the three weeks that lay ahead and so he had taken it to the dry cleaners.

Novak's trial was due to start on Monday; the case had been assigned to Mr Justice Sherdley. His own case was to begin the following Monday; no judge had yet been assigned, and the week after, the case of McKechnie versus McKechnie and Bateman was listed for hearing. He had instructed his clerks to put in no new work. He had much to prepare. But in three weeks' time, one way or another, it would be over.

It would be over. He felt a pang of sadness at the finality of those words. It was already over. He was fooling himself. It was over between him and Julia. The pain he felt at the thought of her had dimmed to a constant throb. He thought of her walking away from the church that morning, of that vision he had of her rising from her pew and then disappearing into air, and a host of other memories crowded in on him without warning. That first kiss in Middle Temple Gardens; the romantic (he shuddered slightly at the word) way they found to communicate; those days in Green Park before Agnes could speak, and all the afternoons in the Stafford. Times spent in a private universe. But now he could hardly remember the sound of her laughter or the way her voice tinkled when she was happy. It was as though all those memories belonged to someone else. And, in a sense, they did. They were no longer his. And he was going to tell a court that there were no such times, no such memories.

It was already over for him. His marriage would surely end and he would be ruined financially. Blytheway, who had carefully avoided endorsing Adam's protestations of innocence, had told him that these things would pass and be forgotten, that his career and his life would carry on. But it did not feel that way to him. He looked around his room. The cat still slept, the remains of some fish-paste in a bowl on the floor. Blytheway had lent him some ornaments, pictures and peacock feathers, and this had imported an elegance to his surroundings which he was unused to. The crystal paper-weight was in its usual place on his desk. His collection of paperbacks took up several of his shelves but now, on the bottom shelf, there was a small row of briefs for the weeks ahead, suggesting that life would indeed continue after the end of Pemberton's claim against him.

He shook himself. He had to get on with his work. But first he would go down to the Clerks' Room to check that there was nothing in his tray that needed to be dealt with.

His tray was empty save for a plain white envelope with familiar hand-writing across the front. It was from Deborah. He slit the envelope open with a paper-knife and headed back to his room, unfolding the Basildon Bond as he went. It was, for his daughter, a lengthy letter. She wrote at length about her lessons, her day-to-day activities and the friends that she had made. She told him how much she missed him and how she hoped that he and Catherine would get back together soon. And how she missed London and their home in Dulwich. Her writing became increasingly scrawled as the letter continued and Adam realised that she must have been setting her thoughts down late into the night.

... And Daddy. When I do come back can we get a new kitten? I know that you were sorry about Socks and that Mummy was angry with you about it. But I don't blame you for it. Really I don't.

Oh Daddy, I really want to come home. Mummy says that the bombing has got a lot less bad in the past few weeks and I'm sure I'll be safe. I don't want to be here anymore. I don't <u>like</u> it here. My room is really cold and dark and I get scared here at night. I don't like all the people here either.

I'm really tired, Daddy, so I better finish now. Please write to me soon. I miss you.

All my love,
Deborah xxxx

Adam stared at the final pages of the letter for a long time. He felt his shoulders sagging and he sat down heavily behind his desk. Then he read the whole letter again. He didn't know what to do. He would write a long letter back that evening.

He put the letter into his middle drawer and opened his notebook. On the first blank page he wrote the word "Novak". He wrote himself an inventory of the case. He had all the evidence that the prosecution was going to rely upon. He had his notes, taken in his old room, on the cardboard cylinder containing the plans of the waterworks, and the bomb-making instructions. He had the statements of Novak and Milo Hoffer and the unsigned statement of Katya Hoffer. Jones had been able to arrange a further meeting at which he, Jones, alone attended with Novak and showed him these documents, but that meeting had yielded nothing of value. Novak was still angry about Adam's determination to call Katya, and stated again that he forbade it.

Adam drew a line under these notes and in large bold letters he wrote out the words "KATYA HOFFER". How did she fit in? Why wasn't she telling the truth? What had she done? And if she hadn't done anything, who was she protecting? And why were Novak and her husband protecting her? Adam was convinced that they were. And so, regardless of Novak's protestations, he had instructed Jones to go ahead and have a witness summons served on her. Jones, with considerable misgivings, had done so, and had taken it upon himself to go out again to Leytonstone. For good measure he had taken a sub-poena addressed to her husband as well. By Jones's (very detailed) account it had not been a pleasant task.

The day after his final visit to Novak, Jones had taken the train out to Leytonstone again. It was still light and he detoured into the street where Novak had been arrested. It was part of a non-descript red brick terrace. Looking at the façade shed no light for him on the situation. After staring up at the building for several minutes he proceeded on to Old Kings Road, counting his steps as he went. The two addresses were no more than four hundred paces apart.

Jones had knocked on the door and stood back a few yards from the front door. It had been opened cautiously by Milo Hoffer, peering timidly from behind the latch stile. Seeing Jones, he had let out a deep breath and opened the door more fully. Jones saw Katya in silhouette behind him, her hair thick and loose.

– Come in. Come in. Have some tea. What news? What news?

– Thank you. But no tea for me. I can't stay long.

Jones had allowed himself to be shown into the room where some weeks earlier he had interviewed Katya Hoffer. It was unchanged. Katya had not followed them into the room and had moved instead towards the kitchen.

– Mrs Hoffer. I'm afraid I need to speak to you again. But I will be very brief, I promise you.

– Come on, Katya. Mr Jones says he won't be long.

Katya Hoffer had sidled into the room and, when the light from the window caught her face, Jones was taken aback again by her delicate beauty. She hovered by the door. Jones, who had not taken a seat, went over to her and, with his arm behind her shoulders, ushered her further into the room before closing the door behind him. At the sound of it clicking shut, Katya had started and spun round, a look of panic and fear across her features.

Jones had taken the summons from his pocket and handed it to her. She took it, bewildered, looking first at the heavy paper and then at Jones before looking back again at the document lying unopened in her hands, cradling it as though it were a wounded bird. Milo Hoffer came across the room to have a look at it, and at that point Jones handed him the second sub-poena. He, as confused as his wife, was the first to speak.

– What is this?

– I'm afraid I've just served you and Mrs Hoffer with witness summonses.

He felt himself reddening.

– It was on the express instructions of Mr Falling, Mr Novak's barrister.

– I'm sorry. But I am not understanding you. What does this mean?

– These documents require you and Mrs Hoffer to come to the Central Criminal Court – the Old Bailey – between Monday 3rd March and Wednesday 5th March to give evidence on behalf of the defence. For Mr Novak.

Katya screamed and dropped the summons, as though it carried a plague.

– No! No! I cannot go. I will not go. You cannot make me go!

Her hands went up to her hair and she began pulling and twisting it. Her shoulders hunched and she bent almost double, letting out a long moan which ended in a sob.

– I'm afraid you must. If you do not come, you will be forced to attend. The tipstaff will be sent to collect you and you can be put in prison if you do not obey the summons.
– Prison?

The word emerged like the pipe of a flute from the hunched-up body. And then

– Prison!!!

This time like the bellow of a horn. She straightened up and looked straight into Jones's eyes. Her face had drained of colour and was contorted with hatred.

– Prison!!!

And she ran at Jones and started clawing at his face, trying to get at his eyes. Jones brought his hands up to protect himself and she started pulling at what remained of his hair, screaming and swearing. She had lapsed into Czech and he did not understand what she was saying. Meanwhile, Milo Hoffer was pulling at her, trying to get him off him and saying "Katya" "Katya" again and again.

Finally, he was free of her. He looked up. Milo had pinned her arms against her sides and she was breathing heavily, her whole body lifting with every breath. Her eyes, red in that white mask, were full of tears.

– I'd better leave.

Jones went out into the hall and then left the house. He felt his heart pounding and his body began to shake. He stood for a while to see whether either of them would emerge but the door remained open and neither Milo nor Katya came to say goodbye or even to close the door. Then, after a few minutes, he turned around and headed back to the station. He would have to prepare two affidavits of service. He would keep the details as prosaic as possible and save the full story for Adam Falling. He felt a deep sense of unease at what had just happened. He would tell Falling that as well.

Jones's unhappiness had been so palpable that, as he related the story, Adam was seized by uncertainty. He remembered Blytheway's tutting disapproval of that course of action. But a decision had to be made and he was the one who had to make it. Milo and Katya Hoffer would be at court on Monday. He needn't call them to give evidence. That final decision could wait. And if he hadn't sub-poenaed them and Novak were to change his mind on the day of the trial, there would have been no way that Adam could have ensured their attendance at such late notice. On balance, despite the disapproval of Jones and Blytheway, he felt he had done the right thing. He would have one last conversation with Novak in the cells under the Central Criminal Court and try, then, to make him change his mind.

He looked at the page of the notebook on which he had written and circled the words "Katya Hoffer" and realised that he had made no notes but had simply been doodling. He'd sketched out the matchstick outline of a scaffold and noose. His heart lurched and he reached for another Pasha, pinned it and lit it. Then drawing deeply on the offensive cylinder of tobacco, he hurriedly crossed through his scribblings. It looked hopeless for Novak. His defence was that he was innocent. But he had no answer to the body of circumstantial evidence that would, no doubt, be deployed with great skill by Peter Preston KC as he sought to extend his hundred per cent conviction record.

He turned to a fresh page in his notebook and wrote down the words "Arnold Bateman". Adam was convinced that Bateman had been having an affair with Mrs McKechnie. If Pemberton persuaded the judge that this was indeed the case, Bateman would have to pay all the costs of an extremely expensive legal battle. The damages could also be astronomical. Only three weeks earlier, in a case called Penny v Penny & Spackman, a doctor had been ordered to pay £1,000 in damages after a twelve-day trial.

And ordered to pay the costs of three KCs and four junior barristers. That case had lasted twelve days. Bateman's costs would not be so high; there was only one KC and three junior barristers. And Falling was doing it for free. But the damages could easily be as high, if not higher. Bateman had £10,000 at his disposal. The fruits of the insurance policy on his wife's life.

Roly's instinct had been to follow the money. But he freely admitted that he knew far less about the case than Adam did. Follow the money? Why not "Cherchez la femme"? In this case "la femme" was Victoria McKechnie. She was McKechnie's wife and Bateman had been sleeping with her. End of story. So why did Blytheway favour the former analysis? Adam thought back to the night of his dinner. It was at the story of the inquest notes that Blythway's attention picked up. It wasn't the lie. It was the reason for the lie. Which was the lie and which was the truth? Was it in the timing of when Marjorie Bateman was run over? Was it in the fact that the Batemans and the McKechnies had been out together that night? Arnold Bateman and the McKechnies had told precisely the same story to the coroner. Had they told the truth? Or were they conspiring together to tell a false story about the timing, or even the cause of her death? Suddenly Pemberton's throwaway words came back to him:

– Poor Bateman. His dear wife is lying dead in the road and he's in bed with Mrs McKechnie.

And suddenly a cloud cleared in his mind. McKechnie hadn't told Pemberton, or any of his legal team, about what was in the inquest notes. Whatever he had said about the death of Marjorie Bateman, if anything, he hadn't told his lawyers the story that he had told the coroner. Adam was as sure as he could be that Victoria McKechnie's version of events on that night would also differ from what she had said at the inquest. He, Jones and Blytheway were the only ones who knew about this. And Bateman, of course. But Bateman had done all he could to prevent him finding out. There had been a collective lie. But what was the reason for the lie? Could it be that Marjorie Bateman was murdered, by her husband, or McKechnie, or all three of them? Killed by Bateman because she had found out about his affair with Victoria McKechnie? Or simply killed for the insurance money? He saw now why Blytheway had immediately concluded that he should be following the money. But how did that help him on giving

Bateman a defence? It was hardly a defence to a claim of adultery to pray in aid murder or conspiracy to murder. The evidence still pointed to adultery and that was all that the court was being asked to determine: did Arnold Bateman have sex with Victoria McKechnie?

Adam pulled out the notes he had written at Romford Town Hall and turned to the last page, where he had scribbled out Marjorie's injuries. A massive injury to the head, crushing injuries to the spine and legs and multiple lacerations. Death, so the coroner had concluded, must have been almost instantaneous. It didn't sound like murder. Unless Marjorie had been pushed into oncoming traffic? However, if Marjorie Bateman had not died, Arnold Bateman would not have received the insurance money. And if Arnold Bateman hadn't received the insurance money, would McKechnie have gone to the expense of these proceedings? And if it was only because Bateman now had money, when did McKechnie find out about the adultery? Pemberton had implied that it was on the night of Marjorie Bateman's death that his client had discovered the adultery. Indeed, that they were having sex at the time of Marjorie's death. If Blytheway was right, then Adam needed to know a lot more about Marjorie Bateman if he was to find his way to the truth. He remembered Blytheway's laughter over pre-prandial drinks. How was truth supposed to help him anyway?

Under the words "Arnold Bateman" he wrote "ask him about Marjorie". And then drew a line across the page and turned over to a fresh sheet and wrote the words "Julia Pemberton" before crossing this out and putting simply "Pemberton" in capital letters. The final hearing was only ten days away now. Jones had tracked down Betty, met her by arrangement in a Lyons' tea house and got her to sign a statement. He had a photostatic copy of it. She had been as good as her word and corroborated his story. There had been no mention of the death of her husband or of when she began working as a prostitute. That represented a worrying glitch in the timing for him. But – he took a deep breath – that was only one lie amongst a whole pattern of dishonesty on his part. He was getting ready to perjure himself, to try and pervert the course of justice. And he was using Betty to help him, to conspire with him. She had been sub-poenaed to attend on the second day of the trial. He had little doubt that she did not realise how serious were the consequences of lying on oath for money. What right did he have to put her in that position?

Then there was all Pemberton's circumstantial evidence against them.

If Pemberton's Counsel persuaded the Court that Adam had indeed been going to the Stafford with Julia, the corollary of that was that he, and Julia, and Betty, had been lying to the court. He wrote on the otherwise blank page "Jenny Pemberton". If she gave evidence on behalf of Julia that would carry enormous weight. Pemberton would have to argue that his own daughter was lying. But would she? Adam remembered Blytheway's instinctive doubts about her evidence. What had Blytheway found out? What was he withholding from his client? Why hadn't Jenny signed a statement?

He felt something rubbing against his legs. It was Delia. She mewed plaintively. He looked at his watch. It was already 4 p.m. He had missed lunch again and his ashtray was again overflowing with butts. The room was acrid with the smell of Turkish cigarettes. He opened a drawer and brought out the remains of the tin of fish-paste, took it across the room and scooped it into the saucer with the serrated edge of the lid. The smell made him hungry. Delia crouched down beside her bowl and began eating, oblivious to Adam's presence. He stretched his arms out towards the ceiling and gave a silent yawn. His back ached. He ought to find something to eat, have a cup of tea.

He went back to his desk and closed the notebook, then headed for the door. Someone knocked before he reached it. It was Caldwell, slightly out of breath from the stairs and holding a dinner jacket and trousers, wrapped in cellophane.

- Come in. Come in. Good to see you, Caldwell. How can I help you?
- Mr Blytheway asked me to come and see you, sir. He asked that I give you this.

Caldwell handed over the suit. It was the one he had worn when dining with Blytheway.

- I don't understand.
- Mr Blytheway asked that you try it on. I am happy to wait outside until you are ready.
- Look, Caldwell. This is very kind of him. But I don't have any braces in chambers.
- Please try it on.

Then Caldwell excused himself and left the room. Adam felt he had little alternative but to do as he was asked. He placed himself to the side of the window, slipped off his shoes and climbed out of his suit trousers. He pulled on the new pair and, to his surprise, they fitted him perfectly. There was no need for braces. The jacket, similarly, had been taken in so that it felt as though it had been made for him. He understood now why Blytheway had scrutinised him so carefully, had put a forefinger into the front of his trousers and said "three inches" to himself. He went to the door and let Caldwell back in. Then did a turn so that the butler could see the dinner jacket from all angles.

– It's a perfect fit!

Caldwell smiled and the scar on his face creased as he did so.

– Mr Blytheway was confident that it would, but he wanted to be sure. He asked me to convey his compliments to you and his apologies for being so busy of late. He has a number of suits that, for reasons of age, he can no longer fit into as comfortably as he would wish. He has arranged for them to be altered in the same way as this one but wanted to be sure that the measurements were right before commissioning the other alterations.
– That's extremely kind … and quite unnecessary. Please pass on my enormous thanks for this suit but it would not be right for me to trespass further on Mr Blytheway's kindness.
– But I'm afraid Mr Blytheway was quite insistent. He asked me to say that with the weeks ahead that are awaiting you, you will need to look your very best. I will come back on Friday with the other suits. Goodbye now, sir. Until Friday.

And with that he slipped out of the door and was gone.

Chapter Fifty-three
(Monday 3rd March 1941)

Tomas Novak was standing to attention under a spotlight. Then Katya shrieked and ran towards him, entwining him in her arms. And suddenly she was a kitten rubbing herself up against his calves.

 – On the count of three, I will tell you everything. One … two …

There was an almighty bang. Novak and the kitten disappeared through the floor. There was a sickening snap and all that remained in the spotlight was a black square hole in the ground and a thick rope, swinging slowly and creaking over the abyss with the weight it carried. Two white hands emerged and Katya pulled herself back into the room. She said:

 – You should have listened more carefully.

The blue mist that had been swirling around the room coagulated into a human form and shimmered towards him.

 – The evidence. Sweetheart. Always start with the evidence. And don't forget to polish your shoes.
 – Have you got a cigarette, Roly? I'm dying for a cigarette.

The cobalt ghost lost shape, becoming iridescent. It became a seething mass of shifting colours gradually resolving into crimson. Pemberton's bloody ghost stood before him.

Don't drink anymore. And I've never smoked. Bad for the health in my view. Don't care what they say in their advertising. But the last time around cigarettes were better than money.

Adam woke with a start. It was cold and everything was black. Slowly the contours of his bed became visible. Delia was curled up next to him sharing the warmth of his body. He raised himself into a sitting position and fumbled for his cigarettes. The flare of the match lit up the room briefly. After lighting up he held it over his watch. It was 3 a.m. He took a long drag, sucking the smoke deep into his lungs, then let out a violent rasping cough. His eyes adjusted to the glow from the tip so that more of his room emerged from the shadows. The "all clear" had sounded just before midnight and then he had fallen asleep. Dawn was still a long way off. He had not slept in an air raid shelter or underground since early December.

He had been having that nightmare, or variations on it, for days but it was becoming more immediate as the trial approached. He thought of Novak, who was probably lying awake in his cramped cell; and Milo and Katya huddled together, or not, perhaps, in their bed, worrying. He finished his cigarette and lay flat again. Delia had not stirred. He placed a hand on her back and felt her rhythmic breathing. Then he turned on his side and tried to go back to sleep. He needed to be rested for the morning.

Sleep would not come, so he went through his inventory for the morning. He had polished his shoes. He had five sets of starched high collars and bands. Caldwell had arrived with five well-fitting suits on Friday afternoon and one of these was hanging from a door frame, wrapped in its cellophane against any dust. His papers were in a tidy pile at the centre of his desk in Lamb Building. Blytheway had lent him a copy of Archbold on Criminal Procedure and Practice. His wig and gown were in his blue bag, hanging behind the door. He began to go through the witness statements in his head. He had read them so many times.

Slivers of light appeared around the edges of the blackout material. He reached over to his watch. It was five in the morning. In less than five hours he would have to be at the Old Bailey. The statue of Justice, a sword in one hand and scales in the other, glimmered gold in his mind before finally he drifted back to sleep.

Chapter Fifty-four

(Monday 3rd March 1941)

Peter Preston KC was standing in the front row in Court 6, his hands resting on the wooden lectern, studying his notebook. Behind him his junior, Phillips, was arranging books and files. With more drama than was necessary he placed the cardboard cylinder and its coiled contents on a spare area of his desk.

Adam watched from junior counsel's row. There was a strong smell of furniture polish and fresh paint. He could smell the starch on his collar, which was biting into his neck. He looked down at his hands, holding them out in front of him. The left one trembled, so he put it down quickly on the oak desk and stroked a finger across the smooth varnished surface.

He allowed himself to look around. The courtroom was cavernous. Designed to inspire awe and fear. Far above him was the raised seat reserved for the Judge. To his right was the still-vacant jury box. He turned around to look at the empty dock; a bevelled wooden hand rail topped a garrison of iron bars. At the back of the court in the far right-hand corner as he looked there was a large metal door. Novak would be produced from there. Adam had never been in the holding area behind that door.

His alarm had gone off at 7 a.m. and he'd jumped out of bed. He washed himself as well as he could in the hand basin and checked his hair. He had had it cut on the Saturday. Then he pulled on the new suit trousers and a clean white shirt, struggling as always with the collar studs. He stroked Delia, being careful not to get any hairs on his clothing, and then fed her some milk and fish-paste. Slipping on his jacket and overcoat he descended to Inner Temple Lane and made his way to Lamb Building.

His papers were where he had left them, but a small white note had been placed on top of them:

– Good luck, sweetheart!

He leafed through his papers and notes for an hour or so before leaving for court. It was a mere fifteen minute walk down Fleet Street and across Ludgate Circus. Jones was waiting on the first floor and strode over to greet him. He was not smiling. Adam found himself staring at the lines around the other man's eyes. They were deeper than he remembered them, and the eyes were red-rimmed. Adam seemed to be seeing everything in microscopic detail, hearing every creak in the old building.

– Mr and Mrs Hoffer are over here.

There was a ghost of reproach in his voice that he was not entirely able to conceal. The Hoffers were seated on one of the many benches that dotted the hall. They were huddled in heavy coats with their heads down, like the refugees they were. Milo Hoffer had his arm around his wife's shoulders. Adam, as counsel, was permitted only limited contact with witnesses or potential witnesses. But he was allowed to say hello.

– Mr and Mrs Hoffer. This is Mr Falling, Tomas's barrister.
– Good morning. Thank you very much for coming along today.

Not the most tactful thing he could have said in the circumstances. The Hoffers raised their heads and looked mournfully up at him. Neither spoke. Katya Hoffer was as beautiful as Jones had said she was. Even the dark shadows under her eyes could not conceal that. He looked into those eyes with what he hoped was a kindly expression. She tried to remain impassive as she stared back at him. Lurking in her eyes he saw something that unnerved him. Terror. He turned to Milo Hoffer.

– I'm going to do everything I can for Tomas. Trust me.

Milo Hoffer sniffed and gave the barest acknowledgement to his words. Adam looked at his watch. 9.15. He had to go to the robing room and change, then he and Jones would go and see Novak in the cells. He left Jones with the Hoffers and made his way up to the top floor. Preston was already there, adjusting his wig in one of the full-length mirrors. He did not acknowledge Adam's presence.

Ten minutes later he and Jones stood together in front of a large metal door and waited to be admitted. The door clanked open and they went through. There was a maze of cells under the court rooms. Novak had a cell to himself, for his own protection. Adam peered through the spy-hole and saw him sitting hunched in the near darkness. The guard unlocked the door, let them through and closed and locked the door behind them. Adam let his eyes adjust to the gloom for a moment before making his way across to his client.

Novak was thinner than ever. He was wearing a suit and tie and he had been given a haircut that made him look almost dapper. But his eyes were dark and showed no ray of hope. He held up a loose hand to shake Adam's, then gripped it firmly and would not let go. The grip was not friendly.

- You must not make Katya give evidence. I forbid it.
- It is in your interests that she gives evidence for you. Your life may depend upon it.
- I forbid it! I forbid it!
- Your life is at stake, Mr Novak.

Novak gave out a roar and threw aside Adam's hand.

- I would rather die than that she give evidence!
- You're not thinking clearly, Mr Novak.
- Not thinking clearly?! I have done nothing but think for the past three months. I would rather die!
- Listen, Mr Novak ... Tomas ... we have limited time. Is there anything that you haven't told us? Is there anything we should know that you have not passed on to us?
- I would rather die!
- I must just run through what is going to happen over the next two or three days.

Novak slumped back down onto the bench against the wall. He no longer appeared to be listening. Adam carried on anyway.

- You will be taken from here to a holding room behind the court itself and then brought into the dock. It's a very big room but do not be intimidated by that. The charge will be put to you and you must plead not guilty. A jury will be chosen to hear your case. Then counsel for the prosecution, Mr Preston, will outline the Crown's case to the court and after that he will call his witnesses. Jones has some paper and a pen for you to use. If there is anything that is said that you disagree with, write it on the paper and he will hand it to me. I will ask his witnesses questions, and when they have finished I will call you to the witness box to give evidence. You will have to make an affirmation that you will tell the truth. I will ask you questions and then Mr Preston will cross-examine you. After that I will call witnesses in your defence. Mr and Mrs Hoffer are here and will be available to give evidence for you.

– I do not permit it.
– You can always change your mind.
– I would rather die.
– After the evidence is finished Mr Preston will sum up his case to the jury. Then I will do the same and finally the judge will also sum up. Then the jury will retire to consider their verdict.

Novak sat still and looked at his hands. He said nothing for a long time and it became clear that he had no more he wished to say. He allowed each of them a limp handshake before they returned to the main hall.

The courtroom was filling up. A clerk had come in to sit at the desk in front of the judge's seat and one or two members of the public had come into the public gallery high above Adam on his right. Preston was sitting down, legs crossed and staring into the middle distance. He had made no eye contact with Adam. Adam looked back again at the metal door leading to the holding room. Novak should be in there by now.

Adam heard a rustling of anticipation at the front of the court and saw an usher moving towards the judge's door. People began to stand in readiness. Suddenly, from behind the metal door, there was the sound of running footsteps and rattling keys. The usher froze and everyone else turned to look at the back of the court, and then chaos erupted as the metal door was flung open. A guard emerged, his face white and eyes bulging, his mouth an O of shock. He was shouting something but in the crescendo of panic Adam could not make it out. Then he realised that the man was pointing at him and beckoning him urgently to come over. Adam dropped his notebook and ran to the back of the court with Jones fast on his heels. The guard opened a door in the panelling and almost pushed Adam into the holding room.

Novak was sitting on a bench and breathing heavily, his head down. His arms were being held at his sides by two other guards, also blowing hard. Adam noticed that he was no longer wearing a tie. As he got closer he saw a harsh and ragged rope mark across Novak's neck.

– Stupid bastard!

one of the guards shouted. And then to Adam:

– Bloody idiot tried to top himself.

He loosened his grip a little on Novak's arm and sat down heavily next to him.

– We found him with his tie in a noose round his throat. He was going red and his neck was bulging over the tie so we couldn't untie it. Had to cut the bloody thing off. Then we found this.

The guard held up a short piece of flex.

– He tied that just as tight under the tie but with the knot on the other side. Bloody nearly got away with it.

Adam put a hand on Novak's shoulder.

– Tomas. Are you all right?

Novak shrugged the hand away and said nothing. The usher poked her head around the door to find out what was going on. Mr Justice Sherdley had been stalled in the outer hallway and was becoming impatient. Adam said to the guards:

– He's not fit to stand trial. Look at the condition he is in.
– No bloody chance. He's standing trial all right.

368

– I'm going to ask to have the case adjourned.
– No you're bloody not!

Then Adam and the guards were all shouting at once, Jones tugging at Adam's sleeve.

– Stop it! Stop it! Shut up! I want the trial to go ahead!

It was Novak.

– Are you sure, Tomas?
– Don't call Katya.

Novak was breathing more normally now. He looked up at Adam and Jones.

– I'm ready.

They bundled their way back through the metal door and down into the well of the court. Adam's wig was lopsided and he adjusted it as he made his way back to counsel's row.

– Fine client you've got there, Falling.

Preston smiled icily in his direction.

– Not a very good hangman though is he? Never fear. We have a very good one waiting for him.

Adam said nothing and resumed his seat. Jones behind him did likewise, smoothing the remains of his hair and trying to make himself look invisible. The public gallery had filled up – no official secrets were going to be divulged in open court – since the ruckus had broken out. Adam heard behind him the sound of Novak shuffling into court between the two guards.

The usher, back by the judge's door, opened it and barked out "Court rise," and in a flow of crimson and white Mr Justice Sherdley entered, looked at the assembly, slight puzzlement playing across his features, bowed, and sat down. The assembly bowed back and resumed their seats.

Peter Preston KC stood up to address him but was waved back into his seat. The judge looked in Adam's direction.

– Mr Falling. Would you mind telling me what is going on?
– My Lord, I apologise for the inconvenience to your Lordship. As you know I represent Mr Novak. Mr Novak has found these proceedings extremely stressful and I am afraid that he attempted just now to take his own life.

The judge leaned forward and removed his spectacles.

– And how, may I ask, did he do that?

Adam explained as the judge listened intently.

– Mr Falling. These are, of course, very serious charges. One can completely understand that your client must be under considerable pressure. I want to ensure that his trial is as fair as it can possibly be.

He was looking down at the shorthand writer as he spoke.

– Is Mr Novak in a fit condition to continue?
– My Lord, he wishes to do so.
– Do you have that in writing from him – endorsed on your brief?
– My Lord, no. This only happened in the last few minutes.
– I think, if he wants to continue, he should put that wish down in writing.

Before Adam could reply, Novak shouted out from the dock.

– I want this trial to continue!
– Will you control your client, Mr Falling?! He must speak through you or not at all! Very well. There is an official note of what Mr Novak has told me. Bring in the jury panel.

A jury was selected and sworn in. Adam used two out of the three objections that he was allowed so as to exclude two potential jurors who he thought looked inimical to his client. Novak was told to stand and the indictment put. He pleaded not guilty in a clear voice. Adam looked for a reaction on the faces of the jury when they heard his strong Czech inflection. It was clear that, for some of them, Novak's accent was the first piece of evidence for the prosecution.

Then Peter Preston KC stood, bowed to the judge, and smiled warmly in the direction of the jury as he began his opening address.

Chapter Fifty-five

(3rd March 1941)

The jury were looking straight past Adam, fixing all of their attention on Preston, so that he was able to study each of them unobserved. One could learn a lot about the jurors just from the way in which they came forward and took the oath: their accents, their names, their standing. The rest one was free to invent. There were two women, one young and one old, from the East End. An elderly labourer, also from the East End. A veteran from the last war, his medals across his chest – Adam had considered making an objection to him but felt that this would be seen by the man's colleagues as an unpatriotic thing to do. One very well-dressed lady who spoke with aristocratic assurance. Next to her was a man whom Adam thought to be a grocer. There was a wealthy-looking man of retirement age, a Bloomsbury type, a man who was probably from the railways, two men from the city and a Jewish lady. She had been called forward as Feinstein but insisted that she had changed her name to Finlay when she made her affirmation. All in all they were a mixed group of people. But they had one thing in common: they were listening with rapt attention to every word Preston uttered, occasionally allowing themselves a hostile glance in the direction of Novak in the dock.

Adam had never been against Preston before and, grudgingly, he had to accept that he was very good. His voice was friendly but not overly so. It embraced his whole audience and it told them that he was one of them. He was courteous in his introduction of Adam, as if to say, he is also on our side but someone has to defend the man in the dock. It was not the voice Preston had used when he and Adam had met briefly in Stirrup Court in January when the latter had come to look at the plans. An actor's voice, thought Adam. He could have challenged Olivier or Gielgud for their crowns.

He had begun his speech in a conventional way, introducing the players in the case and reminding the jury of the technical terms of the indictment before saying by way of explanation:

– In common parlance the Crown alleges that Tomas Novak was trying to help Herr Hitler and to put our lives … yours and mine … in danger. You will have noticed that he was also charged with conspiring with others … although he is alone in the dock …

He had turned with a flourish to point at Novak, who was sitting with his head down and his hands clenched together between his knees as though he was praying.

– … I will return to our allegation of conspiracy in a moment. But first let me tell you what the Crown alleges to be the history of this matter.

He then set out to them the circumstances of Novak's arrest in the early hours of Monday 16th December and of the lifting of the floorboards in his bed-sitting room.

– And what did the officer find, members of the jury? He found *this!*

He had turned with theatrical slowness to the cardboard cylinder sitting in front of his junior and picked up with exaggerated care, as though he was lifting up gelignite. He'd held it up to the jury, turning it slowly between his fingers so that the seam spiralled in front of them.

– What is so important about *this?* Why does it bring us all to this great building today? But before I turn to the contents of this … canister … perhaps I can give you a brief history of one of the wonders of our city.

And he had proceeded to tell them about the days when sewage spilled unchecked into the Thames, the outbreaks of cholera and the *accidental* (he added emphasis) deaths of *thousands* of *innocent* Londoners. He provided a thumbnail history of the establishment of the sewage system and the creation of the pumping stations dotted around the capital that cleansed the water and made it safe to drink again.

– That purified water would be sent to our great reservoirs and from there it would flow out into our taps, our glasses and our pots and

373

pans. We use it for drinking, for cooking and for washing. Ladies and gentlemen, we all know that we are now engaged in a terrible war which is not of our making. In this war we are all warriors now. The enemy throws death down on us from on high. We are all now on the front line. We are all part of England's armies. We have all of us lost friends ... members of our families ... here and abroad ... or we fear such losses in the dark days ahead. Yes. We are all part of an army. And an army needs food, yes, but it also needs water.

Preston then moved on to describe the Abbey Mills Pumping Station and to explain how it was responsible for their water. Then he paused for a long time and looked each member of the jury, one by one, in the face.

– But what has any of this to do with Mr Novak? I will tell you now what was found in this container.

He held it aloft again for them all to see and they stared at it with renewed intensity.

– This tube contained plans of the Abbey Mills Pumping Station ... and this tube also contained detailed plans for the making of bombs!

The aristocratic lady gasped and covered her mouth whilst all the other jurors turned and gave Novak looks of undisguised hatred.

– The Crown says that it is clear beyond any reasonable doubt that whoever possessed these documents, whoever tried to hide them under the floorboards, was planning to sabotage our drinking water. To poison us from the innocent taps in every kitchen and to cause the deaths of many innocent Londoners.

He paused for effect and looked at the faces of his now captive audience.

– Just as Goering and his aircrews are bombing us from above, the Crown says that Mr Novak wished to attack us from below. To kill us in our own homes.

He turned slowly again towards the dock and looked without speaking at Novak, then turned back to face the jury.

- So. What can I tell you about Mr Tomas Novak? Well, you will have already heard from the way in which he entered his plea to this court that he is *not* one of us. He is a foreigner in our city. He is from Czechoslovakia. He is a Jew.

Mrs Finlay, formerly Feinstein, lowered her head and tried to make herself invisible in the jury box.

- He came to us, so he says, as many did, to escape from the Germans. Our country has shown great compassion and trust and has taken in many who have been persecuted abroad. And we are entitled to have their trust and loyalty in return. But sometimes, members of the jury, our trust has been abused.

Preston then told the jury of the Crown's belief that Novak had entered the country only days before his arrest, of the fact that he had initially stated that this was the case before making up a story that he had been in England for some ten months. Not one witness interviewed by the police, not even his landlord, supported this fairy tale. The truth, he said, was that Novak had entered the country with the intention of causing sabotage and death on behalf of Hitler. Preston then turned to a different subject.

- A little earlier I told you that the Crown accuses Mr Novak of conspiring to make us lose this war. "Who with?" you might ask. Mr Novak is alone in the dock. Unfortunately, we have enemies in our presence, not all of whom are known. Mr Falling will say to you "Ah, but none of Mr Novak's fingerprints have been found on the tube so how can it be that he handled it?" That is perhaps the strongest part of his defence. But the point is illusory, members of the jury. For there were other fingerprints on the tube, not yet identified. Does this not show that, far from Mr Novak being innocent as he insists, he is part of a wider conspiracy of people aiming to destroy our way of life? Mr Falling will tell you that Mr Novak has always denied any involvement in a plot. But, members of the jury, he would say that, wouldn't he?

It was clear that Preston was coming to the end of his speech. He had created an electricity, a bond, between him and each member of the jury. There was no doubt now that they were on his side. Adam looked from the jury across at leading counsel for the Crown. He was standing erect and he was speaking now with a greater familiarity than he had allowed himself at the beginning of his address, as though he and the jury now knew one another well and were almost friends. He held no notes.

– I want to finish, members of the jury, by reminding you of what we are fighting for in this terrible war. We are fighting for our survival of course. But we are also fighting for more than that. We are fighting for our history, our heritage and for everything that over many centuries has made Britain the great country it is. Our composers, our poets, our inventors and our leaders. Ours is a country which has not been defeated for almost a millennium. Ours is the country of Lord Horatio Nelson, of Isaac Newton, Dr Johnson and Sir Francis Drake. Ours is the country of William Shakespeare, the greatest writer the world has ever produced. How did Shakespeare describe us? I will remind you: Act II, Scene i of *Richard the Second*:

> *"This royal throne of kings, this sceptred isle,*
> *This earth of majesty, this seat of Mars,*
> *This other Eden, demi-paradise ...*

And then with great emphasis:

> *This fortress built by Nature for herself*
> **Against infection and the hand of war,**
> *This happy breed of men, this little world,*
> *This precious stone set in the silver sea.*
> *Which serves it in the office of a wall*
> *Against the envy of less happier lands*
> *This blessed plot, this earth, this realm, this England!*

Members of the jury, you, we, are all part of that happy breed. It is this England that you are today called upon to protect. The Crown will be asking you to listen carefully to all of the evidence, for and against, and to convict Tomas Novak of treachery.

How often had Preston used that quotation when addressing a jury in a treason trial? He allowed his words to sink in – in other circumstances Adam felt he would have won a round of applause – and then turned to the judge and said:

– My Lord, I will now call my first witness.

Preston called the officers who confirmed the circumstances of the arrest, the notes of interview and Novak's conflicting stories as to when he arrived in England. He called a fingerprint expert who confirmed that Novak's fingerprints had not been found on the cardboard container. Then he called someone from the London Metropolitan Water Board who confirmed the accuracy of the plans of Abbey Mills Pumping Station and explained its history and the areas of London that it serviced. After that he called an expert witness who confirmed that the instructions for the creation of bombs were viable. Adam asked what questions he could but he had so little to go on. He relied, inevitably, very heavily on the absence of any fingerprint evidence to connect Novak to the plans and bomb instructions, but Preston's reliance on the possibility of a wider conspiracy meant that the jury were not particularly impressed with that aspect of the evidence. He challenged the evidence of the landlord but was met with a vehement rejection of the suggestion that Novak had been his tenant for more than a matter of days. Of course, he put to the arresting officers that Novak had always denied any involvement with a plot to sabotage the water supply, but, again, Preston's words were hanging in the air: *he* would *say that, wouldn't he?* Above all, he was hampered by his conviction that Novak was not telling him the truth.

By the middle of the afternoon the prosecution case had been completed. The jurors, who by the end of the opening were smiling at Preston, avoided Adam's eyes. There could be no doubt but that they wanted to convict.

As easy as shelling peas, Adam thought grimly.

There was half an hour of court time left. Adam rose to his feet, looking over his shoulder at the dock behind him.

– My Lord, I call Tomas Novak.

Chapter Fifty-six

(Tuesday 4th March 1941)

– Thank you very much, Mr Novak. If you could wait there, Mr Preston will have some questions for you.

Adam sat down and drank back a glass of water. His left hand was trembling and he felt sweat running down his back. Preston rose gracefully to his feet and directed a conspiratorial smile towards the jury before turning his attention to Novak, standing forlorn in the witness box. This was a disaster!

Novak had jumped when Adam mentioned his name, and had looked up, bewildered, at his counsel. Slowly, painfully, he had risen to his feet in the dock and was ushered across the court by one of the guards.

Adam had watched as Novak, in his crumpled blue suit, made his way down to the front of the court. He passed close by Preston who was watching him like a pink-faced falcon, his pen to his lips. He climbed into the witness box and, disorientated, looked around him, first at the jury, then up at the judge and finally down towards counsel. His eyes did not seem to be focusing.

– Tomas Novak!

Novak jumped and then looked down into the well of the court for the source of the command. The clerk to the court, in wig and gown, was standing facing him.

– How do you wish to take the oath?
– Affirm.

His voice was barely louder than a whisper.

– Raise your right hand and repeat after me.

He raised his hand to give the affirmation and tried to stand up straight. His shoulders were hunched and his hair unruly. Tie-less, he had buttoned his shirt up to conceal the vivid red wheal across his neck. Suddenly he seemed very small against the majesty of the court room. Adam thought back to the erect and arrogant figure he had first met in December. The haughtiness was gone. He muttered the affirmation following the words of the court clerk. His hand, held up before him, was shaking.

Adam went through the formalities of name and address and of his homeland of Czechoslovakia. There was an audible gasp from several members of the jury when Novak said that his training had been as a physicist. This was an intelligent educated man who would have no difficulty with the construction of a bomb. As he confirmed his previous occupation something of the earlier swagger came back to him, as though this was some validation of his worth. He shook himself, as though waking up, and looked around the court room again, with renewed awareness.

– When did you come to this country, Mr Novak?
– At the beginning of 1940, January.
– How did you get here?
– I took a boat from Gibraltar to Liverpool.
– Did you make friends with anyone on the journey?
– Yes. With Milo Hoffer.
– Mr Milosevich Hoffer is a doctor, is that right?
– So I understand.
– Did you befriend anyone else on the boat?
– No.
– Mr Hoffer had a wife, Katya. Did you meet her?
– I did not. (*A lie, thought Adam.*)
– Mr and Mrs Hoffer presented themselves to the Aliens Tribunal for registration. Why did you not do so?
– Mr Hoffer persuaded me not to.

There was another murmuring from the jury and Adam felt they were adding Hoffer to the list of conspirators and fifth columnists.

- Why would Mr Hoffer wish to do that?
- He persuaded me that I, as a physicist, would be treated differently to him … and his wife.
- How did you live between February and December 1940?
- I survived. I found what work I could. I had very little money.
- When you were arrested you were living in Queen's Road in Leytonstone?
- Yes.
- And how did you find that address.
- Mr Milo Hoffer found it for me. He recommended it to me.

There was another susurration from the jury at the second mention of the name.

- How long had you been living there?
- For about nine months.
- You have heard your landlord tell this court that you had only been living there for a matter of days?
- Well, of course. He is lying. He knows the truth.

Novak's voice, louder now, echoed around the court room. It all sounded so desperately thin. Adam had virtually no ammunition with which to defend his client. At that point Mr Justice Sherdley called a halt to proceedings for the day and, before rising, reminded the jury that they should not discuss the case with anyone and reminded Novak similarly that he could not discuss his evidence or the case with anyone, including his lawyers, whilst he was in the witness box.

Dusk was beginning to fall when Adam and Jones came out onto the streets. Adam had left his robes in the robing room whilst Jones had told Mr and Mrs Hoffer to return again tomorrow, reminding them of the power of the witness summons.

- Preston's going to have a field day.
- Novak's not telling the whole truth, the stupid idiot.
- We're going to have to call Katya, Mr Jones. As things stand there's no way that jury are going to acquit him.
- We can't do that, Mr Falling.

- We may have to.
- I'm not happy about this.
- I'll see you back here at 9.30 tomorrow. I want to get back to chambers before Blytheway leaves.

The hearing had resumed at 10.30 the following day but things didn't improve. The jurors, when they reassembled, pointedly avoided looking at Adam as they filed into court whilst exchanging morning greetings and smiles with Preston. Their mood had hardened overnight. Adam had resumed asking questions but nothing seemed to warm them to him or Novak. The fact that he was of previous good character meant nothing. Novak denied all knowledge of the plans and said he had neither seen nor touched them. He denied all knowledge of any conspiracy. *But he would say that.* Adam had asked him about Katya Hoffer but he categorically denied having any knowledge of her and denied even meeting or speaking with her. Adam was sure that was another lie. But he couldn't cross-examine his own client and to have done so would only make matters worse. And so he sat down and handed the floor to Preston, fearing the worst. Adam refilled his glass from the carafe and looked over at his opponent.

Preston stood silently for at least half a minute, gazing down at his notes. He was carrying a Hunter pocket watch in his waistcoat and the gold chain hung in small crescents across his stomach. He took it out, opened it and looked ostentatiously for the time. Then he bowed to the judge and, turning slightly, smiled at the jury. A smile that said "Welcome to the show". Then he turned to face Novak.

- Mr Novak. You are a liar, is that not right?
- I am telling the truth.
- You ... are ... a ... liar!

Preston practically shouted the words at the man. Novak replied so quietly he was hardly audible.

- I am not a liar.
- When you were questioned by the police you told them you had only just arrived in the country, did you not?
- That was a mistake. I'm sorry.

– You have spent some time telling the ladies and the gentlemen of the jury that you arrived in this country in January 1940.
– That is true.
– If that is true, then when you originally spoke to the police you lied, is that right?
– It was a mistake.
– If what you have told this court is true, then what you told the police was a lie.
– No.
– Your evidence is that you had not just come to this country, is that right?
– Yes.
– So it would not be true to say that you had only just arrived.
– No.
– Thank you. But you see, I must put it to you that you had only just come to this country and your ... story that you came here in January of last year is the real lie. Is that right?
– It is the truth.
– Even your landlord says that you had only just arrived here.
– He is lying.
– So, everyone is lying except you.
– My landlord is not telling the truth.

Preston was again silent for a long thirty seconds. He looked over again at the jury. He was giving them every reason they could possibly need for disbelieving Novak. Then he turned back to Novak.

– Mr Novak, you have no respect for the laws of our country do you?
– But of course I respect the laws of this country.
– You knew that, according to our laws, you were under an obligation to report yourself to the authorities on your arrival, is that right?
– Yes.
– And you did not report yourself did you?
– No.
– So you broke one of the laws of our country?
– That is not how it was.

Again the exchange went backwards and forwards until Novak had to admit he had broken the law. Preston had now established that he did not tell the truth and did not obey the laws of his adopted country. Novak's attempts to evade answers that were ultimately inevitable did not endear him to the jury. Having landed two major blows Preston began toying with his witness. Gradually and with no great haste he took Novak through each stage of the prosecution case and pointed out the absence of any real positive defence to it. Of course, most of the evidence against him was circumstantial but it demanded a better explanation than Novak seemed capable of giving. And, said Preston, in an almost rhetorical question, why should the jury not believe that he had only just entered the country? He had done enough to convict Novak but still he asked question upon question. Adam was wondering why he didn't sit down and let him re-examine, and then he looked up at the clock and realised what Preston was doing.

He wanted to keep Novak in the witness box until 1 o'clock when the court would rise. That way Adam would not be able to speak with him over the short adjournment. There could be no doubt but that Preston had noticed Milo and Katya Hoffer waiting outside court. He wanted to make Adam's decision about whether to call them as difficult as possible.

Mr Justice Sherdley announced that the court would be breaking for lunch and gave the customary warning about discussing the case, then everyone rose. Novak was ushered from the witness box and back through the dock to the cells. Over the one-hour break Adam and Jones again went over whether or not to call any witnesses and if so whom. They both agreed that there would be dangers in calling Milo Hoffer as the jury had clearly formed a negative view of him. Although Hoffer had admitted to Jones that he told Novak not to report, there was little guarantee that he would be prepared to say that in court. Adam returned to the question of calling Katya. Jones was opposed to this. They did not know what she would say and Novak had forbidden it. They could not ride rough-shod over their client's instructions. But Novak's instructions were going to be the death of him.

Preston only had a few minutes of questions when the Court resumed at two o'clock and, in re-examination, there was little Adam could do to repair the damage. Novak walked, head bowed, back to the dock. If the defence case were to end at that point, there was little doubt but that he would be convicted and sentenced to death.

– Yes, Mr Falling?

It was Mr Justice Sherdley. Adam felt a panic rising in his chest. He looked up at the judge and then across at the jury. They were looking at him. Their faces blurred as he looked from left to right. Preston muttered something underneath his breath to Phillips who sat behind him. Jones was tugging at his gown. The usher was standing in the well of the court ready to bring in the next witness. Should he call Milo Hoffer? No. It would not help. He could speak of Novak's good character. No use. Should he call Katya Hoffer? She held the secrets in this case. He heard Blytheway tut-tutting in his ear. He had no instructions to do so. It would be completely wrong. Unprofessional. Novak was facing death. He did not believe that Novak was guilty. The jury were going to convict.

– Mr Falling?

The judge again. More insistent this time. Adam made a decision.

– My Lord. I now call Mrs Katya Hoffer.

A gasp went out around the courtroom and then there was a bellowing from the dock. It was Novak.

– No!

Chapter Fifty-seven

(Tuesday 4th March 1941)

– Mr Falling! Please keep your client in order!

If the usher heard Novak's roar she ignored it and headed out into the vestibule. Seconds later she reappeared shepherding Katya Hoffer in front of her. She had taken off her heavy overcoat and was wearing a dark purple dress, high-waisted so that it showed off her figure. There was muted embroidery on her skirt. She paused at the back of the court, then took a deep breath, which accentuated the fullness of her breasts, and strode towards the witness box, eyes fixed straight ahead of her.

There was a sense of grace about her. Adam saw that the jurors, men and women alike, were following her with their eyes. He understood why Jones had been mesmerised by her. Preston turned obliquely towards Adam and said under his breath:

– Well, she's a pretty little thing, Falling.

Looking over his shoulder he saw Novak sitting bolt upright, his mouth open, transfixed. He had made no further sound. It was his eyes, the pupils dilated, which gave him away. Adam realised that in all his weeks and months in prison this was the sight that he dreamt of night and day. He remembered Novak's despair, on their second visit to him, that Katya had not come to see him. Now here she was, only yards away from him. Her presence seemed to stifle his earlier vehement objections. If he was to face the gallows, better that he should do so after seeing her one last time.

Katya Hoffer climbed into the witness box and peered around her, her luxuriant dark hair framing her face. She looked first at the Judge and made a respectful nod of her head in his direction. Mr Justice Sherdley was also engrossed. Then she looked across at the jury and smiled shyly at them. Finally, she looked at Preston and then at Adam. She did not look towards Novak. The terror that he had seen lurking in her eyes appeared to have gone. Instead, she presented herself as humble and eager to assist.

She raised a dainty hand and repeated the affirmation after the Court Clerk. Her voice was clear and musical, though faintly accented. Adam rose to his feet, introduced himself to her, and took her through the preliminaries.

- When did you come to England?
- In January of last year.
- Who did you come with?
- My husband, Milo.
- How did you get here?
- We came by boat from Gibraltar. I thought we were going to America.

Adam took a deep breath. He indicated to Tomas Novak sitting gaping at her in the dock.

- Did you meet this man on your voyage?

Katya turned to look at the back of the court, her eyes narrowing as if attempting better to focus. There was a long pause.

- No I did not.

Adam, over his shoulder, saw Novak's body slump.

- Are you quite sure of that?
- Yes. I am.

Adam changed tack and realised, as soon as the question was out of his mouth, that he had broken one of the cardinal rules: don't ask a question that you don't know the answer to:

When did you and Milo get married?

Why had he asked that question? Why didn't he ask Jones to find this out when he went to see her? Katya hesitated and for the first time seemed unsure of herself.

- I don't see why that is relevant.
- I think you'd better answer the question, Mrs Hoffer.

It was the judge intervening. She looked at him and then back at Adam, and then, in a far lower voice:

- In October 1939.

October 1939? She had only married Milo Hoffer shortly before they left the country. There is an age difference between them of more than twenty years. Her answer begged a lot of other questions which he did not want to investigate. Realising he had made an error, he returned to his previous line:

- Tell me about the journey from Gibraltar.
- What is there to tell?
- How long did it take, what were the seas like, did you make any friends?
- The journey was ten days. We headed straight out to sea so I thought we were going to America. But the captain was just avoiding mines. We were hunted by German submarines, but fortunately they did not find us. I was very frightened …

The last part was said in little more than a whisper and Adam could tell that she was winning over the jury, who sympathised with her, wanted to like her and wanted to believe her.

- How did Milo Hoffer find the trip?
- He has no sea legs. He was very sick. He stayed below deck.
- Where did you sleep during the journey?
- Mr Falling. I really don't see where this line of questions is taking us. Can we move on please?

Mr Justice Sherdley was becoming impatient.

- I'm sorry, my Lord. I am nearly finished. Mrs Hoffer, where did you sleep?
- I slept under one of the lifeboats.

– Do you remember anything else of significance during the journey?

Adam caught a quick sideways glance from her in the direction of Novak.

– No.

He was getting nowhere.

– When did you first become aware of Mr Novak?
– My husband … Milo told me he had been arrested. My husband met him while he was working in a bookshop near to our home.
– You knew nothing of him before then?

Another almost imperceptible sideways glance.

– No.
– No further questions, my Lord.

Adam was not allowed to cross-examine his own witness. He sat down and then, looking up, saw that the Judge's eyes were fixed on him.

– Mr Falling.

Adam stood at once.

– Yes, my Lord.
– Where does this take us? No doubt you will be addressing the jury in due course on Mrs Hoffer's evidence but I have to say that, from where I sit, it appears to have absolutely no bearing on Mr Novak's case *whatsoever!* I suspect, Mr Preston, that you will have no questions arising out of this evidence.

Katya Hoffer made to leave the witness box as Preston stood up to reply.

– On the contrary, my Lord, there are some questions that I would wish to put to Mrs Hoffer. Please stay where you are just for the moment, madam.

Katya Hoffer froze and then slowly turned back and stood where she had been standing before. Preston turned to face her

- You come from Czechoslovakia do you not, Mrs Hoffer?
- Yes, I do.
- Were you aware that Mr Novak also comes from Czechoslovakia?
- I now know that, yes.
- You gave your address as the Old King's Road in Leytonstone?
- Yes.
- And you have lived there since about March 1940 perhaps?
- About that, yes.
- Are there many refugees from Czechoslovakia living in Leytonstone?
- A few I suppose.
- And you Czech people stick together, I suppose?

Katya Hoffer hesitated.

- Milo and I keep to ourselves.
- Did you meet up with other Czech refugees in your area?
- I don't see the point of this question.

Her first mistake. Preston's voice was moving from the courteous to the forceful.

- It is not for you to see the point of my questions, Mrs Hoffer. Did you meet up with other Czech refugees in your area?
- Yes … I suppose so.
- You would have known about the existence of other Czech refugees in your area?
- Probably.
- Mr Novak was arrested in Queen's Road, Leytonstone. Were you aware of that?
- Yes.
- You must keep your voice up Mrs Hoffer, please answer my question again.
- Yes.
- Do you know where Queen's Road is?

Katya looked around for help but none could be forthcoming. After a long pause:

- Yes.
- It is no more than a quarter of a mile from where you yourself are living, is that not right?
- Yes.
- Are you really expecting this court to believe that you had no knowledge of Mr Novak's existence before he was arrested?

She was becoming flustered and her hands began to flutter around her face. Adam was watching her keenly now and saw again the first hint of fear in her eyes.

- I did not.
- Mr Novak told this court that it was your husband who found him his lodgings in Queen's Road. Are you really telling this court that he did this without telling you anything about it?
- I ... I ... Milo does not tell me everything.

Her voice cracked and Adam could see that the jury, still watching intently, were shifting their views about her. He looked up at the Judge and saw that he was writing furiously, taking a note of everything she said.

- You're not telling this Court the truth are you, Mrs Hoffer?

Preston was aggressive and accusatory now, intimidating the frail young woman in the witness box. He paused and slowly turned to the jury – Adam caught the pink aquiline profile – and gave them a sad conspiratorial look.

- How old are you, Mrs Hoffer?
- I am twenty-eight.
- And how old is Mr Hoffer?
- He is fifty-four.
- Fifty-four? So he is twenty-six years older than you are?
- It does not concern me.

    – And you only married him in October 1939.
    – Yes.
    – Just four months before you came to this country?
    – That is my business.

There was a catch in her voice, which gurgled now with emotion. Her cheeks had gone red and there was a hint of a tear in her eyes. Preston shouted at her.

    – Mrs Hoffer! This is a serious matter! Mr Novak stands accused of treachery and faces a death sentence from this court if he is convicted. You *must* answer my questions.

His tone made her jump.

    – Tell me about your courtship.
    – What?
    – How did you meet Mr Hoffer? When did you start courting? When did you decide to get married? *Why* did you decide to get married?

Preston had let out a stream of questions and it was plain that he was attempting to confuse and upset her. She put her hands to her face and began to sob. Her shoulders began to shake, then she said to the Judge, through tears:

    – Your Worship. I do not see the point of these questions. These are personal things.
    – Mr Preston?
    – My Lord.

Preston was suddenly solicitous. He took out his Hunter and studied the time and then looked behind him at the Court clock on the rear wall. It was 3.30 p.m.

    – I am very sorry, Mrs Hoffer. I did not want to upset you. My Lord, looking at the time it may be that the best course would be to adjourn a little earlier than usual so that Mrs Hoffer can recover herself.

– A commendable approach, Mr Preston.

– I think Mrs Hoffer would be assisted by a drink of water.

Preston produced an unused glass from in front of him and, holding it delicately between thumb and finger, filled it from the carafe before leaving counsels' row to hand it to Katya Hoffer. She took it and drank it back before putting it down in front of her.

– 10.30 tomorrow then,

said Mr Justice Sherdley giving the usual warnings about discussing the case. The court rose and Katya Hoffer was shown out of the court by the usher. Adam took off his robes and wrapped his wig in them.

He gathered up his notes and prepared to leave counsels' row. As he was doing so he turned to have a quick word with Jones.

He did not see Preston's junior, Phillips, walk down to the witness box and, very gingerly, picked up Katya Hoffer's water glass and take it back to Preston.

Chapter Fifty-eight
(Wednesday 5th March 1941)

The day's hearing was about to begin. The jurors were all sitting in the jury box, a new mood of seriousness hanging over them. Preston was writing some notes to himself and Novak was sitting silently in the dock behind Adam. He looked over at Katya Hoffer. She wore a blue dress today. There were dark circles under her eyes and he guessed that she had not slept much the night before. It was 10.28. Adam risked his first glance up to the public gallery. The two rows of seats were full of expectant spectators. They were a mixed bunch. Two old women sitting at the front and next to them a Chelsea Pensioner in his bright red uniform. Various men in suits, aged, Adam guessed between forty-five and seventy. He scoured the back row. There was the same general mix. And then he saw him. As he'd promised, Roland Blytheway was sitting in the far corner of the back row, his eyes hooded.

When the court had risen the previous day it was Adam's first duty to go and speak with Tomas Novak. He and Jones made their way down to the cells. He was not looking forward to the interview. He had specifically gone against clear instructions and it was plain that he had placed Katya Hoffer in a potentially vulnerable position. He wasn't sure where Preston was taking his cross-examination but he had been unnecessarily brutal with her – and then surprisingly concerned for her welfare. It was particularly odd that he should suggest that the court rise early when he appeared to have Katya on the ropes.

Novak was in a strange mood. On the one hand he was angry that his instructions had been disobeyed. On the other he appeared pleased – though he did not say it in so many words – that he had had an opportunity to see Katya. When Adam tried to discuss with him what she was saying, how she was providing no support for him, he seemed almost indifferent, as though he had given up hope. A decision still needed to be made about whether or not to call Milo Hoffer but Adam told Jones and Novak that he wanted to think about that issue overnight. They said their goodbyes and left the cell. The warder turned an enormous key and the bolts slotted into place with a metallic clang. Adam took one last look through the spy-hole and in the gloom saw Novak, sitting as they had left him, staring into space.

Adam had gone straight back to Blytheway's room in chambers, where Roly was waiting for him. The latter had agreed to meet with Adam for a debriefing session on each day of the treason trial, realising how stressful he was finding it. On the Monday evening Blytheway had shaken his head as Adam related the day's events, concluding, as Adam had done, that the case was not going well. Adam had raised the question of calling Katya Hoffer on day two – after all there was nothing to lose –and again Blytheway had counselled against it.

Adam had knocked on Blytheway's door and entered. A pot of tea was sitting on the side table with two cups and saucers.

- You're back sooner than I expected.
- We rose early today.
- So the evidence is finished? You didn't call Milo or Katya Hoffer?
- Er, no. I did call Katya Hoffer.

Blytheway lost his habitual cheerfulness and his expression became grim.

- Oh dear. But, I suppose, no harm's been done. If she has already finished her evidence then she can't have added anything too unexpected into the mix.
- She's not finished her evidence.
- Not finished?!
- She was getting upset so Preston suggested that we rise early so that she could compose herself.

Blytheway's became grimmer.

- I don't like the sound of that at all. Give me your notebook.

Adam handed it over and waited whilst Blytheway read his transcript of the cross-examination.

- This is very helpful but of course it does not give me the *flavour* of how the questions were put.
- That was what was slightly odd. Preston actually whispered to me before she started giving evidence how pretty she was. It was almost the first time he'd addressed a word to me. And then he was very courteous to begin with but got more and more aggressive.
- Hmm.
- It was almost as though he wanted to make her cry. But as soon as she started sobbing he completely changed and was apologetic and friendly and suggested that we rise early for her benefit. He even poured a glass of water for her to drink.

Blytheway, who had been putting his cup to his mouth, put it down so suddenly that the crockery clattered.

- I beg your pardon?
- He completely changed and became apologetic and friendly …
- No, not that bit. You say he poured her a glass of water?
- Yes. I don't see why that is so important.
- He didn't suggest that the usher pour her a drink of water?
- I suppose that's what would normally happen.
- Instead he poured a glass that was in front of him on the bench and then, I assume, gave it to the usher to pass on to Katya Hoffer?
- Now that you mention it, he didn't do that. He actually went out of his way to give it to her himself.

Blytheway leaned back in his chair and stared at the ceiling for a long time. Then:

- Tell me, Adam. How did he hold the glass?
- Between his thumb and forefinger.
- Up near the rim I suppose.

Adam saw abruptly saw the way Blytheway's mind was working.

- Yes. But I don't think we can read too much into it. It was a fairly spontaneous gesture. A kindness.

- Do you think so?
- Why shouldn't it be?
- And would I be right in supposing that he didn't place it in her dominant hand, so that when she drank from the glass she had to change hands?
- I … I … I can't say that I noticed.
- Whatever it was, Adam, it wasn't spontaneous. Did you drink water during the day?
- Yes. Of course.
- And how many glasses did you have in front of you?
- One, of course …
- So why did Peter Preston have two?

Adam shuddered and felt himself going white. He looked up at Blytheway, who was staring intently into his eyes.

- Why for that matter would he want to rise early? I suspect dirty tricks, Adam. There's little I can do but I will come along to Court tomorrow and see what happens.

And so it was that Roland Blytheway now sat discreetly at the back of the public gallery.

- Court rise!

Everyone rose to their feet and Mr Justice Sherdley entered bowed and sat down. Preston rose to continue his cross-examination and threw a malicious smile in Adam's direction before smiling broadly to the jury. Katya Hoffer, in the witness box, tried to ready herself for the onslaught. She was very pale and she swayed away from Preston as if expecting a physical blow. Preston again waited for thirty seconds before asking his first question. His tone was aggressive.

- Mrs Hoffer. Yesterday you told this court a pack of lies did you not?
- I told only the truth.
- You will have to speak more loudly than that. The jury must hear what you say. I repeat, you lied and you lied and you lied.
- It's not true.

Preston turned slowly and picked the cardboard cylinder off the desk behind him. Then, with a forefinger at either end he held it up for her and then the jury to see. Katya's eyes widened and her mouth was a black hole in her white face. The judge was leaning forward in his seat, his pen upraised. The jury too were sitting expectantly. Adam felt his heart sinking. Roly had been right.

- Have you ever seen this before, Mrs Hoffer?
- No. I have not.
- Do you know what it is?
- Of course I do not.
- It contained plans of a water pumping station and bomb-making instructions.
- Then of course I know nothing about such things.

Preston lowered the cylinder and, very delicately, replaced it on the desk behind him.

- I want to go through your evidence with you from yesterday, Mrs Hoffer. First of all you said that you did not know Mr Novak prior to his arrest?
- Yes.
- Then you said that you did not know where he lived prior to his arrest?
- That is true.
- And you told us that you had never been to his room at that address?
- Again that is true.

Preston paused and looked around the courtroom. Adam began counting the seconds. He had got to seventy-five before Preston suddenly shouted out at Katya Hoffer:

- Then how, Mrs Hoffer, do you account for the fact that *your* fingerprints are on the cardboard cylinder behind me?

It was as though an electric charge had gone through the room. All eyes focused on Katya Hoffer as she attempted to come to terms with the question she had been asked. Adam sneaked a look at Novak and saw a look of astonishment on his face, mouth wide open and shaking his head in disbelief. He noticed that some of the jurors too had looked and seen Novak's reaction. He looked back at Katya. There was no disguising the look of terror in her eyes now.

- That cannot possibly be!
- It can and it is, Mrs Hoffer. We obtained your fingerprints from the glass that you drank of yesterday afternoon. The ladies and gentle-men of the jury know, indeed Mr Falling has made great play of it, that Mr Novak's fingerprints are not on the tube but there were cer-tain unidentified fingerprints there. The fingerprints on your glass matched some of the fingerprints on the tube that is sitting behind me – *then to the Judge* – My Lord, we took advantage of the additional time available yesterday afternoon to conduct an urgent forensic analysis of Mrs Hoffer's glass.

Katya looked at her hands and made to wipe them against her dress. It was as though she had shrunk physically. She pressed herself to the back of the witness box, and her eyes, filled with entreaty, darted round the court room looking for help which, so plainly, was not coming to her. Adam put his head in his hands. If he hadn't called her none of this would have hap-pened. Eventually Preston broke the silence.

- Can you please explain, Mrs Hoffer, how it is that your fingerprints are on this tube?

Again, a long silence. Adam stood up and addressed the Judge. Preston sat down.

- My Lord, this line of questioning comes as a complete surprise to the defence. I was given absolutely no notice of it and, as is clear, neither was the witness. It would only be fair if she was given time to com-pose herself as Mr Preston purported to do yesterday.
- I absolutely object, my Lord. The witness must answer these questions.

Both counsel were now standing. Mr Justice Sherdley looked at Preston and then back at Falling.

- I think Mr Falling has a point, Mr Preston. It does seem that your show of solicitude to this witness yesterday was something of a charade.
- My Lord!
- I think I will rise for thirty minutes. Mrs Hoffer. I must remind you that you are not allowed to discuss your evidence with anyone during the break. When you come back I expect you to answer Leading Counsel's question.

Adam rushed up towards the public gallery and bumped into Blytheway, who was moving quickly down the stairs

- You were right.
- We can talk as we are walking … You were also right. Katya Hoffer *does* hold the key. But this is very serious. Preston has caught her red-handed. I was watching Novak from the second that Preston picked up that cardboard tube. It was quite plain to me that he knew nothing about this. He was trying to keep her out of it because she plainly *wanted* him to keep her out of it. But I don't think he knew what she had done.
- What should I do?

They were heading towards the robing room. Blytheway pulled his red bag off a hook and began detaching the collar from his shirt and putting on a high one and bands. He smoothed down his hair in front of the mirror as he talked.

- Well, sweetheart. There's very little you can do at this stage. The cross-examination will have to proceed. But it seems to me that you would be mad to call Milo Hoffer now.

Adam flushed and was immediately grateful for the tip.

- As to what will happen next – well, it depends upon whether or not

Katya decides to speak. But whatever happens, she is likely to be charged with, and equally likely to be convicted of, treason. And we all know what that is likely to mean. Preston is, however, prosecuting Novak today and he will no doubt attempt to enmesh the two of them in a conspiracy together. So, convict Novak and then deal with Katya Hoffer later.

– Oh God!

– I would remind you, Adam, that your client is Novak. Katya Hoffer is *not* your client. You must do what you can to save him. If I am right and he knew nothing of what Katya had done, it is in his interests that you pin as much of the guilt on her as is possible. Row Novak clear. Look at Novak's lies to you and find the reasons for those lies. "Cherchez la femme" would be my bloodhound of choice. As for Katya, she must fend for herself – or get whatever help she can from Providence.

– Thank you, Roly.

– If she chooses to defend herself by seeking to put all the blame on Novak, then that is her right. You must deal with that.

– You're due back on in just under fifteen minutes. I think you ought to go and have a word with your client … and Mr Jones of course.

Chapter Fifty-nine

(Wednesday 5th March 1941)

Adam hurried back down to the Court room, where he found Jones and Novak in a huddle, Novak leaning out from the dock. Jones turned to him and said:

- He doesn't believe a word of it. She's been framed.
- I don't think so. Of course, if she denies that the fingerprints are hers then they'll have to apply to call new evidence and that will be difficult for them because the Crown has closed its case. We'll have to hear what she has to say.

Adam turned to Novak.

- Why would they frame her? They could just as easily have framed you and didn't do so. Your fingerprints weren't on the tube. Did you know that she had planted the tube in your room?
- Of course not. She would not do such a thing. I would have noticed her doing it.
- Then she *has* been to your room.

Novak had slipped up.

- I ... No. Of course she has not.
- I can't help you, Mr Novak, if you don't tell me the truth.
- I have nothing to say.

Novak drew back from the edge of the dock, returned to his chair, folded his arms and looked away. At that point the usher called everyone to attention. The hearing was about to resume. Adam returned to Counsels' row.

Mr Justice Sherdley entered the court and bowed to the assembly before sitting down. Preston rose to his feet to continue his cross-examination. A pale-faced Katya Hoffer swayed in the witness box before him.

– Can you please explain to the jury how your fingerprints came to be on this cardboard tube?

There was another long silence, which Preston allowed to continue. Eventually the judge leaned forward towards the witness and said:

– Mrs Hoffer. I'm afraid that you must answer the question.

Still Katya Hoffer said nothing. The jury were leaning forward in their seats. Preston retained his theatrical silence. Suddenly a loud voice said from the back of the Court:

– With the greatest of respect, my Lord, I must disagree with you.

Everyone turned in surprise at this declaration. To his utter astonishment Adam saw Blytheway striding towards Counsels' row, his tapes flapping and his robes billowing out behind him. Preston was looking at the newcomer with a mixture of amazement and irritation at the interference with his performance. He hissed:

– Blytheway! What the hell do you think you're doing?!
– Good morning, sweetheart.
– Mr Blytheway! This is most irregular!

Mr Justice Sherdley was very red in the face. Blytheway slipped into the row next to Adam and replied:

– My Lord, if I have done anything irregular it will be on the transcript and I will be taken to task in due course. I am sure the shorthand writer has taken down everything that has occurred this morning.

The reference to the transcript pulled the Judge up short.

– Very well, Mr Blytheway. You had better explain yourself.

The jurors were confused. Some were looking at Katya Hoffer, others at the Judge or at Preston now seated and seething, and the rest were focusing on Blytheway.

– Well, my Lord, I just happened to be watching this morning's proceedings from the public gallery.

He motioned up to it with his right hand and everyone craned up to where he was indicating, abruptly aware of the other spectators on the drama.

– And I was watching Mr Preston's cross-examination of this witness and felt that an injustice was being perpetrated.
– An injustice?! In my court?! Mr Blytheway. I don't like what I am hearing. And I must ask: what right have you to be addressing me at all?
– My Lord. In the first place I put myself forward as an amicus curiae. A friend to the Court for the benefit of the jury.

The judge threw down his pen in anger. That wouldn't be caught on the transcript. He spoke coldly and with controlled fury.

– In other words, Mr Blytheway, you have come into my court with the intention of telling me how I should be running it?
– My Lord, yes.
– How dare you …!

But Blytheway continued before the Judge could finish his sentence.

– You see, my Lord, it seems to me that, before this witness answers the question that has been asked of her, she should be reminded, preferably by the Court, that she has a privilege against self-incrimination. She does not need to answer questions that may tend to incriminate her. And yet, unless I missed something, I do not believe that she was given such a reminder, by your Lordship or anyone else, including Mr Preston.
– Ah …

Mr Justice Sherdley realised that Blytheway had caught him out. He looked down at the shorthand writer as she patiently recorded his exchange with counsel.

- It seemed to me also that whilst Mr Preston's underhand methods of trying to entrap this vulnerable young woman might attract the opprobrium of this Court –

He paused and gazed down at Preston with something approaching condescension.

- it seems to me that he has also committed a cardinal error.

Preston was on his feet.

- My Lord! I must object to these attacks on my professionalism!

Blytheway looked at him and with a languid waving motion of his left hand bade him sit down. To Adam's surprise, Preston subsided.

- You see, my Lord, although I was not here yesterday, it seems to be comparatively clear that the prosecution has closed its case. Mr Preston cannot willy-nilly attempt to introduce *further* evidence.
- Yes. Mr Blytheway. I see the point you are making.
- But it goes further than that, my Lord. It was not just a matter of attempting to introduce further evidence. Mr Preston made no application to your Lordship to do that and, worse than that, he purported to *give evidence himself*. He told the jury that fingerprints had been taken from the glass. He told the jury that those fingerprints matched those on the cardboard tube. But we have seen no forensic evidence of this. It was, with respect to Mr Preston, entirely improper for him to put such thoughts into the mind of the jury without doing so properly. *Particularly* in a capital trial.

Blytheway spoke with charming reasonableness. Adam stole a glance at the jury. If they had been looking in all directions a few moments earlier, they were now entirely concentrating on Roly. One or two of them threw a suspicious glance in the direction of Preston – was it right that he had been attempting to cheat? Adam sensed the beginnings of a shift in their allegiance from Preston to this surprising newcomer. The Judge looked down at Preston.

- Well, Mr Preston. I think Mr Blytheway has a point. Several points in fact. What do you say?
- My Lord. This is preposterous. There is no doubt in my mind that if Mrs Hoffer were to answer my question it would become clear that her fingerprints were indeed on the cardboard. Mr Blytheway is relying on legal technicalities.
- But we have "legal technicalities" for a reason, Mr Preston, particularly in cases such as the present. And it is right that neither you nor I reminded Mrs Hoffer of her right to remain silent. Should she choose to do so there would be no admissible evidence that her fingerprints were on the cardboard and yet you have put that thought into the minds of the jury *without* admissible evidence.

For the first time in the trial – for the first time since he had known Preston – Adam saw him becoming flustered. The Judge turned back to Blytheway.

- Well, Mr Blytheway. May I ask you … in your role as amicus … where we go from here?
- My Lord, it is not simply a matter for me, or for the Court. It seems to me – and I am sure that this is the point that Mr Falling is waiting to make – that Mr Novak would be entitled to have a new trial. He would be entitled to have this jury discharged. For Mr Preston has, quite wrongly, put it into their minds that Mrs Hoffer is a conspirator with Mr Novak in the commission of the crimes that are alleged.
- Yes. I see. Mr Falling?
- Before Mr Falling addresses you, my Lord – *Blytheway hurried quickly on* – there is another possibility that should be addressed. That is that the trial could continue on the basis that *I* represent Mrs Hoffer.
- But Mr Blytheway, she is not on trial. She is a mere witness.
- A witness whom Mr Preston seeks to incriminate with the most serious of crimes out of her own mouth.
- But she has not sought you out as her counsel. She has no solicitors. You, as you have told me, are here merely as amicus to the court.

Roly looked for the first time towards Katya Hoffer and everyone else followed his gaze. It was as though in all this drama they had forgotten that she was still standing there. Bewildered, she looked at Blytheway and then at the jurors behind him, not saying a word.

– When I addressed you earlier, my Lord, I said that "in the first place" I put myself forward as an amicus.
– And how else do you propose "putting yourself forward"?
– It seems to me, my Lord, that in the unusual position we find ourselves in, Mrs Hoffer might be entitled to the benefit of a dock brief. I would be prepared to represent her on the usual basis for a nominal fee. If it pleases her, that is.

Mr Preston was losing control of the situation. He climbed to his feet again.

– But my Lord. This cannot be accepted. Mrs Hoffer is in the middle of her evidence. She cannot discuss her evidence with anyone until she is finished.

Blytheway, who had seated himself during Preston's latest intervention, rose languidly to his feet once more and, in a manner that treated Preston's comments as those of a schoolboy, said:

– My Lord. If Mr Preston is to take such a stance then it seems to me that there is no alternative to this whole trial being abandoned. We must start all over again with a new jury and Mrs Hoffer will be released from her testamentary oath at which point I will speak with her – if it pleases her of course. There's more than one way to skin a cat, if you'll forgive the vernacular. If Mr Preston is not prepared to let me speak with this witness, then so be it. But it is very much in his interests to let me do so.
– Before we go any further, Mr Blytheway, it is probably sensible to discover whether Mrs Hoffer actually *wants* your assistance.

The judge turned his attention to the witness.

– Mrs Hoffer. Have you been able to follow these exchanges? Mr

Blytheway is making the extremely generous offer to represent you if these proceedings continue. Would you like him to do so?

Katya Hoffer's eyes looked bruised. Her face was white. She bit her lip and nodded mutely.

– For the benefit of the transcript, the witness is nodding her head,

said the Judge; and then to Adam:

– Mr Falling. I haven't heard from you yet. Are you asking for this trial to be abandoned and the jury discharged?

Adam rose to his feet. Next to him Roly had written in large letters on a spare sheet of paper "Not Yet!"

– My Lord, I would like to reserve my position on that. Obviously, if Mr Preston does not agree to Mr Blytheway speaking with Mrs Hoffer, I will have no alternative but to do so. It may be that, even if he is allowed to do so, I will want to make that application. I would prefer to see whether or not Mr Preston will indeed permit Mr Blytheway to speak with Mrs Hoffer at this stage.

The Judge turned to Preston.

– Well, Mr Preston, are you prepared to let Mr Blytheway speak with the witness, notwithstanding the fact that she is still on oath? It does seem to me that the only alternative is the abandonment of the trial.
– My Lord, reluctantly, yes.

Preston was furious. The jury were enthralled. Novak was confused. Katya was weeping. Adam's head was spinning. Blytheway stood again.

– I'm grateful to Mr Preston, my Lord. May I therefore ask, on behalf of Mrs Hoffer, that the Court adjourns until 2 p.m.

Chapter Sixty

(Wednesday 5th March 1941)

It was quarter to two. Adam was sitting in the corner of the robing room, face to the wall, chain-smoking and going over his notes. He and Jones spent the first hour after the adjournment going over things with Novak. The latter was sticking to his story although it was becoming increasingly untenable. Finally, Adam had retreated to the robing room. Blytheway had swept out of court and as Adam emerged he saw him disappearing down the corridor, one arm on Katya Hoffer's elbow whilst Milo Hoffer looked on bemused. He felt a hand on his shoulder and jumped. Startled, he turned to find himself face to face with Roly, wig in hand. He sat down next to Adam.

- Adam, I must speak quickly.
- Roly. I'm sorry. I should never have called Katya.
- It's done. We must deal with the consequences. One of those is that, if things remains as they are Novak will be convicted, Katya will be arrested and most likely she will also be convicted. If you apply for an adjournment – and I appreciate that is wholly a matter for you – we will have succeeded in embarrassing Preston but we will be no further forward. On the contrary, he will get his evidential tackle in order and most probably ensure that in any new trial my client is in the dock with your client. And they may well both go down.
- What are you proposing?
- There have been too many lies in this case, Adam. The truth has to come out – sooner rather than later.
- I thought you believed that truth had nothing to do with anything.
- That's not *quite* the way I put it. In any event, I have had a long discussion with Katya Hoffer. She's a very bright young lady. I have persuaded her that the time has come to tell the truth. It will help that Mr Hoffer will not be in court to hear what she has to say. It may

then be necessary for you to ask for permission to recall your client. I think that if Katya tells the truth then your client may no longer feel constrained to lie.

– Her fingerprints are on the tube aren't they?

– But of course. That is a fact that I cannot get round. But it will be more difficult to deal with in the future, if it is not grasped now.

– But how can it be in your client's interests for her to tell the truth if that will mean that she is then arrested and tried?

– She will be anyway now. I have a far better chance of getting her off any subsequent charges if she tells the truth now and she is not … hampered … in any further trial by the presence of Novak. So we shall do what the prosecution have been trying to do: divide and rule. I would suggest that you don't apply to have the jury discharged. Now I must go.

– But Roly, you know virtually nothing about the case.

– On the contrary, you have been showing me your notes of the evidence and I took an opportunity – forgive me – to read through your papers in an idle hour last week.

Blytheway stood up, put his wig back on and began adjusting it. As he was about to leave, Adam said:

– Roly. Why are you doing this?

– A spontaneous decision, dear boy.

– No, I mean why are you representing Katya for practically nothing – representing *me* for absolutely nothing for that matter?

He sat down again, looked into Adam's eyes, a look of deep seriousness on his face, and put his hand on Adam's shoulder.

– It's something I am rather ashamed of. If I tell you will you treat everything I say in complete confidence?

– Of course.

– The fact is, Adam … I've been *dreadfully* bored! Look at my situation. I have been able to earn an enormous amount of money over the years and have no familial obligations. I have little to spend it on now – and they'll be introducing clothes rationing next! People are continuing to pay enormous amounts of money for something that I enjoy but find *too* easy. I will never be promoted to silk. I will never become a judge. What would you do in my situation?

– Well. I'm very grateful.

– And besides, I don't like Pemberton and I don't like Preston.

Blytheway got up again and was walking towards the exit when Adam shouted after him:

– Roly if your decision was so spontaneous, why had you put your robes in the robing room?

– *Tactical* spontaneity, dear boy. *Tactical* spontaneity.

Chapter Sixty-one

(Wednesday 5ᵗʰ March 1941)

Everyone rose when Mr Justice Sherdley came back into court. Blytheway remained standing when everyone else had resumed their seats. Preston, his head down, looked listless.

- Yes, Mr Blytheway.
- If it please, your Lordship, I have taken instructions and spoken with Mr Falling. I understand he will not be applying to discharge the jury. He tells me he has complete faith in their impartiality and inde- pendence of mind – *Adam had said nothing of the kind but wished he had* – and I feel that, subject to your Lordship's views, the best way forward would be to let Mrs Hoffer tell her story in her own words.
- Very well, Mr Blytheway, please continue.

Blytheway turned to face Katya Hoffer and with an encouraging smile said:

- Mrs Hoffer. Were you telling the Court the truth this morning?
- No. I was not.
- You appreciate that lying to the court is a very serious matter?
- Yes. I am very sorry.
- Why did you lie?
- Because I was frightened.
- Do you understand that you need not say anything that may incrim- inate you?
- I do.
- Are you prepared to tell the court the truth now, even if it might incriminate you?

411

Katya Hoffer took a deep breath, looked up at the Judge and then across at the jurors.

– Yes, I am.
– Please proceed.

She began to speak, softly at first, but with increasing vigour and speed.

– I come from Prague, in Czechoslovakia. I was born Katya Vrabec. When the Germans took over our country they began arresting and murdering our people. I and my brother and my mother and father tried to escape the country but they caught us on the border. They killed my parents … but they said that they would spare my brother and me.

Katya stifled a sob. Blytheway handed a glass of water to the usher.

– Have some water, Mrs Hoffer. Don't worry. I've made sure that my fingerprints are all over the glass.

There was some quiet laughter from the jury.

– They would spare us on one condition. They told me that I must go to England and that I must do as they tell me. If I do not they will kill my brother. They had also arrested Milosevich Hoffer. He is a good man and a doctor. They allowed him to leave for England on condition that he married me. They wanted to be sure that when I reached England I was not interned by the English. They released us but kept my brother and allowed us to make our way to Gibraltar. They had told us that when we got to England we should go to a "safe house" in Queen's Road, Leytonstone and that I would be told what to do and that when I did it I would most probably be arrested by the English police at the safe house. I was very unhappy and very frightened for my brother.

There was a rapt silence in the courtroom as she spoke, broken only by the sound of scribbling pens.

– The ship was heading to the west and I thought that we were sailing to America and I was filled with happiness. If I was taken to America I would not be able to do what they asked me – and it would not be my fault. But the ship was just avoiding mines and then it began to sail north again.

Adam watched Blytheway as he led her through her evidence. He had no notes in front of him and Adam guessed that everything Katya Hoffer had told him was filed in his memory. Roly bent forward slightly when she came to the end of a sentence and said softly:

– Tell me about Tomas Novak.

Looking over his shoulder, Adam saw that Novak was leaning almost out of the dock, his wide eyes fixed on the frail-looking woman in the witness box. At the mention of his name a number of the jurors looked in his direction. Katya took a deep breath and looked directly into Novak's eyes, her gaze softening as she did so.

– Tomas was on the ship.
– This is January / February 1940?
– Yes.
– When you were giving evidence earlier today you told the court that you first became aware of Tomas Novak when he was arrested in December of last year, was that answer true?

She bowed her head again.

– No. It was not true.
– When did you first become aware of Mr Novak?
– On the ship from Gibraltar.
– How did you meet him on the ship?
– We were trying to sleep under the same lifeboat. Milo was sick down below … but it was impossible to sleep. We had to be so quiet … there were submarines … and we started to talk to one another in a whisper … and tell each other about our lives. I told him that my family was all dead. I did not mention my brother … or what I had been

told to do. We whispered all through the night ... and the next night. And the sky was so clear and full of stars. And suddenly I felt ... what might be next to come in my life ... that I was happy ... and as the sky was brightening on the second night and the stars all faded into the blue ... we kissed ... and I was looking forward to the next night ... even if there were submarines below us. To be happy ... even for a little while ... and all the next day looking out at the sea ... I thought of lying again under the lifeboat ... with Tomas ... and on the third night we lay again together under the stars and embraced and ... in a whisper ... talked and talked and talked ...

Katya's voice faded away and she gazed across at Tomas Novak – a look filled with entreaty and sorrow.

- And did Tomas say anything to you on that third evening?
- Yes. He told me that he loved me.

Adam saw, behind him, that Novak now had his head in his hands.

- And what was your reaction?
- I was surprised ... and I was happy.
- Did you say anything in reply?
- Yes. I told him that I loved him as well.
- Why did you say that?
- We were in the middle of the ocean. I was happy for the first time in so long. And our ship could be sunk at any time. And I might not ever reach England. And I believed that I loved him as he loved me, but ...
- But what?

Blytheway asked his question before she could continue.

- But I loved my brother more than I loved Tomas. And I wanted to have the chance to see my brother again one day.
- What happened when you reached England?
- I wanted to see Tomas again ... but also I wanted to help my brother – to see my brother again one day. I did not want to be arrested.
- So what did you do?

- I persuaded Milo that we should give Tomas the safe house to live in. I persuaded Milo to tell him not to report himself.
- Why did you do that?
- If Tomas reported himself he may have been interned. I would not be able to see him ... and Milo and I would have to live in the safe house.
- But you were not interned?
- But part of me *wanted* to be interned. It would be like going to America. I would be able to do nothing.
- So you came to London. Did you see Tomas after you came to London?
- Yes. I would go and visit him at Queen's Road. We ... we became very close.
- Tell me about the cardboard tube that Mr Preston was showing us earlier. He has suggested to you that it carries your fingerprints. Is that correct?

Katya Hoffer bowed her head again and spoke so softly that all who listened strained forward to hear.

- It is true.
- It was left at the bookshop where Milo works with a note for me that it must be left at Queen's Road by Friday 13th December, which was the day after. So I hid it under the floorboards.
- Did you look at what was in the tube?
- I didn't want to know what was in the tube. But I did open it and look.
- What did it contain?
- Just some old plans. I didn't open them.
- Did Tomas Novak know about the plans?
- No. He did not.
- How were you able to hide them without Tomas seeing you?
- I had my own key.

A loud sobbing broke out from the dock. Novak was bent double and bawling. His breath came in great broken gasps as though a dam had broken and months of pent-up emotion was bursting through it. The jurors switched their attention from Katya Hoffer to Novak and looked at him in a new light. Katya shouted across his sobbing:

 – Tomas! Tomas! I'm sorry, Tomas. I'm sorry.
 – Did you not appreciate that you would be putting his life in danger?
 – No. Of course not!
 – Why ever not?
 – Because the English police would know about it all along.

Preston started at what she said and stopped writing, whispering to Phillips to take a very full note.

 – Why do you say that?
 – Because they told me all along that I would be arrested. They told me that if I was arrested very soon after I was told to put the plans in the safe house, then it would prove that the English had broken their codes.
 – My Lord!

Preston was shouting almost before he had got to his feet and all eyes, Blytheway's included, were on him.

 – My Lord (*he said again*), a matter of law has arisen which I would wish to address you on in the absence of the jury.

Mr Justice Sherdley was suddenly very alert. The jurors looked even more confused than at Blytheway's intervention. Only Blytheway, now seated, appeared to be serene.

 – Mr Blytheway, have you anything to say about Mr Preston's intervention?
 – No, my Lord, I am content to hear what Mr Preston has to say on the law.

The jurors were ushered out into the jury room. On their departure Preston asked that the public gallery be cleared and this too was duly done. The Judge looked down at leading Counsel for the Crown.

 – Yes, Mr Preston?
 – My Lord. This witness's evidence is now touching on matters of

416

national security. This was completely unexpected. She has touched upon the question of whether or not our country is able to break German codes. Speaking hypothetically, if we had broken enemy codes and our enemies became aware of that fact, then they would change the codes. English lives may be at stake.

Adam remembered his exchange with Cara about Preston's treason trials at Pemberton's party:

- *It must be a lot of work.*
- *Not really. I've seen the briefs. They're wrapped in white tape and marked secret but they're never very bulky. It seems that we're catching them as soon as they land so they're usually red-handed. I don't know how we're managing to find out about them so quickly. Peter says it's just good luck but I think there is more to it than that. That's one thing I haven't been able to prise out of him.*

Mr Justice Sherdley looked worried for the first time during the trial. Things were spinning out of his control.

- What do you say, Mr Blytheway?
- Well, my Lord, speaking hypothetically, as my learned friend has done, if the evidence that Mrs Hoffer has given to the court is true, it would appear that we have cracked the German codes ... and with Tomas Novak's arrest, the Germans will be aware of the fact.

He let the enormity of what he had said sink in before adding:

- I, of course, have only a limited role in this hearing. And I haven't been present throughout. However, my understanding of the background to this matter, as very kindly provided to me by Mr Falling, is that my learned friend Mr Preston has not adduced any evidence as to how precisely police officers came to raid a bedsit in Leytonstone in the middle of the night. May I ask, has Mr Preston enlightened your Lordship as to that evidence?
- No, Mr Blytheway. He has not.
- Well, my Lord, then it may be that the answer to this little riddle

is simple. All Mr Preston has to do is to tell your Lordship and his learned friends how it was done. If there is nothing in what Mrs Hoffer has told the court then, in due course, Mr Preston can adduce that evidence in any trial that there may be in respect of her actions.

The judge looked from Blytheway to Preston and back again. Adam kept his head down.

– Well, Mr Preston. Mr Blytheway's suggestion seems eminently reasonable. How *was* it that the police came to raid that particular address on that particular night?

Preston was whispering urgently to Phillips, the two leaning towards one another. He looked daggers at Blytheway as he rose to his feet.

– My Lord, I am not at liberty to tell you how it came to be.
– I *beg* your pardon.
– My Lord, these are matters of state security.
– Are you telling me that I, a Judge of the High Court, am not to be allowed to know what is going on in my own court?

Blytheway again intervened

– Well, my Lord, it is bad enough that the Defence is not provided with the evidence that is in the hands of the Crown, but to withhold it from the Judge? I have never heard such a thing.
– Shut up, Blytheway.

Preston spat the words out, all decorum temporarily forgotten. Blytheway shrugged him off.

– But in any event, my Lord, Mrs Hoffer's evidence is almost at an end. There should be no need for this element of her testimony to be touched upon again. The trouble is that, by Mr Preston's evasions, we in the absence of the jury know that she must be telling the truth. How is our knowledge to be communicated to the jury without worrying Mr Preston about national security? It may be, my Lord, that if you were to express yourself in summing up in such a way as to pass on your belief in her testimony that would deal with the problem.

– You mean that I should perhaps sum up with a view to an acquittal of Mr Novak?

– Precisely, my Lord. That is plainly, on the evidence that we have heard this afternoon, the appropriate outcome.

The judge asked that all counsel stand.

– Mr Preston and Mr Phillips, Mr Falling, Mr Blytheway. There has been enough drama for one day. I am going to invite the jury back in and discharge them until tomorrow. There is a lot I need to think about overnight. Mr Blytheway, I think, in addition, that your client must be remanded in custody overnight. Can you oppose that?

– I don't think I can, my Lord.

– Very good.

The jury were called back in and then released for the day. The Judge rose and left the court. Katya Hoffer was escorted by two guards up through the dock to the cells, her expression fixed. As she passed Novak she reached out a hand to him and their fingers touched.

Chapter Sixty-two
(Thursday 6th March 1941)

Eric Jones was sitting immediately behind Adam Falling. In front of him and to his left were, first, Desmond Phillips, and in front of him, Peter Preston KC. Preston was rolling his pen along the backs of his fingers: from the little finger to the forefinger and then back again. Roland Blytheway was still in court but was no longer in counsels' row. He sat at the back, still robed, filing his fingernails and examining his cuticles one by one. His client, Katya Hoffer, was in the cells beneath the building, as was her husband, Milo Hoffer, who had been arrested where he was sitting on his bench in the main hallway. Novak was impassive in the dock, a faraway look on his face. There was a strong smell of furniture polish mixed with the odour of bleach from the mops that, overnight, had been used to clean the courtroom floor. It was late in the afternoon. Jones looked up at the electric lights that gave the room a sickly glow. He listened to the ticking of the clock on the rear wall of the courtroom. They were waiting for the jury to file in with their verdict.

A lot had happened since the court rose the previous afternoon. Down in the cells, Novak had been shocked and confused. Katya, whom he had trusted, had betrayed him. He had known that he was innocent but had been prepared to go to the gallows to protect her, however tangential her involvement may have been. Despite the afternoon's revelations, he still valued her life above his own. Now, as a result of the extraordinary events of Wednesday afternoon, he stood a chance of being acquitted whilst Katya and Milo Hoffer were now in at least as much jeopardy as he was. "What did Blytheway think he was doing?" he had asked. "He was meant to be protecting her but he has put her life in danger." Then, eventually and inevitably, he turned his anger on Falling. If Falling had not disobeyed his instructions, Katya's life would not have been put in such danger. Adam had had no useful answer to this. It was plain to Jones that he was mortified by his mishandling of the case. Jones took no comfort from the fact that he had opposed the course of action taken by his barrister. Adam dealt with the tumble of questions with contrition:

- Whatever else I can say, Mr Novak, Katya is in good hands. Roland Blytheway is the best barrister I have ever seen. He has a clear strategy. His best chance of helping Katya is to ensure that you are acquitted of the charges you face. Her best hope is for you to be acquitted.
- He certainly tied Peter Preston in knots (*added Jones*) – the Judge as well for that matter.

Novak had grudgingly accepted that analysis. Jones and Falling had said their goodbyes for the evening.

On the Thursday morning Adam had briefly recalled Novak and the latter had confirmed the truthfulness of Katya's testimony.

- Mrs Hoffer said yesterday that you told her that you loved her. Is that true?
- Yes. I love her very much. I would do anything for her.
- Why did you tell the court that she had never been to your home?
- She had said that she did not know me.
- Did you know that she had placed the cardboard tube under your floorboards?
- No.
- What did you feel when you heard her evidence yesterday?
- I do not know what to say.

The jury looked at Tomas Novak with new eyes. Preston, clearly still rattled from the day before, was ineffectual in his cross-examination, as one often is when trying to dislodge a witness who is patently telling the truth. His closing speech to the jury lacked the assurance of his performance on the first day of the trial. Blytheway was permitted to address the jury on behalf of Katya Hoffer. His contribution was brief, a mixture of humour, erudition and deadly seriousness.

- Members of the jury, this then is a story of love and betrayal. Tomas Novak loves Katya Hoffer and she loves him. But she loves her brother more. Tomas Novak loved her enough to die for her, though he did not know the extent of her betrayal. Katya Hoffer is not on trial today. You must decide whether she is telling the truth. If she is, she does herself no favours for she puts herself at risk of standing one day where Mr Novak stands. But that is not your concern. That is for another day and perhaps for another jury. You may conclude that, though she loved her brother more, she loved Tomas Novak enough, at the end, not to let him die as a result of her actions.

Mr Justice Sherdley had summed up the case in a way that was favourable to Novak and the jury had been sent out to deliberate at 12.30 that morning. He and Falling had accompanied Novak to the cells and waited with him whilst the jury considered their verdict. It had been a gloomy occasion with talk overshadowed by the wait for the knock on the cell door. Every footstep, every rattle of keys brought conversation to a standstill. After the usual "what ifs" and "if onlys", Novak had subsided into silence. Falling, Jones could tell, was worried not just about the verdict, but about Katya Hoffer, who was incarcerated because of his actions, and about his own upcoming trial. It was Thursday afternoon and on Monday next he would be in the Royal Courts of Justice as a Party Cited in a divorce. And still there had been no signed statement from Jenny. Jones saw these latter concerns flickering across Adam's face but neither of them felt able to discuss a different case in front of a man under the shadow of the noose. Jones worried about preparing the Pemberton case, about the McKechnie trial that was to proceed during the following week, and about the necessity to prepare grounds for appeal if Novak was to be sentenced to death. And then the knock on the door came, summonsing them back up to Court 6. The jury had reached a verdict.

And now they sat awaiting the arrival of Mr Justice Sherdley and the jury.

– All rise!

The jury filed in. Jones noticed that several of them looked in Adam's direction and even in towards the dock. Mrs Finlay, formerly Feinstein, managed a shy smile. Everyone sat down again and Blytheway continued to file his nails. The jury foreman was asked to stand. It was the war veteran, who stood to attention, chest out, a row of medals. The other jurors looked up at him, tension on their faces though they knew the outcome. Preston had stopped playing with his pen and was looking intently at his notebook.

- What is your verdict?
- Not Guilty!

The jury foreman barked it out like a sergeant major. Preston closed his notebook and looked away. Adam, who had been leaning forward, his forearms flat on the desk, slumped forward and put his hands to his face momentarily before recovering himself. Blytheway continued to stare at his cuticles. Adam stood and asked that Novak be released. The Judge granted his application. The jury was discharged and the court rose.

Outside court, Adam went to shake Novak's hand. The gesture was refused.

- What will happen to Katya? Can I see her now?

His client stood before him in his crumpled blue suit. Before Adam could reply, police officers appeared on either side of Novak and he was re-arrested for breach of the Aliens Act and led away again. Falling and Jones watched as he was taken back to the iron door leading down to the cells.

Chapter Sixty-three
(Saturday 8ᵗʰ March 1941)

When the tulips began to fade and drop their pink petals Annie had replaced them with crocuses. Buttery yellow with deep maroon streaks on the outside of each petal. Julia sat in her armchair and watched as the colours faded with the dusk until only silhouettes were left. It was nearly time to put the blackout curtains in place. She looked around her dressing room. She spent more time here than in any room other than the cellar, where her single bed lay next to Jeremy's. On her writing desk were the papers provided to her by her solicitors for the trial that was to begin on Monday. Next to them was the brown envelope containing Jenny's witness statement, still unsigned and un-witnessed. She had put all her financial papers in the middle drawer. A freshly cleaned and pressed two-piece suit hung on the door of the wardrobe. That was for Monday. Annie had made sure there were three other suits in similar condition for Tuesday, Wednesday and Thursday. If the case lasted until Friday she would wear Monday's suit again. There was a pile of starched and pressed blouses on a shelf inside the wardrobe. Demure and unostentatious as her lawyers had advised her they should be. She would wear her pearls.

Annie had been surprisingly sympathetic over recent weeks and, when bringing in the dry-cleaned court outfits, was bold enough to wish her good luck for the week ahead. Julia had been taken aback. She had voiced her suspicions about her maid's motives to Jenny on more than one occasion, but Annie seemed to be sincere. Perhaps she was saying similar things to Jeremy? Samuels hadn't wished her luck or anything like that. He treated her with a wan courtesy appropriate for necessary but unwanted guests.

She walked over to the escritoire and picked up the manila envelope, sliding out its contents in one movement, before returning to her seat with the draft statement. Her last meeting with her solicitor and counsel had been the previous evening. They pressed upon her the urgency of getting the statement signed and witnessed, and she had promised she would do so

– over the weekend. They asked her why she hadn't already done so. Sitting in her armchair now she asked herself the same question. There had been opportunities. She and Jenny had been to the Ritz for tea on two further occasions since she gave her Joan's ring.

On each occasion she had waited for an opening to raise the subject, but could not. Jenny would talk relentlessly about Captain Simon Jenkins. They were writing to one another incessantly. Every morning there would be a new white envelope on the silver tray in the hall. Captain Jenkins used a fountain pen and Jenny's name and address would be there in blue-black curvy writing. They corresponded about everything: their childhoods, their families, every dusty corner of the past and every shiny prospect for the future. Where would be a good part of London to live? What sort of jobs would Simon take once the war was over? What sort of education would be best for children after the war? Perhaps it would be better for children to grow up in the country rather than the town? And their letters, so Jenny had told her, had moved gradually from the hypothetical to the concrete so that the questions changed to "Where shall we live together?", "What shall we do after the war?" "Where should our children be educated?" And on all of these topics Jenny would seek Julia's views.

Above all Jenny wanted to talk about marriage. Of course, Simon hadn't proposed. They hadn't been able to see one another since that last visit to the Café de Paris in January. But she felt sure that he would – and she would accept. Julia had tried gently to suggest that Jenny was being hasty. She hardly knew him. Knew him properly, that was. She was still very young and very beautiful, with a bright future ahead of her. So much could change even in the months ahead. The future was too uncertain. But Jenny was impervious to Julia's caution. She might be young but she knew herself well. And she knew that she loved Simon Jenkins and that he loved her. Their love would overcome all obstacles. After all, Julia married young. Then the conversation would lurch onto why Julia married so young and whether it had been the right thing to do. And although this might have given Julia the opportunity to bring up the question of the witness statement, it never felt right and she would steer the conversation back to Jenny's concerns – and to Captain Simon Jenkins.

– I really think that next time we see one another Simon's going to propose.
– Oh Jenny. It's far too early.

– Well, I think he will anyway.
– Don't forget that he'll need Daddy's permission.
– We've been talking about that. You don't think Daddy will object?
– Daddy's got a lot on his mind at the moment. The truth is I really don't know what he would do.

Then the conversation would swing round back to the beginning again. And still she did not raise the subject of the witness statement. Her lawyers had asked her more than once why she had not obtained Jenny's signature. In her heart she knew the answer. It was because the statement was untrue. If Jenny signed it she could be compelled to swear to its truth in court. She was an adult now. She would be committing perjury even if that perjury was not discovered. Julia had remembered Jenny's distress when the subject had been raised over tea in January. And yet, if she did sign the statement it could well be that Jeremy would drop the case, even at the doors of the court. He would not want to see Jenny, of all people, put through the ordeal of giving evidence against her father and being cross-examined by his KC – or Roland Blytheway for that matter.

And Julia still believed that Jeremy might withdraw his petition. He had become less certain of himself since Jenny's revelations about the diary. And he seemed distinctly unnerved at the prospect of being cross-examined by Adam's counsel, Blytheway. She noticed the little things that pointed towards the possibility of a reconciliation. He wasn't as gruff with her. Their beds, behind the wine-racks that were their makeshift bedroom, were moving closer together. Seeds of doubt were sprouting in his mind. If she could only satisfy him that Jenny was prepared to give evidence, his resolution might well crack.

The crocuses had gone from being silhouettes to formless dark shadows. She peered at her watch, then stumbled over to the window to put up the blackout shades. The sky over Eaton Square was bright and clear. The moon was rising and stars were beginning to prick holes in the darkness. She would go to bed early tonight and take a sleeping draught. She lit a lamp and her room was suffused with soft light. What to do next?

She opened the middle drawer, took out her financial papers and, sitting at her desk, began to arrange them in categories in front of her. She picked up her handwritten summary of her situation and looked at the bottom line. The last time she had reviewed the position she had four hundred guineas. She crossed that figure out and reduced it to three hundred and fifty. She had written a cheque for Mr Alnwick's brief fee. If she lost the case she would be poor. She would have nowhere to live – she could not remain under the same roof with Jeremy, he would not allow it. She would lose her children. Her children! Stephen, Sebastian and Agnes, they were so far away from her. Safer, of course, and she was still able to speak to them on the telephone every evening. They still needed her. She would have to find a new home for herself whilst they would remain in the Cotswolds or in Eaton Square. She would start looking in the personal columns for somewhere to rent, not too far away.

There was a frenzied knocking at the door and Julia jumped. Jenny came rushing in without waiting to be asked. Her mascara was running and her cheeks were flushed. She held her diary in both hands in front of her.

– Jenny! What is it?

Jenny threw herself down in the armchair, put her head in her hands and began sobbing. Julia went over to her and began to stroke her hair; it had been carefully pinned into place and there was a large ivory hairclip holding the tresses at her nape. Jenny was wearing a beautiful red silk dress that flowed down her shoulders. Julia could make out the shape of her knees beneath it. They quivered with her weeping. She was struggling for breath through her tears, and it was several minutes before her shoulders stopped shaking. Eventually, she straightened up and Julia went round to look into her eyes. They were puffy and her complexion was blotched. Her diary was in her lap with her hands lying on top of it. Julia noticed that she was wearing the emerald ring that had belonged to Joan on her left ring finger.

– It's Daddy!

Julia looked at her watch – it was quarter to seven – and waited. Captain Jenkins was due to collect Jenny at seven. She had talked of little else all week.

– I went to his study to ask him what he would think if I got engaged and … and … and he got so *angry*. He said I was too young to leave home and that I had to stay *here!* And he wouldn't *agree* to me getting married. And then he said that I was *infatuated* with Simon … and I *knew* … I just *knew* …

- Knew what, darling?
- *Knew* he'd been reading my diary … and he *promised* me he wouldn't! So I called him a silly old man and grabbed my diary from his desk and ran out.
- Jenny!
- Well, he is a silly old man!

Julia took both of her step-daughter's hands in her own and squeezed them gently.

- But Jenny. You mustn't talk to your father like that. He does mean well, you know. He's under a lot of stress at the moment.
- With his silly petition!

Julia sensed that this might be her only chance. Jenny was going out for the evening and that would leave only Sunday in which to get the witness statement signed. It was unlikely to be easier to broach tomorrow when she would be full of talk of Simon and the Café de Paris. She would hardly be more antagonistic to her father then than she clearly was this evening. Julia spoke in a halting, diffident way.

- Jenny. I'm sorry to raise this but, now you've mentioned the petition, well … all those entries in your diary that proved that Daddy was being silly … my solicitors have prepared a statement for you to sign, just to prove that Daddy's being silly … I've got it here. All you have to do is sign it in front of a witness …
- Oh, Julia. I won't have to give any evidence will I?
- I'm *sure* you won't – *said soothingly* – here it is – *handing over the still open document*. I'll ring for Annie to come and witness it.
- But it's Annie's night off, she won't be back until late.

Damn it!

- Never mind. Why don't you just sign it anyway, and we can get Annie to witness your signature tomorrow.
- Is that allowed?
- I'm sure it is. Just give it a quick read through. Use my pen.

428

Jenny had stopped crying. She ran a finger under every line of type and then, with a deep breath, took up the pen and signed. Then she looked up into Julia's eyes.

   – Will you do me a favour as well?
   – Of course. Anything.

Jenny handed over the diary.

   – Look after this for me. Keep it in your room. I'm *so* angry with Daddy for reading it. I know he won't come in here for it. Promise you won't read it.

Julia turned the bound leather book over in her hands and felt the cold of the little metal lock.

   – Don't you worry ... I'll take care of it for you. I really don't think Daddy will try and read it again. Now, let's sort out your make-up. You're going to look lovely tonight. Forget about me and Daddy, for this evening at least. Just enjoy your evening with Simon ... and don't be too disappointed if he doesn't propose. There's all the time in the world for him to do that.
   – I really want you to meet him. Will you? Next time he's in London.
   – I'd love to meet him.

And using some blusher and face powder Julia hid away all signs of Jenny's tears. She went over to the full-length mirror to admire herself and smiled her thanks to Julia. Samuels knocked on the door and announced the arrival of Captain Jenkins. Jenny beamed.

   – Have a wonderful evening, Jenny.
   – I'll tell you all about it in the morning. Wish me luck.

And then she was out of the door and Julia heard her footsteps clattering down the stairs to the hall.

Chapter Sixty-four

(Saturday 8th March 1941)

There were two packets of ten Embassy cigarettes on his dresser and a note in Blytheway's now familiar handwriting:

"A little treat for you ahead of Monday. Don't worry, sweetheart, everything is under control. I'll see you on Sunday."

Adam smiled to himself and picked up one of the cartons, caressing the cardboard, flipping back the top, and pulling away the tin foil protecting the contents. The blackout shades were already down and the small lamp beside his bed gave the room a warm glow and drew refractions of light from the crystal obelisk next to his bed. Delia had grown and was no longer a kitten. She was sleeping soundly in her basket. He looked around his little home. He had been here over two months now and his natural untidiness had been tempered by Blytheway, who had insisted on being given a key and who would drop by with little gifts.

Blytheway had come round to see Adam on the Thursday evening, after Novak's acquittal, and had been appalled to find a suit jacket on the back of Adam's chair with the trousers draped haphazardly over the top of it. Adam had tried to thank him once more for what he had done at the Old Bailey, but Blytheway's mind had been elsewhere.

- I sometimes think that I am making *absolutely no progress* with you! Will you *never* learn?!
- I'm sorry, Roly. Truly I am. I've learnt a great deal, and after what has happened over the last few days I feel that I will be in very safe hands when the trial begins on Monday. I promise you. I have learnt from my mistakes.
- I'm not talking about Novak. Or about next Monday. I'm talking about the way you treat your clothing! How can you *possibly* succeed in life if you don't look after your suits?

Adam wanted to speak with him about Pemberton's petition, which was due to be heard in a matter of days, but Blytheway would have none of it.

- You don't even appear to have an *iron.* And I noticed that during the Novak trial you wore one of your shirts *two days in a row!*
- Please, Roly, won't you talk to me about the trial. I trust you but I am getting very nervous … scared even … as it gets closer.
- I'm sorry, Adam. First things first. There will be plenty of time to talk of the trial. I must find you a proper rail for your suits and I'll get Caldwell to bring around a spare iron … and an ironing board. This will not do you know!

Then, after a pause:

- And don't worry about the trial. Everything is under control. I have a feeling it may collapse under its own weight. But I'll speak to you about that again over the weekend. Now, I must go. I have rather a lot of documents to read for my conference tomorrow morning.

And he left. Adam did not know what exactly Blytheway was alluding to, and although Roly's sang-froid calmed him down to some extent, it did not do so entirely. Nothing seemed to stress him. He had nerves of ice.

He had not seen Roly on the Friday, although when he returned to his room at the top of Dr Johnson's Building towards the end of the day he found that the five suits that had been given to him had been placed on a small coat rail; and there was an ironing board leaning against the wall in the little kitchen, and a steam iron with a little pink bow made out of the legal tape more usually used to tie up briefs to counsel.

On the Saturday morning Adam had tried to do some preparation for the Bateman case. He'd slipped into Lamb Building and worked steadily in his room there. The Bateman trial was due to begin a week on Monday, and whilst on one level he could not imagine surviving the week immediately ahead, he reminded himself, as all barristers do, that even the worst week of a professional career will come to an end.

It was an unseasonally warm morning, and as lunch-time approached he decided to go out and treat himself to a pint of beer in one of the Fleet Street pubs. He stood up and stretched, closed his notebook, picked up a

novel and pulled on his jacket. Very few people were about and his footsteps echoed on the fading yellow stone as he made his way towards the
Tudor Street exit. A heavy layer of dust lay across the ground and broken
glass crunched under his feet. The Punch Tavern was on the junction of
Fleet Street and Ludgate Circus and was named after the satirical maga-
zine that was published from that place.

The bell tinkled as he pushed open the door, made his way into the
smoky interior and ordered a pint of bitter, putting his coins on the marble
bar. The beer was slightly weak. He took it to a quiet corner and opened
his novel – *Eyeless in Gaza* by Aldous Huxley. A group of journalists were
at a nearby table, talking loudly and drinking heavily. Adam overheard
snatches of their conversation and it became clear that they were expecting a heavy raid that night. Their copious consumption was fuelled by a
tangible anxiety. He had no idea where they could have got such intelligence from, but, he thought, if you trade in bananas you have access to
cheap bananas, if you work in the City you have access to cheap money,
and so, he supposed, if you worked in gossip and news it was reasonable to
assume you would have readier access to information. He tried to concentrate on his novel but the loud and gloomy pronouncements kept intruding. A worm of worry burrowed into his mind. He drained the pint, closed
the novel and trudged back to the Temple. He needed distraction, not that.

The sky was clear and blue and, as he passed Lamb Building and headed
up Inner Temple Lane he heard carefree laughter floating over from
Temple Gardens.

Delia was running around in little circles and mewling. She had spent
too much time shut in the room. He picked her up, put her in her cage
and took her down the stairs. She attempted to put her claws through the
bars and made little sighs of apprehension. Adam made his way through
Cloisters and past Crown Office Row down to the Gardens. Children and
families were playing there. Although the lawns were still carefully tended
there were bomb craters, and trees, smashed and uprooted, lying upon the
grass. The Thames was drifting muddily by beyond the Embankment. He
made his way to the middle of the garden and opened Delia's cage. She
came out cautiously, looking around and sniffing the air. Adam had never
taken her into the Gardens before. He found a twig and began trailing it
around her paws, making her pounce on it, then swirling it around her
in circles so that she jumped and ran after it. Two of the children came

running over to play with his cat and so he handed over the twig, lay back on the grass and pulled a Turkish cigarette from its flimsy packet.

Finishing his cigarette he closed his eyes, listened to the sound of the children playing with Delia, and felt a slight breeze drifting across his face. Then he fell asleep. The air, turning colder, eventually woke him and he opened his eyes to find that the children were gone and the sky was darkening. Delia was asleep in her unlocked cage. He rose slowly to his feet and brushed himself down. He felt a twinge in his back. A full moon was beginning to rise like a spectre in the turquoise sky. He stretched and yawned before picking up Delia and the cage and making his way back to his room.

It had been on his return there that he found Roly's note and the two packets of Embassy. He put up the blackout shades, turned on the lamp and lit the electric fire. Delia had worn herself out. Then he picked up one of the packets, pulled back the foil and made to put a cigarette in his mouth. Before he could do so there was a knock at the door. It was Barry, wearing blue overalls and a helmet and carrying a bucketful of sand and a little jug of milk. Adam's shoulders sagged. He had completely forgotten that he was on fire-watching duty that night.

- I've bought some milk for the cat. But you better get a move on, sir. We're late as it is. Save the fag till later.

Adam climbed into his overalls and put on his regulation-issue helmet whilst Barry fed the cat. Ruefully, he put the cigarette back in its carton and tucked it in his pocket.

He, Barry and an elderly porter by the name of Roberts made up the fire-watching team responsible for looking after Hare Court. They made their way onto the roof and organised their buckets of sand and water and the stirrup pump, and then tried to make themselves comfortable between the cold slate valleys. It was getting dark. Adam made to light a cigarette but was shouted down by Roberts.

- Oi! You can't light that. There's a blackout on!
- But no one will be able to see me. We're completely hidden from the ground.
- It's being seen from the air that I'm thinking of.

433

- Look. Everyone smokes. I'll put it out if any planes start coming over. But we haven't even had a siren yet.
- It's not right, sir.

Adam sighed and put away the cigarette, then stood up to look out on the city. It was a clear night and the sky was full of stars. Moonlight reflected down onto the Thames, and although no electric lights could be seen across the ghostly, smouldering district the river shone like a bright ribbon laying bare the structure of the target. He sighed again and slumped back down against the slate. Thank goodness Roberts had a weak bladder!

It was getting on for 7 p.m. now and still there had been no sirens or signs. Roberts excused himself and went down into Hare Court to use one of the toilets. Adam lit up almost before Roberts had left the rooftop. Barry looked on.

- Are you sure you should be doing that, mate?
- Roberts is a fool. No one can see me and I'll put it out if I have to. But look at the river. Look at the sky. We're sitting ducks whether I smoke or I don't smoke.
- If you don't mind me asking, sir, what's happening with your trial?

Adam sighed again.

- I thought everyone knew what was happening with my trial.
- Well, sir, I suppose we do. It's been the main topic of conversation amongst the Benchers for weeks. Can't help overhearing things.

Adam started, before realising that it had been inevitable that this would be the case. He had been too much immersed in his own problems – and the Novak and Bateman trials – to think it through. Of course, he had been aware of the looks he received, some censorious and some quietly approving, but he had not thought that the Benchers of the Inner Temple would be discussing him over dinner.

- It starts on Monday – I think. I have Mr Blytheway representing me. I'm sure you know of him?
- Who doesn't, sir? He's got himself quite a reputation one way and another.

- What do you mean by that?
- Well, sir. They may have been talking a lot about you in the last few weeks but they've been talking about Mr Blytheway for years and years.
- Oh really? And what have they been saying about him?
- It's mostly not very nice, sir, though Mr Storman seems to like him. Mr Blytheway's all right as far as I'm concerned. Always been polite to me. And doesn't have any airs and graces like some of them do.
- And why don't they like him?
- Well … you know … sir. Well … it's just that … I'm not sure it's my place to say, sir.
- Do they think he's no good? Or dishonest? Something like that?
- Not at all, sir. They couldn't say that. They can't help but say he's good at what he does and that he doesn't cheat. It's just, well, his way of life that they seem to object to. I know this: they'd never let him become a King's Counsel – or a Bencher for that matter.

Adam imagined how Blytheway would smile, insouciantly, at this gossip, but then corrected himself when he realised that of course Blytheway would be perfectly aware of it – as he seemed to be of everything.

- Well. I think he's an excellent barrister, and if we get a chance tonight I'll tell you how he helped me out last week. The funny thing is, though, I don't feel I know that much about him at all. I don't suppose *you* know much about him?
- Not really, sir, no. But there is one bloke in the kitchens – Eric – who did know him quite well during the Great War. He told me the story once but I can't rightly remember it properly. All I know is that he and Pemberton had some big falling out in the trenches. It was about saving someone, a private, who was stuck in No-Man's Land. Well, Blytheway went out there and pulled him back. But Pemberton wouldn't help. That's it as far as I can remember.

Adam shuddered.

- I don't think that I could ever do anything heroic. It's probably just as well I got invalided out.

- Your chest, was it?
- 'Fraid so.
- You're looking a lot better than you were a couple of months ago.
- Fingers crossed. Have you been working in the Temple long, Barry?
- Three or four years. Used to be a cabbie but business was poor in the mid-thirties. Still got the cab garaged up in Norwood just in case. Jean – my wife – and I live down that way still – when I can get home that is.

Heavy breathing on the steps alerted them to Roberts's return, so Adam stubbed out his cigarette and made some ineffectual waving movements to try and dispel the smell of the smoke. Roberts wrinkled up his nose and would have said something, but at that moment the sirens began to sound and a heavy ack-ack bombardment began. Searchlights were coning the air, and the insistent ominous drone of the bombers rumbled high above them and to the east. Adam saw enormous flares of light carpeting in their direction, followed by the aftershock of explosions. The sound intensified. Artillery from the ground, the sound of the planes, the explosions as they approached, and all around the wail of sirens. It was going to be a long night.

Roberts adjusted his helmet.

- All right, lads. Let's get ready.
- Let's hope we don't cop a direct hit.

Barry put into words what they were all fearing. If, however, Adam had had the time to think about it, he would have realised that an indirect hit – or even something that missed them altogether – could still have enormous consequences.

- By the way, Barry.
- Yes, sir.
- Call me Adam.

Chapter Sixty-five
(Saturday 8th March 1941)

Snakehips Johnson took to the small stage again and his West Indian Orchestra struck up behind him. He had been there the last time Jenny and Simon had come to the Café de Paris in January. He was tall and slim and wore an elegant white suit with a bright flower in his lapel.

Their table was close to the dance floor but still felt intimate. Jenny was almost unaware that anyone else was there. She ran her fingers over the crisp white linen tablecloth, then looked into Simon's smiling eyes and raised her glass. They clinked glasses and took another sip of champagne. The bottle stood empty in its ice bucket. All through dinner Jenny had had this sense of expectation, but so far Simon had said nothing to suggest that he would in fact pop the question that evening. Neither of them dared to talk about the future or their plans for it. Simon seemed uncertain, and perhaps a little apprehensive. Her champagne flute, as she put it down, hit her side-plate and toppled over and it was all she could do to stop it falling to the ground and smashing. But she had spilt the last mouthful.

- I'm so sorry. I've never drunk more than one glass before.
- Don't worry. I'll get us another bottle.
- But Simon. No. It's too expensive. You can't possibly afford that on top of dinner and everything else.
- Oh, I can afford it. I'll happily live off bread and water until I can see you again!

Jenny relaxed and smiled warmly at him as he raised his hand to attract a waiter. His words were all the proof she needed. She looked at her watch. It was only twenty past nine. There was another bottle of champagne to drink. There was still plenty of time.

Another bucket and bottle arrived, with fresh flutes, and Simon poured for them both. He gazed into her eyes and she caught a glimpse of his heart.

437

– Here's to us,

he said, and smiled.

– Yes. Here's to us!
– Come on. Let's dance.

He rose from their table and helped Jenny to her feet. She was a little unsteady and he took the chance to hold her around her waist. Her body, warm under the soft red silk of her dress, relaxed into him and his heart leapt. He felt in his jacket pocket for the little casket that he planned to offer to her before the evening was finished.

She was so beautiful, he thought, and *so* good. And he was the luckiest man alive.

Several miles away in the Temple a firestorm was threatening. Adam saw massive fires out towards West Ham and along the docks. There were high explosive bombs, and small one-kilogram incendiaries that rattled in their hundreds down onto the rooftops like malevolent autumn leaves being blown along a gutter. The noise was deafening and the bright moon-lit sky was filled with the man-made stars – shell-bursts – and searchlights attempting to catch the bombers in their cones. So far they had been able to extinguish any incendiaries that fell on their patch, or kick them off the roof into the courtyard below where they fizzled out. But the attack was getting fiercer and the bombs continued to drop.

– Barry! We need more sand!
– We've run out! I'll have to go down and break open some sandbags.
– Roberts! Go and fetch some more water. I'll try and deal with any that land while you're both away.
– Very good, sir.

As Barry and Roberts headed back down into the building Adam took the opportunity to have his second Embassy. What possible difference could his match and the glow of his cigarette make tonight? Looking out from the parapet across the City he saw sheets and curtains of flame cascading down into the streets, the little silhouettes of firemen holding hoses and aiming tons of water into the fires. So great was the noise that he felt as though he heard nothing and was watching a silent film; but in black and red rather than black and white. An incendiary clattered into his valley of slate and he ran across and booted it down into the courtyard before it could catch. He felt his chest constricting and had to sit down and recover his breath. We can't survive much more of this, he thought. I certainly can't!

But in the Café de Paris, safely below ground, the crash of the bombs around Coventry Street was no more than background noise. Snakehips Johnson led the band into "Oh, Johnny" and played a little louder to drown out the sounds of war. Simon and Jenny were dancing cheek to cheek and he had his arm around her waist again. He could feel her ribs moving under the thin silk. They looked into one another's eyes and smiled again as though the future was bright and endless. Jenny danced a little away from him, still touching him by her fingertips, as though to let him have a better view of her. Her red silk dress swayed as she moved her hips and her long dark hair gleamed under the chandeliers. She was smiling at him.

Had he heard something before it happened? He was never entirely sure. Did he hear a screaming noise like metal in agony ripping down towards them? It all happened so fast. There was a massive double bang. Jenny was still holding onto his fingers. In his memory at least she was still smiling. But the explosion didn't stop and just seemed to get louder. Time slowed down and everything was engulfed in an eerie silence. He tried to pull Jenny towards him and watched as the ceiling collapsed in on them in slow motion. He saw Snakehips Johnson take the full force of the ceiling across the side of his head before the singer disappeared under the rubble. Jenny was blown into him and on top of him and her body, as it hit him, felt as boneless and as lifeless as silk. Then everything went dark as he lost consciousness lying under the body of his beloved.

Chapter Sixty-six

(Sunday 9ᵗʰ March 1941)

Julia struggled into wakefulness from a fitful dream. It was dark and still and it took her a few seconds to realise that she was in her bed behind the wine racks. What had woken her? There was a once-familiar smell floating in the air around her. Whisky! She strained to see around her and gradually her eyes became accustomed to the gloom. There was the shadow of a man on the bed next to her. It was Jeremy. She was able to make out that his shoulders were hunched and his head bowed. Something was not right.

– Jeremy. Is that you? Is everything all right?

Her husband tried to speak but began sobbing and bawling uncontrollably. As he wept the stench of whisky grew stronger. Julia began to panic.

– Jeremy! What is it? Please tell me what has happened.
– Our daughter! Our daughter!

He bellowed and moaned these same words again and again. Julia screamed as a growing hysteria gripped her.

– What is it? Please tell me?!
– She's dead!

Julia screamed again and fell across her bed, wailing.

– Oh no! No! No! No! Please tell me it's not true!

Annie came into their part of the cellar holding a lamp and Julia saw for the first time her husband's ravaged features. It was if he had aged ten years since earlier that day. She knew, too, that her tear-streaked face must have looked similarly devastated. She climbed to her feet, as did Jeremy, and they hugged one another. She clung tightly to him as though this would make the nightmare go away. He tried to soothe her.

- She was always so loving and so beautiful. When she went out this evening she seemed to be so full of life?
- Went out this evening?

Jeremy looked at her strangely. He looked befuddled by the drink. He spoke to her slowly, slurring slightly, as if grief had taken away her reason.

- Yes ... don't you remember? ... she went out to the Café de Paris with that man Jenkins?
- You're talking about Jenny? Jenny? So Agnes is still alive? Oh thank God! Thank God!

And to her eternal shame she began to laugh hysterically. Agnes was still alive! Agnes was alive! She hardly heard her husband's roar of anger and grief; hardly saw his fist as it slammed into her jaw. She dropped to the floor where she stood. Two thoughts reverberated through her mind as she lost consciousness: that Agnes was their daughter and that Jenny was Jenny and that now any hope that he would not proceed with his petition was truly lost.

PART THREE

Chapter Sixty-seven

(Sunday 9th March 1941)

The "all clear" sounded at 12.30 a.m. Cordite and the garlicky smell of phosphorus filled the air. Roberts collapsed, wheezing heavily, at the sound of the siren. They had survived. Barry straightened up and looked across the rooftops at the fires burning all around him. The bombers had departed but searchlights still swung around the sky. Beyond the Temple he heard the bells of emergency vehicles rushing in all directions; the sound of glass falling and breaking. He stretched and felt a layer of sweat shifting against the coarse fabric of his uniform. Then he looked down to where Adam was lying, his body a dark bundle, in the valley of slate. His face was briefly illuminated by a side light from the skies and Barry saw the thick red ooze joining his pale lips to the blackened blue overalls. It was beginning to coagulate. He and Roberts had all but forgotten Adam during the last three frantic hours. He leaned down over him and listened to his laboured breathing before moving him into more of a sitting position.

They had returned to the roof with sandbags and water to find him sprawled and unconscious, a cigarette in the bloodied hand that was clutching at his chest. There was no time to take him down and so they had moved him, as carefully as they could, into the valley before continuing their incessant battle with the incendiaries. Barry slumped down beside his stricken friend and looked up at the sky. The full moon had shifted in its orbit but still covered everything in a silvery sheen. For long minutes neither he nor Roberts moved or spoke. This was worse than the 29th December. Roberts had fallen asleep and began snoring. Barry looked over at the older man. His tin hat was awry and sprouts of unruly white hair framed his sooty face. He let him sleep.

It was almost an hour before he stirred and then shook himself awake, confused as to where he was.

– We need to carry him down.

Roberts looked over at Adam and groaned.

Barry took his shoulders and Roberts his feet. He had forgotten how little Adam weighed. His head was lolling to the right and his arms hung limply at his sides, swinging gently as they manoeuvred him down the stairs. He seemed to be at peace. It had been less than five hours earlier that they had been chatting together on the roof.

Roberts was blowing hard by the time they reached Hare Court, and stumbled over an unexploded incendiary, so they put Adam on the ground and recovered their breath. Barry looked at his watch. It was past two in the morning. They picked Adam up again and dragged themselves to Dr Johnson's Buildings. The climb to the top-floor apartment was even more arduous than the descent from the rooftop and they had to pause at every floor. Barry fumbled in Adam's pockets until he found the key.

They laid him on his bed and Roberts took his leave, shuffling to the door and closing it quietly behind him. The blackout shades were in place and so Barry lit a lamp and looked down at Falling. The blood was dry now and Adam's breathing seemed a little easier. His face was very pale. Barry got him into a sitting position, cradled him, then began unbuttoning his overalls. Blood on the buttons came away on his hands. As he pulled off the blouson Adam stirred and said, "Julia?" He laid Adam out flat and took the garment to the sink. There was more blood than he had thought. He put in the plug and turned on the tap. It creaked into life and he held the heavy material under the guttering stream. Kneading it made great red blossoms bloom out and stain the water until it was a deep crimson. He turned off the tap, dipped his hands in the sink to clean them, and then went back to Adam.

He loosened the belt on Adam's trousers and gently pulled them off. The bed had been made up crisply and tightly and he had to pull back the counterpane and the blankets and sheet underneath, dragging them down under the motionless body before pulling them up over him and tucking him in. He emptied the trouser pockets: two packets of Embassy cigarettes, one full and the other with three gone, and a little crystal paperweight. He put them on the sideboard. It was almost three in the morning. He didn't want to leave Adam alone so he found a cushion for his head, turned off the electric light, lay down next to the bed and fell asleep.

Someone was shaking his shoulders. His head was full of strange dreams as he swam back to consciousness. The blackout shades had been removed and he heard the desultory spatter of drizzle against the window and the familiar sound of glass being swept. A thin breeze crept in and feathered his cheeks. He opened his eyes and as he brought them into focus he remembered where he was. Blytheway was looking down at him, his face full of urgency and concern. Dust and ash drifted heavy in the air as sunrays caught them.

- What time is it?
- Ten o'clock. What happened?

Barry told him of the previous night's events. He had never seen Blytheway look so grave. As he spoke, Adam began coughing in his sleep. They both looked over at him. He looked so thin under the protective pea-green blanket.

- We must get him to a doctor.
- This has happened before you know.
- I know all about that. Do you want to be relieved of your vigil?
- No. I want to stay.
- Very well. I'll make some tea for us. And then I must go and make a telephone call.

Blytheway's reputation was well known to all those who worked in the Temple, but although he was always scrupulously polite he gave very little of himself away. If he was honest with himself Barry would say that he, and most of the others, were in awe of him. After they had taken their tea Blytheway exchanged some coppers for a shilling and then left the room. He returned twenty minutes later.

- Why is it almost impossible to find a telephone box that works? The telephone is a good invention but it has got a long way to go before it works properly!

They sat in silence next to the bed for the next hour, Blytheway looking disconsolately around the room.

- This place is a mess!

Blytheway said eventually.

– He'd forgotten he was on duty. I don't think he gets many visitors.
– That's absolutely *no* excuse.

Barry had draped the overall trousers over a chair and Blytheway went over and picked them up, slapping them to get the dirt out.

– These haven't been ironed! I went to the trouble of getting him an iron *and* an ironing board!

He folded them and put them on a hanger, then sat down again and went back into his reverie.

– Why are you here so early on a Sunday morning?
– I'm afraid I had to come here to bring Adam some rather bad news.
– That's the last thing he needs.
– It can't be helped.

Blytheway put his head in his hands, then he turned and looked so deeply into Barry's eyes that he felt almost frightened.

– You see, Jeremy Pemberton's daughter – Jenny – was killed last night ... at the Café de Paris.

He put his head back in his hands. Barry hardly knew Jenny but he had heard of her. Pemberton had brought her to a Ladies' Dining Night during the last Michaelmas term and everyone had told him afterwards how lovely she was. It didn't seem possible. Blytheway did not elaborate and so he respected the ensuing silence. Instead they both concentrated on Adam. He lay there without moving. Only the slight movements of his chest showed that he was still alive. Barry wondered at Blytheway's stillness.

At around 11.30 there was a knock on the door. Barry opened it to find a man he had never seen before: a tall man wearing a dark jacket, striped trousers and a bowler hat. He had a scar down one side of his face. Blytheway shouted across to him.

- Caldwell! Many thanks. You have the jalopy?
- Parked outside King's Bench Walk, sir.
- Excellent. Help me lift him. Will you lend a hand, Barry?
- I don't think he would want to be moved, Mr Blytheway.
- He needs medical attention. And my physician should already be on the way to my home.
- He'd prefer to be here, sir. I don't think you should be taking him against his will.
- I'm sorry, Mr Funge … I mean Barry … we're going to have to use force.
- He doesn't want to go, sir.
- Look, Mr Funge … I mean Barry. I know he will complain. But I also know what I am doing. This is no place for a sick man. Nor is it a place for someone to be when the man he is alleged to have cuckolded – who works less than a hundred yards away – has just lost his daughter. Can you understand that?
- How did you know my name?
- I've always liked you, Barry. Do you think you'll go back to being a cabbie?
- How do you know *that*?!
- You gave me a ride in your taxi about fifteen years ago. Don't you remember talking to me about football and Mr Turnbull? Do you still support the Pensioners?
- Yeah. I'm still a Chelsea fan.
- If you take his feet then Caldwell can take his shoulders …

They dressed him, and as they were buttoning up his jacket Adam stirred.

- Julia? Is that you?

Blytheway looked sternly at Barry.

- I think we shall both forget he said that.
- No, sweetheart. Only me. And some friends.

Adam opened his eyes.

- What happened?
- We need to get you to a doctor. You're going to have to stay with me for a few days.
- No! I want to stay here!
- Adam. I'm going to have to be firm. I don't suppose anyone has any morphine?
- We need to talk about my case.
- Don't worry about that. Just for now. You're in no fit state.
- But it starts tomorrow. I'm not ready.
- Don't worry, sweetheart. It's been put off.
- Put off?
- We'll talk about that later.

At Blytheway's instruction Barry and Caldwell manhandled a protesting Adam down to Inner Temple Lane, Barry holding his feebly kicking legs and Blytheway supervising events from behind and carrying Delia the cat, in her cage, and a change of clothes. From there they heaved him, sagging, between them past the church and Lamb Building and towards King's Bench Walk. Blytheway sneezed and held Delia's cage at arm's length.

- As far as I'm concerned cats should have stayed in Egypt! Do you mind coming with us, Barry? I'll give you the fare for the ride back.
- All right, mate ... sir.

The "jalopy" was a large and rather luxurious black car.

I'm afraid we don't tend to use it much. It's usually more convenient to take a taxi. I keep it fuelled and garaged in case of emergency. This counts as an emergency so we can give it a spin!

They climbed in, Caldwell in the driver's seat and Blytheway on his left with Adam and Barry in the rear. The car park would usually be full of cars for the Sunday service but it was virtually empty. There was a light drizzle so Caldwell started the windscreen wipers off as he headed for the Tudor Street exit. The car purred as it moved up to Fleet Street and then Chancery Lane. Within fifteen minutes they had arrived at Bedford Square. The brakes crunched comfortably as Caldwell drew up and parked behind a large Bentley before limping out to open the passenger doors. As he did so the driver's door of the Bentley opened and paunchy grey-haired man, wearing a dark suit with a gold watch-chain across his belly, pulled himself out.

- Boult! Lovely to see you! Thank you so much for coming.

Blytheway sashayed over to him and shook his hand. Behind him Barry and Caldwell were lifting Adam out of the car and then supporting him on their shoulders.

- May I introduce Dr Boult? A fine physician whom I have used for many years. He was introduced to me by a friend who would have nosebleeds at the most *inopportune* moments!
- Why has my case been ... put off?
- Unhappy news, sweetheart. Jenny Pemberton was killed last night.
- What?!
- There's nothing to be done I'm afraid. Alnwick, Julia's barrister, rang me at some ungodly hour this morning to tell me about it.
- This changes everything doesn't it?
- I would think so. Apparently, Pemberton went on a whisky-blinder and knocked Julia out cold.
- Bastard!
- Alnwick was gabbling and it was all rather garbled as a result. I think we must reserve judgment. Help him into the house. A room has been made up on the first floor and Dr Boult can examine him there.
- Did she sign the statement?
- Yes and no. Apparently she signed it before she left the house. But it wasn't witnessed so we may have some evidential problems in relying upon it. But that's for another day.

Adam tried to stand free of them.

- Thank you for the cigarettes.
- I'm afraid you've managed to get them covered in blood. I'm sure Caldwell can make them usable.
- Has the case been postponed or abandoned?

– Postponed, sweetheart, I'm afraid. If Pemberton has resorted to violence it augurs very badly.

They grabbed back hold of him and half-carried him, half-pulled him into the house and up the stairs to the same first-floor bedroom he had occupied a few weeks previously. Blytheway continued to carry Delia in her cage, his arm at a right-angle from his body and the look of a bad smell across his face. A large towel and some purple silk pyjamas were lying on the bed. Blytheway put the cat down and then retreated whilst Barry and Caldwell changed Adam into his bed-wear.

After about five minutes Caldwell opened the bedroom door and Blytheway re-entered with Dr Boult. Barry came over to them.

– The last doctor who looked at him said that it could be TB.
– I know about that.

Barry had no idea how Blytheway could possibly know.

– Caldwell, would you mind getting some milk for the cat? Dr Boult. Thank you again for coming on this day of rest. Would you mind examining our patient?

Barry watched as the doctor unbuttoned the purple top and pressed his stethoscope against the feeble chest. Doctor Boult listened for a while and then forced Adam into a sitting position before taking the top off altogether and tapping various parts of his back. Then he laid him back down, produced a magnifying glass and used it to look deep into Adam's eyes. He looked over at Barry.

– You mentioned another doctor. Tell me about that.

Barry told him of the events of 29th December – of the vomited blood and the discovery of white grains amongst the brick dust. Dr Boult looked at Blytheway and then at Adam.

– Yes. It is probably tuberculosis. You are lucky to be alive, I think. But you are an infection risk. In my own opinion you should be in isolation. You need at least three weeks' complete rest. Another attack like this would probably kill you.

He handed over some morphine, signed a prescription, and left.

Chapter Sixty-eight
(Saturday 15ᵗʰ March 1941)

Bluebells and bright yellow daffodils were beginning to push their way
yearningly out from the deep green grass around the gravestones. A breeze
made their heads sway. Julia's face, behind her mourning veil, carried yel-
lowish-blue marks that had not been entirely concealed by her foundation
cream, one on the right side of her jaw and the other on her left temple. A
gust of wind made her mantilla gust and pout, cooling her cheeks. Her eyes
had filled with tears, but the wind was not to blame. Ahead of her, under a
colourless sky, the funeral procession in black smudgy imprecision made
its way to the fresh-cut grave, piles of deep soil on either side. She walked
in slow-step, like a guardsman, the limping figure of Simon Jenkins on her
left. Jenny's coffin swayed and tilted in its own irregular and final dance.
In her nostrils she caught the scent of freshly turned loam and the beginnings of the greenness of a new spring.

Jeremy had chosen to take the rear right-side weight. To his left walked
Preston. At the front were Storman and Chips Channon, perhaps, she
thought, feeling guilty about introducing Jenny to the Café de Paris – perhaps because he had to be there anyway for the burial of Poulsen, he of
the twenty-five thousand bottles of champagne and safe haven, who had
also been killed that night. Ahead of Pemberton was Samuels. She did not
know the sixth pall-bearer. Behind the coffin trailed Agnes, Stephen and
Sebastian, separated from her now as they had been in the cortege from
Eaton Square. A pre-figurement of what Jeremy intended for the years
ahead. After the funeral she would have to move out. She fixed her eyes on
Jeremy's back and saw the bones of his shoulders moving in an exhausted
rhythm under his mourning coat. The ground beneath his feet was smooth
and bland and could not account for the way he stumbled and swayed as
he walked. The mahogany coffin that he was helping to carry looked light
and easy.

Julia took a sideways glance at Simon Jenkins from beneath her veil. She had never seen him before that dreadful night (and only once afterwards) but Jenny, in all their conversations at the Ritz, had captured him well. He did not, however, resemble the photograph Jenny had shown her. That showed Julia a care-free young man with dark tousled hair and an enormous white smile, eyes dancing into the camera. The boy, for he was only a boy, next to her was not smiling. All his features were drawn inwards and his eyes – his whole being – had been hollowed out. He should still have been in the Westminster Hospital but he had insisted on being released for this. Julia watched him as he limped along next to her, his right arm encased in thick white plaster holding onto the crutch that he was using to support his right leg. He was wearing his uniform, the same one he had been wearing that night. He had attempted to clean it but Julia saw traces of dust and plaster on his back. The right trouser leg had been cut away to accommodate the plaster that ran up to his thigh, and he winced with every step.

The coffin was approaching the grave now and the men began to unburden themselves, lowering it onto the waiting ropes. The headstone for Joan's grave, black marble with gold lettering, had been balanced against a tree:

Joan Pemberton (formerly Swift)
b. 18ᵗʰ June 1895
d. 6ᵗʰ December 1924

Beloved wife of Jeremy and loving mother of Jenny

"Death lies on her, like an untimely frost
Upon the sweetest flower of all the field."

Julia felt her cheeks reddening as she thought back to the awful events of the previous Sunday morning. She had gone down into the cellar almost immediately after Jenny had left and read for a while. The bombardment was already very loud and she had been worried that she would not sleep that night and so had taken an extra dose of her sleeping draught at around nine in the evening. Everything that happened after that she heard from Annie. Jeremy had stayed upstairs for a little longer but by nine thirty he too was down in the cellar, as were Samuels and Annie. Annie said that he had been wearing blue and white striped flannelette pyjamas. She described how he had doused the gaslight from behind the curtains and everything became dark. Annie could not sleep and watched as that little bedroom behind the wine racks came back into some sort of gloomy focus. And she told Julia of the noise of the heavy bombardment, of which Julia had been totally unaware.

Then, about an hour or so later, there had been a frantic banging on the front door, which no one had wanted to answer. It would not stop. Eventually Samuels stirred himself, put on his dressing-gown and made his way up to the relentless hammering. If he had been drowsy and resentful as he slouched up the narrow steps, his lamp making grotesque shadows on the walls, that soon changed. Annie had heard shouts and expletives, and then heard rather than saw Samuels, with Preston close behind him, rushing down into the cellar. Preston was shaking Pemberton awake. Initially fuzzy and angry at being disturbed, Jeremy had quickly realised that something unimaginable had happened. Julia had slept through all of this.

Annie had heard some reference to the Café de Paris and to a bomb and then Pemberton was out of bed and heading upstairs in his pyjamas. He left his gold-rimmed spectacles next to the bed. Samuels had grabbed a dressing-gown for him as they left. How did Preston know that Jenny might be there? Julia tried to imagine all the conversations she was no longer part of. Preston had come by car and they had all tumbled in and headed towards Procter Street. The bombing was still going on but Pemberton had insisted they use the headlights to increase their speed.

Of course, there had been nothing that they could do. By the time they arrived the area had been cordoned off and demolition workers were inside. The injured were being taken to Charing Cross Hospital and the dead were being lined up on the street outside. Samuels had told Annie how they had gone past the bodies and tried to get into the ruins of the night club only to be prevented by emergency crews. They saw enough though, even through the dust-cloud. Supper tables had crashed down onto the dancers, and you could see the reflection of starlight in the broken glass. Some of the dead were slumped around their tables with un-spilt glasses in front of them.

Then they had been pulled out by the rescue workers, Jeremy in his pyjamas shouting, "Do you know who I am?" and demanding to be allowed back down the stairs. But then, as this fruitless argument raged, two members of the demolition squad started up the stairs carrying a stretcher. The body on it was lying face down but despite the thick dust one could see that the dress had once been red; despite the heavy plaster around the head and the swiftly coagulating pool of blood there, one could see that the hair had once been glossy and auburn.

– Jenny!

Pemberton had shouted at the corpse.

– Jenny! Are you all right?

And he had tried to hold her, to take her in his arms. The stretcher was still at an angle on the stairs and the carriers attempted to wrest it away from his grasp. Pemberton, thirty years older than they, squared up for a fight and it took Preston to wrap his arms around the older man and pull him away. Pemberton was forced to watch as Jenny's body was laid down, face-up now, outside next to all the others before they were moved to the nearest mortuary in Procter Street. He saw her lying in line with so many beautiful people. Samuels told her that Pemberton had said, through tears, that Jenny was the most beautiful of them all. Julia had tried so many times in the last several days to imagine this. She had seen Jenny's body lying in its coffin in the drawing room, where not so long ago they had a party, and she wondered how different what she saw was from the horror of late on that Saturday night.

She had looked beautiful. Her hair had been washed clean and there was the smell of shampoo and of something acrid. Julia had found a quiet time to go and see her there, although it was not forbidden to go at other times. She needed to be alone with her. She – it – was beautiful. But it was no longer Jenny. This thing could no longer smile. It could not open its eyes. There was no love left inside it. All that was left were memories, her diary, Jeremy and Simon – perhaps her letters? She could not talk with it. There was no play of emotion across it as she thought these things. There would be no further discussion of areas to live or how and where to bring up children.

Jeremy had tried to insist that she be brought "forthwith" to Eaton Square but Preston persuaded him that there were some bureaucratic necessities that required fulfilment. Julia attempted to imagine how ridiculous he would have looked railing against the war in his pyjamas, Preston trying to hold him back.

Eventually Preston pulled him away. Samuels, according to Annie, said that he finally agreed to leave her if he were to be allowed to pick her up "one last time" and hold her in his arms. Pemberton had lifted the body up in his arms and held her "like Fay Wray". Jenny's limbs hung loosely and swung about as he spoke to her. He smoothed her hair and kissed her cheeks. Then he said sorry. Samuels said that he would not have let her go but for Preston's insistence. They pulled him back to the car and made their way back home. There was blood on the flannelette pyjamas.

It was after midnight before they returned and Pemberton was already wailing. Preston clearly needed an early night. By this time Pemberton had rounded on Preston for failing to warn him of this large attack. Preston blamed Blytheway for the debacle of a trial the previous week. Pemberton blamed Blytheway for distracting him with the upcoming contested divorce. This hopeless conversation of blame could have carried on all night and so, to end it, Preston, for the best of possible motives, suggested that Pemberton should have a whisky.

It was almost three hours later that Julia had awoken to the sounds of his grief. She realised, in retrospect, that she had still been befuddled by the sleeping draught. She had not, to her shame, recognised in her befuddled state that if you love one person slightly more than you love another then you might as well not love the first person at all if their interests come into conflict. Because she did love Jenny. Or rather she had loved her more than anyone other than her own children. She had begun to understand how, insidiously, Jenny was replacing her in Jeremy's affections. But that had never been Jenny's fault or her intention. Jenny was probably entirely unaware of it.

It was, obviously, impossible that the trial should begin on the following Monday. They had both been devastated by Jenny's death, and, according to rumour at least, Adam was not fit to deal with a contested divorce hearing. Jeremy was clearly unwell although she was not able to assess the extent of this. In addition, she had heard that his trial for the following week had also been postponed.

He no longer spoke to her at all, even at breakfast. But she could smell the whisky on his breath. She could also smell cigarette smoke and she knew that he was raiding his black-market supplies. Annie had told her that, after he knocked her unconscious, she had pulled her into her bed and then guided him upstairs. By now the raid was over. She tried to put him in the marital bedroom but he had become aggressive and argumentative and had insisted on sleeping in Jenny's small single bed. He had slept there ever since, surrounded by photographs of Joan and of Jenny – and by empty whisky bottles and overflowing ashtrays.

And so, on the Thursday after Jenny's death, he had succeeded in bringing her body home. She lay in an open coffin, with incense candles burning behind the shades of the blackout. That was where Julia went to look at her beautiful corpse.

And then the funeral itself. Jeremy must have spent all of the money he had been saving for her (approved) marriage on this. The cortege consisted of three Rolls Royces. The first, of course, contained Jenny's coffin and led the procession, the roof topped up with flowers. White lilies with heavy scent. In the next car were Jeremy, Preston and Storman, together with Agnes, Stephen and Sebastian (brought up from the country), and finally there were Julia, Simon Jenkins, Annie and Samuels in the car behind. Jeremy had blamed Simon for Jenny's death and had to be persuaded to allow him to be part of the cortege. Everyone else would take the tube to West Brompton and meet them there.

The cortege had moved along Sloane Square and right into Sloane Street before turning left into Brompton Road, then Old Brompton Road, towards Brompton Cemetery. For a moment Julia forgot everything and saw the small line of black cars ahead of her, the car-roof flowers swaying in the wind, as taxis and other vehicles slipped by in the other direction. They had arrived at the North Entrance and headed, in a stately fashion up the Central Avenue to the chapel. Jeremy had somehow organised a string quartet and some singers to perform Stabat Mater by Pergolesi. Not an obvious choice for a non-Catholic, but beautiful nonetheless. He gave a halting eulogy, his voice cracking and his tongue stumbling over his words.

And now the coffin was on the ropes and the last act in Jenny's drama was happening. She had loved Jenny so much; but not enough. And she began to cry again and everything blurred out.

Chapter Sixty-nine

(Saturday 15ᵗʰ March 1941)

The pall-bearers had put the coffin down and the grave-diggers were pulling on the ropes to make a cradle for it. Slowly they lifted it and, after positioning it, swaying slightly, over the hole, they began to lower it down and out of sight. Simon began to sob uncontrollably and covered up his face with his free left hand. Julia put her arm around him and hugged him to her side. Through her clothing he felt the warmth of her breast against his shoulder and subsided into her, still weeping. Gently she stroked his hair. Through his tears he saw the ropes now being pulled out from the grave and Jeremy Pemberton reaching for the shovel standing upright in a mound of soil. Simon felt a shooting pain run up his leg as he came to a halt for the burial.

Jenny had spoken and written much to Simon about her father – and about the woman who was now holding him. He remembered that wonderful first time that they had gone to the Café de Paris. Jenny had told him of her father's obstinate stupidity in thinking that Julia had betrayed him; of how, strangely, her father had called her "Joan" more than once during her interview with him that evening before she had met him on the steps of the house. Jeremy stumbled and nearly fell as he sought to make a shovel-full. He seemed older and frailer than the vigorous man Jenny had described, and his gold-rimmed spectacles sat lopsidedly on his nose. Steadying himself, he slid the shovel blade into the soil and then lifted it slowly, rivulets of earth falling from it as he turned to face the grave. He looked confused – as if he did not know where he was – before shaking himself erect, advancing to the grave's edge and tilting the shovel. The soil thudded softly onto the lid as Jeremy turned slowly away and dropped the shovel. He stumbled again and fell to his knees, putting his hands to his face and bowing his head. Simon felt Julia holding him more tightly, so tightly that he could feel her heart beating. Behind Pemberton the gold lettering on Joan's grave-stone glittered slightly in the apologetic sun. A little further away he saw a slim figure in a top hat gliding between the trees.

She had been looking into his eyes when it had happened – looking into his eyes and smiling. He was the last thing she would ever see. He rippled his fingers along the handle of his crutch and tried to retrieve the sensory memory of the last time they had touched.

He was unsure how long he had been unconscious although it had probably not been that long. The weight of Jenny's body upon him had been far greater than he expected until he realised that a substantial part of the ceiling was lying on top of them both. He tried to move but his right arm and leg were pinioned. Above him he could see stars shining in, and the edge of the treacherous moon. Slowly he became aware of the screaming and moaning. He heard a woman saying again and again, "Take me to a hospital, take me to a hospital." People were running across his body and a high heel punctured his ankle, causing him to gasp with pain. He felt an enormous panic rising with him and he had closed his eyes and tried to concentrate on Jenny. He felt her legs lying across his, her chest upon his stomach. He could sense no breathing; feel no heartbeat. Blood was beginning to ooze and drip from her down on to his arm.

He had lain there for an age before what at first he thought a miracle began to happen. Jenny's left arm began to move, slowly at first but then with increased intensity so that it was almost thrashing against him.

– Jenny!

He had called out her name and almost at once the movement stopped. There was a slight pause and then he heard a distinctive crack which he realised, almost instinctively, was that of a bone breaking, and then Jenny's arm fell back down against him.

– It's all right, mate. We'll get you out of there.

It was a demolition crew. They pulled the remains of the rubble off Jenny's body and dumped her unceremoniously face-down onto a stretcher. Even now he wished he had not looked. The back of her head was a dreadful mess and blood was dripping into her still-open eyes. The back of her red silk dress was torn and bloody and almost black from the debris that had hit her. They lifted the stretcher and her left arm swung free. He saw that her ring finger had been broken and the emerald ring that she had been wearing had gone.

461

Eventually he had been placed on a stretcher and taken to the Rialto Cinema, which was being used as a place for sorting out the dead and the dying from those who might still live. The man on the stretcher next to him had a leg so damaged that it swung like a pendulum as emergency staff tried in vain to fix a tourniquet. He looked down at his own damaged limbs and thanked providence that, with luck, he would be able to keep them. Then out of the mist that floated over his eyes he was able to make out a figure in dirty white approaching with a hypodermic syringe. He felt his trousers being pulled down and then a metallic sting in his left thigh, a warming sense of something, and then nothing at all.

They had taken him to the Charing Cross Hospital, and, after a day or so, on to the Westminster Hospital. It was there that they fixed his upper arm and placed pins in his shin and thigh, although he had no memory of these things. He knew, of course, that Jenny was dead.

On the Thursday he had received an unexpected visitor. A pretty nurse announced that Julia Pemberton was here to see him. She was wearing a dark purple tweed twin-set and had an emerald scarf covering her hair and temples. Her eyes were red-rimmed from crying and there were dark shadows under them. Her face had been heavily made-up but he could make out the bluish swelling on her jaw. She sat down by his bed and reached out to touch the fingers of his uninjured left hand, then looked into his eyes.

– I'm so terribly sorry.

And then she began to cry again. Haltingly she told him what she knew of what had happened that night.

– So – *she had concluded* – Jenny would hardly have felt a thing. She didn't suffer.

And as she said these words Simon realised that she was trying as much to convince herself as she had been to convince him. She had told him of the plans for the funeral and Simon had insisted that he wanted to be there. She promised him she would arrange it. Then, after about forty-five minutes she rose to her feet, stroked his hair and bent over him to kiss his forehead. Then she left.

They had almost finished filling the grave with soil and it heaped up into a mound. Under there lay Jenny. There was an uncertain silence as the sound of metal chopping into earth ended. Wreaths were laid. Simon began to sob again.

– Are you all right?

Julia asked softly. Simon nodded and wiped his face with his hand. They turned and began to walk back to the cars, Julia still holding onto him. He realised that, unwittingly, Jenny had saved his life, and he vowed to her that he would try and help her step-mother.

****

Julia helped Simon into the third Rolls and climbed in after him. The doors closed with a reassuring clunk and the cortege headed back down the Avenue retracing the route to Eaton Square. Simon looked awkwardly over his shoulder until Jenny's grave was out of sight, and then turned and watched the two black cars ahead of them as they moved slowly back to the main road.

As the cars left through the North Gate of the cemetery the man in the top hat whom Simon had noticed earlier emerged from behind the statue of an angel and walked unhurriedly towards the grave. He leaned down slightly to read the inscription on the grave-stone and ran an elegant fore-finger delicately along the gold letters before picking up the wreath that Pemberton had placed on the grave, bringing it up to his face and sniffing at it carefully. Then he straightened up and stood for a while deep in thought. And after a few minutes Roland Blytheway began to walk briskly towards the South Gate.

Chapter Seventy

(Saturday 15ᵗʰ March 1941)

Adam pulled himself up to a sitting position in his luxurious bed, groaning heavily as he did so. He plumped up the downy white pillows behind his head, picked up again *Tropic of Cancer* by Henry Miller and began again to read its shockingly lubricious prose. He had known of the book's existence as Orwell had written kindly of it, but as it had been banned and only smuggled copies had entered the country, he had never expected to have the opportunity to read it. There was a knock at the door and Caldwell entered with a tray of tea and toast. Adam looked at his watch and wondered when Blytheway would return.

He had not been invited to attend Jenny's funeral, but then again he had been in no fit state to do so, even surreptitiously. Blytheway had talked him out of attempting it. And so he had persuaded Blytheway to go in his place. Roly had not thought much of the idea.

- It would be bad enough if *I* was to be spotted hovering round the statuary – but think how it would look if you were caught scurrying about!
- But it would be worth the risk.
- That's precisely my point! – *there was a hint of exasperation in Roly's voice* – nothing can be gained from this caper.
- Please, Roly!
- Oh, very well. The postponement of your trial means that I have time on my hands. I shall go in disguise.

This conversation had taken place on the evening before the funeral. Although the trial had been postponed – and despite what Blytheway said – he seemed as busy with other work as he had always been and would often leave home before Adam awoke, not returning until seven or eight in the evening. However, he always found time to give Adam a potted summary of the day's developments and to tell him more, as he discovered them, of the events of the 8th March. There had been no mention of the Café de Paris in the press but it seemed to be common knowledge around the Temple, as was Pemberton's tragic loss. There was, said Roly, a ground-swell of sympathy for him, and Adam realised, belatedly, that Blytheway's anticipation of this was probably another reason why he wanted to get him away from the Temple for a while.

There had been another development, however. There was growing chatter to the effect that Pemberton had returned to the bottle. There had been stories of him staggering as he walked down Inner Temple Lane. He had been seen in El Vino's for the first time in almost twenty years, drinking alone. Whilst his initial, and continuing, indisposition was due to bereavement it appeared that his heavy drinking was not helping. When Jones, at Blytheway's bidding, had telephoned McKechnie's solicitor to suggest an adjournment of the upcoming trial, this had been readily accepted. Mrs McKechnie's solicitors were also quick to agree to this.

By the end of the week Adam was beginning to feel a little better and was becoming bored of looking at the counterpane. Blytheway had given him *Tropic of Cancer* to read.

– The Renshaws gave it to me as a "thank you" present whilst we were out at the Dorchester after their triumph in the literary cause célèbre. I haven't had time to read it yet but they told me it was decidedly louche!

And so, on the Saturday morning of the funeral, Adam was reading a banned book in a first-floor bedroom in Roly's house in Bedford Square. There was a knock at the door and Blytheway entered.

– What do you think?

He gave a twirl. He was wearing a dark frock coat with a black waistcoat underneath. The linings were made of purple silk and it had been tailored to accentuate his waist. Under his wing collar he wore an oyster-coloured cravat and on his head was a tall black silk top-hat.

– Roly! I thought you said that you were going in disguise! You'll stand out like a sore thumb!

– Context is everything, dear boy. Context. I shall be invisible. I still think this is a *complete* waste of time. I shall see you later and report.

He swished out of the room saying "imbecile de course" in a stage whisper. And he had been gone now for almost four hours. Adam finished off his toast, put the tray to one side and returned to the novel. Before he had read more than a page the door swung open and Blytheway entered with a flourish, his top hat in one hand and a bunch of daffodils and bluebells in the other.

– Flowers for the invalid!

He began arranging them in a vase, topping it up with water from the large porcelain carafe in the corner of the room.

– How's the *Tropic of Cancer* coming along?
– I can see why it was banned. All those rude words! I'm glad no one's looking over my shoulder.
– Then I simply *must* read it as well.
– Tell me about the funeral.
– Well, as I suspected, there isn't much to tell. I got close enough to the chapel during the service to hear that Pemberton had chosen Pergolesi. He went up in my estimations with that.
– Were you seen?
– Yes. I'm afraid I was seen. But I wasn't noticed.

Blytheway proceeded to describe the funeral and burial to Adam exhibiting once again the peculiarity of his "photographic" memory. He was able to identify to Adam everyone who was there, what they were wearing (some inevitable sartorial criticism), what they were carrying and where they were standing around the grave. He described how Agnes, Sebastian and Stephen had been kept separate from Julia, and how Julia had walked at the back with a young man with a crutch. He described the cars as they arrived and as they left – the sun glinting on the black paintwork – and who was in which car.

– It was a lovely morning. You could almost feel spring in the air. That's where I got your flowers.

– Is that it?

– Well, I told you that I thought it would be a wild goose chase. And largely it was. But there were two points of interest.

– Go on.

– Well, first, it was the way Pemberton was walking. There was a tendency to splay out his right leg – not with every step but quite frequently. And he stumbled more than once. I'd seen him walk this way before in his drunken days after Joan. I wanted to be sure, however, and when the cars had all gone I went and had a sniff at his wreath. There was a distinct whiff of whisky on it – as though he had been drinking that morning and spilt some on his hands. He also looked thinner than before.

– And what else?

– There seemed to be a surprising closeness between Julia and the boy with the crutch. She put her arm around him and it stayed there, from the grave all the way back to the car, and she helped him.

Adam was taken aback.

– Do you think there is something going on there?

– No, sweetheart. At least not in the way I *think* you mean. I think the young man is Simon Jenkins, Jenny's sweetheart, and that Julia was trying to comfort him. I was too far away to make out whether this was genuine but when I attempted to get a little closer the boy looked straight at me so I slipped out of sight.

– Why would it not be genuine?

– I really don't know, Adam. On the one hand there can be little doubt but that Jenny confided in him and wrote copious letters to him. She probably also spoke to him about her evidence. On the other hand it may well be no more than guilt.

– Guilt?

– Yes. You see I've found out why Pemberton hit Julia that night. It seems that when she discovered that it was Jenny rather than, as she had thought, her own daughter who had died, she began laughing hysterically in Pemberton's face. I think I can understand now why he reacted as he did. And why he is continuing with the petition.

– I had no idea.

And if Julia is counting on help from Simon Jenkins, I suspect he will be less likely to come to her aid if he finds out about that.

Chapter Seventy-one
(Monday 17ᵗʰ March 1941)

Jones arrived to work early. He had taken the previous Thursday and Friday off to spend at home with Mrs Jones. But after four days discussing the ration book he was glad to be back at work once again. Sonia had barely taken her coat off when he walked into his office. Beyond the frosted glass his room seemed to be as he had left it.

   – Mr Bateman called on Friday to make an appointment. He'll be here at ten o'clock.

Jones sighed. He had been expecting this.

   – Thank you, Sonia.

And without more words he opened the door and went over to his desk. Sonia had laid out Thursday's and Friday's correspondence, opened and date-stamped, together with his diary noting that morning's appointment. The Novak file was where he had left it next to the telephone. He picked it up and opened it. All his loose-leaf handwritten notes fell onto the floor and he scrabbled around to pick them up. He hadn't got round to archiving the file. He leafed through his notes and the memories of that strange week came alive again. It was, he thought, the most surreal few days he had ever experienced in a court room. Falling, he supposed, had acquitted himself adequately in the end. But Blytheway had been a revelation. He thought back on the many put-downs he had heard repeated by his colleagues and tried to square these with the performance he had seen. He couldn't. Was it envy, malice or prejudice? It could not possibly touch upon his abilities. In thirty years he had seen nothing like it. Blytheway, although distant and somewhat frivolous on a superficial level, had always been civil – at least to those upon whom he could have unleashed his powerful scorn. He had reserved this for the powerful, like Preston. And when Blytheway had approached him after the trial and asked whether he would be prepared to instruct him on a pro bono basis to defend Katya Hoffer he was so flattered that he accepted without a second thought.

He shuffled the papers and put them back in the file. Then he wrote a note to Sonia asking that she file them in such a way that he could retrieve them quickly when he needed them. There was little new in last week's correspondence. The dramatic things had happened before he took his unprecedented days off.

Everyone knew by Sunday morning that the Café de Paris had been hit. Late on Sunday evening Blytheway had called him at home. How he got the number Jones did not know. Jenny Pemberton was dead and Adam was seriously ill. The trial would not be starting the following day. Jones had felt a great rush of relief followed immediately by shame at the fact that the death of an innocent young woman could provoke such feelings in him. He had mapped out long nights of work that now could be postponed. It took a little while for the implications for the trial itself to sink in. Blytheway had told him that Jenny had signed the statement prepared for her but it had not been witnessed.

Later that week Blytheway had told him to contact McKechnie's lawyers and ask for a postponement of that trial as well. All the lawyers were in agreement that this had to be so. After this had been achieved he dictated a letter to Bateman telling him that the trial was being put off by reason of the indisposition of Pemberton and Falling. Blytheway's call had come on the Wednesday morning. The cancellation of the Pemberton trial meant that he had been able to catch up with his paperwork. The postponement of the McKechnie trial, probably until after Easter, meant that he was ahead of himself. And so he decided to take a couple of days off, forgetting briefly about the tyranny of the ration book.

It was a relief to be back in his office. He put thoughts of minuscule quantities of bacon, cheese and beef out of his mind and called Sonia into his room. Sitting behind his desk he began dictating his responses to the correspondence as she took a diligent note. He glanced at his watch. It was five to ten. He called a halt to his dictation and handed the Novak file to her with the instructions for it, and asked her to bring in Bateman when he arrived.

He pulled out the McKechnie file and was leafing through it when Sonia knocked on his door and ushered in Bateman.

- What's wrong with Pemberton?
- What do you mean?
- Has *he* been injured? I wanted this thing over.
- No. He hasn't been injured. But that's not the point.
- Why did you agree to it being put off without talking to me first then?
- He's just buried his daughter for Christ's sake!
- I should have been consulted.
- Did you know that she had died?
- Yes I did. Everyone in the office knows. But why should that stop him from doing his job? Everyone else has to!

Any lingering sympathy Jones had for Bateman dwindled away at this point.

- You heartless bastard!

He regretted it almost as he said it, but it had the desired effect.

- I'm sorry, mate. It's just I'm under a lot of strain with all of this.

Jones softened.

- I shouldn't have said that. I'm sorry.
- Don't get me wrong. I'm really sorry for the poor gal. But I don't know where I am. I've arranged a week off work.
- I can write a letter to your boss explaining everything.

Bateman laughed rather hollowly.

- That's a good one! My boss is McKechnie. He's taken a week off as well.
- Then he should be sympathetic.
- Look. When *is* this thing is going to happen?
- I don't know exactly. But as soon as I know I'll make sure you know.
- Thanks, mate.
- The other thing is that, even if we had wanted to go ahead we couldn't have.

– Why not?

– As I said in my letter Mr Falling is ill again as well. He was fire-watching that night and had another attack.

– I didn't take that in.

– As soon as I know about the new date I will tell you.

– Thanks, mate.

Bateman got up to leave and the two shook hands. Jones ushered him
out of the office and left it to Sonia to show him back down into Fetter
Lane. He rather liked the man even though he was convinced that he was
not telling the truth.

He went back to considering the remains of the correspondence, ready
to start dictating again. Sonia re-entered carrying the morning's post, still
held together by an elastic band. He slipped off the elastic and shuffled
his way quickly through the unopened letters. It was the usual Monday
stuff: expensive envelopes, some bearing the identity of the sending solicitor with his name and address neatly typed onto them. Then he came to
something out of the ordinary. Near the bottom of the pile there was a
smaller envelope – Basildon Bond – and his name and address had been
written in a rather poorly formed blue ink. He put it down in front of him
and shuffled the remainder of the pile into a tidy stack before placing them
on the corner of his desk. Then he picked up his paper-knife and motioned
to Sonia to leave his room.

There were two pale blue rectangles of writing paper, folded in the
middle. He slipped them out of their envelope and spread them out before
him. Written in the same ink as the envelope, his correspondent had not
used joined-up writing; instead vowel and consonant appeared to have
been painstakingly formed. He turned to the final sheet to find the identity of the sender and felt a surge of alarm tighten across his chest. It was
from Betty Sharples. With everything else that had been happening over
the past week or so he had not given her a single thought. He had sub-poenaed her to attend at the Royal Courts of Justice, Strand, on Tuesday 11th
March. Whatever else he had succeeded in doing after Blytheway's late-
Sunday-night telephone call, he had failed to stand her down.

Dear Mr Jones,

This is a letter from me Mrs Betty Sharples. Do you remember you came to see me about making a statement? I am writing because I am very upset at the way I have been treated.

You got a court order against me to make me come to court this Tuesday to give evidence in Mr Falling's case.

I came to court which wasn't easy and I wore my best dress but when I got there nobody knew what was going on.

I had to ask a lot of people before somebody could tell me that the case was <u>not</u> happening! I was so upset I was crying. So I went home again.

You nor nobody else has told me what is going on!

Well I hope it is over now. I would of gone into the dock for Mr Falling on Tuesday but I do not think I could go back to that place again.

I am sorry for writing to you because I know you are a solicitor. But I had to let somebody know that I was very upset.

Yours faithfully,

Betty Sharples.

Jones finished reading the letter and then read it through twice more. He stared at his frosted glass window and the blurred mauve shape of Sonia moving around beyond it. He got up and walked over to his window, looked down on the damaged streets and thought of this woman whom he had only seen once, wearing her best dress and wandering lost around the echoing cathedral that was the main hall of the Royal Courts because he hadn't told her not to come.

After a long while he returned to his desk and slumped down in his chair. He picked up the letter for a fourth time and read it through again. He could not simply dictate a reply to it; he would have to write out his response long-hand for Sonia to type. He read it through again and his eyes snagged on the reference to "Mr Falling's case". Why would she refer to Adam so formally? "I had to let somebody know". Why not contact Adam to find out what had happened? There was nothing to suggest that she had done so. Nor did it sound as though she would be willing to come to court again.

He called Sonia through and asked her to get him a line through to Lamb Building and to Roland Blytheway.

Chapter Seventy-two

(Wednesday 19ᵗʰ March 1941)

Storman was sitting at a small table in Gordon's Wine Bar near Charing Cross. Under the cavernous arches of the Embankment all was dark, lit only by candles perched in bottles at every table. Their flickering lights threw up ghostly shadow-play on the old brick walls. It was early but already the place was filling up with the evening crowd. A bottle of red wine was open on the table. He lifted the glass to his lips and took a cautious sip. Not bad. The other glass was still empty, as was the seat opposite him. He felt an almost impious thrill, which he was quick to suppress. It was only half past five. He was trying to read the evening paper through the gloom but it was not easy; at least he had brought something to read this time. He glanced again at his watch. He had only been there ten minutes.

Catherine Falling was coming down the stairs. He knew that before she reached the bottom of them. He was beginning to recognise the sound of her footsteps. She walked into the room, her eyes narrowing as she adjusted to the darkness, and then she saw him, smiled and made her way over to the table. She had come straight from the office and was wearing a tidy two-piece cotton navy suit under a pink raincoat. She had a book in her right hand – *Planning Under Socialism* by Beveridge. Storman had never heard either of it or him. He stood to shake her hand but she gave him a warm hug instead and kissed him on the cheek.

- Thank you so much for agreeing to meet with me, Jack.
- Oh, it's a pleasure. It's always good to see you.

They sat down and he began to pour out a glass for her.

- A whole bottle? Are you expecting company?
- Not at all. It just seemed like a good opportunity to try and forget the war for an hour or so.

- Well, you'll have to drink most of it. I get squiffy even after a glass. And I'm not sure I'll be able to stay for an hour. I want to be home before it all starts up again. How's Margaret?
- Oh, very well … Actually, not so good … these raids are beginning to get to her. Last week was bloody. We were in and out of our shelter like yo-yos what with the warnings and then the "all clears" and then the warnings again. Our near neighbours got badly hit and two or three houses got burnt out. It's affecting her nerves.
- I'm very sorry. Please give her my best.
- Of course. I can't stay too long either – for the same reasons.

They clinked glasses. Catherine seemed more assured even than last time – happier too. He hadn't realised how beautiful she was and understood why she thought Adam "a bloody fool".

- I see that you've finished with that other book?
- The Keynes? Oh no. I'm still only half way through it but it's a bit much for the train. Everyone at the office seems to be reading *this* and so I borrowed a copy.
- It doesn't look very racy.
- It's not. But very interesting. All being well I think we'll be hearing a lot more from Mr Beveridge.
- So work's going well?
- Oh, very well. I've been promoted! I'm not tied to a typewriter anymore and they're letting me make decisions.

Storman was looking for the word that described her and it came to him: "liberated". She seemed to have been liberated. He wondered whether she would go back to Adam now even if he wanted her to. It was as though her work had given her intellect a focus, as a magnifying glass intensifies sunlight. She had telephoned him at home the previous evening and left a message with Margaret. She needed to see him urgently.

- I expect you want to know what's going on with Adam's trial?
- I knew you'd realise. It's just that when we met last month you told me that it would all be over by now. But I've seen nothing in the

papers about it and I couldn't believe it would pass without a single mention. What happened?

– It hasn't happened yet.

– What!? What do you mean it hasn't happened yet? I'm sure you told me that it would happen last week. That by now it would all be over?

Storman felt his shoulders slump. The story had been so hot as it swirled around the Temple that he had just assumed everyone would know. He had forgotten that Catherine had severed contact with that world, with Adam, and would have had no way of knowing. He hadn't thought to contact her about it. There were so many small worlds in London spinning around in ignorance of one another. He put his head in his hands.

– What's happened Jack?

– I'm sorry. I didn't think. I just thought that you would know about it.

– About what?

– Did you know that the Café de Paris was bombed about ten days ago?

– Yes, of course. Everyone knows about that. What's that got to do with anything?

– Pemberton's daughter – Jenny – was there. I'm afraid she was killed outright.

There was a long silence. Storman took his hands away from his face and looked into Catherine's eyes. She looked shocked and her mouth, in her pale features, was open in a little "o" of surprise as though she had lost the ability to speak. Candle-shadows flickered like wraiths across her face. When she picked up her glass her hand was shaking. She downed it in one and gestured for it to be refilled. Her voice when she spoke was very quiet:

– She was at that party wasn't she? She was very young ...

– It happened just before the trial was due to start. It couldn't go on. Everyone was devastated. And Pemberton's gone back on the drink.

– What do you mean "back on the drink"? I didn't know he had ever been a drinker.

– It was before you knew him. When his first wife died. He was notorious for a few years before Julia came along.

– Bloody Preston!

Catherine was suddenly loud and vehement.

– He was the one who was saying that it was the safest place in London! Bloody, bloody man!

Storman cleared his throat.

– And I'm afraid there's another problem.
– Another?
– I'm afraid Adam is ill again. He collapsed during the same air raid. More bleeding from the lungs.
– Is he all right?
– He'll be fine. Blytheway has taken him under his wing.
– What a bloody mess! Is there any chance that Pemberton will stop all this?
– Quite the reverse I'm afraid. Julia has moved out.

The bottle was more than half drunk. It was quarter past six now and the place was filling up with people and noise. Storman poured out some more and they clinked glasses in silence and tipped back a little more wine.

– Jack?
– Yes.
– It's about Deborah. I'm really not happy about her being out in Edenbridge. I want to bring her back to London.
– Catherine! We've just been talking about Jenny! It would be madness.
– I'm not happy Jack. It's her letters. They're so long and her writing has deteriorated. It's more of a scrawl. That's not like Deborah. I *know* something's not right.
– Wait until Easter. This is no place for her now.

Catherine reluctantly subsided. She was getting ready to leave. She spoke as she rose to her feet.

– So what's going to happen to this trial?
– It's being rearranged. So is the McKechnie case. It looks as if it's going to happen on the 5th May. The other one will apparently start on 28th April. So it looks as though Pemberton wasn't able to get finished by Easter after all.

Chapter Seventy-three

(Friday 21st March 1941)

Julia stood looking out of her new window. The evening sun turned her into a silhouette: elegant and stylish. The light was beginning to fade but she wanted to see the square properly for the first time. She had moved to Mecklenburg Square near to the heart of Bloomsbury. Buds of spring were beginning to green the central garden although many of the surrounding buildings had been crushed and cratered. A heavy dust hung in the air. Annie and Julia's friend Antonia had helped her to ferry her belongings across from Eaton Square. Annie told her she would look after her room until she came back.

She had not taken much and now it had been largely tidied away. Only one thing remained to be sorted out. She held Jenny's diary in her hands. The leather-bound book felt smooth and comforting. Julia turned the key in its lock and ran her fingers over the creamy smoothness of the flyleaf, where she saw in Jenny's hand:

"Please don't read the contents of my journal. It is <u>very</u> private!"

She let the pages riffle through her fingers from the first to the last and individual words hit her retinas, shorn of context, as Jenny's inner life flickered past on paper: *"sad ...happy ... cross ... sad ... unfair ... cross ... love ... love ... love ..."*

Julia turned from the window and closed her eyes, wiping away little traces of tears. Her shoulders sagged and she made her way to the armchair that came with the apartment. She closed the diary, locked it and placed it in her lap, looking again at her new surroundings. The furniture was ugly and makeshift but she had shared access to a cellar in the event of any bombings. It had also been cheap.

There was a reason for this. Caught in the inaccurate cross-hairs that targeted Kings Cross, Euston and Waterloo stations, Holborn area had been subject to appalling damage. Julia had moved into the most dangerous part of central London. Buildings had been turned inside out and gaped. Everywhere there were lines of men in uniform wearing hard hats passing endless wicker baskets of rubble away from the damage. Cranes with metal buckets were swinging through the sky around broken buildings. Signs set down in the roads warned of danger from escaping gas and unexploded bombs. Some houses and shops had disappeared altogether leaving only a mess of footings and debris. There were vast gaps, and from time to time an occasional building would be standing untouched in the middle of the devastation.

Jenny's name had been embossed in gold on the cover of the diary. She was holding the inner life of someone who no longer lived. The hopes and expectations it contained would never be fulfilled. And scattered through its pages she knew there were crosses added in by Jenny in her innocent conspiracy with her step-mother.

She took it through and, unlocking the drawer in her escritoire that held her private papers, she slipped it in with them and then locked the drawer again, placing the key in her pocket. It was time for her to leave.

Locking the front door behind her she walked off towards Rosebery Avenue. It had no longer been feasible for her to continue her war work in the Westminster Report Centre and, through contacts, she had been able to procure a similar position with the Metropolitan Water Board. They too needed to chart the fall of the bombs, although their primary concern was with maintaining the water supply rather than the immediate protection of human life. Some volunteers had died and others had left under the ferocity of the onslaught upon central London, so that her offer to assist was gratefully accepted.

Walking to Mount Pleasant and looking at all the destruction as she passed, she thought back to the day of the funeral. The cortege had finally arrived back at Eaton Square where a modest wake had been arranged. It was very clear that Julia was not welcome and that Simon was merely being tolerated. She had only the briefest conversations with her children before they were whisked away and sent back to the country. They were all that was left now of Jeremy's flesh and blood, and he intended to keep them for himself. Pemberton, who had abjured drink for the whole time she had known him, had ensured that there were three large bottles of whisky standing on the tray next to the obligatory sherry. He had immediately opened the first of these, poured himself a large glass and knocked it back in one before refilling it. He was also smoking.

At a convenient moment she had excused herself and, looking towards Simon Jenkins, indicated with her eyes that he should follow her. This he gladly did, limping awkwardly towards her, with the heel of his crutch rasping along the parquet flooring. They exited the house and Julia hailed a cab to take them back to Westminster Hospital. Neither of them spoke during the journey or on the difficult route back up to his hospital bed. Julia had so many questions in her mind about Jenny, about her letters, but something inside her held her back from asking.

They had said their goodbyes. She did not know whether she would ever see him again. As he subsided into his blankets she hovered over him, and once again kissed him on the forehead.

– I'm so sorry, Simon.

And then she turned and left, her high heels clicking on the marble floor.

She had reached New River House now and walked into the Water Board. When she had told Antonia that she was leaving Eaton Square and moving to Bloomsbury, Antonia had told her she was mad. Why would anyone want to go somewhere so dangerous?

Julia had simply shrugged her shoulders. Perhaps it *was* guilt and shame at her reaction to Jenny's death? Perhaps it was the sense of a certainty, now, that she would never see her children again in the same way, in which case whether she lived or died scarcely mattered anymore. But whilst both these things were true, she knew that, at bottom, she wanted to be near the Temple. There were other things she wanted; but when one is forced by circumstance into a world of deception, one can also end up deceiving oneself just to keep safe that underlying lie. Sometimes these lies might last a lifetime.

Chapter Seventy-four

(Saturday 22ⁿᵈ March 1941)

The blackout screens were down and a three-bar electric fire glowed in the corner of his bedroom. Tiny lamps gave the room a subdued glow. Half-sitting, half-lying in an armchair, Adam was breathing heavily as he struggled to pull on his black-tie trousers. When finally he had them up round his waist he paused for a few moments before buttoning them up. Eventually he struggled to his feet; a giddy sensation made him sway. In the full-length mirror his chest was pale and hollow under his vest and the trousers drooped, puckering out around the front buttons. He saw, in the reflection behind him, the peacock colours of the silk pyjamas that Roly had lent him lying in a mess across his bed.

Caldwell had put some braces on his dressing table and so he fixed them, somewhat awkwardly, into the trouser buttons until they hung properly. He pulled a freshly ironed dress shirt out of the wardrobe and wrestled the studs through the buttonholes. He fixed the black bow-tie and pulled on his jacket, slipping a white kerchief into the breast pocket, then smoothed down his hair. This was to be the first time he had been down for dinner since arriving. Prior to this all meals had been brought to him in bed by Caldwell. A farewell dinner. Blytheway had assured him that he could stay in Bedford Square as long as he wanted to, but Adam was anxious to return to Dr Johnson's Buildings.

- If I didn't know you better I would be affronted at your choice of accommodation!
- Oh, Roly! Don't get me wrong. I've loved being here. And you've been very kind and generous. I just think I should be nearer to Chambers.
- Nonsense! And anyway I had your diary cleared.
- You did what!?
- You're in no fit state. The doctor said three weeks at least.
- When did you do that?

- Immediately after your arrival.
- But you didn't say anything to me!
- If I told you *everything*, sweetheart, I would never stop talking. If I were at the Board of Trade I would ration pointless conversations.

Adam had thought that rather rich.

- I still feel I ought to go back.
- It's quite a while now since there have been any services in the church.
- I know that, Roly.
- Very well. I'll let you have one of our electric fires. And will you agree to leave your cat behind?
- Delia? I thought you didn't like cats? – *Blytheway had insisted that Delia be kept in Caldwell's rooms.*
- I don't. Cat hair gets everywhere. However, Caldwell has taken quite a shine to it and he can keep it in his quarters. He's even suggested putting in a cat-flap so that it can play around in our vegetable patch. You'll get it back, I promise.
- I suppose Delia would be happier here.
- Even a cat shouldn't be kept cooped up all day. And besides, you are going to be very busy in the coming weeks.

And so Blytheway accepted Adam's decision to return to the Temple and Adam agreed to leave Delia behind.

There was a knock on the door and Caldwell slipped in to announce that there would be drinks in the Salon in fifteen minutes. Adam thanked him and he withdrew, closing the door behind him. He heard the butler limping down the stairs.

He had got to know Caldwell relatively well over the previous two weeks. Always immaculately dressed in striped trousers, grey waistcoat and black frock-coat and wearing white gloves, he would bring Adam breakfast, lunch and dinner, sometimes preparing a separate bedside table so that Roly could share a meal with him. He would bring him the morning paper, and tea at four, as well as assembling and taking down the blackout shades at the appropriate hours. He also advised Adam which of Roly's books he should read next. Caldwell was surprisingly knowledgeable about these – and about literature, art and culture generally.

As the days had gone by the perfunctory courtesies attending the delivery of plates, glasses and cups became more discursive. Occasionally Caldwell would even take a seat by the bed, lowering himself awkwardly down and manhandling his damaged right leg until it was comfortable. He could not bend it. He would sit for perhaps ten minutes and chat before rising with difficulty to his feet again, using the arms of his carver chair as leverage to get him upright.

Blytheway was still an enigma to Adam and he had tried, by oblique questions and targeted generalities, to glean from Caldwell a fuller picture of the man. However, Caldwell's inevitable answer would be that Adam should ask Mr Blytheway. He was only a little less revealing when Adam asked him questions about himself. Whilst he was prepared to discuss art, literature, rationing, the war, he would not be drawn. Adam had asked him about the scarring to his face and the damage to his leg, and Caldwell said that these were things that he would rather not discuss. This was to become the stock reply, politely delivered, to any questions Adam put to him about his past. He did, though, open up briefly on one point.

- Mr Blytheway told me when I visited last month that he had a "photographic memory". Is that your experience?
- Well, if Mr Blytheway has told you of it, sir, I can see no harm in commenting on it. He has a complete recall of everything. I found this quite disconcerting at first. There are, I suspect, some things that it would be better to forget. But I do not think Mr Blytheway is able to do that.
- What sort of things?
- Things, I am afraid, that I would rather not discuss. But I would say that he remembers, word for word, our every exchange. He remembers every meal I have ever prepared for him, every guest and precisely what he or she was wearing on any given day. That alone keeps me on my toes, so to speak, sir.

The sound of the dinner gong shimmered up to them from the ground floor. Adam made his way slowly down the stairs, shuffling a step at a time and pausing several times for breath. Caldwell was waiting at the Salon door and opened it for him. The Salon was as he remembered it: the armchairs, coffee table and cocktail cabinet, the Meissonier table, the glass-fronted bookcases, and a profusion of burning candles giving everything a honeyed glow. And against the far wall was the chaise longue upon which Blytheway was reclining.

He uncoiled elegantly and came over to greet him smiling warmly. Roly was wearing a single-breasted dinner jacket cut long, his dress shirt was the stiff stippled type, and the studs glittered with small diamonds. Around his waist was a narrow pearl-white cummerbund artfully highlighted with discreet splashes of yellow and green. Adam noticed a line of a similar green on the lower edges of Roly's bow tie.

They moved to the armchairs and Caldwell brought in an ice-bucket and two flutes. There was a watery clinking of ice against metal as he pulled out the bottle. As before he eased the cork off with a sigh rather than a pop, poured out two sparkling glasses for them, and then withdrew.

– A quarter to eight and no sirens. I think we may be in for another night's reprieve. Here's to your safe return to the Temple.

They clinked glasses and drank.

– And to your kindness and hospitality. Roly, last time we were here you said that it was all right to smoke?
– I'm not sure that's a good idea.
– But, Roly, it's been nearly two weeks.
– And you're still alive. Cigarettes aren't indispensable to happiness you know.
– But they're harmless enough. They're meant to be good for clearing the chest.
– I *know* what their advertisements say. However, it doesn't tally with my own observations of those who smoke.
– Please!
– Oh, very well. You're an adult, I suppose, and able to make your own choices.

Blytheway leaned over towards the table, opened a drawer and pulled out the two packets of Embassy that he had given him a fortnight earlier. They were still spattered with Adam's dried blood. He handed them over and placed an ashtray within reach.

- I thought I'd leave the blood where it was as a grim warning. It set me to thinking. I wouldn't be surprised if one day it becomes compulsory to decorate cigarette packets with blood or some such, just so that people know the risks they are taking.
- Now you *are* being frivolous, Roly. That's absurd – and besides I'm not taking a risk at all.

Adam lit up and took in a deep lungful of smoke. As he blew it out he was overcome with a spluttering fit that left him red-eyed.

- How nice to hear that sound again! It's been *such* a while.
- Sorry about that. I'm sure that was good for me. Clearing out my system.
- If you say so. Are you really sure it is sensible for you to return to living alone in your condition?
- How long have you been living here?

He saw Blytheway register this evasion.

- Since the end of the Great War. It has always been a very pleasant part of town, and such interesting neighbours. Bombs permitting, I think I shall stay here.
- Did you entertain much?
- Entertain and be entertained. But it's a younger man's game and, if I am honest – which of course I always am – I'm tired of it. That very nice lady Otteline Morrell, who died several years ago, lived just down the street and could always be counted on for an interesting soirée.
- The Bloomsbury Set?
- Oh, there was always an interesting crowd and I don't deny that it was exciting at first to have them all come round here from time to time.
- But you tired of it?
- Please don't get me wrong, Adam. I greatly admired a lot of their writings and their art, but after a while I found their conversations to be essentially frivolous.

Adam tried and failed to smother a laugh and ended up coughing and laughing at the same time.

– Now, Adam! But it wasn't just that. I felt that they had an innate sense of their own superiority over the rest of society, and such an attitude is one that I have never been able to stomach. My memory was also something of a curse. I would always know when someone was misquoting something. I would put to a person something flatly contradictory that he or she had said at an earlier occasion and they would emphatically deny having said it. The arts of cross-examination and logic are utterly useless in such circumstances – and, worse, would be seen as bad manners.

– So they stopped inviting you?

– Not at all. I think they regarded me as something of an inoffensive gad-fly. But I had had enough and in the end there was an amicable parting of the ways and we all remained on good terms. Anyway, when the war came and the bombing started, those who were left all seemed to move out to the country.

– Weren't you tempted to do the same?

– I wouldn't dream of it. I want to be here. I want to see what happens. I'm not going to be taking silly risks, but if I did move out whilst all of this was going on I would never forgive myself.

– You mentioned that you had a place in the country?

– A lovely little place in Wiltshire with beautiful formal gardens and a small lake. That's where I keep those peacocks I mentioned. I would go there for a few weeks in the summer and for the occasional weekend away. But that was enough for me. Believe me, Adam, if I am feeling so bored in London I would be utterly unbearable on an indefinite stay in the country. My housekeeper is looking after the place for me and she sends me regular reports.

Caldwell entered to say that dinner was ready and they made their way through to the dining room. The room was laid out as before.

By ten o'clock they were back in the Salon taking their coffee with some port. There had been no sirens or bombs. The meal, as before, had been excellent given the constraints: tinned vegetable soup, grilled and buttered Dover sole with potatoes and spring green cabbage from the garden, followed by steamed chocolate pudding made with milk powder. As before they shared just over a decanter of claret. Conversation was perfunctory but this did not concern Adam. He had been kept up to date with most developments (or at least those which Roly felt it relevant to impart). Any more serious discussions would be left for after dinner.

- Where have you been all day, Roly?
- Portobello Road in the morning, looking for antiques – I managed to pick up a rather good piece of Chinese porcelain – and then in the afternoon I thought I would amble around Bloomsbury. I try and do this about once a month to look at the bomb damage so that I have a record of how things are progressing. Perhaps deteriorating would be a better word.
- Is it bad?
- Very bad I'm afraid. The whole area around here and Holborn has taken a frightful battering. I won't give you chapter and verse on every square but it is decidedly worse than it was in February. The raids over the last three weeks or so, including the one that got you, appear to have tipped an unseemly proportion of their loads right down on top of us. So many lovely buildings have just disappeared. It's a tragedy. It is also absolutely *filthy!* Dust, soot and ash every-where. I think I ruined the clothes I was wearing, and I had to spend over half an hour in the bath scrubbing away afterwards.
- Do you think we are getting near to the end of it?
- If I were Hitler – or should I say Goering – I would take one look at the reconnaissance photographs of all the destruction and I would press on until everything was gone. I don't think London can take much more of this. Mind you, he made a *complete* mess of the Battle of Britain so we must live in hope.

Blytheway stretched and yawned and then cupped his pocket watch to look at the time.

- I rather like the Portobello Road. It's rather seedy, I'll admit. But lovely big houses. I've always wondered why the area is called Notting Hill. When I have a little more time on my hands I may look into that.

He went off into a reverie, leaning back in his armchair and looking at the ceiling before taking a languid sip of port and closing his eyes. Adam thought he was about to drop off without telling him anything about his case.

– Have there been any developments?

Blytheway immediately sat upright and looked into Adam's face. His eyes were alert and smiling.

– I thought you were never going to ask.
– I've learned my lesson,

Adam said ruefully before continuing.

– You said earlier that if you told me everything you would never stop talking. Have you told me everything about my case?
– Of course not. It would be *impossible* to tell you everything.
– Surely I have a right to know everything?
– That depends upon what you mean by "everything". There are facts, there are rumours and there are speculations, some of them mine. I really don't think you are *entitled* to know all these things, particularly matters of speculation and rumour … and leaving such questions aside, whatever your "entitlement" I'm not sure it is actually in your *interest* to know everything.

Adam sighed and slumped back in his armchair. On the one hand Blytheway had obviously been waiting for him to ask, and on the other he was holding out on answers. He had learned, however, that Roly would take things in his own way and at his own pace.

– Tell me about Pemberton at least.
– He doesn't appear to have improved since the funeral. If anything he is drinking more. Last Thursday I was walking down Inner Temple Lane as he was walking – if that is a proper word to use – up. He was staggering in fact. His hair was a mess and he looked as though he had slept in his clothing, which to me is the surest sign of decadence. His spectacles were smeared and I am sure he did not recognise me until we were almost level with one another. I made to tip my hat when he recognised me and he let off a stream of abuse which took the breath away, some of it personal and unrepeatable. I must say he has a wonderful turn of phrase, even when drunk. Quite reminded me

of the old days. The trouble was he was so *loud*, and quite venomous. Heads popped out of windows. I thought it best not to reply and went on my way followed by a fairly fluent bout of cursing – some fairly commendable alliteration if I might say so. I rounded the corner of the church, waited a moment and then stepped back to have another look. He was standing in a daze with people staring at him, as though he'd forgotten where he was going; then he turned and tottered back down the Lane to Stirrup Court.

– He sounds as though he was in a terrible state.

– If anything worse than when Joan died. I think Julia was an enormous help to him when Jenny was a baby, but when she began to grow up he took all the love that he had had for Joan and poured it all into Jenny. He put all his chips into one pocket of the wheel.

– All of them?

– A good question, and I am not sure that I am qualified to answer it. However, I can hazard a guess. If I am right (and I am rarely wrong) and to continue with my roulette analogy, if it is true that Jenny came more and more to resemble Joan as she grew up he may have started to transfer chips from Julia to Jenny, and this of course could lead to a very unhappy change in the balance of affections. Julia is not, I understand, a stupid person. She would have been aware, sooner or later, of what was happening. It wasn't Jenny's fault of course ...

Blytheway paused and looked across at him with that pitiless stare. Adam felt his eyes widening and his face colouring. This was not a hypothesis that had occurred to him – he had been so concentrated on Julia that he had not looked at the wider picture: at Pemberton and Jenny. He found himself searching his memory for any scrap or tittle from his locked store of forbidden memories that might confirm or refute what was being said.

– You've gone strangely quiet, Adam. And you seem miles away. I won't ask what you are thinking, and obviously you know Pemberton better than you knew either Julia or Jenny. But it seems to me that, even with your *limited* knowledge of the characters concerned, my hypothesis does not sound so far-fetched?

– I'd never thought of things in that way.

– If I'm right, Pemberton has bet everything on one person, and now that one person is gone. That is why I think it is even worse for him to lose Jenny. He has not only lost her and all the love he held for her, but he has also lost the posthumous investment of his love for Joan. He's lost all his chips. And if all the love has been lost, then hate, I am afraid, can be quick to fill the vacuum. I can only say that the look that hit me from his murky pools was pure hatred – as though I personally was responsible for Jenny's death. In fact, now that I think of it, he *did* blame me for her death.

– He's gone mad!
– Oh, don't underestimate him. He is no fool and I am sure he will try and pull himself together. But his hatred appears to be all-embracing. There are two silver linings to this cloud. I cannot believe he will be as challenging an opponent in McKechnie, or as difficult a witness in his own case. That can only be to your advantage ... More port?

Blytheway reached for the decanter and filled their glasses.

– 1922 Fonseca. I couldn't resist having it decanted although I am sure it would have outlasted the war. What do you think?

Adam took another sip of the ruby and savoured the play of flavours across his tongue.

– Very good.
– I'm glad you like it. Perhaps we should try and finish it? It's a Saturday after all.

Blytheway also took a sip, rolled it around his mouth, swallowed and let a silence descend on the room.

– You said there were *two* silver linings?
– Oh? So I did. You see, I am not the only member of the Bar that Pemberton has taken to abusing. I am not sure he is always aware that he is doing it. There was an enormous reservoir of sympathy for him after Jenny died but he has performed *superhuman* feats to ensure that this has all now almost drained away. You don't think I would have let you go back to Dr Johnson's Buildings if it were otherwise, do you?

490

– I see.
– You should trust me more, Adam.
– But if he's behaving like that in public he must be abusing Julia terribly at home?
– Oh, Julia moved out several days ago.
– Moved out? Why didn't you tell me?
– I'm terribly sorry. It must have slipped my mind.
– Nothing slips your mind. Where has she gone?
– I'm afraid I really don't know. Somewhere more central I believe.
– Can you find out?
– I am sure I could. But I don't believe it is in your interests to know.
– What right –?
– Trust me, Adam.

He realised again that Blytheway could not be pushed and that he should get what he could out of the man and be grateful for it.

– What does Jenny's death mean so far as her statement is concerned?
– Well. I have seen a copy of it. It is fairly short, and although it would appear that she signed it, it was not witnessed. That creates some evidential difficulties, as you yourself must understand. It would not have mattered so much if she were alive: her statement was for the use of Mrs Pemberton's lawyers, it was not for submission to the court or to the other legal teams. In the ordinary course of things it would have remained with the files of Randall, Beams and Purefoy, Jenny would have given her evidence, and then she would have been cross-examined on it. It was never intended to be an affidavit. Now that she is ... dead, of course, she cannot give that evidence. If it had been witnessed, it would have been that much easier to get it admitted into evidence in her absence. That is considerably more difficult now.
– But that would be disastrous!
– Oh, it doesn't help. Then again, as I said to you once before, I was never entirely happy, instinctively, with this evidence. And there is another problem.
– Another?
– Yes. You see, her statement is rather meaningless as it stands.

– But I thought it provided Jul – Mrs Pemberton with a complete alibi?

Adam saw that Blytheway had noted the slip, and realised that this would be filed away in his photographic memory.

– In one way it does. But it is very short, as I said. All it does is make reference to a number of crosses in her diary. It cannot be understood without being cross-referenced to this. And the current whereabouts of the diary are unclear. If it is still in Eaton Square I do not believe it will be seen again. Not, at least, until long after your trial is over. I cannot believe Pemberton would be able to bring himself to destroy it but it would be very easy for it to go missing.
– So Pemberton has it?
– To be honest, I don't believe he has. I understand from Alnwick that Mrs Pemberton may have smuggled it out of the house when she left. But whether that is true or not remains to be seen. So you see we have a double hurdle.

Adam felt the remains of any hope left in him draining away. He was slightly befuddled by drink and felt himself casting about for another life-line. Blytheway read his mind.

– I think we should have a slight pause now whilst I recharge you with Fonseca 1922.

He poured and they drank in silence. Adam sensed that Blytheway was waiting for him to speak.

– Betty! There is still Betty Sharples! She supports my story.
– I thought you should have another glass before we got onto Betty, Adam. I would like you to read this and then explain it to me.

Blytheway reached into his inside pocket, pulled out a pale blue Basildon Bond envelope addressed in blue ink to Eric Jones, and handed it to an unsuspecting Falling.

Chapter Seventy-five
(Sunday 23rd March 1941)

It was getting late now. The lamps and candles in the Salon cast a circle of light around the armchairs where Adam and Roly were sitting and made the port decanter gleam. All was quiet in the Square outside. Adam took the envelope from Blytheway's hand and turned it over in his hands. He did not recognise the child-like handwriting, but the W1 postmark was identification enough. He noticed that it had been posted on Friday 14th March, over a week ago. He looked over at Roly, who was watching him intently, then opened the flap and pulled out the letter. The date receipt stamp was Monday 17th March. He looked over again at his friend, who said nothing. Then he read it through twice, starting again the first time when he reached the end.

- Why didn't you tell me about this earlier?
- I could see no profit in it. You've been very unwell.
- But I *ought* to have been told about it!
- And what, pray, could you have done about it other than worry? Have another glass of port.

Blytheway reached for the decanter and in a fluid movement lifted it and positioned it over the rim of Adam's glass, letting the ruby-red liquid trickle slowly into it. Adam immediately put it to his mouth.

- And besides, I have been very busy this week and I wanted to be present when you read the letter. *Equally* important, I didn't want anyone else to be present.
- Why ever not?
- Oh Adam, please!
- Did Jones reply to her letter?
- With my assistance, yes. He was mortified, to be frank. Jones is a

493

good solicitor and he feels he has let everyone down – particularly Betty – wandering about the Royal Courts lost and in her best dress. He apologised profusely to her and explained what had happened to you and to Jenny and all of the last-minute panics. He told her that the trial had been refixed for the 5th May and that she would be needed on the 6th, and he included a postal order to cover her conduct money – with a little bit extra to cover her inconvenience and upset. We haven't received a reply.

– I still don't see why you had to wait until now to show it to me.

Blytheway sighed.

– Because I wanted to hear from you an unvarnished and unrehearsed explanation for this letter.
– I would have thought that was obvious. She wrote the letter because no one told her that the trial wasn't happening. And she was upset.
– Please don't be obtuse, Adam. I've read and re-read that letter and it simply doesn't fit. It's privileged, of course, so Pemberton and his lawyers aren't entitled to see it, but it gives me a far clearer picture of Betty than her witness statement did – and a far better idea of how she is likely to perform on oath (if she is called). It also raises a number of questions that I would like you to answer for me.

Suddenly the room felt so cold that Adam was surprised he couldn't see his own breath. It would be bad enough being cross-examined by Roly when he was telling the truth! He didn't want to lie to him, but if he explained to Blytheway what he had agreed with Betty back in December, then Blytheway would have to cease to act for him. He understood now why his friend had waited; why he wanted to conduct this interview alone. He steadied himself and looked down at his glass, unable to catch Blytheway's eye, took a deep breath, and said:

– Of course! I would be happy to answer any questions you have.
– When did you first meet this girl?
– About May or June of last year. *Lie.*
– Was she working as a prostitute at that time?
– Yes. *Lie.*

- Had you ever seen a prostitute before then?
- No.
- What made you decide to start seeing prostitutes?
- I don't really know.
- So tell me, what made you decide – in May or June of last year – to start seeing prostitutes?
- Umm …

There was a long silence whilst Adam grappled with this simple question. Blytheway said nothing, and although Adam was avoiding his eyes he could feel them boring into him. Eventually Roly broke the silence:

- "Umm" isn't actually a very good answer, Adam.
- Err … I was just looking for some excitement, something different. I wanted to try the thrill of it. *Lie.*
- So, all was not well in that department at home?
- Yes it was … I mean, no, it wasn't really.
- Well. Which was it?
- I suppose it was and it wasn't.
- And is that the reason why you decided to go to see a prostitute?
- Yes. *Lie.*
- And what made you choose Betty Sharples?
- I don't know really. She was the first person I found. *Lie.*
- Would you mind describing her to me?
- Not at all. She's in her mid-twenties, about five foot five with blonde hair and rather pretty.
- Would it be fair to say, then, Adam, that *if* she does appear at your hearing, a neutral observer *might* conclude that she does not look dissimilar to Julia Pemberton?
- I suppose they might, yes.

Adam was not enjoying this – and Blytheway had only just begun.

- Was there any reason why you would always seek out Betty?
- Not really.
- I mean, in that area of town it can't be difficult to find someone else for a change? Was she offering preferential rates for repeat customers?

- I just liked her that's all. We got on.
- And what particularly did you like about her? Why did you get on with her so well? What did you talk about?
- Oh, this and that.
- This and that? So when Betty is asked what you talked about is she going to say "this and that"?
- I suppose so.
- I'll move on I think. Is she married or single? Does she have children?

Adam breathed more easily. He knew the answer to this one.

- She's a widow.
- A widow? She sounds very young to be a widow. How and when did her husband die?

Adam opened his mouth to reply. He was about to tell Roly how Joe had been killed in the Blitz after getting back from Dunkirk but remembered just before he spoke that this would upset the whole chronology.

- Um… Accident at work I think. *Lie.*
- And *when* did this accident happen?
- Beginning of 1940 from memory. *Lie.*
- So presumably Betty brought a claim for compensation for his death?
- I don't know.
- You don't know!? You're supposed to be a lawyer! Presumably you would have given her the benefit of your knowledge and experience? Tried to help her out?
- We didn't really talk about that?
- Then I'll ask you again. What *did* you talk about?
- Day-to-day things really.
- I'll move on I think. Why did you choose to take Betty to an expensive hotel like the Stafford when, presumably, she has her own boudoir?
- It just seemed more romantic, I suppose.
- Romantic!? You're *paying* someone you hardly know for sexual intercourse and you take her to a place like that?
- I'd never done anything like that before and I suppose I just felt safer – cleaner.

– When did you first take her to the Stafford Hotel?

– May or June of last year from memory.

– So, if I understand our case correctly, you didn't go to see any prostitutes until about May or June 1940. At the same time, by unhappy coincidence, Winston Churchill introduced regulations requiring anyone who checked into a hotel to provide identification. That notwithstanding you chose this moment to take someone other than your wife to the Stafford Hotel? Don't answer that. We're down to the dregs. I'm sure Caldwell will have left another decanter in the hall just in case.

Roly sprang lithely to his feet and was out of the room almost before Adam looked up. He took a deep breath. It was plain that Blytheway did not believe a word of it. After a while he had stopped counting his own lies. Every time Roly had had him on the ropes he had backed away from pressing home his advantage. It would not be like that when Sir Patrick Tempest eventually cross-examined him. He wondered how Betty would cope with the onslaught. He thought back to that first conversation he had with Roly in this room. He had said that the truth mattered to him enormously and that he would never mislead the court. What he had said next was engraved on Adam's mind:

> *"You should know by now that the courtroom is not a theatre for truth. Or for justice for that matter. Would you really want the truth to come out in every case? And anyway, let us assume that Novak loves this woman. Is he not entitled to say to himself I will sacrifice my life for that love even if the truth must remain hidden? Assuming he actually knows the truth. People do the strangest things in the name of love, as we all know."*

At the time he had thought these remarks rather barbed. It was only now that he realised how sharp the hook that lay within them was. He looked at his watch. It was past two in the morning.

Blytheway re-entered carrying a fresh decanter, a biscuit tin and a bag of candles. Adam had not noticed that, one by one, the existing candles had guttered and gone out.

– Cream crackers. I thought we needed a bit of sustenance if we were to avoid bad heads. Take these and light them up please. And when you've done that why don't you have another cigarette? You don't seem to have touched one for over an hour and you look as though you could do with one.

After the candles had been lit, the port poured and the biscuit tin opened, the two sat down again.

– Roly, I'd like to explain about Betty Sharples.
– I don't want to hear any more about her for now, if you don't mind. Unless you are going to tell me that your defence to the petition is untrue?
– I'm telling the truth.
– And that is what you will say at the trial?
– Yes.
– Then we shall leave it there shall we? Have that cigarette.

Relieved, Adam picked up the packet of Embassy and shucked out a cigarette, lighting it from the flame of one of the candles. If Blytheway had been affecting tiredness earlier there was no sign of it now. His languid form crackled, nonetheless, with energy. Adam thought it wise to change the subject.

– Do you have any news of Catherine?
– I'm pleased to say she is doing very well. Storman managed to get her a job at the Board of Trade, and by all accounts she is thriving. Earning forty-eight shillings a week, which is not at all bad considering, and reading avidly about Keynes and Beveridge.
– Who are they? And how can you possibly know about her reading habits?
– Jack Storman's been looking after her. He appears to have been meeting her fairly regularly for drinks and meals. He lets me know what he thinks he can tell me without compromising Catherine's confidences.
– Storman? But he's married!
– My! That wasn't jealousy was it? I don't think, given our recent conversation, you are in a position to complain.

Adam thought back to the Pembertons' party, where Storman had attended alone, and wondered how long it was since he had actually seen Margaret Storman. He had always admired the man and it was he who had recommended Blytheway to him.

- How long have you known Jack?
- Almost since the outset of my career at the Bar.
- I do find that odd. You see, I have known him since I started out, and he has never even mentioned your existence – let alone the fact that you are friends.
- That is precisely why he and I get along so well together. He is a compartmentaliser. He has no difficulty at all in living with separate worlds and keeping them apart. I saw a kindred spirit almost from the start. I mentioned before dinner that I used to join in the soirées of the Bloomsbury set and their friends. When it was my turn to entertain, Jack was the only member of the Bar I ever invited – and Margaret of course.
- Why do we never see Margaret these days?
- Well, I wouldn't want to be breaking confidences but I know that Jack wouldn't mind me mentioning this. Margaret was always a lovely lady, intelligent, considerate and pretty, particularly in her youth. Indeed, on some occasions when Jack was indisposed I would stand in for him as her consort. A lovely lady. But as the years have gone by the poor thing has been increasingly afflicted with agoraphobia. For several years now, certainly since 1937, she has been reluctant even to leave home. She has become increasingly dependent upon Jack, which has been something of a strain. The war has made it all much worse: to have a fear of open spaces when people are trying to kill you in your home! It hasn't been easy for him.
- Jack told me that he thought you were a far better barrister than he was.
- That's very kind of him because he is extremely good. It's another thing I like about him: he is capable of making an objective appraisal of his talents as against someone else.
- Then you agree with him?
- I have little choice other than to agree with him. False modesty is egregious and he would agree on that. Neither he nor I regard

ourselves as competitors for some non-existent prize. We are friends.
- You obviously still see quite a lot of him?
- Yes. He is perhaps the one member of the Bar – although you may have some future claims – whom I can trust. He knows more about me than anyone else. But he would never tell *you* what he knows. He would regard that as *my* prerogative. Well, it's almost three thirty. One more glass of port and a few more crackers and then I think we should both turn in.

Blytheway reached for the new decanter and poured out two more glasses, then proffered the cream crackers again. Adam lit a final cigarette. The evening – or rather early morning – subsided into something approaching calm. Blytheway looked as fresh as he had when the evening began. His pearl-white cummerbund with the yellow and green splashes looked as though it had only just been put on and his dress shoes twinkled blackly.

- There's something else I don't understand, Roly.
- Fire away, sweetheart.
- With all your intelligence – and your photographic memory – why are you working as a fire watcher? Why haven't you been seconded to military intelligence?
- A very good question, Adam. I often ask myself that. I did apply but I was turned down.
- Turned down!?
- Unfortunately, yes. Look at Preston. He has landed himself a prestigious position at the Ministry. Would you really say that he is a match for me? He has friends in high places. I, however, it would seem, only have enemies there. Come on, let's blow out these candles and call it a day.

Chapter Seventy-six

(Friday 28th March 1941)

Julia Pemberton emerged from the Temple Church, as she always did, at about 9.15 a.m. and headed through Cloisters down towards Fountain Court. She walked with her head low, a dark blue scarf covering her hair, avoiding the looks of any who crossed her path. Watching from his window in Lamb Building Adam was close enough to her to hear the rapid staccato click of her heels. He looked at his watch. He could afford to give her a ten-minute start. He inserted a pin into a cheap cigarette and, lighting it, took a long drag, holding onto the smoke for as long as he could before blowing it in a dirty cloud into the mild spring morning air.

He was bored and lonely. As Blytheway had predicted, there was no work waiting for him when he returned to Chambers – he wondered if Roly had engineered this – and he was running short of money. His rooms felt emptier without Delia, although he realised it would have been selfish to hold her captive there.

It had been almost noon before he awoke from his night talking with Blytheway. Caldwell brought him brunch of tinned salmon and reconstituted egg together with a cup of coffee. Roly, he was told, had been up for many hours (if he had been to bed at all) and had gone out to meet someone for lunch. He would be back at around three to help with moving Adam back to the Temple. The porcelain carafe in the corner of the room had been filled with water. Adam downed most of it, fighting off the pick-axe pain of a port hangover, and holding onto the side of his head to prevent it falling off.

The blackout shades had been taken down and a greenish light, heavy with dust, drifted in from the square and lay in a bright band across his rumpled sheets. He pulled off his silk pyjama top and threw it onto the bed. Opening his wardrobe he was surprised to find it almost empty, with only one set of clothes left in it. Blytheway had arranged for all the substantive removals to take place whilst he slept. He dressed slowly, stopping more than once to get his breath back.

As promised Blytheway returned at three. Caldwell had the jalopy ready and drove them down to the Savoy where Blytheway had made a reservation for two. Over tea Roly told him all the things that had not been covered the night before. The McKenzie trial was just over five weeks away and was followed immediately by the Pemberton trial. If he was to be properly ready for his own trial he needed to be on top of Bateman's case sooner rather than later. Easter Sunday was on the 13ᵗʰ April – just over three weeks away – and there would be a hiatus. Betty Sharples's position needed to be clarified. Was she going to be prepared to give evidence, and, if so, what was she actually going to say when cross-examined by Sir Patrick Tempest? The whereabouts of Jenny's diary needed to be confirmed definitively. If Adam was insistent on returning to the Temple he should keep his head down. Sentiments were in flux and his presence would likely do more harm than good. Adam had attempted again to press Blytheway on Julia's whereabouts but the man would not budge. Roly called for the bill.

- There is one other thing I should have mentioned last night.
- Yes?
- It's about Catherine. She told Jack that she is not at all happy about Deborah being up in Edenbridge. She wants to bring her back to London.
- Bring her back!? Is she mad?
- I know, Adam. I know. But all may not be well out there. Jack has persuaded her to wait, at least, until Easter.

Caldwell had been waiting outside the Savoy and drove them to the Temple. Adam's accommodation was not quite how he had left it. It was plain that Caldwell had been around to tidy and clean it. His clothes had all been placed on hangers and there was a pair of silk pyjamas folded on the bed for him. On the sideboard there were two more packets of Embassy. Blytheway had written "no blood yet!" on the cardboard cartons. By six o'clock he was alone. There had been no air raids since the previous Wednesday and so Adam had climbed into bed and had an early and undisturbed night.

On the Monday he had turned up in chambers to a generally warm welcome and an empty tray: no work. He had been able, however, to watch from his window as Julia entered and exited the church. Blytheway had said that she had moved further into central London but had professed ignorance as to her whereabouts. Adam simply did not believe him. He had watched as she disappeared through Cloisters and a plan had come to him. He had not spoken to her since their unhappy meeting in Hamleys all those months ago. He had been able to watch her, but only at a distance. A long time ago she had told him that she loved him. Perhaps it still wasn't too late? They needed to talk.

The following morning he had not watched her leave the Temple Church but had instead found himself a hiding place amongst the alcoves around Fountain Court. He was able to watch which way she went: through Judges' Gate. On the Wednesday morning he had taken up a hiding place near to the front of the Royal Courts of Justice. Julia, heels clicking and head down, had emerged onto the Strand before crossing and, walking within fifteen yards of him, heading north up Carey Street. He had waited a couple of minutes and then followed to see her turning right towards Chancery Lane. On the Thursday morning he had taken up a position near the Silver Vaults by Southampton Buildings. Julia had walked up Chancery Lane without noticing him and, after a minute or two, discreetly, he had followed her. He saw her enter Gray's Inn by the main gate (where not long ago he had hidden in the dark from Richards, the gabardine snoop). He gave her a head start and then ran laboriously after her. He was just in time to see her leaving the Inn through the Eastern Gate onto Gray's Inn Road.

He had smoked the cigarette down to the pin and so he dropped it in his ashtray and made for the door. If he walked quickly he could be ahead of her on Gray's Inn Road and see where she was heading. He left Lamb Building at a run – which lasted little more than twenty paces before he was forced to stop and gasp for breath. He had forgotten how unwell he was. He walked as briskly as he could; he was taking a direct route whereas hers was more of a digression. He headed up Inner Temple Lane and then across onto Chancery Lane, limping sweatily up towards High Holborn. He saw her entering the Main Gate of Gray's Inn. He had left it too late. He forced himself to run again and felt his chest aching. He was blowing hard when he reached the bottom of Gray's Inn Road, and looking up he saw her emerging from the East Gate and heading north. He continued to run until she was no more than fifty yards ahead of him. And then he stopped, caught his breath and walked on again in her wake.

Julia reached the junction with Theobald's Road and turned left. By the time Adam reached the same point she was crossing the road and heading into John Street. He tried to run again and he entered John Street before she left it. She was walking up the left-hand pavement. At the top she crossed over Guildford Street and into Mecklenburg Square.

Adam was proceeding more cautiously now. He sensed that he was close to where she lived, but at the same time he had suddenly become aware of the potential spectacle he had made of himself, running and walking blindly after her through these devastated streets. It would not look well for him to have been seen following her. If the worst came to the worst he could camp out on Monday in Mecklenburg Square itself and watch from there where she was headed. He looked around him. There were no familiar faces. There was a broken building on the corner, cordoned off, and he concealed himself within it, watching her covertly from a distance of about seventy-five yards.

She had stopped and was reaching inside her handbag. She pulled out what she was looking for and headed for a front door, turned the lock and disappeared inside. He knew where she lived! He felt his heart thumping against his rib-cage. There was a catch in his throat. If only she could have had such a place for them to meet before. He made to leave his hiding place and go to her door, and then he hesitated. He must look wet-faced and unruly. His suit was covered in dust and ash. There might also be dust on his face and his hair; he had no mirror. Perhaps it would be better to wait?

But he couldn't wait. He would approach her house from the other side of the square. Slowly he emerged onto Guilford Street, checking that he was not being watched, and then headed for Mecklenburg Place, the other entrance to the square. Slowly he made his way around to where her door was; there was no need to hurry now. He got to the corner. Her door was less than twenty-five yards away. She was inside and alone. No one would be expecting them to meet there. There would be no other time as propitious. She was only a door's knock away. He moved to the edge of the pavement and was on the point of crossing when something caught his eye that made him rush back into the shadows and shrink from sight.

Jeremy Pemberton was marching up the road. His hair was dishevelled and his right leg splayed out as he walked. He reached her door and began hammering on it.

– Julia! Julia! I know you're in there! Let me in! You bitch! Let me in!

Chapter Seventy-seven

(Friday 28th March 1941)

Julia closed the door behind her and put her keys back into her handbag. She took off her scarf and draped her coat over a hook in the hall. She asked herself, as she had done many times, why she continued to go to the church after the services had stopped in January. She would go in and take her usual seat, pick up one of the prayer books and read from it almost at random. The morning service had been her ritual for so many years, enriched by that now-gone period of intrigue and romance, and she could not bring herself to give it up. It was a place of calm, in a world that was becoming increasingly hostile … even without more. There were no longer white notes within the shields of the knights.

She had followed Adam's story after he had been taken ill and then expelled from Stirrup Court: his move to Lamb Building and the beginnings of a brief renaissance in his professional life. She had heard about his friendship with Roland Blytheway, and learnt with dismay about that man's apparently devilish powers and unseemly private life. He was a man to avoid.

And after Jenny's death and her reaction to it (something for which she felt nothing but remorse and shame), she had learned of Adam's illness. He was such a simple soul, she had decided. It was not long after he moved to Lamb Building that, on emerging from the church, she had glanced up and noticed him watching her. On succeeding days it had always been possible, as she walked with her head down, to take a furtive glance in his direction and see that familiar shape against the window, smoke drifting out into the Temple.

Then he was ill again and it stopped. She had heard that he was recuperating with Blytheway in Bedford Square. There could be no reason for him to return to Dr Johnson's Buildings. After Jenny's death the burgeoning sympathy around the Temple for her husband was palpable and the eyes that had previously scanned her as she went in and out now scraped at her.

She was glad to be away from Eaton Square. Although it was inevitable that she should leave and she grieved it, Jeremy's behaviour was increasingly intolerable. Even before she left there were empty bottles everywhere, the pervasive smell of cigarettes, and an undercurrent of malice and blame, as though she had pressed the bomb-release button that extinguished Jenny.

Then on Monday of this week she had looked up as she disappeared under Cloisters and saw that familiar figure, perhaps thinner, and a puff of smoke as she disappeared from view. Something in her heart leapt, and then was equally swiftly imprisoned. Adam was back! But then he had disappeared again and for the rest of the week she had seen no sign. It had been a good week nonetheless. There had been no raids for over a week and work at New River Head had been uneventful and easy. People were beginning to say that, perhaps, the worst was over.

She headed into the little room that she called her study, sat at her escritoire and pulled out some writing paper. It was time to write to her children, separate letters to each that she sent every day. She would write to Agnes first. Spring sunlight was pouring in on her. She opened the window an edge and caught the clean green smell of spring. Returning to her desk, she smoothed out a sheet of writing paper, uncapped her pen and wrote the date in the top right-hand corner – she would have to order some personalised notepaper. What to speak about? Her days were monotonous, punctuated only by her uneventful evenings at New Bridge Head. The weather, perhaps? A series of questions about life in the Cotswolds? She would think of something.

She began carefully to write the first "D". At that point there was a thunderous hammering on the door. She jumped with shock and the pen skewed across the page in a jagged line of ink.

– Julia! Julia! I know you're in there! Let me in! You bitch! Let me in!

The words were slightly slurred. She put down her pen and took a deep breath. She would do nothing.

– Julia! Julia! I know you're in there! I saw you come back from church!

Beyond her slightly opened window she could hear the scrape of other windows opening. She went over to it and opened it more widely, leaning out. Standing on her doorstep was her husband. He was swaying slightly and he looked thinner, even, than at the funeral.

– Leave me alone, Jeremy! Go away!

His head jerked round in the direction of her voice and he seemed to struggle to focus.

– You know why I'm here, Julia! Let me in!
– Go away!

Her husband jerked his head forward again and concentrated on the front door. She saw him take a deep breath, adopt a sideways-on position, and then charge at the door. There was a massive thumping noise from the hall. She ran through and saw, as he charged again, the door flex concave around the lock as he hit again and then again. It was only a matter of time before the lock burst.

– Stop it! Stop it! I'll let you in.

There was a pause as Julia ran back to her study to find the key in her bag, and then, with fingers trembling, unlocked the door.

– Where is it?
– Where's what?
– Jenny's diary.
– It's none of your business.
– She was my daughter! It *is* my business. Where is it!?
– She gave it to me. She didn't want you to look at it. You broke her trust. She was really upset.

Julia's words tumbled out and stopped her husband dead. He looked confused.

– I upset her?
– You told her she couldn't marry Simon Jenkins. She was crying. She said that she called you "a silly old man".

Jeremy was suddenly silenced and Julia saw tears forming in his eyes. He looked broken.

– I upset her?
– That was her last memory of you before she went out. And she gave me the diary because of it.

He let out a dreadful roar.

– It's in your escritoire! I'll find it!

And he ran from room to room until he found it. The drawer was locked and he began pulling at it.

– Give me the key!
– No!

Still holding onto the drawer handle, he looked around the room until he saw Julia's handbag sitting on a chair. He ran over and grabbed it then emptied it out onto the floor looking vainly for the key. Julia tapped the pocket of her jacket to satisfy herself it was where she had put it. Jeremy noticed what she did and ran at her with his fist flailing.

– Give me your jacket!
– No!
– Give it to me now!

She tried to run away from him but he grabbed the rear of her skirt and pulled her back before delivering a heavy punch to the back of her head. Everything went black and when she came to, after perhaps a few seconds, she saw him opening the drawer, her jacket lying in a heap on the floor next to him. He had the diary. She tried to stop him taking it away, throwing herself at him, but he hit her again. This time it was a glancing blow and she was able to hold onto his legs. He was kicking at her head trying to make her let go, but, somehow, she held on. Now he was in the hallway, staggering under her weight at his feet. She felt his shoe make contact with her head with sickening power, and the wet and salt of blood on her lips. But she would not let go.

508

He was almost down the steps now, the diary in his hand; her body juddered down the concrete and she felt shooting pains along her shoulder, hip and thigh. But she would not let go. They were out on the street and she was covered in mortar dust and soot. He kicked her in the head again and she felt her grip loosening. Looking up she saw the early morning sky and heads peeping out from windows. A sort of silence was descending upon her and everything was becoming blurred.

Suddenly, the kicking stopped. Pemberton had fallen. As she closed her eyes she heard shouting and swearing and the sound of fists; of bodies rolling on the pavement. Then, from a distance:

– You'll regret this, Falling.

She felt the leather diary being placed into her hands and then the sensation of someone trying to lift her and failing. Then there were other hands that lifted her up and carried her inside.

When eventually she awoke she was lying on her bed, the diary still in her hands and a makeshift bandage around her head. She raised herself slightly and looked across the room to see Adam, covered in dust, watching her intently.

– A doctor's on the way.
– Get out! Get out! You'll ruin everything!
– You've still got the diary.
– Get out!

And she began to weep.

Chapter Seventy-eight

(Friday 28th March 1941)

Adam closed the door behind him and walked back down into the square. It was barely half past ten in the morning. The signs of the scuffle were still visible in the scattered dust upon the pavement. His suit was filthy with it. He made to brush himself down and saw that his blood-stained handkerchief was still balled up in his right hand.

It had all happened so quickly. When Pemberton had emerged, shouting, from the house with Julia clinging to his legs and the diary in his hand, Adam had hung back. He had watched in a daze as Julia's supine body was pulled down the steps, bumping heavily on the stone, and still he did nothing. Everything had seemed unreal and a strange silence descended upon him. He looked up to see people looking out of windows at the spectacle below. And then Pemberton started kicking Julia in the head in an effort to make her let go, and something inside Adam snapped.

He was running towards them and barrelled into Pemberton, shoulder first. Pemberton, his feet tethered, had fallen like a tree, with Adam landing on top of him. Their faces were only inches apart. Adam saw the hatred in his eyes and smelt the whisky on his breath. Entangled as they were they had traded punches before people from the surrounding houses intervened. And Pemberton had run off, shouting his threat to Adam over his shoulder as he went. The diary was in the dust and Adam had picked it up and put it back in Julia's hands. She was only semi-conscious and blood was oozing from her mouth. Her right eye was beginning to swell up and there were traces of blood on her scalp.

He had tried to lift her but couldn't. Other hands picked her up and carried her inside, laying her down on her bed. One of the neighbours, a lady, fetched a piece of bed-sheet and tied it round Julia's head. Another said he would phone for a doctor. Adam took up a chair by her bed and watched as the others ministered to her. Their voices floated over him:

– Bloody madman … he could of killed her … oo does he think he is?

Someone asked if he was all right and he nodded. He could taste blood in his mouth and so he took out his handkerchief to wipe it away. Then they left him with Julia to await the doctor.

Her outburst when she had come round had unnerved him. He had approached her to try and comfort her but she had shrugged off his hands and turned away from him, telling him again to leave.

So here he was back on the street. He did not know what he should do next and decided eventually that he should head back towards the Temple. He had reached Guilford Street and was about to head back down John Street when someone grabbed him from behind, pulling firmly on his collar. Pemberton had been lying in wait! He started to struggle.

– Calm down, sweetheart. I'm dusty enough as it is.
– Roly! What are you doing here?
– Shall we say I just happened to be passing?
– Well, that's highly unlikely, isn't it?
– No more unlikely than *you* being here.
– Why *are* you here?
– I blame myself really. I should *never* have let you go back to the Temple. And I should have been even more opaque about Mrs Pemberton's current location.

Adam thought back to his conversation with Blytheway the previous weekend. He had said that he had gone to Portobello Market and then taken an amble around Bloomsbury and visited every square.

– You knew where she was living all along?
– I may have done.
– Then why didn't you tell me?
– It was for your own good. And look what knowing has done for you!
– I was just passing. It was just a coincidence.

Blytheway laughed.

- Yes. Of course it was, dear boy. But you'll have to do *a lot* better than that if there are repercussions.
- What do you mean?
- Oh, I don't know. You get yourself into a street fight with Pemberton, a man who has cited you as a Co-Respondent, apparently over Mrs Pemberton, who happens to be the Respondent in the same petition. I can't see what *possible* repercussions there could be. If you'll forgive my language, you behaved like a bloody fool!
- He was trying to steal Jenny's diary.
- I saw that.
- And he kicked Julia unconscious.
- I saw that as well.
- What was I supposed to do?
- Let us just say that you put yourself on the horns of a dilemma which, had I better control over you, would not have presented itself.

They were walking westwards along Guilford Street.

- So what are the repercussions likely to be?
- Sometimes I think you are going out of your way to make my job as difficult as possible ... In the first place you've made an even bigger enemy of Pemberton than he was before, if that is possible.

They crossed the road to avoid the debris of a bombed building that spilled out into the road. Blytheway was brushing at his clothing as he walked.

- You will also have to explain how you happened to be outside Mrs Pemberton's house when the fracas erupted. *If* Pemberton chooses to rely upon this incident it will create a rather difficult question for you to answer.
- Do you think he will?
- Actually, I doubt it. How he managed to be drunk at nine in the morning I do not know. But he was. And he will be aware of that. The objective evidence is that he burst into his wife's home, assaulted her and attempted to steal a diary in her possession. That assault carried on into the street where a host of onlookers were in a position to

witness it. I allowed myself to get close enough – after Pemberton had run off and Julia was safely back in the house – and the general mood was not favourable to our friend. It would hardly look good for a senior KC to be seen acting in that way. I doubt that he will look back on it with any pride, and we must hope he will think it better to leave it out of account.

– Where are we going?
– I'm taking you back to Bedford Square. I think it best that you spend at least the next two nights with me.
– I'm perfectly fine.
– Your handkerchief tells me you're not. And besides, Pemberton will be looking for you. No doubt he is waiting for El Vinos to open as we speak. It's far better to wait until he sobers up.

They were walking along Bedford Square now. Roly reached into his pocket and pulled out his house key.

– I will ask Caldwell to go down and fetch you some clean clothes.
– Roly? Why were you there?
– You ask far too many questions! Let us just say that, from my window, I am still able to see Mrs Pemberton going in and out of the church – why, I *do not* know – and to watch you as, between Tuesday and Thursday of this week, you left chambers in her wake. I am sure there is a perfectly innocent explanation for it but part of me wondered whether perhaps you were trying to find out where she lived ... Then this morning you gave her a longer start and then attempted to run up Inner Temple Lane. I would have left you to it, but a matter of minutes later I saw Pemberton stomping up from Stirrup Court in the same direction. I thought it might be wise to see what was going on. Come on in. Caldwell will prepare an early luncheon for us.

Chapter Seventy-nine

(Wednesday 2nd April 1941)

His room was as dark as night and he had no idea what time it was. Adam rolled onto his side and fumbled for the bedside lamp. It was almost ten o'clock. He had grown used to Caldwell coming in and taking down the blackout shades and now, back in Dr Johnson's Buildings again and with no need to set his alarm, he had slept on. Although still weak he felt refreshed. He hauled himself out of bed and started to dismantle the shades. The weather outside was bleak and a thin drizzle was spraying the side of the church.

It had been his first night back in the Temple since Blytheway had hauled him away the previous Friday. Roly had administered a stiff scotch and after a light lunch had bundled him back up to the first-floor bedroom before returning to chambers muttering about work to be done. Adam spent the rest of the day and much of the weekend in bed. He was still weak; there was no work for him to do and his desire to watch the comings and goings from the church had been blunted by his altercation with Pemberton. He was happy to lie low for a while, and so he stayed in bed and read.

Blytheway had been preparing a case that was due to start on the Wednesday and had a conference out of chambers on the Tuesday. Adam was plumped up on his pillows eating toast when Blytheway came to see him before heading out. A cold breeze crept in through the slightly opened window.

– I should be back by mid-afternoon and then Caldwell and I will take you back to the Temple.

And then he was gone. Adam had chewed on the last few pieces of toast, finished his tea and gazed out of the window at the greening branches swaying there. Then he went back to reading his latest book, Montaigne's *Essays*, which Blytheway had pressed upon him the previous day.

– Sometimes I think we should all be Pyrrhonian Sceptics: "all I know is that I know nothing, and I'm not even sure about that."

Later that day Caldwell and Blytheway had taken Adam back to the Temple. Caldwell had made some sandwiches as an evening meal. He had put up the blackout shades and then they had left him alone. Adam had opted for another early night. And now it was after ten on the Wednesday morning and he was still not dressed. He took off his pyjama top and went over to the sink to wash his chest and face. Caldwell had cleaned his dusty suit and so he put it on and made his way down to Lamb Building for another day of idleness.

His tray in the Clerks' Room was empty but for a white envelope addressed to him and marked "By Hand, Confidential". It was from Jones, who had received a letter from Betty Sharples that morning. She was not prepared to come to court again. He had tried to telephone Adam but he had not been in Chambers. He would be out at court all day but it might be possible to contact him this evening. Adam ran two steps at a time up to Blythway's room – his defence was falling apart – but Roly had already left for court. He fumbled for his cigarettes and headed across to his own room. It was almost eleven o'clock.

He opened the window and gazed down on the church. Julia had been and gone – if she dared to go there anymore. The drizzle persisted and a few black-jacketed barristers were scurrying up towards the courts or across towards Inner Temple Library. He fixed his pin into a cheap cigarette, lit up, took in a deep mouthful of smoke, spluttered awhile, and then blew what was left out onto the masonry around his window. His left hand was trembling again. He lit another and then three more in succession as he leaned out of the window and decided what to do next. There had been no sign of Gabardine for the last few days.

By noon he had made up his mind. He grabbed his raincoat from a hook by the door, took a paperback from his bookshelf and headed out of Chambers and down towards Temple Tube. On the platform he let three trains go before boarding. He wasn't being followed. He changed to the Piccadilly line at South Kensington before alighting at Green Park. He came back into daylight on the park side. The rain had stopped but heavy grey cloud, like a dirty snowdrift, hung over the gardens. He had no appointment. He was in no hurry.

This was where he and Julia had met that first time. The railings had gone. He stepped down onto one of the pathways and walked towards the tree where they had first embraced without caution. It was still there. He wanted to carve their initials into it. Instead he walked on. The wind through the wires of the barrage balloons made high-pitched singing noises, and there were trenches cut into the lawns surrounded by sand-bags. He had last been here in December. Then it was sparse and bare. Now life was returning to the trees – and to the walkways, as young lovers and mothers with prams promenaded aimlessly about. Fifty yards to his left was the park-side entrance to the Stafford. He walked on by. Finally, at the other end of the park he found a large tree and leaned back against it, looking towards the tube from where he had come. There was no sign of Jackson or Gabardine. No one else seemed to have any interest in him. He waited there for half an hour. It was past one in the afternoon. Why couldn't Blytheway have been in Chambers? He was no doubt out earning big money on some fashionable but frivolous brief somewhere.

He walked off around the perimeter of the park taking an indirect route towards Shepherd Market. It was the first time he had been there in day-light. He knew his way now. It was after two in the afternoon. He found his way to Clarges Street and pressed the bell to her flat.

****

Betty was still in her dressing-gown. It had been over a week since the last raid and that had been good for business. She was not expecting company. The ringing started again, more insistently this time. She was up to date with the rent. She smoothed down her hair in the looking-glass, wrapped her gown more tightly round her, put her key into the pocket and nudged her slippers onto her feet. She yawned as she made her way slowly down the stairs. She decided she was quite hungry.

Adam Falling was framed in the doorway when she opened the door. The pale white light from the street made him half-silhouette. He was better dressed than she remembered him, but thinner again. Her eyes were drawn to his face. He was pale and his skin was pulled tight over his cheekbones; the cheeks hollow, the eyes a pleading blue, staring into hers.

She tried to close the door on him but he was too quick for her and, with unexpected strength, pushed it open again and then stepped inside, closing the door behind him.

– Betty, we need to talk!
– I'm scared, Mr Falling.
– And you *must* call me Adam!

He bundled her up to her room. It was unlocked. He edged her in ahead of him before closing the door behind them. Weak sunlight was shining through the window onto her unmade bed. There was one chair in the room and she collapsed into it and started to cry. Adam looked around. He remembered the small chest of drawers. It had a looking-glass above it – he saw Jones's letter still lying open there – a basin with some toiletries balanced on it, a large clay jug and a small wardrobe where, no doubt, she kept her clothes. Betty was sobbing.

– I don't want to go to that place no more, Mr Falling. It frightened me.
– I'm really sorry about what happened, Betty. There was nothing I could do. Jones will have told you about it. I got hurt and my boss's daughter was killed. She was only eighteen.
– I had to buy some writing paper and borrow a pen.
– I'm sorry …
– It ain't right!
– I know. I'm sorry. You should have been told.
– No! *This* ain't right! You want me to go to that … that … *place* and tell lies. That ain't right!

Falling started coughing and slumped down on the unmade bed. He pulled out a cigarette and pin, lit up and started smoking. He looked so thin. He cupped the ash in his hand and reached out to put it the bin. He was gazing at her intently now. His voice when he spoke was soothing and calm. She remembered it from the first time she had met him. Warm and mellow. He reached inside his jacket and pulled out his wallet. Splaying it open, he pulled out a ten-pound note and held it out to her.

– This is to say sorry. You can have this as well as the other ten pounds I promised you if you give evidence.

- I really don't want to …
- There's nothing to worry about. It will be easy. Over before you know it. Can I take you out for a spot of lunch?
- I really shouldn't, Mr Falling …
- You *must* call me Adam. Just a bit of lunch? I'd like to talk to you. Get to know you better.

Betty was looking at the ten-pound note. It would take a lot to earn that much money. And she would get another ten on top. Her stomach rumbled under her dressing-gown. She looked into Adam's eyes again. A free meal as well?

- Come on! Get dressed!

She hugged her dressing-gown more tightly around her and looked from Adam towards the door. He did not move. She went over to her little wardrobe and pulled out her best dress. Still he did not leave the room. His eyes flickered from her face to her hips, and then back to her eyes. She sighed and undid the rope that wrapped her, letting her gown fall to the floor. She was standing naked before him apart from some pink nylon panties. Adam was still holding the ten-pound note out towards her. She opened a drawer, pulled out a brassiere and hitched it over herself. Then, imagining she was no longer being watched, she pulled her best dress on over her head. Adam was still sitting on the bed and smoking. She smoothed herself down, went over to her looking-glass, brushed her long blonde hair back into shape and looked again at Adam. Apart from her dignity, she was still naked.

- You look beautiful!
- I don't go out for many meals.
- We're a bit late for a proper lunch but I'm sure I can find somewhere.

He helped her on with her coat and offered his arm and she took it. Then, arm in arm, they made their way slowly down the stairs. She opened the door and they stepped out into Clarges Street and a chilly April afternoon.

****

Adam guided her round the corner into Curzon Street. There was a Lyons' Corner House in Coventry Street, only ten minutes' walk away. They would keep to the back streets. He had been shaken more than he had realised by Blytheway's gentle cross-examination the previous week. He needed to know more about Betty. She had to stop calling him Mr Falling. Sooner or later he would have to persuade her to say that Joe was killed in January 1940 rather than in May. He would also have to come up with a convincing explanation for (and description of) this earlier, fictitious death.

Chapter Eighty

(Thursday 3rd April 1941)

This time he had set his alarm clock. It rattled into life at about 8.30 in the morning. The bedside table had been moved by someone, Caldwell probably, when he had been putting up the blackout shades. The hammer was swinging backwards and forward between the two chimes and, reaching for the button to silence it, Adam fell out of bed, landing heavily on his side. Winded, he lay on the floor for a while, the bells still ringing, and contemplated climbing back into bed. He had no particular reason to go into Chambers. There was nothing in his diary.

It had been a late night. He and Betty had walked to Coventry Street and it was only as they got close to the Corner House that he had remembered that this was where the Café de Paris used to be. They had turned a corner and come upon the devastation. The rubble had been tamed to some extent but still it protruded into the road. There were barriers and warning signs; pieces of brick and scorched plaster still lay in the street. The temporary morgue had been closed but one could still see where it used to be.

– This is where she died isn't it?
– Yes.
– Was she pretty?
– She was very pretty. She was a good person. She was going to help us.
– Us?
– Sorry me and Ju … me and my boss's wife, her father.
– What do you mean?
– She was going to give my boss's wife an alibi. She was going to give evidence against her father about this affair.
– But you told me it was all true!
– What's true and what's not true doesn't matter anymore. Look at this mess.

They stepped across an overflow of rock. Adam caught his trousers on some barbed wire and had to stop to detach himself.

– What is true is that this young woman felt so strongly about the justice of it all that she was prepared to give evidence against her father in support of her step-mother. What is also true is that her body is now lying in the ground in Brompton Cemetery.
– I don't know what you're going on about.
– I'm sorry, Betty. I'm rambling. Here we are. Let me take your coat. I'm famished.

They had had a long late lunch and it was almost six before he got back to Chambers. Blytheway had already left for the evening and so he had gone back to his room. He had been preparing for an early night when Barry knocked to remind him he was on fire duty again that night. It had been another quiet night and he had been able to sleep several hours at his post before, at 4 a.m., he Barry and Roberts had decided to call it a day and return to their beds.

Why not just climb back into bed? Then he remembered. He needed to talk to Blytheway before he went off to court again. He stumbled to his feet, pulled off his pyjamas, washed and then put on a different suit. There was an air of normality around the Temple, despite the brick dust and the smell of burning. He hurried to Lamb Building but he was too late. Roly had already left. He put a call through to Jones but he was also out at court. Adam returned to the Clerks' Room.

– Do you mind telling me where Mr Blytheway is today?
– He's in court, sir.
– I *know* he is in court. But which court?
– Old Bailey, sir. He's doing a treason trial.

Adam froze. He felt the air escape from his lungs so that, for a few seconds, he could not speak.

– A treason trial?
– Yes, sir. I'll just get the diary.

His senior clerk picked up the heavy leather book and leafed through to the 3rd April and ran his finger down the initials of his barristers, arranged in descending orders with silks first.

– Let me see …

Adam knew what he would say before he looked up.

– Hoffer, sir. He started it yesterday.
– Which Court? Which Court!?
– Six, sir.

Adam was out of the door without saying thank you, goodbye or where he was going.

He ran, walked, ran down Fleet Street and across Ludgate Circus. Security was minimal at the Central Criminal Court. He took the stairs two at a time up to the public gallery. A crowd of disgruntled people was milling around the entrance and a security guard was keeping them at bay.

– How long before we can get in, then?
– I don't know, sir. As soon as I am told anything I will pass it on.

Familiar with the building, Adam went down to the main entrance to the court. There were swing doors on either side of the well of the court. In his time, as Counsel, he had passed through one or other of these doors. On either side, beyond them was another set of glazed doors. Counsel for the prosecution would sit on the left of the court, nearer the witness box. Counsel for the defence would be on the right, nearer the jury. Adam went to the left-hand window first. He saw the familiar silky shape of Peter Preston KC sitting somewhat slumped over his notebook. Beyond him, in the witness box, was a man in an expensive suit whom he had never seen before. He was in his early forties, and despite the comparative cold he appeared to be sweating as he answered questions. Every now and then he would turn towards the trial judge with a look of entreaty on his face, his arms held out as though begging. Adam took the widest angle he could in order to see who the judge was. It was Mr Justice Sherdley. The same judge who had presided over Novak's trial. With some reluctance the judge was waving down the witness's pleas. On more than one occasion Preston rose a little unsteadily to his feet to make a point, only to be told to sit down.

Adam moved to the right-hand window. Blytheway in his less glamorous junior's robes was on his feet asking questions with that obvious precision which Adam had cause to fear. The jury appeared to be enraptured by the exchange. Eventually, Blytheway bowed deferentially to the judge, gave the jury what Adam could only imagine was a complicit look, and then slid back into his seat. Adam returned to the left-hand window. Preston was on his feet. Watching his body language from behind it was all too clear that he was trying, unsuccessfully, to undo some great damage to the case for the prosecution.

The witness was released and after a brief exchange the judge made some sort of an announcement to the ushers before rising, nodding to counsel and leaving the court room. Someone shouted something up to whoever was in the public gallery. He heard a shuffling of feet on the floor above him, realised that the public gallery was again being opened to the public, and ran for the stairs.

It was virtually full by the time he got there, so he had to squeeze himself in. It was 11.15 a.m. His view from the back row was restricted. He could see the witness box and the judge's seat. He could see Leading Counsel's row. But junior counsel's row and the dock were out of sight. Blytheway and Katya Hoffer, if she was in the dock, were beyond his view. Why hadn't Blytheway mentioned anything of this to him?

There was a murmur of gossip in the public gallery. It became apparent that Preston had presented the case for the prosecution the previous day. He had adduced, properly this time, evidence to the effect that Katya's fingerprints were on the cardboard cylinder under Novak's floorboards. He had told the jury, as he was of course obliged to do, that Novak had been acquitted of all charges, that he knew nothing of the cylindrical tube. And then, at about 3.30 p.m. the previous day the public gallery had been cleared. The people around him were in no doubt as to Katya's guilt.

– Court rise!

There was a shuffling noise and the sound of wooden chairs flapping backwards as counsel rose and Mr Justice Sherdley entered again and bowed at counsels' rows. There was a settling noise as everyone sat down again. Adam heard Blytheway's familiar voice, calm as ever, from beyond his sightline.

– My Lord, I call Mrs Katya Hoffer.

People in the public gallery were straining to see her. Adam only saw her as she reached the witness box. She seemed thinner and paler than before. She had been in prison for less than a month and, to Adam's shame, he had temporarily forgotten of her existence. He tried to imagine what the last few weeks would have been like for her. She was on trial as a traitor, facing the death penalty whilst overhead the state that she was alleged to be supporting was trying to kill those down below: judge, counsel, jury and even those in the public gallery. If that were not enough she had been plotting to kill them using their own water supplies. Katya took a deep breath and looked out on the court room, dignity and self-belief recovered. She looked down into the well of the court and Adam imagined her eyes locking with those of Roland Blytheway.

He asked her to give her full name and address. Then:

– Mrs Hoffer, would you mind telling the jury of your nationality?
– I am from Czechoslovakia.
– And, if you don't mind, your religious persuasion.
– I am a Jew.

A rustle ran through the gallery. Weren't the Jews as bad as the Germans?

– You are not German?
– No.
– Are you a supporter of the Nazi party?
– No! I am not!

Her vehemence echoed down to her from the ceiling.

– Why is that?
– The Nazis! They killed my mother and my father! They are holding my brother hostage!

– Now, Mr Preston, King's Counsel, says that your fingerprints were found on that tube, the one that was found under the floorboards of Mr Novak's room. Do you accept that?

– Yes.

– So do you accept that you placed the tube where it was found by the police?

– I placed it there.

– Where did you get it from?

– I was told before I left Czechoslovakia that I would receive it. It was left for me at the bookshop where my husband was working. There was a note which said that it had to be placed under the floorboards by the next day. So I put it where I was told to put it.

– Under the floorboards in Mr Novak's room?

– Yes.

– Why did you do this?

– They had my brother. They said they would kill him if I did not.

– I'm sorry, Mrs Hoffer, who do you mean by "they"?

– The Nazis!

She spat out the words.

– Did you know what was in the tube?

– Yes. It contained some old plans.

– How did you know this?

– I wanted to see what it was that I was putting there.

– And how were you able to get into Mr Novak's rooms?

Katya lowered her head and her voice dropped to a whisper.

– It was supposed to be a room for me and Milo.

– Milo?

– My husband.

– If it was supposed to be your room what was Mr Novak doing living there?

– I persuaded Mi ... my husband to give the room to Tomas ... to Mr Novak.

– I'm sorry, Mrs Hoffer. That is a partial explanation, of course. But if

525

you gave the keys to Mr Novak, how was it that you were able to gain access to the room?

There was a long pause. Katya Hoffer looked around the court room, first down at Blytheway, then at the judge, then Preston, then over at the jury and on to the public gallery – Adam cowered away from her gaze – then back at Blytheway. Her lips quivered and her chin began to wobble. Her eyes filled with tears and she brushed a hand through her gorgeous mop of auburn hair.

– Because I loved him … I love him!

There was a long silence. Adam imagined Blytheway standing still and erect, perhaps chancing a slight sympathetic glance in the direction of the jury, allowing them to think what the word "love" meant in this context, and then taking several beats before his next question.

– Did you have any idea that you might be putting his life in danger?
– No! No! I did not! It was just some old plans!
– Why then did you not simply occupy the rooms yourself?
– I was scared.
– Scared of what?
– I don't know. I was scared of getting into trouble.
– So you *knew* it was wrong?
– It was just some old plans!
– But if you loved him why did you put him in a place where you were scared to go?

Katya bowed her head.

– I loved my brother more than I loved Tomas.
– Do you know how to make a bomb, Mrs Hoffer?
– No. I do not.
– To your knowledge, did Mr Novak know how to make a bomb?
– No.
– Then … what was the purpose of putting the plans under the floorboards?

Before she could answer Adam saw Preston rising to his feet.

– My Lord. At this point a matter of law arises. I would appreciate the
opportunity to discuss this in the absence of the jury. I would also
ask that the public gallery be cleared.
– Do you have any objections, Mr Blytheway?
– No, my Lord.

The jury was ushered out and the door into the public gallery opened
and everyone there was also asked to leave. They shuffled out, grumbling
and complaining. More than one person said "Not again". Adam went to
the Bar Mess for a cup of tea. It was only 11.45 a.m. He wished he had
brought something to read. How long would this "point of law" last?

It was almost one o'clock and there had been no indication that the trial
had started up again. Bored of sitting around, he went back up to the public
gallery only to find the door guarded. This was taking a long time! He went
down the stairs to the entrance to Court Six. He could look in through
the windows and at least see whether the court was in session. He looked
through the right-hand window first and was able to see Blytheway sitting
in junior counsel's row. To Blytheway's right Adam saw the jury. The trial
was continuing but the public gallery remained closed. The jury were all
staring intently across the court room. Mr Justice Sherdley was also visible, listening intently to something. He did not appear to be looking in the
direction of Peter Preston KC.

Adam went to the left hand window. Peter Preston KC was on his feet.
Looking beyond Preston, Adam saw Katya Hoffer in the witness box.
She was being cross-examined. It was she who the judge and jury were
looking at.

Lunch time arrived and the court rose. For some reason Adam didn't
want to confront Blytheway. He probably had enough on his plate. Instead
he left the building and found the nearest public house, ordering a pint
of bitter and a fish-paste sandwich. The bread was stale and scratched his
lips as he chewed. Why hadn't Roly told him what was going on? He had
been living under his roof for the previous few days – and for a fortnight
prior to that. Was he not trusted? He remembered Roly's comments about
"compartmentalisation". Was this simply part of his desire to keep things
separate? Didn't he want or need Adam's help?

It was two o'clock. Adam headed back into the Old Bailey. He didn't trouble with heading up to the public gallery but went directly to the left-hand court room door. Preston was still on his feet. He could only see his long silk gown and the head bowed under the grey wig, looking at his notes rather than the witness as he spoke, his junior rattling into a blue notebook behind him. Mr Justice Sherdley hardly looked at Leading Counsel but appeared to be reserving all of his attention for the witness.

Adam moved to the right-hand window. Blytheway, in junior counsel's row, appeared to be making a languid note. He turned suddenly to speak to his solicitor and in that instant caught Adam's eye through the glass. He flickered and smiled and then concentrated on his solicitor. To his surprise Adam saw Jones leaning forward to speak with his counsel. After a few moments Blytheway turned back to his notebook. The jury were straining forward, gripped by the drama that was unfolding before them and fixed with a sense of responsibility that, perhaps, only the unexpected necessity of signing the Official Secrets Act could impart. Adam returned to the left-hand window and looked up towards the witness box. Katya Hoffer was giving her answers vehemently.

The cross-examination was coming to an end. Preston slumped back into his seat. The sign of an unsuccessful cross-examination. No meaningful glances in the direction of the jury. There was no elegant slide from being upright to being seated. Preston looked behind him and shrugged at his junior. He did not notice Adam watching him.

He rushed back to the right-hand window to see Blytheway asking a few perfunctory questions of Katya. Mr Justice Sherdley had no questions. Katya nodded in the direction of the judge and then of the jury, and allowed herself a shy smile. Then she stepped down and returned to the dock.

Blytheway stood again and said something to the Judge. The attention of those in court then shifted to the very back of the court. Something was happening beyond Adam's line of sight. He felt a sense of anticipation rippling silently around the room. He couldn't see what was happening and so returned to the left-hand window. And then all became clear. Tomas Novak was being brought up from the cells to testify. He recognised his old client, also thinner and still wearing the same suit as before, being escorted to the witness box.

The usher handed him a card and he held it up in his right hand. He pulled some spectacles out of his breast pocket and balanced them on his nose before picking up the card and reading the affirmation. He stumbled over the words. When he had finished he handed the card back to the usher and looked directly at where the dock must have been. He stared for a long time and Adam imagined Katya returning his gaze, her face a mixture of entreaty and contrition. Finally, he looked in the direction of Blytheway, listened to a question and gave his name and address – Adam was able to lip-read that much.

In profile Novak was as thin as a stick. His suit hung off him and his shoulders were stooped with the effort of carrying his head. It cost him an effort to look up, and his eyes when answering questions flickered between Blytheway, the judge and Katya – but mostly Katya. Adam was able to pick up bits of the familiar story. Novak was speaking of the boat trip from Gibraltar and made references to lifeboats and stars. He waited for, and caught, Novak saying "happy" more than once, looking over at Katya as he said it. Mr Justice Sherdley was rapt in his attention, taking a careful note and asking the occasional question of the witness.

Adam needed to see how the jury were taking it. He went to the right-hand window and saw Blytheway standing languidly as he asked his questions. The men and women of the jury were leaning forward in their seats, apparently oblivious to one another as they stared across at Novak and occasionally slipped a glance in the direction of Katya. None of them seemed to look at Blytheway. It was as though he had made himself invisible – a disembodied voice asking questions. Adam looked at his watch. It was a half past three. Blytheway turned towards the jury – Adam imagined a brief smile in their direction – and then looked at Mr Justice Sherdley, bowed and sat down.

Returning to the right-hand window he saw Preston climbing to his feet. His body language was aggressive, and, for the first time, Adam actually heard something of what was going on. Preston was pointing his finger and shouting at Novak. Adam could not make out what was being said. Novak became angry in return. His eyes blazed as he answered the questions asked of him. On more than one occasion he curled his lip in contempt of his inquisitor and Adam remembered the arrogant man he had first met in the prison cells at Brixton. He appeared to be beside himself with rage and he began gesticulating as he answered: stretching out both his hands, placing them over his heart, hammering the top of the witness box with his fist. And all the time his main attention was not upon Preston but on Katya. It was impossible to tell how effective Preston was being. Adam went back to the left-hand window. Blytheway did not appear to be taking a note of the exchanges although he appeared to be concentrating deeply on something. The jury now were alternating their gazes between Novak, Katya and Blytheway and looking more and more frequently in Roly's direction. Adam caught a flash of silver and saw Blytheway admiring his right hand, the fingers splayed out. He had been filing his nails.

The cross-examination was winding down. Novak appeared to be unbowed and, if anything, a little pleased with himself. Preston sat down and Novak transferred his gaze to Blytheway, answering a couple of perfunctory questions. Then he was being escorted back to the cells, his eyes fixed on the dock as he was taken out and down. That was the end of the case for the defence, then, and Preston began rising to his feet to make his closing address to the jury. Suddenly his head jerked round in the direction of Blytheway. He stood for about half a minute before sitting down again. Adam could sense his irritation.

Blytheway was on his feet and addressing the judge. He spoke for about two minutes before Mr Justice Sherdley turned to the jury and, plainly, asked them to leave the court room. When the jury box had been vacated Blytheway stood again and continued to address the judge. Mr Justice Sherdley betrayed first impatience, then irritation and finally resignation. Blytheway sat down and Mr Justice Sherdley turned to Preston. Leading Counsel for the prosecution was plainly even more irritated than the judge. He was shouting again, gesticulating furiously and shooting angry glances in Blytheway's direction. Blytheway had returned to filing his nails. When Preston had finished Roly stood up briefly to reply. Mr Justice Sherdley gave a brief judgment on the issue and then stood and bowed to counsel, who stood and bowed in return. It was four thirty. The court was rising for the day and would resume on Friday. Adam decided to make himself scarce.

Chapter Eighty-one
(Thursday 3rd April 1941)

Adam let himself into Blytheway's room. A clerk was busy putting the blackout shades in place, lighting his electric fire and switching on the Tiffany lamps. He looked up as Adam entered and asked whether he would like a cup of tea. Adam nodded and the clerk left, returning fifteen minutes later carrying a tray with a pot, two cups and a little jug of milk. Adam helped himself and then looked around the room that he had first seen as a client. On one wall was a complete leather-bound collection of the *English Reports*. Beneath these were the recently launched *All England Reports*. There were first editions of Sir Edward Coke's *Institutes of the Lawes of England* and Sir William Blackstone's *Commentaries on the Laws of England*. Blytheway's active cases were laid out neatly on another shelf. Adam rifled through them and found his own case about three from the top. He undid the pink ribbon and leafed through the pages of the brief. Remarkably, it was devoid of any pen or pencil marks: no underlining, no comments in the margins. He tied up the brief, took a seat on the client side of the desk and waited. Blytheway would be back before the tea went cold.

The door opened as he was lifting the cup to his lips.

– I thought I might find you here.

Blytheway hung his red bag and his overcoat on the coat stand.

– Tea.

he said, and went over to pour himself a cup. Then he took his place behind his desk and looked quizzically at Adam.

– So, what was going on today?

– I would have thought that fairly obvious.

– Why didn't you tell me it was happening?

– You have enough to worry about, sweetheart.

– But I could have helped you …

– Oh, I don't think so, dear boy. It was better that you stayed as far away as possible. I was pleased to see that you had disappeared before Preston came out of court. He was *not* in a good mood.

– Why? What happened?

– Well, strictly of course I shouldn't tell you as we were all obliged to sign the Official Secrets Act before the trial could continue in camera. But you know so much of the story anyway and I am sure I can count on your discretion.

– The court went into camera because of that stuff about secret codes I suppose?

– Yes. That was inevitable. It started on Wednesday actually.

– That's why the public gallery had been cleared when I arrived?

– Precisely. Do you remember, last time around, how aerated Preston had become when I asked how it was that the police were able to target Novak's floorboards? We got around that last time by soft-pedalling. *This* time around I made great play of the fact that no explanation had been proffered. No jury likes being kept in the dark.

– And Preston went for it?

– Hook, line and sinker. He sought permission to call someone from Military Intelligence on the basis that we all, jury included, would have to sign the Official Secrets Act.

– And you were happy to go along with it?

– Of course. There's no point in preparing a trap and then warning someone to step around it.

– A trap?

– Preston wanted to adduce the "top secret" evidence about how our code-breakers had intercepted enemy messages identifying these plans. I, on the other hand, wanted to have an opportunity to ask this man from Military … "Intelligence" what they knew about Katya Hoffer beyond this.

– That must have made you popular!

– Not particularly. The judge was very irritated and Preston was very cross – although it's hard to know. He hasn't spoken a civil word to me at any stage during this trial. In fairness, he hasn't spoken an uncivil word.

– Did it work?

– I was able to suggest to our man from "Intelligence" that Katya was no more than a tethered goat. Unfortunately for him he agreed. "Tethered goat." I may use that in my closing submissions.

– What happened just before the end of the day?

– Well, Preston wanted to get on with his closing submissions there and then. I was able to persuade our judge that, at 4.30 in the afternoon, it was unfair on the jury. It would be far better if closing submissions from prosecution and defence – and our judge's summing up – were heard tomorrow. Mrs Hoffer is facing the death penalty and the matter should be considered with proper decorum and respect for her rights. The judge ultimately agreed, although Preston was less than happy. I think he has become too used to quick and easy convictions. Perhaps he had a lunch party arranged for tomorrow? Furthermore, Preston knows she's innocent. I am fairly clear in my mind about that. He's just far more concerned with his wretched success rate. Two losses in a row would make him extremely unhappy.

– Is there any way I can get into court with you tomorrow, as your junior or something?

– Absolutely not! I am playing a dangerous game, Adam, and a young woman's life is at stake. However, come and meet me in the Bar Mess at around 2 p.m. I suspect that all speeches will by then be over and the jury will have retired. We can have a nice chat then. Would you mind organising some more tea?

Adam slipped out and down to the Clerks' Room. Blytheway was silent whilst they waited for the tea to arrive. He stared moodily into the bottom of his cup and swilled the tea leaves around as he thought.

– There's another thing.

– Yes?

– Preston was the one who took Pemberton to the Café de Paris that night. He was there when they came across her body being freighted out from the basement. From all accounts it was a terrible sight. I have seen some horrible things in my time but I'm glad that I didn't have to witness that. To see the effect on Pemberton. I'm not surprised that it rather unhinged him. But we must not lose sight of the effect it must have had on poor Preston. After all, as I understand it he was the one who said it was the safest place in London. Pemberton lashed out at him and blamed him for Jenny's death – which I think was hardly fair. However, it was no less fair that he has blamed me and you.

– Us?

– So I have heard. If we hadn't given Preston such a hard time in the Novak trial he might have warned Pemberton of the approaching raid – I am convinced that he has access to the secret codes and messages; and if Pemberton had not been so preoccupied with the upcoming petition, which of course we are both involved in, he may have been more careful of his daughter's interests, of her life.

– But that's absurd!

– But I think it is true. I confess to feeling some shreds of pity for Preston. Not that I would let that interfere with my professional duties.

Chapter Eighty-two
(Friday 4th April 1941)

Adam left Lamb Building at about 12.30 and headed down Fleet Street towards the Old Bailey. By one o'clock he was ordering sausage and potatoes in the Bar Mess. (Blytheway had said two o'clock, but he was impatient.) By five past one barristers, wrapped in their gowns, some with their wigs in their hands, were filing in. Suddenly Adam felt vulnerable. Blytheway had suggested two o'clock for a reason. If the speeches and summing up had ended by one – and even if they hadn't – it would be Blytheway's duty to go down to the cells and speak with Katya. Preston, on the other hand, had no such obligation. It was inevitable, therefore, that Preston would enter the Mess first. Cutting up his potatoes with one eye on the door, he felt suddenly cold.

He was swiping half a potato around his plate, mopping up the thin gravy, when he saw Preston enter. He was carrying his wig and a copy of Archbold in one hand and his papers in the other. His hair had been smeared across his scalp by the wig and he looked harassed. He spotted Adam, sitting in his suit, almost as he entered. Adam suddenly realised how he must have stuck out; he was not wearing a robe or bands. Preston's eyes widened and he hesitated before turning on his heel and leaving the room. It was almost fifteen minutes before he returned.

Preston now queued up with his tray and, having obtained a plate of food, looked carefully around the Mess before making his decision. He headed towards Adam with a look of suppressed fury on his face. Adam noticed sweat trickling down his cheek before staring down at his empty plate and reaching for his glass of water. He heard the scrape of the chair opposite him and the rattle of cutlery as Preston dumped his tray opposite him.

– You've got a bloody nerve coming here!
– I don't know what you're talking about. I'm entitled to eat here if I choose to.

- I hope Blytheway hasn't been spilling any secrets to you?
- You're going to lose again, aren't you?
- I knew it! That man's a disgrace.
- I was watching you yesterday through the door. I didn't need to know any secrets to know that it was going badly for you. So, no, Blytheway hasn't told me anything he shouldn't. I know a little about this case anyway, remember?

Preston harrumphed and concentrated on his lunch. Adam watched him as he ate. He seemed somehow diminished. When he had finished Adam cleared his throat and spoke again.

- Look, Preston. I heard about Jenny. That you were there when she was found. I'm really sorry.

Preston started and pushed his tray away. Then he looked straight into Adam's eyes for what seemed to be a long time. Adam stared back, fascinated. He saw an inner dialogue unfolding. Preston registered anger, horror, what seemed to be remorse, and then horror again. His shoulders slumped slightly.

- It was terrible.

His voice was low and quavering. There was another long silence as Preston's eyes bored into him. Eventually Adam bowed his head and looked down at the table.

- I can't imagine how terrible it was. I am very sorry.
- And people like you and Blytheway are prepared to take the shilling and defend the criminals who are doing this to our country ... to our friends and families!

Adam remembered what Roly had said the previous evening: that Katya was a tethered goat and that Preston knew she was innocent of the charges made against her. He thought of his prescience about upcoming raids.

- You know more about these codes and messages than you're letting on, don't you?

- Keep your voice down!
- You do though?
- I know no more than I am entitled to know. I've signed the Act. And as far as I am concerned my conscience is clear. I have done nothing dishonourable.

Neither of them heard Blytheway gliding over to join them until he set down his tray.

- My dear Preston. How good it is to see you speaking with Adam!
- I don't want to talk with you!
- Oh, sweetheart! Why ever not?

Adam noticed that Blytheway had visited the robing room and spruced up his hair before joining them. There was a faint smell of pomade.

- Sausage and potatoes! Delicious!
- I was telling Preston how sorry I was about Jenny.

Blytheway put down his knife and fork and looked at Preston. He raised a hand towards him and stroked his shoulder. Preston flinched.

- No one should have to witness what you were obliged to see.
- And yet you defend these people?!
- Surely it has occurred to you, my friend, that if we allow our legal system to be corrupted by this war then we will be the losers. We shall have handed them an unnecessary victory on a plate. I am *so* glad that we are speaking again, even in this rather antagonistic context.
- Your problem is that you cannot take anything seriously. You're irredeemably frivolous, Blytheway!
- On the contrary. You should know by now that I am deadly serious about things that matter – about things that I can affect. The trouble is that there is very little that I – or you for that matter – *can* actually affect.
- Whilst I accept that you, as junior counsel and a fire watcher, which I acknowledge is obviously useful, have little influence, my position is entirely different. Being one of His Majesty's Counsel brings all

sorts of access that you would not have any awareness of. And my job in the Ministry in my (limited) spare time does allow me to make a real difference.
– A low blow, if you don't mind me saying. But it is so good that we can have a chance to chat whilst we're waiting for the jury to come back. I expect we'll have most of the afternoon to catch up.

Preston was about to reply when a black-suited usher approached them to say that they were wanted in Court Six. The jury had a verdict and it was unanimous. Preston and Blytheway rose to leave.

– That was quick. Stay here, Adam, I want to speak with you after it's over.
– Yes, Falling. Stay here. I think it is where you are meant to be.

With slightly forced courtesies they made for the exit. Adam went and got himself a cup of tea. Was an early verdict good or bad for Katya? He didn't know but he would find out soon enough. As he regained his seat and lifted the cup to his lips the door to the Mess opened and Pemberton stormed in, looking in all directions until he saw Adam. Adam's day had suddenly got worse.

****

– Where's the diary, Falling?
– I have no idea. How did you know I would be here?
– Preston called me after he saw you. Where is it?
– Ask Julia. I certainly haven't got it.

Adam looked at Pemberton. He was standing over him, his arms braced against the table, and he had not sat down. He was thinner still than the last time he had seen him but his eyes were clear. There was a heavy whiff of after-shave. Adam remembered that the last time he had seen him was when they were rolling round in the dust punching one another. There was no scent of alcohol this time.

– It belongs to me! I'm her father!
– She's dead, Pemberton.

Pemberton punched him hard on the side of the face. The Mess was almost empty again as everyone, apart from those waiting for a jury to return, had gone back to their courts. Those that remained looked up at the sound of the blow. Adam suddenly remembered that he and Pemberton were notorious. He cupped his hand around his jaw and felt the beginnings of a swelling under the warmth of the pain.

- No one wanted her to die, Pemberton. I'm really sorry.
- Rot in hell! It's all your fault that this has happened!
- I thought she was lovely.
- You're going to suffer, Falling.
- What are you talking about?

Pemberton eased himself down into the seat opposite.

- You're a failure, Falling. You don't have a clue about what is going on around you. If I had been head of chambers all those years ago I would have made sure you didn't get a space with us.
- It's taken you a long time to say that.
- Finest traditions of the Bar and all that. I was stuck with you and had to make the best of it.
- I've been far happier since I left.
- Of course you are! Sleeping with that amoral reprobate Blytheway!
- I beg your pardon?
- Well, there can't be any other reason for it, can there? He can't possibly be impressed by your mind.
- This is outrageous!

The few heads remaining in the Mess were now turned in their direction.

- He's corrupt! And so, evidently, are you.
- So you think that I slept with your wife and then moved on and slept with Blytheway?
- You know that you slept with her. I'm going to prove that, Falling. And damn the pair of you! Damn Blytheway as well.
- You're mad. I haven't slept with Julia. And I certainly haven't slept with Blytheway!

- When this is over I intend to institute criminal proceedings against you and him. If necessary it will be a private prosecution.
- That's why you want the diary, isn't it? It shows that you're talking nonsense.
- We'll see, Falling, we'll see. But in less than four weeks you and I will be facing each other across a court. Bateman is as guilty as sin and only an idiot could persuade him to carry on with defending that petition. Fortunately for me he *is* being represented by an idiot. I'm going to humiliate you, Falling. And then, the following week, I'm going to humiliate you again.
- We'll see.
- And the best thing about it is that in the first trial I'm going to be well paid for my efforts and Bateman will have to fork out. And in the second trial you will have to pay my costs and pay me damages on top.
- You're jumping the gun.
- And Falling. Don't you worry. I won't be drinking. That's behind me now.
- I'm glad to hear that.
- I could beat you hollow even if I was drunk. But I'm going to make you pay for killing Jenny.

The man was deranged. But before Adam could reply Blytheway came back into the Mess, Preston following, to announce that Katya had been found not guilty.

- So that's good news all round! I'm sorry Pemberton, are you leaving?

Pemberton was already slouching towards the door.

- What a pity. I was hoping we could have a chat. Adam, I'm sorry to be a bore but I need to go down and see Mrs Hoffer. She's still in custody I'm afraid but I am hoping to broker a meeting between her and Mr Novak.

Chapter Eighty-three

(Wednesday 16th April 1941)

The nearest working telephone box was about ten minutes' walk from Julia's apartment and frequently one had to queue up to use it. It was quarter past seven in the evening before she was able to step inside, take some coins from her purse and put a call through to her children. She had last been able to see them over the previous long weekend, the Easter weekend, when she had taken Easter eggs down to the Cotswolds for them. Dusk was falling by the time she stepped out. There had been a rap on the glass from the next in line to use the kiosk and she had been obliged to say hurried goodbyes to Agnes.

People were already hurrying towards Holborn underground station as she made her way back to Mecklenburg Square. In just over half an hour the blackout was due to begin. Inside her apartment she switched on the main light and put the blackout shades in place. She had laid out her nightdress on the bed, and her overnight bag, filled with toiletries should she need to decamp to the cellar, lay next to it. She opened a tin of tomato soup and poured it into a pan on the hot-plate.

While it was bubbling up she went to her tiny bathroom and, with a piece of cotton, began removing her foundation. There were dark shadows under her eyes and her face was gaunt. The smell of cream of tomato drifted in on her and she went back to the little kitchen and poured the soup into a bowl.

As she was lifting her spoon to eat there was a knock on the door. Placing the chain in the security latch she cautiously pulled the door open and peered out into the gloom. It was Audrey Fisher, a fresh-faced woman in her early thirties who lived around the corner and worked with her at the Water Board.

– Sorry to disturb, Julia, but we need to go back to work.

Julia looked at her watch.

- It's my night off.
- Mine too. I've had a call. Bad things are about to happen. We've got no choice.
- Give me a minute.

Julia unlatched the door and let Audrey in. She poured her soup into a Thermos flask, picked up her overnight bag and put on her overcoat. They were out of the door within minutes.

- I'm really sorry to have to do this. We've both been working double shifts lately.
- Did anyone call for me?
- A man named Jack Storman rang to find out how you were. He asked if you could call him.
- How long do you think this is going to last?
- All night I think.

They hurried along the darkening, almost deserted streets.

Down in the bunker they took their places at the usual desks. Ladies in twin-sets took seats by the maps of the city, ready to move markers around. And then the sirens and the drone of planes began.

This had been her life now for several weeks. The postponement of the trial and the heavy, if erratic, bombing had allowed a strange normality to emerge. In the room there had been growing talk of invasion, which served to contextualise her problems and diminish them. Jenny's death, equally, had, in an odd way, made her more sanguine.

This raid was different. As the clocked clicked through to nine the sound of planes overhead was loud, oppressive and unending, as was the sound of explosions. Occasionally the building they were in jumped and rocked as if it were on springs.

Then the reports began to come in. Bombs were falling everywhere in a manner that had not been experienced before. It was as though everywhere and everything in London was being hit that night: the Temple, the West End, Mayfair, the Docks, Islington, Farringdon, Camden and even Kent: Shortlands, Bromley and Beckenham. One accurate bomb, and her trial (and perhaps her life) would be over. She felt a strange omnipotence about her friends, and enemies, as the reports came in and she unscrewed the Thermos to drink the hot tomato soup.

****

On the roof of 1 Hare Court, Blytheway was standing in for Adam who, still unwell, continued to insist on staying in his room in Dr Johnson's Buildings. Incendiaries, high explosives and parachute mines were falling and he, Barry and Roberts were kicking the incendiaries off the roof and watching for fires. Blytheway's overalls had been tailored to accentuate his figure. Barry turned to him in a lull.

– This is worse than anything we've seen so far, sir.
– Roly! Please!

Blytheway wiped away some sweat from his face. He was breathing heavily.

– I'm afraid you are right, Barry. If this carries on much longer we shall all be obliged to cash in our chips ... Look out!

A rattle of incendiaries landed in the gutter. The three men moved quickly to avoid them.

– Kick them hard! Oh, how I hate having to shout!

And they managed to get them all off the roof.

****

In Dr Johnson's Buildings, Adam remained in bed sleeping fitfully despite the roar of the planes and the sound of explosions. His mind was filled with images of the coming trials, and when sleep occasionally came to him Blytheway's cobalt ghost would shimmer around the room.

****

In the basement in Eaton Square Pemberton sat on his bed. The electric light flickered against the wine racks and blankets. Samuels and Annie sat on the bed opposite, Julia's bed, and listened to the bombardment overhead. Occasionally they looked one another in the eye and saw how large were the whites: this felt like the end. Then they would look across at their employer, whose eyes were inward and seeing something completely different. The interminable rumble continued and the cellar shook as bombs exploded nearby.

Pemberton was thinking of Julia, in that bomb-wrecked part of London. He hoped that she might perhaps die now and he could seal his grief over. There was nothing left for him. He gazed fretfully at the whisky bottle that he had placed on the bedside table and willed himself not to open it. Or not yet at least.

****

Jack Storman and his wife, Margaret, were hugging one another in the darkness of their Anderson shelter. He had lit a candle, which flickered, sending shadows over the walls. His wife was still beautiful, in a way that many women were not, but the fear and anxiety that had been growing in her over the years had creased her beauty. It was 2 a.m. now and the bombs had been falling for five hours. The incessant noise and the sound of encroaching explosions seemed to intensify. He made himself admit that he was terrified. He held his wife closer and she looked deeply into his eyes with the look that she had given him twenty-five years ago on their wedding day.

- I'm so thirsty.
- This can't go on much longer.
- I know. We'll see it through – as we always do.
- Do you want me to get you some water?
- No. It's too dangerous. Stay here with me.

Storman pulled himself away from her.

- I won't be a minute.
- You shouldn't. I love you so much!
- I love you too!

It was a ritual that they had insisted on, implicitly, since the Blitz began. Storman climbed out of the shelter and stumbled up their long, narrow garden back to the house. He fumbled his way to the cupboard and then to the kitchen tap and, like a blind man, trickled water into a glass for his wife. In daylight it would have taken less than a minute. In these circumstances it took him five. The glass was cool in his hand, and on a whim he drank it down. He edged the glass back to the spout of the tap and slowly turned the tap back on. When the glass was heavy enough he turned off the flow and felt his way to the back door.

Opening the kitchen door he could see, in a fire-cracker of explosions, their gardens, the little stone path and, at the end of it, the shelter. He stepped out into a maelstrom of sudden noise, and a burst of hot wind blew him backwards into the house.

When he came to his clothing was soaked with steaming water, and fragments of glass littered him. The kitchen windows had all been blown out. Lifting his head to look outside, he saw that the shelter was no longer there.

Chapter Eighty-four

(Thursday 17ᵗʰ April 1941)

Someone was shaking him insistently by the shoulders. He didn't want to wake up. The previous night's bombardment had broken his sleep comprehensively by 1 a.m. and although he had no thought of going down to the shelter the noise from outside was of cataclysmic proportions. Dawn was edging round the corners of the blackout shades by the time he eventually fell asleep. The silent shaking continued and he turned his head away and tried to burrow down under his blankets.

– Need to sleep …

he said drowsily.

He felt a hand on his face, a thumb in one cheek and fingers in the other and his head was wrenched back to where it had been.

– I am afraid you cannot sleep. You must wake up!

It was Roly. The urgency in his voice was something Adam had never heard before and it woke him with a start. Opening his eyes, he saw Blytheway leaning over him. He was again dressed in a frock coat but, unusually, the rest of his clothing was lacking in colour. The last time he had seen him he had been wearing his specially tailored overalls in readiness for a night of fire-fighting.

– What is it? What time is it? What day is it?
– I let myself in when you didn't respond to my knocking.
– What's going on?
– Terrible news, I am afraid.

Alarmed, Adam hauled himself quickly into a sitting position. Blytheway looked distraught. As his eyes came fully into focus he could tell that Roly had been weeping. There was none of the usual jauntiness. No "sweethearts". No "darlings". No "hey-hos". His hair was out of place as though he had been running his hands through it obsessively. Adam did not know what to think. He had never before seen Blytheway without a ready answer, Blytheway helpless.

He had taken down the blackout shades before shaking Adam awake. The window had been pulled open and green scents mingled with the smell of smoke and fire that wafted in. The urgent bells of emergency vehicles were clattering along in the streets outside the Temple.

- What is it?
- Margaret Storman.
- Jack's wife?
- Their Anderson shelter took a direct hit. I am afraid she was killed instantly. Poor Margaret. Poor Jack.
- My God! How's Jack.
- In a terrible way. I didn't find out until 6 a.m. when I got home. He had telephoned at three in the morning and Caldwell took a message. He couldn't get hold of me to pass it on. But he knows me very well. I knew something was wrong when I saw our car sitting outside the house.

Adam noticed that he did not refer to it as his "jalopy".

- He had laid out a change of clothes in my dressing room. Sub-fusc. And we were on our way to Shortlands by twenty past. Adam, I have never seen such destruction. So many roads were closed that it took us an hour and a half to get to Storman. Al Bowley was killed as well … and Baron Stamp and his wife and son – nice man. I fear that we are losing this war.
- What about Jack?
- He was in a terrible state by the time we got there. Catatonic with grief. Margaret was still in what was left of their shelter. He had made calls to the emergency services of course but had to tell them that she was beyond hope … so she wasn't a high priority.

- But he survived? Is he very badly injured?
- They had been in their sad shelter for five hours and he had gone to get Margaret a glass of water because she was thirsty. He was just going back into the garden when the bomb struck. Blew him backwards and blew out all the windows. He still had fragments of glass all over his pyjamas. I think he might have been concussed. Caldwell made some tea for us all.
- This is dreadful.
- You see, Jack poured Margaret a glass of water and then drank it himself. And so then he had to pour another glass – and that took a little time with the blackout on. He kept saying to me that, if he had just taken the first glass out to her, he could have been with her at the end. I don't think he wants to go on living.

Blytheway stifled a sob.

- Jack knew she was dead. The shelter was utterly demolished but he hadn't been able to pluck up the courage to try and get her out. He said that, with our help, we could take her back to the house and lay her out with some dignity there. Of course, that was *absolutely* not on! We forbade him to try, and ushered him back into the kitchen when he tried …

He put his head in his hands and squeezed on his eyes before running his fingers through his grey hair again and again. Adam remained silent. There was nothing he could say. For the first and the last occasion in the time that he spent with Blytheway, his friend looked old and tired and vulnerable. He reached out a hand and stroked his shoulder.

- So Caldwell and I had to deal with the situation. We gathered up some sheets and made our way down his beautiful garden. It was a lovely morning. There had been a curved roof of corrugated metal but it had been completely obliterated. I've seen a great deal of death, Adam. God knows. I try, as Yeats would have it, to "cast a cold eye" on it. But this was a woman I loved. Just as I love Jack.

Adam had a mental picture of the two men walking unsteadily towards the devastation. Jack watching them from the blown-out kitchen windows.

– She must have died instantly. That is a small comfort. I cast my cold eye. The bomb must have landed on the back of her neck. She was probably cowering in fear. What a terrible mess! Of course, the woman I knew as Margaret was gone; but so much of her body had been destroyed as well. There was blood everywhere and her clothes had been scorched off her. Thank goodness we took sheets to cover her! She was stuck through with pieces of corrugated iron and we had to do our best to remove it. I've had training in this sort of thing.

Adam remembered that Blytheway had been in the ambulance corps in the last war.

– Her body was still in one piece. But dreadfully disfigured. She was a lot lighter to carry than she should have been. Once we had got her out and wrapped her in our sheets we persuaded Jack that he should not look and waited until the ambulance arrived so that she could be taken to the morgue. We brought Jack back into London. He is staying with us for the time being. We gave him your room. I hope that's all right?
– I'm so sorry, Roly.
– You see. I have very few people who I can count as real friends. People who have the ability to take me as I am. And Margaret and Jack were two of the very few who could. I can hardly imagine what Jack is going through. And for once in my life there is absolutely nothing I can do to make things better.
– You said that she had developed agoraphobia. Why did that happen?
– I'm afraid that I don't know. It was a source of great anxiety to Jack but I was never able to pin it down to any particular incident or cause – though goodness knows I tried.
– I never felt I knew her that well.
– She was a delightful – beautiful – lady. And she made Jack very happy. As I think I mentioned, she and Jack were the only friends that I felt able to introduce to the Bloomsbury Set.
– And you stood in for Jack at various functions?
– He sometimes had problems with his back. It was not something I would normally do. I tend to hate these black-tie balls that the Inns throw each summer. They weren't organised with people like me

in mind. But for Jack and Margaret I was happy to make an exception. Of course, after 1937, when her condition deteriorated, I was no longer required to fulfil that function. I will miss her.
– So what happens next?

Blytheway shook himself, as though he were reminding himself who he was. When next he spoke it was almost as though the old Roly was back.

– I told Storman that we would deal with the funeral arrangements. After Caldwell dropped me here he went back to the house to get on with it. It may take a little time. A lot of people were killed last night. That is one of the reasons I needed to see you. I suspect that the funeral will take place a week on Saturday. I am sure you would want to be there, health permitting. But I know that you are likely to be worried about the Bateman trial, which is due to begin on the following Monday.
– I'll be there, Roly. Whatever the cost.
– Think about it, Adam, before you commit yourself to it.
– Why on earth would I need to think about it?
– Jack Storman is a member of your old chambers. They will all be there. He is also a good friend of your wife. She no doubt will also be there. Julia Pemberton will be there. I, of course, will be there, as will Caldwell. Are you really sure that you're up to it?
– I must.
– All right, Adam. But if I were you I would turn up a few minutes late rather than a few minutes early.

Blytheway stood up to leave.
– It's nearly time for luncheon, sweetheart, and I don't want to keep Jack waiting.
– Stay. Have another cup of tea.
– Sorry, sweetheart. I need to go. I will walk back. I need to clear my head. I'm sorry about the state I've been in. I think I dropped my guard. I rarely do that.

And with a slight bow he let himself out.

Chapter Eighty-five

(Tuesday 22nd April 1941)

Adam lit a match and looked at his alarm clock. It was four in the morning. Sleep was slow in coming. The blackout was not due to end for another ninety minutes but the air was quiet. He climbed out of bed and went over to the window. Slowly he pulled down the shades. The air was clear and bright. He pulled open the window and looked down at Inner Temple Lane.

He had found it difficult in getting to sleep, and as he looked down at the moon-washed alleyway he was unsure if he had slept at all. He had been thinking of Jack and Margaret Storman again. Blytheway's description of her terrible injuries. He remembered that Roly had a "photographic memory" – everything he saw that morning would remain with him forever. He had also been assailed by dreams. Blytheway, inevitably, was present asking questions. Betty was telling her old stories and other voices were invading. Jones was talking about Bateman's insurance policy and its ultimate rewards; and Pemberton was talking about Mrs Bateman lying dead in the street whilst Bateman was in bed with Mrs McKechnie. And finally there was Betty, from an earlier dream, telling him that the insurance company wouldn't pay out because she had been wearing a flashing straw hat at the time of her husband's death. There was a message in there somewhere. *Look at the evidence, darling.*

He had met Betty the previous evening in the same Lyons' tea shop as they had met in before. He had paid for dinner and the purpose, for him, of their evening was to learn more about her husband, Joe, and the circumstances of his death. He had been unhappy about the fact, as teased out by Blytheway, that he knew so little about her life. He needed to know much more.

Joe was a good, good-looking, man. He had loved Betty dearly and they had talked about setting up in business together when all of this was over. He had had a limited education but he was clearly intelligent and ambitious. He wanted them to have a big family and they had married just before he joined up for the British Expeditionary Force. He knew that he might die and that, in such circumstances, he would leave her without material support. In those circumstances, he had taken out some life insurance. He knew that it would be no good to him or to her if he was killed in France, because of the "enemy action" exclusion, but neither of them had any idea that it would apply if he actually got killed in her parents' house in Islington.

He liked music hall and he liked George Formby (even though Formby was from the North) and he would take her out on a boat on the Serpentine when he had the opportunity. He would write her poems in a touching doggerel that spoke of her beauty and kindness. He thought the war would be over soon and perhaps they would be able to move out of London to somewhere cleaner like Hertfordshire. She, for her part, made dresses and gloves, and, when they had evenings apart, would knit.

He was from Haringey and she was from Islington. He got down on one knee when he asked her to marry him and he also asked her father's permission and told him that his prospects, after the war, were good.

He made it back from Dunkirk and was on leave when a bomb hit the house, destroying it and killing him. Her mum and dad were killed too. She tried to make a claim on the insurance policy but the circumstances of his death meant that the insurance company had a get-out clause. And so, with nowhere to live, no family and no source of income, she had, after much soul-searching, turned to prostitution. She showed Adam a picture of him in his uniform, posed in a studio. He looked like a decent sort of man.

He learnt a lot more about Betty and Joe, but there was something in her story that continued to niggle at him, something important in there which he had not grasped.

Looking down onto Inner Temple Lane, he breathed in the air and sensed the first green blush of spring.

And then it hit him, with the force of a punch to the stomach. He was gasping for air at the realization. He needed to speak to Jones, urgently.

Chapter Eighty-six
(Wednesday 23rd April 1941)

Adam waited in his room in chambers. Jones and Bateman were about to be shown up. This was an almighty gamble but, for the first time, he felt that Bateman might have a defence. He looked around his room, at the Chinese prints and the peacock feathers in vases, and he thought to himself – again for the first time – that he had got somewhere without Blytheway's overt help. He had helped him in his dreams and in his approach to things, but he had left him alone to work it all out. And he felt that now, he had done so.

He had been unable to sleep again that Tuesday morning, and as soon as it was proper to do so he had put a call through to Jones and asked for an urgent conference to be arranged in Lamb Building. He had been insistent that Jones bring a copy of the insurance policy that had paid out £10,000 on the death of Marjorie Bateman, and a photograph of her. He had a copy of the policy in his hands, which he read through as Jones and Bateman were being shown up to his room. It was all there. The documents ultimately told him everything in this case.

Jones and Bateman were shown in. Adam stood and shook hands with them. He felt more assured than he had ever done. He enjoyed the way that his expensive suit moved in the right way as he moved his body. Understanding a situation gave him control. He was beginning to realise why Blytheway had so much self-possession. Perhaps he might be learning something from him?

- Good evening, Mr Bateman, Mr Jones.
- What's going on? Why did you need to see the insurance policy all of a sudden?
- You haven't been telling me the truth, Mr Bateman.
- Bloody cheek!
- Tell me about the insurance policy. Why are you so upset about me looking at it?

– Well, because it's irrelevant, isn't it? What has *it* got to do with anything?
– It has an exemption in it, doesn't it? An exemption for death from enemy action?
– And?
– Does Mr McKechnie have a similar policy for Victoria?
– What if he does?
– It just occurred to me that, if you worked for the same insurance company you'd have the same insurance policy.
– Yeah. Well. Probably … we did. But I don't see what that has to do with anything.
– Please forgive me, Mr Bateman, for this, but it seems to me that, under the terms of the policy, if, for example, Marjorie had been killed in a house that was hit by a bomb you would not have got any insurance money, but if she had been killed by a car during the blackout you would.
– What are you trying to say?
– Mr McKechnie's home was destroyed on the night of Marjorie's death, wasn't it?
– Oh! I see! I see what you're getting at!
– May I indulge in a little theory, Mr Bateman? It goes like this: you fell in love with Victoria McKechnie. To be honest it doesn't matter when. Everything about you – forgive me – tells me that you love her. But at the same time Mr McKechnie fell in love with Marjorie … though it may not have been love; I don't know enough about either of you.
– I don't see where all this is going?
– Bear with me. I think each of you loved your wives but – here's the tragedy of it all – you loved the other woman more.
– This is nonsense!
– Bear with me again. Let us assume again, on the basis that I am right, that the four of you would go to the ABC cinema, would shrink down in the back row and then would leave before the second feature to be with each other's spouses. If that hypothesis were right, then you would be at home with Victoria and Mr McKechnie would be at home with Marjorie.
– What rot!
– Have you brought a photograph of Marjorie?

Adam watched Bateman closely. He was wearing the same loud pinstripe as at their first conference. He was sweating profusely and getting redder and redder as Adam spoke. He seemed relieved at the change of subject as he reached into the inside pocket of his jacket and pulled out his wallet.

It was a small black and white studio framed shot. Marjorie was wearing a dark blouse and a delicate string of pearls. The picture caught her in profile; she was looking to her right. She had long dark hair and full lips held in a slight, amused smile. Adam gasped. She was beautiful.

- How long ago was this taken?
- Last summer.
- How old was she when she died?
- Thirty-one.
- Had you seen this photograph before Mr Jones?

Jones did not know where all this was heading and he did not like it. He looked up from his hastily scribbled notes and took the photograph.

- No.
- This changes my whole perception of your case, Mr Bateman. I confess I had overlooked Marjorie's role in all of this.
- I don't know what you're talking about, mate.
- I'm just wondering, if the four of you were in the habit of going to the pictures as regularly as Victoria's diary suggests, what was going on with Mr McKechnie and Marjorie whilst you were, allegedly, with Victoria?
- I thought you were on my side!
- Oh, but I am! But if I am going to be able to help you you're going to have to tell me the truth.

Adam looked over at Jones and saw a smile dawning on his face. The tenseness went out of his shoulders and he slapped his hand down on Adam's desk with a sudden shout.

- Of course!

Bateman was angrier now than he had been when he had first met Adam in Stirrup Court.

- What's got into you two?
- Mr Jones, why don't you explain it?

Jones was more than happy to oblige.

- What Mr Falling is getting at is that if you were having an … um … intimate relationship with Victoria whilst, at the same time, Mr McKechnie was carrying on with Marjorie, then you may well have a defence to the petition.
- What?!
- If it is right that Mr McKechnie was, um, carrying on with Marjorie, then it can be said that he connived in your relationship with Victoria. He condoned it. In those circumstances, even if adultery is proven, he may not be entitled to a decree of divorce.

Bateman's mouth fell open as he looked from Jones to Adam and then back to Jones. Confusion struggled with hope and relief across his features.

- You mean I won't have to pay damages and I won't have to pay his legal fees?
- Probably not. In fact, he may have to pay *your* costs – and those of Victoria.
- And he won't be able to take Ernest and Susan away from her?
- No. My only concern is that all three of you are at risk of prosecution for fraud.
- What are you talking about?

Adam took a deep breath and was overcome by a fit of coughing.

- Here's what I think happened that night: all four of you went to the pictures, as usual. Then before the second feature you and Victoria went back to your house and McKechnie and Marjorie went back to his. His house was demolished by a bomb that night. I believe he and Marjorie were inside and that was what killed her. She wasn't hit by a car at all!
- Where's this leading?
- McKechnie came and found the two of you, and between you all you

decided to move Marjorie's body into the road and you concocted a story for the coroner. You and McKechnie are both in the insurance business. You both knew about the exemption clause.

– Why would we do such a thing?

– For ten thousand pounds. McKechnie assumed you would share the money with him.

– Marjorie was *my wife!*

– That's what really hurt, wasn't it? She was your wife. You were the one with an "insurable interest" in her life. But she loved McKechnie. And he loved her. He helped you process the claim and when the money came through you kept it all for yourself. It was only after that that McKechnie started making the allegations of adultery. I'm right aren't I?

Bateman's shoulders slumped and he looked down at his knees. When he spoke it was no more than a whisper.

– Yes. It wasn't *my* idea. Honest. But she *was* my wife!

– Mr Bateman, I can only defend you now if you tell the truth to the court as you have told it to us now. You have a choice: either you do that and you can retain us as your lawyers or you persist in your story that you and Victoria were not having an affair. In those circumstances, I am afraid that we will have to cease to represent you.

– Well, if it means one in the eye for McKechnie, I'll happily tell the truth.

– There is a risk that the fraud will emerge but it is not inevitable.

– As far as I'm concerned it's worth the risk. Easy come, easy go. Let's give it a go!

– Mr Jones, this changes everything. I must speak urgently with Victoria's counsel. Mr Bateman, I want you to put your instructions to us in writing and sign them off. I will need you to provide the full story of your relationship with Victoria and McKechnie's relationship with Marjorie.

Adam brought the conference to a close, and as Jones and Bateman were leaving the room he put a call through to David Farquarson, Victoria's barrister, and organised an urgent meeting for the following morning.

Chapter Eighty-seven

(Thursday 24th April 1941)

Jones was as good as his word, and by the following morning a large buff envelope arrived. Inside were ten typed pages that set out the full story starting with an office party on 22nd December 1936 when Marjorie first met McKechnie and Bateman first met Victoria. A friendship developed between the four and then things took a turn for the worse. McKechnie had taken a shine to Marjorie and they had started an affair. Victoria found out what was happening and, distressed, had confided in Bateman and they had comforted one another. There had been arguments and tantrums, but over time the four had reached an accommodation that satisfied them all. A German bomb brought that to an end at the beginning of the Blitz.

David Farquarson was five years senior to Adam and so it was necessary for him to go around to 3, Paper Buildings to see him. It was a short walk from Lamb Building, and after a brief wait he was shown up to Farquarson's room. The tall, slightly stooped man greeted him with old-fashioned courtesy and listened quietly as Adam told his tale. When he had finished, Farquarson rose from his desk without speaking, and went over to the window to look out over Inner Temple Gardens, his silhouette still against the light. Adam began to think he would never speak. Finally, he turned back into the room.

- I see.
- I think he's telling the truth at last. But I need to know what your client has to say about this.
- I confess that I have been concerned about what she has told me, to date. To be honest, I sensed that she was becoming increasingly reluctant to stick to it.
- I need her to confirm Bateman's account. If she does, we both have a lot of work to do.
- I'll get my solicitor onto her and get back to you as soon as I can.
- Try and call me later today.

The two men stood and bowed slightly to one another, handshakes being out of the question, and Adam took his leave.

Adam spent the rest of the day in his room in chambers waiting for Farquarson to call. It was almost five o'clock before the telephone rang.

- She confirms everything.
- Which of us should call Pemberton?
- I think, in the circumstances, it should come from you. Let me know how he reacts.

Adam put the phone down and stared at it for a long time. Finally, he picked it up and put a call through to Stirrup Court. At the other end of the line, Pemberton growled:

- What do *you* want, Falling?
- Bateman intends to change his case. He now accepts that he was conducting an affair with Mrs McKechnie and that adultery occurred on the dates set out in the petition.
- Seeing sense at last! I knew that you would be too scared to fight against me! I take it your client will also be paying all my client's costs?
- Oh, I didn't say that the petition was no longer defended. Farquarson and I will both be applying to amend our Answers. We shall be pleading condonation.

There was a long pause.

- Go rot in hell, Falling!

And Pemberton put the phone down.

Chapter Eighty-eight

(Friday 25th April 1941)

McKechnie was angry.

- I thought we had had all the meetings we needed to have!
- Mr Pemberton said that it was urgent.
- He told us it was an open and shut case! He just wants to squeeze more money out of me. Him and that other useless bloke!
- I've told you. You'll get your costs back if you win.
- "IF?!" You've never said "if" before! What's going on?
- There may have been some developments.
- How could there be developments!? We're talking about something that happened months ago.

McKechnie's solicitor was not enjoying this. He had told Mr Pemberton KC that it was extremely difficult for him to drop everything and come to a consultation just like that. He was extremely busy and he had the final preparations to do for the trial, which was due to begin on Monday. But Pemberton had been adamant.

- Couldn't it wait? We are nearly there and surely we could have a consultation on the morning. Before the case begins. They haven't got a leg to stand on after all.
- I spoke to Falling last night. They are changing their case. He and Farquarson intend to admit adultery and plead condonation. They're saying McKechnie knew about it all the time. And if McKechnie knew about it, the only explanation I've been able to come up with is that he was having an affair with Bateman's wife.
- Oh shit! ... Sorry for the obscenity, sir.
- Never mind about that! I need to see McKechnie right now! And don't tell him *why* I need to see him.

That had been all he needed! They had been seated for less than five minutes before Arthur breezed in and invited them to follow him to Mr Pemberton's room. It was two in the afternoon. Sunlight drifted in and the sound of birdsong could be heard from the open window. The supernumerary Perkins was sitting at his little desk – *cowering, more like*, McKechnie thought. Jeremy Pemberton KC had all the papers ranged out across his desk. He did not look particularly happy.

– What's all this about? I had piles of work to get through! I've got to be out of the office most of next week, d'you remember?

Pemberton raised his hands in a way that was almost defensive and tried to fan his client into silence. When McKechnie had subsided he leant forward and said, in what was an attempt to be consolatory and unconcerned:

– Mr Falling telephoned me last night. He may have raised a problem for us. I mean for you.
– For me, not us?! I thought we were on the same side.
– It is just a small point and I am sure that we will be able to sort it out very quickly.
– Falling's raised a problem? A problem that means I have to drop everything? You've been telling me all along that he is hopeless! How could he have raised a problem that means I have to come here at the last minute?
– I'm sure it is nothing. But Falling tells me that he and Victoria's barrister are intending to amend their cases.
– What does that mean?
– They are both going to admit that he and Victoria were having an affair.

McKechnie took a deep breath and sighed with relief. He began to smile.

– Well then. There's nothing to worry about is there?
– Not exactly.

McKechnie's smile faded.

– Why ever not?

– Apparently, they are going to be pleading condonation.

– "Pleading condonation"? Speak to me in English for Christ's sake!

– Look. I'm sorry. What they are saying, in essence, is that they were having an affair but that you knew all about it and didn't do anything about it. That you let it happen.

– But that's ridiculous! And anyway, even if I did know, he was still screwing my wife!

– But did you know?

McKechnie was no fool. He realised that the question was loaded. Collins had told him about how barristers had to pull out if you changed your story. He paused for a long time. Probably slightly too long a time.

– Of course I didn't! Why would I let something like that go on? Under my nose. Here. Look.

He produced a photograph of Victoria McKechnie and handed it to Pemberton, who took it and studied it carefully. Mrs McKechnie was without doubt an attractive woman although, in his view, she looked slightly common.

– Very pretty …

– Why would I let another man have his way?

– Well. I have been wondering about that. Even without seeing such an attractive portrait. I was pretty much stumped, I must confess. I looked at all the possibilities and almost none of them made any sense …

– *Almost* none of them?

– The only one that made any sense at all – forgive me, Mr McKechnie – was that you were engaged in a relationship with Mrs Bateman, and, in such circumstances, allowing Mr Bateman to "carry on" with your wife may have seemed like, shall we say, an adequate quid pro quo.

– What's a "quid pro quo" for fuck's sake?!

McKechnie was becoming increasingly agitated. Pemberton needed a drink – quickly.

– A "quid pro quo" is Latin. It means "something for something". "A favour for a favour".
– What the hell are you talking about?
– I am saying that, next Monday, it may be suggested that you were content for your wife to sleep with Bateman if in return he did not kick up about you sleeping with Mrs Bateman ...
– Well. This is absurd. You told me I had a good case.
– You still *do* have a good case ... unless you knew about the affair all along, particularly if you were sleeping with Marjorie Bateman. Were you sleeping with her?

McKechnie felt something cold enter into his stomach. He had to choose his words carefully. A lot might depend upon what he said next. Bateman's barrister knew about the inquest and what was said at it. He said nothing for a long time.

– Come on, Mr McKechnie. It is not a difficult question. The answer is either "yes" or "no".
– NO!!

The word roared out of him as though it had been wrenched from deep inside him. He could sense Pemberton and Collins beginning to relax as the tension of the previous minutes passed. Even Perkins looked up from his desk and gave a little smile. There was relief in his voice when the smiling KC eventually spoke.

– Well. That's all right then.
– So, I've still got a good case then?
– Yes, Mr McKechnie. *If* you are telling us the truth.
– Why would I lie?

Pemberton could think of many reasons why he would lie about this. But he had done his duty. He had given his client the opportunity to change his story and that opportunity had not been taken. His conscience was clear. If he was lying – and was found out in the lies – he was going to lose. But it wouldn't be his fault. The only embarrassment for him would be that Falling would have beaten him in a case that Pemberton had told his client it was impossible to lose. A splinter of shame entered his heart at the thought. And he abruptly stopped smiling. He stood and ushered everyone out of his room. He had a lot to do and tomorrow he had to go to St Luke's Cemetery in Bromley for the funeral of Margaret Storman.

Chapter Eighty-nine

(Saturday 26th April 1941)

Magpie Hall Lane consisted of a series of Mock Tudor villas designed to accommodate the prosperous middle class. St Luke's Cemetery was there but it was just over a mile from St Luke's Church. Adam knew this because he had taken an early train from Victoria to Bromley South and then walked along Bromley Common so that he could see both the church and the cemetery. Roly had counselled that he should arrive a little late at the service, and this he intended to do. Throughout the short time he had known Blytheway his advice had been faultless, and although he had ignored it in the past he had no intention of repeating those mistakes. However, just because he intended to join the service a few minutes late did not mean that he had to be late in getting to Bromley.

The train journey had taken him through Dulwich and he had thought with a pang of all that he had lost. His wife was still there. His daughter was in Suffolk for the duration of the war. Or at least for the duration of the Blitz – assuming London survived it. Blytheway, true to his word, had taken over the organisation of the funeral. He had heard little of Storman, nor had he even seen him. The word was that he was in a bad way. Roly had provided him with a copy of the Order of Service. Thick cream high-quality card, edged in black, that Adam turned over and over in his hands as he walked back towards the church. There were to be a number of pieces of music and a eulogy in the middle. It was not clear who was going to make that eulogy.

He retraced his steps along Southborough Lane and onto Crown Lane Spur. Then back into Bromley Common. He would be at the funeral service but he would be the last to enter the church. He stood by a privet hedge about a hundred yards from the entrance. He was wearing a black mourning suit that Blytheway had given to him (after it had been suitably taken in) and his shoes had been polished to a high shine. Blytheway's influence upon him went beyond the court and the conference room. He intended to stand by the privet hedge, stock-still, and watch the people entering the church. Roly had taught him that you did not need to hide to be hidden.

The service, according to the programme in his hands, was due to begin at 11a.m. He had stepped off the train just before ten. It was now 10.45. He watched as the mourners arrived. First, to his surprise, was Barry with an attractive blonde lady whom he assumed to be his wife, Jean. They were wearing their formal best and took copies of the Order of Service from the liveried man waiting on the door. Then came Pemberton, in company with Peter and Cara Preston. They were all dressed in black and an air of sincere sadness hung off them. Then, a few minutes later, came Julia Pemberton. His heart leapt at the sight of her. Her head was bowed and she was wearing a black mantilla, probably the same veil that she wore to Jenny's funeral only about a month ago – and to her aunt's funeral the day after they had begun their affair.

Where was Catherine? He had been certain that she would be there. Blytheway had told him that Storman had left her a message to call him just hours before Margaret was killed. That he had been concerned about how she was getting on. The service was due to begin in about ten minutes and still there was no sign of her. On the other hand, unless they were already inside, there was no sign of Blytheway, Storman, or Margaret's coffin. Then he saw her. Marching along Bromley Common he could recognise her from her silhouette, from the way she walked: that urgent, thrusting walk. She was wearing a black overcoat and had a small black cloche hat on. Her face was so pale it was almost white and she seemed thinner than when he had last seen her. At first he did not think that it could be her because she was pulling someone along behind her. A child. He realised with a shock that it was Deborah, his daughter. What was she doing in London?

At five minutes to eleven he heard the clip-clop of hooves. A horse-drawn hearse pulled up outside the church. There were four black Friesians, each wearing a head-dress of ostrich feathers, dyed black. The door to the carriage opened and Blytheway climbed out. He was wearing a dark outfit: a frock coat covered by a black damask cloak which covered his arms. He was followed by Storman and then Caldwell. Two other men, neither of whom were known to Adam, also emerged, and then the coach-driver himself – who, from the way he held himself, did not seem like someone who did this for a living – climbed down. All the men were wearing black

566

silk top hats. The horses neighed and stamped their feet and Adam saw their breath rising steamily. Then they were still.

The six men reached inside the hearse and pulled out the coffin. Carefully, it was lifted onto their shoulders with Storman and Blytheway at the front. It was topped with white lilies and it did not appear to weigh much. They made their way into the church and as they approached the organ struck up. A slow continuo. Then the strings joined in, following the main theme. The music carried a sense of quiet completion tinged with sadness. Everything was now done. Then the strings began to improvise on the initial theme. Adam sensed an Italianate grandeur underlying it all. But, ultimately, it was the music of tranquillity. Of heaven. The coffin-bearers entered the church and closed the door behind them and the music became more muffled. There did not seem to be anyone else expected and so he made his way to the door, opened it and entered. There was an overpowering smell of fresh flowers. The music was still going on. He looked down towards the nave and saw that there was a string quartet playing. Looking up, he had the slightest view of the organist and his mirror. Lilies and white roses spilled out from large ornamental vases on either side of the nave. The coffin had been placed on a dais between the north and south transepts. In front of it there was a large framed photograph of Margaret Storman in a ball gown. The picture was garlanded with tiny pink and white roses. Adam saw Blytheway's hand at work in this unconventional flourish.

The place was full. He had been so much concentrating on certain individuals that he had failed to register how many people had entered. There was nowhere to sit, but he was happy to stand at the back. Looking around the church, his eyes sought out Catherine before he looked for Julia. She was standing near the back. Deborah was holding her hand and looking around in every direction. He knew that she must be looking for him. He cowered. Then he saw Julia and he realised that, for everything – for whatever he wanted – he still loved her. He did not want to, but he felt a physical lurch just at the sight of her. This was something he could not understand. But as a physical reality it was there. How do you deal with that sort of thing? That ache?

He let his eyes leave her and move on to Pemberton, Preston and the Stirrup Court crowd. They were sticking together. He sensed small talk between the two silks, although the overall atmosphere was one of mourning. They all knew and respected Storman. They were there to pay their respects to the ending of his true life. Adam sensed that this was not going to be a place for recrimination and blame, and he felt a part of himself relax.

Looking at the programme, he saw that the music was the Canon in D Major by Pachelbel. It had been beautiful. The coffin seemed very small. As he looked at the forlorn box the music struck up again. More ephemeral beauty. The timelessness of the music drew all eyes to the sad coffin sitting in the middle of everything: the ruins of the woman within – the woman who had been everything to Jack Storman, who was now gone and who would not be able to come back again. Adam looked again at the programme. It was "Salut d'Amour" by Edward Elgar, a song he had written as a wedding gift for his wife. "Love's Greeting". "Hello, my love". The violin soared over the other instruments telling its sinuous story of love and yearning before fading out on a long sustained high note as the rest of the quartet subsided beneath it.

These two pieces of music seemed to have drained everyone present of anything but pity for Jack Storman and his adored wife. They filled the church with a sense of forgiveness and regret. Adam had no doubt but that this would fade away quickly; but for now, at least, the petty problems he had felt washed away. He looked around again. To Preston, who had told him he was out of his depth; to Pemberton, who thought he was an idiot and told him so; to Catherine, who told him that he didn't know the difference between articulacy and eloquence; and to Julia, who had made it very clear that she did not love him anymore, whatever they had previously shared. And he felt a strange sort of peace. This would all be over soon. He need not worry. Then he saw his daughter in a dark duffle-coat, looking over her shoulder, searching around and around until she saw him. And when she did her face lit up and with an enormous smile she shouted, "Daddy! Daddy!" so that everyone turned around and looked at Deborah and then at him. And Catherine glanced briefly in his direction – her face a mask – and then patted his daughter on the head and told her to be quiet.

There was a brief period of rustling from the congregation as people adjusted their seats and studied their programmes. Then all was silent. The eulogy was to follow. Roland Blytheway stood up and walked to the centre of the church, his precise footsteps on the slate floor echoing through the silence. He stood to one side of the coffin and began to speak. He had no notes. His voice was grave.

— Jack asked me to say a few words on his behalf and for his beloved wife, Margaret. It is a profound honour to be able to do so. I have known Jack for almost thirty years and I knew Margaret for twenty-seven of those years. Margaret and Jack for all that time were two of my dearest and truest friends. We are a small profession and for many years Jack has been one of our great stars. It is a tribute to him — and to Margaret — that so many have made the difficult journey here this morning to share his grief at her loss. As I look around this church I see so many of our number from all around the Temple — from all of the Inns of Court. Barristers ... Judges ... solicitors ... and, of course, *everyone* from Stirrup Court.

He cast a kind eye over Pemberton, Preston and all the rest.

— You must feel his loss particularly keenly, and all of us here understand that and extend to you all our greatest sympathy. I, of course, never shared chambers with Jack, but such is his standing with all of us that I feel as though somehow I have done. Yes. He is, and always has been a brilliant barrister. We all know that. But he is far greater than that. I only began to realise this when I met Margaret for the first time. For — forgive me Jack — she was more than your equal.

— Margaret was a very private person. I doubt that many of us had the privilege to get to know her well. I was one of the fortunate few who was given that opportunity. Margaret scintillated in conversation. She seemed to know everything. I can think of very few people who could demonstrate her depth and breadth of learning. She also had a wicked sense of humour. On one occasion at the breakfast table, Jack came in with his face bleeding. She asked what had happened and he said that he had been practising his closing speech to the jury whilst shaving and had cut himself. He urged her to come and watch him at the Old Bailey and she did. Although his client was acquitted his speech was — forgive me Jack — overlong and ponderous. There was a heavy silence between them on the train back to Shortlands, and eventually Jack asked her what he thought of the speech.

— "Well," she said, "if you want my honest opinion you should have concentrated on shaving and cut your speech!"

A murmur of laughter susurrated around the church.

– I had the good fortune to dine with Jack and Margaret on many occasions. Sometimes we shared tables with people who regarded themselves as "the intellectual elite". Their view of themselves, not mine. She was their equal in every way. She and Jack shared interests that went well beyond the narrow confines of the Bar. She brought out the best in him, and, as someone who felt he knew her – and loved her – I understand only too well how devastating is his loss. I had also the great privilege to escort her to various events over the years when Jack was indisposed. Margaret was one of my favourite people. Her company was always a delight, and when she walked or danced she appeared to float a little above the ground. I shall miss her enormously and I, as a mere friend, cannot begin to fathom the depths of our dear friend's loss."

He motioned towards the rose-rimmed photograph in front of the coffin.

– This is how I remember Margaret and how I would ask you to remember her. It is a portrait taken at a Middle Temple Ball in the thirties when I had the luck to be her partner for the evening. She had beauty, poise and grace. She had style *and* she had substance. Margaret – *he said addressing the photograph* – we shall never forget you.

Blytheway fell silent. Adam felt an urge to applaud but stifled it. There was a deep silence after he had finished speaking, and after a long pause and one last look at the photograph Blytheway click-clicked his way back to his seat. The music began again: Adagio in G Minor by Albinoni, according to the Order of Service – the violins keening over a muted funereal organ.

According to the programme the final piece of music was to be "Solemn Melody" by Henry Walford Davies, who had himself died the previous month and had once been the organist at the Temple Church. However, when the Albinoni came to an end and the string quartet began changing their scores, Adam saw Roly put out a delaying hand. Jack Storman KC rose to his feet and shuffled over towards the coffin. He was stooping and breathing heavily.

- Thank you, Roly. Thank you to everyone who has taken the trouble to come here this morning. I know that there is nothing in the Order of Service about a second speech. That is because I really did not think that I would be capable of saying anything. I will be brief. I have been very blessed – just in knowing Margaret, let alone being with her ... being married to her for twenty-five years. I confess. I really do not know how I will be able to carry on now. But I will find a way. And, I think, the beginning of the way lies in front of me now. You. All my friends. I will find a way, with your help. None of us can afford the luxury of giving up. We must go on. The pain I am currently feeling is almost unbearable. But I am no different from so many, some of them who are here with me today, who are feeling similar, perhaps even worse pain.

Adam looked across at Pemberton and saw that he had his head in his hands.

- We must support one another through this. This war will end. We will, somehow, survive it. I would like to invite you all to join me afterwards at Sunbridge Park Manor. Unfortunately, our ... my home is uninhabitable at the moment. I must tell you about the last exchange I had with Margaret. We were in the Anderson shelter at the bottom of our garden. It was the early hours of the morning and we had been in there, hugging one another, for almost five hours. Margaret said that she was thirsty and I insisted on going to get her a glass of water. She tried to persuade me not to. It was too dangerous, she said. But I went anyway. How I wish I had stayed with her. Her last words to me, before I left the shelter, were, "I love you so much!" My last words to her were, "I love you too."

That fire-cracker moment when he saw his garden illuminated and she had one more second to live.

Storman bowed his head. There was a long silence punctuated by sobs from the congregation. Eventually, Storman struggled back to his seat and the string quartet began to play. After about a minute Blytheway helped Storman back to his feet and the two of them joined the other pall bearers and lifted Margaret's coffin off its dais. The white lilies on top of it swayed. They placed it on their shoulders and began a slow, stately walk back up the aisle. Storman was at the front on the right and, as he passed by, Adam reached out a hand and squeezed his shoulder. The older man looked at him and grimaced.

By the time the congregation had emerged from the church the coffin was in the hearse and the horses were clip-clopping towards the cemetery. This had been the moment Adam had been dreading. All those people who did not want to speak to him, who hated him, or with whom he did not want to converse. It would have to be endured. He would walk at the back of the cortege and keep out of the way.

- Daddy!"
- Hello, sweetheart. What are you doing here? Aren't you supposed to be in the country?
- Oh, but I couldn't, Daddy. I was really unhappy there. There was a man who I thought was nice to begin with but he wasn't. He used to try and come into my room at night because, he said anyway, that he wanted to talk to me. I had to start locking the door. I was going to write to you to tell you I was coming back but I wanted it to be a surprise.
- Well. It is certainly a surprise, Deborah. And it is absolutely lovely to see you. I've missed you so much! But it's not safe here. People are being killed. People we love.
- I know, Daddy. But I was so lonely. And I missed you and Mummy. *And* I was *so* unhappy. Mummy's agreed that I can come back. I can be with my old friends again. So many of them are still living around the corner. So many of them have come back.

He bent down and kissed her on the cheek. She took his hand and together they walked at the back of the cortege as the hearse made its slow journey towards the cemetery.

- Will you come and play with me? At home? Soon? Please?
- Yes. Of course.
- And can we get another cat?
- Of course we can!
- I miss Socks but we can't bring her back, can we?

– No. We can't. I am so sorry about Socks.
– It's not your fault, Daddy. You did what you thought was right. I really don't blame you for that.

He squeezed her hand and looked ahead to the mourners in front of him. Pemberton and Preston and the assorted members of his old chambers were immediately behind the hearse. Catherine walked along behind them. She had not made any attempt to greet him, but he could hardly blame her for that. Julia too was alone within the crowd. Her veil had made it impossible for him to work out what was going through her mind.

– I want to tell you about *all* of my adventures. Everything I've learned.
– And I want to hear them all. Everything!
– You and Mummy *will* get together again, won't you?
– I don't know, sweetheart.
– But you must! I've been thinking about that more than anything. I can help. I'm sure I can help!

They were beside the open grave now. The coffin had been placed on the ropes and was being manoeuvred gingerly over the hole in the ground. And then it was released and the ropes were drawn out. Storman threw in the first handful of soil. Adam squeezed his daughter's hand again.

– I've got to leave now, darling. But I will see you soon.
– You can't.
– I must.

He picked her up and gave her a big hug. Then he put her down, kissed her and began to walk away.

– Daddy!
– I'll see you very soon, sweetheart.

There was no way that he could go to the wake. Storman would understand, as would Roly. He would be an unnecessary and unhelpful distraction. The Bateman trial began on Monday and he needed to know, urgently, whether Jones had been able to get the documents he had asked for. And what they said.

Chapter Ninety

(Monday 28th April 1941)

Jones was beginning to see the possibility of another improbable success. He and Adam were sitting with Bateman on a bench outside Court Fifteen on the first floor of the Royal Courts of Justice. Barristers and their solicitors and clients were milling around the other courts making their final preparations for the day ahead. Dressed in their black gowns and wearing their off-white horsehair wigs, they were flicking through their papers and writing final scribbles in their blue books. The dark stone flooring and heavy wooden panelling outside the court rooms gave everything a gloomy air. Jones looked across at his counsel and thought about how much he had changed in the four months since he had first taken Bateman to see him. Adam too was wearing his black robe and horsehair wig. His winged collar and white bands were pristine and highly starched. He was, thought Jones, better dressed than he used to be – and had a great deal more self-confidence. However, at the same time, he appeared to have lost all hope so far as the future was concerned. It was only a week now before the rearranged Pemberton trial was due to begin, and he could understand Falling's apprehension.

It was 9.30 a.m. The scandal sheets had at last got hold of the story and it was beginning to circulate. That was hardly surprising, he thought. You couldn't make it up! A KC is cuckolded by a junior member of his chambers with his glamorous younger wife. On top of that, Falling was representing a co-respondent in an unrelated matter and his Head of Chambers was representing the petitioner. The cuckolded KC representing the cuckold, and the cuckolding junior representing the person accused of being a cuckold. Everything was sub-judice of course. The press had to be careful what they said about pending trials. However, they were doing their best within those constraints. He looked over to the bench to his right. Various accredited members of the press had gathered. The proceedings were going to be in open court and so they could not be stopped. It was not as though it were a spy trial, after all. On the bench to his left were Jeremy Pemberton KC, Perkins, Collins and McKechnie. Beyond them were Farquarson, Mrs McKechnie and her solicitor.

Adam was looking again at the new documents. Jones had brought them to him on the Sunday afternoon. Draft amended pleadings alleging condonation had been prepared and they would need the permission of the judge, but that should not be a problem. The truth would out. Mr Justice Caraway was a great believer in the truth. It was 9.45 a.m.

– All right!

Adam said.

– I think that we should do it now.

He got up and walked across to Jeremy Pemberton with the documents, his gown swaying behind him as he walked. Pemberton did not stand up as he approached.

– What do you want, Falling?!
– I have some new documents for you, Jeremy.
– Well! It's a bit late isn't it?
– I didn't receive them myself until yesterday.
– You'll need leave.
– Oh, I think I will get leave.
– What are they?
– Here.

Adam handed Pemberton two separate bundles of documents.

– I think you ought to take Mr McKechnie's instructions on these. The ones in the buff envelope are the notes of the inquest into the death of Marjorie Bateman. You may want to ask your client why he – and Mrs McKechnie – and Mr Bateman – all gave evidence about her death. Why, in particular, they appeared to be all in harmony with one another. It does seem a bit odd, don't you think, if Bateman had only recently discovered his wife in bed with my client?

575

- Is that the best that you can do, Falling? This is absolute nonsense! A
  woman had died. Surely something like that comes first. You were
  there on Saturday. A terrible tragedy takes precedence over these ...
  "everyday" concerns.
- Oh, I entirely agree with you. These quotidian – *Roly would have been
  pleased with that word* – woes are as nothing compared to a death.
- What else do you want to show me?

Adam handed over the other documents. They were the result of a shot
in the dark, he had to confess to himself. But he had hit the target.

- First of all there is the application for payment out on the insurance
  policy. You will see that it is all in your client's handwriting. Apart
  from my client's signature. Mr McKechnie completed the whole
  thing. I understand that it was your client's idea to make a claim.
- And what if it was? Mrs Bateman had been run over and your client
  was entitled to make a claim.
- But if your client was aware of the fact that Bateman was sleeping
  with Victoria McKechnie, why didn't he say something at that stage?
  There was no ranting about "ABC" then, as we know. I have tens of
  witnesses, if necessary, who can say that the ... the "diary outburst"
  ... did not happen until about eight weeks after your client completed
  this application form. In fact, he did not say a thing about it until
  seven days after my client received his insurance money. This is the
  remaining document.

Adam handed over the letter which had enclosed the £10,000. He let
Pemberton read it.

- You see, Jeremy, all this suggests to me – and I think it will suggest to
  Mr Justice Caraway – that your client knew exactly what was going
  on. He knew all about his wife's affair. He condoned it. Because he
  was having an affair with Marjorie Bateman.

The gentlemen of the press had roused themselves and were gathered in
a semi-circle around the bench. Pemberton was irritated.

– We need to speak somewhere away from these people. Come with me to the Robing Room.

Once there, Pemberton let rip.

– You've got a bloody cheek! This is completely unprofessional!
– I don't know what you mean.
– Springing this on me literally at the doors of the court!
– As I said, I only found out about the insurance claim yesterday.

Adam was careful not to include any sort of reference to the inquest notes, but then again he had not until recently had permission to make reference to those.

– If what you say is true, Falling, your client is guilty of an insurance fraud. He will have to go to prison … and pay the money back.
– I fully appreciate that, as does my client. However, he will not also be guilty of perjury, if the court accepts that what he is saying is true. Your client was the prime mover in this fraud. Bateman will be saying that he was undone by his overbearing superior. That will look good in the press before our own hearing next week, won't it? You are still going to lose this case, Pemberton. My client would be prepared to meet his own costs if your client is prepared now to accept the inevitable. I can't speak for Farquarson or Victoria McKechnie of course. He won't do better than my offer. I think you had better take your client's instructions.

Chapter Ninety-one

(Monday 28ᵗʰ April 1941)

Pemberton asked Mr Justice Caraway for an hour on the basis that this might shorten the trial, and took Mr McKechnie back to Stirrup Court so that they could go through the new documents in the absence of the press.

– What are you saying to me?
– If these documents are true documents then I think that you're almost bound to lose this case.
– But you said that this was a case that it was impossible to lose!
– Well, Mr McKechnie, that was on the basis that you were telling me the truth. These new documents suggest to me that you were not.

Mckechnie let out an empty laugh.

– So this Falling bloke. The one you said was useless. Has got us beat?
– Not necessarily. If you are telling me the truth now and you weren't having an affair with Mrs Bateman and you didn't know that Bateman was having an affair with your wife, this case can still be won. I think, however, that it is unlikely. Take another look at these documents and then tell me whether or not you were having an affair with Marjorie Bateman ... and whether or not you knew about Bateman's relationship with your wife.

Pemberton handed over the documents to an unwilling McKechnie. He turned them over in his hands and his shoulders slumped.

– It's all true. I didn't know about ... about ... condonation ... she was still my wife after all. Can't we just carry on with the case? Why should he get to keep the money?
– Of course we can carry on. But only on the basis that you admit to the

court what you have just told me. Otherwise we must withdraw. And if we lose, you will have to pay even more in costs than you would have to pay today. And you won't get any of that insurance money. I don't think it is worth it.

McKechnie reluctantly agreed and they made their way back to court.

Mr Justice Caraway was content to accept the settlement. The Petition would be dropped. There would be no order as to costs between Bateman and McKechnie although he would have to pay Victoria's costs. She could keep her children. Everything before the Judge was conducted with the utmost courtesy as was the tradition, but Adam could sense Pemberton's rage and frustration.

****

- I think I owe you an apology, Mr Falling.
- I don't know what you're talking about.
- That first time I met you I thought you were just a pervert with nothing but adultery on your mind. I was wrong about that. Can we have that pint now?
- Of course. I would be delighted. We can go to the Seven Stars. On condition, however, that Mr Jones comes with us.
- Absolutely! This trial may have cost me a bit of money but it has all been worthwhile. I could have lost the lot – and more; I'll be paying for the drinks. Do you mind if Victoria comes with us?

Adam began to chuckle and had to stifle a cough.

- Not at all. Why don't you invite her barrister to join us as well? We may have to wait a little while until opening time.

Chapter Ninety-two
(Wednesday 30ᵗʰ April 1941)

Adam looked at his watch. It was 11.30. He took his jacket from the back of the chair and put it on as he was leaving his room in chambers. It was a half an hour's walk and he did not need to be there until 12.30, but he was nervous. He pulled out a cigarette as he descended, and lit up as he left the building. Today and the day before were free days. The precipitate ending to the Bateman trial meant that he had been able to have two lie-ins in a row and, for all his anxiety, he felt refreshed.

In the end he had stayed in the Seven Stars until about seven in the evening. The recent raids meant that no one wanted to stay in the pub much later than that. Victoria and her legal team had joined them all, and Bateman had insisted on buying all the drinks. Adam had drunk two pints of bitter. Bateman was in ecstasy.

- It hasn't been cheap but it's been worth every penny!
- Thank you, Mr Bateman ...
- It was worth it just to see that look on McKechnie's face.

Bateman turned to Victoria McKechnie.

- I think we should get married now.
- But we can't get married!
- Why ever not?
- Because I'm not divorced. Graham's petition was dismissed, remember? And he had to pay all my costs.

Bateman had laughed with delight and Adam and Jones had joined in. For Adam, it had represented, with the Novak acquittal, one of the two highest points in his career. Bateman turned to him.

– Here, Mr Falling. I'm thinking of getting some tickets to the Cup Final at Wembley on Saturday week, would you and Jones like to come?
– I don't know. Who's playing?
– Arsenal and Preston North End.

By then his ordeal would be over and he would have nothing else to look forward to.

– Why not. Thanks.

He turned to Jones with a quiet aside.

– Thank you sincerely for all your help on this. I couldn't have done it without you.
– I'm not sure I did that much.
– I'm afraid I left it very late to work out what was going on.
– You worked it out. That was the main thing.
– I mean I left you with precious little time to find the documents.
– Oh, it wasn't too difficult. We all knew about the inquest notes, and once Mr Bateman gave us his authority it was relatively straightforward. And, of course, he had kept the letter enclosing the cheque, and he had a copy of the insurance policy. Said he had plans to frame it. The only potential headaches were in getting hold of the application form that McKechnie had filled out. That had been sent to archive and sometimes they can take several days, if not weeks, to get hold of.
– Well, it was a stroke of luck that you could get hold of it so quickly.

Jones had been on the point of putting his pint mug to his lips when Adam said this. He paused abruptly and put the glass down and looked into Adam's eyes, confused.

– But I thought you knew ...
– Knew what?
– Blytheway telephoned me about ten days ago. He said that he thought you were doing a marvellous job on Bateman's case and that you would probably be asking me to get hold of the application form. He

581

told me to say to Bateman that it was routine but that sometimes
these things take time. And so I did.
- Why didn't you say anything to me about it?
- I thought you knew.
- Didn't you have any idea *why* he thought you should get hold of it?
- Listen, Mr Falling. I've seen enough of what he can do. I didn't feel
any need to ask questions.

****

Adam had almost reached Trafalgar Square. He looked at his watch again.
It was almost noon. He made his way down Whitehall until he reached the
Red Lion, and stepped inside. He needed a drink. Sitting at one of the tables
with a weak pint of bitter in his hand, he thought again about Blytheway's
intervention in the Bateman case. Why hadn't he said anything? He was
clearly following the money. He had been thinking about this question
ever since that exchange with Jones and the only explanation he could
come up with was that Roly had trusted him to get there in the end.

It was 12.25 and time to leave. He took his glass back to the bar, lit up
another cigarette as he was leaving and headed for the little restaurant.

He had put a telephone call through to Catherine on the Monday evening. The elation from the day's events had given him the necessary confidence to do so. She had been preparing to bed down for the night. Deborah
was already asleep so he was not able to speak with her. The conversation was inevitably stilted but he persuaded her to meet him. He needed
to discuss Deborah. Was it wise to allow her to come back to London?
Catherine's tone was cold but polite. She would meet him during her lunch
hour on the Wednesday. She could only manage forty-five minutes. It was
very busy at the Board of Trade.

He pushed open the door and entered. The place was already almost full
and the noise of conversation and the sound of knives, forks and plates hit
him. He struggled to locate her within the crowded room. Then he saw
her, sitting in a half-hidden alcove towards the back. Once he had found
her it was as though there was no one else in the room. She was wearing
an elegant dark twin-set. Mauve. Her legs were crossed at the knee and she
was reading. Before her was a plate of bangers and mash and a cup of tea.
Untouched. In the place opposite her was the same lunch. She had not seen

him come in. She was reading something. He had almost reached the table before she looked up and saw him.

She folded the book closed and placed it on her side plate before rising to her feet. He tried to kiss her on the cheek but she moved her head out of the way. She was not smiling.

- I ordered us both some lunch. You never used to arrive anywhere on time.
- I thought I was a few minutes early.
- Look. I haven't got much time. Can we get this over with please?
- What are you reading?

She sighed and held up the book so that he could see the cover – *Political and Economic Democracy* by Max Ascoli and Fritz Lehman – and scooped her fork into the mashed potato.

- I hope it's got a good plot. It doesn't look as though it has.
- It's a selection of essays. Someone was able to get it from New York. Roosevelt's New Deal and all that,

she said with her mouth full.

- I don't know much about that. Tell me about it.
- I'm sure you don't, Adam. And no, I won't. I don't have the time or the inclination. What do you want?
- Here's some more money for you and Deborah.

He handed over fifteen pounds.

- A pay-rise?

she said, raising an eyebrow as she chewed on a sausage.

- Look. I'm sorry that I haven't been giving you more but you know what our finances are like. But I am expecting a cheque on a case very soon. It has eased the pressure.
- Yes. I heard about that. Apparently, you have not only beaten Preston

in a case but you got one over on Pemberton earlier this week. If things weren't as they are between us I could almost have been proud of you. Arrogant, conceited snobs!
- How do you know about that?
- Jack told me. Seems that whatever else your colleagues think about you they are universally pleased that they both got their comeuppance.
- When did you see Jack?
- Eat your bangers and mash. It's getting cold and I want to get back to work. You wanted to talk about Deborah?

Catherine had almost finished her meal and he hadn't even started. She did not look at him as she waited for him to answer. The outfit she was wearing was new, he thought, and although she had lost a little weight she appeared to be in good health. She had not been so assertive since they were at Cambridge together. Since they had married. She looked less pale than she had done at the funeral. And younger than he remembered. She had emptied her plate and was starting on her tea.

- Is that a new suit?
- Eat your lunch!
- I don't think I've seen it before.
- I treated myself. Get on with it.
- Do you think it is altogether wise for Deborah to come back to London? Why couldn't it wait until the blitz was over, one way or another?

Catherine put down her cup and sighed and looked properly into his eyes for the first time. Deep brown. He had forgotten how lovely they were.

- She's my daughter too, you know. I only want what's best for her. You know what happened to Jenny. And now to Margaret. I'm just worried for her safety.
- Has she told her about what was happening out there?
- I think so. She was telling me about it at the funeral.
- I suspect she was giving you the potted version – or you would be more worried about that than you sound.
- I don't know what you're talking about.

584

– It was that man we used to call "the gypsy". Of course, he wasn't a gypsy at all; he just looked a bit wild and so that's where we found the nickname for him.

Adam groaned and put his head in his hands, looking through his fingers at his rapidly cooling meal.

– Oh, God! What has been happening?
– I think it could have been worse. Did she tell you the story she told me at first? That he wanted to come into her room to talk with her after she had gone to bed so that she had to lock the door?
– Yes. That isn't good. But it could have been worse.
– Our daughter is too sensible to be overly disconcerted by something like that, but I didn't believe her. I had told Jack about my concerns and he said I should wait until Easter. And so I did. I went up there on Good Friday.

She looked as though she might begin to cry. Adam waited her for to continue.

– He was always letting her ride his horse. And it started off innocently enough. And then he wanted to help her into the saddle. For Christ's sake! She isn't thirteen yet! He was touching her where he shouldn't touch her. And then he started coming around to her bedroom after she had turned the light out and saying he wanted to read her bedtime stories or give her a cuddle.
– I can't believe this.
– Dear Deborah didn't know what was going on – why should she? – but she knew that it wasn't right. The man's almost forty for heaven's sake! So now do you understand why I brought her back?
– Yes. But can we talk about putting her somewhere else away from this place?
– Perhaps.
– And may I see her?
– I don't believe I have any entitlement to stop you. If I did, you can rest assured that there is no guarantee that I would allow it.
– May I buy her a new kitten? She wrote to me saying she wants one.

– We'll have to wait and see. Look, I must go now. You haven't eaten a thing! I was hoping you would pay.

Catherine began to rise and put her book in her bag.

– How was Jack?
– Fine.

She clipped her bag shut.

– You are going to pay, aren't you?
– Of course. Tell me about Jack. When did you see him?
– Yesterday, if you must know. He's staying with that friend of yours. I'm tempted to say that none of this is any of your business.

She was turning to leave.

– Does Deborah know about the trial?
– Of course not!
– Thank you, Catherine.
– I can't believe it! I don't think you have *any* understanding of how much you have humiliated me!

Then she turned her back on him and walked out.

Chapter Ninety-three

(Thursday 1ˢᵗ May 1941)

Jeremy Pemberton KC edged his way into the narrow cubicle that was the chambers toilet, turned on the light, then closed and locked the door behind him. He pulled his fob watch out from his waistcoat and flipped it open. It was ten to eleven. He took off his gold-rimmed spectacles and polished the lenses with his handkerchief before settling them back on his nose and peering closely at himself in the mirror. He had lost weight and he had aged. The skin of his cheeks lay in folds, but since the last time he had studied himself closely it had also begun to look puffy and unhealthy. He put his watch back in his pocket and lifted his hand to his face, tugging at it. He was fifty-five. He looked into his eyes. They were bloodshot behind his spectacles. Not very. But sufficiently so for anyone with more than average powers of observation. There was nothing average, however, about Sir Patrick Tempest KC.

There had been a small mention of the Bateman case in Tuesday's *Times*: "Before Mr Justice Caraway. HIS LORDSHIP gave judgment for the Respondent and Co-Respondent, by consent, in this action in which Mr Graham McKechnie petitioned his wife, Mrs Victoria McKechnie for divorce on the grounds of adultery citing Mr Arnold Bateman. The Respondent and Co-Respondent had, by late amendment, admitted adultery but pleaded condonation. Mr McKechnie agreed to pay Mrs McKechnie's costs. There was otherwise no order as to costs. Mr Jeremy Pemberton KC with whom was Mr R. Perkins for the Petitioner, Mr D. Farquarson for the Petitioner and Mr A. Falling for the Co-Respondent."

The press had been all over it and, although the report was short, Pemberton knew that it would have been noted by everyone around the Temple. They all read the law reports, however brief. It wasn't as though the case warranted any sort of mention. There was only one reason why so many journalists had come to this ... to this ... *non-event*: a bigger story lay behind it. He felt again that bitter humiliation and remembered

587

McKechnie's caustic criticism as they parted company at the entrance to the Royal Courts of Justice.

  – *I'm the one that's got to pay for this mess, remember!*

So Jeremy Pemberton KC hailed a cab, went home and opened a bottle of whisky.

He took out his watch to check out the time again. It was five to eleven. He pulled a heavy glass bottle out of his trouser pocket and knocked back a shot of Listerine, gargling for thirty seconds before spitting it into the sink. He turned on the cold tap and splashed his face before drying off with the hand towel. Pemberton smoothed his lapels in the mirror. From his other pocket he took out a bottle of Four Seven Eleven and dabbed the eau de cologne onto his cheeks. Leaving the toilet he returned to his room, put both bottles in a drawer, and then went downstairs and exited Stirrup Court. The sun was shining out of a blue sky and a gentle breeze caressed his face.

It was a short walk to 11, King's Bench Walk and the chambers of Sir Patrick Tempest KC. Tempest was sixty-one and six years Pemberton's senior, but he had been in silk since 1919, ten years before Pemberton himself received his Letters Patent from the Lord Chancellor. Sir Patrick Tempest KC was a legend. He had been brought up on the advocacy of Sir Edward Carson, Rufus Isaacs and Henry Duke. He had sparred frequently with Sir Edward Marshall Hall KC and did much work for whichever party formed the government of the day. It was this work that had led to his knighthood. However, he was equally at home in the criminal courts, the Chancery Division, fashionable libel actions and, of course, the divorce courts. He was also very expensive. Sir Patrick Tempest KC had not succumbed to the convention of acting for nothing for other members of the Bar. And Pemberton had to accept that it was not a convention that he himself tended to observe.

Pemberton had been more shaken at losing the Bateman case that he could even admit to himself. He questioned his judgment and fretted about the ordeal that awaited him under Blytheway's cross-examination. Blytheway had made a fool out of Preston, who had seemed shell-shocked on his return to chambers after Novak's acquittal – more so after Blytheway secured a "not guilty" verdict for Katya Hoffer several weeks later. And so he had asked for an urgent consultation with his legal team to go through everything one final time before the trial began on Monday. Tempest had agreed, perhaps out of sympathy for a fellow member of the profession, for he was a very busy man.

Pemberton entered 11, King's Bench Walk and walked up to the first floor. Mr Franklin, his solicitor, of Franklin, Warnock and Cattermole, was already sitting in the waiting room. He had barely had time to shake hands and sit down before the senior clerk entered and invited them to follow him to Tempest's room. He opened the door into a room that was spacious and bright. The walls were lined with the law reports and text-books and the lower shelves with a multitude of briefs, some tied in pink ribbons and others – his government work – tied in white. They bore testimony to his great popularity.

Tempest rose from behind his large desk as the door opened and came round to greet them. He was a tall, rangy man with a full head of silvery hair. Expensive chalk-striped suit and brightly polished shoes. His junior, a Mr Eliot, also rose from a far smaller desk, but said nothing.

– Jeremy!

he said, proffering his hand.

– I know we are not supposed to shake hands or address one another so informally but you and I have known each other so long – crossed swords so often – that it would feel wrong to do otherwise.
– Thank you, Pat. And thank you for letting me come to see you at such short notice. It is good to see you.
– I saw the report of the Bateman case. That must have hurt. But I wouldn't take it too hard. We are only ever as good as our cases. Every member of the Bar, me included, has lost a case because a client has lied to us. There's nothing we can do about that. Or rather, there is. One must simply get back into the saddle and write it off to experience. We are not magicians after all.
– Thank you, Pat. You have obviously realised that was one of the reasons I wanted to see you.

Pemberton could feel the other man's eyes boring into him. There was a quizzical look on his mobile features as he gazed first into Pemberton's eyes and then down across his face and his clothing. However, Tempest did not reveal his thoughts to his client or his solicitor.

- I think I'm on top of everything but would be happy to go over any points that are giving you particular concern. I do, also, have some questions of my own. But let us deal with your points first.
- I brought the inventories. I couldn't remember whether you actually had an opportunity to consider them?
- I did. And I think I have their details firmly in my mind. But let us go through them again.

Pemberton pulled out four sheets of foolscap from an inside pocket and unfolded them.

- These first two pages are an inventory I took of Falling's books before he moved out. The other two are a list of Julia's books that I compiled with the assistance of Samuels – he is my butler – when Julia was out. We went into her dressing room. I kept a key.
- A key?
- We had an unspoken convention between us that she would not come into my study and I would not go into her dressing room. Both of us locked the doors when we were out. But we both had keys to the other's rooms.
- Forgive me, Jeremy, but that does seem to me a little … caddish?
- I know. I felt bad about it until I realised that she was doing exactly the same to me. I changed all the locks.
- Mr Franklin told me about that. Well let's have a look at them.

The four men stood around the desk looking down at the papers that documented the literary interests of the Respondent and the Co-Respondent. There were more books on Adam's list than there were on Julia's. However, the similarities were striking. Adam's list included *Vile Bodies, Decline and Fall, Black Mischief,* and *A Handful of Dust* and *Scoop* by Evelyn Waugh. Julia's included only *Vile Bodies* and *Scoop*. Adam had the collected works of Sir Arthur Conan Doyle whilst Julia only had *A Study in Scarlet* and *The*

Sign of Four. Adam had *Chrome Yellow, Antic Hay, Those Barren Leaves, Brave New World* and *Eyeless in Gaza*, whilst Julia only had *Antic Hay* and *Brave New World*. Both had the collected poetry of Wilfred Owen and Siegfried Sassoon. They both had *The Great Gatsby* by F. Scott Fitzgerald. Adam had nearly everything that had been published by George Orwell: *Down and Out in Paris and London, Burmese Days, Keep the Aspidistra Flying* and *Coming up for Air*. All were first editions. Julia had only *Down and Out in Paris and London* and *Coming up for Air*. Both first editions. The rest of Julia's collection was more conventional and old-fashioned. Sir Patrick Tempest KC picked up the two lists and studied them more carefully.

– So, if you are right Falling gave her at least one, two, three … eleven books as gifts? I looked up the publication dates of these books and I think the most recently published was *Coming up for Air*, which came out in June 1939.
– It's no wonder the scoundrel didn't have a practice! Seems to have spent all his time reading obscure novels.
– Oh, they are not all that obscure. I have read many of these books myself – in my spare time. But I have to say, it is a rather flimsy basis upon which to mount a petition for adultery. I have certainly never come across such a case before.

Pemberton's shoulders slumped.

– So you think I'm going to be in difficulties?
– No. I didn't say that. I only said that it was rather unusual. It is not as though it is the only point that you have. There is the watermark, of course.
– I didn't bring that with me. It's rather a fragile piece of evidence.
– I'm surprised it survived being burnt at all.
– Well, that was a bit of luck, I suppose. I don't know how it happened. But how are we going to prove that Falling received a letter from my wife?
– We don't need to.
– Why ever not? If it is important surely we should be getting it into the evidence.
– Oh, we will. It is just that we don't need to prove it. I took the liberty

of ringing up Blytheway yesterday. Said that we hadn't served a notice to admit but that I took it he would not be disputing that the watermark was consistent with your stationery. He admitted it right away. If anything, he seemed rather blasé about it. He told me that he felt that I should ring Alnwick for the sake of propriety but that he didn't think Alnwick would disagree with him. And Alnwick also confirmed that there would be no issue as to provenance.
– Well. That's good news.
– Not really. If your wife told you she had sent a letter to Falling there would be something seriously amiss if they did not all tell the same story. I want to come back to that before we finish. But I would rather deal with the things you want to talk about first.

There was a silence, lasting almost a minute, whilst Pemberton thought about what was troubling him.

– I think I wanted to ask you about Blytheway.
– I had assumed as much.
– We all know he is a bit of a dilettante – a frivolous lightweight – but he got one over on Preston recently and I wondered what you thought of him?
– Let us all return to our seats.

When they were all sitting down Tempest looked across his desk at Pemberton for a long moment before continuing:
– I'm afraid that I have never regarded Blytheway as a lightweight. Quite the contrary – and I have been against him many, many times.
– I didn't realise.
– I know that many of my cases have been reported, and if you look back through them you will not find many, particularly in recent years, where opposing counsel was Roland Blytheway. However, if you look back to an earlier time there are quite a few reports of cases when we were both junior counsel. I don't go out of my way to advertise them, to be frank.

Pemberton's heart sank.

– Why. What happened?

– He gave me a number of bloody noses. And so, in recent years, if I think that he has a good case, I have settled. Settled cases don't tend to get into the law reports unless of course – *giving Pemberton a particularly telling look* – they are settled at the doors of the court in the midst of a swarm of journalists. To be fair to myself I do think Blytheway shows me equal respect and if he has a poor case he will be the first to sue for peace.

– If he is such a good barrister why did he never take silk? You can't be saying that he is as good as we are?

Pemberton immediately regretted that remark. Although he had never really admitted it to himself he knew that he and Tempest were not in the same league.

– Jeremy, Jeremy. We both know why that is, really, don't we?

Pemberton chose not to answer that question and pressed on.

– So you think I have a good case, and Blytheway thinks Falling has a good case. Well, you can't both be right, can you?

– I wasn't saying that every case we had against one another settled. We have fought cases in recent years and some of them I have won and some of them he has won. However – and I have naturally been thinking about this a great deal in recent weeks – those have all been cases where everything turned on *credibility*. If *his* client was believed, he won. If *my* client was believed, I won.

– Well, if it is just a matter of credibility we are all right, aren't we? What judge is going to prefer his evidence – Julia's for that matter – to that of one of His Majesty's Counsel?

– Oh, Jeremy, please! Don't be pompous, I beg you! That's the last thing we need. You must not *presume!* You see, there is one other point – and it favours our opponents.

– What's that?

– This is your case. You are the one making the allegations. You are the one who has something to prove. The burden of proof is on us. They don't have to prove anything. Again, when I went back through my encounters with Blytheway – those cases that ended up in court – whilst credibility was important and probably decisive we both did better when it was the other who carried the burden of proof. We, I am afraid, are carrying that burden. And it would be extremely remiss of us if we did not take that into account.

– This is all sounding rather gloomy!

– Not at all. It is a cardinal rule, that so many younger members of Bar forget – not you of course – that it is far more important to look carefully at one's own weaknesses than to concentrate on the perceived weaknesses in the other side's case. That is all I am doing.

They had been with Tempest for the better part of an hour. Mr Franklin and Tempest's junior, Eliot, had been scribbling frantically without making any contribution to the debate. Tempest asked his client if he had any further questions.

– There is one another point I would like to discuss with you. It is about my late daughter Jenny's diary.

– I was deeply saddened to hear what had happened. I can't imagine what you have been going through since then.

– Thank you, Pat. And thank you for your letter, which was greatly appreciated. I am sorry I didn't reply to it. There were so many letters and I was in something of a state for quite a while after that.

– Oh, don't worry about that. I think I said in my letter that you shouldn't trouble to reply.

– Well. Anyway. Thank you.

– What did you want to discuss about the diary?

– Have you seen it?

– And read it. Eliot and I were able to borrow it from Mrs Pemberton's solicitors on the usual undertakings. I married up those little crosses with the dates in the petition. If those were indeed days when Jenny went to the Ritz with Mrs Pemberton, then, taken together with Falling's case that he was seeing a prostitute and not your wife, she may have a defence. It's definitely Jenny's writing in the diary isn't it?

– Yes. I am afraid I read sections of it even though she had asked me not to. I feel very bad about that. She and I had a terrible argument about it just before she went out to the Café de Paris with that Jenkins chap. That's why she took it away from me and gave it to Julia.

Pemberton was silent for a moment, his shoulders hunched as he looked down at his shoes. He thought about telling his counsel about the rather unseemly incident in Mecklenburg Square when he tried to wrench it away from Julia and got into a fight with Falling, but decided against it. Tempest said nothing and waited for him to continue.

– You see … I don't know how to say this but … now that Jenny is … is dead … can't we try and stop this evidence going in?
– I wondered if you would ask me that. I suspect you know the answer to your own question as well as I do. Jenny may be gone but the diary remains. The crosses are all still there and I have no doubt Mrs Pemberton will give evidence to the effect that these correspond with occasions when she was with Jenny at the Ritz. It will be a question of whether or not she is believed about that. In addition, it may be that Mrs Pemberton's solicitors have been able to obtain a witness statement that is admissible in evidence so that Jenny may be able to assist her step-mother from beyond the grave. Do you know whether a statement was obtained?
– No. I don't. I have asked all of my staff if any of them actually witnessed her signing off a statement but they have all denied it.
– So, the options are either that she did not sign a statement, for whatever reason, or she did sign one but, in all probability, it wasn't witnessed; and if the latter eventuality proves to be the case that will affect the evidential weight that it can be given. But we must wait and see whether anything is produced. I don't think there is anything more we can do about this aspect of the case, certainly for the present. Is there anything else in connection with the diary or Jenny's evidence?

Pemberton was silent for a long minute, studying his shoes and wiping his eyes with his handkerchief. He shook his head.

– Good. Now I have some questions that I would like to put to you. Questions that, no doubt, Blytheway will be putting to you. First of all, have you ever seen your wife alone with Falling?

595

- No. Well, not exactly.
- Not exactly?
- As you can imagine, I have given this a lot of thought.
- What do you mean by "not exactly"?
- There was one time. It was at the Middle Temple Ball in 1936. He marked her card. When I remembered this – at the same time that I was looking through her books – I looked out her dance card. It was the seventh dance. A slow waltz. She was supposed to be dancing the eighth dance, a foxtrot, with Peter Preston in my chambers, but when I asked him about this recently he told me he had looked for her but couldn't find her. She was supposed to be dancing the ninth dance with me, and she did. I didn't see anything out of the ordinary at the time. But for about four minutes she was missing.

Tempest leaned back in his leather chair. There was a long silence.

- Hmmm. It's not much to go on but it may help. Have you still got the dance card?
- It's in her room. I am fairly sure she didn't take it with her. No one realised the potential significance of it.

Pemberton did not want to draw unnecessary attention to the fact that he himself had not spotted that potential significance.

- Good. But that brings me back to my central question. Leaving aside a four-minute absence at a ball in 1936, have you on any other occasion seen your wife with Mr Falling?

After a long pause:

- No. The next time I saw them together was at our home and that was only when he and his wife were taking their leave – and he was only there because I invited them – because I wanted to talk to him – to observe him – to see how he reacted to being in the presence of my wife.
- Well. I think that may be a problem. And it brings me to my next question. If the occasions when you have seen them together are as

limited as you say they are, what made you suspect that there was anything between them at all?

– Well, again – and I know that this may sound silly in the cold light of day – but on two occasions in late 1940, after her children had been evacuated, she spoke in her sleep. She was evidently distressed. She was writhing a little in the bed.

– And what did she say?

– Not much. The first time I didn't place much store by it. She said "Not now. One day, perhaps."

– "Not now, one day, perhaps"?

– I know. As I say, I didn't put much on it. But several nights later the same thing happened. She said again, in exactly the same words and exactly the same tone of voice, "Not now, one day perhaps." Well, for it to happen again worried me. I wondered whether or not she was thinking of the children, that one day, perhaps, they could come back and be with us. And so the following morning, in an effort to help, I told her what she had been saying in her sleep and asked her what it meant. I thought she would be grateful to me and start talking about Agnes, Stephen and Sebastian but instead she became seriously alarmed. She asked me what else she had said, and of course I said nothing because there had been nothing else. But when I asked her what her dream was all about she said she didn't remember ...

– Carry on.

– And so I thought back. I noticed that she had a certain happiness that was independent of me. That there was a certain ... guardedness ... when she talked about her days. And I tried to trace back to where it had begun. I had been so busy that I hadn't noticed before. And it took me back to 1936. Then I searched through all my memories and the nearest thing I could find was Julia dancing a slow waltz with Adam Falling. And when I pictured that dance in my mind's eye I felt as though there was a ... a ... bat's squeak of an intimacy that went a little too far. And so I began watching Falling and my wife more carefully.

– Is that really all that pointed in the direction of Falling?

– Well, there was one other thing. Falling is a chain smoker. His room always stank of cigarette smoke. It wasn't as if he smoked anything decent. Wretched Woodbines.

- How is this relevant?
- I realised that sometimes when Julia had come home there was a whiff of cigarette smoke on her clothing. Of course, that could have been completely innocent. So many people smoke, although I can't stand the habit myself.
- That is not much to go on.
- After my suspicions were raised I waited for her to come home from her ... "war work" ... and when she took off her coat and hung it up in the hall I went over to smell it. I picked up one of the sleeves and held it to my nose. There was a definite reek of tobacco. Cheap tobacco. Unfortunately, I was still holding the sleeve up to my face when Julia came back into the hall and saw me. She looked alarmed again, and rather than say "Why are you behaving so ridiculously?" or something like that, she made no comment at all.
- It is not the strongest evidence, I'm afraid.
- But here's the thing: when I got home from chambers, I learnt from Samuels, my butler, that she had arranged for all of her clothing to be dry-cleaned.

Tempest steepled his fingers and gazed up at the ceiling whilst everyone waited for him to say something.

- Well. I *might* be able to make something of that. But you never actually saw them together?
- No.
- That brings me to my last question: you have *never* – or almost never seen them together.
- No.
- So how did they communicate with one another? I have been giving this a lot of thought. I take it there were no letters sent either to your home by him or to your chambers by her?
- No. I'm absolutely sure of that.
- What about the letter that she says she sent to him last December?
- I've asked Arthur about that and he has no recollection of such a letter, but he can't be sure.
- We'll need a statement from him to that effect. What about telephone calls? Surely, if he had telephoned her at home a member of staff

would have answered, and if she rang him one of the clerks would have taken it? Is there any indication that either telephoned the other?

– No – *said Pemberton glumly.*

– So. I ask my question again: how did they communicate?

– I don't know.

– Hmm ...

Tempest's response betrayed a sliver of doubt.

Still, we have some very good positive evidence and, having looked at the down side, I will spend the rest of the time between now and Monday looking at the better parts of our case.

He brought the meeting to an end and everyone stood to leave. He shook Pemberton's hand again and told him to feel free to call him over the weekend if necessary. Pemberton had his home number. And they all made their way out and descended back into the grounds of the Inner Temple.

"Not now. One day, perhaps."

Chapter Ninety-four

(Friday 2nd May 1941)

A peacock feather is a thing of beauty, Adam thought as he took one out from its Chinese vase and walked over to the window of his room. Holding it by its stem, he waved it gently so that the green feathery barbs swayed to and fro. Turning slightly so that the eye of the feather could catch the late afternoon sun, he gazed at its iridescent shimmer – bronze, blue, dark purple and green. The Temple was quiet. He looked down at the Temple Church. It glinted dustily in the bright sunlight. A clock struck four and brought him out of his reverie.

He returned the feather to the vase on his desk and arranged it into a fan of colour with the others. There was nothing else on his desk apart from the two vases of feathers. His room was empty apart from the desk and chairs and his collection of paperbacks. There were no briefs waiting to be done. He had sent the Bateman papers back to Jones on Tuesday. He patted his jacket and felt the reassuring shape of a folded cheque in the inside right breast pocket. Twenty guineas! As a good solicitor should do, Jones had taken money on account and the cheque had arrived that morning.

Adam was not concerned by the fact that he had no work to do. The early conclusion of the case had meant that he had unexpected free days to get up to date. It wasn't as though there was no work out there. After the brief report of the case in Tuesday's paper several solicitors had telephoned his new clerk asking to book him for cases and conferences, but he had given instructions for such requests to be turned down, for the time being at least. He needed to have a clear diary until the Pemberton case was over. And so his clerk told those that called that Adam was unable to take any new work prior to the 12th May. No further explanation was necessary. The fact that Adam was co-respondent in divorce proceedings was well known now, and, after his success in the McKechnie trial, the notoriety he had gained was tinged with respect. He had noticed this around the Temple as well. Many members of the Bar who had averted their eyes when he passed no longer did so, and some allowed themselves a half-smile in his direction as he went by. To his surprise he felt at peace with himself.

After Catherine left the restaurant Adam had eaten his tepid lunch and paid the bill. The tea was too cold to drink. On a whim, because he had nothing else of importance to do that day, he had decided to walk up to Bedford Square and call on Jack Storman, whom he assumed would still be at Blytheway's house. Caldwell answered his knocking and showed him in. Roly was at work but Storman was sitting in the back garden. It was large, well-tended and a trap for sunlight. Blue irises and pink and yellow roses filled the borders, and there was a weeping cherry tree in the middle of what had been a lawn but was now a vegetable patch. Adam wondered where Blytheway had kept his peacocks. At the far end was a small greenhouse and a wooden bench. Jack Storman was sitting in the middle of the bench, his head down and his shoulders slumped. He was wearing an unseasonal overcoat, and to Adam he looked shrunken up inside it. He did not notice Adam approaching until he was less than ten feet away. Storman looked up with a start at the sound of footsteps.

- Adam! I'm sorry. I was miles away.
- I hope you don't mind, Jack, I thought I would drop by.
- No, no. Of course not. Not at all.

Storman moved over on the bench to make room for Adam. He sat next to him and neither of them said anything for a companionable five minutes. Adam did not know whether Storman wanted to talk. Instead, they gazed up the ornamental path towards the rear of Blytheway's home. A gentle breeze made the heads of the irises sway and the scent of sweet peas and tomatoes drifted from the greenhouse. Eventually Storman stirred.

- Thank you for coming on Saturday, Adam.
- I'm so sorry.

They lapsed into silence again. Adam gazed at the shadows that the rose bushes made. There was a pink petal next to the bench and he bent down to pick it up. It wasn't uniformly pink. It was almost white at its heart and grew darker in colour towards its edges. Concave. He held it up to the sun and studied the veins in it.

- I'm sorry that I didn't join everyone at the hotel afterwards – or have a proper conversation for that matter.
- I was pleased that you were able to come at all. And I understand why you didn't want to stay.
- It was a surprise seeing Deborah there.
- Yes. I'm sure. I should have warned you but I've not been myself.
- I had lunch with Catherine today.
- Yes. She told me she was seeing you.
- I can't believe she's brought Deborah back.
- I told her not to. Or at least I told her to wait until Easter.
- It's not safe here.
- You don't need to tell *me* that, Adam.
- I'm sorry.
- She came round here yesterday.
- She's been in Roly's house?
- Caldwell made up some tomato sandwiches and we ate them in the garden – sitting on this bench actually. I tried to persuade her to get Deborah away from London but she was fairly adamant about it.
- Did she meet Roly?
- Not here. He was at work.
- So she met him after the funeral?
- At Sunbridge Park Manor. They had quite a long discussion. He was very nice to Deborah.
- What were they talking about?
- Oh Adam! *You* know Roly. In a room containing Julia, Pemberton and Preston? Me, for that matter. When she came over to speak with him, after pleasantries, he was careful to usher her well away from everyone. He asked me to look after Deborah.
- Could you at least get an idea of what they were saying?
- Oh, she was being very vehement. I caught Jeremy and Julia looking over at them. They seemed to be attracting a lot of attention. But no one could hear what was being said.

Storman lapsed into silence again. Adam looked at his watch. It was getting on for five. Then he thought suddenly of what Blytheway had told him – that Jack had been meeting Catherine fairly regularly for drinks and meals (he had seen her, after all, yesterday), and that Storman would let him know what he thought he could as long as it didn't compromise Catherine's confidences.

– Hang on a minute! You know exactly what she said. She confides in you, I know. If you didn't hear what she said after the funeral I'm sure she would have told you yesterday.

Storman sighed.

– I want to keep out of this, Adam.
– If she told my counsel something, surely I am entitled to know what it was?

Another sigh.

– She told him what she has told me every time we have met one another.
– Which is?
– She doesn't believe a word of your story. That you've made up this prostitute business to protect Julia.
– You don't accept what she says, do you?
– Adam. *Please* don't ask me to cross-examine you on your story. I am finding all of this very uncomfortable as it is.

Adam decided not to take it any further. He took another look at his watch and said that it was time he left. Both men stood and Storman escorted him back through the house to the front door. They shook hands on the doorstep.

– It's funny. I lived here for a while as well.
– I know.
– Roly has been a marvel. Thank you so much for recommending him to me. For him to put me up and provide me with his cast-offs was more than I could possibly expect.
– You know he disapproves of your accommodation – and your tidiness generally?
– He can be quite forthright.

- He has a bee in his bonnet. Goes on about the fact that you only have a basin and worries that you aren't keeping yourself properly clean.
- He insisted on bringing me an iron and ironing board.
- Well, now he is worried about your bathing habits. He asked me to tell you – on the off chance that we met up – that you should feel free to come round here for a bath if you need one.
- Oh, really! He is quite peculiar.
- Yes. But a good friend. He handled all of the funeral arrangements – right down to putting a notice in the *Times*. Insisted on paying for everything. Caldwell has been very supportive as well.
- I'll see you soon.
- Good luck for next week.
- Thanks.

Adam walked down the steps and headed back towards the Temple. He heard the front door shutting quietly behind him.

****

He looked around his empty room in chambers again. Storman hadn't believed his story. Catherine plainly did not. What did Roly think? He went over to the window again and looked down on the church. At that point the door burst open and Blytheway rushed in, still wearing his wing collar and bands from a day in court.

- I have some terrible news!
- Why? What is it? What's happened?
- The Limitation of Supplies (Miscellaneous) Order of 1940.
- What?
- It's due to expire on the 31st May!
- I'm sorry. What has that got to do with anything?
- I *knew* this would happen!
- What would happen?
- Adam, I have this on very good authority but I think that this may not yet be in the public domain so what I am about to tell you must be treated with the utmost confidentiality. Is that understood?
- Yes. Of course.

Blytheway subsided into a chair and motioned for Adam to do likewise.

– It would be better if you are sitting down.
– What's going on?
– Now I don't want you to be *too* upset, but what I have feared for many months is about to come to pass.
– Yes?

Roland Blytheway took a deep breath.

– As of the 1st June they are going to introduce *clothes rationing!*

Chapter Ninety-five

(Friday 2nd May 1941)

Adam laughed out loud.

- I don't believe you are treating this with the seriousness it deserves. I'm disappointed in you.
- I thought it was going to be something to do with my case.
- Oh, that!
- Aren't you at all concerned about it?
- Of course I am, sweetheart. But that is something I can do something *about*. I can't do anything about clothes rationing.

Blytheway pulled a feather out of one of the vases and studied it carefully.

- I wonder how my peacocks are faring. I haven't seen them in months!
- Oh, Roly! Be serious for a moment.
- I must put a call through to my housekeeper. I'm sure they must be all right. She would have called me if they weren't.

He stood and took a turn around the room, running his finger along the mantelpiece to check for dust.

- I hear that you have stopped taking new work for the time being?
- I'm not like you, Roly. I need to have a clear head to deal with next week.
- I've never seen a room of yours looking this tidy. Well done! Are you hanging up your suits properly?
- Tell me about Sir Patrick Tempest.

Blytheway returned to his seat and looked deeply into Adam's eyes. He saw again that fierce intelligence that had unnerved him the first time they met.

- Pat? A formidable opponent.
- Does he scare you?
- Not at all. But he does worry me.
- Do you think you are equal to him?
- I'm *more* than equal to him. I'm worried about you. I'm also worried about Mrs Pemberton's counsel, Alnwick. The man's a fool!
- I hear that you had an opportunity to speak with Catherine after the funeral?
- Delightful lady! Smarter than most of our colleagues. And you have a lovely daughter. I hope you have taken the time to see her.
- We went out for tea yesterday. There's a shortage of kittens.
- If you like I could try and persuade Caldwell to give up Delia. He has become rather attached to the wretched thing but I would be glad to get shot!
- It's all right. I think she would prefer a kitten. Catherine told you that she didn't believe my story about Betty. That I was doing it to protect Ju ... Mrs Pemberton, didn't she?
- She did.
- Do you think she's right?

Once again Blytheway gave him that intimidating stare.

- Are you intending to change your instructions?

Adam stared back at him until he could no longer stand his piercing eyes. He lowered his head.

- No.
- Then what does it matter what I think?
- What worries you about Alnwick?
- Besides the fact that he is a blithering idiot, not much. I went to see him yesterday. He has got this case completely the wrong way round.
- In what way?
- Well, first of all, he doesn't intend to use Jenny's statement because it was not witnessed. Nor does he intend to put Jenny's diary to Pemberton because it was a record of what she was thinking, feeling and doing and not something that Pemberton had any direct knowledge of.

- But the statement wasn't intended to be used, in any event. She was supposed to give evidence and now she can't. It was for her solicitors. Not for the court. And why would it be so important to put the diary to Pemberton? Hasn't Alnwick got a point?
- I sometimes think you are as bad as he is! And he has got his tactics completely wrong. He intends to cross-examine Pemberton about the fact that he punched Julia in the face and knocked her out.
- Surely that would put Pemberton in bad odour with the court – with the press.
- Only until Pemberton tells everyone that it was because she was laughing hysterically about the death of the only daughter he had with Joan.
- I see your point.
- Now. I want you to think very carefully about something.
- What?
- You've told me how you were invited to Pemberton's Christmas party and that you thought it odd at the time.
- Yes.
- That he went out of his way to speak with you? Could you please try and remember what he spoke about?

Adam closed his eyes.

- It's hard to recall in detail. He spoke about how he had seen all this coming and stocked up so that he could take advantage of the black market.
- I knew about that. Despicable!
- He talked about the Bateman case. Which was hardly surprising. He said Julia was doing her "war work" but would be along later.
- He offered me a packet of cigarettes and told me he thought it was unhealthy to smoke whatever the advertising said. And that was about it.
- Nothing more?
- No. I don't think so. Oh, wait a minute. He said something about … Mrs Pemberton having all of her clothing dry-cleaned.

Blytheway sat upright in his chair.

- Interesting. Did he say that before or after he mentioned smoking?
- I can't rightly remember.
- I want you to think about this. I must go now. I've spent five shillings on a season ticket for the Summer Exhibition at the Royal Academy and I want to catch the private view tonight before it closes. Here.

Blytheway handed Adam a ticket. It was for a concert the following evening at the Queen's Hall.

- Bach, Beethoven and Brahms! It should be a splendid occasion. Why don't you come round to the house about six and we can have a glass of something before we head off?

And with that he stood up, smiled, turned and left. Adam studied the ticket. It would be a welcome distraction. Then the door to his room opened and Blytheway leaned in, holding onto the door handle.

- There was one other thing.
- Yes?
- Tempest telephoned me yesterday evening, as a courtesy. He said that he is likely to be relying on a dance card that belonged to Mrs Pemberton.
- A dance card?
- From the 1936 Middle Temple Ball.
- I don't understand.
- Apparently, it shows that you marked Mrs Pemberton's card for the seventh dance, which was a slow waltz, and Preston had booked himself in for the eight, which was a foxtrot.

Adam felt his insides lurch.

- I don't see what that has to do with anything.
- Pemberton saw you dancing with his wife, and when recently he asked Preston about the slow waltz it appears that Julia had gone missing. He looked around for her but she was nowhere to be seen,

apparently. Although she was back in time for the ninth dance, which was with her husband. Tempest intends to call Preston to vouch for that fact. Attention, it seems, is likely to be focused on those missing five or so minutes.

– I'm sure, given a little time, I can explain everything.

Roly's voice suddenly became very stern.

– No, Adam. I forbid it.
– It was entirely innocent.
– I do not intend to ask any questions of you or Mrs Pemberton about it.
– What if I insist? You are supposed to act on my instructions.
– If you insist then we must part company. You have trusted my judgment so far – by and large at least. I would ask that you do so once more.
– Very well.
– Tomorrow at Bedford Square, sweetheart?

And he closed the door and departed, this time not to return. Adam was filled with a sense of grim foreboding.

Chapter Ninety-six

(Monday 5th May 1941)

Double summer time started over the weekend so that the sun rose very early. Corresponding changes had been made to the hours of blackout. There was hardly any point in enforcing it when the sun was still shining. The sun rose at 6.26 a.m. – which a week earlier would have been 5.39 a.m. Sunlight edged the blackout shades and brought Adam to consciousness. His debut role as a co-respondent was due to begin in just over four hours. Roly was going to meet him with Jones in chambers at nine and, after a conference, he planned to be at court by quarter to ten.

He climbed out of bed, pulling up his sagging flannel pyjama bottoms as he made his way wearily to the window to pull away the blackout. There was little more, now, that he could do. He was in Blytheway's hands. He had, however, been unnerved by his Friday meeting with Roly, for two particular reasons. First of all Blytheway clearly saw Tempest as a real threat. The case turned on credibility and, if Blytheway was right, Tempest was likely to unmask him. The second point of concern was the dance card. How could a case like this turn upon the fact that Julia went missing for five minutes or so? Roly could have dismissed the point as ridiculous. He could have asked Adam what had happened next. But he had done neither. Instead he made further discussion of the point a resigning matter. Why would he do such a thing? It was hardly the largest problem in the case. Julia could have had all sorts of reasons for avoiding a dance with Preston. Blytheway would have understood that. He had told Adam that he did not like either Pemberton or Preston. Why was he unwilling to take the easy way out and support whatever version of events Adam put forward? He did not understand and it worried him.

After Roly left his room, Adam had felt a deep sense of panic engulf him. The reality of facing one of the country's most formidable cross-examiners was becoming tangible. Whatever Roly knew or believed, he was getting ready to tell a series of lies under oath to protect a woman who no longer loved him. Worse than that, he had enmeshed Betty in his scheme. They were on the point of attempting to pervert the course of justice. He was sure that she had no idea of the seriousness of the situation. And he could not tell her in case she withdrew. He had lain awake most of that night thinking of all of the ways in which he and Betty could be tripped up. He hadn't thought it through at all. When he took Betty back to the Stafford he had no idea that it would actually end up with a fully contested trial. Or that Pemberton would employ someone as daunting as Sir Patrick Tempest. There were too many holes in his story. Too many things that he had not fully discussed with Betty. He needed to see her again. To give her the ten-pound note in advance of the trial. No matter how well *he* lied, if she was caught out he – and Julia – were finished.

Betty would have been working that night, on the Friday. From his conversations with her he knew that she rarely surfaced before noon. He had realised that he had to go round and see her again in her flat on the Saturday morning. He couldn't take the risk of being seen in public with her just before the trial was due to begin. He waited until eleven o'clock before leaving Doctor Johnson's Buildings. Stepping out into Inner Temple Lane, he looked to his left and right. There was no one in sight. He made his way down to Temple tube. The platform was empty apart from him. It did not look as though he was being followed. He took the District Line to Victoria, and leaving the station he made his way on foot to Green Park and on past the trenches and sandbags. It was ten to twelve before he reached Green Park tube. Barrage balloons, their wires humming in the breeze, drifted above him in the clear blue sky.

He crossed to the northern side of Piccadilly and made his way indirectly, via Bolton Street, to Clarges Street. He found her address, rang the bell and waited. Presently the door was opened and Betty stood before him, fully dressed this time.

– Mr Falling? What do you want?
– It has to be Adam remember? Can I come in?

She stood aside and let him pass and followed him up to the second floor. The room was as he remembered it. She sat down in the only chair and looked up at him expectantly. He produced a ten-pound note, leaned over and handed it to her. She took it without saying anything.

– What do you want?
– What do you want, *Adam*.
– Adam.

He went over to her bed, sat down on it and gazed over at her. Those were not her working clothes. She appeared prim. Proper. Like the seamstress she used to be. She was also pretty. He lit a cigarette and she got up to open a window. The faint breeze that made the cables in the park hum slipped into the room. Adam reminded her that she needed to be at the Royal Courts of Justice on Wednesday – and possibly Thursday. He had come to see her, he said, to make sure they would be telling the same story. They had started seeing one another in May. Her husband, Joe, died in January 1940 and his death left her penniless. He had been an electrician and died in an accident at work. She used to be a seamstress. Adam had insisted on going to the Stafford – she did not know why – although from time to time he would meet her at her flat. It was important that they both said the same thing about how her flat was furnished. They both looked around and, rather than making a mental inventory, Adam insisted on reciting everything that was in the room, from the large clay jug to the photograph of her late husband that was facing the wall. He produced a copy of the petition and showed her the dates on which he was alleged to have committed adultery with Julia. It was not necessary that she tell the court that she remembered all these dates. That would be far-fetched. As long as she could say that they sounded about right, that would do. They talked for over two hours whilst Adam dealt with every potential eventuality, and they debated the final form of their story.

It had been almost two thirty by the time he had finished.

– I'm famished!
– I'm sorry. I hadn't been thinking. Look. Here's five shillings for you to get something to eat.
– Ta.

He rose to leave.

– There's one last thing.
– What?

- I think I am almost certain to be asked why I was seeing you so frequently – and taking you to a posh hotel when you had this perfectly satisfactory room.
- Even *I* can see *that* question coming!
- I want you to tell the court that you thought I was falling in love with you.

She laughed loudly and suddenly.

- Come off it!
- And I want you to say you were falling in love with me as well.
- Why would you fall in love with someone like me?

It was a good question. Adam looked into her intelligent blue eyes and realised that he was fonder of her than he had ever expected to be.

- *Please!* Can you do that?
- I think so.
- Will you kiss me one more time?

She stood and came over to him and they embraced. Once more they were kissing. Once more he felt her tongue, her hands squeezing his back and holding him very tight. The moment lasted a long time before slowly, almost reluctantly, she pulled her face away from his. He was breathless. She stroked his cheek as he turned to leave.

- Thank you, Betty. I'll see you next Wednesday.
- Funny, ain't it?
- What?
- I'll be telling the court we've been having sex regular for months and apart from two kisses we ain't done nothing.

He smiled at her, pecked her cheek and made his way out.

✱✱✱✱

It had been almost four o'clock before he got back to Doctor Johnson's Buildings. He was due at Bedford Square for 5.30, so he rinsed his face and put on the black-tie outfit Blytheway had given him, and by 5.25 he was knocking at the door. He noticed that Blytheway's car was parked outside. Caldwell opened the door and ushered him in. Blytheway had been reclining on the chaise longue in the salon with a bottle of champagne waiting on ice. Two flutes were set out on the mahogany coffee table. He had looked Adam up and down as he entered.

- I worry about you, Adam.
- Don't fret about me. I have complete faith in you.
- Oh, don't be silly. I'm not talking about the trial.

Adam sighed.

- What is it this time?
- I don't know why you insisted on moving out of here and back to the Temple.
- I didn't want to overstay my welcome.
- You know perfectly well what I am talking about!
- You've lost me.
- All you've got there is a basin. When was the last time you had a bath? It's beginning to show you know.
- I can manage.
- Nonsense! A gentleman will bathe regularly. You must feel free to come and use our facilities – whenever you please.

They had finished the champagne and, at quarter past six Caldwell entered wearing a chauffeur's uniform complete with peaked cap. They rose and he led them to the car, dropping them off in Langham Place. The "three Bs": Bach's Brandenburg Concerto Number 1, Beethoven's Piano Concerto Number 1 and Brahms's Second Symphony. Adam tried, during the interval, to make Roly open up about the issue of the slow waltz but he refused to be drawn and became quite stern on the issue. Instead, he insisted on talking about music.

- I do love the Queen's Hall. Such a good orchestra! And I never miss the Proms. Did you notice that they are performing Elgar next Saturday?

The Enigma Variations and the Dream of Gerontius! I'm minded to get some tickets. Would you like to join me?
- Roly! I'm afraid I can't even begin to think about next Saturday. It's hard enough thinking about next week.
- Well. I'll get two tickets anyway and if you don't want to come I'll take Storman. I know how much he likes Elgar.

After the concert had finished they had emerged into the late evening twilight; Caldwell was waiting with the car. He had driven Adam back to the Temple before heading north to Bedford Square. Adam had been no clearer about the significance of the dance card.

✳✳✳✳

Sunday had been an idle day. He had gone through the (false) evidence he was intending to give and tried to think of anything he had not covered with Betty. There was nothing else that he could think of. He checked his watch. It was 7.30 double summer time, and he needed to wash and dress. Fifteen hours until it all began.

Chapter Ninety-seven

(Monday 5th May 1941)

The case had been listed in Court Twelve. The three of them had come in through the front entrance and walked across the black and white marble tiles, first to the Robing Room, where Roly put on his wig, gown, wing collar and bands, and then onto the concrete steps that took one to the first floor. He had been typically frivolous, even by his high standards, in conference.

- Your tie's not straight!
- Can't we talk about my case?
- Trust me, sweetheart. It is more important that you look the part.

Blytheway eyed him up and down and brushed down his lapels.

- You really *do* need a bath!
- Can't we talk even a *little* about the case? I think that, as my friend, you owe me that at least.

Blytheway sighed heavily.

- Very well. I suppose you have a point. And in view of what I am about to say, you do, I suppose, have a right of veto.
- Why? What are you intending?
- I am sure you know. I have no doubt that you have been thinking as deeply about all this as I have.

Somehow Adam doubted the accuracy of this last remark.

- Go on.
- Forgive me Adam. But the more I have thought about your situation

the clearer it has become to me that you wish this petition to be dismissed whatever the personal cost to you yourself.

– I'm telling the truth!

– Let's leave the truth to one side just for now, sweetheart. It has become increasingly apparent to me that the only way to satisfy your instructions is if I portray you to the court as, forgive my language … a *four-letter man!*

– What do you mean?

– It seems to me that your instructions, when looked at objectively, require the court to paint you blacker than black. The blacker you are painted, the whiter will Mrs Pemberton appear. We must distance your evident lack of morality from Mrs Pemberton's evident goodness. We need to divide and rule, albeit not in the conventional sense that the expression is used. The more unattractive your character appears to be, the less plausible it would be for Mrs Pemberton to want to have anything to do with you.

– What about the dance card? Won't you at least hear my explanation for it? I've been thinking about it a lot.

Blytheway had become very stern once more. When he spoke he almost frightened Adam.

– Adam! I thought I had made it absolutely clear that I do not want to go near the dance card! Come. It is time for us to head off.

****

On the first floor of the Royal Courts of Justice, the various legal teams were assembled on the wooden benches outside Court Twelve. To their left sat Alnwick and Mr Purefoy with Julia Pemberton. The sight of her still made him gasp internally and he felt that inevitable physical longing. She was dressed demurely in a modest twin-set of pale grey. Her eyes were lowered and she looked at the floor as Alnwick and Purefoy discussed tactics. To the right were Pemberton, Franklin and Sir Patrick Tempest. Counsel were all wearing their robes and wigs. Sir Patrick Tempest was standing as he addressed his professional and lay clients. He was an imposing figure in his early sixties. There wasn't an ounce of fat on him and his rapidly moving aquiline features betrayed a rare intelligence. Adam was frightened by him. He was obviously discussing last-minute details of their strategy. In addition to the lawyers there was a ruck of journalists hovering about. Adam recognised many of the faces from the previous week when he and Pemberton had faced one another as barristers rather than litigants. Some of them were scribbling furiously in their notebooks.

Tempest said something to his solicitor, who handed over a small rectangular piece of card. He took it and headed in their direction. Roly saw him coming and rose to his feet. Adam noticed for the first time that he had foundation powder on his face.

– Roly! Good to see you. It is always a delight to be against you.
– And you, Pat.
– I thought it would be polite to let you see the dance card I mentioned last week.
– Thank you. I knew that you would. Finest traditions of the Bar. Shouldn't you be showing it to Alnwick before giving it to me?
– I'm sure you will pass it on to him. Fair, I think, to let you see it first.

Blytheway took the card and Tempest retreated. It was yellowing with age. He and Adam studied it together. He saw the cross and his name, written in his own hand, which had precipitated everything that had led them to these benches. Beneath it, against the slow waltz, was Preston's neat writing – blue-black ink. And the next dance was marked out for Jeremy Pemberton.

– This is too ridiculous!
– All of life can be seen as ridiculous from a particular perspective.
– If they are reduced to relying on old dance cards, they clearly haven't much to go on. Can't we use this to show how absurd this whole charade is?
– I don't want to warn you again, Adam.

Blytheway stood up and took the card over to Alnwick. As he was handing it over Adam saw, just beyond the two barristers, a man emerging from the stairs and onto the first floor. He was young and handsome and limped unsteadily with the aid of a crutch towards Julia Pemberton and her lawyers. Adam realised immediately that this must be Simon Jenkins. The man whom Jenny Pemberton had loved. The man with whom she had been dancing when she died.

An usher came out through the swing doors of court twelve and declared loudly that Mr Justice Wilkinson was ready to begin and that everyone should come into court.

Chapter Ninety-eight

(Monday 5th May 1941)

They filed into the cavernous oak-panelled court room and began arranging their papers. There was a strong smell of wax polish. Journalists pushed and shoved their way into the box reserved for them, at right angles to everyone else. Members of the public were beginning to fill the benches at the back. Looking over his shoulder, Adam saw Simon Jenkins ease himself awkwardly into a sitting position. There was no sign of Catherine. Sir Patrick Tempest made his way to the front row and set up his lectern. He was wearing a frock coat under his long silk gown. His junior, Eliot, sat in the row behind him whilst Pemberton and his solicitor, Mr Franklin, sat at a table in front of him. Alnwick sat alongside Eliot, and Blytheway took his place at the right of the same bench. Adam and Julia took their places with their solicitors behind their respective counsel. She was so close to him he could almost reach out and touch her. Only Jones was between them. He could hear her breathing and, from the corner of his eye, saw her breasts moving up and down under the grey tweed. He reached into his trouser pocket and curled his fingers around the little crystal obelisk that she had given him as a Christmas present in 1936. He could feel the cracks and fissures in it. He rolled it around in his hand. Julia was avoiding any sort of eye contact with him. It all seemed a long time ago.

The convention that both the client and the solicitor of leading counsel sit in front of the silk whereas all other clients sit behind junior counsel was a matter of practicality. If they were to sit behind junior counsel it would make direct and confidential communication difficult, if not impossible. Leading counsel leaned discreetly forward to take instructions. Junior counsel would get a tug on the gown and had to turn their backs on the court. Pemberton had turned to speak to Tempest. Adam was able to study him unobserved as he whispered to leading counsel. It was exactly a week since they had been in the court next door. He looked tired and angry. His eyes were bloodshot behind the familiar gold-rimmed spectacles.

– All rise!

Everyone stood, the door at the back of the court swung open and Mr Justice Wilkinson strode in, bowing perfunctorily towards counsel before taking his seat in front of the carved royal crest.

– Pemberton versus Pemberton and Falling!

the clerk said as everyone apart from Tempest resumed their seats. Mr Justice Wilkinson had played rugby for his county in younger days and was reputed to be a concert-standard pianist. Blytheway had told Adam that he was a very good musician but that his arpeggios when playing Chopin's Preludes were a bit arthritic. *All that scrummaging, I suspect.* He was in very good physical shape for a man in his fifties and it was clear that he had no intention of taking any nonsense.

– Yes, Mr Tempest?
– May it please your Lordship ...

His voice was a thing of beauty. He spoke sufficiently loudly for every-one to hear every syllable, but at the same time the tone was almost con-versational. It was apparent that every word had been chosen with care and for maximum effect. He began by introducing counsel and, with a wave of his hand towards Pemberton and then over his shoulder towards Julia and Adam, identifying the parties. Then he began to outline his case. In the press box the journalists were writing frenetically.

– As your Lordship probably knows this trial was originally fixed to commence on the 10th March of this year. Sadly, a tragedy of terrible proportions befell my client on the weekend before. Jenny, the only daughter he had with his first wife Joan, was killed by enemy action at the Café de Paris. I *know* that your Lordship, along with very many at the Bar, knew Joan Pemberton, who was taken away in an influ-enza epidemic at the age of twenty-nine?"

Mr Justice Wilkinson nodded sombrely.

   – For several years my client was severely distraught at this *first* grievous loss. However, in due course, he met and married his current
wife, Julia, who is the respondent to this petition and with whom
he had three children: Stephen, Sebastian and Agnes. He had felt
that this union was a happy one but during the course of last year
he formed the view that the situation was far from happy. In short,
he came to the conclusion that his wife was conducting an affair.
He will give evidence to the effect that his suspicions were first
aroused after Stephen, Sebastian and Agnes had been evacuated to
the Cotswolds and the respondent spoke in her sleep. The words she
spoke were: "Not now. One day perhaps." My Lord, I would be the
first to accept that these words are on one level innocuous. The obvious interpretation would be that the respondent was dreaming of her
children. However, several nights later, Mr Pemberton will say that,
again in her sleep, she repeated the self-same words in exactly the
same sad tone of voice. Mr Pemberton was of course concerned at
his wife's evident distress and so the following morning over breakfast he asked her about what she had said. He wanted to soothe her
concerns about her children and assumed that she would turn to that
topic. However, to his great surprise and consternation she became
seriously alarmed, he will say, and asked what else she had said in
her sleep. There was no mention of her children, and when he asked
her what she had been dreaming about she effected not to remember.
This may seem to your Lordship to be a small and trivial point. But
we submit that it is quite the opposite. Your Lordship is faced with a
case which is made up of innumerable small points but they all point
to the almost inevitable conclusion that the respondent was conducting an affair with the co-respondent, Mr Adam Falling.

Adam felt a scorching heat across his face. He bent his head and gripped
tightly the crystal obelisk in his pocket. *Talking in her sleep? Acting suspi-
ciously when confronted? Why hadn't she told him about this?* He looked across
at Julia, who was gazing down at the floor. Her eyes were blank. A murmur
was running through the press box and he began to picture the following
day's headlines.

   – Mr Falling …

Tempest continued with a half glance over his shoulder in Adam's direction.

- I must tell you something about Mr Falling. He has been a member of the Bar for some fifteen years and was until recently a member of the chambers of which my client is the head. When my client became aware of Mr Falling's affair he gave him seven days to leave. Has your Lordship come across Mr Falling, either in your years of practice or since your ascension to the Bench?

Mr Justice Wilkinson averted his gaze from Tempest and stared into Adam's eyes. Adam did his best to stare back. Then the judge looked back at Tempest and shook his head.

- I hope Mr Falling won't mind me saying this, but his has not been a successful career at the Bar. And yet, as a good Head of Chambers would do, my client did his best to help him out. For example, he recommended him for a position on the Aliens Tribunal. All this when he was in absolute ignorance of Mr Falling's dishonesty and deceit.

Adam bowed his head.

- So, what does the case for the Petitioner consist of? I want to make it clear at the outset that, with two qualifications, we do not have any evidence that the two were together or that they ever communicated with one another. We can point to no witness who can make up that apparent deficit in the case. We do not have, as is so often the case in matters such as this, damning evidence from a private detective. However, what we *do* have on both these issues condemns the respondent and co-respondent absolutely. Mr Falling is a man from the lower middle class. He comes from the north of England although he does have a degree from Cambridge. Whilst he may have been unsuccessful at the Bar he is plainly intelligent and, we will say, he is a cunning dissembler. The respondent, equally, is no fool. It is our case that these two *again motioning over his shoulder* have attempted, largely successfully, to cover their tracks. That is, after all, the way of the adulterer throughout history.

It was clear that the judge's curiosity had been pricked. The press were lapping it up.

- But, I want to turn now to the two qualifications to the concession that I have just made. Being seen together? They were seen by my client dancing the slow waltz at the Middle Temple Ball in the summer of 1936. That they did dance the slow waltz that evening is admitted by both of my Learned Friends. In reality, however, they could hardly deny it. I will be introducing into evidence Mrs Pemberton's dance card. The slow waltz was the seventh dance and it is plain from Mr Falling's own handwriting that he partnered Mrs Pemberton. Why is this germane, relevant or material? Well, of course, it may not be. However, when we examine the dance card we see that the next dance was to be a foxtrot and that Mrs Pemberton's card had been marked by Mr Peter Preston, now one of Her Majesty's Counsel. You are, I believe, familiar with Mr Preston KC?
- I know him very well. He has often appeared in front of me.
- When my client asked him recently about that slow waltz, Mr Preston was quite clear in his recollection. After the slow waltz came to an end and everyone began to regroup in preparation for the next dance, he went looking for Mrs Pemberton but she had disappeared; although when the time came for the *next* dance she was back in the Hall. So, for five minutes Mrs Pemberton was missing. "Five minutes?" your Lordship may ask. To which I would reply, *How long does it take to strike a match? How long does it take for gasoline to ignite? For a man and woman to kiss?* I shall be calling Mr Preston KC to confirm this small point of evidence. I had hoped that this would not be necessary, but although Mr Blytheway for Mr Falling was prepared to accept that evidence without contradiction, Mr Alnwick insisted that he be called to answer questions.

The press were loving it. Adam looked at Blytheway, who was sitting in front of him looking bored. He wasn't even taking a note. Why had he simply accepted the evidence of Preston without asking him for his instructions? This was getting out of hand. What was Roly playing at? He looked across at Alnwick. Roly had said that Julia had been sold a pup. The man had a look of complacent endeavour on his face as he wrote furiously in his blue notebook. He was beginning to doubt Blythway's judgment again.

– We will see where that takes us. I now turn to the question of communication. There is evidence of one act of communication. It is common ground that Mrs Pemberton wrote to Mr Falling in December of last year. We do not know what her letter said because Mr Falling had set it on fire and left the residue in his ashtray where Mr Pemberton found it. Although it had been burnt, by some piece of alchemy the watermark survived and my client recognised it. Why was Mrs Pemberton communicating with Mr Falling at all? A man who, on her case (on both of their cases for that matter), she hardly knew? We understand that she will say that it was a letter of apology for the unwarranted suspicions that her husband had been voicing. *We* say that, with respect, this is utter nonsense. In the first place there is little evidence that my client voiced his suspicions to Mr Falling. Secondly, we ask: If this was entirely innocent, why did Mrs Pemberton ask Mr Falling to destroy the letter? If it still existed and it said what she said it said, then it would be a powerful piece of evidence in her *favour*. Why destroy something that actually helps the case? We say that the answer is an obvious one: the letter said nothing of the sort! We must speculate on the contents of that communication, but our speculation leads us to this conclusion: that Mrs Pemberton had realised that her husband had worked out what was going on and was seeking to warn her lover.

Lover? thought Adam. We weren't lovers by then anyway.

– So we say that in these two instances we can point to the two brackets that wrapped up this adulterous association. The beginning and the end. It started with a dance and it ended with a letter of warning. You may ask: *Is that all you have?* I will answer that likely question. No. It is not. Unfortunately, it will be necessary, during the course of this hearing, to delve into Mrs Pemberton's earlier life and to things such as her finances. Now I must ask Mrs Pemberton to forgive me, but she would have to admit that she is not an educated woman. Like so many women she did not go to University. That is not a criticism.

Very few women do. It does not suggest that she is lacking in intelligence. It does mean, however, that for example her literary palette is narrower than that which one would expect from a man. And yet, a consideration of her bookshelves demonstrates an almost ... *avant-garde* taste in literature. That, again, cannot be entirely a criticism. It is good to see a woman seeking to improve herself. The problem is this: her literary tastes mirror so closely those of Mr Falling that the coincidence becomes extraordinary. We will present evidence, by way of inventories of their books, that sets out the entire collection of Mr Falling's books at Stirrup Court and Mrs Pemberton's books in her private room in Eaton Square. That these two people who are outwardly so different in education and social standing should walk so closely together – one is tempted to say "hand in hand" – through the field of literature beggars belief. And so we ask, how did this coincidence come to pass? We say that the obvious conclusion must be that where their literary tastes converge what we are seeing is gifts from him to her.

Adam cursed himself again for being so stupid.

– Finally, we have the evidence of cigarette smoke. Again, you may think this is an ephemeral point. However, we will be adducing evidence to the effect that Mr Falling was a man who chain-smoked cheap Woodbine cigarettes. That these are regarded as "working-class" cigarettes is scarcely the point. They have their own distinctive smell. Mr Pemberton, as he explored in his mind who it was that his wife was consorting with – to whom in her dreams she had said "Not now, one day perhaps" – remembered that his wife's clothing had of late been smelling heavily of cigarette smoke. He became convinced that this must be the smell of Woodbines. Indeed, he took the opportunity to smell closely the sleeve of her coat. It was hanging in the hall. You may think what an absurd, almost paranoid thing to do. The objective observer would certainly think so. The objective observer would ask: *Why are you behaving in such a ridiculous manner?* But the objective observer in this case was Mrs Pemberton. She came unexpectedly into the hall and found her husband with his nose to the sleeve of her coat. And how did she ridicule him? What did she say? Nothing.

Instead the following day she had all of her clothing dry-cleaned! Why didn't she say something about her husband's apparently strange behaviour? Why did she take the first possible opportunity to have everything dry-cleaned? We say: to remove every trace of the evidence that my client was sniffing out. In the course of this trial we shall be seeking clear answers to those questions.

– My Lord. I must deal briefly with what may be described as the defences being put forward on behalf of the respondent and co-respondent. We do not accept either, although it has to be said that Mrs Pemberton's defence does her more credit than that put forward on behalf of Mr Falling. It is her case that on practically all of the dates that are set out in the petition she was in fact having innocent tea at the Ritz with her late step-daughter, Jenny, and that they were discussing "women's issues". Jenny, of course, very sadly cannot now vouch for that, but we anticipate that either Mr Alnwick or Mr Blytheway or both of them will rely upon Jenny's diary, which contains crosses against most of the relevant dates. It is deeply sad that Jenny is no longer with us. It is a lesser sadness that she cannot answer questions about her diary. There is nothing, unfortunately, that can be done about that sad fact. Our client does not accept that, notwithstanding Jenny's filial loyalty, this affair did not happen. Then there is the case put forward on behalf of Mr Falling. He admits to adultery. But not with Mrs Pemberton. It is his – rather unbelievable – case that he *was* committing adultery but with a prostitute named Betty. That he went to the Stafford Hotel off Green Park will be clear from the testimony of Mr Jackson, a private detective. On behalf of the Petitioner we say that this is no more than a late-invented subterfuge to put this court off the scent. Why would he spend money on a hotel room when, in all probability, this lady of the night had her own room to go back to? It makes no sense. It is not as though Mr Falling had the finances, judging from the state of his practice, to indulge in such excess. We shall have questions to ask of him on this.

Adam looked over at the press box. Those who were not writing were smiling at one another. This was going to be a great story!

- My Lord, that is all I have to say at this stage. Does your Lordship have any questions?
- No, Mr Tempest.
- In that case I will call Mr Jeremy Pemberton KC.

Chapter Ninety-nine

(5th May 1941)

Pemberton rose and made his way to the witness box. This was reached by climbing several wooden steps so that he was on a level with the judge and looked down on everyone else in the court room. He was wearing a dark, expensively tailored three-piece suit, a white shirt and a blue tie. A white handkerchief peeped out from his breast pocket. He was facing the press box. His eyes moved from the journalists onto counsel, his gaze lingering with evident distaste on Roland Blytheway. From there he turned his gaze to Julia, and then finally to Adam. The look was withering. He took the oath and answered the usual questions about his full name, his address and his occupation, addressing all his answers to the judge, who took a diligent note. Adam took the opportunity during these preliminaries to steal a look in Julia's direction. Her eyes were locked on her husband.

Jeremy Pemberton spoke smoothly and mellifluously in answer to Tempest's questions. More in sorrow than in anger was his tone. Tempest took him methodically through his evidence. His education, his marriage to Joan, his impressive war record. Armistice Day. The birth of Jenny. The death of Joan. The years of sorrow. Meeting and marrying Julia. Taking silk. Their three children. Then, the background having been established, he dealt with all the matters that Tempest had outlined.

- – I want to ask you about something that I have already described to the learned Judge. About the occasions when Mrs Pemberton talked in her sleep.
- – Yes?
- – We all talk in our sleep from time to time and usually it does not mean anything. It is the fragment of a good – or bad – dream?
- – I accept that.
- – Had Mrs Pemberton ever spoken in her sleep before?
- – From time to time, yes.

– And did you ever, with any of these other episodes, feel a need to ask her about them?

– No.

– Why was it different this time?

– It was the *way* she said what she said.

– Could you perhaps explain to the court?

– It was ... it was ... I didn't tell her this at the time ...

Pemberton faltered and then began to weep.

– Would you like a glass of water, Mr Pemberton?

– No thank you. I'll be all right.

– What was it about the way she said what she said?

– After she said the words "One day perhaps" she let out a terrible sob. She sounded dreadfully unhappy. I thought she was thinking about her children.

– And it happened again?

– Several days later. It was exactly the same. "Not now. One day perhaps." And then she sobbed in her sleep.

Adam allowed himself to look surreptitiously in Julia's direction. Her head was down and a hand hid her eyes. She could not, however, hide her tears. Large drops falling down her cheeks and onto the floor. He had known nothing of this. Tempest took his client through the conversation at the breakfast table, her alarm, her apparent inability to remember her dream, and then all the rest of the evidence about books, watermarks and the smell of Woodbines on clothing. Apart from the questions from a silk and the answers from another silk there was an eerie silence to the proceedings. The public gallery was full. The press were writing down everything they could. The judge, too, was filling his judicial notebook. By the time Pemberton's evidence in chief had finished it was plain to all that the sympathies of press, public and judge were with him. *I can't see how this can get any worse*, Adam thought to himself as Alnwick stood up to cross-examine. But it was about to get a lot worse.

Alnwick hauled himself to his feet. Before turning to Pemberton he looked first at the press box. With a little shock Adam realised the man was looking forward to the publicity; to his name being printed in the following day's papers. Then he turned towards Pemberton – an imperceptible bow to the judge en route. After a routine "May it please your Lordship" he embarked on his cross-examination. It was entirely predictable. He laboured his points: Adam and Julia had been seen together only once in the last five years or so, there had only been one letter from his client to Falling and she gave an immediate explanation for this when Pemberton asked. He didn't deal with the dream. He didn't deal with Jenny's evidence or the evidence in her diary. Instead he moved onto the evidence in relation to the books. Blytheway had his head in his hands.

- You and your counsel have made great play of the contents of my client's bookshelves?
- Yes.
- You would accept, however, wouldn't you, that your wife is a very intelligent lady?
- Of course. I would be the first to accept that proposition.
- She is a woman with an independent, questioning mind?
- That I also accept.
- Why, then, can you not accept that she sought out these books of her own free will? Out of intellectual curiosity?
- I know my wife. We have been married for over fifteen years. Yes, she is intelligent. But I am now forced, against my will and desire, to the conclusion that she is also calculating and sly. Yes. I accept that she has independence of mind. But I am now forced to conclude that her independence of mind is linked to an independence of heart that means she has been prepared to forsake the vows she made to me all those years ago and to follow her heart, whatever the cost. Nothing that you have put to me has, *in any way*, dented my beliefs about the situation between her and … and *Falling!*

He gave Adam a look that dripped hatred. And then Alnwick fired his blunderbuss.

- It is right, is it not, that you have been violent to your wife? That you have assaulted her?

632

Adam felt a collective intake of breath around the court room. Perhaps, the sympathy of the court and the observers should not be with Pemberton? Blytheway, sitting in front of him, shook his head.

- What are you talking about?
- Is it not right that in the early hours of 9th March 1941 you hit your wife so hard that she was knocked unconscious?

Adam allowed himself a glance over his shoulder. Simon Jenkins was leaning forward in his seat waiting expectantly for the answer.

- Yes. Yes. And, of course, I regret it. But she provoked me terribly.

Alnwick should have stopped there but he ploughed on.

- There can't be any excuse for hitting a woman so hard that she is rendered unconscious?
- The only daughter I had by Joan had just been killed! And when Julia realised that it was Jenny that had died rather than our daughter together, Agnes, she began laughing hysterically! She said "Thank God!"

There was a hush and all eyes were on Julia.

- No!

Shouting from the rear of the court. It was Simon Jenkins.

- I can't believe it! You bitch! You horrible bitch! You lying two-faced bitch!
- Silence!

Mr Justice Wilkinson was not impressed.

- Get that man out of my court! I will not have such contempt.

Simon was wearing a uniform, and this probably tempered the judge's disapproval.

– Young man. Get out of my court! Immediately! You must think yourself fortunate that I have not decided to throw you in prison for such
manifest contempt.

Jenkins eased his way to his feet and edged his way out of the court
room. Blytheway leaned over to Alnwick and said in little more than a
whisper,

– Well done, darling.
– No further questions, my Lord.

And Alnwick subsided into his seat red-faced. The press were still scribbling to catch up. Mr Justice Wilkinson looked at the clock at the back of
the court.

– It is almost one o'clock. We shall resume at five past two.

And with that he rose, bowed to counsel and marched out.

****

Adam, Blytheway and Jones crossed the Strand to the café for a cup of tea
and a sandwich.

– Well. I did say he was a blithering idiot.
– Why didn't you want to cross-examine Preston?
– I had made it perfectly clear that I would not do and that this was a
resigning issue. Will you please ask no further questions about it?
– Let me tell you what happened.
– Adam, you are coming close to making me angry. I have only ever
been angry once in my life.
– How do you think it's going?
– Well, I think that is perfectly obvious. I was ready for the evidence
about the cigarette smoke but I have to confess the "dream sequence"
took me by surprise. I didn't see that coming.
– Would it help if I gave you my thoughts about what that may have
been about?

– No. Alnwick in his incompetent way has dealt with a lot of the "jury points" and so I suspect that my cross-examination will necessarily be brief.

And Roly lapsed into silence and did not say anything for the remainder of the short adjournment until, looking at his watch:

– It's time we made our way back.

Everyone else was already in court by the time they entered. Adam noticed that Simon Jenkins had also slipped back into the public gallery. Pemberton was back in the witness box and they had only just resumed their places when they were ordered to rise and Mr Justice Wilkinson entered. All stood. Roly had told Adam that he had frequently been against the judge before he took judicial office. *No fool.* Everyone sat down except for Blytheway.

– Yes, Mr Blytheway?
– May it please your Lordship.

He turned to face Sir Jeremy Pemberton KC.

– Mr Pemberton, many of the questions that I would have asked have been put to you *very ably* by my learned friend Mr Alnwick, and so you will be pleased to hear that my questions will, I hope, be very brief.

Adam sensed the man relaxing almost imperceptibly. His shoulders sagged with the sense of a reprieve.

– I want to ask you a few questions about your daughter Jenny.

Tempest was on his feet immediately.

– My Lord, I do not see the relevance of such a line of questioning.
– I tend to agree, Mr Tempest. Where is this going, Mr Blytheway? How is it going to help me?

Roly, who had slipped back into his seat when Tempest intervened, rose languidly to his feet.

- My Lord, you will recall that, in Mr Pemberton's evidence in chief, there was a rich passage about both his daughter Jenny and his late wife, Joan. If it is relevant evidence for the Petitioner I must surely be entitled to ask questions about that evidence?
- Very well, Mr Blytheway. But if I feel that you are taking liberties with the court I will intervene.
- Of course, my Lord. Now; on reflection, Mr Pemberton, I think I will begin by asking some questions about your first wife, Joan Pemberton.
- This is outrageous!
- Forgive me, Mr Pemberton, but you have made very serious allegations about my client – and about your present wife. They are both entitled to have their defences explored. I am sure you will have no difficulty in answering – in agreeing with most of my questions. Joan Pemberton was a very beautiful woman was she not?
- Yes. Everyone knew that.
- And she was also, and more importantly, a very good woman?
- The best woman I ever had the good fortune to meet.

He looked across at Julia as he answered this question and tried unsuccessfully to conceal a sneer.

- She was also an honest woman? Honest and kind?
- I don't see where this is going.
- I tend to agree, Mr Blytheway.

The judge had intervened. Blytheway had to be careful, Adam thought.

- I was merely setting the scene, my Lord. So many of us remember Joan Pemberton with great fondness.
- Get to the point, Mr Blytheway!

Roly was unperturbed and fixed his attention again on Pemberton.

- As I said, I really wanted to ask you about your daughter Jenny.

636

- Very well.
- Would you accept that she was as beautiful as Joan?
- Yes. Of course.
- Would you also accept that as she grew older she began to resemble more and more her mother?
- Yes.
- Would you also accept that she was as good and honest as her late mother?
- She was a wonderful child.
- Would you accept that she loved you very deeply?
- I believe she did.
- Would you accept, also, that she trusted you?
- Yes.
- To the extent that she entrusted you with her private diary for 1940?
- Yes, of course.

Adam looked over at Tempest, who was beginning to fidget. He did not seem as relaxed with this cross-examination as he had been when Alnwick was questioning Pemberton. It was almost as though he was anticipating the next question, and when it came Tempest had to restrain himself from intervening. It was after all a perfectly fair question.

- Would you also accept that you betrayed your daughter's trust?
- How dare you! I don't know what you are talking about!
- She lent you her diary for one particular purpose, didn't she?
- And what might that have been?
- She wanted you to see the crosses she had marked against certain dates? The dates on which she said she had met with Mrs Pemberton at the Ritz. The dates on which you allege she was with Mr Falling at the Stafford Hotel?

Pemberton looked over helplessly at his leading counsel, who looked away. His shoulders slumped.

- Yes.
- She gave you the diary for the express purpose of showing you those crosses. Is that not right?

- Yes.
- But she also told you not to read the individual entries that she had made. Is that right?
- Yes.
- So she trusted you so much that she left her private diary with you. Would that be fair?
- I really don't know where this is going Blytheway.

A mistake. The judge intervened.

- Mr Pemberton! Answer counsel's question! And show some respect to him. I will not have you referring to him in that off-hand way in my court!
- I'm sorry, my Lord.

Roly continued.

- The point I am making, Mr Pemberton, is that you betrayed her trust. You read her diary when she had told you expressly not to do so. That is right, isn't it?
- Yes. Of course, I regret it enormously. Every night I think of this in light of what happened.
- That is the reason, is it not, why she gave the diary to Mrs Pemberton?
- Yes.
- You read her diary and you saw that she was in love with Simon Jenkins – the young man who was recently expelled from this court by his Lordship – and you told her that you would not countenance their relationship becoming more serious. Would that be fair?
- Yes.
- You read her diary and you knew how much in love she was?
- Yes.
- And you disapproved?
- Yes.
- You knew that the *only* reason that she had entrusted you with her intimate diary was because she wanted to lend her support to her step-mother?

    – Yes.
    – And reading her diary you saw that she loved you?
    – Yes.
    – And that she also loved her step-mother?
    – Yes.
    – And she did not want you to divorce?
    – Yes.
    – And that her step-mother loved her?

There was a long pause.

    – Laughing hysterically at her death does not suggest she loved her.
    – Mrs Pemberton had taken a sleeping draught that night, had she not?
    – I believe she had.
    – She was disorientated?
    – Probably.
    – She thought you were telling her that your daughter Agnes had died?
    – I believe that was probably the case.
    – She was full of remorse the following morning?
    – Yes.
    – You are on oath, Mr Pemberton. Do you really believe that Mrs Pemberton did not love Jenny?

There was a long pause. Adam looked over his shoulder. Simon Jenkins was listening intently to the exchanges.

    – No. But how she reacted hurt me deeply.

Roly was immediately conciliatory.

    – I know that, Mr Pemberton. And we are also sincerely sorry about what happened to Jenny. But I must ask these questions. I would like you to have a look at Jenny's diary.

He handed up the leather-bound book with the key still in the lock.

    – It is all right. She is gone now. Unlock it and consider its contents. We are, after all, on a quest for the truth. Would you please confirm that it is written in her hand?

Pemberton stroked the sheets of paper.

- Yes. I would recognise that lovely handwriting anywhere.
- Look at the frontispiece. From memory it reads, "Please don't read the contents of my journal. It is very private." I believe she underlined the word "very"?
- Yes.
- And she signed it underneath. That is her signature is it not?

He stroked Jenny's declaration.

- Yes. That is her signature.

Blytheway turned and took a document from his solicitor, studied it and handed it across to Tempest via Alnwick. Receiving it back, he gave it to the usher so that she could pass it up to Pemberton. Tempest rose to his feet.

- Forgive me, my Lord, but Mr Blytheway is trying to put in evidence a witness statement allegedly signed by Miss Jenny Pemberton. But unwitnessed.

The judge intervened.

- This is not evidence, Mr Blytheway.
- Not yet, my Lord.
- What do you mean?
- I mean that I am entitled to put this document to Mr Pemberton, and depending on his answers to my questions it may or may not become evidence.
- Very well.

The document was handed up to Pemberton. It was the statement Jenny had signed without a witness on the evening of her death. He studied it and again began to weep.

- Would you accept, Mr Pemberton, that the signature on this unwitnessed statement is the same as that in the diary?
- Yes. I can't deny that.
- My Lord, in those circumstances I think I am entitled to have this document entered into the evidence. Mr Pemberton, can you think of any reason why your daughter, who is honest and true, would put her name to a statement that was dishonest and false?

Pemberton paused for a long time and looked around the court room. There was a palpable tension in the room. The journalists had their pens poised. The witness seemed to have shrunk. After a minute of the silence Blytheway spoke again.

- I'm sorry, Mr Pemberton. I know this is very painful for you. But is it your case that your daughter is a liar and was attempting to pervert the course of justice before her untimely and tragic death?

Again no response and a long silence.

- Mr Pemberton! Was your daughter a liar? Was your daughter about to embark on an escapade that would involve her in attempting to pervert the course of justice?

Another long pause.

- Mr Pemberton. *Please.*

The judge intervened.

- I think you should answer this question, Mr Pemberton.
- No! She was my daughter. She wouldn't lie! She was the most beautiful, the best girl in the world!
- So how do you explain why she was prepared to go on oath and state that on most of the dates when Mrs Pemberton was alleged to have been committing adultery with my client she was actually with Mrs Pemberton?
- I don't know. She must have been wrong. Or misguided.

– I want to ask you about something else that is said in the diary. In her entry for 31ˢᵗ December 1940 Jenny speaks of a meeting with you during which you repeatedly referred to her as Joan. Is what she said correct?
– Yes.

Pemberton bowed his head. Blytheway paused and took a sip from his glass of water.

– It is right, is it not, that you threw a party at your home in Eaton Square on 13ᵗʰ December 1940?
– Yes.
– And you invited my client and his wife to that party?
– Yes.
– At a time when you had already decided that he was having an affair with your wife?
– Yes.
– And you had a conversation with them when they arrived?
– Yes.
– And you made no mention whatsoever of your suspicions?
– No.
– And this was the first time you had ever invited Mr Falling to one of your parties even though he had been a member of your chambers for some fifteen years?
– I don't see where this is going or what it has to do with anything.
– When I use the expression "the black market" do you know what I am referring to?

Tempest leapt to his feet.

– My Lord! I cannot see how this has anything to do with the issue before you.

Mr Justice Wilkinson looked enquiringly at Roly.

– Yes, Mr Blytheway?
– My questions will be very brief and, as is often the case, their relevance ought to become clearer as this matter continues.

– Very well, but I will warn you again that if I think that you are taking me on a wild goose chase I will intervene.
– Of course, my Lord.

Blytheway returned his gaze to Pemberton. Adam thought the witness looked worried.

– Do you know what I am referring to when I mention the black market?
– I believe I do.
– Would it be fair to describe it as a market in which goods are traded illegally?
– Yes. I think that that is fair.
– Do you recall that the subject of the black market came up in your conversation with Mr Falling at your party?
– I really don't recall.
– I want to put to you part of the conversation which, according to my client, took place that evening. Mr Falling will say that you said that you had stocked up on cigarettes and alcohol and with the aid of your senior clerk, Arthur, you released these onto the black market for your mutual benefit. I am going to ask a question about this in a moment, but before you answer it I am obliged to tell you that you have a privilege against incriminating yourself. You are under no obligation to answer any question that might tend to incriminate you. Now ... my question is ... do you agree that this is a fair representation of that part of your conversation with Mr and Mrs Falling?

Pemberton's fury was palpable. His face had become bright red and the veins in his forehead were visibly pulsing. He gripped and released the edge of the stand. When he looked across at Blytheway pure hatred blazed out of him.

– Do you want to answer this question?
– No!

Blytheway turned to the bench –

– No further questions, my Lord

643

and sat down. There was no re-examination from Tempest. Pemberton returned to his place and Sir Patrick Tempest KC called for Peter Preston KC to be brought into court. Preston looked dapper as he gave the oath although he eyed Blytheway with resentment and suspicion. He gave the mandatory details and explained how at the Middle Temple Ball of 1936 he had marked Julia's card for the foxtrot and how, when the time came for the dance, he had looked everywhere but had been unable to find her. Alnwick rose to cross-examine.

- Would you accept that there are all sorts of reasons why a woman might miss a dance?
- There could have been, of course, I accept that.
- She could, for example, have gone to the Ladies' room?
- She did not give me any explanation when I saw her later as to why she had missed the dance. She was always a lovely lady and I was surprised that there was not even an apology from her, let alone an explanation. That was most unlike her.

Alnwick, who had clearly not learned a thing from the morning session, let off his blunderbuss again and caught himself squarely in the foot.

- Were you aware that Mrs Pemberton had an aversion to you?
- I don't know what on earth you are talking about!
- She had the view – I will try to put this delicately – that your hands had a tendency to wander.
- This is outrageous!

Blytheway turned round to Adam and then looked at the ceiling with an air of gloom. The judge interrupted the cross-examination.

- Mr Alnwick. Are you making a positive case that your client accepted a dance from Mr Preston and then chose not to honour that because of her views about Mr Preston's proclivities? Is that the evidence she is going to be giving?
- No, my Lord.
- This is most improper!

Alnwick sat down and the judge looked at Blytheway.

– No questions, my Lord.

Tempest then called Jackson, the private detective. He explained how he had made enquiries about expensive hotels within an easy radius of Eaton Square and how he had discovered that Adam Falling had been frequenting the Stafford. He told how he followed him to Shepherd Market and witnessed him picking up a prostitute whom he took back to that hotel, and how he subsequently interviewed her. Alnwick asked him whether he had ever seen Falling with Mrs Pemberton, and he answered, as he had to, that he had not. Blytheway rose to cross-examine.

– Just one question, Mr Jackson. It is right that, in addition to speaking with the prostitute you also spoke to the man working on reception?
– Yes.
– Is it not right that in answer to your questions he confirmed that Mr Falling always brought the same lady to the hotel?
– That is what he told me.
– And that lady was the person he had picked up in Shepherd Market?
– Yes.

Blytheway turned to face the judge.

– No further questions, my Lord.
– Very well. It is almost 4 p.m. I think we will rise now and we can start afresh with the evidence, I think, of Mrs Pemberton tomorrow.

Sir Patrick Tempest rose to his feet.

– My Lord, before the court rises may I introduce one very brief witness?
– What is the nature of the evidence you wish to call?
– I wish to call Mr Arthur Kean. He is the senior clerk at Stirrup Chambers. His evidence goes to the issue of the letter that Mrs Pemberton says she sent to Mr Falling.
– Very well.

645

Arthur entered the witness box and took the oath. The suit he was wearing looked more expensive even than that worn by his Head of Chambers. He stated that all correspondence that came into chambers was sifted by him and the other clerks and then placed in the relevant tray. He confirmed that neither he nor any of his staff had any recollection of such a letter being received. When he had given this evidence, Mr Justice Wilkinson turned to Alnwick.

– Do you have any questions?
– No, my Lord.

Alnwick had apparently at last learnt his lesson.

– And you, Mr Blytheway?
– One or two, my Lord.
– Very well.

Blytheway turned to face Arthur Kean.

– In light of your answers to Mr Tempest's questions would it be right to say that you have never seen any letters arriving for Mr Falling that came from Mrs Pemberton?
– No, I have not.
– Or taken any telephone calls from Mrs Pemberton in which she asked to speak with Mr Falling?
– No.

Roland Blytheway paused and looked over at the press box before returning his gaze to Arthur Kean.

– Mr Kean, when I use the expression "the black market", do you know what I am talking about?

Adam looked across at Tempest, who was struggling with the temptation to rise to his feet again. He resisted.

– Everyone's *heard* of the black market.

  – Dealing on or with the black market is illegal, isn't it?

This time the judge intervened.

  – Mr Blytheway! This is not a trial about illegal trading. What is the relevance of this?

Roly was unperturbed.

  – Mr Kean is giving evidence in support of his employer. If it be the case that he and Mr Pemberton have been engaged together in illicit activity that may have had some impact on the evidence he was prepared to give on behalf of his employer. I put it no higher than that.
  – Carry on.
  – Mr Kean, I should make it clear that before you answer my next question there is in our courts a privilege against self-incrimination. You do not therefore have to answer my next question. Do you understand?
  – Yes.
  – Were you and Mr Pemberton working together to exploit the black market using cigarettes and alcohol provided to you by Mr Pemberton and sharing the profits?
  – I don't want to answer that question.

Blytheway turned to the judge, said he had no further questions and slipped back into his seat. Tempest said he had no re-examination.

  – Court rise!
  – 10.30 tomorrow,

said the judge before striding out of court.

****

Adam and Blytheway parted company with Jones on the Strand and headed back to Lamb Building.

– You were brilliant, Roly! I think the afternoon went far better than the morning.

Blytheway remained gloomy.

– Unfortunately, I don't think that black market stuff is going to make a shred of difference.
– Why introduce it then?
– I *disapprove* of the black market. And I wanted to tweak Pemberton's tail. Listen, Adam, would you like to come and dine with me tonight? I think we need to try and lift Storman's spirits.
– Thank you. I'd love to.
– On one condition however.
– Which is?
– I don't want any talk of this case. It is the last thing Storman needs.

Chapter One Hundred

(Tuesday 6th May 1941)

– Court rise!

Sir Patrick Tempest formally closed his case. Alnwick stood up and called Julia. She was wearing a demure cream outfit. In order to get to the witness box she had to squeeze past Jones and then Adam. He stood to get out of her way. Her leg touched his as she passed and he smelt her perfume. She did not look at him.

Although the report in the *Times* had been an unsensational recitation of the events of the previous day, the tabloids had been more lurid: "The dance card mystery", ran the *Daily Sketch*'s headline; "Unlocking the secret diary" was the *Daily Mirror*'s title; "Barristers in alleged love triangle" was the *Daily Mail*'s take on it. None of the journalists had been complimentary about Alnwick's contribution. Adam looked over at him as his client made her way up the steps to the witness box. He appeared subdued.

Julia was composed as she took the oath. Adam allowed himself to luxuriate in the sound of her voice. The last time he had heard it was in Hamley's on the 20th December.

If you love … loved me … you'll tell the world you hate me. If you love me you'll understand why I must tell everyone that I have never cared for you. You will find a way to explain why all the bloody books on my shelves are the same as the ones you have in chambers … to explain why you were going to the Stafford on free afternoons. A way that doesn't involve me. New Year's Day is on a Wednesday. We'll both receive the Petition on the Thursday. I can't see you again.

Alnwick got her to introduce herself to the court and, the formalities out of the way, took her through her evidence. He took her through her early life, her meeting Pemberton, his problem with drink (dealt with euphemistically), their marriage and children and her relationship with Jenny. Then he dealt with the evacuation of Stephen, Sebastian and Agnes to the Cotswolds.

- Do you miss your children?
- Dreadfully.
- Did you ever considering joining your children away from London?
- Never.
- Why was that?
- My place was with my husband. He is a very brave and noble man. I believed that if he had the courage to stay here I had to be there at his side.
- Do you love your husband?

Julia gave Pemberton a long look of melting softness before she answered.

- I love Jeremy with all my heart. I have loved him since the day I met him.
- Have you ever loved anyone else?
- No. That would be impossible.
- Do you love Mr Adam Falling?

Julia looked affronted at the question and glanced dismissively in his direction. *At least our eyes have met at last*, he thought.

- No! Of course not! I hardly know the man!
- Did you ever love him?
- No!
- Much has been made of the fact that you had a dance with him at a ball in 1936.
- I had completely forgotten about that to be honest. Until my husband produced that dance card. I remembered that his first name was Adam but I hadn't remembered his surname until Jeremy started mentioning him to me in the months before last Christmas. Until that card was produced I had forgotten all about the fact that we had shared one dance over four years ago. I left it in my room when I moved out.

- After that dance did you have any further contact with him?
- No.
- It has been said that you missed the next dance.
- I really can't remember. But if Mr Preston says that he couldn't find me for it I have no reason to doubt that. He is an honourable man.
- Did you offer him any explanation for your absence?
- I don't believe I did. On the other hand I don't believe he ever asked me. He is a very popular man and I doubt that the fact that he and I missed our dance mattered much to him.
- After that dance did you have any further contact with Adam Falling?
- No.
- Did you want to have anything more to do with him?
- No!
- Was there any reason for that?

She looked offended.

- Well. That is a very stupid question! – *Adam tended to agree* – I am a married woman. I love my husband and, besides, one dance was enough for me. He is a lesser man than my husband. I didn't care for him at all!
- But you wrote him a letter?
- I did. Poor Jeremy had been going through a very difficult time. For some mad reason he clearly got it into his head that something was going on between me and Mr Falling. I don't know why.
- What sort of things would he say?
- Jeremy has always talked to me about chambers and about the members of his chambers. He is a good and conscientious Head of Chambers and I am proud of him for that. But he hardly *ever* mentioned Adam Falling. And if he did, it was almost always in a disparaging way. Then in the last few months of 1940 Jeremy changed. He started talking about Mr Falling all the time. I was baffled by this to be honest. And he would give me such odd looks when he did so – as though he was getting at something and I was supposed to understand what it was.
- Carry on.
- I racked my brain. I thought Jeremy was behaving really strangely

about this. But I put that down to the fact that everyone was finding life very difficult with all the bombing from the Germans. He had a lot of responsibilities: to Jenny, to me, to Stephen, Sebastian and Agnes. To our staff. But he also had to think of Stirrup Court and the members of his chambers. He would come home in the evening and tell me of another building in the Temple that had been destroyed. He worried terribly about what would happen if Stirrup Court was destroyed. He was under a great deal of strain and I put it all down to the war.

– Did there come a time when you realised that Mr Pemberton was in reality suggesting that you were having an affair with Mr Falling?

– It was such a ridiculous notion that it took a while to sink in. But about a week before our Christmas party Jeremy made a point of telling me over breakfast that he intended to invite Mr and Mrs Falling to come along.

– Did that surprise you?

– Well. Yes, really. He had never invited the man, or his wife, before, and suddenly, after making all these rather strange comments he went out of his way to tell me that they had been invited, and then went on to say that he was sure I would welcome the opportunity to speak with him and get to know him better! I had to put down my teacup. *"Why would I want to get to know Mr Falling better? Or even speak to him?"* I asked. And then he said something that really shocked me. He said, "Come on, my dear, you know what I'm talking about." And then I realised. The silly man had got it into his head that I was having some sort of relationship with Mr Falling. I couldn't believe it.

– What happened next?

– I told Jeremy that I didn't know what he was talking about and he said that I knew perfectly well.

– When you realised that he was indeed suggesting to you that you were having an affair with Mr Falling, what did you do?

– Well. Obviously, I was shocked and embarrassed. I assumed Jeremy was inviting Mr and Mrs Falling to our party so that he could cause some sort of scene. I hardly knew the man and I felt it would be dreadfully unfair on him to do what Jeremy appeared to be intent on doing in front of Mr Falling's wife. And so I wrote a polite letter to him, marked "private and confidential", setting out what I understood was being alleged and apologising for it. Because it was completely wrong.

- Did you ask that Mr Falling destroy the letter?
- Yes, I did. I was frightfully embarrassed. It was humiliating.

Alnwick turned to the question of her books. She explained that this was nothing more than an unhappy coincidence. She may not have had as full an education as Jeremy but she wasn't stupid and she didn't have a job. The days were long, especially after her children were evacuated, and she didn't need all day to read the paper so she started buying herself books to read.

Why had she decided to have all her clothing dry-cleaned?

- My life had changed since the war began and I had taken up voluntary work as part of the war effort.
- Can you tell the court the nature of that work?
- I do not know if I am liberty to do so.

She looked inquiringly at the Judge, who nodded for her to continue.

- Whilst I lived at Eaton Square I was able to help by going to Westminster and helping to chart the falling of the bombs so that we could ensure that the emergency services knew where they needed to go.
- I see.
- Since I moved out I've been doing the same job for the Water Board, in Rosebery Avenue.
- What has this got to do with getting your clothing dry-cleaned?
- I don't smoke. And neither does Jeremy. I agree with him that it is a filthy habit. I was not often around cigarette smoke before but everyone I was working with seemed to smoke. I agree that I did see Jeremy smelling my coat in the hall and I realised immediately what he was thinking. That my coat smelt of smoke. I had just got back from my work, after all. Jeremy is a very fastidious man who abhors dirt. I felt I had let him down and so I decided the proper thing to do was to get everything cleaned. I never dreamed that it would be suggested that this was in some way sinister.

Alnwick then turned to deal with Julia's relationship with Jenny. She explained how Jenny had been very small when she first met Pemberton and she had always regarded her as a younger sister rather than a step-daughter. Although Jeremy would refer to Jenny as "our daughter" – and she thought it very considerate of him to do so – she always considered her as just "Jenny". Agnes was their daughter.

- What were your feelings towards Jenny?
- I loved her. We were very close. I used to let her borrow my dresses.
- We heard Mr Pemberton say yesterday that you laughed hysterically when you realised that it had been Jenny who had been killed and not Agnes.

Julia paused in her evidence and looked around the court room. Her complexion was mottled. She put her hand to her eyes and pinched the bridge of her nose between finger and thumb. She tried to speak but her voice cracked. A glass of water was passed up to her and she took a sip before continuing. She bowed her head.

- It's true. It is the incident in my life that I am most ashamed of. I don't blame Jeremy for hitting me. My reaction was awful and I felt positively *wretched* the following morning. I apologised to Jeremy over and over again and I have been filled with remorse ever since. I completely understand why he has found it hard, if not impossible, to forgive me. I made a dreadful situation even worse. I hurt the man I loved grievously and I have to live with that.

She looked over to the public gallery and Adam sensed her seeking out Simon Jenkins.

- And I want to apologise to Mr Jenkins as well. I know Jenny loved him and I believe that he loved her too. I am deeply sorry.

The judge was taking a careful note of her evidence and the journalists continued to scribble furiously. Blytheway took no notes.

- Tell me about your trips to the Ritz with Jenny.

654

– We used to go together quite regularly. I enjoyed her company.

– What did you talk about?

– "Women's things" mostly. She used to talk about Mr Jenkins a lot. I think she was hoping that he would propose. The last time we went there for tea I gave her a lovely ring that Jeremy had given to Joan. He had passed it onto me when we married but I always felt that it should go to Jenny. She was wearing it the night she … the night she died.

– Did you keep a note of the dates of your meetings?

– No. There was no reason to do so.

– We have heard about Jenny's diary. Did she ever show it to you?

– No. Not until after I received Jeremy's petition.

– Tell the court what happened next.

– Jenny couldn't believe what Jeremy was doing. She thought he had gone mad. She didn't believe I had been having an affair. In all of our conversations, she told me, I had never even mentioned Mr Falling, which was true. Why would I? And she demanded that I show her the petition.

– Did you?

– I refused. I told her that she should not get involved in what was happening between me and Daddy. But she insisted.

– So you showed it to her?

– Eventually. I didn't want to.

– And what was her reaction?

– She immediately said that the petition was wrong and that she could prove it – she was very excited – and that is when she showed me her diary. She asked that I didn't read the actual entries but pointed to all these crosses that she had put on particular days.

– Did you know what she was trying to show you?

– I was confused to be honest. Then she explained that she had put crosses in her diary for the days that we had our trips to the Ritz. She hadn't put anything in about what we had discussed because it was all very personal and private. And sure enough, on nearly every occasion when I was supposed to have been conducting an affair with Mr Falling I was in fact having tea or lunch with Jenny.

– Did you know Jenny was putting crosses in her diary to mark the days that you met?

– I had absolutely no idea. I knew she enjoyed our little get-togethers but I didn't know she was keeping this record.

– Can you confirm that the crosses in her diary *do* mark days on which you and she met?
– Of course I can't! I had no reason to keep my own records.
– No further questions, my Lord. If you wouldn't mind staying in the witness box, there may be some more questions for you.

Alnwick had been ponderous and slow but at least he had performed better than on the previous day. On reflection, however, Adam concluded that Julia had given a superb performance. Blytheway rose to his feet to begin his cross-examination. Before he could begin, the judge leaned forward.

– Mr Blytheway. It is almost one o'clock. Mr Alnwick's examination in chief was rather lengthy – that is not a criticism; we will begin again at five past two.

****

After they had installed themselves in the cafeteria and obtained their tea and sandwiches, Adam wanted to press Blytheway on his view of the morning's hearing.

– Not while we're eating, Adam. I thought Jack was on rather good form last night, in all the circumstances.
– I'm becoming very fond of cod.
– After you left I had another try at persuading him to get out of London for a while – say hello to the peacocks – but he is hell-bent on staying here. I hope he doesn't do anything stupid.
– How often, exactly, has Catherine been round to the house?
– Once or twice I believe.
– Why didn't you tell me that you had spoken with her after the funeral?
– It would have served no purpose. Eat up. We need to be getting back.

Blytheway wiped his mouth with a paper napkin and stood up to leave.

– Now that you have finished eating there is a question about the case I would like to you to answer. Have you any idea why Tempest didn't call the receptionist at the Stafford? If they had such a good case and I had been taking Mrs Pemberton back to the hotel they would only have to call him.

- I suspect they were uncertain about what he was likely to say and decided not to take the risk. It is elementary, sweetheart, that one should not ask a witness a question when you do not know what the answer will be.
- But there would be no reason why Pemberton couldn't have arranged for Jackson to go and speak to him. To find out what he would say.
- Of course, you are right, Adam. And I am sure he did.
- So that suggests that whatever he said was unhelpful to Pemberton's case?
- I am sure you are right.
- So if that is the case, shouldn't we be getting a statement from him?

Blytheway was on his feet now. He shot a look in Jones's direction. The solicitor looked embarrassed. Roly sighed.

- We already have one, Adam. I asked Mr Jones to carry out that commission.
- Why didn't you tell me? What did he say?
- Two questions! Answering the second first, the receptionist said that you always brought the same woman back and that woman was Betty.
- So, we will be calling him?
- No. To answer your first question: I have no doubt that he gave the same answers to Jackson. You would not call, as your own witness, someone who could put a hole in your case.
- That's why we should call him.
- Don't be dense, Adam! You should know better. We are talking about a fundamental point here. If Tempest called him he would be stuck with the answers he had given to Jackson. He is not allowed to cross-examine his own witness. If, on the other hand, *we* called him, Tempest could challenge his story. He is very good at that you know.
- But why should we worry? He would be telling the truth.
- Trust me, Adam. I have an unerring instinct in these matters. If it is any consolation Mr Jones's initial view was the same as yours. That is why I decided that it would serve no purpose to discuss the evidence

of the receptionist with you. Come. We shall be late. It would not do
to keep Mr Justice Wilkinson waiting. Punctuality is all.

And he headed out of the café and was crossing the Strand almost before
the bell on the door had rung.

****

– Yes, Mr Blytheway?
– May it please your Lordship.

The court was full. Simon Jenkins was still in the back of the court with
the rest of the public. Blytheway swivelled towards Julia Pemberton.

– Mrs Pemberton. As you know, I ask questions on behalf of Mr Falling,
  who sits behind me. You have probably gathered from the evidence
  so far that Mr Falling is a heavy smoker and he tended to Woodbines,
  which are cheap and ill-smelling?
– Yes.
– You told this court that you can't abide smoking?
– It is a filthy habit!
– Would you countenance a relationship with such a man? A married
  man who smokes heavily – and smokes an inferior brand of cigarette? You may not know this but he has graduated to rather smelly
  Turkish cigarettes.
– Never! It is a most *unattractive* habit!
– You will also have heard evidence that Mr Falling is a man who con-
  sorts with prostitutes – he has admitted as much. When you wrote
  your letter to him were you aware of that fact?
– I was absolutely disgusted! It made me understand why Jeremy disapproved of him so. If I had known that, I would *never* have sent a
  letter to him. He deserves all he gets! I'm only sorry that Jeremy came
  to the conclusion that I was in some way involved. It makes me feel
  sick just to look at him!

Adam chanced a glance in the direction of the press box. They stared
back at him as they formulated their pen-portraits of a despicable human

being. He bowed his head and tried to look, without being noticed, at the Judge. Judicial eyes bored into him. The expression on the face of Mr Justice Wilkinson left no doubt as to the view he took of this particular member of the Bar.

- I want to ask you briefly about Jenny Pemberton. You have expressed your deep remorse over your reaction to learning that it was Jenny and not Agnes who had been killed.
- Yes.
- You have also told the court that you loved her and knew that she loved Mr Jenkins.
- Yes.
- It is right, is it not, that you went to visit Mr Jenkins in hospital after that terrible incident?
- Yes.
- And that you went out of your way to ensure that he could attend her funeral, and supported his limping damaged body as he made his way to her grave?
- How could you *possibly* know that?
- I'm sorry, Mrs Pemberton, but it is not for you to ask me questions. You must merely answer mine. Is what I have put to you true?
- Yes.
- Why did you do that?
- I knew how much Jenny loved Simon. And if what she told me was right, he loved her as well. I was distraught at Jenny's death but I also knew that Jeremy's suffering was greater and that for Simon to lose the love of his life would have been intolerable. I was trying to make amends.
- No further questions, my Lord.

Blytheway coiled smoothly back into his seat. Sir Patrick Tempest rose to his feet to begin his cross-examination of Mrs Julia Pemberton

Chapter One Hundred and One

(Tuesday 6th May 1941)

Tempest was always going to get an easier ride than the other barristers. He had achieved more than most High Court Judges, he had beaten them frequently before they had been appointed and he had a reputation for sharp put-downs when a judge, injudiciously, intervened; all this meant that the man sitting under the royal coat of arms thought twice before challenging him. That was particularly so when the gentlemen of the press were out in force. He rose to his feet.

- Mrs Pemberton. I would like to ask you first about your background. About the time before you met Mr Pemberton. What did your father do for a living?
- I don't rightly know. He went out to work every day in his suit and carrying his briefcase and then he would come home in the evening. Something to do with money.

Tempest affected surprise.

- You mean that you don't know what your father did for a living?
- He and I didn't get on.
- He wasn't enormously successful, was he? Financially, I mean?
- I never really thought about it.
- You confided about your parents to Mr Pemberton at the outset of your courtship, did you not?
- I don't know what you are talking about.
- You said that they were poor and mean-spirited?
- It is all a long time ago.
- They wouldn't even let you have a dolls' house for Christmas?
- That is true.
- You didn't really like them, did you?

660

- I really don't understand what you are getting at.
- Are they here today?
- My father died some years ago.
- And your mother?
- She is not here.
- It is customary, is it not, for the bride's family to finance the wedding?

Mr Justice Wilkinson intervened.

- How is this helping me, Mr Tempest?
- Bear with me, my Lord.

The judge subsided.

- Would you accept that proposition?
- Yes.
- But my client, Mr Pemberton, paid for everything did he not?
- He did.
- You received no financial settlement– there was nothing established in your favour in the event of the marriage failing?
- I married for love.
- But the reality is that you have no independent fortune?
- I do not.
- So, if your husband, my client, proves that you committed adultery with Mr Falling you will be left with nothing?
- I suppose that is true.
- And you love Stephen, Sebastian and Agnes.
- Of course.
- And you will lose them too?

Julia bowed her head and covered her eyes. Her voice burbled with emotion.

- Yes.
- So if you lose this case – if I satisfy the court that you did indeed commit adultery with Mr Adam Falling – you will lose all your possessions and you will lose the custody of your children. Were you aware of that?

- I suppose I was, yes.
- So you have two very good reasons for resisting you husband's petition. You don't want to lose all the money and financial security and you don't want to lose your children?
- I don't want to lose my husband! I love him!

She shouted this and wept as she said it.

- Now I want to ask you about your education. This is not a criticism but you did not go to university did you?
- No.
- You have limited formal education, would that be fair?
- I didn't have much choice.
- What do you think, aesthetically, of the works of Evelyn Waugh?
- I don't know what you are talking about. He wrote good stories. All I want from a book is a good story.
- What about Orwell? He's a socialist isn't he?
- He writes about the poor. I don't see what is wrong about *reading* about the poor.

Julia was coping quite well with the questions she was being asked. She made it all seem so credible.

- Do you remember talking in you sleep?
- Of course I don't!
- "Not now, one day perhaps" – and then you sobbed. Can you tell the court what you were dreaming about?
- Mr Tempest. We all have dreams when we are sleeping. Most of them we don't remember. I was so shocked by what Jeremy said at breakfast that I tried very hard to remember what I had been dreaming about. But I could not.

Tempest was very good but he was not able to crack his witness. On the issue of Jenny's diary his approach was subtle.

- You fully accept that you have kept no personal records of the dates when you met with Jenny?

- Why should I?
- So, if she is wrong about those dates then your alibi explodes?
- I suppose so.
- What time of the day did you meet Jenny?
- It varied. But it was usually at around four.
- So, that doesn't preclude a possible meeting before or after you met Jenny?
- I suppose it doesn't. Although usually we would leave the house together and come back home again together. I spend most of my days at home. There was only one occasion when we didn't leave the house together and that was the last time we went there. I went to her room to collect her and she was busy writing a letter to Mr Jenkins so I went ahead and she caught me up. The only times we didn't go home together were when I had to go to Westminster and help chart the bombs.
- Is it possible that Jenny was mistaken as to the dates she marked in her diary with a cross?

Julia paused before answering, and cocked her head to one side as she gave the question some thought.

- Yes. I suppose she could have been mistaken. I can't really say one way or the other. As you know, I have no independent record. On the other hand she is … was … always so meticulous.
- You have been married to Mr Pemberton for around fifteen years, haven't you?
- I have.
- Would you say that you know your husband well?
- I think so.
- I hope he will forgive me for stating this but he is a very intelligent man, is he not?
- I can certainly agree with that.
- And astute?
- Very.
- Level-headed?
- Yes.
- Balanced?

– That's why he is so good at his job.
– He's not a man given to making outlandish allegations?
– No. Which is why all of this …

She threw a look, which encompassed the judge, counsel, the press and the public, around the courtroom.

– … is so baffling to me.
– Would you also accept that he has always been discreet?
– I believe so.
– He is not a man who likes "scenes"?
– I am sorry?
– He is not a man who is in the habit of having loud arguments in public?
– I suppose not.
– Washing dirty linen in public?
– No.
– You told the court that he would frequently come home from work and speak of the members of his chambers to you, albeit you say that he rarely mentioned Mr Falling until recently.
– Yes. He liked to let off steam. I think he liked to bounce things off me.
– These were cosy evening conversations between husband and wife?
– Yes.
– Although nothing was said between you about them, you both understood that what was said was confidential?
– I don't understand.
– He was confiding in you was he not?
– When you put it that way I suppose he was.
– Would it be fair to say that the things he told you about members of chambers were his private views and reactions?
– Yes.
– By and large the things he said to you about them were not the sort of things that he would say to their faces?
– I suppose not.

Sir Patrick Tempest paused and moved his gaze from Julia and onto Adam. His eyes betrayed a ferocious intelligence but not, thought Adam, quite as intimidating as Roly's on the few occasions he had chosen to unleash it. Tempest turned his attention back to Julia.

- Did you have any evidence that Mr Pemberton had voiced any of his suspicions to Mr Falling?

She bowed her head.

- No.
- I want to ask you about the Christmas party we have heard a little about. A lot of people were invited, were they not?
- Yes.
- Many members of the Bar, many High Court Judges, even a Cabinet Minister?
- Yes.
- You knew that there was absolutely *no* likelihood that Mr Pemberton would cause a scene with Mr Falling at that Christmas party didn't you?
- I wasn't sure.

Tempest feigned astonishment and looked at the press box.

- You weren't *sure!*
- He'd been acting so strangely.
- Did you, at *any* stage, ask your husband why he had invited Mr and Mrs Falling?
- No.
- Did you at any stage ask him whether he was intending to put what you describe as "outlandish" allegations to Mr Falling?
- No.
- So, to recap, your husband had told you in confidence about his suspicions about Mr Falling; he told you these things in confidence and there was nothing to suggest that he had communicated his suspicions to Mr Falling. You would agree with all of that would you?
- Yes.
- Your husband is a discreet man who does not like there to be scenes and, on this occasion, notwithstanding your alleged concerns, you

did not raise with him the possibility that he intended to create such a scene?
- No.
- So, Mrs Pemberton, the question I must ask you, in light of the above, is why did you write to Mr Falling at all?

There was a very long pause whilst Julia considered her answer. Blytheway, still not taking a note, was watching intently. Adam remembered what he had said in that first conference: *A little piece of evidence can make a big hole. I fear that this one lies below the water line. It could sink you.*

- If I had known what a dreadful man he was I would not have written it. It was foolish. I can see that now. At the time I just wasn't thinking straight. I couldn't believe that the man that I loved was capable of believing that I could betray him.
- But it goes further than that, Mrs Pemberton. You asked him to destroy your letter and he did.
- I felt humiliated.

Adam feared that Julia was beginning to crumble.

- As members of the Bar we are often told that it is useful to stand back from the bare facts and consider them in a wider context. That is what I want to do now. We have established on your case that you met Mr Falling only once, for a short dance in 1936; that you disappeared – or at least could not be found for four or five minutes after that dance; that you had no regard for Mr Falling; that your husband voiced certain suspicions to you, in confidence, about Mr Falling and his relationship with you; that you had no good reason to think that he would "create a scene" when Mr and Mrs Falling came to your Christmas party; that you made no attempt to clarify that with your husband at the time; and that, ultimately, you wrote this letter to Mr Falling.
- Yes.
- And you told him to destroy it after he had read it?
- Yes.

Tempest paused again and looked at the judge and then slowly turned towards the press box before continuing.

- This is where I want to stand back. This is the position as I understand it: there is a member of the Bar, whom you hardly know and who happens to be a member of your husband's chambers. You do not like him and you hardly even know him. Your husband makes completely unfounded allegations of adultery against you, citing Mr Falling. You don't try and explain why it is not so. Instead you write to the person being accused and you ask him to destroy the letter after reading it. That is the position, is it not?
- You're rearranging the facts to make it seem suspicious. But it isn't!
- Let us look at it from the perspective of Mr Falling. This is a member of the Bar who one must assume has a modicum of intelligence. He receives *out of the blue* a letter from the wife of his Head of Chambers, someone he has only met once. This letter sets out completely false allegations about you and him and at the end of it you ask him to destroy the letter.
- I should never have written the letter.
- You heard in my opening remarks to the judge that this letter, if it had been preserved, would have been of considerable assistance to you and to Mr Falling?
- When I wrote it I wasn't thinking that I would have to explain my actions in this court.
- But this member of the Bar, who was entirely innocent of the allegations made against him, obeyed your request to destroy the only evidence which, if you are telling the truth, could have supported your respective defences. Can you give me any good explanation why he should do such a thing?
- Because I asked him to I suppose.
- Mrs Pemberton, we are standing back, remember. I must put it to you that any innocent member of the Bar receiving a letter like that would have preserved it. There is only one explanation for his actions. That he knew you well and that he trusted you. Is that not right?
- No!

Julia was indeed crumbling. She began to weep and her body crumpled in the witness box.

– I will put it again. He knew you and he trusted you?
– No,

she said quietly.

– And he loved you?
– No.
– And you loved him too?

She could not resist looking in Adam's direction. Their eyes locked briefly and this time he saw a tender sadness in her eyes.

– No! I love my husband! I could not love anyone else!
– No further questions, my Lord.

Alnwick had no re-examination and Julia was allowed to resume her seat. She had to make her way past Adam and Jones and they stood to let her through. As she passed him, in a movement that would have been imperceptible to all but him she pushed back her bottom so it rested for a fraction of a second against his groin. All the main players were in the rows in front of them. Tempest's junior, Eliot, was obstructed by Jones. *What did it mean? The last time he had that sensation was in October 1940 when it all ended.* He looked at her questioningly as she sat down. But she did not look in his direction. Then the clerk announced that the court was rising.

✳✳✳✳

The tepid champagne bottle. The view over Green Park from the second floor of the Stafford. The knock on the door, The peacock headscarf. Blond curls escaping.

– Four years. Our lives are flying away from us.

Then the champagne

– To us.
– Yes. To us.

668

- What's upsetting you?
- I got a lovely letter from Agnes this morning. Well … not so much a letter … but she had drawn a picture of a house, a boxy thing, with a line of blue crayon at the top – that was the sky – and a line of green crayon at the bottom which was the grass.
- When did you last see them?
- And she had written, scrawled really, "To Mummy and Daddy, love Agnes", and then put a line of crosses under her name.
- They'll be able to come back soon, I'm sure.
- I couldn't bear to lose them, Adam
- Why should you lose them? They're much safer where they are.
- I've been sleeping very badly. I'm so tired…. Top-up please … Thank you … So much has changed in the last four years.
- *We* haven't changed though.
- Would you like some more?
- Let's leave a glass each for afterwards.

He remembered undressing her at her request until she was only wearing her panties.

- Shouldn't we move away from the window?
- No, Adam. Put your hand inside.

And they had made their way to the bed.

- I want this to be memorable.
- I love you so much!
- I love you too. I mean it, you know.
- Why should I not believe you?
- I mean it, you know.

And afterwards

- Let's have that last glass of champagne.
- Do you want me to cover you with a sheet?
- Come to the window, Adam.

And then they were sitting naked at the little table.

– Julia. What's wrong?
– I don't think we can carry on any longer.
– Why ever not?
– It's this war. We're taking enormous risks.

She had started to cry.

– Do you remember that time when I asked you whether, if we weren't both happily married with children, you would marry me and you said yes?

She was sobbing.

– Yes.
– Do you think that will ever happen?
– Not now, one day perhaps.

And she had sobbed again.

– When?
– Maybe in twenty years.
– Twenty years?

And she had climbed back into the bed and fallen asleep. He had watched her as the light disappeared and, when it came time to wake her she had acted almost like an automaton as she stood up and dressed herself then opened the hotel room door to leave.

– Goodbye, Adam.
– Please don't leave me!
– Goodbye, Adam.

And she turned and was gone and Adam felt that his life had come to an end at that moment.

Chapter One Hundred and Two

(Wednesday 7th May 1941)

Betty was waiting dutifully outside court and Adam, when he saw her, went across and, rather incongruously, shook her hand.

- Thank you for coming.
- I'm really scared.
- You'll be fine. Just remember what we agreed.

He looked up as he was taking his leave and heading into court to see Catherine approaching. She looked dismissively at Betty, glared at Adam and headed into the public gallery. As he entered the row behind Blytheway, Roly turned and smiled and said

- Keep it short, sweetheart.

Roland Blytheway rose to his feet.

- I call Mr Adam Falling.

He ascended to the witness box and took the oath. He looked around the court room. Catherine seemed far away. Julia avoided his eyes when he looked in her direction. The only person who seemed capable of meeting his eyes was Roland Blytheway. Roly took him through his evidence in a conventional way. He dealt with his comparatively poverty-stricken background, his parents, his scholarships to a local Grammar school and then to Cambridge, and then, without touching upon the matter in hand, to his expulsion from Stirrup Court.

- I want to ask you briefly about two cases that you conducted since you left Stirrup Court. The first was a treason trial, was it not?

671

- Yes.
- And I understand that counsel for the prosecution was Peter Preston KC, who was a member of your former chambers and who gave evidence to the court on Monday.
- Yes.
- And I think it is a matter of record that you successfully defended your client?
- Yes.
- And that was the first dent in Mr Preston's otherwise unblemished record of prosecuting alleged traitors?
- So I understand.
- And then, last week, you represented a co-respondent in a case that was very similar to this one?
- Yes.
- And counsel for the Petitioner was Jeremy Pemberton KC?
- Yes.
- Indeed, as I understand the position, Mr Pemberton recommended that you be appointed as counsel for the co-respondent?
- Yes.
- Had he ever recommended you for a case before?
- No.
- What was your reaction to that?
- I was surprised. Grateful, of course, but slightly baffled.
- And on top of that he also invited you to his Christmas party?
- Yes.
- Was that something that happened often?
- No. It was very rare for Jeremy ... for Mr Pemberton to invite my wife and me to a party.
- Why, then, did you think he invited you?
- Beyond receiving that unexpected letter from Mrs Pemberton, I had no idea.
- I will come to the letter presently. By the end of that evening did you have any theories as to why he invited you?
- He was making all sorts of strange, heavy hints when he spoke to me.
- And did they bring you to any potential conclusions?
- I know it seems crazy but it tied in with what Mrs Pemberton's letter

had said and I formed the impression that he thought I had been having an affair with her ... with Mrs Pemberton.

– Had you?

– Of course not! And, anyway, I was married.

Adam glanced towards Catherine who was shaking her head vehemently. He hoped no one had noticed.

– Can you tell the court what happened in the case you conducted against Mr Pemberton? Who won?

– I suppose I did.

– Suppose?

– His client's petition was dismissed and I agreed on *my* client's behalf not to seek costs.

– So, in the relatively short time since you left Stirrup Court you have joined battle with two of the silks and beaten them both?

Adam looked down at Pemberton, who had lowered his head.

– I suppose so.

– I want to ask you about the books you read.

– Yes.

– They have been described as "avant-garde", whatever that means.

– I don't think so. Anyone with a love of literature would find them interesting.

– Do you have many law books on your shelves?

– Not many.

– Would it be fair to say that you enjoy literature more than you enjoy law?

– I think I wanted to be a writer but came to the conclusion that I did not have the talent.

– Were you aware that Mrs Pemberton shared many of your tastes in books?

– How could I be?

– It has been suggested that you gave these books to Mrs Pemberton. What do you say to that?

– It's ridiculous! She is in a different class to me, for one thing. I was barely out of the working class when I went up to Cambridge.

– Anything else?

– Well, I am married. And so is she.

Blytheway paused and looked around the court. In the press box the journalists were beginning to take a different view of Adam Falling. He was a working-class boy who through dint of intelligence had managed to get into Cambridge and then to find a place at the Bar. He had shown his mettle by beating two of his former colleagues, both silks, in court. He might be a bounder but there may be some good back-stories here, in the gutter press at least.

– I need now to turn to the question of Betty Sharples.

This was where it was going to get difficult. He glanced over at Catherine, who was watching him keenly.

– Yes.

– It is your case, is it not, that on all of the dates, between May and October, when you booked a room and went to the Stafford it was for the purpose of having an … an assignation with Mrs Sharples?

– Yes.

– One might ask, as Sir Patrick has asked …

A languid wave of the hand in the direction of Sir Patrick Tempest KC.

– … why it was necessary to go to the expense of hiring a hotel room when Betty Sharples almost certainly had a room of her own to take you back to?

– When I first met Betty I had never done anything like that before. I didn't want to go back to her room because … well, because I didn't want it to appear to be what, I acknowledge, I know it was.

– This leads to two – sorry – three questions, and I will ask them one after the other. The first is: Did Betty have her own room and did you ever go there?

– She did. And I have been there once or twice.

Adam looked up. Catherine had a hand over her mouth, appalled.

- The second is: Why, after the first time, when I assume you were able to acknowledge what you were doing, you didn't simply take advantage of her room? You didn't simply go there?
- I wanted it to be more romantic than that. I thought that if I had gone to the trouble of paying for a room in an expensive hotel she would stay with me longer – and she did.
- And my third question is this: Why go to the same ... lady of the night ... on each occasion?
- I suppose ... I mean ... from that very first time I became fond of her. I believe now, looking back, that I was beginning to fall in love with her.

Adam, who had been addressing all his answers to Mr Justice Wilkinson, glanced up and across the court room. Catherine looked furious, Julia had her head down and the press were scribbling away.

- I want to turn to the letter Mrs Pemberton wrote to you in December of last year. You have heard her account of it. Do you agree or disagree with her description of its contents?
- It is exactly as she told the court.
- Why did you destroy it?
- Because she asked me to.
- What was your reaction to receiving such a letter?
- Obviously, I was surprised. And more than a little concerned at its contents.
- Why were you concerned?
- Well, there was no truth in what Mr Pemberton suspected but I was concerned about the implications for me in chambers. I was also worried, to be frank, that the facts and the nature of my relationship with Bet ... with Mrs Sharples would come out.
- Did you mention any of this to Mr Pemberton when you met him at that Christmas party?
- No.
- Why not?
- I hoped that it was all no more than speculation. After all, I had not been having a relationship with Mrs Pemberton.

- And I want to ask you clearly and so that there can be no doubt about the basis of your case. Have you ever been in any sort of intimate relationship with Mrs Pemberton?
- No.
- No further questions, my Lord.

And to Adam's surprise Blytheway abruptly sat down. He hadn't asked any questions about the Middle Temple Ball in 1936, or the slow waltz or the dance card.

Alnwick was the first to cross-examine and Adam relaxed into this. There was nothing to worry about. Alnwick was keen to deflect the fire from Julia. His questioning was predictable and pedestrian and lasted little more than forty-five minutes. By the time he had finished the fingers of the court clock were edging towards one. Mr Justice Wilkinson gave him the customary warning not to talk to anyone about his evidence and then the court rose. He watched from the witness box as the courtroom emptied. The judge had been polite but severe, but from almost everywhere else in the court he felt nothing but antipathy. Julia again avoided his glance. Catherine stared long into his eyes before turning abruptly and making her way out. Withering contempt. Jeremy Pemberton KC's expression was one of pure hatred. He had lifted himself unsteadily from the table in front of Tempest and limped out of court. He looked ten years older than he was and his suit hung off him. Adam waited until the court was empty before descending. *The area outside the court should be empty by now.*

But he was wrong. Blytheway and Jones were standing in front of Betty Sharples having an animated discussion with her. She was cowering. He walked towards them but Blytheway, seeing him approach, shooed him away. So he went down into the main hall and then left the building by the Carey Street exit at the rear. He wasn't hungry. He wasn't allowed to talk to anyone. He would instead walk around Lincoln's Inn Fields in the early summer sunshine.

****

Adam stood when the court was ordered to rise. When everyone else had resumed their seats Sir Patrick Tempest KC remained on his feet. There was an expectant silence. *Keep it short and stick to what Betty and I have agreed,*

Adam thought to himself. *Don't vary off my script.* His supreme test awaited him. This was what had been worrying him ever since he had learnt that Tempest was to lead for Mr Pemberton. Tempest, tall and slim, raised his silvery head and bowed gently to the court – *May it please your Lordship* – before turning to Adam and adjusting his spectacles. Behind him the journalists sat with pens and pencils poised, their eyes on Adam.

– How old are you, Mr Falling?
– Thirty-eight.
– And how old is Mrs Pemberton?
– Thirty-seven.

Bugger!

– How, pray, do you know Mrs Pemberton's age?
– Thirty-seven or thirty-eight, I'm not sure.
– You were quite correct the first time. How is it that you know how old Mrs Pemberton is?
– It was a guess.
– A very good guess, Mr Falling. Do you know the day on which her birthday falls?
– No.
– I may come back to that. How old is Mr Jeremy Pemberton of Her Majesty's Counsel?
– I don't know. Mid-fifties?
– He is fifty-five, Mr Falling. So that there is an age difference of almost twenty years between him and his wife and a one year age difference between you and Mrs Pemberton. Would you accept that?
– Well … yes. If the ages you gave to me are correct it is a matter of simple mathematics.
– You are a married man?
– Yes.
– And your wife, Catherine, is in the public gallery?

He glanced in that direction and saw Catherine attempting to shrink away from the attention.

- Yes.
- In what year did you marry?
- 1924.
- So you have been married for around sixteen years and you have one daughter, Deborah, who is now twelve years old rising thirteen?
- Yes.
- I believe that you and Catherine met at Cambridge, where she was also a student?
- Yes.
- So she is a very intelligent lady?
- Yes.
- A good mother?
- Of course.
- I'm sorry to have to ask you this but, if you were pushed to point to a deficiency in her character as a wife, what would it be?

Adam had been dreading this question. He closed his eyes and rocked backwards in the witness box, and then took a deep breath.

- I cannot point to any deficiencies in Catherine. She is a better, a more intelligent person than I am.
- Again, I must apologise for my indelicacy, but were there any difficulties in your intimate relationship together?

Adam reddened. He could not bear to look at Catherine.

- Do I have to answer this question, my Lord?
- Yes, Mr Falling.
- There are ... were ... no difficulties in that part of our relationship.

Tempest paused and shuffled through his papers. He looked in the direction of the press box.

- As you are aware, Mr Falling, in 1939 the Government introduced National Registration Identity Cards. Everyone over sixteen must have one.
- I accept that.

- And you have one?
- Of course.
- And when Mr Churchill came to power in May of last year it became an obligatory requirement that anyone who checked into a hotel should produce his identity card.
- Yes.
- And it is your case, is it not, that you first met with Mrs Sharples just after the requirement to give proof of identity was introduced?
- Yes.
- So, by taking Mrs Sharples back to the Stafford you were, at the same time, producing verifiable evidence of an act of adultery? An act of infidelity to your wife?
- Yes.

There was a long pause. Tempest looked up at the judge, who returned his gaze.

- So, to recap, you had been married for sixteen years to a good and intelligent woman with whom you are unable to find any fault. You have a daughter of twelve and there are no problems in your private life. Yes?
- Yes.
- And would I be right in saying that it is your case that prior to your … dalliance … with Mrs Sharples you had never been unfaithful to your wife?
- No.
- So, to continue my summary with that background in mind, you chose to take a prostitute to an expensive hotel *immediately after* it became compulsory to provide evidence of identity?
- Yes.
- When she had a perfectly respectable room to go back to?
- Yes.

Tempest's tone turned suddenly from comparatively polite but sceptical enquiry to the fierceness Adam had heard so much about.

- This is *absolute nonsense* is it not, Mr Falling?!

– No.
– Because, I put it to you, there is a far simpler explanation. You had been visiting the Stafford for many months, years perhaps, with Mrs Pemberton and you signed the register under a false name.
– I hardly know Mrs Pemberton.
– Is Mrs Sharples here?
– Yes. She will support what I have said.
– Is she the young lady who has been waiting outside court?
– Yes.
– Just so it is on the record, would it be fair to say that she is about five foot five and has blonde hair of a similar length to Mrs Pemberton's?
– She's only twenty-three.
– But everything else I have put to you is accurate?
– Yes.
– And you say that the reason for going to an expensive hotel in the first place was because you did not want to acknowledge what you were doing?
– Yes.
– And that after that it was to ensure she spent more time with you.
– Yes.
– But this is more nonsense, is it not? I apologise for being direct but prostitutes are, I understand, paid according to the time and, forgive my indelicacy, for the services provided. If you wanted to stay with her longer you simply had to pay her more. To pay her more would have cost less than the cost of a prestigious hotel?
– Now that you put it that way, I suppose so. I hadn't thought of it in that way.
– You say that you thought you were beginning to fall in love with her?
– Yes.
– Did you think that she was reciprocating your feelings?
– I believe so, yes.
– And yet she continued to accept payment from you for … for her services?
– Yes.
– That doesn't sound like a love match to me, Mr Falling. It sounds to me like something altogether more … more mercenary.
– I don't know what you are talking about.

- Have you paid her to give evidence on your behalf?
- Of course I haven't! That's ridiculous!
- Did you ever do anything other than sleep with her?
- We went out for meals once or twice to the Lyons Corner House in Coventry Street.
- And who paid?
- I did.
- And anything else?
- As I said to Mr Blytheway, I went back to her flat once or twice.
- And where is that?
- In Clarges Street.
- And what did you talk about on these occasions?
- The things that people who like one another talk about.
- I would like it if you could tell us something about Mrs Sharples please, Mr Falling. We know that she is blonde and five foot five (as is Mrs Pemberton) and that she is twenty three years of age. What else can you tell us?
- Well. That she used to be a seamstress and that she had been married. Her husband was unfortunately killed in an accident at work at the beginning of last year. He was uninsured. She had no money and so she felt she had no alternative to beginning work as a prostitute. She's a very good person really.
- The real reason you were meeting with her in places like the Lyons Corner House – if indeed you were – was so that you could get your stories straight. That's right isn't it?
- Not at all.

Adam looked at the court clock. It was almost quarter to four. The day's ordeal would soon be over. He was still alive.

- I want to ask you, Mr Falling, why you didn't join up?
- I tried to but I failed the medical.
- And what was the reason for your failure?
- I failed the medical. I have problems with my chest. I was told in January that it was probably tuberculosis.

Tempest then turned to the similarity between Adam's books and those on Julia's shelves. Adam kept it simple. He had his literary tastes and he had no idea about Mrs Pemberton's. He could not be held responsible for the preferences of others. Yes, it was a surprising coincidence now that he had been made aware of it; but it was nothing to do with him. He was not cross-examined about his smoking. Finally, he was asked about Julia's letter.

- Prior to the receipt of Mrs Pemberton's letter, had Mr Pemberton done anything or said anything to suggest that he suspected you of having an affair with his wife?
- No.
- Did you not then think it extraordinary, if what you say is true, that Mrs Pemberton wrote to you at all?
- I was bemused, I confess.
- Here is the wife of your Head of Chambers writing to you, out of the blue, and apologising for the completely misguided allegation that you and she were having an affair when in the first place you were not, and secondly he had made no mention of such suspicions to you?
- No.

It was five past four. Betty would not have to give evidence until tomorrow.

- You see. I must put to you, as I will put to the learned Judge at the conclusion of this hearing, that you have been telling a pack of lies.
- I have not.
- That for whatever reason, you are trying to protect Mrs Pemberton from the fact of your adultery with her.
- No.
- That you had been going with Mrs Pemberton to that hotel for months or years before it was necessary to provide proof of identity.
- No.
- That she and you continued to go there after Mr Churchill came to power but it was only at that time that you gave the hotel your true identity.
- No.
- And that in order to protect Mrs Pemberton, when it became apparent

that Mr Pemberton had worked out what was going on, you took Mrs Sharples there as a subterfuge to try and put Mr Pemberton off the scent.

– No.

– And you say Mrs Sharples will support your version of events?

– Yes.

– I will look forward to asking her some questions. One final question. The last time you went to the Stafford was on Monday 23rd December 1940, is that right?

– Yes.

– And the penultimate time you visited was on the 21st October 1940?

– Yes.

– So there was a gap of over two months when prior to that you had been going there once or twice a week.

– If you say so.

– And we know that, by Friday 13th December 1940, you were aware of Mr Pemberton's suspicions?

– I was.

– And you knew, did you not, that Mr Pemberton tended to employ a private detective, Mr Jackson, a man with whom you are familiar?

– I suppose so.

– You knew that there was a likelihood that Mr Jackson would be following you that day?

– I really didn't think my Head of Chambers would do such a thing.

– You said in answer to Mr Blytheway that one of your concerns was that Mr Pemberton's suspicions might bring into the open the fact that you were consorting with a prostitute?

– I was obviously worried about my reputation.

– And yet, in the full knowledge that you may well have been followed, you went to the Stafford Hotel with Miss Sharples on the evening of 23rd December 1940?

– I wasn't thinking straight.

Tempest turned towards the judge and then across at the press box.

– I must put it to you, Mr Falling, that you were in a long-standing and intimate relationship with Mrs Pemberton.

683

Adam looked in Julia's direction. She had been watching him anxiously but immediately looked away.

– *I had a dream about you last night, Adam.*
– *What did you dream?*
– *I dreamt I was lying naked on your bed and you began kissing my neck, and then my breasts, and then my tummy.*
– *And how did the dream end?*
– *With you fucking me senseless.*

He turned to face the judge.

– It is not true, my Lord.
– No further questions, my Lord.

Blytheway rose to re-examine.

– You say you were diagnosed with tuberculosis in January of this year?
– Yes.
– Have you told your wife?
– No.
– Why not?
– My behaviour towards her has been dreadful. I cannot say how deeply sorry I am about what I have done. I want her to know how much remorse I feel for this terrible series of events. She certainly did not deserve it. I am so sorry.

He looked up into the public gallery but Catherine had gone. Blytheway turned to the judge.

– That is Mr Falling's case.

And then he sat down. The judge leaned towards him.

– Mr Blytheway, I understood from your client's evidence that Mrs Betty Sharples was waiting outside and was to be called as a witness on his behalf.

Blytheway uncoiled.

- She is, my Lord, but that won't be necessary. I think Mr Falling's case, albeit that it does him little credit, is sufficiently clear without any further evidence.
- Very well. It is twenty past four now and I will rise. Speeches tomorrow.

Chapter One Hundred and Three

(Thursday 8th May 1941)

– Court rise!

It was five past two. Mr Justice Wilkinson strode into court and sat down to give his judgment. Twenty-four hours ago Sir Patrick Tempest had been about to begin his cross-examination. It had not exactly been the most pleasant day of Adam's life. When he and Blytheway got back to Lamb Building and took their leave of Mr Jones he could hardly contain his anger.

– You didn't call Betty!
– I took an executive decision, sweetheart.
– But you didn't ask me before you did it!
– How could I? You were on oath.
– She was ready and willing to give her evidence to the court! We would have been home and dry if you had done.
– I think we should go upstairs for a cup of tea.

The tea had been poured and they were sitting on either side of Roly's desk. The peacock feathers still stood in their vases and one of the Tiffany lamps was alight. It was too early for the blackout. Blytheway raised his cup to his lips and took a sip.

– You will recall that during the short adjournment today Jones and I were speaking with Miss Sharples? Actually, that is not quite accurate. Apart from a few pleasantries on my part all the important questions were asked by Mr Jones, although, I confess, I did tell him what questions I wanted asking.
– And what was the nature of those questions?
– I wanted to find out more about her poor husband.

- And she no doubt told you that he died in an industrial accident in the early part of 1940?
- Indeed she did. However, when we asked her the nature of that industrial accident, when exactly it happened, what injuries he sustained, who his employer was and whether she had contemplated making a claim against that employer, whether there were any letters that had been written by her or by the employer and whether she could produce any of those letters, she was altogether vague. I am not saying, of course, that she was not a good and truthful witness. After all, it has been your consistent instruction to me that her account is an accurate one. But I took the view that the risks of her being befuddled by Tempest were too great. It would have been like putting a minnow in a pool with a shark.

Adam resisted the temptation to argue further.

- How did I do?
- It could have been worse. On the other hand, it could have been far better.
- Why?

Blytheway sighed and refilled his cup.

- More tea, while I'm holding the pot? *Adam shook his head.* Whilst, of course, I am not doubting your veracity, Tempest did illustrate the apparent absurdity of your defence.
- You don't believe me, do you?
- And when he went on to lay down the possibility that you had concocted a story with Mrs Sharples *and* had paid her to say what she was about to tell the court, it seemed to me that the risk of her saying the wrong thing was too great. Are you sure you won't have another cup?

With a sinking heart, Adam held up his cup and allowed Blytheway to fill it.

- So you think we're sunk?

- I didn't say that, sweetheart.
- I remember you saying that if I was holed below the waterline I would sink.
- I confess, I don't know what will happen tomorrow. But we have one special card on our side.
- But we've closed our case! We can't call any more evidence.
- I'm talking about the burden of proof, sweetheart. Tempest is as aware of that as I am – even if you have taken your eyes of the ball.
- How is that going to help?
- You don't have to prove anything. Neither does Mrs Pemberton. Jeremy Pemberton KC has to prove his case. Of course, he can prove that you are – forgive me – rather disreputable. But he should not be allowed to use your bad character to bring down Mrs Pemberton. It does not assist him to show the world what an awful man you are. It doesn't, I accept, do you many favours, particularly with your wife, but it should not be allowed to blacken Mrs Pemberton's name on what on any view is a flimsy circumstantial case.
- Tomorrow's going to be pretty bloody isn't it?
- Yes.

And so it proved. If Adam's spirits had been on a low ebb after his discussions with Roly they were not made any better by the press reports. "Barrister 'consorted with a prostitute'"; "Barrister denies adultery with Head of Chambers' wife – but admits to adultery with a prostitute"; "Barrister's Defence to Adultery Petition 'absolute nonsense'"; "Barrister's wife walks out of court". The articles were also supplemented by unflattering portraits of the sort of person Adam Falling was. Both his defence and the allegations against him had been placed in inverted commas. Catherine was absent from the public gallery when the court assembled for final speeches.

All of the closing addresses, even that from Roland Blytheway, concentrated on the vileness of Adam Falling. The emphasis differed, however. Alnwick was outright in his condemnation of the co-respondent; Tempest, who was of course asserting that the defence was merely a façade, concentrated on the moral degradation of a man who could stoop to the depths of inventing a liaison with a prostitute in most improbable circumstances as a way of hiding his affair with a respectable woman; and Roly took a more ambivalent stance: yes, this was something that was right for moral condemnation, but on the other hand it did little to prove that Mr Falling had an intimate relationship with Mrs Pemberton. Even taking Jeremy Pemberton's case at its highest – that Mr Falling had been having an adulterous relationship with Mrs Pemberton and had interposed a prostitute as a way of deflecting attention from her – how could he satisfy the court, on the balance of probabilities, that the woman with whom he was unfaithful was Mrs Pemberton? Blytheway had ripped through the evidence for the Petitioner.

– The evidence that has been presented to the court does not paint my client in a good light. That is something that I must accept. He has condemned himself out of his own mouth and that shame is something that he will have to live with for the rest of his professional career ... and beyond. But he is not before this court because he has consorted with a prostitute. He is here because it is alleged that he had a relationship with the wife of a *much esteemed* member of the Bar. The court may well conclude that my client has consorted with prostitutes and equally may take a very dim view of his conduct. But that is nothing to the point – *nihil ad rem*, as some lawyers continue to say to confuse their clients; and if that is all that the court can find it is not enough to condemn Mrs Pemberton. The court has heard from her and will have formed its own impression of her as a person and as a witness. She is a mother of three children and a wife to Mr Pemberton. She has professed her love for him repeatedly in her evidence. Whilst she could have retreated to the country with her children, whom she loves dearly (that last point does not appear to be in dispute) she has stayed by her husband's side and, in addition, engaged in vital war work in London, putting her own life at risk in so doing. She is, these abhorrent allegations being put to one side, a respectable woman. And what is being asked of this court is that her respectability should be taken away from her solely on the basis of some books she chose to buy, her decision to have her clothing dry-cleaned – she says to please her husband – and the fact that she wrote a letter to Mr Falling which, in the light of what she now knows of him, she would not have written.

And then Blytheway turned again to the evidence and to the burden of proof. *The evidence, darling, always start with the evidence.* The burden of proof was always on Pemberton. If Mr Pemberton could not satisfy the court that there had in fact been an intimate relationship between Julia and Adam, then the petition must fail.

– And it goes further than that, my Lord. The more unlikely an allegation is, the more cogent should be the evidence should be to prove it. If, for example, it was known to all, including the court, that my client was a man convicted of grievous bodily harm, then it would not be such a jump to be persuaded that he had gone further and committed murder. If on the other hand my client was a clergyman who had espoused a credo of non-violence in his life, then concluding that the latter client was guilty of murder would be a far larger leap. The evidence would have to be far more cogent. Leaving my client and his self-evident faults to one side for a moment and looking at Mrs Pemberton, she is, I would ask you to accept, nearer to the clergyman than to the man convicted of GBH. And, therefore, the evidence needs to be the more cogent.

And then Blytheway sat down. The press was continuing to scribble when Alnwick stood up to address the court, but, as his turgid address continued, their pens and pencils were holstered. They were unsheathed again when Tempest stood to address them. Sir Patrick Tempest had made all his points eloquently and had enlarged on the points that had been made in his opening. However, unlike Blytheway, he had been interrupted by the judge frequently. It was clear that Mr Justice Wilkinson had been concerned about the burden of proof and about Mr Pemberton's obligation to shift it onto his wife. It was equally apparent that this was causing him considerable concern. How could he condemn a woman and ruin her reputation on such flimsy evidence? Why should the fact that Mr Falling had been shown to be a person of the blackest character be allowed to tarnish the reputation of an otherwise blameless woman? Surely, he needed to have more evidence than he had been given to take a decision to grant her husband a divorce, with all the domestic and financial consequences that this would entail, on no more than her literary interests, the fact that she had all her clothing dry-cleaned, and the fact that she had written an ill-judged letter to Mr Falling? Tempest tried gamely to deal with these points, but when eventually he sat down Adam sensed something approaching defeat in the way his body sank into his seat.

From where he was he was also able to observe, unnoticed, Jeremy Pemberton's reaction to the speeches. From appearing mildly confident before they began, he had become increasingly agitated. He was writing a lot of notes and passing them back to Tempest. Every now and again he would turn to his silk and engage him in detailed conversation, looking from time to time over Tempest's shoulder towards Adam. That look of pure hatred. As Blytheway's address continued, Adam noticed that, increasingly, that hatred was tinged with worry.

****

Mr Justice Wilkinson picked up a sheaf of papers containing his handwritten notes.

– This is the judgment of the court.

He began. He then went through the allegations and the counter-allegations before getting onto the evidence. Adam could see Pemberton fidgeting. Julia stared at her feet. *Why can't they tell us what their conclusion is at the beginning rather than making us wait in suspense until the end?* And then, as the clock reached three, Mr Justice Wilkinson reached the end.

– And, so, I have come to the conclusion, not without some doubts and some uncertainty as I considered the evidence and the submissions of counsel, that Mr Pemberton has failed to prove his case. Whilst in the course of my deliberations, as I have said, I had anxious doubts, I am now absolutely sure that there has been no adultery between Mr Falling and Mrs Pemberton. I accept the submissions of Mr Blytheway, who, as usual, in his characteristically frank way, has not tried to underplay the deplorable moral faults in his client, and yet, whatever those faults may be, it would be quite wrong of me, on the evidence I have heard, to taint the character of Mrs Pemberton. I therefore dismiss this petition.

Pemberton was on his feet. His face was red and his white hair was standing on end. His spectacles were less than straight. He looked dishevelled.

- No!!! This outrageous! This is not justice! I cannot accept this judgment!
- Sir Patrick, I must insist that you control your client. His behaviour in my court is completely unacceptable!

Tempest was out of his row and was doing his best to calm his client down and make him sit.

- I apologise, my Lord. As you can see, my client is distraught at the outcome.
- I'm afraid that is absolutely no excuse!

Tempest succeeded in wrestling his client back into his seat and then Alnwick stood up to ask that Mr Pemberton pay his wife's costs. That application succeeded. Then Blytheway stood up to make the same request.

- I have granted Mr Alnwick's application for costs but I am not convinced that Mr Falling, who comes out of this matter with no merit whatsoever, should receive his. Enlighten me.
- My Lord, my client has said all along that he had been seeing a prostitute. Equally, he had denied all along that he had been having a relationship with Mrs Pemberton. This court has now accepted his evidence on that latter point. That was the only point before the court. He has been vindicated. He must, therefore, be entitled to his costs. I should also say that, in view of Mr Falling's straitened circumstances, I have been acting on a *pro bono* basis. All that a costs order will mean is that Mr Jones will be paid for his services. I myself will gain no benefit from it. So, a costs order in favour of Mr Falling will be a considerably smaller sum than that which Mr Pemberton will have to pay for the inestimable services of Mr Purefoy and Mr Alnwick.

There was some toing and froing but eventually Mr Wilkinson agreed that Jeremy Pemberton KC should pay Mr Jones's costs. And then the court rose. The petition had failed. Adam's ordeal was over.

Chapter One Hundred and Four
(Thursday 8th May 1941)

Pemberton was shouting and screaming as the court dispersed. He cursed Julia. He cursed Adam. But most of all he cursed Blytheway. Tempest tried in vain to calm him down but the task was beyond him. He was still yelling abuse in the corridor, surrounded by the lawyers for all three sides and by Julia and Adam. Blytheway said nothing and simply watched. Picking out Adam in the circle around him, Pemberton advanced on him. His limp was more pronounced, and, as he began bellowing in Adam's face, Adam smelt the vestiges of whisky.

– This isn't over, Falling. I'll take it to the Court of Appeal! Your name will be dirt for ever more. Don't you worry. I'll ...

Then Jeremy Pemberton KC staggered and, with a cry, holding his hand to his chest, he collapsed unconscious. Almost all the lawyers, Purefoy and Jones included, rushed over to assist him. Only Julia, Adam and Blytheway stood back. The journalists had their notepads open and continued to scribble.

– Time to make ourselves scarce, sweetheart.

The two men headed quickly down the stairs and started walking over the marble tiles to the exit onto the Strand. Behind him Adam heard the clattering of high heels.

– Adam! Adam!

He turned, and to his surprise he saw Julia running towards them. She ran into his arms and hugged him closely before kissing him on the lips. There were tears in her eyes.

– I'm so very, very sorry. I will explain everything. Seven o'clock on
Saturday.

And then she ran back the way that she had come. With the drama that
was unfolding upstairs, the whole thirty-second incident appeared to have
been missed. Adam turned to Blytheway bemused.

– What was all that about?
– I'm sorry, Adam. I feel that I have completely let you down.
– What are you talking about?
– I also feel that I have done a disservice to Alnwick in what I have been
  saying to you about his abilities.
– He was hopeless.
– Then again, in my defence, I was acting for a member of the Bar and
  so I could have been forgiven for assuming that you would under-
  stand the implications of today's verdict.
– Roly. I'm lost. What on earth are you talking about?
– *Res judicata*, sweetheart.
– *Res judicata?*
– It refers to a matter already judged. The case against you and Mrs
  Pemberton has now been judged upon and, subject to any appeal –
  and any appeal would be absolutely hopeless in the current circumstances – the matter, the allegations cannot be reopened. As far as
  the courts in this country are concerned, wherever the truth may
  lie, you have never had a relationship with Mrs Pemberton, you have
  never been intimate with her and any suggestion that you have can
  be met with the plea of *res judicata*. Of course this is academic because
  you have made it entirely clear to me, throughout your instructions,
  that you did not have a relationship with Mrs Pemberton; but in the
  hypothetical circumstance that you *had*, the verdict of the court is
  that as a matter of law you have never been close to Mrs Pemberton,
  you have never made love to her and you have certainly not committed adultery with her. You certainly never loved her. And she never
  loved you.

PART FOUR

Chapter One Hundred and Five

(Saturday 10ᵗʰ May 1941)

It was almost five in the evening when Adam rang the bell at Blytheway's home in Bedford Square. He had gone to the first half of the cup final at Wembley with Jones, Bateman, Victoria McKechnie, and sixty thousand others, but had made it clear that he would have to leave at half time. Caldwell opened the door.

- Good afternoon, sir. How can I assist?
- Is Mr Blytheway in?
- I'm sorry sir, he and Mr Storman have gone to the Queen's Hall to see the Elgar concert.
- Oh, I'd forgotten about that. Listen, would there be any problem if I took a bath here?
- Not at all, sir. Why don't you come into the Salon and I'll make you a pot of tea. Your bath should be ready within fifteen minutes.

Adam had finished his tea in the bath. Naturally he had supported Preston North End. The score had been one all when he made his apologies and left. Surrounded by so many people and what with the dirt, sweat and excitement, he felt unclean afterwards. He needed a bath and a good suit. He was going to meet Julia on terms that might possibly be as they had been before everything went wrong. Jeremy had suffered a heart attack but was apparently recovering well at St Bart's. Adam knew that he still loved Julia but, for his peace of mind if not for anything else, he needed her explanation of what had happened to them over the last six months. He climbed out of the bath and rubbed his newly washed hair with a rough towel before combing it down and brushing his teeth. It was quarter to six. This could be the most important moment of his life.

****

In Mecklenburg Square Julia climbed out of her bath, pulled on her towelling robe and dried herself. She had laid out the clothing she had chosen across her bed. Saturday was her night off from the Water Board so she didn't need to be dowdy: a pervenche-blue frock pulled in at the waist to emphasise her figure, and silk brassiere, panties and stockings. The sun was streaming into the room and she opened the window to allow in a slight breeze. She dressed quickly and glanced at her watch. It was 6 p.m. Going over to her little dressing table, she sat down and opened a drawer. There was a limited choice and so she picked a pale blue eye shadow which would be set off by her dress, and applied it. Then her mascara, and finally some pale pink lipstick. There was an antique perfume atomiser on her table and she picked it up and directed a gentle spray onto her neck.

Turning around in her seat, she looked at the room and the limited collection of possessions she had been able to bring with her. It had always been a temporary home and now its time was almost done. Jeremy had no entitlement to keep her out of their home in Eaton Square and in a few days she would be back in her old environment. He could no longer threaten to interfere with her relationship with her children. After dashing down to speak with Adam she had returned immediately to his side and accompanied him to St Bartholomew's. Bart's was the nearest hospital and he had been placed on an open ward. All the way she told him how much she loved him and how sorry she was that they had gone through this awful ordeal. She could tell, just by looking into his vague and faded eyes, that he no longer knew what to believe. The fight had gone out of him. The doctors said that it was likely to be a long convalescence. She was able to arrange, for a little money, for him to have a private room. When she visited him on Friday and on Saturday morning he was asleep and she was advised not to wake him.

She glanced at her wrist again: 6.15. She took one last look in the mirror, smoothed down her hair and went to the wardrobe to pick out a coat, a three-quarter-length unlined garment in pale honey linen with shells embroidered on the pockets. She had purchased it the previous season from Bradleys of Chepstow Place for twelve and a half guineas in the days when she did not worry about money. Then she went to leave. She took the chain out of the security latch and pulled open the door, only to find Audrey Fisher on her doorstep. Her colleague from the Water Board had been on the point of knocking.

- Hello. This is a surprise. What are you doing here?
- I got a call from the Water Board. We all have to go into work tonight. They're expecting a big raid.
- But it's my night off. I've arranged to meet someone.
- Apparently, all leave's been cancelled.
- Can't you say that you weren't able to contact me?
- I don't think so.

Julia stalled her friend and tried to think of a way to avoid going to Rosebery Avenue that evening.

****

At exactly the moment when Julia was confronted by Audrey on her doorstep Adam opened the door of the Temple Church and went inside. He took a seat in a poorly lit part of the building. Julia had given a time but not a place but he knew that she had intended them to meet in the Temple Church. He was wearing the best of the suits Roly had gifted to him, and he had polished his shoes. A late afternoon sun sent weakening rays through the higher windows. He picked up a prayer book and tried to read from it. Insufficient light. So instead he looked around the ancient building and tried once more to work out where Julia used to kneel and say her prayers in the days when she would leave him a note. He had no idea. And then he heard the approach of footsteps outside. Someone was coming towards the door of the church. He looked over and saw it gradually opening. His heart was in his mouth. Now, at last, he would have Julia's explanation for what had been going on. He got to his feet and smoothed down his hair.

It was Blytheway, dressed in his tailored fire watcher's outfit.

- Roly! What on earth are you doing here? I thought you and Storman had gone to see some Elgar?
- It was an absolutely wonderful concert! I think it went some way to lifting Jack's spirits.
- You didn't go to the concert dressed like that?
- Of course not. I took Jack back home and changed out of my black tie into my evening garb. I'm on duty tonight. I suggested that Jack have an early night and Caldwell agreed to look after him.

- But that doesn't explain why you've come into the church.
- When I found you weren't in your room I took a wild guess and came here.
- So you were looking for me?
- Do you mind if I join you, sweetheart?

He took the pew next to Adam's, wiped away at the dirt and sat down. The two men sat next to one another in silence for a while. Eventually, Adam spoke.

- I don't feel as though I have thanked you properly for what you did for me last week.
- Not at all, darling. It was quite fun wasn't it? I always like crossing swords with Pat. He is in a different league to Pemberton and Preston.
- Something's been troubling me. I don't know if you feel you can talk about it.

Blytheway's tone became sombre.

- I am very worried, Adam. I don't think our city can take much more of this. I feel that we have reached the end-game.
- What do you mean?
- That raid that killed Margaret was horrific. They only need to muster the planes to do that once or twice more and we will be finished, for all of Churchill's oratory. I am beginning to wonder which day will be my last.
- Why don't you escape to the country? No one would criticise you.
- Ah. And see my peacocks one last time. That would be nice. But I couldn't, Adam. I would never be able to forgive myself. I need to be here. We all have our allotted time and we should not allow fear to distract us from that.
- Would you be prepared to answer my questions, please, Roly?
- You have chosen a very good time to ask them. I'm feeling rather fatalistic this evening.
- I'd completely understand if you felt you couldn't answer me but why did you avoid all reference to the 1936 Ball? The slow waltz and the dance card and all of that?

- I suppose it can't do any harm now. Julia Pemberton was wearing a white backless dress that evening, wasn't she?
- How could you possibly know that?
- Because I was there.
- Why didn't you say anything?
- Think about it, sweetheart … That was one of those evenings I mentioned at Margaret's funeral when I stood in for Jack. The photograph on the altar was taken that night. I told her she should pose alone as it would be something of a fraud if I was part of that. I think I have told you before that I am blessed – or cursed – with a photographic memory. I remember that Jeremy and Julia were three back behind her in the queue. I don't think you and Catherine had your photographs taken.
- We couldn't afford it to be honest.
- Well, I couldn't have every dance with Margaret. That would have been unchivalrous. And for some reason I was disinclined to ask any of the ladies there to dance with me. I don't think any of them thought of me as an ideal partner. If I hadn't wanted to help out Margaret and Jack I *certainly* wouldn't have been there. Wild horses and all of that. Anyway, an old Bencher had marked Margaret's card for the slow waltz, and as it started I went out into the garden for a bit of fresh air. I noticed as I was leaving that you were dancing with Mrs Pemberton …
- I thought I'd seen someone in the garden!
- It was me. "I've been wanting to do that for a long time," you said. And she replied, "We'll be missed," and back in you went. I made myself scarce.

Adam realised that his mouth had dropped open. It was at last dawning on him.

- So the reason you avoided all reference to that part of the events was because you knew what had happened during the missing five minutes?
- I couldn't mislead the court Adam. And I was there as an advocate. I was not there to give evidence but rather to make my submissions on the evidence as it emerged. I, of course, do not know what, if any,

701

significance that moment had. But what I could not *possibly* do was to put forward some half-baked, un-thought-through version of events that you might have been tempted to put to me.

Adam was reeling.

- So you thought all along that I was having an affair with Julia?
- What I thought does not matter. It was for Pemberton to prove it. And he failed.
- Why do you dislike him so much? I remember asking you that question a few months ago and you wouldn't answer. Someone at the Inner Temple said it was something to do with the Great War.
- I wondered whether you would ask me that and I have been in two minds as to whether or not I should tell you. But, again, I think that tonight may be the right time for me to tell you my secrets. There may not be another time. It was the fourth of November 1918, a week before the Armistice and I, with my co-driver, was operating an ambulance.
- Who was your co-driver?
- Muriel.
- Muriel?
- She was a dark-haired suffragette who took no nonsense from anyone. She hated the name Muriel and insisted that I call her "M".
- "M"?
- We made a good team. I wasn't particularly attracted to women and she had a certain ambivalence – very choosy about men – although she liked horses unreservedly. So we got on together very well.
- We found ourselves at the front at the Sambre-Oise Canal. It was to prove to be the last great battle of the war. We weren't to know that things were so close to an end.
- Where does Pemberton come into this?
- He was there as well. He was something of a legendary figure. All that bravery. That incredible luck he had throughout his campaigns. But there was a private I was rather fond of. A young lad who was perhaps ten years my junior. Fred, he was called. A fresh-faced blond boy who was kind and sensitive and was neither deferential nor arrogant. He used to come and sit with me and M in the back of the ambulance and we'd

all play whist. Although we were to win the battle the Germans got our range, and whilst Fred was out in no-man's land he got caught by a shell just as night was falling. I had been keeping an eye out for him and I was convinced he had been killed, or if not killed grievously injured.

Adam glanced across at Blytheway. There was a far-away look in his eyes.

- A photographic memory is a curse as well as a blessing, Adam. I am forced to remember everything in minute detail. There are many things I would rather forget. That night was certainly one of them. They were raining shells down on us and throwing up flares so that the mud flats where Fred was lying were lit up spasmodically. Even if he was alive it would be almost impossible to save him. I was hunkering down in a trench with M and the person next to us was Jeremy Pemberton. He looked terrified and I think he had been drinking.
- So what happened?
- There was a brief break in the shelling and I heard Fred calling for help. He must have been less than a hundred yards away. Of course, I had no alternative but to try and save him. But I couldn't do it on my own. It would take two people to drag his body back. I asked Pemberton to help me bring back Fred but he refused point blank. "He's only a private," he said. I think he was frightened that his luck might run out just as the war was coming to an end.

Adam looked at his watch. It was after seven. Sirens were beginning to sound.

- I don't think she will be coming, Adam. I think she intended to, but, as always, we are being overtaken by events.
- What are you talking about?
- Eyes and ears, Adam.

Adam's shoulders slumped.

- Can I speak to you hypothetically?
- Hypothetically?

– Working on the outlandish hypothesis that you were having a relationship with Mrs Pemberton and she suddenly broke it off giving no
reason, and that she was intending to come here tonight to explain
herself?
– Okay.
– Love is such a strange thing. Can one love two people at the same
time? It's a perennial question. Well, I think one can. But, at the same
time, when it comes to that sticking point one has to acknowledge
that one can love two or more people and yet one can love one or
more people more than one loves another person.
– What are you getting at?
– Katya loved Tomas but she loved her brother more. Tomas loved Katya
more than he loved his life. I think Bateman loved Marjorie but he
loved Victoria more. In this hypothetical situation you loved Catherine
but, ultimately, loved Julia more. Julia loved you – and she loved Jeremy
and Jenny – but, ultimately, she loved her children the most.
– Go on.
– If, for example, when Julia said in her sleep "Not now, one day perhaps", she was reliving a conversation with you and not remembering something that she had said or felt about her children, it would
suggest that she loved them more than she loved you. And more than
she loved you, Pemberton and Jenny. Well, the latter proposition is
borne out by her reaction on learning that it was Jenny and not Agnes
who had been killed. And again, speaking hypothetically, if you loved
Julia more than anyone else in the world it would make perfect sense
that you would be prepared to sacrifice your marriage, your reputation and your career by creating a false story that linked you to a
prostitute who bore a remarkable resemblance to Julia Pemberton.
These are of course just my musings on an outlandish hypothesis.

The sirens were becoming more insistent and the sound of enemy bombers could now be heard clearly.

– This is all rot!
– Of course it is, sweetheart. An idle speculation.
– Tell me more about Pemberton.
– I have to confess that, for I think the only time in my life, I became

angry. Fred was stuck in no-man's land and Pemberton refused to help. And his only excuse was that the man was "only" a private. For about fifteen minutes I remonstrated with him but he was adamant. Eventually, M agreed to come with me. We folded rolls of bandages into our clothing and then covered ourselves in mud. You can *imagine* how distasteful I found that! Then we waited for a pause in the shelling and, when no flares were above, crawled out to try and find him. I can remember every single second of this. Every time a flare went up we had to lie still. M's courage filled me with admiration. She never complained and seemed to know instinctively what to do.

Bombs were beginning to fall and they sounded close.

– It took us about an hour to reach him. And every time we heard the whistle of a shell we thought that this could be the end. The stench was terrible and we had to crawl past a lot of corpses. Fred had managed to pull himself into a crater full of water. He had dreadful facial injuries and it was a wonder that he had not lost his leg. We bandaged him up as best we could and then dragged him back to the trench. There were shells falling around us and flares overhead. He screamed once in agony but I was very firm. No more screaming or we would all be dead. And after that, somehow, he limited himself to groaning. Well, we got him back and the following day we got him to a field hospital.
– What happened to M?
– I don't know, I'm afraid, sweetheart. I lost touch with her after the war.

The floor of the church was shaking and the loud percussive roar was closing in.

– I think we should be getting out of here now.
– And did Fred survive? Did you ever see him again?
– Fred? Oh yes. I see him every day. His surname is Caldwell.

Chapter One Hundred and Six

(Saturday 10th May 1941)

Julia was still wearing the outfit that she had put on for Adam when she and Audrey entered the Water Board building in Rosebery Avenue. They went straight down into the bunker and took up their usual places. It was not long before reports began coming in of the bombings and they began charting them. Hundreds of planes were flying overhead.

- Bombs are falling in Kingsway.
- Smithfield has been hit.
- Westminster is being pounded.
- St Clement Danes has taken a direct hit and it looks as if it has been destroyed.
- They're targeting the Law Courts and the Temple.

Julia looked up horrified from her note book. *Oh God! They're dropping bombs on the place I asked Adam to meet me!* But there was no time for her to warn him, to save him or to do anything other than continue with her duties. She watched and listened in horror as more and more reports came in of bombs hitting the Temple.

****

Adam and Roly climbed to the top of Hare Court and made ready to deal with the incendiaries as they had done on so many occasions in recent months. Barry appeared and joined them. The incendiaries were raining down on them and as night drew in the sky was lit by an eerie glow. They were surrounded by fire and the noise of bombs. And the Temple was beginning to burn.

- They've hit Inner Temple Hall!

706

Roly said as the flames leapt up. Adam was caked in sweat and was having difficulty breathing. His chest constricted.

– We need to get down there!

They rushed down from the roof, but by the time they reached the Temple Church the flames on the roof of the Hall were out of control and were beginning to leap in the wind towards Lamb Building. And then the roof of Lamb Building caught fire. A ferocious blaze began eating into the structure until the wood began to crumple and masonry fell down on the men below. Cloisters had been hit and was falling apart.

The flames leapt again, from Lamb Buildings and onto the roof of the Temple Church. It was consumed by fire. A structure that had been consecrated in 1185 was being destroyed and they were helpless observers.

– Let's try and save what we can,

said Roly, and rushed into the building. Adam and Barry followed along with others. One of them was Storman. Adam looked at him in astonishment.

– What are you doing here? I thought you were in bed.
– Caldwell told me what was happening. He and I came down here together.

Over Storman's shoulder he saw Caldwell – Fred – picking up a crucifix and carrying it to safety. They were all trying to remove the artefacts inside, Victorian or otherwise, before the building collapsed. The heat was so intense that the lead was beginning to melt and dropping ominously amongst the rescuers. He saw Barry running out with a painting under his arm. A piece of masonry fell and knocked him down without pinioning him. He was unconscious inside the church and big glowing drops of molten lead had begun to fall on him. He was going to die in there. Adam's chest was no longer cooperating. He could hardly breathe. He rushed over to Barry and half pulled, half lifted him to his feet. He knew he was on the verge of collapse but he had to get Barry out. Barry put an arm around his shoulder and the two of them stumbled out of the building. Adam took him as far away from the fires as he could and then went back towards the church. Blytheway, in his tailored fire-watching suit, was shouting.

- We need to be organised. We need to deal with this as logically as we can in the circumstances. We need –

But he never finished that sentence. A piece of masonry fell down and hit him on the side of the head, crushing him. Adam ran towards him.

- No! No!!

Roly was unconscious. His body was stuck under a large piece of stone. Adam tried to remove it but it was too heavy for him and his strength was beginning to fail.

- Here. Let me help.

Strong arms reached across and, somehow, removed the masonry. Adam looked over his shoulder. It was Peter Preston KC. And then everything went black.

Chapter One Hundred and Seven

(Sunday 11th May 1941)

Julia had watched in horror as the bombs continued to fall on the place where she had asked Adam to meet her. Every new report battered her heart. But there was nothing she could do. When the "all clear" sounded she walked straight down to the Temple. Everywhere was burning and the smell of smoke was overwhelming. She knew, because of her work, that the Houses of Parliament had been severely damaged, that St Clement Danes had been destroyed, that Smithfield and Kingsway had been badly damaged and that more than a thousand people had been killed. But she didn't know what had happened to Adam. She picked her way through the rubble. She stumbled and fell more than once and her face was black with soot. Her left knee was bleeding and the pain caused her to limp. It was almost six in the morning before she reached the Temple. She entered from Mitre Court. The pungent smell of smoke and burning was almost too much to bear. Making her way towards the Temple Church, she saw with a shock that it had been virtually destroyed. Flames were still rising from it. She fell again. Lamb Building was in ruins. She approached the smouldering wreckage and saw amongst the scorched and broken stone some peacock feathers and fragments of Tiffany lamps. There were also some Penguin paperbacks, by Waugh and Huxley. Scorched.

Eventually she was able to find someone who could tell what had happened. Adam was still alive but in a very poor condition. He had been taken to St Bart's. And so she set off.

****

Falling was on an open ward. She limped along it, pushing her hair out of her eyes and doing the best to get the ash off her clothing. She wiped the blood from her knees with her coat. It was ruined anyway. The shells embroidered on the pockets had turned black. Two beds away from Adam she saw Roland Blytheway, his head swathed in bandages, and a man she didn't know with a deep scar on his cheek, holding Blytheway's hand and weeping. Blytheway's eyes were open but uncomprehending. Storman was standing on the other side of the bed. He looked infinitely sad.

And then she reached Adam. He was delirious. A nurse was standing by the bed.

– It's his chest. We don't know if he will survive.

Julia pulled a chair up to the bed and took his hand.

– Oh, Adam! I'm so very sorry. I treated you abominably. I thought we would both survive all of this.

He grunted and squeezed her hand. She looked over at his bedside table. The crystal obelisk was sitting there, covered in blood.

– We found it in his pocket, Miss. He wouldn't let us take it away from him – or clean it up.

Storman came over and put his hand on her shoulder.

– Blytheway is going to live. But he has lost his memory.

Adam looked up at Julia and Storman. The light was fading. But she was with him at the end. He could feel the texture of her palm. Its warmth. He squeezed her hand again. And then he lost consciousness.

Epilogue

(Sunday 18th May 1941)

Julia had moved back into Eaton Square. After Adam lost consciousness she had, in a fit of guilt, gone to see her husband. He was still alive and was due to be moved to a private nursing home. No one was able to say how long he would be there or whether he would ever come out. Adam, meanwhile, was recovering. Blytheway was rambling about a black eye someone gave him at the Dorchester as he struggled to regain his memory. Everything in her private room was as it had been. Annie came in with a fresh bowl of flowers.

– It's so good to have you back, Miss. Shall I put these in the window?
– Thank you, Annie, yes.

Annie placed the pot there and departed. How much had changed in the last six months? She walked over to the window and looked out. And then she looked down at the fresh bowl of flowers. There was a piece of paper sticking out from them. Puzzled and alarmed she pulled it out.

"TRUST ME. I love you."

So Annie had known all along!

She opened the window and put Pergolesi on the gramophone, the music blaring out at the sky. Then she put the note in her pocket and went down to the garden. Surveying the vegetable patch that used to be their lawn, she took out the note and read it again. Then she took out the golden locket she always wore around her neck, the double locket that contained in the front a lock of Agnes's hair whilst the second chamber had always been empty. She clicked it open and put Adam's note into the second chamber. Then she made her way back into her home. And *Stabat Mater* carried on from the gramophone.

711

Lightning Source UK Ltd.
Milton Keynes UK
UKHW01f0614240718
326190UK00001B/163/P